The Sixth Cadfael Omnibus

Ellis Peters

The Sixth Cadfael Omnibus

The Heretic's Apprentice
The Potter's Field
The Summer of The Danes

sphere

SPHERE

First published in this omnibus edition in Great Britain in 1996 by
Warner Books
Reprinted 1996, 1997, 1999, 2001
Reprinted by Time Warner Paperbacks in 2004
Reprinted by Sphere in 2009 (twice), 2010, 2012 (twice)

A CIP catalogue record for this book
is available from the British Library.

ISBN 978-0-7515-1589-3

Photoset in North Wales by
Derek Doyle & Associates, Mold, Clwyd.
Printed and bound by CPI Group (UK) Ltd, Croydon, CR0 4YY

Papers used by Sphere are from well-managed forests
and other responsible sources.

MIX
Paper from
responsible sources
FSC   FSC® C104740
www.fsc.org

Sphere
An imprint of
Little, Brown Book Group
100 Victoria Embankment
London EC4Y 0DY

An Hachette UK Company
www.hachette.co.uk

www.littlebrown.co.uk

The Heretic's Apprentice

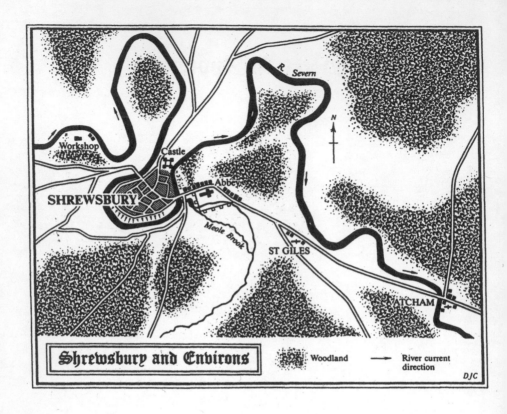

Shrewsbury and Environs

Woodland — River current direction

DJC

Chapter One

N THE nineteenth day of June, when the eminent visitor arrived, Brother Cadfael was in the abbot's garden, trimming off dead roses. It was a task Abbot Radulfus kept jealously to himself in the ordinary way, for he was proud of his roses, and valued the brief moments he could spend with them, but in three more days the house would be celebrating the anniversary of the translation of Saint Winifred to her shrine in the church, and the preparations for the annual influx of pilgrims and patrons were occupying all his time, and keeping all his obedientiaries busy into the bargain. Brother Cadfael, who had no official function, was for once allowed to take over the dead-heading in his place, the only brother privileged to be trusted with the abbatial blossoms, which must be immaculate and bright for the saint's festival, like everything else within the enclave.

This year there would be no ceremonial procession all the way from Saint Giles, at the edge of the town, as there had been two years previously, in 1141. There her relics had rested while proper preparation was made to receive them, and on the great day, Cadfael remembered, the threatened rain had fallen all around, yet never a drop had spattered her reliquary or its attendants, or doused the candles that accompanied her erect as lances, undisturbed by the wind. Small miracles following wherever Winifred passed, as flowers sprang in the footsteps of Welsh Olwen in the legend. Great miracles came more rarely, but Winifred could manifest her power where it

3

was deserved. They had good reason to know and be glad of that, both far away in Gwytherin, the scene of her ministry, and here in Shrewsbury. This year the celebrations would remain within the enclave, but there would still be room enough for wonders, if the saint had a mind to it.

The pilgrims were already arriving for the festival, in such numbers that Cadfael hardly spared a look or an ear for the steady bustle far up the great court, round the gatehouse and the guest-hall, or the sound of hooves on the cobbles, as grooms led the horses down into the stable-yard. Brother Denis the hospitaller would have a full house to accommodate and feed, even before the festival day itself, when the townsfolk and the villagers from miles around would flood in for worship.

It was only when Prior Robert was seen to round the corner of the cloister at the briskest walk his dignity would permit, and head purposefully for the abbot's lodging, that Cadfael paused in his leisurely trimming of spent flowers to note the event, and speculate. Robert's austere long visage had the look of an angel sent on an errand of cosmic importance, and endowed with the authority of the superb being who had sent him. His silver tonsure shone in the sun of early afternoon, and his thin patrician nose probed ahead, sniffing glory.

'We have a more than ordinarily important visitor,' thought Cadfael. And he followed the prior's progress into the doorway of the abbot's lodging with interest, not greatly surprised to see the abbot himself issue forth a few minutes later, and set off up the court with Robert striding at his side. Two tall men, much of a height, the one all smooth, willowy elegance, carefully cultivated, the other all bone and sinew and hard, undemonstrative intelligence. It had been a severe blow to Prior Robert when he was passed over in favour of a stranger, to fill the vacancy left by the deposition of Abbot Heribert, but he had not given up hope. And he was durable, he might even outlive Radulfus and come into his own at last. Not, prayed Cadfael devoutly, for many years yet.

He had not long to wait before Abbot Radulfus and his visitor came down the court together, in the courteous and wary conversation of strangers measuring each other at first meeting. Here was a guest of too great and probably too private significance to be housed in the guest-hall, even among the nobility. A man almost as tall as Radulfus, and in all but the shoulders twice his width, well-fleshed and portly almost to

4

fat, and yet it was powerful and muscular flesh, too. At first glance his was a face rounded and glossy with good living, full-lipped, full-cheeked and self-indulgent. At second glance the lips set into a formidable and intolerant strength, the fleshy chin was seen to clothe a determined jaw, and the eyes in their slightly puffy settings had nevertheless a sharp and critical intelligence. His head was uncovered, and wore the tonsure, otherwise Cadfael, who had never seen him before, would have taken him for some baron or earl of the king's court, for his clothing, but for its sombre colours of dark crimson and black, had a lordly splendour about its cut and its ornament, a long, rich gown, full-skirted but slashed almost to the waist before and behind for riding, its gold-hemmed collar open in the summer weather upon a fine linen shirt, and a gold-linked chain and cross that circled a thick, muscular throat. Doubtless there was a body-servant or a groom somewhere at hand to relieve him of the necessity of carrying cloak or baggage of any kind, even the gloves he had probably stripped off on dismounting. The pitch of his voice, heard distantly as the two prelates entered the lodging and vanished from sight, was low and measured, and yet held a suggestion of current displeasure.

In a few moments Cadfael saw the possible reason for that. A groom came down the court from the gatehouse leading two horses to the stables, a solid brown cob, most likely his own mount, and a big, handsome black beast with white stockings, richly caparisoned. No need to ask whose. The impressive harness, scarlet saddle-cloth and ornamented bridle made all plain. Two more men followed with their less decorated horseflesh in hand, and a packhorse into the bargain, well loaded. This was a cleric who did not travel without the comforts to which he was accustomed. But what might well have brought that note of measured irritation into his voice was that the black horse, the only one of the party worthy to do justice to his rider's state, if not the only one fitted to carry his weight, went lame in the left foreleg. Whatever his errand and destination, the abbot's guest would be forced to prolong his stay here for a few days, until that injury healed.

Cadfael finished his clipping and carried away the basket of fading heads into the garden, leaving the hum and activity of the great court behind. The roses had begun to bloom early, by reason of fine, warm weather. Spring rains had brought a good hay crop, and June ideal conditions for gathering it. The shearing was almost finished, and the wool dealers were reckoning up hopefully the value of their clips. Saint Winifred's modest pilgrims, coming on foot, would have dry travelling and warm lying, even out of doors. Her doing, perhaps? Cadfael could well believe that if the Welsh girl smiled, the sun would shine on the borders.

The earlier sown of the two pease fields that sloped down from the rim of the garden to the Meole brook had already ripened and been harvested, ten days of sun bringing on the pods very quickly. Brother Winfrid, a hefty, blue-eyed young giant, was busy digging in the roots to feed the soil, while the haulms, cropped with sickles, lay piled at the edge of the field, drying for fodder and bedding. The hands that wielded the spade were huge and brown, and looked as if they should have been clumsy, but in fact were as deft and delicate in handling Cadfael's precious glass vessels and brittle dried herbs as they were powerful and effective with mattock and spade.

Within the walled herb-garden the drowning sweetness hung heavy, spiced and warm. Weeds can enjoy good growing weather no less than the herbs on which they encroach, and there was always work to be done at this season. Cadfael tucked up his habit and set to work on his knees, close to the warm earth, with the heady fragrance disturbed and quivering round him like invisible wings, and the sun caressing his back.

He was still at it, though in a happy languor that made no haste, rather luxuriating in the touch of leaf and root and soil, when Hugh Beringar came looking for him two hours later. Cadfael heard the light, springy step on the gravel, and sat back on his heels to watch his friend's approach. Hugh smiled at seeing him on his knees.

'Am I in your prayers?'

'Constantly,' said Cadfael gravely. 'A man has to work at it in so stubborn a case.'

He crumbled a handful of warm, dark earth between his hands, dusted his palms, and Hugh gave him a hand to help him rise. There was a good deal more steel in the young sheriff's slight body and slender wrist than anyone would suppose. Cadfael had known him for five years only, but drawn nearer to him than to many he had rubbed shoulders with all the twenty-three years of his monastic life. 'And what are you doing here?' he demanded briskly. 'I thought you were north among your own lands, getting in the hay.'

'So I was, until yesterday. The hay's in, the shearing's done, and I've brought Aline and Giles back to the town. Just in time to be summoned to pay my respects to some grand magnate who's visiting here, and is none too pleased about it. If his horse hadn't fallen lame he'd still be on his way to Chester. Have you not a drink, Cadfael, for a thirsty man? Though why I should be parched,' he added absently, 'when he did all the talking, is more than I know.'

Cadfael had a wine of his own within the workshop, new but fit to drink. He brought a jug of it out into the sunshine, and they sat down together on the bench against the north wall of the garden, to sun themselves in unashamed idleness.

'I saw the horse,' said Cadfael. 'He'll be days yet before he's fit to take the road to Chester. I saw the man, too, if it's he the abbot made haste to welcome. By the sound of it he was not expected. If he's in haste to get to Chester he'll need a fresh horse, or more patience than I fancy he possesses.'

'Oh, he's reconciled. Radulfus may have him on his hands a week or more yet. If he made for Chester now he wouldn't find his man there, there's no haste. Earl Ranulf is on the Welsh border, fending off another raid from Gwynedd. Owain will keep him busy a while.'

'And who is this cleric on his way to Chester?' asked Cadfael curiously. 'And what did he want with you?'

'Well, being frustrated himself – until I told him there was no hurry, for the earl was away riding his borders – he had a mind to be as busy a nuisance to all about him as possible. Send for the sheriff, at least exact the reverence due! But there is a grain of purpose in it, too. He wanted whatever information I had about the whereabouts and intentions of Owain Gwynedd, and especially he wished to know how big a threat our Welsh prince is being to Earl Ranulf, how glad the earl might be to have some help in the matter, and how willing he might be to pay for it in kind.'

'In the king's interests,' Cadfael deduced, after a moment of frowning thought. 'Is he one of Bishop Henry's familiars, then?'

'Not he! Stephen's making wise use of the archbishop for once, instead of his brother of Winchester. Henry's busy elsewhere. No, your guest is one Gerbert, of the Augustinian canons of Canterbury, a big man in the household of Archbishop Theobald. His errand is to make a cautious gesture of peace and goodwill to Earl Ranulf, whose loyalty – to Stephen's or any side! – is never better than shaky, but might

7

be secured – or Stephen hopes it might! – on terms of mutual gain. You give me full and fair support there in the north, and I'll help you hold off Owain Gwynedd and his Welshmen. Stronger together than apart!'

Cadfael's bushy eyebrows were arched towards his grizzled tonsure. 'What, when Ranulf is still holding Lincoln castle, in Stephen's despite? Yes, and other royal castles he holds illegally? Has Stephen shut his eyes to that fashion of support and friendship?'

'Stephen has forgotten nothing. But he's willing to dissemble if it will keep Ranulf quiet and complacent for a few months. There's more than one unchancy ally getting too big for his boots,' said Hugh. 'I fancy Stephen has it in mind to deal with one at a time, and there's one at least is a bigger threat than Ranulf of Chester. He'll get his due, all in good time, but there's one Stephen has more against than a few purloined castles, and it's worth buying Chester's complacence until Essex is dealt with.'

'You sound certain of what's in the king's mind,' said Cadfael mildly.

'As good as certain, yes. I saw how the man bore himself at court, last Christmas. A stranger might have doubted which among us was the king. Easy going Stephen may be, meek he is not. And there were rumours that the earl of Essex was bargaining again with the empress while she was in Oxford, but changed his mind when the siege went against her. He's been back and forth between the two of them times enough already. I think he's near the end of his rope.'

'And Ranulf is to be placated until his fellow-earl has been dealt with.' Cadfael rubbed dubiously at his blunt brown nose, and thought that over for a moment in silence. 'That seems to me more like the bishop of Winchester's way of thinking than King Stephen's,' he said warily.

'So it may be. And perhaps that's why the king is using one of Canterbury's household for this errand, and not Winchester's. Who's to suspect any motion of Henry's mind could be lurking behind Archbishop Theobald's hand? There isn't a man in the policies of king or empress who doesn't know how little love's lost between the two.'

Cadfael could not well deny the truth of that. The enmity dated back five years, to the time when the archbishopric of Canterbury had been vacant, after William of Corbeil's death, and King Stephen's younger brother, Henry, had cherished

8

confident pretensions to the office, which he certainly regarded as no more than his due. His disappointment was acute when Pope Innocent gave the appointment instead to Theobald of Bec, and Henry made his displeasure so clear and the influence he could bring to bear so obvious that Innocent, either in a genuine wish to recognise his undoubted ability, or in pure exasperation and malice, had given him, by way of consolation, the papal legateship in England, thus making him in fact superior to the archbishop, a measure hardly calculated to endear either of them to the other. Five years of dignified but fierce contention had banked the fires. No, no suspect earl approached by an intimate of Theobald's was likely to look behind the proposition for any trace of Henry of Winchester's devious manipulations.

'Well,' allowed Cadfael cautiously, 'it may suit Ranulf to be civil, seeing his hands are full with the Welsh of Gwynedd. Though what Stephen can offer him by way of help is hard to see.'

'Nothing,' agreed Hugh with a short bark of laughter, 'and Ranulf will know that as well as we do. Nothing but his forbearance, but that will be worth welcoming, in the circumstances. Oh, they'll understand each other well enough, and no trust on either side, but either one of them will see that the other will keep to his part for the present, out of self-interest. An agreement to put off contention to a more convenient time is better at this moment than no agreement at all, and the need to look over a shoulder every hour or so. Ranulf can give all his mind to Owain Gwynedd, and Stephen can give all his to the matter of Geoffrey de Mandeville in Essex.'

'And in the meantime we must entertain Canon Gerbert until his horse is fit to bear him.'

'And his body-servant and his two grooms, and one of Bishop de Clinton's deacons, lent as his guide here through the diocese. A meek little fellow called Serlo, who goes in trembling awe of the man. I doubt if he'd ever heard of Saint Winifred, for that matter – Gerbert, I mean, not Serlo – but he'll be wanting to direct her festival for you, now that he's halted here.'

'He had that look about him,' Cadfael admitted. 'And what have you told him about the small matter of Owain Gwynedd?'

'The truth, if not the whole truth. That Owain is able to keep Ranulf so busy on his own border that he'll have no time to

9

make trouble elsewhere. No need to make any real concessions to keep him quiet, but sweet talk can do no harm.'

'And no need to mention that you have an arrangement with Owain,' agreed Cadfael placidly, 'to leave us alone here, and keep the earl of Chester off your back. It may not restore any of Stephen's purloined castles in the north, but at least it keeps the earl's greedy hands off any more of them. And what's the news from the west? This uneasy quietness down there in Gloucester's country has me wondering what's afoot. Have you any word of what he's up to?'

The desultory and exhausting civil war between cousins for the throne of England had been going on for more than five years, in spasmodic motion about the south and west, seldom reaching as far north as Shrewsbury. The Empress Maud, with her devoted champion and illegitimate half-brother Earl Robert of Gloucester, held almost undisputed sway now in the south-west, based on Bristol and Gloucester, King Stephen held the rest of the country, but with a shaky and tenuous grip in those parts most remote from his base in London and the southern counties. In such disturbed conditions every baron and earl was liable to look to his own ambitions and opportunities, and set out to secure a little kingdom for himself rather than devote his energies to supporting king or empress. Earl Ranulf of Chester felt himself distant enough from either rival's power to feather his own nest while fortune favoured the bold, and it was becoming all too plain that his professed loyalty to King Stephen took second place to the establishment of a realm of his own spanning the north from Chester to Lincoln. Canon Gerbert's errand certainly implied no confidence in the earl's word, however piously pledged, but was meant to hold him quiescent for a time for his own interests, until the king was ready to deal with him. So, at least, Hugh judged the matter.

'Robert,' said Hugh, 'is busy strengthening all his defences and turning the south-west into a fortress. And he and his sister between them are bringing up the lad she hopes to make king some day. Oh, yes, young Henry is still there in Bristol, but Stephen has no chance in the world of carrying his war that far, and even if he could, he would not know what to do with the boy when he had him. But neither can she get more good out of the child than the pleasure of his presence, though perhaps that's benefit enough. In the end they'll have to send him home again. The next time he comes – the next time it may be in earnest and in arms. Who knows?'

10

The empress had sent over into France, less than a year ago, to plead for help from her husband, but Count Geoffrey of Anjou, whether he believed in his wife's claim to the throne of England or not, had no intentions of sending over to her aid forces he himself was busy using adroitly and successfully in the conquest of Normandy, an enterprise which interested him much more than Maud's pretensions. He had sent over, instead of the knights and arms she needed, their ten-year-old son.

What sort of father, Cadfael wondered, could this Count of Anjou be? It was said that he set determined store upon the fortunes of his house and his successors, and gave his children a good education, and certainly he had every confidence, justifiably, in Earl Robert's devotion to the child placed in his charge. But still, to send a boy so young into a country disrupted by civil war! No doubt he had Stephen's measure, of course, and knew him incapable of harming the child even if he got him into his hands. And what if the child himself had a will of his own, even at so tender an age, and had urged the venture in his own right?

Yes, an audacious father might well respect audacity in his son. No doubt, thought Cadfael, we shall hear more of this Henry Plantagenet who's minding his lessons and biding his time in Bristol.

'I must be off,' said Hugh, rising and stretching lazily in the warmth of the sun. 'I've had my fill of clerics for today – no offence to present company, but then, you're no cleric. Did you never fancy taking minor orders, Cadfael? Just far enough to claim the benefit if ever one of your less seemly exploits came to light? Better the abbot's court than mine, if ever it came to it!'

'If ever it came to it,' said Cadfael sedately, rising with him, 'the likelihood is you'd need to keep your mouth tight shut, for you'd be in it with me nine times out of ten. Do you remember the horses you hid from the king's round-up when—'

Hugh flung an arm round his friend's shoulders, laughing. 'Oh, if you're to start remembering, I can more than match you. Better agree to let old deeds rest. We were always the most reasonable of men. Come on, bear me company as far as the gatehouse. It must be getting round towards Vespers.'

They made their way along the gravel path together without haste, beside the box hedge and through the vegetable garden to where the rose beds began. Brother Winfrid was just coming over the crest from the slope of the pease-field, striding springily with his spade over his shoulder.

'Get leave soon, and come up and see your godson,' said Hugh as they rounded the box hedge, and the hum and bustle of the court reached out to surround them like the busy sound of bees in swarm. 'As soon as we reach town Giles begins asking for you.'

'I will, gladly. I miss him when you go north, but he's better there through the summer than here shut within walls. And Aline's well?' He asked it serenely, well aware that he would have heard of it at once if there had been anything amiss.

'Blooming like a rose. But come and see for yourself. She'll be expecting you.'

They came round the corner of the guest-hall into the court, still almost as lively as a town square. One more horse was being led down to the stables, Brother Denis was receiving the arriving guest, dusty from the road, at the door of his domain; two or three attendant novices were running to and fro with brychans and candles and pitchers of water; visitors already settled stood watching the newcomers throng in at the gatehouse, greeting friends among them, renewing old acquaintances and embarking on new; while the children of the cloister, oblates and schoolboys alike, gathered in little groups, all eyes and ears, bouncing and shrilling like crickets, and darting about among the pilgrims as excitedly as dogs at a fair. The passing of Brother Jerome, scuttling up the court from the cloister towards the infirmary, would normally have subdued the boys into demure silence, but in this cheerful turmoil it was easy to avoid him.

'You'll have your house full for the festival,' said Hugh, halting to watch the coloured chaos, and taking pleasure in it as candidly as did the children.

In the group gathered just within the gate there was a sudden ripple of movement. The porter drew back towards the doorway of his lodge, and on either side people recoiled as if to allow passage to horsemen, but there was no sharp rapping of hooves striking the cobbles under the arch of the gateway. Those who entered came on foot, and as they emerged into court the reason for making such generous way for them became apparent. A long, flat handcart came creaking in, towed by a thickset, grizzled countryman before, and pushed by a lean and travel-stained young man behind. The load it carried was covered by a dun-coloured cloak, and topped with

12

a bundle wrapped in sacking, but by the way the two men leaned and strained at it it was seen to be heavy, and the shape of it, a man's height long and shoulder-wide, brought mortality to mind. A ripple of silence washed outward from it, and by degrees reached the spot where Hugh and Cadfael stood watching. The children looked on great-eyed, ears pricked, at once awestricken and inquisitive, intent on missing nothing.

'I think,' said Hugh quietly, 'you have a guest who'll need a bed somewhere else than in the guest-hall.'

The young man had straightened up wincingly from stooping into the weight of the cart, and looked round him for the nearest authority. The porter came towards him, circling the cart and coffin with the circumspect bearing of one accustomed to everything, and not to be put out of countenance even by the apparition of death intruding like a morality play into the preparations for a festival. What passed between them was too soft, too earnest and private to be heard beyond the two of them, but it seemed that the stranger was asking lodging for both himself and his charge. His bearing was reverent and courteous, as was due in these surroundings, but also quietly confident. He turned his head and gestured with his hand towards the church. A young fellow of perhaps twenty-six or twenty-seven years, in clothes sun-faded and very dusty from the roads. Above average tall, thin and sinewy, large-boned and broad-shouldered, with a tangle of straw-coloured hair somewhat fairer than the deep tan of his forehead and cheeks, and a good, bold prow of a nose, thin and straight. A proud face, some-what drawn with effort just now, and earnest with the gravity of his errand, but by nature, Cadfael thought, studying him across the width of the court, it should be an open, hopeful, good-natured countenance, ready to smile, and a wide-lipped mouth ready to confide at the first friendly invitation.

'One of your flock from here in the Foregate?' asked Hugh, viewing him with interest. 'But no, by the look of him he's been on the roads from somewhere a good deal more distant.'

'But for all that,' said Cadfael, shaking his head over an elusive likeness, 'it seems to me I've seen that face before, somewhere, at some time. Or else he reminds me of some other lad I've known.'

'The lads you've known in your time could come from half the world over. Well, you'll find out, all in good time,' said Hugh, 'for it seems Brother Denis is giving his attention to the matter, and one of your youngsters is off into the cloister in haste to fetch somebody else.'

The somebody else proved to be no less than Prior Robert himself, with Brother Jerome trotting dutifully at his heels. The length of Robert's stride and the shortness of Jerome's legs turned what should have been a busy, self-important bustle into a hasty shamble, but it would always get Jerome in time to any spot where there was something happening that might provide him with occasion for curiosity, censure or sanctimony.

'Your strange visitors are acceptable,' observed Hugh, seeing how the conference was proceeding, 'if only on probation. I suppose he could hardly turn away a dead man.'

'The fellow with the cart I do know,' said Cadfael. 'He comes from close under the Wrekin, I've seen him bringing goods in to market. Cart and man must be hired for this delivery. But the other has come from far beyond that, for sure. Now I wonder how far he's brought his charge, hiring help along the way. And whether he's reached the end of his journey here.'

It was by no means certain that Prior Robert welcomed the sudden appearance of a coffin in the centre of a court thronged with pilgrims hoping for good omens and pleasurable excitement. In fact Prior Robert never showed an approving face to anything that in any way disrupted the smooth and orthodox course of events within the enclave. But clearly he could find no reason to refuse whatever was being requested here with due deference. If only on probation, as Hugh had said, they were to be permitted to remain. Jerome ran officiously to round up four sturdy brothers and novices, to hoist the coffin from the cart and bear it away towards the cloister, bound, no doubt, for the mortuary chapel within the church. The young man lifted the modest roll of his possessions, and trudged somewhat wearily along behind the cortège, to vanish into the south archway of the cloister. He walked as if he were stiff and footsore, but bore himself erect and steadily, with no studied show of grief, though his face remained thoughtfully solemn, preoccupied rather with what went on in his own mind than what those around him here might be thinking.

Brother Denis came down the steps from the guest-hall and walked briskly down the court after this funereal procession, presumably to retrieve and house with decent friendliness the

14

living guest. The onlookers stared after for a moment, and then returned to their interrupted occasions, and the hum and motion of activity resumed, at first softly and hesitantly, but very soon more vociferously than before, since they had now something pleasurably strange to talk about, once the moment of awe was over. .

Hugh and Cadfael crossed the court to the gatehouse in considering silence. The carter had taken the shafts of his lightened cart and hauled it back through the arch of the gatehouse into the Foregate. Evidently he had been paid for his trouble in advance, and was content with his hire.

'It seems that one's job is done,' said Hugh, watching him turn into the street. 'No doubt you'll soon hear what's afoot from Brother Denis.'

Hugh's horse, the tall grey he perversely favoured, was tethered at the gatehouse; no great beauty in looks or temperament, hard-mouthed, strong-willed and obstinate, with a profound contempt for all humanity except his master, and nothing more than the tolerant respect of an equal even for Hugh.

'Come up soon,' said Hugh with his toe in the stirrup and the reins gathered in his hand, 'and bring me all the gossip. Who knows, in a day or so, you may be able to fit a name to the face.'

Chapter Two

ADFAEL CAME out from the refectory after
supper into a light, warm evening, radiant with
reflected brightness from a rosy sunset. The
readings during the meal, probably chosen by Prior
Robert in compliment to Canon Gerbert, had been from the
writings of Saint Augustine, of whom Cadfael was not as fond
as he might have been. There is a certain unbending rigidity
about Augustine that offers little compassion to anyone with
whom he disagrees. Cadfael was never going to surrender his
private reservations about any reputed saint who could
describe humankind as a mass of corruption and sin proceeding
inevitably towards death, or one who could look upon the
world, for all its imperfections, and find it irredeemably evil. In
this glowing evening light Cadfael looked upon the world, from
the roses in the garden to the wrought stones of the cloister
walls, and found it unquestionably beautiful. Nor could he
accept that the number of those predestined to salvation was
fixed, limited and immutable, as Augustine proclaimed, nor
indeed that the fate of any man was sealed and hopeless from
his birth, or why not throw away all regard for others and rob
and murder and lay waste, and indulge every anarchic appetite
in this world, having nothing beyond to look forward to?

In this undisciplined mood Cadfael proceeded to the
infirmary, instead of to Collations, where the pursuit of Saint
Augustine's ferocious righteousness would certainly continue.
Much better to go and check the contents of brother Edmund's

16

medicine cupboard, and sit and gossip a little while with the few old brothers now too feeble to play a full part in the order of the monastic day.

Edmund, a child of the cloister from his fourth year and meticulous in observation, had gone dutifully to the chapter-house to listen to Jerome's reading. He came back to make his nightly rounds just as Cadfael was closing the doors of the medicine-cupboard, and memorising with silently moving lips the three items that needed replenishment.

'So this is where you got to,' said Edmund, unsurprised. 'That's fortunate, for I've brought with me someone who needs to borrow a sharp eye and a steady hand. I was going to try it myself, but your eyes are better than mine.'

Cadfael turned to see who this late evening patient might be. The light within there was none too good, and the man who came in on Edmund's heels was hesitant in entering, and hung back shyly in the doorway. Young, thin, and about Edmund's own height which was above the average.

'Come in to the lamp,' said Edmund, 'and show Brother Cadfael your hand.' And to Cadfael, as the young man drew near in silence: 'Our guest is newly come today, and has had a long journey. He must be in good need of his sleep, but he'll sleep the better if you can get the splinters out of his flesh, before they fester. Here, let me steady the lamp.'

The rising light cast the young man's face into sharp and craggy relief, fine, jutting nose, strong bones of cheek and jaw, deep shadows emphasising the set of the mouth and the hollows of the eyes under the high forehead. He had washed off the dust of travel and brushed into severe order the tangle of fair, waving hair. The colour of his eyes could not be determined at this moment, for they were cast down beneath large, arched lids at the right hand he was obediently holding close to the lamp, palm upturned. The young man who had brought with him into the abbey a dead companion, and asked shelter for them both.

The hand he proffered deprecatingly for inspection was large and sinewy, with long, broad-jointed fingers. The damage was at once apparent. In the heel of his palm, in the flesh at the base of the thumb, two or three ragged punctures had been aggravated by pressure into a small inflamed wound. If it was not already festering, without attention it very soon would be.

'Your porter keeps his cart in very poor shape,' said Cadfael. 'How did you impale yourself like this? Pushing it out of a

17

ditch? Or was he leaving you more than your share of the work to do, safe with his harness in front there? And what have you been using to try and dig out the splinters? A dirty knife?'

'It's nothing,' said the young man. 'I didn't want to bother you with it. It was a new shaft he'd just fitted, not yet smoothed off properly. And it did make a very heavy load, what with having to line and seal it with lead. The slivers have run in deep, there's wood still in there, though I did prick out some.'

There were tweezers in the medicine cupboard. Cadfael probed carefully in the inflamed flesh, narrowing his eyes over the young man's palm. His sight was excellent, and his touch, when necessary, relentless. The rough wood had gone deep, and splintered further in the flesh. He coaxed out fragment after fragment, and flexed and pressed the place to discover if any still remained. There was no telling from the demeanour of his patient, who stood placid and unflinching, taciturn by nature, or else shy and withdrawn here in a place still strange to him.

'Do you still feel anything there within?'

'No, only the soreness, no pricking,' said the youth, experimenting.

The path of the longest splinter showed dark under the skin. Cadfael reached into the cupboard for a lotion to cleanse the wound, comfrey and cleavers and woundwort, which had got its name for good reason. 'To keep it from taking bad ways. If it's still angry tomorrow, come to me and we'll bathe it again, but I think you have good healing flesh.'

Edmund had left them, to make the round of his elders, and refill the little constant lamp in their chapel. Cadfael closed the cupboard, and took up the lamp by which he had been working, to restore it to its usual place. It showed him his patient's face fully lit from before, close and clear. The deep-set eyes, fixed unwaveringly on Cadfael, must surely be a dark but brilliant blue by daylight; now they looked almost black. The long mouth with its obstinate set suddenly relaxed into a wide boyish smile.

'Now I do know you!' said Cadfael, startled and pleased. 'I thought when I saw you come in at the gatehouse I'd seen that face somewhere before. Not your name! If ever I knew that, I've forgotten it years since. But you're the boy who was clerk to old William of Lythwood, and went off on pilgrimage with him, long ago now.'

'Seven years,' said the boy, flashing into animation at being remembered. 'And my name's Elave.'

'Well, well, so you're safe home after your wanderings! No

wonder you had the look of having come half across the world. I remember William bringing his last gift to the church here, before he set out. He was bent on getting to Jerusalem, I recall at the time I half wished I could go with him. Did he reach the city indeed?'

'He did,' said Elave, growing ever brighter. 'We did! Lucky I was that ever I took service with him, I had the best master a man could have. Even before he took the notion to take me with him on his journey, not having a son of his own.'

'No, no more he had,' agreed Cadfael, looking back through seven years. 'It's his nephews took over his business. A shrewd man he was, and a good patron to our house. There are many here among the brothers will remember his benefits...'

He caught himself up abruptly there. In the flush of recollection of the past he had lost sight for a while of the present. He came back to it with a sudden recoil into gravity. This boy had departed with a single companion, and with a single companion he now returned.

'Do you tell me,' Cadfael asked soberly, 'that it's William of Lythwood you've brought home in a coffin?'

'It is,' said Elave. 'He died at Valognes, before we could reach Barfleur. He'd kept money by to pay his score if it happened, and get us both home. He'd been ill since we started north through France, sometimes we had to halt a month or more along the way till he could go again. He knew he was for dying, he made no great trouble about it. And the monks were good to us. I write a good hand, I worked when I could. We did what we wanted to do.' He told it quite simply and tranquilly; having been so long with a master content in himself and his faith, and unafraid of his end, the boy had grown into the same practical and cheerful acceptance. 'I have messages to deliver for him to his kin. And I'm charged to ask a bed for him here.'

'Here in abbey ground?' asked Cadfael.

'Yes. I've asked to be heard tomorrow at chapter. He was a good patron to this house for all his life, the lord abbot will remember that.'

'It's a different abbot we have now, but Prior Robert will know, and many others among us. And Abbot Radulfus will listen, you need not fear a refusal from him. William will have witnesses enough. But I'm sorry he could not come home alive to tell us of it.' He eyed the lanky young man before him with considered respect. 'You've done well by him, and a hard road you must have had of it, these last miles. You must have been

19

barely a grown man when he took you off overseas.'

'I was nearly nineteen,' said Elave, smiling. 'Nineteen and hardy enough, strong as a horse I was. I'm twenty-six now, I can make my own way.' He was studying Cadfael as intently as he was being studied. 'I remember you, Brother. You were the one who soldiered in the east once, years ago.'

'So I did,' acknowledged Cadfael, almost fondly. Confronted with this young traveller from places once well known, and sharp with memories for him, he felt the old longings quickening again within him, and the old ghosts stirring. 'When you have time, you and I could have things to talk about. But not now! If you're not worn out with journeying, you should be, and there'll be a moment or two to spare tomorrow. Better go and get your sleep now. I'm bound for Compline.'

'It's true,' owned Elave, heaving a long, fulfilled sigh at having reached the end of his charge. 'I'm main glad to be here, and have done with what I promised him. I'll bid you goodnight, then, Brother, and thanks.'

Cadfael watched him cross the width of the court to the steps of the guest-hall, a tough, durable young man who had packed into seven years more journeying than most men saw in a lifetime. No one else within these walls could follow in spirit where he had been, no one but Cadfael. The old appetite stirred ravenously, after contented years of stability and peace.

'Would you have known him again?' asked Edmund, emerging at Cadfael's shoulder. 'He came once or twice on his master's errands, I remember, but between eighteen or so and his middle twenties a man can change past recognition, especially a man who's made his way to the ends of the earth and back. I wonder sometimes, Cadfael, I even glimpse sometimes, what I may have missed.'

'And do you thank your father for giving you to God,' wondered Cadfael, 'or wish he'd left you your chances among men?' They had been friends long enough and closely enough to permit such a question.

Brother Edmund smiled his quiet, composed smile. 'You at least can question no one's act but your own. I am of a past order, Cadfael, there'll be no more of me, not under Radulfus, at any rate. Come to Compline, and pray for the constancy we promised.'

The young man Elave was admitted to chapter next morning,

20

as soon as the immediate household affairs had been dealt with.

The numbers at chapter were swelled that day by the visiting clerics. Canon Gerbert, his mission necessarily delayed for a while, could not but turn his frustrated energies to meddling in whatever came to hand, and sat enthroned beside Abbot Radulfus throughout the session, and the bishop's deacon, committed to faithful attendance on this formidable prelate, hovered anxiously at his elbow. This Serlo was, as Hugh had said, a meek little fellow with a soft, round, ingenuous face, much in awe of Gerbert. He might have been in his forties, smooth-cheeked and pink and wholesome, with a thin, greying ring of fair hair, erased here and there by incipient baldness. No doubt he had suffered from his over-powering companion along the road, and was intent simply on completing his errand as soon and as peaceably as possible. It might seem a very long way to Chester, if he was instructed to go so far.

Into this augmented and august assembly Elave came when he was bidden, refreshed and bright with the relief of reaching his goal and shedding his burden of responsibility. His face was open and confident, even joyful. He had no reason to expect anything but acceptance.

'My lord,' said Elave, 'I have brought back from the Holy Land the body of my master, William of Lythwood, who was well known in this town, and has been in his time a benefactor to the abbey and the church. Sir, you will not have known him, for he left on his pilgrimage seven years ago, but there are brothers here who will remember his gifts and charities, and bear witness for him. It was his wish to be buried in the cemetery here at the abbey, and I ask for him, with all respect, his funeral and grave within these walls.'

Probably he had rehearsed that speech many times, Cadfael thought, and shaped and reshaped it doubtfully, for he did not seem like a man of many or ready words, unless, perhaps, he was roused in defence of something he valued. However that might be, he delivered it from the heart. He had a pleasant voice, pitched agreeably low, and travel had taught him how to bear himself among men of all kinds and all fortunes.

Radulfus nodded acknowledgement, and turned to Prior Robert. 'You were here, Robert, seven years ago and more, as I was not. Tell me of this man as you remember him. He was a merchant of Shrewsbury?'

'A much respected merchant,' said the prior readily. 'He

kept a flock folded and grazed on the Welsh side of the town, and acted as agent for a number of other sheep-farmers of the middle kind, to sell their clips together to the best advantage. He also had a workshop preparing vellum from the skins. Of good repute, very fine white vellum. We have bought from him in the past. So do other monastic houses. His nephews have the business now. Their family house is near Saint Alkmund's church in the town.'

'And he has been a patron of our house?'

Brother Benedict the sacristan detailed the many gifts William had made over the years, both to the choir and the parish of Holy Cross. 'He was a close friend of Abbot Heribert, who died here among us three years ago.' Heribert, too gentle and mild for the taste of Bishop Henry of Winchester, then papal legate, had been demoted to give place to Radulfus, and had ended his days quite happily as a simple choir-monk, without regrets.

'William also gave freely in winter for the poor,' added Brother Oswald the almoner.

'It seems that William has well deserved to have what he asks,' said the abbot and looked up encouragingly at his petitioner. 'I understand you went with him on pilgrimage. You have done well by your master, I commend your loyalty, and I trust the journey has done great good to you, living, as to your master, who died still a pilgrim. There could be no more blessed death. Leave us now. I will speak with you again very soon.'

Elave made him a deep reverence, and went out from the chapter-house with a buoyant step, like a man going to a festival.

Canon Gerbert had refrained from comment while the petitioner was present, but he cleared his throat vociferously as soon as Elave had vanished, and said with weighty gravity: 'My lord abbot, it is a great privilege to be buried within the walls. It must not be granted lightly. Is it certain that this is a fit case for such an honour? There must be many men, above the rank of merchant, who would wish to achieve such a resting-place. It behoves your house to consider very gravely before admitting anyone, however charitable, who may fall short of worthiness.'

'I have never held,' said Radulfus, unperturbed, 'that rank or trade is valued before God. We have heard an impressive list of this man's gifts to our church, let alone those to his

22

fellow-men. And bear in mind that he undertook, and accomplished, the pilgrimage to Jerusalem, an act of devotion that testifies to his quality and courage.'

It was characteristic of Serlo, that harmless and guileless soul – so Cadfael thought long afterwards, when the dust had settled – to speak up with the best of intentions at the wrong moment, and in disastrously wrong words.

'So good counsel prevailed,' he said, beaming. 'A timely word of admonishment and warning has had this blessed effect. Truly a priest should never be silent when he hears doctrine misread. His words may turn a soul astray into the right path.'

His childlike gratification faded slowly into the heavy silence he had provoked. He looked about him without immediate understanding, and gradually perceived how most eyes avoided him, looking studiously far into the distance or down into folded hands, while Abbot Radulfus viewed him steadily and hard but without expression, and Canon Gerbert turned on him a cold, transfixing glare. The beaming smile faded sickly from Serlo's round and innocent face. 'To pay good heed to stricture and obey instruction atones for all errors,' he ventured, trying to edge away whatever in his words had caused this consternation, and failing. His voice ebbed feebly into silence.

'What doctrine,' demanded Gerbert with black deliberation, 'had this man misread? What occasion had his priest had to admonish him? Are you saying that he was *ordered* to go on pilgrimage, to purge some mortal error?'

'No, no, not ordered,' said Serlo faintly. 'It was suggested to him that his soul would benefit by such a reparation.'

'Reparation for what gross offence?' pursued the canon relentlessly.

'Oh, none, none that did harm to any, no act of violence or dishonesty. It is long past,' said Serlo gallantly, digging in his heels with unaccustomed bravery to retrieve what he had launched. 'It was nine years ago, when Archbishop William of Corbeil, of blessed memory, sent out a preaching mission to many of the towns in England. As papal legate he was concerned for the wellbeing of the Church, and thought fit to use preaching canons from his own house at St. Osyth's. I was sent to attend on the reverend Father who came into our diocese, and I was with him when he preached here at the High Cross. William of Lythwood entertained us to supper afterwards, and there was much earnest talk. He was not

23

contumacious, he did but enquire and question, and in all solemnity. A courteous, hospitable man. But even in thought – for want of proper instruction...'

'What you are saying,' pronounced Gerbert menacingly, 'is that a man who was reproved for heretical views is now asking for burial within these walls.'

'Oh, I would not say heretical,' babbled Serlo in haste. 'Misguided views, perhaps, but I would not say heretical. There was no complaint ever made of him to the bishop. And you have seen that he did as he was counselled, for two years later he set out on this pilgrimage.'

'Many men undertake pilgrimages for their own pleasure,' said Gerbert grimly, 'rather than for the proper purpose. Some even for trade, like hucksters. The act is no absolution for error, it is the sincere intent that delivers.'

'We have no reason,' Abbot Radulfus pointed out drily, 'to conclude that William's intent was less than sincere. These are judgements which are out of our hands, we should have the humility to acknowledge as much.'

'Nevertheless, we have a duty under God, and cannot evade it. What proof have we that the man ever changed those suspect beliefs he held? We have not examined as to what they were, how grave, and whether they were ever repented and discarded. Because there is here in England a healthy and vigorous Church, we must not think that the peril of false belief belongs only to the past. Have you not heard that there are loose preachers abroad in France who draw the credulous after them, reviling their own priests as greedy and corrupt, and the rites of the Church as meaningless? In the south the abbot of Clairvaux is grown much concerned about such false prophets.'

'Though the abbot of Clairvaux has himself warned,' interjected Radulfus briskly, 'that the failure of the priesthood to set an example of piety and simplicity helps to turn people to these dissenting sects. The Church has a duty also to purge its own shortcomings.'

Cadfael listened, as all the brothers were listening, with pricked ears and alert eyes, hoping that this sudden squall would slacken and blow over just as nimbly. Radulfus would not allow any prelate to usurp his authority in his own chapter-house, but not even he could forbid an envoy of the archbishop to assert his rights of speech and judgement in a matter of doctrine. The very mention of Bernard of Clairvaux, the apostle of austerity, was a reminder of the rising influence of the Cistercians, to which order Archbishop Theobald was sympathetically inclined. And though Bernard might put in a word for popular criticism of the worldliness of many high churchmen, and yearn for a return to the poverty and simplicity of the Apostles, by all accounts he would have small mercy on anyone who diverged from the strictly orthodox where dogma was concerned. Radulfus might sidestep one citation of Bernard by countering wth another, but he was quick to change the subject before he risked losing the exchange.

'Here is Serlo,' he said simply, 'who remembers whatever contention the archbishop's missioner had with William. He may also recall whatever points of belief had arisen between them.'

Serlo, by the dubious look on his face, hardly knew whether to be glad of such an opportunity or sorry. He opened his mouth hesitantly, but Radulfus stopped him with a raised hand.

'Wait! It is also only fair that the one man who can truly testify to his master's mind and observance before death should be present to hear what is said of him, and answer it on his behalf. We have no right to exclude a man from the favour he has asked without a just hearing. Denis, will you go and ask the young man Elave to come back into council?'

'Very gladly,' said Brother Denis, and went out with such indignant alacrity that it was not difficult to read his mind.

Elave came back into chapter in all innocence, expecting his formal answer and in no doubt what it would be. His alert step and confident face spoke for him. He had no warning of what was to come, even when the abbot spoke up, choosing his words with careful moderation.

'Young sir, there is here some debate concerning your master's request. It has been said that before he departed on his pilgrimage he had been in some dispute with a priest sent by the archbishop to preach here in Shrewsbury, and had been reproved for certain beliefs he held, which were not altogether in accord wih Church doctrine. It is even suggested that his pilgrimage was enjoined upon him almost as penance. Do you know anything of this? It may well be that it never came to your ears at all.'

Elave's level brows, thick and russet, darker than his hair, drew together in doubt and bewilderment, but not yet disquiet.

'I knew he had given much thought to some articles of faith,

25

but no more than that. He *wanted* his pilgrimage. He was growing old but still hearty, there were others and younger could manage here in his stead. He asked me if I would go with him, and I went. There was never any dispute between him and Father Elias that I know of. Father Elias knew him for a good man.'

'The good who go astray into wrong paths do more harm than the evil, who are our open enemies,' said Canon Gerbert sharply. 'It is the enemy within who betrays the fortress.'

Now that, thought Cadfael, rings true of Church thinking. A Seljuk Turk or a Saracen can cut down Christians in battle or throw stray pilgrims into dungeons, and still be tolerated and respected, even if he's held to be already damned. But if a Christian steps a little aside in his beliefs he becomes anathema. He had seen it years ago in the east, in the admittedly beleaguered Christian churches. Hardpressed by enemies, it was on their own they turned most savagely. Here at home he had never before encountered it, but it might yet come to be as common as in Antioch or Alexandria. Not, however, if Radulfus could rein it in.

'His own priest does not seem to have regarded William as an enemy, either within or without,' said the abbot mildly. 'But Deacon Serlo here is about to tell us what he recalls of the contention, and it is only just that you should afterwards speak as to your master's mind before his death, in assurance that he is worthy to be buried here within the precinct.'

'Speak up!' said Gerbert as Serlo hesitated, dismayed and unhappy at what he had set in motion. 'And be precise! On what heads was fault found with the man's beliefs?'

'There were certain small points at issue,' Serlo said submissively, 'as I remember it. Two in particular, besides his doubts concerning the baptism of infants. He had difficulty in comprehending the Trinity...'

Who does not! thought Cadfael. If it were comprehensible, all these interpreters of the good God would be out of an occupation. And every one of those denies the interpretation set up by every other.

'He said if the first was Father, and the second Son, how could they be co-eternal and co-equal? And as to the Spirit, he could not see how it could be equal with either Father or Son if it emanated from them. Moreoover, he saw no need for a third, creation, salvation and all things being complete in Father and Son. Thus the third served only to satisfy the vision

26

of those who think in threes, as the song-makers and the soothsayers do, and all those who deal with enchantment.'

'He said that of the Church?' Gerbert's countenance was stiff and brow black.

'Not of the Church, no, that I do not believe he ever said. And the Trinity is a most high mystery, many have difficulty with it.'

'It is not for them to question or reason with inadequate minds, but to accept with unquestioning faith. Truth is set before them, they have only to believe. It is the perverse and perilous who have the arrogance to bring mere fallible reason to bear on what is ineffable. Go on! Two points, you said. What is the second?'

Serlo cast an almost apologetic glance at Radulfus, and an even more rapid and uneasy one at Elave, who all this time was staring upon him with knotted brows and thrusting jaw, not yet committed to fear or anger or any other emotion, simply waiting and listening.

'It arose out of this same matter of the Father and the Son. He said that if they were of one and the same substance, as the creed calls them consubstantial, then the entry of the Son into humankind must mean also the entry of the Father, taking to himself and making divine that which he had united with the godhead. And therefore the Father and the Son alike knew the suffering and the death and the resurrection, and as one partake in our redemption.'

'It is the Patripassian heresy!' cried Gerbert, outraged. 'Sabellius was excommunicated for it, and for his other errors. Noetus of Smyrna preached it to his ruin. This is indeed a dangerous venture. No wonder the priest warned him of the pit he was digging for his own soul.'

'Howbeit,' Radulfus reminded the assembly firmly, 'the man, it seems, listened to counsel and undertook the pilgrimage, and as to the probity of his life, nothing has been alleged against it. We are concerned, not with what he speculated upon seven years and more ago, but with his spiritual wellbeing at his death. There is but one witness here who can testify as to that. Now let us hear from his servant and companion.' He turned to look closely at Elave, whose face had set into controlled and conscious awareness, not of danger, but of deep offence. 'Speak for your master,' said Radulfus quietly, 'for you knew him to the end. What was his manner of life in all that long journey?'

27

'He was regular in observance everywhere,' said Elave, 'and made his confession where he could. There was no fault found with him in any land. In the Holy City we visited all the most sacred places, and going and returning we lodged whenever we could in abbeys and priories, and everywhere my master was accepted for a good and pious man, and paid his way honestly, and was well regarded.'

'But had he renounced his views,' demanded Gerbert, 'and recanted his heresy? Or did he still adhere secretly to his former errors?'

'Did he ever speak with you about these things?' the abbot asked, overriding the intervention.

'Very seldom, my lord, and I did not well understand such deep matters. I cannot answer for another man's mind, only for his conduct, which I knew to be virtuous.' Elave's face had set into contained and guarded calm. He did not look like a man who would fall short in understanding of deep matters, or lack the interest to consider them.

'And in his last illness,' Radulfus pursued mildly, 'he asked for a priest?'

'He did, Father, and made his confession and received absolution without question. He died with all the due rites of the Church. Wherever there was place and time along the way he made his confession, especially after he first fell ill, and we were forced to stay a whole month in the monastery at Saint Marcel before he was fit to continue the journey home. And there he often spoke with the brothers, and all these matters of faith and doubt were understood and tolerated among them. I know he spoke openly of things that troubled him, and they found no fault there with debating all manner of questions concerning holy things.'

Canon Gerbert stared cold suspicion. 'And where was this place, this Saint Marcel? And when was it you spent a month there? How recently?'

'It was in the spring of last year. We left early in the May, and made the pilgrimage from there to Saint James at Compostela with a party from Cluny, to give thanks that my master was restored to health. Or so we thought then, but he was never in real health again, and we had many halts thereafter. Saint Marcel is close by Chalons on the Saône. It is a daughter house of Cluny.'

Gerbert sniffed loudly and turned up his masterful nose at the mention of Cluny. That great house had taken seriously to

28

the pilgrim traffic and had given aid and support, protection along the roads and shelter in their houses to many hundreds not only from France, but of recent years from England, too. But for the close dependants of Archbishop Theobald it was first and foremost the mother-house of that difficult colleague and ambitious and arrogant rival, Bishop Henry of Winchester.

'There was one of the brothers died there,' said Elave, standing up sturdily for the sanctity and wisdom of Cluny, 'who had written on all these things, and taught in his young days, and he was revered beyond any other among the brothers, and had the most saintly name among them. He saw no wrong in pondering all these difficult matters by the test of reason, and neither did his abbot, who had sent him there from Cluny for his health. I heard him read once from Saint John's Gospel, and speak on what he read. It was wonderful to hear. And that was but a short time before he died.'

'It is presumption to play human reason like a false light upon divine mysteries,' warned Gerbert sourly. 'Faith is to be received, not taken apart by the wit of a mere man. Who was this brother?'

'He was called Pierre Abelard, a Breton. He died in the April, before we set out for Compostela in the May.'

The name had meant nothing to Elave beyond what he had seen and heard for himself, and kept wonderingly in his mind ever since. But it meant a great deal to Gerbert. He stiffened in his stall, flaring up half a head taller, as a candle suddenly rears pale and lofty as the wick flares.

'That man? Foolish, gullible soul, do you not know the man himself was twice charged and convicted of heresy? Long ago his writings on the Trinity were burned, and the writer imprisoned. And only three years ago at the Council of Sens he was again convicted of heretical writings, and condemned to have his works destroyed and end his life in perpetual imprisonment.'

It seemed that Abbot Radulfus, though less exclamatory, was equally well informed, if not better.

'A sentence which was very quickly revoked,' he remarked drily, 'and the author allowed to retire peacefully into Cluny at the request of the abbot.'

Unwarily Gerbert was provoked into snapping back without due thought. 'In my view no such revocation should have been granted. It was not deserved. The sentence should have stood.'

29

'It was issued by the Holy Father,' said the abbot gently, 'who cannot err.' Whether his tongue was in his cheek at that moment Cadfael could not be sure, but the tone, though soft and reverent, stung, and was meant to sting.

'So was the sentence!' Gerbert snapped back even more unwisely. 'His Holiness surely had misleading information when he withdrew it. Doubtless he made a right judgement upon such truth as was presented to him.'

Elave spoke up as if to himself, but loudly enough to carry to all ears, and with a brilliance of eye and a jut of jaw that spoke more loudly still. 'Yet by very definition a thing cannot be its opposite, therefore one judgement or the other must be error. It could as well be the former as the latter.'

Who was it claimed, Cadfael reflected, startled and pleased, that he could not understand the arguments of the philosophers? This lad had kept his ears open and his mind alert all those miles to Jerusalem and back, and learned more than he's telling. At least he's turned Gerbert purple and closed his mouth for a moment.

A moment was enough for the abbot. This dangerous line of talk was getting out of hand. He cut it short with decision.

'The Holy Father has authority both to bind and to loose, and the same infallible will that can condemn can also with equal right absolve. There is here, it seems to me, no contradiction at all. Whatever views he may have held seven years ago, William of Lythwood died on pilgrimage, confessed and shriven, in a state of grace. There is no bar to his burial within this enclave, and he shall have what he has asked of us.'

Chapter Three

S CADFAEL came through the court after dinner,
to return to his labours in the herb-garden, he
encountered Elave. The young man was just
coming down the steps from the guest-hall, in
movement and countenance bright and vehement, like a tool
honed for fine use. He was still roused and ready to be
aggressive after the rough passage of his master's body to its
desired resting-place, the bones of his face showed polished
with tension, and his prow of a nose quested beligerently on
the summer air.

'You look ready to bite,' said Cadfael, coming by design face
to face with him.

The boy looked back at him for a moment uncertain how to
respond, where even this unalarming presence was still an
unknown quantity. Then he grinned, and the sharp tension
eased.

'Not you, at any rate, Brother! If I showed my teeth, did I
not have cause?'

'Well, at least you know our abbot all the better for it. You
have what you asked. But as well keep a lock on your lips until
the other one is gone. One way to be sure of saying nothing
that can be taken amiss is to say nothing at all. Another is to
agree with whatever the prelates say. But I doubt that would
have much appeal for you.'

'It's like threading a way between archers in ambush,' said
Elave, relaxing. 'For a cloistered man, Brother, you say things

31

aside from the ordinary yourself.'

'We're none of us as ordinary as all that. What I feel, when the divines begin talking doctrine, is that God speaks all languages, and whatever is said to him or of him in any tongue will need no interpreter. And if it's devoutly meant, no apology. How is that hand of yours? No inflammation?'

Elave shifted the box he was carrying to his other arm, and showed the faded scar in his palm, still slightly puffed and pink round the healed punctures.

'Come round with me to my workshop, if you've the time to spare,' Cadfael invited, 'and let me dress that again for you. And that will be the last you need think of it.' He cast a glance at the box tucked under the young man's arm. 'But you have errands to do in the town? You'll be off to visit William's kinsfolk.'

'They'll need to know of his burying, tomorrow,' said Elave. 'They'll be here. There was always a good feeling among them all, never bad blood. It was Girard's wife who kept the house for the whole family. I must go and tell them what's arranged. But there's no haste, I daresay once I'm up there it will be for the rest of the day and into the evening.'

They fell in amicably together, side by side, out of the court and through the rose garden, rounding the thick hedge. As soon as they entered the walled garden the sun-warmed scent of the herbs rose to enfold them in a cloud of fragrance, every step along the gravel path between the beds stirring wave on wave of sweetness.

'Shame to go withindoors on such a day,' said Cadfael. 'Sit down here in the sun, I'll bring the lotion out to you.'

Elave sat down willingly on the bench by the north wall, tilting his face up to the sun, and laid his burden down beside him. Cadfael eyed it with interest, but went first to bring out the cleansing lotion, and anoint the fading wound once again.

'You'll feel no more of that now, it's clean enough. Young flesh heals well, and you've surely been through more risks crossing the world and back than you should be meeting here in Shrewsbury.' He stoppered the flask, and sat down beside his guest. 'I suppose they won't even know yet, that you're back and their kinsman dead – the family there in the town?'

'Not yet, no. There was barely time last night to get my master well bestowed, and what with the dispute in chapter this morning, I've had no chance yet to get word to them. You know them – his nephews? Girard sees to the flock and the sales, and fetches in the wool clips from the others he deals for. Jevan always managed the vellum making, even in William's day. Come to think of it, for all I know things may be changed there since we left.'

'You'll find them all living,' said Cadfael reassuringly, 'that I do know. Not that we see much of them down here in the Foregate. They come sometimes on festival days, but they have their own church at Saint Alkmund's.' He eyed the box Elave had laid down on the bench between them. 'Something William was bringing back to them? May I look? Faith, I own I'm looking already, I can't take my eyes from it. That's a wonderful piece of carving. And old, surely.'

Elave looked down at it with the critical appreciation and indifferent detachment of one to whom it meant simply an errand to be discharged, something he would be glad to hand over and be rid of. But he took it up readily and placed it in Cadfael's hands to be examined closely.

'I have to take it by way of a dowry for the girl. When he grew too ill to go on he thought of her, seeing he'd taken her into his household from the day she was born. So he gave me this to bring to Girard, to be used for her when she marries. It's a poor lookout for a girl with no dowry when it comes to getting a husband.'

'I remember there was a little girl,' said Cadfael, turning the box in his hands with admiration. It was enough to excite the artist in any man. Fashioned from some dark eastern wood, about a foot long by eight inches wide and four deep, the lid flawlessly fitted, with a small, gilded lock. The under surface was plain, polished to a lustrous darkness almost black, the upper surface and the edges of the lid beautifully and intricately carved in a tracery of vine leaves and grapes, and in the centre of the lid a lozenge containing an ivory plaque, an aureoled head, full-face, with great Byzantine eyes. It was so old that the sharp edges had been slightly smoothed and rounded by handling, but the lines of the carving were still picked out in gold.

'Fine work!' said Cadfael, handling it reverently. He balanced it in his hands, and it hung like a solid mass of wood, nothing shifting within. 'You never wondered what was in it?'

Elave looked faintly surprised, and hoisted indifferent shoulders. 'It was packed away, and I had other things to think about. I've only this past half-hour got it out of the baggage-roll. No, I never did wonder. I took it he'd saved up

33

some money for her. I'm just handing it over to Girard as I was told to do. It's the girl's, not mine.'

'You don't know where he got it?'

'Oh, yes, I know where he bought it. From a poor deacon in the market in Tripoli, just before we took ship for Cyprus and Thessalonika on our way home. There were Christian fugitives beginning to drift in then from beyond Edessa, turned out of their monasteries by mamluk raiders from Mosul. They came with next to nothing, they had to sell whatever they'd contrived to bring with them in order to live. William drove shrewd bargains among the merchants, but he dealt fairly with those poor souls. They said life was becoming hard and dangerous in those parts. The journey out we made the slow way, by land. William wanted to see the great collection of relics in Constantinople. But coming home we started by sea. There are plenty of Greek and Italian merchant ships plying as far as Thessalonika, some even all the way to Bari and Venice.'

'There was a time,' mused Cadfael, drawn back through the years, 'when I knew those seas very well. How did you fare for lodging on the way out, all those miles afoot?'

'Now and then we went a piece in company, but mostly it was we two alone. The monks of Cluny have hospices all across France and down through Italy, even close by the emperor's city they have a house for pilgrims. And as soon as you reach the Holy Land the Knights of Saint John provide shelter everywhere. It's a great thing to have done,' said Elave, looking back in awe and wonder. 'Along the way a man lives a day at a time, and looks no further ahead than the next day, and no further behind than the day just passed. Now I see it whole, and it is wonderful.'

'But not all good,' said Cadfael. 'That couldn't be, we couldn't ask it. Remember the cold and the rain and the hunger at times, and losses by thieves now and then, and a few knocks from those who prey on travellers – oh, never tell me you met none! And the weariness, and the times when William fell ill, the bad food, the sour water, the stones of the road. You've met all that. Every man who travels that far across the world has met it all.'

'I do remember all that,' said Elave sturdily, 'but it is still wonderful.'

'Good! So it should be,' said Cadfael, sighing. 'Lad, I should be glad to sit and talk with you about every step of the way, when your time's free. You go and deliver your box to Master

Girard, and that's your duty done. And what will you do now? Go back to work for them as before?'

'No, not that. It was for William I worked. They have their own clerk, I wouldn't wish to displace him, and they don't need two. Besides, I want more, and different. I'll take time to look about me. I've come back with more skills than when I went, I'd like to use them.' He rose, and tucked the carved box securely under his arm.

'I've forgotten,' said Cadfael, following the gesture thoughtfully, 'if indeed I ever knew – how did he come by the child? He had none of his own, and as far as I know, Girard has none, and the other brother has never married. Where did the girl come from? Some foundling he took in?'

'You could say so. They had a serving maid, a simple soul, who fell foul of a small huckster at the fair one year, and brought forth a daughter. William gave houseroom to the pair of them, and Margaret cared for the baby like her own child, and when the mother died they simply kept the girl. A pretty little thing she was. She had more wit than her mother. It was William named her Fortunata, for he said she'd come into the world with nothing, not even a father, and still found herself a home and a family, and so she'd still fall on her feet lifelong. She was eleven, rising twelve,' said Elave, 'when we set out, and grown into a skinny, awkward little thing all teeth and elbows. They say the prettiest pups make the ugliest dogs. She'll need a decent dowry to make up for her gawky looks.'

He stretched his long person, hoisted his box more firmly under his arm, dipped his fair head in a small, friendly reverence, and was off along the path, his haste to discharge all the final duties with which he had been entrusted tempered somewhat by a sense of the seven years since he had seen William's family, and the inevitable estrangement time must have brought about, until now scarcely realised. What had once been familiar was now alien, and it would take time to edge his way back to it. Cadfael watched him disappear round the corner of the box hedge, torn between sympathy and envy.

The house of Girard of Lythwood, like so many of the merchant burgages of Shrewsbury, was in the shape of an L, the short base directly on the street, and pierced by an arched entry leading through to the yard and garden behind. The base of the L was of only one storey, and provided the shop where Jevan, the younger brother, stored and sold his finished leaves

35

and gatherings of vellum and the cured skins from which they were folded and cut to order. The upright of the L showed its gable end to the street, and consisted of a low undercroft and the living floor above, with a loft in the steep roof that provided extra sleeping quarters. The entire burgage was not large, space being valuable within so enclosed a town, in its tight noose of river. Outside the loop, in the suburbs of Frankwell on one side and the Foregate on the other, there was room to expand, but within the wall every inch of ground had to be used to the best advantage.

Elave halted before the house, and stood a moment to take in the strangeness of what he felt, a sudden warmth of homecoming, an almost panic reluctance to go in and declare himself, a mute wonder at the smallness of the house that had been his home for a number of years. In the overwhelming basilicas of Constantinople, as in the profound isolation of deserts, a man grows used to immensity.

He went in slowly through the narrow entry and into the yard. On his right the stables, the byre for the cow, the store shed and low coop for the chickens were just as he remembered them, and on his left the house door stood wide open, as it always had on such summer days. A woman was just coming up from the garden that stretched away beyond the house, with a basket of clothes in her arms, crisp washing just gathered from the hedge. She observed the stranger entering, and quickened her step to meet him.

'Goodday, sir! If you're wanting my husband...' She halted there, astonished, recognising but not believing at first what she saw. Between eighteen and twenty-five a young man does not change so much as to be unrecognisable to his own family, however he may have filled out and matured during that time. It was simply that she had had no warning, no word to indicate that he was within five hundred miles of her.

'Mistress Margaret,' said Elave, 'you've not forgotten me?'

The voice completed what his face had begun. She flushed bright with acceptance and evident pleasure. 'Dear, now, and it *is* you! Just for a moment there you had me struck out of my wits, thinking I was seeing visions, and you still half the world away, in some outlandish place. Well, now, and here you are safe and sound, after all that journeying. Glad I am to see you again, boy, and so will Girard and Jevan be. Who'd have thought you'd spring out of nowhere like this, all in a moment, and just in time for Saint Winifred's festival. Come within,

36

come, let me put this laundry down and get you a draught to drink, and tell me how you've fared all this long time.'

She freed a hand to take him warmly by the arm and usher him within, to a bench by the unshuttered window of the hall, with such voluble goodwill that his silence passed unnoticed. She was a neat, brown-haired, bustling woman in her middle forties, healthy and hardworking and a good and discreet neighbour, and her shining housekeeping reflected her own strong-willed brightness.

'Girard's away making up the wool clip, he'll be a day or so yet. His face will be a sight to see when he comes in and sees Uncle William sitting here at the table like in the old days. Where is he? Is he following you up now, or had he business below at the abbey?'

Elave drew breath and said what had to be said. 'He'll not be coming, Mistress.'

'Not coming?' she said, astonished, turning sharply in the doorway of her larder.

'Sorry I am to have no better word to bring you. Master William died in France, before we could embark for home. But I've brought him home, as I promised him I would. He lies at the abbey now, and tomorrow he's to be buried there, in the cemetery among the patrons of the house.'

She stood motionless, staring at him with pitcher and cup forgotten in her hands, and for a long moment she was silent.

'It was what he wanted,' said Elave. 'He did what he set out to do, and he has what he wanted.'

'Not everyone can say as much,' said Margaret slowly. 'So Uncle William's gone! Business below at the abbey, did I say? And so he has, but not as I supposed. And you left to bring him over the sea alone! And Girard away, and who's to tell where at this moment? It will grieve him if he's not here to pay the last dues to a good man.' She shook herself, and stirred out of her brief stillness, practical always. 'Well, now, no fault of yours, you did well by him, and have no need to look back. Sit you down and be easy. You're home, at least, done your wanderings for the time being, you can do with a rest.'

She brought him ale, and sat down beside him, considering without distress all that was now needful. A competent woman, she would have everything ordered and seemly whether her husband returned in time or not.

'He was nearing eighty years old,' she said, 'by my reckoning. He had a good life, and was a good kinsman and a

37

good neighbour, and he ended doing a blessed thing, and one that he wanted with all his heart, once that old preacher from St. Osyth's put the thought in his mind. There,' said Margaret, shaking her head with a sigh, 'here I am harking back like a fool, and I never meant to. Time's short! I should have thought the abbot could have sent us word of the need as soon as you came in at the gatehouse.'

'He knew nothing of it until this morning at chapter. He's been here only four years, and we've been gone seven. But everything is in hand now.'

'Maybe it is, down there, but I must see to it that all's ready up here, for there'll be all the neighbours in to join us, and I hope you'll come back with us, after the funeral. Conan's here, that's lucky, I'll send him west to see if he can find Girard in time, though there's no knowing just where he'll be. There are six flocks he has to deal with out there. Sit you here quietly, while I go and bring Jevan from the shop, and Aldwin from his books, and you can tell us all how it was with the old man. Fortunata's off in the town marketing, but she'll surely be back soon.'

She was off on the instant, bustling out to fetch Jevan out of his shop, and Elave was left breathless and mute with her ready volubility, having had no chance as yet to mention the charge he had still to deliver. In a few minutes she was back with the vellum-maker, the clerk, and the shepherd Conan hard on her heels, the entire core of the household but for the absent fosterchild. All these Elave knew well from his former service, and only one was much changed. Conan had been a youngster of twenty when last seen, slender and willowy, now he had broadened out and put on flesh and muscle, swelling into gross good looks, ruddy and strong with outdoor living. Aldwin had entered the household in Girard's service, and stepped into Elave's shoes when William took his own boy with him on pilgrimage. A man of past forty at that time, barely literate but quick with numbers as a gift of nature, Aldwin looked much the same now at nearing fifty, but that his hair had rather more grey in it, and was thinning on the crown. He had had to work hard to earn his place and hold it, and his long face had set into defensive lines of effort and anxiety. Elave had got his letters early, from a priest who had seen his small parishioner's promise and taken pains to bring it to fruit, and the boy had shamelessly enjoyed his superiority when he had worked in Aldwin's company. He remembered now how he had happily passed on his own skills to the much older man, not out of any genuine wish to help him, but rather to impress and dazzle both Aldwin and the observers with his own cleverness. He was older and wiser now, he had discovered how great was the world and how small his own person. He was glad that Aldwin should have this secure place, this sound roof over his head, and no one now to threaten his tenure.

Jevan of Lythwood was just past forty, seven years younger than his brother, tall, erect and lightly built, with a cleanshaven, scholarly face. He had not been formally educated in boyhood, but by reason of taking early to the craft of vellum-making he had come to the notice of lettered men who bought from him, monastics, clerks, even a few among the lords of local manors who had some learning, and being of very quick and eager intelligence he had set himself to learn from them, aroused their interest to help him forward, and turned himself into a scholar, the only person in this house who could read Latin, or more than a few words of English. It was good for business that the seller of parchments should measure up to the quality of his work, and understand the uses the cultured world made of it.

All these came hurrying in on Margaret's heels to gather familiarly around the table, and welcome back the traveller and his news. The loss of William, old, fulfilled, and delivered from this world in a state of grace and to the resting-place he had desired, was not a tragedy, but the completion of an altogether satisfactory life, the more easily and readily accepted because he had been gone from this household for seven years, and the gap he had left had closed gently, and had not now been torn open again by his recovered presence. Elave told what he could of the journey home, of the recurring bouts of illness, and the death, a gentle death in a clean bed and with a soul confessed and shriven, at Valognes, not far from the port where he should have embarked for home.

'And his funeral is to be tomorrow,' said Jevan. 'At what hour?'

'After the Mass at ten. The abbot is to take the office himself. He stood by my master's claim for admittance,' said Elave by way of explanation, 'against some visiting canon there from Canterbury. One of the bishop's deacons is travelling with him, and let out like a fool some old business of falling out with a travelling preacher, years ago, and this Gerbert would have every word dragged out again, and wanted to call William

39

a heretic and refuse him entry, but the abbot set his foot firmly on that and let him in. I came close,' admitted Elave, roused to recollection, 'to sticking my own neck in a heretic's collar, arguing with the man. And he's one who doesn't take kindly to being opposed. He could hardly turn on the abbot in his own house, but I doubt he feels much love for me. I'd better keep my head low till he moves on.'

'You did quite right,' said Margaret warmly, 'to stand by your master. I hope it's done you no harm.'

'Oh, surely not! It's all past now. You'll be at the Mass tomorrow?'

'Every man of us,' said Jevan, 'and the women, too. And Girard, if we can find him in time, but he's on the move, and may be near the border by now. He meant to come back for Saint Winifred's feast, but there's always the chance of delays among the border flocks.'

Elave had left the wooden box lying on the bench under the window. He rose to fetch it to the table. All eyes settled upon it with interest.

'This I was ordered to deliver into Master Girard's hands. Master William sent it to him to be held in trust for Fortunata until her marriage. It's her dowry. When he was so ill he thought of her, and said she must have a dowry. And this is what he sent.'

Jevan was the first to reach out to touch and handle it, fascinated by the beauty of the carving.

'This is rare work. Somewhere in the east he found this?' He took it up, surprised at the weight. 'It makes a handsome treasury. What's within it?'

'That I don't know. It was near his death when he gave it to me and told me what he wanted. Nothing more, and I never questioned him. I had enough to do, then and afterwards.'

'So you did,' said Margaret, 'and you did it very well, and we owe you thanks, for he was our kin, and a good man, and I'm glad he had so good a lad to see him safely all that way and back again home.' She took up the box from the table, where Jevan had laid it down, and was fingering the gilded carving with evident admiration. 'Well, if it was sent to Girard, I'll keep it aside until Girard comes home. This is the business of the man of the house.'

'Even the key,' said Jevan, 'is a piece of art. So our Fortunata lives up to her name, as Uncle William always said she would. And the lucky girl still out marketing, and doesn't yet know of her fortune!'

40

Margaret opened the tall press in a corner of the room, and laid both box and key on an upper shelf within. 'There it stays until my husband comes home, and he'll take good care of it until my girl shows a fancy to get wed, and maybe sets eyes on the lad she wants for husband.'

All eyes had followed William's gift to its hiding-place. Aldwin said sourly: 'There'll be aplenty will fancy her for wife, if they get wind she has goods to bring with her. She'll have need of your good counsel, Mistress.'

Conan had said nothing at all. He had never been a talker. His eyes followed the box until the door of the press closed on it, but all he had to say throughout was said at the last, when Elave rose to take his leave. The shepherd rose with him.

'I'll be off, then, and take the pony, and see if I can find where the master is. But whether or not, I'll be back by nightfall.'

They were all dispersing to their various occupations when Margaret drew Elave back by the sleeve, delaying him until the rest had gone.

'You'll understand, I'm sure, how it is,' she said confidingly. 'I wouldn't say anything but just to you, Elave. You were always a good lad with the accounts, and worked hard, and to tell the honest truth, Aldwin is no match for you, though he does his best, and can manage well enough all that's required of him. But he's getting older, and has no home or folks of his own, and what would he do if we parted with him now? You're young, there's many a merchant would be glad to hire you, with your knowledge of the world. You won't take it amiss...'

Elave had caught her drift long before this, and broke in hastily to reassure her. 'No, no, never think of it! I never expected to have my old place back. I wouldn't for the world put Aldwin's nose out of joint. I'm glad he should be secure the rest of his life. Never trouble for me, I shall look about me and find work to do. And as for bearing any grudge that I'm not asked back, I never so much as thought of it. Nothing but good have I had from this house, and I shan't forget it. No, Aldwin can go on with his labours with all my goodwill.'

'That's like the lad I remember!' she said with hearty relief. 'I knew you'd take it as it's meant. I hope you may get good service with some travelling merchant, one that trades oversea, that would suit you, after all you've seen and done. But you will come up with us tomorrow after Uncle William's burial, and take meat with us?'

He promised readily, glad to have their relationship established and understood. To tell the truth, he thought he might have felt confined and restricted here now, dealing with the buying of stock and paying of wages, the weighing and marketing of wool, and the small profits and expenses of a good but limited business. He was not yet sure what he did want, he could afford to spend a little while looking round before committing himself. Going out at the hall door he came shoulder to shoulder with Conan, on his way out to the stable, and dropped back to let Margaret's messenger go first.

A young woman with a basket on her arm had just emerged from the narrow entry that led to the street, and was crossing the yard towards them. She was not over-tall, but looked tall by reason of her erect bearing and long, free step, light and springy from the ground like the gait of a mettlesome colt. Her plain grey gown swayed with the lissom movement of a trim body, and the well-poised head on her long neck was crowned with a great coiled braid of dark hair lit with shadowy gleams of red. Halfway across the yard towards them she halted abruptly, gazing open-mouthed and wide-eyed, and suddenly she laughed aloud, a joyous, silver sound of pleasurable amazement.

'You!' she said, in a soft, delighted cry. 'Is it truth? I am not dreaming?'

She stopped them both on the instant, brought up short by the warmth of her greeting, Elave gaping like an idiot at this unknown girl who yet appeared not only to recognise him, but to take pleasure in the recognition, Conan fallen warily silent beside him, his face expressionless, his eyes roving from one face to the other, narrowed and intent.

'Do you not know me?' cried the girl's clear bell of a voice, through the bubbling spring of her laughter.

Fool that he was, who else could she be, coming in thus bare-headed from the shops of the town? But it was true, he would not have known her. The thin little pointed face had filled out into a smooth ivory oval, the teeth that had looked far too many and too large for her mouth shone now even and white between dark-rose lips that smiled at his astonishment and confusion. All the sharp little bones had rounded into grace. The long hair that had hung in elflocks round scrawny childish shoulders looked like a crown, thus braided and coiled upon her head, and the greenish hazel eyes whose stare he had found disconcerting seven years ago now sparkled and glowed with pleasure at seeing him again, a very arresting flattery.

42

'I know you now,' he said, fumbling for words. 'But you're changed!'

'You are not,' she said. 'Browner, perhaps, and your hair's even fairer than it used to be, but I'd have known you anywhere. And you turn up like this without a word of warning, and they were letting you go without waiting for me?'

'I'm coming again tomorrow,' he said, and hesitated to attempt the ·explanation, here in the yard, with Conan still lingering on the borders of their meeting. 'Mistress Margaret will tell you about it. I had messages to bring...'

'If you knew' said Fortunata, 'how often and how long we've talked of you both, and wondered how you were faring in those far places. It's not every day we have kinsfolk setting out on such an adventure, do you think we never gave you a thought?'

Hardly once in all those years had it entered his mind to wonder about any of those left behind. Closest to him in this house, and alone significant, had been William, and with William he had gone, blithely, without a thought for anyone left to continue life here, least of all a leggy little girl of eleven with a spotty skin and a disconcerting stare.

'I doubt,' he said, abashed, 'that I ever deserved you should.'

'What has desert to do with it?' she said. 'And you were leaving now until tomorrow? No, that you can't! Come back with me into the house, if only for an hour. Why must I wait until tomorrow to get used to seeing you again?'

She had him by the hand, turning him back towards the open door, and though he knew it was no more than the open and gallant friendliness of one who had known him from her childhood, and wished him well in absence as she wished well to all men of goodwill – nothing more than that, not yet! – he went with her like a bidden child, silenced and charmed. He would have gone wherever she led him. He had that to tell her that would cloud her brightness for a while, and afterwards no rights in her or in this house, no reason to believe she would ever be more to him than she was now, or he to her. But he went with her, and the warm dimness of the hall received them.

Conan looked after them for a long moment, before he went on towards the stable, his thick brows drawn together, and his wits very busy in his head.

Chapter Four

T WAS FULLY dark when Conan came home again, and he came alone.

'I went as far as Forton, but he'd gone on to Nesse early in the day, likely he'd have finished there and moved on before night. I thought it best to come back. He'll not be home tomorrow, not until too late to see old William to his grave, not knowing the need.'

'He'll be sorry to let the old man go without him,' said Margaret, shaking her head, 'but there's nothing to be done about it now. Well, we'll have to manage everything properly on his behalf. I suppose it would have been a pity to fetch him back so far and lose two days or more in the middle of the shearing time. Perhaps it's just as well he was out of reach.'

'Uncle William will sleep just as well,' said Jevan, unperturbed. 'He had an eye to business in his day, he wouldn't favour waste of time, or risk of another dealer picking up one of his customers while his back was turned. Never fret, we'll make a good family showing tomorrow. And if you want to be up early to prepare your table, Meg, you'd best be off to bed and get your rest.'

'Yes,' she said, sighing, and braced her hands on the table to rise. 'Never mind, Conan, you did what you could. There's meat and bread and ale in the kitchen for you, as soon as you've stabled the pony. Goodnight to you both! Jevan, you'll put out the lamp and see the door bolted?'

'I will. When did you know me to forget? Goodnight, Meg!'

The master bedchamber was the only one on this main floor. Fortunata had a small room above, closed off from the larger part of the loft where the menservants had their beds, and Jevan slept in a small chamber over the entry from the street into the yard, where he kept his choicest wares and his chest of books.

Margaret's door closed behind her. Conan had turned to go out to the kitchen, but in the doorway he looked back, and asked: 'Did he stay long? The young fellow? He was for going, the same time I left, but we met with Fortunata in the yard, and he turned back with her.'

Jevan looked up in tolerant surprise. 'He stayed and ate with us. He's bidden back with us tomorrow, too. Our girl seemed pleased to see him.' His grave, long face, very solemn in repose, was nevertheless lit by a pair of glittering black eyes that missed very little, and seemed to be seeing too far into Conan at this moment for Conan's comfort, and finding what they saw mildly amusing. 'Nothing to fret you,' said Jevan. 'He's no shepherd, to put a spoke in your wheel. Go and get your supper, and let Aldwin do the fretting, if there's any to be done.'

It was a thought which had not been in Conan's mind until that moment, but it had its validity, just as surely as the other possibility which had really been preoccupying him. He went off to the kitchen with the two considerations churning in his brain, to find the meal left for him, and Aldwin sitting morosely at the trestle table with a half empty mug of ale.

'I never thought,' said Conan, spreading his elbows on the other side of the table, 'wc should ever see that young spark again. All those perils by land and sea that we hear about, cutthroats and robbers by land, storm and shipwreck and pirates on the sea, and he has to wriggle his way between the lot of them and come safe home. More than his master did!'

'Did you find Girard?' asked Aldwin.

'No, he's too far west. There was no time to go farther after him, they'll have to bury the old man without him. Small grief to me,' said Conan candidly, 'if it was Elave we were burying.'

'He'll be off again,' Aldwin said, strenuously hoping so. 'He'll be too big for us now, he won't stay.'

Conan gave vent to a laugh that held no amusement. 'Go, will he? He was for going this afternoon until he set eyes on Fortunata. He came back fast enough when she took him by the hand and bade him in again. And by what I saw of the

45

looks between them, she'll have no eyes for another man while he's around.'

Aldwin gave him a wary and disbelieving look. 'Are you taking a fancy to get the girl for yourself? I never saw sign of it before.'

'I like her well enough, always have. But for all they treat her like a daughter, she's none of their kind, just a foundling taken in for pity. And when it's money, it sticks close in the blood, and mostly to the men, and Dame Margaret has nephews if Girard has none on his side. Like or not like, a man has to think of his prospects.'

'And now you think better of the girl because she has a dowry from old William,' Aldwin guessed shrewdly, 'and want the other fellow out of sight and mind. For all he brought her the dowry! And how do you know but what's in it maybe worth nothing to boast of?'

'In a fine carved casket like that? You saw how it was ornamented, all tendrils and ivory.'

'A box is a box. It's what it holds that counts.'

'No man would put rubbish in a box like that. But little value or great, it's worth the wager. For I do like the girl, and I think it only good sense and no shame,' vowed Conan roundly, 'to like her the better for having possessions. And you'd do well,' he added seriously, 'to think on your own case if that youngster comes to Fortunata's lure and stays here, where he was taught his clerking.'

He was giving words to what had been eating away at Aldwin's always tenuous peace of mind ever since Elave had showed his face. But he made one feeble effort to stand it off. 'I've seen no sign he'd be wanted back here.'

'For one not wanted he was made strangely welcome, then,' retorted Conan. 'And didn't I just say something to Jevan, that made him answer how *I* had nothing to fret about, seeing Elave was no shepherd, to threaten me. Let Aldwin do the fretting, says he, if there's any to be done.'

Aldwin had been doing the fretting all the evening, and it was made manifest by the tight clenching of his hands, white at the knuckle, and the sour set of his mouth, as though it were full of gall. He sat mute, seething in his fears and suspicions, and this light pronouncement of Jevan's, all the confirmation they needed.

'Why did he have to come safe out of a mad journey that's killed its thousands before now?' wondered Conan, brooding.

'I wish the man no great harm, God knows, but I wish him elsewhere. I'd wish him well, if only he'd make off somewhere else to enjoy it. But he'd be a fool not to see that he can do very well for himself here. I can't see him taking to his heels.'

'Not,' agreed Aldwin malevolently, 'unless the hounds were snapping at them.'

Aldwin sat for some while after Conan had gone off to his bed. By the time he rose from the table the hall would certainly be in darkness, the outer door barred, and Jevan already in his own chamber. Aldwin lit an end of candle from the last flicker of the saucer lamp, to light him through the hall to the wooden stairway to the loft, before he blew out the dwindling flame.

In the hall it was silent and still, no movement but the very slight creak of a shutter in the night breeze. Aldwin's candle made a minute point of light in the darkness, enough to show him his way the width of a familiar room. He was halfway to the foot of the stair when he halted, stood hesitating for a moment, listening to the reassuring silence, and then turned and made straight for the corner press.

The key was always in the lock, but seldom turned. Such valuables as the house contained were kept in the coffer in Girard's bedchamber. Aldwin carefully opened the long door, set his candle to stand steady on a shelf at breast-level, and reached up to the higher shelf where Margaret had placed Fortunata's box. Even when he had it set down beside his light he wavered. How if the key turned creakingly instead of silently, or would not yield at all? He could not have said what impelled him to meddle, but curiosity was strong and constant in him, as if he had to know the ins and outs of everything in the household, in case some overlooked detail might be held in store to be used against him. He turned the little key, and it revolved sweetly and silently, well made like the lock it operated and the box it adorned and guarded. With his left hand he raised the lid, and with his right lifted the candle to cast its light directly within.

'What are you doing there?' demanded Jevan's voice, sharp and irritable from the top of the stairway.

Aldwin started violently, shaking drops of hot wax on to his hand. He had the lid closed and the key turned in an instant, and thrust the box back on to its upper shelf in panic haste. The open door of the press screened what he was about. From where Jevan came surging down the first few treads of the stairs, a

47

moving shadow among shadows, he would see the light, though not its source, a segment of the open cupboard, and Aldwin's body in sharp silhouette, but could not have seen what his hands were up to, apart, perhaps, from that movement of reaching up to replace the violated treasure. Aldwin clawed along the shelf and turned with the candle in one hand, and the small knife he had just palmed from his own belt in the other.

'I left my penknife here yesterday, when I cut a new peg to fasten the handle of the small bucket. I shall need it in the morning.'

Jevan had come the rest of the way down the staircase, and advanced upon him in resigned irritation, brushing him aside to close the door of the press.

'Take it, then, and get to bed, and give over disturbing the household at this hour.'

Aldwin departed with what was for him unusual alacrity and docility, only too pleased to have come so well out of what might have been an awkward encounter. He did not so much as look round, but carried his guttering candle-end up the stairs and into the loft with a shaking hand. But behind him he heard the small, grating sound of a large key turning, and knew that Jevan had locked the press. His clerk's furtive foragings might be tolerated and passed over as annoying but harmless, but they were not to be encouraged. Aldwin had best walk warily with Jevan for a while, until the incident was forgotten.

The vexing thing was that it had all been for nothing. He had never had time to examine what was in the box, but had had to close the lid hastily in the same moment as opening it, with no time to get a glimpse within. He was not going to try that again. The contents of Fortunata's box would have to remain a secret until Girard came home.

On the twenty-first day of June, after mid-morning Mass, William of Lythwood was buried in a modest corner of the graveyard east of the abbey church, where good patrons of the house found a final resting-place. So he had what he wanted, and slept content.

Among those attending, Brother Cadfael could discern certain currents of discontent. He knew the clerk Aldwin much as he had known Elave in his day, as an occasional messenger on behalf of his master, and to tell truth, had never yet seen him looking content, but his bearing on this day seemed more abstracted and morose than usual, and he and the shepherd had their heads together in a conspiratorial manner, and their eyes narrowed and sharp upon the returned pilgrim in a manner which suggested that he was by no means welcome to them, however amiably the rest of the household behaved to him. And the young man himself seemed preoccupied with his own thoughts, and for all his concentration upon the office, his eyes strayed several times towards the young woman who stood modestly a pace behind Dame Margaret, earnestly attentive and very solemn beside the grave of the man who had given her a home and a name. And a dowry!

She was well worth looking at. Possibly Elave was debating reconsidering his determination to look about him for something more and better than could be found in his old employment. The skinny little thing all teeth and elbows had grown into a very attractive woman. One, however, who showed no sign at this moment of finding the young man as disturbing as he obviously found her. She had devoted herself wholly to her benefactor's funeral rites, and had no attention to spare for anything else.

Before the company dispersed there were civilities to be exchanged, condolences to be dispensed by the clerics and gracefully received by the family. In the sunlit court the company sorted itself, for the decent while required, into little groups, kind with kind, Abbot Radulfus and Prior Robert paying due attentions to Margaret and Jevan of Lythwood before withdrawing, Brother Jerome, as the prior's chaplain, making it his business to spend some minutes with the lesser members of the bereaved household. A few words had to be said to the girl, before he moved on to the menservants. The pious platitudes he first offered to Conan and Aldwin showed signs of developing into something much more voluble and interesting, and at the same time more confidential, for now there were three heads together instead of two, and still the occasional narrowed glance darted in Elave's direction.

Well, the young man had behaved impeccably throughout, and since the confrontation with Canon Gerbert had kept a guard on his tongue. Small bait for Brother Jerome there, though the very hint of unorthodoxy, especially when frowned upon by so eminent a prelate, was enough to cause Jerome's little nose to sniff the air like a meagre hound on a scent. The canon himself had not chosen to grace William's obsequies with his presence, but he would probably receive a full account

49

from Prior Robert, who also knew how to value the opportunity to cultivate a close confidant and agent of the archbishop.

Howbeit, this minor matter, which had briefly threatened to blaze up into a dangerous heat, must surely be over now. William had his wish, Elave had done his loyal duty in securing it for him, and Radulfus had maintained the petitioner's right. And once tomorrow's festivities were over, Gerbert would soon be on his way, and without his exalted rigidity, almost certainly sincere, and probably excited by recent embassages to France and Rome, there would be an end here in Shrewsbury of these arid measurings and probings of every word a man spoke.

Cadfael watched the household of William of Lythwood muster its funeral guests and sally forth from the gatehouse towards the town, and went off to dinner in the refectory with the easy mind of a man who believes himself to have seen an important matter satisfactorily settled.

William's wake was well supplied with ale, wine and mead, and went the way of most wakes, from dignified solemnity and pious rememberance to sentimental and increasingly elaborated reminiscence, while discreet voices grew louder and anecdotes borrowed as much from imagination as from memory. And since Elave had been his companion for seven years while he had been out of sight and often out of mind of these old neighbours of his, the young man found himself being plied with the best ale in the house, in exchange for the stories he had to tell of the long journey and the wonders seen along the way, and of William's dignified farewell to the world.

If he had not drunk considerably more than he was accustomed to, he might not have given direct and open answers to oblique and insinuating questions. On the other hand, in view of his habitual and belligerent honesty, and the fact that he had no reason to suppose he had need of caution in this company, it is at least equally probable that he would.

It did not begin until all the visitors were leaving, or already gone, and Jevan was out in the street taking slow and pleasurable leave of the last of them, and being a comfortable, neighbourly time about it. Margaret was in the kitchen with Fortunata, clearing away the remains of the feast and supervising the washing of the pots that had provided it. Elave was left sitting at the table in the hall with Conan and Aldwin,

50

and when most of the work in the kitchen was done, Fortunata came in quietly and sat down with them.

They were talking of the next day's festival. It was only seemly that a funeral should be fittingly observed and tidied away before the day of Saint Winifred's translation, so that everything on the morrow could be festive and auspicious, like the unclouded weather they hoped for. From the efficacy of the relics of saints and the validity of their miracles it was no long way to the matter of William. It was, after all, William's day, and fitting that they should be remembering him well into the dusk.

'According to one of the brothers down there,' said Aldwin earnestly, 'the little anxious grey fellow that runs so busy about the prior, it was a question whether the old man would be let in at all. Somebody there was for digging up that old scuffle he had with the missioner, to deny him a place.'

'It's a grave matter to disagree with the Church,' agreed Conan, shaking his head. 'It's not for us to know better than the priests, not where faith's concerned. Listen and say Amen, that's my advice. Did ever William talk to you about such things, Elave? You travelled a long way and a good many years with him, did he try to take you along with him down that road, too?'

'He never made any secret of what he thought,' said Elave. 'He'd argue his point, and with good sense, too, even to priests, but there was none of them found any great fault with him for thinking about such things. What are wits for unless a man uses them?'

'That's presumption,' said Aldwin, 'in simple folk like us, who haven't the learning or the calling of the churchmen. As the king and the sheriff have power over us in their field, so has the priest in his. It's not for us to meddle with matters beyond us. Conan's right, listen and say Amen!'

'How can you say Amen to damning a newborn child to hell because the little thing died before it could be baptised?' Elave asked reasonably. 'It was one of the things that bothered him. He used to argue not even the worst of men could throw a child into the fire, so how could the good God? It's against his nature.'

'And you,' said Aldwin, staring curiosity and concern, 'did you agree with him? Do you say so, too?'

'Yes, I do say so. I can't believe the reason they give us, that babes are born into the world already rotten with sin. How can

51

that be true? A creature new and helpless, barely into this world, how can it ever have done wrong?'

'They say,' ventured Conan cautiously, 'even babes unborn are rotten with the sin of Adam, and fallen with him.'

'And I say that it's only his own deeds, bad and good, that a man will have to answer for in the judgement, and that's what will save or damn him. Though it's not often I've known a man so bad as to make me believe in damnation,' said Elave, still absorbed into his own reasoning, and intent only on expressing himself clearly and simply, without suspicion of hostility or danger. 'There was a father of the Church, once, as I heard tell, in Alexandria, who held that in the end everyone would find salvation. Even the fallen angels would return to their fealty, even the devil would repent and make his way back to God.'

He felt the chill and the shiver that went through his audience, but thought no more of it than that his travelled wisdom, small as it still was, had carried him out of the reach of their parochial innocence. Even Fortunata, listening silently to the talk of the menfolk, had stiffened and opened her eyes wide and round at such an utterance, startled and perhaps shocked. She said nothing in this company, but she followed every word that was spoken, and the colour ebbed and flowed in her cheeks as she glanced attentively from face to face.

'That's blasphemous!' said Aldwin in an awed whisper. 'The Church tells us there's no salvation but by grace, not by works. A man can do nothing to save himself, being born sinful.'

'I don't believe that,' said Elave stubbornly. 'Would the good God have made a creature so imperfect that he can have no free will of his own to choose between right and wrong? We can make our own way towards salvation, or down into the muck, and at the last we must every one stand by his own acts in the judgement. If we are men we ought to make our own way towards grace, not sit on our hams and wait for it to lift us up.'

'No, no, we're taught differently,' insisted Conan doggedly. 'Men are fallen by the first fall, and incline towards evil. They can never do good but by the grace of God.'

'And I say they *can* and do! A man *can* choose to avoid sin and do justly, of his own will, and his own will *is* the gift of God, and meant to be used. Why should a man get credit for leaving it all to God?' said Elave, roused but reasonable. 'We think about what we're doing daily with our hands, to earn a

52

living. What fools we should be not to give a thought to what we're doing with our souls, to earn an eternal life. *Earn* it,' said Elave with emphasis, 'not wait to be given it unearned.'

'It's against the Church fathers,' objected Aldwin just as strongly. 'Our priest here preached a sermon once about Saint Augustine, how he wrote that the number of the elect is fixed and not to be changed, and all the rest are lost and damned, so how can their free will and their own acts help them? Only God's grace can save, everything else is vain and sinful.'

'I don't believe it,' said Elave loudly and firmly. 'Or why should we even try to deal justly? These very priests urge us to do right, and demand of us confession and penance if we fall short. Why, if the roll is already made up? Where is the sense of it? No, I do not believe it!'

Aldwin was looking at him in awed solemnity. 'You do not believe even Saint Augustine?'

'If he wrote that, no, I do not believe him.'

There was a sudden heavy silence, as though this blunt statement had knocked both his interrogators out of words. Aldwin, looking sidewise with narrowed and solemn eyes, drew furtively along the bench, removing even his sleeve from compromising contact with so perilous a neighbour.

'Well,' said Conan at length, too cheerfully and too loudly, shifting briskly on his side of the table as though time had suddenly nudged him in the ribs, 'I suppose we'd best be stirring, or we'll none of us be up in time to get the work done tomorrow before Mass. Straight from a wake to a wedding, as the saying goes! Let's hope the weather still holds.' And he rose, thrusting back his end of the bench, and stood stretching his thick, long limbs.

'It will,' said Aldwin confidently, recovering from his wary stillness with a great intake of breath. 'The saint had the sun shine on her procession when they brought her here from Saint Giles, while it rained all around. She won't fail us tomorrow.' And he, too, rose, with every appearance of relief. Plainly the convivial evening was over, and two, at least, were glad of it.

Elave sat still until they were gone, with loud and over-amiable goodnights, about their last tasks before bed. The house had fallen silent. Margaret was sitting in the kitchen, going over the day's events for flaws and compensations with the neighbour who came in to help her on such special occasions. Fortunata had not moved or spoken. Elave turned to face her, doubtfully eyeing her stillness, and the intent gravity of her face. Silence and solemnity seemed alien in her, and perhaps really were, but when they took possession of her they were entire and impressive.

'You are so quiet,' said Elave doubtfully. 'Have I offended you in anything I've said? I know I've talked too much, and too presumptuously.'

'No,' she said, her voice measured and low, 'nothing has offended me. I never thought about such things before, that's all. I was too young, when you went away, for William ever to talk so to me. He was very good to me, and I'm glad you spoke up boldly for him. So would I have done.'

But she had no more to say, not then. Whatever she was thinking now about such things she was not yet ready to say, and perhaps by tomorrow she would have abandoned the consideration of what was difficult even for the world's philosophers and theologians, and would come down with Margaret and Jevan to Saint Winifred's festival content to enjoy the music and excitement and worship without questioning, to listen and say Amen.

She went out with him across the yard and through the entry into the street when he left, and gave him her hand at parting, still in a silence that was composed and withdrawn.

'I shall see you at church tomorrow?' said Elave, belatedly afraid that he had indeed alienated her, for she confronted him with so wide and thoughtful a stare of her unwavering hazel eyes that he could not even guess at what went on in the mind behind them.

'Yes,' said Fortunata simply, 'I shall be there.' And she smiled, briefly and abstractedly, withdrew her hand gently from his, and turned back to return to the house, leaving him to walk back through the town to the bridge still unhappily in doubt whether he had not talked a great deal too much and too rashly, and injured himself in her eyes.

The sun duly shone for Saint Winifred on her festival day, as it had on the day of her first coming to the abbey of Saint Peter and Saint Paul. The gardens overflowed with blossom, the eager pilgrims housed by Brother Denis put on their best and came forth like so many more gaily coloured flowers, the burgesses of Shrewsbury flocked down from the town, and the parishioners of Holy Cross in from the Foregate and the scattered villages of Father Boniface's extensive parish. The new priest had only recently been inducted after a lengthy

54

interregnum, and his flock were still carefuly taking his measure, after their unhappy experience with the late Father Ailnoth. But first reactions were entirely favourable. Cynric the verger acted as a kind of touchstone for Foregate opinion. His views, so seldom expressed in words, but so easy for the simple and direct to interpret by intuition, would be accepted without question by most of those who worshipped at Holy Cross, and it·was already clear to the children, Cynric's closest cronies in spite of his taciturnity, that their long, bony, silent friend liked and approved of Father Boniface. That was enough for them. They approached their new priest with candour and confidence, secure in Cynric's recommendation.

Boniface was young, not much past thirty, of unassuming appearance and modest bearing, no scholar like his predecessor, but earnestly cheerful about his duties. The deference he showed to his monastic neighbours disposed even Prior Robert to approve of him, though with some condescension in view of the young man's humble birth and scanty Latin. Abbot Radulfus, conscious of one disastrous mistake in the previous appointment, had taken his time over this one, and studied the candidates with care. Did the Foregate really need a learned theologian? Craftsmen, small merchants, husbandmen, cottars and hardworking villeins from the villages and manors, they were better off with one of their own kind, aware of their needs and troubles, not stooping to them but climbing laboriously with them, elbow to elbow. It seemed that Father Boniface had energy and determination for the climb, force enough to urge a few others upward with him, and the stubborn loyalty not to leave them behind if they tired. In Latin or in the vernacular, that was language the people could understand.

This was a day on which secular and monastic clergy united to do honour to their saint, and chapter was postponed until after High Mass, when the church was open to all the pilgrims who wished to bring their private petitions to her altar, to touch her silver reliquary and offer prayers and gifts in the hope of engaging her gentle attention and benevolence for their illnesses, burdens and anxieties. All day long they would be coming and going, kneeling and rising in the pale, resplendent light of the scented candles Brother Rhun made in her honour. Ever since she had visited Rhun, himself a pilgrim, with her secret counsel, and lifted him out of lameness in her arms, to the bodily perfection of his present radiance, Rhun had made himself her page and squire, and his beauty reflected and testified to hers. For everyone knew that Winifred had been, as her legend said, the fairest maiden in the world in her day.

Everything, in fact, seemed to Brother Cadfael to be working together in perfect accord to make this what it should be, a day of supreme content, without blemish. He went to his stall in the chapter-house well satisfied with the world in general, and composed himself to sit through the day's business, even the most uninteresting details, with commendable attention. Some of the obedientiaries could be tedious enough on their own subjects to send a tired man to sleep, but today he was determined to extend virtuous tolerance even to the dullest of them.

Even to Canon Gerbert, he resolved, watching that superb cleric sail into the chapter-house and appropriate the stall beside the abbot, he would attribute only the most sanctified of motives, whatever fault the visitor might find with the discipline here, and however supercilious his behaviour towards Abbot Radulfus. Today nothing must ruffle the summer tranquillity.

Into this admirable mood a sudden disagreeable wind blew, driven before the billowing skirts of Prior Robert's habit as he strode in with aristocratic nose aloft and nostrils distended, as though someone had thrust an evil-smelling obscenity under them. Such sweeping speed in one so dedicated to preserving his own dignity sent an ominous shiver along the ranks of the brothers, all the more as Brother Jerome was disclosed scuttling in the prior's shadow. His narrow, pallid face proclaimed an excitement half horrified, half gratified.

'Father Abbot,' declaimed Robert, trumpeting outrage loud and clear, 'I have a most grave matter to bring before you. Brother Jerome here brought it to my notice, as I must in conscience bring it to yours. There is one waiting outside who has brought a terrible charge against William of Lythwood's apprentice, Elave. You recall how suspect the master's faith was once shown to be; now it seems the servant may outdo the master. One of the same household bears witness that last night, before other witnesses also, this man gave voice to views utterly opposed to the Church's teaching. Girard of Lythwood's clerk, Aldwin, denounces Elave for abominable heresies, and stands ready to maintain the charge against him before this assembly, as is his bounden duty.'

56

Chapter Five

T WAS SAID, and could not be unsaid. The word, once launched, has a deadly permanence. This word brought with it a total stillness and silence, as though a killing frost had settled on the chapter-house. The paralysis lasted for some moments before even the eyes moved, swerving from the righteous indignation of the prior's countenance to glide sidelong over Brother Jerome and peer through the open doorway in search of the accuser, who had not yet shown himself, but waited humbly somewhere out of sight.

Cadfael's first thought was that this was no more than another of Jerome's acidities, impulsive, ill-founded and certain to be refuted as soon as enquiry was made. Most of Jerome's mountains turned out molehills on examination. Then he looked round to read Canon Gerbert's austere face, and knew that this was a far graver matter, and could not be lightly set aside. Even if the archbishop's envoy had not been present to hear, Abbot Radulfus himself could not have ignored such a charge. He could bring reason to bear on the proceedings that must follow, but he could not halt them.

Gerbert would clench his teeth into any such deviation, that much was certain from the set of his lips and the wide, predatory stare of his eyes, but at least he had the courtesy to leave the first initiative here to the abbot.

'I trust,' said Radulfus, in the dry, deliberate voice that indicated his controlled displeasure, 'that you have satisfied

57

yourself, Robert, that this accusation is seriously meant, and not a gesture of personal animosity? It might be well, before we proceed further, to warn the accuser of the gravity of what he is doing. If he speaks out of some private spite, he should be given the opportunity to think better of his own position, and withdraw the charge. Men are fallible, and may say on impulse things quickly regretted.'

'I have so warned him,' said the prior firmly. 'He answers that there are two others who heard what he heard, and can bear witness as he can. This does not rest simply on a dispute between two men. Also, as you know, Father, this Elave returned here only a few days ago, the clerk Aldwin can have no grudge against him, surely, in so short a time.'

'And this is the same who brought home his master's body,' Canon Gerbert cut in sharply, 'and showed even then, I must say, certain rebellious and most questionable tendencies. This charge must not pass as leniently as the lingering suspicions against the dead man.'

'The charge has been made, and apparently is persisted in,' agreed Radulfus coldly. 'It must certainly be brought to question, but not here, not now. This is a matter for the seniors only, not for novices and the younger brothers among us. Am I to understand, Robert, that the accused man as yet knows nothing of what is charged against him?'

'No, Father, not from me, and certainly not from the man Aldwin, he came secretly to Brother Jerome to tell what he had heard.'

'The young man is a guest in our house,' said the abbot. 'He has a right to know what is said of him, and to answer it fully. And the other two witnesses of whom the accuser speaks, who are they?'

'They belong to the same household, and were present in the hall when these things were spoken. The girl Fortunata is a fosterchild to Girard of Lythwood, and Conan is his head shepherd.'

'They are both still here within the enclave,' put in Brother Jerome, eagerly helpful. 'They attended Mass, and are still in the church.'

'This matter should be dealt with at once,' urged Canon Gerbert, stiff with zeal. 'Delay can only dim the memories of the witnesses, and give the offender time to consider his interests and run from trial. It is for you to direct, Father Abbot, but I would recommend you to do so immediately, boldly, while you have all these people here within your gates. Dismiss your novices now, and send word and summon those witnesses and the man accused. And I would give orders to the porters to see that the accused does not pass through the gates.'

Canon Gerbert was accustomed to instant compliance with even his suggestions, let alone his orders, however obliquely expressed, but in his own house Abbot Radulfus went his own way.

'I would remind this chapter,' he said shortly, 'that while we of the Order certainly have a duty to serve and defend the faith, every man has also his parish priest, and every parish priest has his bishop. We have here with us the representative of Bishop de Clinton, in whose diocese of Lichfield and Coventry we dwell, and in whose cure accused, accuser and witnesses rest.' Serlo was certainly present, but had said not a word until now. In Gerbert's presence he went in awe and silence. 'I am sure,' said Radulfus with emphasis, 'that he will hold, as I do, that though we may be justified in making a first enquiry into the charge made, we cannot proceed further without referring the case to the bishop, within whose discipline it falls. If we find upon examination that the charge is groundless, that can be the end of the matter. If we feel there is need to proceed further with it, then it must be referred to the man's own bishop, who has the right to deal with it by whatever tribunal he sees fit to appoint.'

'That is truth,' said Serlo gallantly, thus encouraged to follow where he might have hesitated to lead. 'My bishop would certainly wish to exercise his writ in such a case.'

A judgement of Solomon, thought Cadfael, well content with his abbot. Roger de Clinton will be no better pleased to have another cleric usurping his authroity in his diocese than Radulfus is to see any man, were it the archbishop himself, leave alone his envoy, twitching the reins away from him here. And young Elave will probably have good reason to be glad of it before all's done. Now how did he come to let down his guard so rashly with witnesses by, after one fright already past?

'I would not for the world trespass upon the ground of Bishop de Clinton,' said Gerbert, hastily jealous for his own good repute, but not sounding at all pleased about it. 'Certainly he must be informed if this matter proves to be true substance. But it is we who are faced with the need to probe the facts, while memories are fresh, and put on record what we

59

discover. No time should be lost. Father Abbot, in my view we should hold a hearing now, at once.'

'I am inclined to the same opinion,' said the abbot drily. 'In the event of the charge turning out to be malicious or trivial, or untrue, or simply mistaken, it need then go no further, and the bishop will be spared a grief and an aggravation, no less than the waste of his time. I think we are competent to probe out the difference between harmless speculation and wilful perversion.'

It seemed to Cadfael that that indicated pretty clearly the abbot's view of the whole unfortunate affair, and though Canon Gerbert had opened his mouth, most probably to proclaim that even speculation among the laity was itself harm enough, he thought better of it, and clenched his teeth again grimly on the undoubted reserve he felt about the abbot's attitude, character and fitness for his office. Men of the cloth are as liable to instant antipathies as are ordinary folk, and these two were as far apart as east from west.

'Very well,' said Radulfus, running a long, commanding glance round the assembly, 'let us proceed. This chapter is suspended. We will summon it again when time permits. Brother Richard and Brother Anselm, will you see all the juniors set to useful service, and then seek out those three people named? The young woman Fortunata, the shepherd Conan, and the accused man. Bring them here, and say nothing as to the cause until they come before us. The accuser, I take it,' he said, turning upon Jerome, 'is already here without.'

Jerome had lingered in the shadow of the prior's skirts all this time, sure of his righteousness but not quite sure of the abbot's recognition of it. This was the first encouragement he had received, or so he read it, and visibly brightened.

'He is, Father. Shall I bring him in?'

'No,' said the abbot, 'not until the accused is here to confront him. Let him say what he has to say face to face with the man he denounces.'

Elave and Fortunata entered the chapter-house together, open of face, puzzled and curious at being summoned thus, but plainly innocent of all foreboding. Whatever had been said unwisely at last night's gathering, whatever she was expected to confirm against the speaker, it was perfectly clear to Cadfael that the girl had no reservations about her companion, indeed the very fact that they came in together, and had obviously been found together when the summons was delivered, spoke for itself. The expectancy in their faces was wondering but unthreatened, and Aldwin's accusation, when it was uttered, would come as a shattering blow not to the young man only, but to the girl as well. Gerbert would certainly have one reluctant witness, if not a hostile one, Cadfael reflected, conscious of his own heart's alerted and partisan sympathy. Conscious, too, that Abbot Radulfus had noted, as he had, the significance of their trusting entrance, and the wondering look they exchanged, smiling, before they made their reverence to the array of prelates and monastics before them, and waited to be enlightened.

'You sent for us, Father Abbot,' said Elave, since no one else broke the silence. 'We are here.'

The 'we' says it all, thought Cadfael. If she had any doubts of him last night, she has forgotten them this morning, or thought them over and rejected them. And that is valid evidence, too, whatever she may be forced to say later.

'I sent for you, Elave,' said the abbot with deliberation, 'to help us in a certain matter which has arisen here this morning. Wait but a moment, there is one more has been summoned to attend.'

He came in at that moment, circumspectly and in some awe of the tribunal before him, but not, Cadfael thought, ignorant of its purpose. There was no open-eyed but unintimidated wonder in Conan's weathered, wary, rosily comely face, and noticeably he kept his eyes respectfully upon the abbot, and never cast a glance aside at Elave. He knew what was in the wind, he came prepared for it. And this one, if he discreetly showed no eagerness displayed no reluctance, either.

'My lord, they told me Conan is wanted here. That's my name.'

'Are we now ready to proceed?' demanded Canon Gerbert impatiently, stirring irritably in his stall.

'We are,' said Radulfus. 'Well, Jerome, bring in the man Aldwin. And Elave, stand forward in the centre. This man has somewhat to say of you that should be said only in your presence.'

The name alone had jolted both Fortunata and Elave, even before Aldwin showed his face in the doorway, and came in with a resolution and belligerence that were not native to him, and probably cost him an effort to maintain. His long face was

61

set in lines of arduous determination, a man naturally resigned and timorous bent on going through with an enterprise that called for courage. He took his stand almost within arm's length of Elave, and jutted an aggressive jaw at the young man's shocked stare, but there were drops of sweat on his own balding forehead. He spread his feet to take firm grip on the stones of the floor, and stared back at Elave without blinking. Elave had already begun to understand. By her bewildered face Fortunata had not. She drew back a pace or two, looking searchingly from one man's face to the other, her lips parted on quickened breath.

'This man,' said the abbot evenly, 'has made certain charges against you, Elave. He says that last night, in his master's house, you gave voice to views on matters of religion that run counter to the teachings of the Church, and bring you into grave danger of heresy. He cites these witnesses present in support of what he urges against you. How do you say, was there indeed such talk between you? You were there to speak, and they to hear?'

'Father,' said Elave, grown very pale and quiet, 'I was there in the house. I did have speech with them. The talk did turn on matters of faith. We had only yesterday buried a good master, it was natural we should give thought to his soul and our own.'

'And do you yourself, in good conscience, believe that you said nothing that could run counter to true belief?' asked Radulfus mildly.

'To the best that I know and understand, Father, I never did.'

'You, fellow, Aldwin,' ordered Canon Gerbert, leaning forward in his stall, 'repeat those things of which you complained to Brother Jerome. Let us hear them all, and in the words you heard spoken, so far as you can recall them. Change nothing!'

'My lords, as we sat together, we were speaking of William who was newly buried, and Conan asked if he had ever taken Elave with him down the same road that got him into straits with the priest, those years ago. And Elave said William never made any secret of what he thought, and on his travels no one ever found fault with him for thinking about such matters. What are wits for, he said, unless a man uses them. And we said that it was presumption in us simple folk, that we should listen and say Amen to what the Church tells us, for in that field the priests have authority over us.'

62

'A very proper saying,' said Gerbert roundly. 'And how did he reply?'

'Sir, he said how could a man say Amen to damning a child unchristened to hell? The worst of men, he said, could not cast an infant into the fire, so how could God, being goodness itself, do so? It would be against God's very nature, he said.'

'That is to argue,' said Gerbert, 'that infant baptism is unneeded, and of no virtue. There can be no other logical end of such reasoning. If they are in no need of redemption by baptism, to be spared inevitable reprobation, then the sacrament is brought into contempt.'

'Did you say the words Aldwin reports of you?' asked Radulfus quietly, his eyes on Elave's roused and indignant face.

'Father, I did. I do not believe such innocent children, just because baptism does not reach them in time before they die, can possibly fall through God's hands. Surely his hold is more secure than that.'

'You persist in a deadly error,' insisted Gerbert. 'It is as I have said, such a belief casts out and debases the sacrament of baptism, which is the only deliverance from mortal sin. If one sacrament is brought into derision, then all are denied. On this count alone you stand in danger of judgement.'

'Sir,' Aldwin took him up eagerly, 'he said also that he did not believe in the need because he did not believe that children are born into the world rotten with sin. How could that be, he said, of a little thing newly come into being, helpless to do anything of itself, good or evil. Is not that indeed to make an empty mockery of baptism? And we said that we are taught and must believe that even the babes yet unborn are rotten with the sin of Adam, and fallen with him. But he said no, it is only his own deeds, bad and good, that a man must answer for in the judgement, and his own deeds will save or damn him.'

'To deny original sin is to degrade every sacrament,' Gerbert repeated forcibly.

'No, I never thought of it so,' protested Elave hotly. 'I did say a helpless newborn child cannot be a sinner. But surely baptism is to welcome him into the world and into the Church, and help him to keep his innocence. I never said it was useless or a light thing.'

'But you do deny original sin?' Gerbert pressed him hard.

'Yes,' said Elave after a long pause. 'I do deny it.' His face had sharpened into icy whiteness, but his jaw was set and his eyes had begun to burn with a deep, still anger.

Abbot Radulfus eyed him steadily and asked in a mild and reasonable voice: 'What, then, do you believe to be the state of the child on entering this world? A child the son of Adam, as are we all.'

Elave looked back at him as gravely, arrested by the serenity of the voice that questioned him. 'His state is the same,' he said slowly, 'as the state of Adam before his fall. For even Adam had his innocence once.'

'So others before you have argued,' said Radulfus, 'and have not inevitably been called heretical. Much has been written on the subject, in good faith and in deep concern for the good of the Church. Is this the worst you have to urge, Aldwin, against this man?'

'No, Father,' Aldwin said in haste, 'there is more. He said it is a man's own acts that will save or damn him, but that he had not often met a man so bad as to make him believe in eternal damnation. And then he said that there was a father of the Church once, in Alexandria, who held that in the end everyone would find salvation, even the fallen angels, even the devil himself.'

In the shudder of unease that passed along the ranks of the brothers the abbot remarked simply: 'So there was. His name was Origen. It was his theme that all things came from God, and will return to God. As I recall, it was an enemy of his who brought the devil into it, though I grant the implication is there. I gather that Elave merely cited what Origen is said to have written and believed. He did not say that he himself believed it? Well, Aldwin?'

Aldwin drew in his chin cautiously at that, and gave some thought to the possibility that he himself was edging his way through quicksands. 'No, Father, that is true. He said only that there was a father of the Church who spoke so. But we said that was blasphemy, for the teaching of the Church is that salvation comes by the grace of God, and no other way, and a man's works can avail him not at all. But then he said outright: I do not believe that!'

'Did you so?' asked Radulfus.

'I did,' Elave's blood was up, the pallor of his face had burned into a sharp-edged brightness that was almost dazzling. Cadfael at once despaired of him and exulted in him. The abbot had done his best to temper all this fermenting doubt and malice and fear that had gathered in the chapter-house like a bitter cloud, making it hard to breathe, and here was this stubborn creature accepting all challenges, and digging in his heels to resist even his friends. Now that he was embattled he would do battle. He would not give back one pace out of regard for his skin. 'I did say so. I say it again. I said that we have the power in ourselves to make our own way towards salvation. I said we have free will to choose between right and wrong, to labour upwards or to dive down and wallow in the muck, and at the last we must every one answer for our own acts in the judgement. I said if we are men, and not beasts, we ought to make our own way towards grace, not sit on our hams and wait for it to lift us up, unworthy.'

'By such arrogance,' trumpeted Canon Gerbert, offended as much by the flashing eyes and obdurate voice as by what was said, 'by such pride as yours the rebel angels fell. So you would do without God, and repudiate his divine grace, the only means to salve your insolent soul—'

'You wrong me,' flashed back Elave. 'I do not deny divine grace. The grace is in the gifts he has given us, free will to choose good and refuse evil, and mount towards our own salvation, yes, and the strength to choose rightly. If we do our part, God will do the rest.'

Abbot Radulfus tapped sharply with his ring on the arm of his stall, and called the assembly to order with unshaken authority. 'For my part,' he said as they quieted, 'I find no fault with a man for holding that he can and should aspire to grace by right use of grace. But we are straying from what we are here to do. Let us by all means listen scrupulously to all that Elave is alleged to have said, and let him admit what he admits and deny what he denies of it, and let these witnesses confirm or refute. Have you yet more to add, Aldwin?'

By this time Aldwin had learned to be careful how he trod with the abbot, and add nothing to the bare words he had memorised overnight.

'Father, but one more thing. I said I heard a preacher tell how Saint Augustine wrote that the number of the elect is already fixed and cannot be changed, and all the rest are doomed to reprobation. And he said that he did not believe it. And I could not keep from asking again, did he not believe even Saint Augustine? And he said again, no, he did not.'

'I said,' cried Elave hotly, 'that I could not believe the roll was already made up, for why then should we even try to deal justly or pay God worship, or give any heed to the priests who urge us to keep from sin, and demand of us confession and

65

penance if we trespass? To what end, if we are damned whatever we do? And when he asked again, did I not believe even Saint Augustine, I said that *if he wrote that*, no, I did not believe him. For I have no knowledge else that he ever did write such a thing.'

'Is that truth?' demanded Radulfus, before Gerbert could speak. 'Aldwin, do you bear out those were the actual words spoken?'

'It may be so,' agreed Aldwin cautiously. 'Yes, I think he did say *if* the saint had so written. I saw no difference there, but your lordships will better judge than I.'

'And that is all? You have nothing more to add?'

'No, Father, that's all. After that we let him lie, we wanted no more of him.'

'You were wise,' said Canon Gerbert grimly. 'Well, Father Abbot, can we now hear if the witnesses confirm all that has been said? It seems to me there is substance enough in what we have heard, if these two persons also can verify it.'

Conan gave his own account of the evening's talk so fluently and willingly that Cadfael could not resist the feeling that he had learned his speech by heart, and the impression of a small conspiracy emerged, for Cadfael at least, so clearly that he wondered it was not obvious to all. To the abbot, he thought, studying the controlled, ascetic face, it almost certainly was, and yet even if these two had connived for their own ends, yet the fact remained that these things had been said, and Elave, even if he corrected or enlarged here and there, did not deny them. How had they contrived to get him to talk so openly? And more important still, how had they ensured that the girl should be present? For it became increasingly plain that on her evidence everything depended. The more Abbot Radulfus might suspect Aldwin and Conan of malice against Elave, the more important was what Fortunata might have to say about it.

She had listened intently to all that passed. Belated understanding had paled her oval face and dilated her eyes into glittering green anxiety, flashing from face to face as question and answer flew and the tension in the chapter-house mounted. When the abbot turned to look at her she stiffened, and the set of her lips tightened nervously.

'And you, child? You also were present and heard what passed?'

She said carefully: 'I was not present throughout. I was

66

helping my mother in the kitchen when these three were left together.'

'But you joined them later,' said Gerbert. 'At what stage? Did you hear him say that infant baptism was needless and useless?'

At that she spoke up boldly: 'No, sir, for he never did say that.'

'Oh, if you stick upon the wording ... Did you hear him say, then, that he did not believe unbaptised children suffered damnation? For that leads to the same end.'

'No,' said Fortunata. 'He never did say what his own belief was in that matter. He was speaking of his master, who is dead. He said that William used to say not even the worst of men could throw a child into the fire, so how could God do so? When he said this,' said Fortunata firmly, 'he was telling us what William had said, not what he himself thought.'

'That is true, but only half the truth,' cried Aldwin, 'for the next moment I asked him plainly: Do you also hold that belief? And he said: Yes, I do say so.'

'Is that true, girl?' demanded Gerbert, turning upon Fortunata a black and threatening scowl. And when she faced him with eyes flashing but lips tight shut: 'It seems to me that this witness has no devout wish to help us. We should have done better to take all testimony under oath, it seems. Let us at least make sure in this woman's case.' He turned his forbidding gaze hard and long upon the obdurately silent girl. 'Woman, do you know in what suspicion you place yourself if you do not speak truth? Father Prior, bring her a Bible. Let her swear upon the Gospels and imperil her soul if she lies.'

Fortunata laid her hand upon the proffered book which Prior Robert solemnly opened before her, and took the oath in a voice so low as to be barley audible. Elave had opened his mouth and taken a step towards her in helpless anger at the aspersion cast upon her, but stopped himself as quickly and stood mute, his teeth clenched upon his rage, and his face soured with the bitter taste of it.

'Now,' said the abbot, with such quiet but formidable authority that even Gerbert made no further attempt to wrest the initiative from him, 'let us leave questioning until you have told us yourself, without haste or fear, all you recall of what went on in that meeting. Speak freely, and I believe we shall hear truth.'

She took heart and drew steady breath, and told it carefully, as best she remembered it. Once or twice she hesitated, sorely tempted to omit or explain, but Cadfael noticed how her left hand clasped and wrung the right hand that had been laid upon the open Gospel, as though it burned, and impelled her past the momentary silence.

'With your leave, Father Abbot,' said Gerbert grimly when she ended, 'when you have put such questions as you see fit to this witness, I have three to put to her, and they encompass the heart of the matter. But first do you proceed.'

'I have no questions,' said Radulfus. 'The lady has given us her full account on oath, and I accept it. Ask what you have to ask.'

'First,' said Gerbert, leaning forward in his stall with thick brown brows drawn down over his sharp, intimidating stare, 'did you hear the accused say, when asked pointblank if he agreed with his master in denying that unbaptised children were doomed to reprobation, that yes, he did so agree?'

She turned her head aside for an instant, and wrung at her hand for reminder, and in a very low voice she said: 'Yes, I heard him say so.'

'That is to repudiate the sacrament of baptism. Second, did you hear him deny that all the children of men are rotten with the sin of Adam? Did you hear him say that only a man's own deeds will save or damn him?'

With a flash of spirit she said, louder than before: 'Yes, but he was not denying grace, the grace is in the gift of choice—'

Gerbert cut her off there with uplifted hand and flashing eyes. 'He said it. That is enough. It is the claim that grace is unneeded, that salvation is in a man's own hands. Thirdly, did you hear him say, and repeat, that he did not believe what Saint Augustine wrote of the elect and the rejected?'

'Yes,' she said, this time slowly and carefully. '*If* the saint so wrote, he said, he did not believe him. No one has ever told me, and I cannot read or write, beyond my name and some small things. Did Saint Augustine say what the preacher reported of him?'

'That is enough!' snapped Gerbert. 'This girl bears out all that has been charged against the accused. The proceedings are in you hands.'

'It is my judgement,' said Radulfus, 'that we should adjourn, and deliberate in private. The witnesses are dismissed. Go home, daughter, and be assured you have told truth, and need trouble not at all what follows, for the truth cannot but be good. Go, all of you, but hold yourselves ready should you be needed again and recalled. And you, Elave...' He sat studying the young man's face, which was raised to him pale, resolute and irate, with set mouth and wide and brilliant eyes, still burning for Fortunata's distress. 'You are a guest in our house. I have seen no cause why any man of us should not take your word.' He was aware of Gerbert stiffening with disapproval beside him, but swept on with raised voice, overriding protest. 'If you promise not to leave here until this matter is resolved, then you are free in the meantime to go back and forth here as you will.'

For a moment Elave's attention wavered. Fortunata had turned in the doorway to look back, then she was gone. Conan and Aldwin had left hastily on their dismissal, and vanished before her, eager to escape while their case was surely safe in the hands of the visiting prelate, whose nose for unorthodoxy was shown to be so keen and his zeal so relentless. Accuser and witnesses were gone. Elave returned his obdurate but respectful gaze to the abbot, and said with deliberation: 'My lord, I have no mind to leave my lodging here in your house until I can do so free and vindicated. I give you my word on that.'

'Go, then, until I ask your attendance again. And now,' said Radulfus, rising, 'this session is adjourned. Go to your duties, every one, and bear in mind we are still in a day dedicated to the rememberance of Saint Winifred, and the saints also bear witness to all that we do, and will testify accordingly.'

'I understand you very well,' said Canon Gerbert, when he was alone with Radulfus in the abbot's parlour. Closeted thus in private with his peer, he sat relaxed, even weary, all his censorious zeal shed, a fallible man and anxious for his faith. 'Here retired from the world, or at the worst concerned largely with the region and the people close about you, you have not seen the danger of false belief. And I grant you it has not yet cast a shadow in this land, and I pray our people may be sturdy enough to resist all such devious temptations. But it comes, Father Abbot, it comes! From the east the serpents of undoing are working their way westward, and of all travellers from the east I go in dread that they may bring back with them bad seed, perhaps even unwittingly, to take root and grow even here. There are malignant wandering preachers active even now in Flanders, in France, on the Rhine, in Lombardy, who cry out

69

against Holy Church and her priesthood, that we are corrupt and greedy, that the Apostles lived simply, in holy poverty. In Antwerp a certain Tachelm has drawn deluded thousands after him to raid churches and tear down their ornaments. In France, in Rouen itself, yet another such goes about preaching poverty and humility and demanding reform. I have travelled in the south on my archbishop's errands, and seen how error grows and spreads like a heath fire. These are not a few sick in mind and harmless. In Provence, in Languedoc, there are regions where a fashion of Manichean heresy has grown so strong it is become almost a rival church. Do you wonder that I dread even the first weak spark that may start such a blaze?'

'No,' said Radulfus, 'I do not wonder. We should never relax our guard. But also we must see every man clearly, with his words and his deeds upon him, and not hasten to cover him from sight with this universal cloak of heresy. Once the word is spoken, the man himself may become invisible. And therefore expendable! Here is certainly no wandering preacher, no inflamer of crowds, no ambitious madman whipping up a following for his own gain. The boy spoke of a master he had valued and served, and therefore tended to speak in praise of him, in defence of his bold doubts, the more loyally and fiercely if his companions raised their voices against him. He had probably drunk enough to loosen his tongue, besides. He may well have said, and repeated to us, more than he truly means, to the aggravation of his cause. Shall we do the same?'

'No,' said Gerbert heavily, 'I would not wish that. And I do see him clearly. You say rightly, here is no wild man bent on mischief, but a sound, hardworking fellow, profitable to his master and I doubt not honest and well-meaning with his neighbours. Do you not see how much more dangerous that makes him? To hear false doctrine from one himself plainly false and vile is no temptation at all, to hear it from one fair of countenance and reputation, speaking it with his heart's conviction, that can be deadly seduction. It is why I fear him.'

'It is why one century's saint is the next century's heretic,' the abbot replied drily, 'and one century's heretic the next century's saint. It is as well to think long and calmly before affixing either name to any man.'

'That is to neglect a duty we cannot evade,' said Gerbert, again bristling. 'The peril which is here and now must be dealt with here and now, or the battle is lost, for the seed will have fallen and rooted.'

70

'Then at least we may know the wheat from the tares. And bear in mind,' said Radulfus gravely, 'that where error is sincere and bred out of misguided goodness, the blemish may be healed by reason and persuasion.'

'Or failing that,' said Gerbert with inflexible resolution, 'by lopping off the diseased member.'

Chapter Six

LAVE passed through the gates unchallenged, and turned towards the town. Evidently the porter had not yet got word of the alarm raised against this one ordinary mortal among the abbey guests, or else he had already received the abbot's fiat that the accused's parole was given and accepted, and he was free to go and come as he pleased, provided he did not collect his belongings and take to his heels altogether, for no attempt was made to bar his way. The brother on the gate even gave him a cheerful good-day as he passed.

Out in the Foregate he paused to look both ways along the highroad, but all the witnesses against him had vanished from sight. He set off in haste towards the bridge and the town, certain that Fortunata in her distress would make straight for home. She had left the chapter-house before he had given his word he had no intention of departing unvindicated, she might well think him already a prisoner, might even blame herself for his plight. He had seen how reluctantly she had borne true witness against him, and at this moment it grieved him more that she should grieve than that his own liberty and life should be in danger. In that danger he found it hard to believe, therefore it was easy to bear. Her evident agitation he believed in utterly, and it caused him deep and compelling pain. He had to speak to her, to reassure her she had done him no wrong in the world, that this commotion would pass, that the abbot was a reasonable man, and the other one, the one who wanted blood, would soon be gone and leave the judgement to saner judges. And more beyond that, that he had understood how valiantly she had striven to defend him, that he was grateful for it, perhaps even hoping in his heart to find in it a deeper meaning than sympathy, and more intimate than concern for justice. Though he must guard his tongue from saying too much, as long as even the shadow of reprobation hung over him.

He had reached the end of the enclave wall, where the ground on his left opened out over the silvery oval of the mill pool, and on the right of the road the houses of the Foregate gave way to a grove of trees that stretched as far as the approaches to the bridge over the Severn. And there she was before him, unmistakeable in her bearing and gait, hastening along the dusty highway with an impetuosity that suggested angry resolution rather than consternation and dismay. He broke into a run, and overtook her in the shadow of the trees. At the sound of his racing feet she had swung round to face him, and at sight of him, without a word said beyond his breathless 'Mistress ...!' she caught him hastily by the hand and drew him well aside into the grove, out of sight from the road.

'What is this? Have they freed you? Is it over?' She raised to him a face glowing and intent with unmistakeable joy, but still holding it in check for fear of a fall as sudden as her elation.

'No, not yet. No, there'll be more debate yet before I'm quit of all this. But I had to speak to you, to thank you for what you did for me—'

'*Thank* me!' she said in a soft, incredulous cry. 'For digging the pit a little deeper under you? I burn with shame that I had not even the courage to lie!'

'No, no, you mustn't think so! You did me no wrong at all, you did everything you could to help me. Why should you be forced to lie? In any case, you could not do it, it is not in you. Nor will I lie,' said Elave fiercely, 'nor give back from what I believe. What I came to say is that you must not fret for me, nor ever for a moment think that I have anything but gratitude and reverence for you. You stood my friend the only way I would have you stand my friend.'

He had not even realised that he was holding both her hands, clasped close against his breast, so that they stood heart to heart, the rhythm of matched heartbeats and quickened breathing shaking them both. Her face, raised to his, was

73

intent and fierce, her hazel eyes dazzlingly wide and bright.

'If they have not freed you, how are you here? Do they know you are gone? Will they not be hunting for you if you're missed?'

'Why should they? I'm free to go and come, as long as I remain a guest in the abbey until there's a judgement. The abbot took my word I would not run.'

'But you must,' she said urgently. 'I thank God that you ran after me like this, while there's time. You must go, get away from here as far as you can. Into Wales would be best. Come with me now, quickly, I'll get you to Jevan's workshop beyond Frankwell, and hide you there until I can get you a horse.'

Elave was shaking his head vigorously before she had ended her plea. 'No, I will not run! I gave the abbot my word, but even if he had never asked it or I given it, I would not run. I will not bow to such superstitious foolishness, it would be to encourage the madmen, and put other souls in worse danger than mine. This I don't believe can come to anything perilous, if I stand my ground. We have not yet come to that extreme of folly, that a man can be hounded for thinking about holy things. You'll see, the storm will all pass over.'

'No,' she insisted, 'not so easily. Things are changing, did you not smell the smoke of it even there in the chapter-house? I foresee it, if you do not. I was hurrying back now to talk to Jevan, to see what more can be brought to bear, to deliver you away out of danger. You brought me something of my own, it must have value. I want to use it to have you away and safe. What better use could I make of it?'

'No!' he said in sharp protest. 'I will not have it! I am not going to run, I refuse to run. And that, whatever it may be, is for you, for your marriage.'

'My marriage!' she said in a wondering voice, very low, and opened wide at him the greenish fire of her eyes, as though the thought was new to her and very strange.

'Never trouble for me, in the end it will all be well. I am going back now,' said Elave firmly, too dazzled to be observant. 'Never fear, I'll take good care how I speak, how I carry myself, but I will not deny what I believe, or say ay to what I do not believe. And I will not run. From what? I have no guilt from which to run.'

He loosed her hand with a gesture almost rough, because at the end it seemed such a hard thing to do. He was turning away through the trees when he looked back, and she had not moved. Her eyes were on him, fixed thoughtfully, almost severely, and her lower lip was caught between even teeth.

'There is another reason,' he said, 'why I will not go. Alone it would be enough to hold me. To run now would be to leave you.'

'And do you think,' said Fortunata, 'that I would not follow and find you?'

She heard the several voices before she entered the hall, voices raised not so much in anger or argument as in bewilderment and consternation. Either Conan or Aldwin had thought it wise to acquaint the household with the morning's sensational turn of events at once on arrival home, no doubt to put the best aspect on what they had done. She had no doubt that they were in collusion in the matter, but whatever their motives, they would not want to appear simply as squalid informers. A gloss of genuine religious revulsion and sense of duty would have to glaze over the malice entailed.

They were all there, Margaret, Jevan, Conan and Aldwin, gathered in an agitated group, baffled question and oblique answer flying at the same time, Conan standing back to be the innocent bystander caught up in someone else's quarrel, Aldwin bleating aloud as Fortunata entered: 'How could I know? I was worried that such things should be said, I feared for my own souls if I hid them. All I did was tell Brother Jerome what was troubling me—'

'And he told Prior Robert,' cried Fortunata from the doorway, 'and Prior Robert told everyone, especially that great man from Canterbury, as you knew very well he would. How can you pretend you never meant Elave harm? Once you launched it, you knew where it would end.'

They had all swung about to face her, startled by her anger rather than by the suddenness of her entry.

'No!' protested Aldwin, recovering his breath. 'No, I swear I only thought the prior might speak to him, warn him, turn him to better counsel ...'

'And therefore,' she said sharply, 'you told him who had been present to hear. Why do that unless you meant it to go further? Why force me into your plans? That I shall never forgive you!'

'Wait, wait, wait!' cried Jevan, throwing up his hands. 'Are you telling me, chick, that *you* were called to witness? In God's name, man, what possessed you? How dared you bring our girl into such a business?'

75

'It was not I who wanted that,' protested Aldwin. 'Brother Jerome got it out of me who was there, I never meant to bring her into the tangle. But I am a son of the Church, I needed to slough the load from my conscience, but then it got out of hand.'

'I never knew you all that constant in observance,' said Jevan ruefully. 'You could as well have refused to name any names but your own. Well, what's done is done. Is it over even now? Need we expect her to be called to more enquiries, more interrogations? Is it to drag on to exhaustion, now it's begun?'

'It isn't over,' said Fortunata. 'They have not pronounced any judgement, but they won't let go so easily. Elave is pledged not to go away until he's freed of the charge. I know it because I have just left him, among the trees close by the bridge, and he's on his way back now to the abbey to stand his ground. I wanted him to run, I begged him to run, but he refuses. See what you've done, Aldwin, to a poor young man who never did you any harm, who has no family or patron now, no safe home and secure living, as you have. Here are you provided for life, without a care for your old age, and he has to find work again wherever he can, and now you have put a shadow upon him that will cling round him whatever the judgement, and turn men away from employing him for fear of being thought suspect by contagion. Why did you do it? Why?'

Aldwin had been gradually recovering his composure since the shock of her entrance had upset it, but now it seemed he had lost it altogether, and his wits with it. He stood gaping at her mutely, and from her to Jevan. Twice he swallowed hard before he could find a word to say, and even then he brought out the words with infinite caution, disbelieving.

'Provided for life?'

'You know you are,' she said impatiently, and herself was struck mute the next moment, suddenly sensible that for Aldwin nothing had ever been known beyond possibility of doubt. Every evil was to be expected, every good suspect and to be watched jealously, lest it evaporate as he breathed on it. 'Oh, no!' she said on a despairing breath. 'Was *that* it? Did you think he was come to turn you out and take your place? Was that why you wanted rid of him?'

'What?' cried Jevan. 'Is the girl right, man? Did you suppose you were to be thrown out on the roads to make way for him to get his old place back again? After all the years you've lived here and worked for us? Did this house ever treat any of its people so? You know better than that!'

But that was Aldwin's trouble, that he valued himself so low he expected as low a regard from everyone else, even after years, and the respect and consideration the house of Lythwood showed towards its other dependants could not, in his eyes, be relied on as applying equally to him. He stood dumbstruck, his mouth working silently.

'My dear soul!' said Margaret, grieving. 'The thought never entered our heads to part with you. Certainly he was a good lad when we had him, but we wouldn't have displaced you for the world. Why, the boy didn't want it, either. I told him how it was, the first time he came back here, and he said surely, the place was yours, he never had the least wish to take it from you. Have you been fretting all this time over that? I thought you knew us better.'

'I've damaged him for no reason,' said Aldwin, as though to himself. 'No reason at all!' And suddenly, with a convulsive moment that shook his aging body as a gale shakes a bush, he turned and blundered towards the doorway. Conan caught him by the arm and held him fast.

'Where are you going? What can you do? It's done. You told no lies, what was said was said.'

'I'll overtake him,' said Aldwin with unaccustomed resolution. 'I'll tell him I'm sorry for it. I'll go with him to the monks, and see if I can undo what I've done – any part of what I've done. I'll own why I did it. I'll withdraw the charge I made.'

'Don't be a fool!' urged Conan roughly. 'What difference will that make? The charge is laid now, the priests won't let it be dropped, not they. It's no small matter to accuse a man of heresy and then go back on it, you'll only end in as bad case as he. And they have my witness, and Fortunata's, what use is it taking back yours? Let be, and show some sense!'

But Aldwin's courage was up, and his conscience stricken too deeply for sense. He dragged himself free from the detaining hand. 'I can but try! I will! That at least.' And he was out at the door, and halfway across the yard towards the street. Conan would have gone after him, but Jevan called him back sharply.

'Let him alone! At the very least, if he owns to his own fear and malice, he must surely shake the case against the lad. Words, words, I don't doubt they were spoken, but words can be interpreted many ways, and even a small doubt cast can alter the image. You get back to work, and let the poor devil go and ease his mind the best way he can. If he falls foul of the priests, we'll put in a word for him and get him out of it.'

Conan gave up reluctantly, shrugging off his misgivings about the whole affair. 'Then I'd best get out to the folds until nightfall. God knows how he'll fare, but by then, one way or another, I suppose we shall find out.' And he went out still shaking his head disapprovingly over Aldwin's foolishness, and they heard his solid footsteps cross the yard to the passage into the street.

'What a coil!' said Jevan with a gusty sigh. 'And I must be off, too, and fetch some more skins from the workshop. There's a canon of Haughmond coming tomorrow, and I've no notion yet what size of book he has in mind. Don't take things too much to heart, girl,' he said, and embraced Fortunata warmly in a long arm. 'If it comes to the worst we'll get the prior of Haughmond to say a word to Gerbert for any man of ours – one Augustinian must surely listen to another, and the prior owes me a favour or two.'

He released her and was off towards the door in his turn, when she demanded abruptly: 'Uncle – does Elave count as a man of ours?'

Jevan swung about to stare at her, his thin black brows raised, and the dark, observant eyes beneath them flashed into the smile that came seldom but brilliantly, a little teasing, a little intimidating, but for her always reassuring.

'If you want him,' he said, 'he shall.'

Elave had gone but a few yards back towards the abbey gatehouse when he saw half a dozen men come boiling out of the open gate, and split two ways along the Foregate. The suddenness of the eruption and the distant clamour of their raised voices as they emerged and separated made him draw back hastily into the cover of the trees, to consider what this hubbub might have to do with him. They were certainly sent forth in a body, and carrying staves, which boded no good if they were indeed hunting for him. He worked his way cautiously along the grove to get a closer view, for they were sweeping the open road first before enlarging their field, and two were away on the run along the further length of the enclave wall, to reach the corner and get a view along the next stretch of the road. Someone or something was certainly being hunted. Not by any of the brothers. Here were no black habits, but sober workaday homespun and hard-wearing leather, on sturdy laymen. Three of them he knew for the grooms attendant on Canon Gerbert, a fourth was his body servant, for Elave had seen the man about the guest-hall, busy and pompous, jack in office by virtue of his master's status. The others must surely have been recruited from among those pilgrims ablest in body and readiest for zealous mischief. It was not the abbot who had set the dogs on him, but Gerbert.

He drew back deeper into cover, and stood scowling at the intent hunters quartering the Foregate. He had no mind to show himself, however boldly, and risk being set upon and dragged back like a felon, when he had not, in his reading of his commitment, ever broken his parole. Maybe Canon Gerbert read the terms differently, and considered his going outside the gate, even without his gear, as proof of a guilty mind and instant flight. Well, he should not have the satisfaction of being able to sustain that view. Elave was going back through that gate on his own two feet, of his own obstinate will, true to his bond and staking his liberty and perhaps his life. The peril in which he could not bring himself to believe looked more real and sinister now.

They had left a single groom, the brawniest of Gerbert's three, sentinel before the gatehouse, prowling up and down as though neither time nor force could shift him. Small hope of slipping past that great sinewy hulk! And a couple of the hounds, having beaten the road, the gardens and the cottages along the Foregate for a hundred paces either way, were crossing the road purposefully towards the trees. Better remove himself from here to a safe distance until they either abandoned the hunt, or pursued it into more remote coverts, and allowed him safe passage back into the fold. Elave drew off hastily through the trees, and followed their dwindling course north-eastward until he came round into the orchards beyond the Gaye, and the belt of bushes that clothed the riverside. They were more likely to search for him westward. Along the border, English fugitives made for Wales, Welsh fugitives for England. The two laws baulked and held off at the dyke, though trade crossed back and forth merrily enough.

There was still a matter of three hours or so before Vespers, when he could hope that everyone would be in church again, and he might be able to slip in either through the gatehouse, if the burly guard had departed, or into the church by the west door among the local parishioners. No point in going back, meantime, to risk running his head into a snare. He found

79

himself a comfortable nest among the tall grass above the river, screened by bushes and islanded in a silence that would give him due warning of any foot rustling the grass or shoulders brushing through the branches of alder and willow for a hundred yards around, and sat thinking of Fortunata. He could not credit that he was in the kind of danger she envisaged, and yet he could not quite put the shadow away from him.

Across the swift and sinuous currents of the Severn, sparkling in sunlight, the hill of the town rose sharply, its long, enfolding wall terminating here opposite his hiding-place in the thick sandstone towers of the castle, and giving place to the highroad launching away to the north from the Castle Foregate towards Whitchurch and Wem. And even now he could have forded the river only a little way downstream and made off at speed by that road, but he was damned if he would! He had committed no crime, he had said only what he held to be right, and there was nothing in it of blasphemy or disrespect to the Church, and he would not take back a word of it, or run away from his own utterances and afford his accusers a cheap triumph.

He had no way of knowing the time, but when he thought it must be drawing near to Vespers he left his nest, and made his way cautiously back by the same route, keeping in cover, until he could see between the trees the dusty whiteness of the road, the people passing along it, and the lively bustle about the gatehouse. He had a while to wait before the Vesper bell rang, and he spent it moving warily from one cover to another, to see whether any of his pursuers were to be noted among the people gathering outside the west door of the church. He recognised none, but in the constant movement it was difficult to be sure. The big man who had been left to guard the gate was nowhere within view. Elave's best moment would come when the little bell was heard, and the gossips passing the time of day there in the early evening sunshine would gather and move into the church.

The moment was on him as fast as the thought. The bell chimed, and the worshippers gathered their families, saluted their friends, and began to move in by the west door. Elave darted out in time to mingle with them and hide himself in the middle of the procession, and there was no outcry, no rough hand grasping him by the shoulder. Now he had a choice between continuing left with the good people of the Foregate into the church, or slipping through the open gate of the

80

enclave into the great court, and walking calmly across to the guest-hall. If he had chosen the church all might have been well, but the temptation to walk openly into the court as from a respectable stroll was too much for him. He left the shelter of the worshippers, and turned in through the gate.

From the doorway of the porter's lodge on his right a great howl of triumph soared, and was echoed from the road he had left behind. The canon's giant groom had been talking with the porter, vengeance in ambush, and two of his colleagues were just coming back from a foray into the town. All three of them fell upon the returning prodigal at once. A heavy cudgel struck him on the back of the head, sending him staggering, and before he could regain his balance or his wits he was grappled in the big man's muscular arms, while one of the others caught him by the hair, dragging his head back. He let out a yell of rage, and laid about him with fist and foot, heaving off his assailant from behind, wrenching one arm free from the big man's embrace and lashing out heartily at his nose. A second blow on the head drove him to his knees, half stunned. Distantly he heard dismayed voices crying out at such violence on sacred ground, and sandalled feet running hastily over the cobbles. Lucky for him that the brothers were just gathering from their various occupations to the sound of the bell.

Brother Edmund from the infirmary, Brother Cadfael from the turn of the path into the garden, bore down on the unseemly struggle with habits flying.

'Stop that! Stop at once!' cried Edmund, scandalised at the profanation, and waving agitated arms impartially at all the offenders.

Cadfael, with a sharper turn of speed, wasted no breath on remonstrance, but made straight for the cudgel that was uplifted for a third blow at the victim's already bloodied head, halted it in midair, and twisted it without difficulty out of the hand that wielded it, fetching a howl from the over-enthusiastic groom in the process. The three huntsmen ceased battering their captive, but kept fast hold of him, hauling him to his feet and pinning him between them as though he might yet slip through their fingers and make off like a hare through the gate.

'We've got him!' they proclaimed almost in unison. 'It's him, it's the heretic! He was for making off out of trouble, but we've got him for you, safe and sound—'

'Sound?' Cadfael echoed ruefully. 'You've half killed the lad between you. Did it need three of you to deal with one man?

Here he was, within the pale, did you have to break his head for him?'

'We've been hunting him all the afternoon,' protested the big man, swelling with his own prowess, 'as Canon Gerbert ordered us. Were we to take any chances with such a fellow when we did lay hands on him? Find and bring him back, we were told, and here he is.'

'Bring him?' said Cadfael, shoving one of Elave's captors unceremoniously aside to take his place, with an arm about the young man's body to support him. 'I saw from the turn of the hedge there who brought him back. He walked in here of his own will. You can take no credit for it, even if you count what you're about as credit. What possessed your master to set the dogs on him in the first place? He gave his word he wouldn't run, and Father Abbot accepted it, and said he was free to go and come as he pleased for the time being. A pledge good enough for our abbot was not good enough for Canon Gerbert, I suppose?'

By that time three or four others had gathered excitedly about them, and here came Prior Robert, sailing towards them from the corner of the cloister in acute displeasure at seeing what appeared to be an agitated and disorderly gathering disturbing the procession to Vespers.

'What is this? What is happening here? Have you not heard the bell?' His eyes fell upon Elave, propped up unsteadily between Cadfael and Edmund, his clothes dusty and in disarray, his brow and cheek smeared with blood. 'Oh,' he said, satisfaction tempered with some dismay at the violence done, 'so they have brought you back. It seems the attempt at flight cost you dear. I am sorry you are hurt, but you should not have run from justice.'

'I did not run from justice,' said Elave, panting. 'The lord abbot gave me leave to go and come freely, on my word not to run, and I did not run.'

'That is truth,' said Cadfael, 'for he walked in here of his own accord. He was heading for the guest-hall, where he's lodged like any other traveller, when these fellows fell upon him, and now they claim to have recaptured him for Canon Gerbert. Did he ever give such orders?'

'Canon Gerbert understood the liberty granted him as holding good only within the enclave,' said the prior sharply. 'So, I must say, did I. When this man was found to have gone from the court we supposed him to have attempted escape. But

82

I am sorry it was necessary to be so rough with him. Now what is to be done? He needs attention ... Cadfael, see to his hurts, if you will, and after Vespers I will see the abbot and tell him what has happened. It may be he should be housed in isolation ...'

Which meant, thought Cadfael, in a cell, under lock and key. Well, at worst that would keep these great oafs away from him. But we shall see what Abbot Radulfus will say.

'If I may miss Vespers,' he said, 'I'll have him away into the infirmary for now, and take care of his injuries there. He'll need no armed guards, the state he's in, but I'll stay with him until we get the lord abbot's orders concerning him.'

'Well, at least,' said Cadfael, bathing away blood from Elave's head in the small anteroom in the infirmary, where the medicine cupboard was kept, 'you left your mark on a couple of them. And though you'll have a devil of a headache for a while, you've a good hard skull, and there'll be no lasting harm. I don't know but you'd be just as well in a penitential cell till all blows over. The bed's the same as all the other beds, the cell's fine and cool in this weather, there's a little desk for reading – our delinquents are meant to spend their time during imprisonment in improving their minds and repenting their errors. Can you read?'

'Yes,' said Elave, passive under the ministering hands.

'Then we could ask for books from the library for you. The right course with a young fellow who's gone astray after unblessed beliefs is to ply him with the works of the Church fathers, and visit him with good counsel and godly argument. With me to minister to your bruises, and Anselm to discuss this world and the next with you, you'd have some of the best company to be had in this enclave, and with official sanction, mind. And a solitary cell keeps out the bleatings of fools and zealous idiots who hunt three to a lone man. Keep still now! Does that hurt?'

'No,' said Elave, curiously soothed by this flow of talk which he did not quite know how to take. 'You think they will shut me up in a cell?'

'I think Canon Gerbert will insist. And it's not so easy to refuse the archbishop's envoy over details. For they've come to the conclusion, I hear, that your case cannot be simply dismissed. That's Gerbert's verdict. The abbot's is that if there is to be further probing, it must be by your own bishop, and nothing shall be done until he declares what he wishes in the matter. And little Serlo is off to Coventry tomorrow morning, to report to him all that has happened. So no harm can come to you and no one can question or fret you until Roger de Clinton has had his say. You may as well pass your time as pleasantly as possible. Anselm has built up a very passable library.'

'I think,' said Elave with quickening interest, in spite of his aching head, 'I should like to read Saint Augustine, and see if he really did write what he's said to have written.'

'About the number of the elect? He did, in a treatise called "De Correptione et Gratia", if my memory serves me right. Which,' said Cadfael honestly, 'I have never read, though I have had it read to me in the frater. Could you manage him in the Latin? I'd be small help to you there, but Anselm would.'

'It's a strange thing,' said Elave, pondering with deep solemnity over the course of events which had brought him to this curious pass, 'all the years I worked for William, and travelled with him, and listened to him, I never truly gave any thought to these things until now. They never bothered me. They do now, they matter to me now. If no one had meddled with William's memory and tried to deny him a grave, I never should have given thought to them.'

'If it's any help to have company along the way,' admitted Cadfael, 'I begin to find my case much the same as yours. Where the seed lights, the herb grows. And there's nothing like hard usage and drought to drive its roots in deep.'

Jevan came back to the house near Saint Alkmund's when it was already dark, with a bundle of new white skins of vellum, of a silken, creamy texture, and very thin and supple. He was proud of the work he did. The prior of Haughmond would not be disappointed in the wares on offer. Jevan bestowed them carefully in the shop, and locked up there before crossing the yard to the hall, where supper was laid, and Margaret and Fortunata were waiting for him.

'Is Aldwin not back yet?' he asked, looking round with raised brows as they sat down only three to table.

Margaret looked up from serving with a somewhat anxious face. 'No, no sign of him since. I was getting worried about him. What can possibly have kept him this long?'

'He'll have fallen foul of the theologians,' said Jevan, shrugging, 'and serve him right for throwing the other lad to them, like a bone to a pack of dogs. He'll be still at the abbey, and his turn to answer awkward questions. But they'll turn him loose when they've wrung him dry. Whether they'll do as much for Elave there's no knowing. Well, I shall lock up the house as usual before I go to my bed. If he creeps back later than that he'll have to lie in the stable-loft for the night.'

'Conan's not back, either,' said Margaret, shaking her head over the distressful day that should have been all celebration. 'And I thought Girard would have been home before this. I hope nothing has happened to him.'

'Nothing will have happened,' Jevan assured her firmly, 'but some matter of business to his profit. You know he can take very good care of himself, and he has excellent relations all along the border. If he meant to be back for the festival, and has missed his day, it will be because he's added a couple of new customers to his tally. It takes time to strike a bargain with a Welsh sheep-man. He'll be back home safe and sound in a day or so.'

'And what will he find when he does get home?' She sighed ruefully. 'Elave in this trouble as soon as he shows his face here again, Uncle William dead and buried, and now Aldwin getting himself still deeper into so bad a business. Truly I hope you're right, and he has done well with the wool clip, it will be some comfort at least if one thing has gone right.'

She rose to clear away the supper dishes, still shaking her head over undefined misgivings, and Fortunata was left alone with Jevan.

'Uncle,' she said hesitantly, after some minutes of silence, 'I wanted to talk to you. Whether I like it or not, I have been drawn into this terrible charge against Elave. He will not believe he is in grave danger, but I know he is. I want to help him. I must help him.'

The solemnity of her voice had caused him to turn and regard her long and attentively, with those black, penetrating eyes that saw deep into her now as in her childhood, and always with detached affection.

'I think this matters to you,' he said, 'more than might appear, when you have barely seen him again, and after years.'

It was not a question, but she answered it. 'I think I love him. What else can this be? It is not so strange. There were years before the years of his absence. I liked him then, better than he knew.'

'And you talked with him today, as I remember,' he said keenly, 'after this hearing at the abbey.'

'Yes,' she said.

'And thereafter, I fancy, he knows better how well you like him! And has he given you cause to be as certain of his liking for you?'

'Cause enough. He said that if there were no other reason I should be reason enough to hold him fast, in despite of whatever danger there may be to him here. Uncle, you know I have a dowry now from William. When my father comes home, and that box is opened, I want to use whatever he has given me to help Elave. To offer for his fine, if a fine is allowed to pay off his debt, to bargain for his liberty if they hold him, yes, even to corrupt his guards if the worst comes, and get him away over the border.'

'And you'd feel no guilt,' said Jevan with his sharp, dark smile, 'at defying the law and flouting the Church?'

'None, because he has done no wrong. If they condemn him, it's they who are guilty. But I mean to ask Father to speak up for him. As one who knows him, and is respected by everyone, law, Church and all. If Girard of Lythwood stood guarantor for his future behaviour, I believe they might listen.'

'So they might,' agreed Jevan heartily. 'At least that and every other means can be tried. I told you – if you want him, then Elave can and shall count as a man of ours. There, you be off to your bed and sleep easy. Who knows what magic may be discovered when William's box is opened?'

Late but not too late, Conan came home just before the door was locked, only a little tipsy after celebrating the end of the day, as he freely admitted, with half a dozen boon companions at the alehouse in Mardol.

Aldwin did not come home at all.

Chapter Seven

ROTHER CADFAEL arose well before Prime, took his scrip, and went out to collect certain waterside plants, now in their full summer leaf. The morning was veiled with a light covering of cloud, through which the sun shimmered in pearly tints of faint rose and misty blue. Later it would clear and be hot again. As he went out from the gatehouse a groom was just bringing up Serlo's mule from the stable-yard, and the bishop's deacon came out from the guest-hall ready for his journey, and paused at the top of the steps to draw deep breath, as though the solitary ride to Coventry held out to him all the delights of a holiday, by comparison with riding in Canon Gerbert's overbearing company. His errand, perhaps, was less pleasurable. So gentle a soul would not enjoy reporting to his bishop an accusation that might threaten a young man's liberty and life, but by his very nature he would probably make as fair a case as he could for the accused. And Roger de Clinton was a man of good repute, devout and charitable if austere, a founder of religious houses and patron of poor priests. All might yet go well for Elave, if he did not let his newly discovered predilection for undisciplined thought run away with him.

I must talk to Anselm about some books for him, Cadfael reminded himself as he left the dusty highroad and began to descend the green path to the riverside, threading the bushes now at the most exuberant of their summer growth, rich cover for fugitives or the beasts of the woodland. The vegetable gardens of the Gaye unfolded green and neat along the riverside, the uncut grass of the bank making a thick emerald barrier between water and tillage. Beyond were the orchards, and then two fields of grain and the disused mill, and after that trees and bushes leaning over the swift, silent currents, crowding an overhanging bank, indented here and there by little coves, where the water lay deceptively innocent and still, lipping sandy shallows. Cadfael wanted comfrey and marsh mallow, both the leaves and the roots, and knew exactly where they grew profusely. Freshly prepared root and leaf of comfrey to heal Elave's broken head, marsh mallow to soothe the surface soreness, were better than the ready-made ointments or the poultices from dried material in his workshop. Nature was a rich provider in summer. Stored medicines were for the winter.

He had filled his scrip and was on the point of turning back, in no hurry since he had plenty of time before Prime, when his eye caught the pallor of some strange water-flower that floated out on the idle current from under the overhanging bushes, and again drifted back, trailing soiled white petals. The tremor of the water overlaid them with shifting points of light as the early sun came through the veil. In a moment they floated out again into full view, and this time they were seen to be joined to a thick pale stem that ended abruptly in something dark.

There were places along this stretch of the river where the Severn sometimes brought in and discarded whatever it had captured higher upstream. In low water, as now, things cast adrift above the bridge were usually picked up at that point. Once past the bridge, they might well drift in anywhere along this stretch. Only in the swollen and turgid floods of winter storms or February thaws did the Severn hurl them on beyond, to fetch up, perhaps, as far downstream as Attingham, or to be trapped deep down in the debris of storms, and never recovered at all. Cadfael knew most of the currents, and knew now from what manner of root this pallid, languid flower grew. The brightness of the morning, opening like a rose as the gossamer cloud parted, seemed instead to darken the promising day.

He put down his scrip in the grass, kilted his habit, and clambered down through the bushes to the shallow water. The river had brought in its drowned man with just enough impetus and at the right angle to lodge him securely under the bank. He lay sprawled on his face, only the left arm in deep enough water to be moved and cradled by the stream, a lean, stoop-shouldered man in dun-coloured coat and hose, indeed with something dun-coloured about him altogether, as though he had begun life in brighter colours and been faded by the discouragement of time. Grizzled, straggling hair, more grey than brown, draped a balding skull. But the river had not taken him, he had been committed to it with intent. In the back of his coat, just where its ample folds broke the surface of the water, there was a long slit, from the upper end of which a meagre ooze of blood had darkened and corroded the coarse homespun. Where his bowed back rose just clear of the surface, the stain was even drying into a crust along the folds of cloth.

Cadfael stood calf-deep between the body and the river, in case the dead man should be drawn back into the current when disturbed, and turned the corpse face upward, exposing to view the long, despondent, grudging countenance of Girard of Lythwood's clerk, Aldwin.

There was nothing to be done for him. He was sodden and bleached with water, surely dead for many hours. Nor could he be left lying here while help was sought to move him, or the river might snatch him back again. Cadfael took him under the arms and drew him along through the shallows to a spot where the bank sloped gently down, and there pulled him up into the grassy shelf above. Then he set off at speed, back along the riverside path to the bridge. There he hesitated for a moment which way to take, up into the town to carry the news to Hugh Beringar, or back to the abbey to inform abbot and prior, but it was towards the town he turned. Canon Gerbert could wait for the news that the accuser would never again testify against Elave, in the matter of heresy or any other offence. Not that his death would end the case! On the contrary, it was at the back of Cadfael's mind that an even more sinister shadow was closing over that troublesome young man in a penitent's cell at the abbey. He had no time to contemplate the implications then, but they were there in his consciousness as he hurried across the bridge and in at the town gate, and he liked them not at all. Better, far better, to go first to Hugh, and let him consider the meaning of this death, before other and less reasonable beings got their teeth into it.

'How long,' asked Hugh, looking down at the dead man with bleak attention, 'do you suppose he's been in the water?'

He was asking, not Cadfael, but Madog of the Dead-Boat,

summoned hastily from his hut and his coracles by the western bridge. There was very little about the ways of the Severn that Madog did not know, it was his life, as it had been the death of many of his generation in its treacherous flood-times. Given a hint as to where an unfortunate had gone into the stream, Madog would know where to expect the river to give him back, and it was to him everyone turned to find what was lost. He scratched thoughtfully at his bushy beard, and viewed the corpse without haste from head to foot. Already a little bloated, grey of flesh and oozing water and weed into the grass, Aldwin peered back into the bright sky from imperfectly closed eyes.

'All last night, certainly. Ten hours it might be, but more likely less, it would still have been daylight then. Somewhere, I fancy,' said Madog, 'he was laid up dead until dark, and then cast into the river. And not far from here. Most of the night he's lain here where Cadfael found him. How else would there still be blood to be seen on him? If he had not washed up within a short distance, face down as you say he was, the river would have bleached him clean.'

'Between here and the bridge?' Hugh suggested, eyeing the little dark, hairy Welshman with respectful attention. Sheriff and waterman, they had worked together before this, and knew each other well.

'With the level as it is, if he'd gone in above the bridge I doubt if he'd ever have passed it.'

Hugh looked back along the open green plain of the Gaye, lush and sunny, through the fringe of bushes and trees. 'Between here and the bridge nothing could happen in open day. This is the first cover to be found beside the water. And though this fellow may be a light-weight, no one would want to carry or drag him very far to reach the river. And if he'd been cast in here, whoever wanted to be quit of him would have made sure he went far enough out for the current to take him down the next reach and beyond. What do you say, Madog?'

Madog confirmed it with a jerk of his shaggy head.

'There's been no rain and no dew,' said Cadfael thoughtfully. 'Grass and ground are dry. If he was hidden until nightfall, it would be close where he was killed. A man needs privacy and cover both to kill and to hide his dead. Somewhere there may be traces of blood in the grass, or wherever the murderer bestowed him.'

'We can but look,' agreed Hugh, with no great expectation

90

of finding anything. 'There's the old mill offers one place where murder could be done without a witness. I'll have them search there. We'll comb this belt of trees, too, though I doubt there'll be anything here to find. And what should this fellow be doing at the mill, or here, for that matter? You've told me how he spent the morning. What he did afterwards we may find out from the household up there in the town. They know nothing of this yet. They may well be wondering and enquiring about him by this time, if it's dawned on them yet that he's been out all night. Or perhaps he often was, and no one wondered. I know little enough about him, but I know he lived there with his master's family. But beyond the mill, upstream – no, the whole stretch of the Gaye lies open. There's nothing from here on could give shelter to a killing. Nothing until the bridge. But surely, if the man was killed by daylight, and left in the bushes there even a couple of hours until dark, he might be found before he could be put into the river.'

'Would that matter?' wondered Cadfael. 'A little more risky, perhaps, but still there'd be nothing to show who slipped the dagger into his back. Sending him down-river does but confuse place and time. And perhaps that was important to whoever did it.'

'Well, I'll take the news up to the wool-merchants myself, and see what they can tell me.' Hugh looked round to where his sergeant and four men of the castle garrison stood a little apart, waiting for his orders in attentive silence. 'Will can see the body brought up after us. The fellow has no other home, to my knowledge, they'll need to take care of his burying. Come back with me, Cadfael, we'll at least take a look among the trees by the bridge, and under the arch.'

They set off side by side, out of the fringe of trees into the abbey wheatfields and past the abandoned mill. They had reached the waterside path that hemmed the kitchen gardens when Hugh asked, slanting a brief, oblique and burdened smile along his shoulder: 'How long did you say that heretical pilgrim of yours was out at liberty yesterday? While Canon Gerbert's grooms went puffing busily up and down looking for him to no purpose?'

It was asked quite lightly and currently, but Cadfael understood its significance, and knew that Hugh had already grasped it equally well. 'From about an hour before Nones until Vespers,' he said, and clearly heard the unacknowledged but unmistakeable reserve and concern in his own voice.

'And then he walked into the enclave in all conscious innocence. And has not accounted for where he spent those hours?'

'No one has yet asked him,' said Cadfael simply.

'Good! Then do my work for me there, will you? Tell no one in the abbey yet about this death, and let no one question Elave until I do it myself. I'll be with you before the morning's out, and we'll talk privately with the abbot before anyone else shall know what's happened. I want to see this lad for myself, and hear what he has to say for himself before any other gets at him. For you know, don't you,' said Hugh with detached sympathy, 'what his inquisitors are going to say?'

Cadfael left them to their search of the grove of trees and the bushes that cloaked the path down to the riverside, and made his way back to the abbey, though with some reluctance at abandoning the hunt even for a few hours. He was well aware of the immediate implications of Aldwin's death, and uneasily conscious that he did not know Elave well enough to discount them out of hand. Instinctive liking is not enough to guarantee any man's integrity, let alone his innocence of murder, where he had been basely wronged, and was by chance presented with the opportunity to avenge his injury. A high and hasty temper, which undoubtedly he had, might do the rest almost before he could think at all, let alone think better of it.

But *in the back*?

No, that Cadfael could not imagine. Had there been such an encounter it would have been face to face. And what of the dagger? Did Elave even possess such a weapon? A knife for all general purposes he must possess, no sensible traveller would go far without one. But he would not be carrying it on him in the abbey, and he certainly had not taken the time to go and collect it from his belongings in the guest-hall, before hurrying out at the gate after Fortunata. The porter could testify to that. He had come rushing straight up from the chapter-house without so much as a glance aside. And if by unlikely chance he had had it on him at that hearing, then it must be with him now in his locked cell. Or if he had discarded it, Hugh's sergeants would do their best to find it. Of one thing Cadfael was certain, he did not want Elave to be a murderer.

Just as Cadfael was approaching the gatehouse, someone emerged from it and turned towards the town. A tall, lean, dark man, frowning down abstractedly at the dust of the

Foregate as he strode, and shaking his head at some puzzling frustration of his own, probably of no great moment but still puzzling. He jerked momentarily out of his preoccupation when Cadfael gave him good-day, and returned the greeting with a vague glance and an absent smile before withdrawing again into whatever matter was chafing at his peace of mind.

It was altogether too apt a reminder, that Jevan of Lythwood should be calling in at the abbey gatehouse at this hour of the morning, after his brother's clerk had failed to come home the previous night. Cadfael turned to look after him. A tall man with a long, ardent stride, making for home with his hands clasped behind his back, and his brows knotted in so far unenlightened conjecture. Cadfael hoped he would cross the bridge without pausing to look down over the parapet towards the level, sunlit length of the Gaye, where at this moment Will Warden's men might be carrying the litter with Aldwin's body. Better that Hugh should reach the house first, both to warn the household, and to harvest whatever he could from their bearing and their answers, before the inevitable burden arrived to set the busy and demanding rites of death in motion.

'What was Jevan of Lythwood wanting here?' Cadfael asked of the porter, who was making himself useful holding a very handsome and lively young mare while her master buckled on his saddle-roll behind. A good number of the guests would be moving on today, having paid their annual tribute to Saint Winifred.

'He wanted to know if his clerk had been here,' said the porter.

'Why did he suppose his clerk should have been here?'

'He says he changed his mind, yesterday, about laying charges against that lad we've got under lock and key, as soon as he found out the young fellow had no intention of elbowing him out of his employment. Said he was all for rushing off down here on the spot to take back what he'd laid against him. Much good that would do! Small use running after the arrow once it's loosed. But that's what he wanted to do, so his master says.'

'What did you tell him?' asked Cadfael.

'What should I tell him? I told him we've seen nor hide nor hair of his clerk since he went out of the gate here early yesterday afternoon. It seems he's been missing overnight. But wherever he's been, he hasn't been here.'

Cadfael pondered this new turn of events with misgiving.

'When was it he took this change of heart, and started back here? What time of the day?'

'Very near as soon as he got home, so Jevan says. No more than an hour after he'd left here. But he never came,' said the porter placidly. 'Changed his mind again, I daresay, when he got near, and began to reason how it might fall back on him, without delivering the other fellow.'

Cadfael went on down the court very thoughtfully. He had already missed Prime, but there was ample time before the Mass; he might as well take himself off to his workshop and unload his scrip, and try to get all these confused and confusing events clear in his mind. If Aldwin had come running back with the idea of undoing what he had done, then even if he had encountered an angry and resentful Elave, it would have needed only the first hasty words of penitence and restitution to disarm the avenger. Why kill a man who is willing at least to try to make amends? Still, some might argue, an angry man might not wait for any words, but strike on sight. *In the back*? No, it would not do. That Elave had killed his accuser might be the first thought to spring into other minds, but it could find no lodging in Cadfael's. And not for mere obstinate liking, either, but because it made no sense.

Hugh arrived towards the end of chapter, alone and, somewhat to Cadfael's surprise, as well as to his profound relief, ahead of any other and untoward report. Rumour was usually so blithe and busy about the town and the Foregate that he had expected word of Aldwin's death to worm its way in with inconvenient speed and a good deal of regrettable embroidery to the plain tale, but it had not happened. Hugh could tell the story his own way, and in the privacy of Abbot Radulfus's parlour, with Cadfael to confirm and supplement. And the abbot did not say what, inevitably, someone else very soon would. Instead he said directly:

'Who last saw the man alive?'

'From what we know so far,' said Hugh, 'those who saw him go out of the house early yesterday afternoon. Jevan of Lythwood, who came enquiring for him here this morning, as Cadfael says, before ever I got the word to him of his man's death. The fosterchild Fortunata, she who was made a witness to the charge yesterday. The woman of the house. And the shepherd Conan. But that was broad daylight, he must have been seen by others, at the town gate, on the bridge, here in the Foregate, or wherever he turned aside. We shall trace his every step, to fill in the time before he died.'

'But we cannot know when that was,' said Radulfus.

'No, true, no better than a guess. But Madog judges he was put into the river as soon as it grew dark, and that he'd lain hidden somewhere after his death, waiting for dark. Perhaps two or three hours, but there's no knowing. I have men out looking for any trace of where he may have lain hidden. If we find that, we find where he was murdered, for he could not have been moved far.'

'And all Lythwood's household are in one tale together – that the clerk, when he heard the young man made no claim to his place, started to come here, to confess his malice and withdraw the charge he had made?'

'Further, the girl says that she had parted from Elave in the trees, there not far from the bridge, and told Aldwin so. She believes he went off in such haste in the hope of overtaking him. She says also,' said Hugh with emphasis, 'that she urged Elave to take to his heels, and he refused.'

'Then what he did accords with what he said,' Radulfus allowed. 'And his accuser set out to confess and beg pardon. Yes – it argues against,' he said, holding Hugh eye to eye.

'There are those who will argue for. And it must be said,' Hugh owned fairly, 'that circumstances give body to what they'll say. He was at liberty, he had good reason to bear a grudge. We know of no one else who had cause to strike at Aldwin. He set off to meet Elave, there in the trees. In cover. It hangs together, on the face of it, all too well, for the body must surely have gone into the water below the bridge, and cover is scant there along the Gaye.'

'All true,' said Radulfus. 'But equally true, I think, that if the young man had killed he would hardly have walked back into our precinct of his own will, as admittedly he did. Moreover, if the dead man was cast into the river after dark, that was not done by Elave. At least we know at what hour he returned here, it was just when the Vesper bell sounded. That does not prove past doubt that he did not kill, but it casts it into question. Well, we have him safe.' He smiled, a little grimly. It was an ambiguous reassurance. A stone cell, securely locked, ensured Elave's personal safety not less than his close custody. 'And now you wish to question him.'

In your presence,' said Hugh, 'if you will.' And catching the sharp, intelligent eye he said simply: 'Better with a witness who

95

cannot be suspect. You are as good a judge of a man as I am, and better.'

'Very well,' said Radulfus. 'He shall not come to us. We will go to him, while they are all in the frater. Robert is in attendance on Canon Gerbert.' So he would be, thought Cadfael uncharitably. Robert was not the man to let slip the chance to ingratiate himself with a man of influence with the archbishop. For once his predilection for the powerful would be useful. 'Anselm has been asking me to send the boy books to read,' said the abbot. 'He points out, rightly, that we have a duty to provide good counsel and exhortation, if we are to combat erroneous beliefs. Do you feel fitted, Cadfael, to undertake an advocacy on God's behalf?'

'I am not sure,' said Cadfael bluntly, thus brought up against the measure of his own concern and partisanship, 'that the instructed would not be ahead of the instructor. I see my measure more in tending his broken head than in meddling with the sound mind inside it.'

Elave sat on his narrow pallet in one of the two stone penitential cells which were seldom occupied, and told what he had to tell, while Cadfael renewed the dressings on his gashes, and bandaged him afresh. He still looked somewhat the worse for wear, bruised and stiff from the attentions of Gerbert's over-zealous grooms, but by no means subdued. At first, indeed, he was inclined to be belligerent, on the assumption that all these officials, religious and secular alike, must be hostile, and predisposed to find fault in every word he said. It was an attitude which did not consort well with his customary openness and amiability, and Cadfael was sorry to see him thus maimed, even for a brief time. But it seemed that he did not find in his visitors quite the animosity and menace he had expected, for in a little while his closed and wary face eased and warmed, and the chill edge melted from his voice.

'I gave my word I would not quit this place,' he said firmly, 'until I was fairly dismissed as free and fit to go, and I never meant to do otherwise than as I said. You told me, my lord, that I was free to come and go on my own business meantime, and so I did, and never thought wrong. I went after the lady because she was in distress for me, and that I could not abide. You saw it yourself, Father Abbot. I overtook her before the bridge. I wanted to tell her not to fret, for she did me no wrong, what she said of me I had indeed said, and I would not for the world have had her grieve at speaking truth, whatever might fall on me. And also,' said Elave, taking heart in remembering, 'I wanted to show her my thankfulness, that she felt gently towards me. For it showed plain, you also saw it, and I was glad of it.'

'And when you parted from her?' said Hugh.

'I would have come back straightway, but I saw them come boiling out of the gate here and quartering the Foregate, and it was plain they were hot on my heels already. So I drew off into the trees to wait my chance. I had no mind to be dragged back by force,' said Elave indignantly, 'when I had nothing in mind but to walk in of my own will, and sit and wait for my judgement. But they left the big fellow standing guard, and I never got my chance to get past him. I thought if I waited for Vespers I might take cover and slip in among the folk coming to church.'

'But you did not spend all that time close here in hiding,' said Hugh, 'for I hear they drew every covert for half a mile from the road. Where did you go?'

'Made my way back through the trees, round behind the Gaye and a fair way down the river, and lay up in cover there till I thought it must be almost time for Vespers.'

'And you saw nobody in all that time? Nobody saw or spoke to you?'

'It was my whole intent that nobody should see me,' said Elave reasonably. 'I was hiding from a hue and cry. No, there's no one can speak for me all that time. But why should I come back as I did, if I meant to run? I could have been halfway to the border in that time. Acquit me at least of going back on my word.'

'That you certainly have not done,' said Abbot Radulfus. 'And you may believe that I knew nothing of this pursuit of you, and would not have countenanced it. No doubt it was done out of pure zeal, but it was misdirected and blameworthy, and I am sorry you should have fallen victim to violence. No one now supposes that you had any intent of running away. I accepted your word, I would do so again.'

Elave peered from beneath Brother Cadfael's bandages with brows drawn together in puzzlement, looking from face to face without understanding. 'Then why these questions? Does it matter where I went, since I came back again? How is it to the purpose?' He looked longest and most intently at Hugh, whose authority was secular, and should have had nothing to do or

97

say in a charge of heresy. 'What is it? Something has happened. What can there be new since yesterday? What is it that I do not know?'

They were all studying him hard and silently, wondering indeed whether he did or did not know, and whether a relatively simple young man could dissemble so well, and one whose word the abbot had taken without question only one day past. Whatever conclusion they came to could not then be declared. Hugh said with careful mildness: 'First, perhaps you should know what Fortunata and her family have told us. You parted from her between here and the bridge, that she confirms, and she then went home. There she encountered and reproached your accuser Aldwin for bringing such a charge against you, and it came out that he had been afraid of losing his place to you, a matter of great gravity to him, as you'll allow.'

'But it was no such matter,' said Elave, astonished. 'That was settled the first time I set foot in the house. I never wanted to elbow him out, and Dame Margaret told me fairly enough they would not oust him. He had nothing to fear from me.'

'But he thought he had. No one had put it in plain terms to him until then. And when he heard it, as they all four agree – the shepherd, too – he declared his intent of running after you to confess and ask pardon, and if he failed to overtake you – the girl having told him where she had left you – of following you here to the abbey to do his best to undo what he had done against you.'

Elave shook his head blankly. 'I never saw him. I was among the trees ten minutes or more, watching the road, before I gave up and went off towards the river. I should have seen him if he'd passed. Maybe he took fright when he saw them beating all the coverts and baying after me along the Foregate, and thought better of repenting.' It was said without bitterness, even with a resigned grin. 'It's easier and safer to set the hounds on than to call them off.'

'A true word!' said Hugh. 'They have been known to bite the huntsman, if he came between them and the quarry once their blood was up. So you never saw and had speech with him, and have no notion where he went or what happened to him?'

'None in the world. Why?' asked Elave simply. 'Have you lost him?'

'No,' said Hugh, 'we have found him. Brother Cadfael found him early this morning lodged under the bank of the Severn beyond the Gaye. Dead, stabbed in the back.'

'Did he know or did he not?' wondered Hugh, when they were out in the great court, and the cell door closed and locked on the prisoner. 'You saw him, do you know what to make of him? Fix him as watchfully as you will, any man can lie if he must. I would rather rely on things solid and provable. He did come back. Would a man who had killed do so? He has a good, serviceable knife, well able to kill, but it's in his bundle in the guest-hall still, not on him, and we know he no sooner showed his face in the gateway than he was set on, and attended every moment after, until that door closed on him. If he had another knife, and had it on him, he must have discarded it. Father Abbot, do you believe this lad? Is he telling truth? When he offered his word, you accepted it. Do you still do so?'

'I neither believe nor disbelieve,' said Radulfus heavily. 'How dare I? But I hope!'

Chapter Eight

ILLIAM WARDEN, who was the longest serving and most experienced of Hugh's sergeants, came looking for the sheriff just as Hugh and Cadfael were crossing to the gatehouse; a big, bearded, burly man of middle age, grizzled and weatherbeaten, and with a solid conceit of himself that sometimes tended to undervalue others. He had taken Hugh for a lightweight when first the young man succeeded to the sheriff's office, but time had considerably tempered that opinion, and brought them into a relationship of healthy mutual respect. The sergeant's beard was bristling with satisfaction now. Clearly he had made progress, and was pleased with himself accordingly.

'My lord, we've found it – the place where he was laid up till dark. Or at least, where he or some other bled long enough to leave his traces clear enough. While we were beating the bushes Madog thought to search through the grass under the arch of the bridge. Some fisherman had drawn up his light boat there, and turned it up to do some caulking on the boards. He wouldn't be working on it yesterday, a feast day. When we hoisted it, there was the grass flattened the length of it, and a small patch of it blackened with blood. What with the dry weather, that ground has been uncovered a month or more, it's bleached pale as straw. There's no missing that stain, meagre though it is. A dead man could lie snug enough under there, with a boat upturned over him and nothing to show.'

'So that was the place!' said Hugh on a long, thoughtful

100

breath. 'And no great risk, slipping a body into the water there in the dark, from under the arch. No sound, no splash, nothing to see. With an oar, or a pole, you could thrust him well out into the current.'

'We were right, it seems,' said Cadfael. 'You have to deal only with that length of the water, from the bridge to where he fetched up. You did not find the knife?'

The sergeant shook his head. 'If he killed his man there, under the arch or in the bushes, he'd clean the knife in the edge of the water and take it away with him. Why waste a good knife? And why leave it lying about for some neighbour to find, and say: I know that, it belongs to John Weaver, or whoever it might be, and how comes it to have blood on it? No, we shan't find the knife.'

'True,' said Hugh, 'a man would have to be scared out of his wits to throw it away to be found, and I fancy this man was in sharp command of his. Never mind, you've done well, we know now where the thing was done, there or close by.'

'There's more yet to tell you, my lord,' said Will, gratified, 'and stranger, if he was in such a hurry as they told us, when he ran off to recant his charges. We asked the porter on the town gate if he'd seen him pass out and cross the bridge, and he said yes, he had, and spoke to him, but barely got an answer. But he hadn't come straight from Lythwood's house, that's certain. It was more than an hour later, maybe as much as an hour and a half.'

'He's sure of that?' demanded Hugh. 'There's no real check there, not in quiet times. He could be hazy about time passing.'

'He's sure. He saw them all come back after the hubbub they had here at chapter, Aldwin and the shepherd first and the girl after, and it seemed to him they were all of them in an upset. He'd heard nothing then of what had happened, but he did notice the fuss they were in, and long before Aldwin came down to the gate again the whole tale was out. The porter was all agog when he laid eyes on the very man coming down the Wyle, he was hoping to stop him and gossip, but Aldwin went past without a word. Oh, he's sure enough! He knows how long had passed.'

'So all that time he was still in the town,' said Hugh, and gnawed a thoughtful lip. 'Yet in the end he did cross the bridge, going where he'd said he was going. But why the delay? What can have kept him?'

'Or who?' suggested Cadfael.

'Or who! Do you think someone ran after him to dissuade him? None of his own people, or they would have said so. Who else would try to turn him back? No one else knew what he was about. Well,' said Hugh, 'nothing else for it, we'll walk every yard of the way from Lythwood's house to the bridge, and hammer on every door, until we find out how far he got before turning aside. Someone must have seen him, somewhere along the way.'

'I fancy,' said Cadfael, pondering all he had seen and known of Aldwin, which was meagre enough and sad enough, 'he was not a man who had many friends, nor one of any great resolution of mind. He must have had to pluck up all his courage to accuse Elave in the first place, it would cost him more to withdraw his accusation, and put himself in the way of being suspect of perjury or malice or both. He may well have taken fright on the way, and changed his mind yet again, and decided to let well or ill alone. Where would a solitary dim soul like that go to think things out? And try to get his courage back? They sell courage of a sort in the taverns. And another sort, though not for sale, a man can find in the confessional. Try the alehouses and the churches, Hugh. In either a man can be quiet and think.'

It was one of the young men-at-arms of the castle garrison, not at all displeased at being given the task of enquiring at the alehouses of the town, who came up with the next link in Aldwin's uncertain traverse of Shrewsbury. There was a small tavern in a narrow, secluded close off the upper end of the steep, descending Wyle. It was sited about midway between the house near Saint Alkmund's church and the town gate, and the lanes leading to it were shut between high walls, and on a feast day might well be largely deserted. A man overtaken by someone bent on changing his mind for him, or suddenly possessed by misgivings calculated to change it for him without other persuasion, might well swerve from the direct way and debate the issue over a pot of ale in this quiet and secluded place. In any case, the young enquirer had no intention of missing any of the places of refreshment that lay within his commission.

'Aldwin?' said the potman, willing enough to talk about so sensational a tragedy. 'I only heard the word an hour past. Of course I knew him. A silent sort, mostly. If he did come in he'd sit in a corner and say hardly a word. He always expected the worst, you might say, but who'd have thought anyone would want to do him harm? He never did anyone else any that I knew of, not till this to-do yesterday. The talk is that the one he informed on has got his own back with a vengeance. And him with trouble enough,' said the potman, lowering his voice confidentially, 'if the Church has got its claws into him, small need to go crying out for worse.'

'Did you · see the man yesterday at all?' asked the man-at-arms.

'Aldwin? Yes, he was here for a while, up in the corner of the bench there, as glum as ever. I hadn't heard anything then about this business at the abbey, or I'd have taken more notice. We'd none of us any notion the poor soul would be dead by this morning. It falls on a man without giving him time to put his affairs in order.'

'He was here?' echoed the enquirer, elated. 'What time was that?'

'Well past noon. Nearly three, I suppose, when they came in.'

'They? He wasn't alone?'

'No, the other fellow brought him in, very confidential, with an arm round his shoulders and talking fast into his ear. They must have sat there for above half an hour, and then the other one went off and left him to himself another half-hour, brooding, it seemed. He was never a drinker, though, Aldwin. Sober as a stone when he got up and went out at the door, and without a word, mind you. Too late for words now, poor soul.'

'Who was it with him?' demanded the questioner eagerly. 'What's his name?'

'I don't know that I ever heard his name, but I know who he is. He works for the same master – that shepherd of theirs who keeps the flock they have out on the Welsh side of town.'

'Conan?' echoed Jevan, turning from the shelves of his shop with a creamy skin of vellum in his hands. 'He's off with the sheep, and he may very well sleep up there, these summer nights he often does. Why, is there anything new? He told you what he knew, what we all knew, this morning. Should we have kept him here? I knew of no reason you might need him again.'

'Neither did I, then,' agreed Hugh grimly. 'But it seems Master Conan told no more than half a tale, the half you and all the household could bear witness to. Not a word about running after Aldwin and haling him away into the tavern in the Three-Tree Shut, and keeping him in there more than half an hour.'

Jevan's level dark brows had soared to his hair, and his jaw dropped for a moment. 'He did that? He said he'd be off to the flock and get on with his work for the rest of the day. I took it that's what he'd done.' He came slowly to the solid table where he folded his skins, and spread the one he was carrying carefully over it, smoothing it out abstractedly with a sweep of one long hand. He was a very meticulous man. Everything in his shop was in immaculate order, the uncut skins draped over racks, the trimmed leaves ranged on shelves in their varied sizes, and the knives with which he cut and trimmed them laid out in neat alignment in their tray, ready to his hand. The shop was small, and open on to the street in this fine weather, its shutters laid by until nightfall.

'He went into the alehouse with Aldwin in his arm, so the potman says, about three o'clock. They were there a good half-hour, with Conan talking fast and confidentially into Aldwin's ear. Then Conan left him there, and I daresay did go to his work, and Aldwin still sat there another half-hour alone. That's the story my man unearthed, and that's the story I want out of Conan's hide, along with whatever more there may be to tell.'

Jevan stroked his long, well-shaven jaw and considered, with a speculative eye upon Hugh's face. 'Now that you tell me this, my lord, I must say I see more in what was said yesterday than I saw at the time. For when Aldwin said he must go and try to overtake that boy he'd done his best to ruin, and go with him to the monks to withdraw everything he'd said against him, Conan did tell him not to be a fool, that he'd only get himself into trouble, and do no good for the lad. He tried his best to dissuade him. But I thought nothing of it but that it was good sense enough, and all he meant was to haul Aldwin back out of danger. When I said let him go, if he's bent on it, Conan shrugged it off, and went off about his own business. Or so I thought. Now I wonder. Does not this sound to you as though he spent another half-hour trying to persuade the poor fool to give up his penitent notion? You say it was he was doing the talking, and Aldwin the listening. And another half-hour still before Aldwin could make up his mind to jump one way or the other.'

'It sounds like that indeed,' said Hugh. 'Moreover, if Conan went off content, and left him to himself, surely he thought he

104

had convinced him. If it meant so much to him he would not have let go until he was satisfied he'd got his way. But what I do not understand is why it should matter so gravely to him. Is Conan the man to venture so much for a friend, or care so much into what mire another man blundered?'

'I confess,' said Jevan, 'I've never thought so. He has a very sharp eye on his own advantage, though he's a good worker in his own line, and gives value for what he's paid.'

'Then why? What other reason could he have for going to such pains to persuade the poor wretch to let things lie? What could he possibly have against Elave, that he should want him dead, or buried alive in a Church prison? The lad's barely home. If they've exchanged a dozen words that must be the measure of it. If it's not concern for Aldwin or a grudge against Elave this fellow of yours has in mind, what is it?'

'You should ask him that,' said Jevan with a slow and baffled shake of his head, but with a certain wondering note in his voice that made Hugh prick up his ears.

'So I will. But now I am asking you.'

'Well,' said Jevan cautiously, 'you must bear in mind I may be wrong. But there is a matter which Conan may be holding against Elave. Quite without provocation, and no doubt Elave would be astonished if he knew of it. You have not noticed our Fortunata? She is grown into a very fresh and winning young woman, since Elave went off with my uncle on this pilgrimage to Jerusalem, and before that, you must remember, they were here familiar in the house some years, and liked each other well enough, he condescending to a child, and she childishly fond of a pleasant young man, even if he did no better than humour her liking. A very different matter he found her when he came back. And here's Conan ...'

'Who has known her as long, and seen her grow,' said Hugh sceptically, 'and could have offered for her long ago if he was so minded, with no Elave to stand in his way. And did he?'

'He did not,' Jevan granted, hollowly smiling. 'But times have changed. In spite of the name my uncle gave to her, Fortunata until now has had nothing of her own, to make her a good match. Young Elave has brought back from the east not only himself, but the legacy my Uncle William, bless his kindly soul, thought to send to his fosterchild when he knew he might not see her again. Oh, no, Conan has no knowledge, as yet, of what may be in the box Elave brought for her. It will not be opened until my brother gets home from his wool-buying. But

105

Conan knows it exists, it is here, it came from a generous man, virtually on his deathbed, when such a man would open his heart. From the looks I've seen Conan giving Fortunata these last few days, he's beginning to look on her as earmarked for him, dowry and all, and on Elave as a threat to be removed.'

'By death, if need be?' hazarded Hugh doubtfully. It seemed too bold and bitter an extreme for so ordinary a man to contemplate. 'It was not he who brought the charge.'

'I have wondered if they did not hatch that rotten egg between them. It suited them both to get rid of the youngster if they could, since it turns out Aldwin feared he might be elbowed out of office. It was like him to think the worst of my brother and me, as of all others. Oh, I doubt if either of them thought of anything so final as a death sentence. It would do if the lad was whisked off into the bishop's prison, or even so harried and ill-used here that he'd make off for healthier places when he was released. And doubtless Conan misread women,' said the cynic who had never married, 'and thought even the threat against Elave would put the girl off him. He should have known better. It has put her on! She'll fight for him tooth and nail now. The priests have not heard the last of our Fortunata.'

'So that's the way of it,' said Hugh, and whistled softly. 'You make a case for more than you know. If that's how it is with him, he might well be alarmed when Aldwin changed his tune, and wanted to get the boy out of the mire he'd thrust him into. It could well be enough to make him go after Aldwin, hang upon him, pour words into his ear, do everything possible to dissuade him. Would it be enough to make him go still further?'

Jevan stood gazing at him enquiringly, and laid down, slowly and almost absently, the edge of vellum he had taken up to fold across to its matching edge. 'Further? How further? What have you in mind? It would seem he had won his argument, and went away satisfied. Nothing further was needed.'

'Ah, but suppose he was not quite satisfied. Suppose he could not rely on it that he'd won? Knowing Aldwin for the whiffle-minded poor soul he was, with a bad conscience, his own fear removed and his grudge with it, and his resolution blown this way and that as the wind changed, suppose Conan stayed lurking somewhere to see what he would do. And saw him get up and walk out of the tavern without a word, and off down the Wyle to the town gate and the bridge. All his words gone to waste, and more than words needed, quickly, before the damage was done. Did it matter to him all that much? Aldwin would think no ill even when he was pursued a second time – by a man he'd known for years. He might even let himself be drawn aside into some quiet place to argue the cause all over again. And Aldwin,' said Hugh, 'died somewhere in cover by the bridge, and lay hidden under an upturned boat until dark, and was slipped into the water under cover of the arch.'

Jevan stood contemplating that in silence for some minutes. Then he shook his head vigorously, but without complete conviction. 'I think it's out of his scope. But agreed, it would certainly account for why he should conceal half the tale, and pretend the last he saw of Aldwin was in our yard, like the rest of us. But no, surely little men with little grievances don't kill for them. Unless,' he ended, 'it was done in a silly rage, almost by accident, instantly regretted. That they might!'

'Send and fetch him back here,' said Hugh. 'Tell him nothing. If you send, he'll come unsuspecting. And if he's wise, he'll tell the truth.'

Girard of Lythwood came home in the middle of the evening, two days later than he had intended, but highly content with his week's work, for the delay was due to his collecting two new clients on his travels, with good clips to sell, and thankful to make contact with an honest middleman and broker, after some less happy dealings in previous years. All the stores of wool he had weighed and bought were safely stowed in his warehouse outside the Castle Foregate before he came home to his own house. His hired pack-ponies, needed only once a year after the annual clip, were restored to the stable, and the two grooms hired with them were paid off and sent to their homes. Girard was a practical man, who dealt with first things first. He paid his bills on time, and expected others to pay what they owed him with as little reluctance or delay. By the end of June or the beginning of July the contract woolman who dealt with the Flemish export trade would come to collect the summer's load. Girard knew his limitations. He was content to spread his net over a quarter of the shire and its Welsh neighbours, and leave the wholesale trade to more ambitious men.

Girard was half a head shorter than his younger brother, but a good deal broader in the shoulders and thicker in the bone, a portly man in the best of health and spirits, round-faced and cheerful, with a thick thornbush of reddish brown hair and a close trimmed beard. His good humour was seldom shaken even by the unexpected, but even he was taken aback at arriving home after a week's absence to find his pilgrim Uncle William dead and buried, William's young companion back safely from all the perils of his travels only to fall headlong into mortal trouble at home, his clerk dead and laid out for burial in one of the outhouses in his yard, the parish priest of Saint Alkmund's probing anxiously into the dead man's spiritual health before he would bury him, and his shepherd sweating and dumbstruck in Jevan's shop with one of the sheriff's men standing over him. It was no help to have three people all attempting to explain at the same time how these chaotic events had come about in his absence.

But Girard was a man who saw to first things first. If Uncle William was dead, and buried with all propriety, then there was nothing to be done about that, no haste even about coming to terms with the truth of it. If Aldwin, of all improbable people had come by a violent death, then that, too, though requiring a just resolution, was hardly within his competence to set right. Father Elias's doubts about the poor fellow's spiritual condition was another matter, and would need consideration. If Elave was in a locked cell at the abbey, then at least nothing worse could happen to him at this moment. As for Conan, he was solid enough, it would do him no harm to sweat a little. There would be time to salvage him, if it proved necessary. Meantime, Girard's horse had done a good few miles that day, and needed stabling, and Girard himself was hungry.

'Come within, lass,' he said briskly, flinging a bracing arm about his wife's waist and sweeping her towards the hall, 'and, Jevan, see to my beast for me, will you, till I get this tale straight. It's too late for lamentation and too soon for panic. Whatever's gone wrong, there'll be a time for putting it right. The more haste, the less speed! Fortunata, my chick, go and draw me some ale, I'm dry as a lime-pit. And set the supper forward, for if I'm to be any use I need my food.'

They did as he bade, every one of them. The pivot of the house, hearty and heartening, was home. Jevan, who had left most of the exclaiming to the women, allowed his brother his position as prop and stay of household, business and all, as from a relaxed and acknowledged distance, having his own separate kingdom among the membranes of vellum. He stabled, groomed and fed the tired horse at leisure, before he

108

went into the house to join the rest at table. By that time Conan had been whisked away to the castle, to answer to Hugh Beringar. Jevan smiled, somewhat wryly, as he shuttered the frontage, and went into the hall.

'Well, it's a strange thing,' said Girard, sitting back with a satisfied sigh, 'that a man can't be off about his business one week in the year but everything must happen in that week. Just as well Conan never caught up with me, or I should have missed two new customers, for I should have set off back with him if he had reached me. The wool of four hundred sheep I got from those two villages, and some of it the lowland breed, too. But I'm sorry, love, that you've had the worry of all this, and me not here to lift it from you. We'll see now what's to be done. The first thing, as I reckon, is this matter of Aldwin. Whatever he may have done and said against another man in his fret – was there ever such a one as Aldwin for fearing the worst and being afraid to ask in case it came true? Well, whatever he may have done, he was our man, and we'll see him properly buried. But Father Elias here is troubled about the funeral.'

Father Elias, parish priest of Saint Alkmund's, was there with them at the end of the table, swept in to supper in Girard's hospitable arm from his conscientious brooding over the dead. Small, elderly, grey and fierce in his piety, Father Elias ate like a little bird, whenever he remembered to eat at all, and ran about among his flock busy and bothered, like a flustered hen trying to round up alien ducklings under her wings. Souls tended to elude him, every one seeming at the time the only one to matter, and he spent much of his time on his knees apologising to God for the soul that slipped through his fingers. But he would not let even that fugitive in upon false recommendation.

'The man was my parishioner,' said the little priest, in a wisp of a voice that yet had an irascible resolution in it, 'and I grieve for him and will pray for him. But he died by violence, and as it were in the act of bringing mortal charges against another in malice, and what can the health of his soul be? He has not been to Mass in my church these many weeks, nor to confession. He was never regular in his worship, as all men should be. I would not ban him for his slackness. But when did he last confess, and gain absolution? How can I accept him unless I know he died penitent?'

'One little act of contrition will do?' ventured Girard mildly. 'He may have gone to another priest. Who knows? The

109

thought could have come upon him somewhere else, and seemed to him a mortal matter there and then.'

'There are four parishes within the walls,' said Elias with grudging tolerance. 'I will ask. Though one who misses Mass so often … Well, I will ask, here within the town and beyond. It may even be that he feared to come to me. Men are feeble, and go aside to hide their feebleness.'

'So they are, Father, so they do! Wouldn't he be ashamed to come to you, if he'd never shown his face at Mass for so long? And mightn't he go rather to another, one who didn't know him so well, and might be easier on his sins? You ask, Father, and you'll find excuse for him somewhere. Then there's this matter of Conan. He's our man, too, whatever he may have been up to. You say he gave evidence, about this lad of William's talking some foolishness about the Church? What do you say, Jevan, did they put their heads together to do him harm?'

'It's likely enough,' said Jevan, shrugging. 'Though I wouldn't say they understood rightly what they were doing. It turns out Aldwin, the silly soul, feared he'd be thrown out to let Elave back in.'

'That would be like him, surely!' agreed Girard, sighing. 'Always one to look on the black side. Though he should have had more sense, all the years he's known us. I daresay he thought the youngster would take to his heels, and be off to find his fortune elsewhere, as soon as he felt the threat. But why should Conan want to be rid of him?'

There was a brief, blank silence and some head-shaking, then Jevan said with his small, rueful smile: 'I think our shepherd has also taken to thinking of Elave as a perilous rival, though not for employment. He has an eye on Fortunata …'

'On me?' Fortunata sat bolt upright with astonishment, and gaped at her uncle across the table. 'I've never seen signs of it! And I'm sure I never gave him any cause.'

'… and fancies and fears,' continued Jevan, his smile deepening, 'that Elave, if he stays, will make a more personable suitor. Not to say a more welcome one! And who's to say he's wrong?' And he added, his black eye bent on the girl in teasing affection: 'On both counts!'

'Conan has never paid me any attention,' said Fortunata, past sheer amazement now, and quick to examine what might very well be true, even if it had eluded her notice. 'Never! I can't believe he has ever given me a thought.'

'He would certainly never make a winning lover,' said Jevan, 'but there's been a change in these last few days. You've been too busy looking in another direction to notice it.'

'You mean he's been casting sheep's eyes at my girl?' demanded Girard, and laughed aloud at the notion.

'Hardly that! I would call it a very calculating eye. Has not Margaret told you, Fortunata has an endowment now from William, to be her dowry.'

'There was a box mentioned that has yet to be opened. Why, does any man think I would let my girl want for a dowry, when she has a mind to marry? Though it's good that the old man remembered her, and thought to send her his blessing, too. If she did have a mind to Conan, well, I suppose he's not a bad fellow, a girl could do worse. He should have known I'd never let her go empty-handed, whoever she chose.' And he added, with an appreciative glance at Fortunata: 'Though our girl might do a great deal better, too!'

'Coin in the hand,' said Jevan sardonically, 'is more worth than all the promises.'

'Ah, you surely do the man an injustice! What's to prevent him waking up to the fact that our little lass has grown into a beauty, and as good as she is pretty, too. And even if he did bear witness against Elave to elbow him out of the running, and urge Aldwin not to recant for the same none too creditable reason, men have done worse, and not been made to pay too highly for it. But this business of Aldwin is murder. No, that's out of Conan's scope, surely!' He looked down the length of the table to Father Elías, sitting small, attentive and sharp-eyed under his wispy grey tonsure. 'Surely, Father?'

'I have learned,' said the little priest, 'not to put any villainy out of any man's reach. Nor any goodness, either. A life is a very fragile thing, created in desperate labour and snuffed out by a breath of wind – anger, or drunkenness, or mere horseplay, it takes no more than an instant.'

'Conan has merely a few hours of time to account for,' Jevan pointed out mildly. 'He must surely have met with someone who knew him on his way out to the sheep, he has only to name them, they have only to say where and when they saw him. This time, if he tells all the truth instead of half, he cannot miscarry.'

And that would leave only Elave. The grossly offended, the most aggrieved, suddenly approached by his accuser, among trees, without witness, too enraged to wait to hear what his enemy wanted to say to him. It was what almost every soul in Shrewsbury must be saying, taking the ending for granted. One charge of heresy, one of murder. All that afternoon until Vespers he was at liberty, and who had seen Aldwin alive since he passed the porter on the town gate? Two and a half hours between then and Vespers, when Elave was again in custody, two and a half hours in which he could have done murder. Even the objection that Aldwin's wound was in the back could easily be set aside. He came running to plead his penitence, Elave turned on him so furious a face and so menacing a front that he took fright and turned to flee, and got the knife in his back as he fled. Yes, they would all say so. And if it was argued that Elave had no knife on him, that it was left in his bundle in the guest-hall? He had another, doubtless at the bottom of the river by now. There was an answer to everything.

'Father,' said Fortunata abruptly, rising from her place, 'will you open my box for me now? Let us see what I am worth. And then I must talk to you. About Elave!'

Margaret brought the box from the corner press, and cleared an end of the table to make room for it before her husband. Girard's bushy brows rose appreciatively at the sight of it, and he handled it admiringly.

'Why, this is a beautiful thing in itself. This could bring you in an extra penny or two if you ever need it.' He took up the gilded key and fitted it into the lock. It turned smoothly and silently, and Girard opened the lid to reveal a neat, thick swathing of felt, folded in such a way that it could be opened to disclose what the box contained without removing it. Six little bags of similar felt were packed within. All of a size, snugly fitted together to fill the space.

'Well, they're yours,' said Girard, smiling at Fortunata, who was leaning over to stare at them with her face in shadow. 'Open one!'

She drew out one of the bags, and the soft chink of silver sounded under her fingers. There was no drawstring, the top of the bag was simply folded over. She tipped the contents streaming out upon the table, a flood of silver pennies, more than she had ever seen at one time, and yet somehow curiously disappointing. The casket was so beautiful and unusual, a work of art, the contents, however valuable, mere everyday money, the traffic of trade. But yes, they might have their uses, urgent uses if it came to the worst.

112

'There you are, girl!' said Girard, delighted. 'Good coin of the realm, and all yours. Nigh on a hundred pence there, I should guess. And five more like it. Uncle William did well by you. Shall we count them for you?'

She hesitated for a moment, and then she said: 'Yes!' and herself curved a hand round the little pile of thin, small silver pieces, and began to tell them over one by one back into the bag. There were ninety-three of them. By the time she had folded the bag closed again and restored it to its corner in the box, Girard was half-way through the next.

Father Elias had drawn back a little from the table, averting his eyes from this sudden dazzling display of comparative wealth with a curious mixture of desire and detestation. A poor parish priest seldom saw even ten silver pennies together, let alone a hundred. He said hollowly: 'I will go and enquire about Aldwin at Saint Julian's,' and walked quietly out of the room and out of the house, and only Margaret noticed his going, and ran after him to see him courteously out to the street.

There were five hundred and seventy pennies in the six bags. Fortunata fitted them all snugly back into their places in the box, and closed the lid upon them.

'Lock it again, and put it away safely for me,' she said. 'It is mine, isn't it? To use as I like?' They were all looking at her with steady, benevolent interest, and the indulgent respect they had always shown towards her, even from her intense and serious childhood.

'I wanted you to know. Since Elave came back, even more since this shadow fell, I have come close to him afresh, closer than ever I was. I think I love him. So I did long ago, but this is love in a different kind. He brought me this money to help me to a good marriage, but now I know that the marriage I want is with him, and even if I cannot have it, I want to use this gift to help him out of the shadow, even if it means he must go away from here, where they can't lay hands on him again. Money can buy a lot of things, even ways out of prison, even men to open the doors. At least I can try.'

'Girl dear,' said Girard, gently but firmly, 'it was you told me, just a while since, how you urged him to run for his life when he had the chance. And he was the one who refused. A man who won't run can't be made to run. And to my way of thinking he's right. And not only because he gave his word, but because of why he gave his word. He said he'd done no wrong, and wouldn't afford any man proof that he went in fear of justice.'

113

'I know it,' said Fortunata. 'But *he* has absolute faith in the justice of Church and state. And I am not sure that I have. I would rather buy him his life against his will than see him throw it away.'

'You would not get him to take it,' warned Jevan. 'He has refused you once.'

'That was before Aldwin was murdered,' she said starkly. 'Then he was accused only of heresy. Now, if he is not yet charged, it's a matter of murder. He never did it, I won't believe it, murder is not in his nature. But there he is helpless under lock and key, already in their hands. It *is* his life now.'

'He still has his life,' said Girard robustly, and flung an arm about her to draw her to his solid side. 'Hugh Beringar is not the man to take the easy answer and never look beyond. If the lad is blameless he'll come out of it whole and free. Wait! Wait a little and see what the law can discover. I won't meddle with murder. Do I know for sure that any man is innocent, whether it's Elave or Conan? But if it comes down to the simple matter of heresy, then I'll throw all the weight I have into the balance to bring him off safely. You shall have him, he shall have the place poor Aldwin grudged to him, and I'll be guarantor for his good behaviour. But murder – no! Am I God, to see guilt or innocence in a man's face?'

Chapter Nine

ATHER ELIAS, having visited all his fellow-priests within the town, came down to the abbey next morning, and appealed at chapter as to whether any of the brothers who were also priests had by any chance taken confession from the clerk Aldwin before the services of Saint Winifred's translation. The eve of a festival day must have found plenty of work for the confessors, since it was natural for any worshippers who had neglected their spiritual condition for some time to find their consciences pricking them into the confessional, to come purged and refreshed to the celebrations of the day, and rest content in their renewed virtue and peace of mind. If any cleric here had been approached by Aldwin, he would be able to declare it. But no one had. It ended with Father Elias scurrying out of the chapter-house disappointed and distrait, shaking his shaggy grey head and trailing the wide, frayed sleeves of his gown like a small, dishevelled bird.

Brother Cadfael went out from chapter to his work in the garden with the rear view of that shabby little figure still before his mind's eye. A stickler, was Father Elias, he would not easily give up. Somewhere, somehow, he must find a reason to convince himself that Aldwin had died in a state of grace, and see to it that his soul had all the consolation and assistance the rites of the Church could provide. But it seemed he had already tried every cleric in the town and the Foregate, and so far fruitlessly. And he was not a man who could simply shut his eyes and pretend that all was well, his conscience had a flinty streak, and would pay him out with a vengeance if he lowered his standards without due grounds for clemency. Cadfael felt a dual sympathy for the perfectionist priest and back-sliding parishioner. At this moment their case seemed to him to take precedence even over Elave's plight. Elave was safe enough now until Bishop Roger de Clinton declared his will towards him. If he could not get out, neither could any zealot get in, to break his head again. His wounds were healing and his bruises fading, and Brother Anselm, precentor and librarian, had given him the first volume of Saint Augustine's 'Confessions' to pass the time away. So that he might discover, said Anselm, that Augustine did write on other themes besides predestination, reprobation and sin.

Anselm was ten years younger than Cadfael, a lean, active, gifted soul with a grain of irrepressible mischief still alive if usually dormant within him. Cadfael had suggested that he should rather give Elave Augustine's 'Against Fortunatus' to read. There he might find, written some years before the saint's more orthodox outpourings, in one of his periods of sharply changing belief: 'There is no sin unless through a man's own will, and hence the reward when we do right things also of our own will.' Let Elave commit that to memory, and he could quote it in his own defence. More than likely Anselm would take him at his word, and feed the suspect all manner of quotations supportive to his cause. It was a game any well-read student of the early fathers could play, and Anselm better than most.

So for some days at least, until Serlo could reach his bishop in Coventry and return with his response, Elave was safe enough, and could do with the time to get over his rough handling. But Aldwin, dead and in need of burial, could not wait.

Cadfael could not but wonder how things were going with Hugh's enquiries within the town. He had seen nothing of him since the morning of the previous day, and the revelation of murder had removed the centre of action from the abbey into the wide and populated field of the secular world. Even if the original root of the case was within these walls, in the cloudy issue of heresy, and the obvious suspect here in close keeping, there outside the walls the last hours of Aldwin's life remained to be filled in, and there were hundreds of men in town and Foregate who had known him, who might have old grudges or new complaints against him, nothing whatever to do with the charges against Elave. And there were frailties in the case against Elave which Hugh had seen for himself, and would not lightly discard in favour of the easy answer. No, Aldwin was the more urgent priority.

After dinner, in the half-hour or so allowed for rest, Cadfael went into the church, into the grateful stony coolness, and stood for some minutes silent before Saint Winifred's altar. Of late, if he felt the need to speak to her in actual words at all, he found himself addressing her in Welsh, but usually he relied on her to know all the preoccupations of his mind without words. Doubtful, in any case, if the young and beautiful Welsh girl of her first brief life had known any English or Latin, or even been able to read and write her own language, though the stately prioress of her second life, pilgrim to Rome and head of a community of holy women, must have had time to learn and study to her heart's content. But it was as the girl that Cadfael always imagined her. A girl whose beauty was legendary, and caused her to be coveted by princes.

Before he left her, though he was not conscious of having expressed any need or request, he felt the quietude and certainty the thought of her always gave him. He circled the parish altar into the nave, and there was Father Boniface just filling the little altar lamp and straightening the candles in their holders. Cadfael stopped to pass the time of day.

'You'll have had Father Elias from Saint Alkmund's after you this morning, I daresay? He came to us at chapter on the same errand. A sad business, this of Aldwin's death.'

Father Boniface nodded his solemn dark head, and wiped oily fingers, boylike, in the skirt of his gown. He was thin but wiry, and almost as taciturn as his verger, but that deferent shyness was gradually easing as he worked his way into the confidence of his flock.

'Yes, he came to me after Prime. I never knew this Aldwin, living. I wish I could have helped him, dead, but to my knowledge I never saw him until the wool-merchant's funeral, the day before the festival. Certainly he never came to me for confession.'

'Nor to any of those within here,' said Cadfael. 'Nor in the town, for Elias asked there first. And your parish is a wide one. Poor Father Elias would have to walk a few miles to find the next priest. And if Aldwin never knocked on the door of any of his own neighbours, I doubt if he made a long journey to seek

117

his penance elsewhere.'

'True, I have occasion to walk a few miles myself in the way of duty,' agreed Boniface, with pride rather than regret in the breadth of his cure. 'Not that I grudge it, God knows! Night or day, it's a joy to know that from the furthest hamlet they can call me when they need me, and know that I'll come. Sometimes I question my fortune, knowing it so little deserved. Only two days ago I was called away to Betton, and missed all but the morning Mass. I was sorry it should be that day, but no choice, there was a man dying, or he and all his kin thought he was dying. It was worth the journey, for he took the turn for life and I stayed until we were sure. It was getting dusk when I got back–' He broke off suddenly, open mouthed and round-eyed. 'So it was!' he said slowly. 'And I never thought to say!'

'What is it?' asked Cadfael curiously. It had been a long and confiding speech for this quiet, reticent young man, and this sudden halt was almost startling. 'What have you thought of now?'

'Why, that there was one more priest here then who is not here now. Father Elias will not know. I had a visitor came for the day of Saint Winifred's translation, one who was my fellow-student, and ordained only a month ago. He came on the eve of the festival, early in the afternoon, and stayed through the next day, and when I was called away that morning after Mass I left him here to take part in all the offices in my place. I knew that would please him. He stayed until I came back, but that was when it was growing dark, and he was in haste then to be on his way home. It's only a short while, from past noon one day to nightfall the next, but how if he did have a penitent come asking?'

'He said no word of any such before he went?' asked Cadfael.

'He was in haste to be off, he had a walk of four miles. I never asked him. He was very proud to take my place, he said Compline for me. It could be!' said Boniface. 'Thin it may be, but it is a chance. Should we not make sure?'

'So we can,' said Cadfael heartily, 'if he's still within reach. But where should we look for him now? Four miles, you said? That's no great way.'

'He's nephew to Father Eadmer at Attingham, and named for his uncle. Whether he's still there, with him, is more than I know. But he has no cure yet. I would go,' said Boniface, hesitating, 'but I could hardly get back for Vespers. If I'd thought of it earlier …'

'Never trouble yourself,' said Cadfael. 'I'll ask leave of Father Abbot and go myself. For such a cause he'll give permission. It's the welfare of a soul at stake. And in this warm weather,' he added practically, 'there's need of haste.'

It was, as it chanced, the first day for over a week to grow lightly overcast, though before night the cloud cover cleared again. To set out along the Foregate with the abbot's blessing behind him and a four-mile walk ahead was pure pleasure, and the lingering *vagus* left in Cadfael breathed a little deeper when he reached the fork of the road at Saint Giles, and took the left-hand branch towards Attingham. There were times when the old wandering desire quickened again within him, and the very fact that he had been sent on an errand even beyond the limits of the shire, only three months back, in March, had rather roused than quenched the appetite. The vow of stability, however gravely undertaken, sometimes proved as hard to keep as the vow of obedience, which Cadfael had always found his chief stumbling-block. He greeted this afternoon's freedom – and justified freedom, at that, since it had sanction and purpose – as a refreshment and a holiday.

The highroad had a broad margin of turf on either side, soft green walking, the veil of cloud had tempered the sun's heat, the meadows were green on either hand, full of flowers and vibrant with insects, and in the bushes and headlands of the fields the birds were loud and full of themselves, shrilling off rivals, their first brood already fledged and trying their wings. Cadfael rolled contentedly along the green verge, the grass stroking silken cool about his ankles. Now if the end came up to the journey, every step of the way would be repaid with double pleasure.

Before him, beyond the level of the fields, rose the wooded hogback of the Wrekin, and soon the river reappeared at some distance on his left, to wind nearer as he proceeded, until it was close beside the highway, a gentle, innocent stream between flat grassy banks, incapable of menace to all appearances, though the local people knew better than to trust it. There were cattle in the pastures here, and waterfowl among the fringes of reeds. And soon he could see the square, squat tower of the parish church of Saint Eata beyond the curve of the Severn, and the low roofs of the village clustered close to it.

There was a wooden bridge somewhat to the left, but Cadfael made straight for the church and the priest's house beside it. Here the river spread out into a maze of green and golden shallows, and at this summer level could easily be forded. Cadfael tucked up his habit and splashed through, shaking the little rafts of water crowfoot until the whole languid surface quivered.

Over the years, summer by summer, so many people had waded the river here instead of turning aside to the bridge that they had worn a narrow, sandy path up the opposite bank and across the grassy level between river and church, straight to the priest's house. Behind the mellow red stone of the church and the weathered timber of the modest dwelling in its shadow a circle of old trees gave shelter from the wind, and shaded half of the small garden. Father Eadmer had been many years in office here, and worked lovingly upon his garden. Half of it was producing vegetables for his table, and by the look of it a surplus to eke out the diet of his poorer neighbours. The other half was given over to a pretty little herber full of flowers, and the undulation of the ground had made it possible for him to shape a short bench of earth, turfed over with wild thyme, for a seat. And there sat Father Eadmer in his midsummer glory, a man lavish but solid of flesh, his breviary unopened on his knees, his considerable weight distilling around him, at every movement, a great aureole of fragrance. Before him, hatless in the sun, a younger man was busy hoeing between rows of young cabbages, and the gleam of his shaven scalp above the ebullient ring of curly hair reassured Cadfael, as he approached, that he had not had his journey for nothing. At least enquiry was possible, even if it produced disappointing answers.

'Well, well!' said the elder Eadmer, sitting up straight and almost sliding the breviary from his lap. 'Is it you, off on your travels again?'

'No further than here,' said Cadfael, 'this time.'

'And how's that unfortunate young brother you had with you in the spring?' And Eadmer called across the vegetable beds to the young man with the hoe: 'Leave that, Eddi, and fetch Brother Cadfael here a beaker of ale. Bring pitcher and all!'

Young Eadmer laid aside the hoe cheerfully, and was off into the house on fine long legs. Cadfael sat down beside the priest on the green bench, and waves of spicy fragrance rose around him.

'He's back with his pens and brushes, doing good work, and

120

none the worse for his journey, indeed all the better in spirit. His walking improves, slowly but it improves. And how have you been? I hear this is your nephew, the young one, and newly made priest.'

'A month since. He's waiting to see what the bishop has in mind for him. The lad was lucky enough to catch his eye, it may work out well for him.'

It was clear to Cadfael, when the young Eadmer came striding out with a wooden tray of beakers and the pitcher, and served them with easy and willing grace, that the new priest was likely to catch any observant eye, for he was tall, well made and goodlooking, and blessedly unselfconscious about his assets. He dropped to the grass at their feet as soon as he had waited on them, and acknowledged his presentation to this Benedictine elder with pleasant deference, but quite without awe. One of those happy people for whose confidence and fearlessness circumstances will always rearrange themselves, and rough roads subside into level pastures. Cadfael wondered if his touch could do as much for other less fortunate souls.

'Time spent sitting here with you and drinking your ale,' admitted Cadfael with mild regret, 'is stolen time, I fear, however delightful. I'm on an errand that won't wait, and once it's done I must be off back. And my business is with your nephew here.'

'With me?' said the young man, looking up in surprise.

'You came visiting Father Boniface, did you not, for Saint Winifred's translation? And stayed with him from past noon on the eve until after Compline on the feast day?'

'I did. We were deacons together,' said young Eadmer, stretching up to refill their beakers without stirring from his grassy seat. 'Why? Did I mislay something for him when I disrobed? I'll walk back and see him again before I leave here.'

'And he had to leave you in his place most of that day, from after the morning Mass until past Compline. Did any man come to you, during all that time, asking advice or wanting you to hear his confession?'

The straight-gazing brown eyes looked up at him thoughtfully, very grave now. Cadfael could read the answer and marvel at it even before Eadmer said: 'Yes. One man did.'

It was too early yet to be sure of achievement. Cadfael asked cautiously: 'What manner of man? Of what age?'

'Oh, fifty years old, I should guess, going grey, and balding. A little stooped, and lined in the face, but he was uneasy and

121

troubled when I saw him. Not a craftsman, by his hands, perhaps a small tradesman or someone's house servant.'

More and more hopeful, Cadfael thought, and went on, encouraged: 'You did see him clearly?'

'It was not in the church. He came to the little room over the porch, where Cynric sleeps. Looking for Father Boniface, but found me instead. So we were face to face.'

'You did not know him, though?'

'No, I know very few in Shrewsbury. I never was there before.'

No need to ask if he had been at chapter, or at the session that followed, to know Aldwin again from that encounter. Cadfael knew he had not. He had too sure a sense of the limitations of his fledgling rights to overstep them.

'And you confessed this man? And gave him penance and absolution?'

'I did. And helped him through the penance. You will understand that I can tell you nothing about his confession.'

'I would not ask you. If this was the man I believe it was, what matters is that you did absolve him, that his soul's peace was made. For, you see,' said Cadfael, considerately mirroring the young man's severe gravity, 'if I am right, the man is now dead. And since his parish priest had reason to wonder about the state of his strayed sheep, he is enquiring as to his spiritual standing before he will bury him with all the rites of the Church. It's why every priest in the town has been questioned, and I come at last to you.'

'Dead?' echoed Eadmer, dismayed. 'He was in sound health for a man of his years. How is that possible? And he was happier when he left me, he would not … No! So how comes it he is dead so soon?'

'You will surely have heard by now,' said Cadfael, 'that the morning after the feast day a man was taken out of the river? Not drowned, but stabbed. The sheriff is hunting for his murderer.'

'And this is the man?' asked the young priest, aghast.

'This is the man who so sorely needs a guarantor. Whether he is the man you confessed I cannot yet be certain.'

'I never knew his name,' said the boy, hesitant.

'You would know his face,' said his uncle, and spared to comment or prompt him further. There was no need. Young Eadmer set a hand to the ground and bounded to his feet, brushing down the skirt of his cassock briskly. 'I will come back

122

with you,' he said, 'and I hope with all my heart that I can speak for your murdered man.'

There were four of them about the trestle table on which Aldwin's body had been laid out decently for burial: Girard, Father Elias, Cadfael and young Eadmer. In this narrow storeshed in the yard, swept out and sweetened with green branches, there was no room for more. And these witnesses were enough.

There had been very little said on the walk back to Shrewsbury. Eadmer, bent on preserving the sacredness of what had passed between them, had banished even the mention of their meeting until he should know that this dead man was indeed his penitent. Possibly his first penitent, and approached with awe, humility and reverence in consequence.

They had gone first to Father Elias, to ask him to accompany them to Girard's house, for if this promise came to fruit it would be both ease for his mind, and due licence to hasten the arrangements for burial. The little priest came with them eagerly. He stood at the head of the bier, the place granted to him as of right, and his aging hands, thin and curled like a small bird's claws, trembled for a moment as he turned back the covering from the dead man's face. At the foot Eadmer stood, the fledgling priest fronting the old man worn but durable, after years of gain and loss in his strivings to medicine the human condition.

Eadmer did not move or utter a sound as the sheet was drawn down to uncover a face now somewhat eased, Cadfael thought, of its living discouragement and suspicion. The sinews of the cheeks and jaw had relaxed their sour tightness, and with it some years had slipped from him, leaving him almost serene. Eadmer gazed at him with prolonged wonder and compassion, and said simply, 'Yes, that is my penitent.'

'You are quite sure?' said Cadfael.

'Quite sure.'

'And he made confession and received absolution? Praise be to God!' said Father Elias, drawing up the sheet again. 'I need not hesitate further. On the very day of his death he cleansed his soul. He did perform his penance?'

'We said what was due together,' said Eadmer. 'He was distressed, I wanted to see him depart in better comfort, and so he did. I saw no cause to be hard on him. It seemed to me he might have done enough penance in his lifetime to be

123

somewhat in credit. There are those who make their own way stony. There's no merit in it, but I doubt if they can help it, and I felt it should count in extenuation of some small sins.'

For that Father Elias gave him a sharp and somewhat disapproving glance, but forebore from reproving what an austere old man might well consider the presumption, even levity, of youth. Eadmer was certainly innocent of having set out to arouse any such reservations. He opened his honest brown eyes wide on Father Elias, and said simply: 'I'm glad out of measure, Father, that Brother Cadfael thought to come looking for me in time. And even more glad that I was there when this man was in need. God knows I have failings of my own to confess, for I was vexed at first when he came stumbling up the stairs. I came near to telling him to go away and come back at a better time, until I saw his face clearly. And all because he was making me late for Vespers.'

It was said so naturally and simply that it passed Brother Cadfael by for a long moment. He had turned towards the open doorway, where Girard was already leading the way out, and the early evening hung textured like a pearl, the westering sun veiled. He had heard the words without regarding them, and enlightenment fell on him so dazzlingly that he stumbled on the threshold. He swung about to stare at the young man following him.

'What was that you said? For Vespers? He made you late for *Vespers*?'

'So he did,' said Eadmer blankly. 'I was just opening the door to go down and into the church when he came. The office was half over by the time I sent him away consoled.'

'Dear God!' said Cadfael reverently. 'And I never even thought to ask about the time! And this was on the festival day? Not the Vespers of the day you arrived? Not the eve?'

'It was the festival day, when Boniface was away. Why, what's in that to shake you? What is it I've said?'

'The moment I clapped eyes on you, lad,' said Cadfael joyfully, 'I knew you had a happy touch about you. You've delivered not one man, but two, God bless you for it. Now come, come with me round the corner to Saint Mary's close, and tell the sheriff what you've just told me.'

Hugh had come back to his house and family after a long and exasperating day of pursuing fruitless enquiries among an apparently unobservant populace, and trying to extract truth from a scared and perspiring Conan, who was willing to admit that he had spent an hour or so trying to persuade Aldwin to let sleeping dogs lie, since it was known already, but insisted that after that he had wasted no more time, but gone straight to his work in the pastures west of the town. And that might well be true, even if he could cite no acquaintance who had met and spoken to him on the way. But there remained the possibility that he was still lying, and had followed and made one more disastrous attempt to sway a mind normally only too easily deflected from any purpose.

Enough and more than enough for one day. Hugh had taken himself off home to his own house, to his wife and his son and his supper, and he was sitting in the clean rushes of the hall floor, stripped down to shirt and hose in the mild evening, helping three-year-old Giles to build a castle, when Cadfael came rapping briskly at the open door, and marched in upon him shining with portentous news, and towing by the sleeve an unknown and plainly nonplussed young man.

Hugh abandoned his tower of wooden blocks unfinished, and came alertly to his feet. 'Truant again, are you? I looked for you in the herbarium an hour ago. Where have you been off to this time? And who is this you've brought me?'

'I've been no further than Attingham,' said Cadfael, 'to visit Father Eadmer. And here I've brought you his nephew, who is also Father Eadmer, ordained last month. This young man came to join his friend Father Boniface at Holy Cross for Saint Winifred's celebrations. You know Father Elias has been fretting as to whether Aldwin died in a fit state to deserve all the rites of the Church, seeing he seldom showed his face at Mass in his own parish church. Elias had tried every priest he knew of, in and out of the town, to see if any could stand sponsor for the poor fellow. Boniface told me of one more who was here for a day and half a day, however unlikely it might be that a local man should find his way to him in so short a time. Howbeit, here he is, and he has a tale to tell you.'

Young Eadmer told it accommodatingly, though hardly comprehending what significance it could have here, beyond what he already knew. 'And I walked back here with Brother Cadfael to see the man himself, whether he was indeed the one who came to me. And he is,' he ended simply. 'But what Brother Cadfael sees in it more, of such moment that it must come at once to you, my lord, that he must tell you himself, for I can't guess at it.'

'But you have not mentioned,' said Cadfael, 'at what time this man came to you with his confession.'

'It was just when the bell had rung for Vespers,' Eadmer repeated obligingly, still mystified. 'Because of him I came very late to the office.'

'Vespers?' Hugh had stiffened, turning upon them a face ablaze with enlightenment. 'You are sure? That very day?'

'That very day!' Cadfael confirmed triumphantly. 'And just at the ringing of the Vesper bell, as I have good reason to know, Elave walked into the great court and was set upon by Gerbert's henchmen and battered to the ground, and has been prisoner in the abbey ever since. Aldwin was alive and well and seeking confession at that very moment. Whoever killed him, it was not Elave!'

Chapter Ten

 HAPTER WAS nearly over, next morning, when Girard of Lythwood presented himself at the gatehouse, requesting a hearing before the lord abbot. As a man of consequence in the town, and like his late uncle a good patron of the abbey, he came confidently, aware of his own merit and status. He had brought his fosterdaughter Fortunata with him, and they both came roused and girded, if not for battle, at least for possible contention, to be encountered courteously but with determination.

'Certainly admit them,' said Radulfus. 'I am glad Master Girard is home again, his househould has been greatly troubled and needs its head.'

Cadfael watched their entry into the chapter-house with fixed attention. They were both in their best, adorned to cut the most impressive figure possible, the ideal respected citizen and his modest daughter. The girl took her stance a pace behind her father, and kept her eyes devoutly lowered in this monastic assembly, but when they opened wide for an instant, to flash a glance round the room and take a rapid estimate of possible friends and enemies, they were very shrewd, fierce and bright. The first calculating glance had noted the continuing presence of Canon Gerbert, and recorded it with regret. In his presence she would contain her grief, anger and anxiety on Elave's behalf, and let Girard speak for her. Gerbert would deplore a froward woman, and Fortunata had certainly primed her father by this time in every detail. They must have spent the remainder of the past evening, after Cadfael's departure, preparing what they were now about to propound.

The significance of one detail was not yet apparent, though it did suggest interesting possibilities. Girard carried under his arm, polished to that lovely dark patina by age and handling, and with the light caressing the gilded curves of its carving, the box that contained Fortunata's dowry.

'My lord,' said Girard, 'I thank you for this courtesy. I come in the matter of the young man you have detained here as a prisoner. Everyone here knows that his accuser was done to death, and though no charge has been made against Elave on that count, your lordship must know that it has been the common talk everywhere that he must be a murderer. I trust you have now heard from the lord sheriff that it is not so. Aldwin was still alive and well when Elave was taken and made prisoner here. In the matter of the murder he is proven innocent. There is the word of a priest to vouch for him.'

'Yes, this has been made known to us,' said the abbot. 'On that head Elave is cleared of all blame. I am glad to publish his innocence.'

'And I welcome your good word,' said Girard with emphasis, 'as one who has a right to speak in all this, and to be heard, seeing that both Aldwin and Elave were of my uncle's household, and now of mine, and the weight of both falls upon me. One man of mine has been killed unlawfully, and I want justice for him. I do not approve all that he did, but I understand his thinking and his actions, knowing his nature as I do. For him I can at least do this much, bury him decently, and if I can, help to run to earth his murderer. I have a duty also to Elave, who is living, and against whom the mortal charge now falls to the ground. Will you hear me on this behalf, my lord?'

'Willingly,' said Radulfus. 'Proceed!'

'Is this the time or place for such a plea?' objected Canon Gerbert, shifting impatiently in his stall and frowning at the solid burgess who stood straddling the flags of the floor so immovably. 'We are not now hearing this man's case. The withdrawal of one charge —'

'The charge of murder was never made,' said Radulfus, cutting him off short, 'and as now appears, never can be made.'

'The withdrawal of one suspicion,' snapped Gerbert, 'does not affect the charge which has been made, and which awaits

128

judgement. It is not the purpose of chapter to hear pleas out of place, which may prejudice the case when the bishop declares his wishes. It would be a breach of form to allow it.'

'My lords,' said Girard with admirable smoothness and calm, 'I have a proposition to make, which I feel to be reasonable and permissible, if you find yourselves so minded. To put it before you I needs must speak as to my knowledge of Elave, of his character, and the service he has done my household. It is relevant.'

'I find that reasonable,' said the abbot imperturbably. 'You shall have your hearing, Master Girard. Speak freely!'

'My lord, I thank you! You must know, then, that this young man was in the employ of my uncle for some years, and proved always honest, reliable and trustworthy in all matters, so that my uncle took him with him as servant, guard and friend on his pilgrimage to Jerusalem, Rome and Compostela, and throughout those years of travelling the lad continued always dutiful, tended his master in illness, and when the old man died in France, brought back his body for burial here. A long and devoted service, my lords. Among other charges faithfully carried out, at his master's wish he brought back this treasury, here in this casket, as a dowry for William's fosterdaughter here, now mine.'

'This is not disputed,' said Gerbert, shifting restlessly in his seat, 'but it is hardly to the purpose. The charge of heresy remains, and cannot be put aside. In my view, having seen elsewhere to what horrors it can lead, it is graver than that of murder. We know, do we not, how this poison can exist in vessels otherwise seen by the world as pure and virtuous, and yet contaminate souls by the thousand. A man cannot prevail by good works, only by divine grace, and who strays from the true doctrine of the Church has repudiated divine grace.'

'Yet we are told a tree shall be known by its fruit,' remarked the abbot drily. 'Divine grace, I think, will know where to look for a responsive human grace, without instruction from us. Go on, Master Girard. I believe you have a proposal to make.'

'I have, Father. At the least it is now known that my clerk's death happened through no fault of Elave, who never coveted his place or tried to oust him, nor did him any harm. Yet there is the place vacant now, nonetheless. And I, who have known Elave and trusted him, say that I am prepared to take him back in Aldwin's place, and advance him in my business. If you will release him into my charge, I make myself his guarantor that

129

he shall not leave Shrewsbury. I engage that he shall remain in my house, and be available whenever your lordships require him to attend, until his case is heard and justly judged.'

'And regardless,' asked Radulfus mildly, 'of what the verdict may be?'

'My lord, if the judging is just, so will the verdict be. And after that day he will need no guarantor.'

'It is presumptous,' said Gerbert coldly, 'to be so certain of your own rightness.'

'I speak as I have found. And I know as well as any man that in the heat of argument or ale words can be spoken beyond what was ever meant, but I do not think God would condemn a man for folly, not beyond the consequences of folly, which can be punishment enough.'

Radulfus was smiling behind his austere mask, though only those who had grown close and familiar with him would have known it. 'Well, I appreciate the kindliness of your intentions,' he said. 'Have you anything more to add?'

'Only this voice to add to mine, Father. Here in this casket are five hundred and seventy silver pence, the dowry sent by my uncle for the girl-child he took as his daughter. As Elave took great pains to deliver it to her safely, so Fortunata desires, in reverence to William who sent it, to use it now for Elave's deliverance from prison. Here she offers it in bail for him, and I will guarantee that when the time comes he shall answer to it.'

'Is this indeed your own wish, child?' asked the abbot, studying Fortunata's demure and wary calm with interest. 'No one has persuaded you to this offer?'

'No one, Father,' she said firmly. 'The thought was mine.'

'And do you know,' he insisted gently, 'that all those who go bail for another do take the risk of loss?'

She raised her ivory eyelids, lofty and smooth, for one brief and brilliant flash of hazel eyes. 'Not all, Father,' she said, uttering defiance in the soft, discreet voice of daughterly submission. And to Cadfael, watching, it was plain that Radulfus, even if he kept his formidable countenance, was not displeased.

'You may not know, Father,' explained Girard considerately, and even somewhat complacently, 'that women stake only on certainties. Well, that is what I propose, and I promise you I will fulfill my part of it, if you agree to release him into my custody. At any time you may be assured you will find him at my house. I am told he would not run from you when he was loose before; he certainly will not this time, when Fortunata stands to lose by him. As *you* suppose,' he added generously, 'for *I* am in no doubt.'

Radulfus had Canon Gerbert on his right hand, and Prior Robert on his left, and knew himself between two monuments of orthodoxy in more than doctrine. The precise letter of canon law was sacred to Robert, and the influence of an archbishop, distilled through his confidential envoy, hung close and convincing at his elbow, stiffening a mind already disposed to rigidity. As between his abbot and Theobald's vicarious presence Robert might be torn, and would certainly endeavour to remain compatible with both, but in extremes he would go with Gerbert. Cadfael, watching him manipulating inward argument, with devoutly folded hands, arched silver brows and tightly pursed mouth, could almost find the words in which he would endorse whatever Gerbert said, whilst subtly refraining from actually echoing it. And if he knew his man, so did the abbot. As for Gerbert himself, Cadfael had a sudden startling insight into a mind utterly alien to his own. For the man really had, somewhere in Europe, glimpsed yawning chaos and been afraid, seen the subtleties of the devil working through the mouths of men, and the fragmentation of Christendom in the eruption of loud-voiced prophets bursting out of limbo like bubbles in the scum of a boiling pot, and the dispersion into the wilderness in the malignant excesses of their deluded followers. There was nothing false in the horror with which Gerbert looked upon the threat of heresy, though how he could find it in an open soul like Elave remained incomprehensible.

Nor could the abbot afford to oppose the archbishop's representative, however true it might be that Theobald probably held a more balanced and temperate opinion of those who felt compelled to reason about faith than did Gerbert. A threat that troubled pope, cardinals and bishops abroad, however nebulous it might feel here, must be taken seriously. There is much to be said for being an island off the main. Invasions, curses and plagues are slower to reach you, and arrive so weakened as to be almost exhausted beforehand. Yet even distance may not always be a perfect defence.

'You have heard,' said Radulfus, 'an offer which is generous, and comes from one whose good faith may be taken for granted. We need only debate what is right for us to do in

131

response. I have only one reservation. If this concerned only my own monastic household, I should have none. Let me hear your view, Canon Gerbert.'

There was no help for it, he would certainly be expressing it very forcibly; as well compel him to speak first, so that his rigours could at least be moderated afterwards.

'In a matter of such gravity,' said Gerbert, 'I am absolutely against any relaxation. It is true, and I acknowledge it, that the accused has been at liberty once, and returned as he was pledged to do. But that experience may itself cause him to do otherwise if the chance is repeated. I say we have no right to take any risk with a prisoner accused of such a perilous crime. I tell you, the threat to Christendom is not understood here, or there would be no dispute, none! He must remain under lock and key until the cause is fully heard.'

'Robert?'

'I cannot but agree,' said the prior, looking studiously down his long nose. 'It is too serious a charge to take even the least risk of flight. Moreover, the time is not wasted while he remains in our custody. Brother Anselm has been providing him with books, for the better instruction of his mind. If we keep him, the good seed may yet fall on ground not utterly barren.'

'True,' said Brother Anselm without detectable irony, 'he reads, and he thinks about what he reads. He brought back more than silver pence from the Holy Land. An intelligent man's baggage on such a journey must be light, but in his mind he can accumulate a world.' Wisely and ambiguously he halted there, before Canon Gerbert should wind his slower way through this speech to understanding, and spy an infinitesimal note of heresy in it. It is not wise to tease a man with no humour in him.

'It seems I should be outvoted if I came down on the side of release,' said the abbot drily, 'but it so chances that I, too, am for continuing to hold the young man here in the enclave. This house is my domain, but jurisdiction has already passed out of my hands. We have sent word to the bishop, and expect to hear his will very soon. Therefore the judgement is now with him, and our part is simply to ensure that we hand over the accused to him, or to his representatives, as soon as he makes his will known. I am now no more in this matter than the bishop's agent. I am sorry, Master Girard, but that must be my answer. I cannot take you as bail, I cannot give you custody of Elave. I can promise you that he shall come to no harm here in my house. Nor suffer any further violence,' he added with intent, if without emphasis.

'Then at least,' said Girard quickly, accepting what he saw to be unalterable, but alert to make the most of what ground was left to him, 'can I be assured that the bishop will give me as fair a hearing, when it comes to a trial, as you have given me now?'

'I shall see to it that he is informed of your wish and right to be heard,' said the abbot.

'And may we see and speak with Elave, now that we are here? It may help to settle his mind to know that there is a roof and employment ready for him, when he is free to accept them.'

'I see no objection,' said Radulfus.

'In company,' added Gerbert quickly and loudly. 'There must be some brother present to witness all that may be said.'

'That can quite well be provided,' said the abbot. 'Brother Cadfael will be paying his daily visit to the young man after chapter, to see how his injuries are healing. He can conduct Master Girard, and remain throughout the visit.' And with that he rose authoritatively to cut off further objections that might be forming in Canon Gerbert's undoubtedly less agile mind. He had not so much as glanced in Cadfael's direction. 'This chapter is concluded,' he said, and followed his secular visitors out of the chapter-house.

Elave was sitting on his pallet under the narrow window of the cell. There was a book open on the reading desk beside him, but he was no longer reading, only frowning over some deep inward consideration drawn from what he had read, and by the set of his face he had not found much that was comprehensible in whichever of the early fathers Anselm had brought him. It seemed to him that most of them spent far more time in denouncing one another than in extolling God, and more venom on the one occupation than fervour on the other. Perhaps there were others who were less ready to declare war at the drop of a word, and actually thought and spoke well of their fellow theologians, even when they differed, but if so, all their books must have been burned, and possibly they themselves into the bargain.

'The longer I study here,' he had said to Brother Anselm bluntly, 'the more I begin to think well of heretics. Perhaps I am one, after all. When they all professed to believe in God,

133

and tried to live in a way pleasing to him, how could they hate one another so much?'

In a few curiously companionable days they had arrived at terms on which such questions could be asked and answered freely. And Anselm had turned a page of Origen and replied tranquilly: 'It all comes of trying to formulate what is too vast and mysterious to be formulated. Once the bit was between their teeth there was nothing for it but to take exception to anything that differed from their own conception. And every rival conception lured its conceiver deeper and deeper into a quagmire. The simple souls who found no difficulty and knew nothing about formulae walked dryshod across the same marsh, not knowing it was there.'

'I fancy that was what I was doing,' said Elave ruefully, 'until I came here. Now I'm bogged to the knees, and doubt if I shall ever get out.'

'Oh, you may have lost your saving innocence,' said Anselm comfortably, 'but if you are sinking, it's in a morass of other men's words, not your own. They never hold so fast. You have only to close the book.'

'Too late! There are things I want to know, now. How did Father and Son first become three? Who first wrote of them as three, to confuse us all? How can there be three, all equal, who are yet not three but one?'

'As the three lobes of the clover leaf are three and equal but united in one leaf,' suggested Anselm.

'And the four-leaved clover, that brings luck? What is the fourth, humankind? Or are we the stem of the threesome, that binds all together?'

Anselm shook his head over him, but with unperturbed serenity and a tolerant grin. 'Never write a book, son! You would certainly be made to burn it!'

Now Elave sat in his solitude, which did not seem to him particularly lonely, and thought about this and other conversations which had passed between precentor and prisoner during the past few days, and seriously considered whether a man was really better for reading anything at all, let alone these labyrinthine works of theology that served only to make the clear and bright seem muddied and dim, by clothing everything they touched in words obscure and shapeless as mist, far out of the comprehension of ordinary men, of whom the greater part of the human creation is composed. When he looked out from the cell window, at a narrow lancet of pale blue sky fretted with the tremor of leaves and feathered with a few wisps of bright white cloud, everything appeared to him radiant and simple again, within the grasp of even the meanest, and conferring benevolence impartially and joyously upon all.

He started when he heard the key grate in the lock, not having associated the murmur of voices outside with his own person. The sounds of the outer world came in to him throughout the day by the window, and the chime of the office bell marked off the hours for him. He was even becoming used to the horarium, and celebrated the regular observances with small inward genuflections of his own. For God was no part of the morass or the labyrinth and could not be blamed for what men had made of a shining simplicity and certainty.

But the turning of the key in the lock belonged to his own practical workaday world, from which this banishment could only be temporary, possibly for a purpose, a halting place for thought after the journey half across the world. He sat watching the door open upon the summer day outside, and it was not opened inch by cautious inch but wide and generously, back to touch the wall, as Brother Cadfael came in.

'Son, you have visitors!' He waved them past him into the small, stony room, watching the sudden brightness flood over Elave's dazzled face and set him blinking. 'How is your head this morning?'

The head in question had shed its bandages the previous day, only a dry scar was left in the thick hair. Elave said in a daze: 'Well, very well!'

'No aches and pains? Then that's my business done. And now,' said Cadfael, withdrawing to perch on the foot of the bed with his back to the room, 'I am one of the stones of the wall. I am ordered to stay with you, but you may regard me as deaf and mute.'

It seemed that he had made mutes of two of the three thus unceremoniously brought together, for Elave had come to his feet in a great start, and stood staring at Fortunata as she was staring at him, flushed and great-eyed, and stricken silent. Only their eyes were still eloquent, and Cadfael had not turned his back so completely that he could not observe them from the corner of his own eye, and read what was not being said. It had not taken those two long to make up their minds. Yet he must remember that this was not so sudden, except in its discovery. They had known each other and lived in the same household from her infancy until her eleventh year, and in another

135

fashion there had surely been a strong fondness, indulgent and condescending, no doubt, on his part, probably worshipping and wistful on hers, for girls tend to achieve grown-up and painful affections far earlier than boys. She had had to wait for her fulfilment until he came home, to find the bud had blossomed, and to stand astonished at its beauty.

'Well, lad!' Girard said heartily, eyeing the young man from head to foot and shaking him warmly by both hands. 'You're home at last after all your ventures, and I not here to greet you! But greet you I do now, and gladly. I never looked to see you in this trouble, but God helping, it will all pass off safely in the end. From all accounts you did well by Uncle William. So far as is in us, we'll do well by you.'

Elave drew himself out of his daze with an effort, gulped, and sat down abruptly on his bed. 'I never thought,' he said, 'they would have let you in to see me. It was good of you to trouble for me, but take no chances on my behalf. Touch no pitch, and it can't stick to you! You know what they're holding against me? You should not come near me,' he said vehemently, 'not yet, not until I'm freed. I'm contagious!'

'But you do know,' said Fortunata, 'that you're not suspect of ever harming Aldwin? That's over, proven false.'

'Yes, I know. Brother Anselm brought me word, after Prime. But that's but the half of it.'

'The greater half,' said Girard, plumping himself down on the small, high stool, which his amplitude overflowed on every side.

'Not everyone within here thinks so. Fortunata has already put herself in disfavour with some because she was not hot enough against me when they questioned her. I would not for the world,' said Elave earnestly, 'bring harm upon her or upon you. Stay from me, I shall be easier in my mind.'

'We have the abbot's leave to come,' said Girard, 'and for all I could see his goodwill, too. We came here to chapter, Fortunata and I, to make an offer on your behalf. And if you think we shall either of us draw off and leave you unfriended for fear of a few over-zealous sniffers-out of evil, with tongues that wag at both ends, you're mistaken in us. My name stands sturdy enough in this town to survive a deal of buffeting by gossips. And so shall yours, before this is over. What we hoped was to have you released to come home with us, on my guarantee of your good behaviour. I pledged you to answer to your bail when you were called, and told them there's now a place for you in my employ. Why not? You had no hand in Aldwin's death and neither did I, nor would either of us ever have turned him off to make way for you. But for all that, it's done! The poor soul's gone, I need a clerk, and you need somewhere to lay your head when you get out of here. Where better than in the house you know, dealing with a business you used to know well, and can soon master again? So if you're willing, there's my hand on it, and we're both bound. What do you say?'

'I say there's nothing in the world I'd like better!' Elave's face, carefully composed these last days into a wary calm, had slipped its mask and flushed into a warmth of pleasure and gratitude that made him look very young and vulnerable. It would cost him something to reassemble his breached defences when these two were gone, Cadfael reflected. 'But we should not be talking of it now. We must not!' Elave protested, quivering. 'God knows I'm grateful to you for such generosity, but I dare hardly think of the future until I'm out of here. Out of here, and vindicated! You have not told me what they answered, but I can guess at it. They would not turn me loose, not even into your charge.'

Girard owned it regretfully. 'But the abbot gave us leave to come and see you, and tell you what I propose for you, so that you may at least know you have friends who are stirring for you. Every voice raised in your support must be of some help. I've told you of what I am keeping for you. Now Fortunata has somewhat to say to you on her own account.'

Girard on entering had sensibly laid down the burden he was carrying upon the pallet beside Elave. Fortunata stirred out of her tranced stillness, and leaned to take it up and sit down beside him, nursing the box on her knees.

'You remember how you brought this to our house? Father and I brought it here today to pledge as bail for your release, but they would not let you go. But if we could not buy your liberty with it one way,' she said in a low deliberate voice, 'there are other ways. Remember what I said to you when last we were together.'

'I do remember,' he said.

'Such matters need money,' said Fortunata, choosing her words with aching care. 'Uncle William sent me a lot of money. I want it to be used for you. In whatever way may be needful. You've given no parole now. The one you did give *they* violated, not you.'

137

Girard laid a restraining hand upon her arm, and said in a warning whisper, which nevertheless found a betraying echo from the stone walls: 'Gently, my girl! Walls have ears!'

'But no tongues,' said Cadfael as softly. 'No, speak freely, child, it's not me you need fear. Say all you have to say to him, and let him answer you. Expect no interference from me, one way or the other.'

For answer Fortunata took up the box she was nursing, and thrust it into Elave's hands. Cadfael heard the infinitesimal chink of small coins shifting, and turned his head in time to see the slight start Elave made as he received the weight, the stiffening of the young man's shoulders and the sharp contraction of his brows. He saw him tilt the box between his hands to elicit a fainter echo of the small sound, and weigh it thoughtfully on his palms.

'It was money Master William sent you?' said Elave consideringly. 'I never knew what was in it. But it's yours. He sent it for you, I brought it here for you.'

'If it profits you, it profits me,' said Fortunata. 'Yes, I will say what I came to say, even though I know Father does not approve. I don't trust them to do you justice. I am afraid for you. I want you far away from here, and safe. This money is mine, I may do what I choose with it. It can buy a horse, shelter, food, perhaps even a man to turn a key and open the door. I want you to accept it – to accept the use of it, and whatever I can buy with it for you. I'm not afraid, except for you. I'm not ashamed. And wherever you may go, however far, I'll follow you.'

She had begun in a bleak, defiant calm, but she ended with contained and muted passion, her voice still level and low, her hands clenched together in her lap, her face very pale and fierce. Elave's hand shook as he closed it tightly over hers, pushing the box aside on his bed. After a long pause, not of hesitation, rather of an unbending resolution that had difficulty in finding the clearest but least hurtful words in which to express himself, he said quietly: 'No! I cannot take it, or let you make such use of it for my sake. You know why. I have not changed, I shall not change. If I ran away from this charge I should be opening the door to devils, ready to bay after other honest men. If this fight is not fought out to the end now, heresy can be cried against anyone who offends his neighbour, so easy is it to accuse when there are those willing to condemn for a doubt, for a question, for a word out of place. And I will

138

not give way. I will not budge until they come to me and tell me they find no blame in me, and ask me civilly to come forth and go my way.'

She had known all along, in spite of her persistence, that he would say no. She withdrew her hand from his very slowly, and rose to her feet, but could not for a moment bring herself to turn away from him, even when Girard took her gently by the arm.

'But then,' said Elave deliberately, his eyes holding hers, 'then I will take your gift – if I can also have the bride who comes with it.'

Chapter Eleven

HAVE A request to make of you, Fortunata,' said
Cadfael, as he crossed the great court between the
silent visitors, the girl disconsolate, her fosterfather
almost certainly relieved at Elave's dogged insistence on remaining where he was and relying on justice. Girard
undoubtedly believed in justice. 'Will you allow me to show
this box to Brother Anselm? He's well versed in all the crafts,
and may be able to say where it came from, and how old it is. I
should be interested to see for what purpose he thinks it was
made. You certainly can't lose by it, Anselm carries weight as
an obedientiary, and he's well disposed to Elave already. Have
you time now to come to the scriptorium with me? You may
like to know more about your box. It surely has a value in
itself.'

She gave her assent almost absently, her thoughts still left
behind with Elave.

'The lad needs all the friends he can get,' said Girard
ruefully. 'I had hoped that now the worse charge has fallen to
the ground those who blamed him for all might feel some
shame, and soften even on the other charge. But here's this
great prelate from Canterbury claiming that over-bold thinking
about belief is worse than murder. What sort of values are
those? I don't know but I'd help the boy to a horse myself if
he'd agreed, but I'd rather my girl had no part in it.'

'He will not let me have any part,' said Fortunata bitterly.

'And I think the more of him for it! And what I can do within the law to haul him safely out of this coil, that I'll do, at whatever cost. If he's the man you want, as it seems he wants you, then neither of you shall want in vain,' said Girard roundly.

Brother Anselm had his workshop in a corner carrel of the north walk of the cloister, where he kept the manuscripts of his music in neat and loving store. He was busy mending the bellows of his little portative organ when they walked in upon him, but he set it aside willingly enough when he saw the box Girard laid before him. He took it up and turned it about in the best light, to admire the delicacy of the carving, and the depth of colour time had given to the wood.

'This is a beautiful thing! He was a true craftsman who made it. See the handling of the ivory, the great round brow, as if the carver had first drawn a circle to guide him, and then drawn in the lines of age and thought. I wonder what saint is pictured here? An elder, certainly. It could be Saint John Chrysostom.' He followed the whorls and tendrils of the vine leaves with a thin, appreciative fingertip. 'Where did he pick up such a thing, I wonder?'

'Elave told me,' said Cadfael, 'that William bought it in a market in Tripoli, from some fugitive monks driven out of their monasteries, somewhere beyond Edessa, by raiders from Mosul. You think it was made there, in the east?'

'The ivory may well have been,' said Anselm judicially. 'Somewhere in the eastern empire, certainly. The full-faced gaze, the great, fixed eyes ... Of the carving of the box I am not so sure. I fancy it came from nearer home. Not an English house – perhaps French or German. Have we your leave, daughter, to examine it inside?'

Fortunata's curiosity was already caught and held, she was leaning forward eagerly to follow whatever Anselm might have to demonstrate. 'Yes, open it!' she said, and herself proffered the key.

Girard turned the key in the lock and raised the lid, to lift out the little felt bags that uttered their brief insect sound as he handled them. The interior of the box was lined with pale brown vellum. Anselm raised it to the light and peered within. One corner of the lining was curled up slightly from the wood, and a thin edge of some darker colour showed there, pressed between vellum and wood. He drew it out carefully with a fingernail, and unrolled a wisp of dark purple membrane, frayed from some larger shape, for one edge of it was fretted

141

away into a worn fringe, where it had parted, the rest presented a clear, cut edge, the segment of a circle or half-circle. So small a wisp, and so inexplicable. He smoothed it out flat upon the desk. Hardly bigger than a thumbnail, but the cut side was a segment of a larger curve. The colour, though rubbed, and perhaps paler than it had once been, was nevertheless a rich, soft purple.

The pale lining in the base of the box seemed also to have the faintest of darker blooms upon its surface here and there. Cadfael drew a nail gently from end to end of it, and examined the fine dust of vellum he had collected, bluish rose, leaving a thin, clean line where he had scratched the membrane. Anselm stroked along the mark and smoothed down the ruffled pile, but the streak was still clear to be seen. He looked closely at his fingertip, and the faintest trace of colour was there, the translucent blue of mist. And something more, that made him look even more closely, and then take up the box again and hold it in full sunlight, tilting and turning it to catch the rays. And Cadfael saw what Anselm had seen, trapped in the velvety surface of the leather, invisible except by favour of the light, the scattered sparkle of gold dust.

Fortunata stood gazing curiously at the wisp of purple smoothed out upon the desk. A breath would have blown it away. 'What can this have been? What was it part of?'

'It is a fragment from a tongue of leather, the kind that would be stitched to the top and base of the spines of books, if they were to be stored in chests. Stored side by side, spine upwards. The tongues were an aid to drawing out a single book.'

'Do you think, then,' she pursued, 'that there was once a book kept in this box?'

'It's possible. The box may be a hundred, two hundred years old. It may have been in many places, and used for many things before it found its way into the market in Tripoli.'

'But a book kept in this would have no use for these tongues,' she objected alertly, her interest quickening. 'It would lie flat. And it would lie alone. There is no room for more than one.'

'True. But books, like boxes, may travel many miles and be carried in many ways before they match and are put together. By this fragment, surely it did once carry a book, if only for a time. Perhaps the monks who sold the box had kept their breviary in it. The book they would not part with, even when

142

they were destitute. In their monastery it may have been one of many in a chest, and they could not carry all, when the raiders from Mosul drove them out.'

'This leather tongue was well worn,' Fortunata continued her pursuit, fingering the frayed edge worn thin as gauze. 'The book must have fitted very close within here, to leave this wisp behind.'

'Leather perishes in the end,' said Girard. 'Much handling can wear it away into dry dust, and the books of the office are constantly in use. If there's such a threat from these mamluks of Mosul, the poor souls round Edessa would have little chance to copy new service books.'

Cadfael had begun thoughtfully restoring the felt bags of coins to the casket, packing them solidly. Before the base was covered he drew a finger along the vellum again, and studied the tip in the sunlight, and the invisible grains of gold caught the light, became visible for a fleeting instant, and vanished again as he flexed his hand. Girard closed the lid and turned the key, and picked up the box to tuck it under his arm. Cadfael had rolled up the bags tightly to muffle all movement, but even so, when the box was tilted, he caught the very faint and brief clink as silver pennies shifted.

'I'm grateful to you for letting me see so fine a piece of craftmanship,' said Anselm, relaxing with a sigh. 'It's the work of a master, and you are a fortunate lady to possess it. Master William had an eye for quality.'

'So I've told her,' Girard agreed heartily. 'If she should wish to part with it, it would fetch her in a fair sum to add to what is inside.'

'It might well fetch more than the sum it holds,' Anselm said seriously. 'I am wondering if it was made to hold relics. The ivory suggests it, but of course it may not be so. The maker took pleasure in embellishing his work, whatever its purpose.'

'I'll go with you to the gatehouse,' said Cadfael, stirring out of his private ponderings as Girard and Fortunata turned to walk along the north range on their way out. He fell in beside Girard, the girl going a pace or two ahead of them, her eyes on the flags of the walk, her lips set and brows drawn, somewhere far from them in a closed world of her own thoughts. Only when they were out in the great court and approaching the gate, and Cadfael halted to take leave of them, did she turn and look at him directly. Her eyes lit on what he was still carrying in his hand, and suddenly she smiled.

'You've forgotten to put away the key to Elave's cell. Or,' she wondered, her smile deepening and warming from lips to eyes, 'are *you* thinking of letting him out?'

'No,' said Cadfael. 'I am thinking of letting myself in. There are things Elave and I have to talk about.'

Elave had quite lost by this time the sharp, defensive, even aggressive front he had first presented to anyone who entered his cell. No one visited him regularly except Anselm, Cadfael, and the novice who brought his food, and with all these he was now on strangely familiar terms. The sound of the key turning caused him to turn his head, but at sight of Cadfael re-entering, and so soon, his glance of rapid enquiry changed to a welcoming smile. He had been reclining on his bed with his face uplifted to the light from the narrow lancet window, but he swung his feet to the floor and moved hospitably to make way for Cadfael on the pallet beside him.

'I hardly thought to see you again so soon,' he said. 'Are they gone? God forbid I should ever hurt her, but what else could I do? She will not admit what in her heart she knows! If I ran away I should be ashamed, and so would she, and that I won't bear. I am not ashamed now, I have nothing to be ashamed of. Do *you* think I'm a fool for refusing to take to my heels?'

'A rare kind of fool, if you are,' said Cadfael. 'And every practical way, no fool at all. And who should know everything there is to be known about that box you brought for her, so well as you? So tell me this – when she plumped it in your arms a while ago, what did you note about it that surprised you? Oh, I saw you handle it. The moment the weight was in your hands it jarred you, for all you never said a word. What was there new to discover about it? Will you tell me, or shall I first tell you? And we shall see if we both agree.'

Elave was gazing at him along his shoulder, with wonder, doubt and speculation in his eyes. 'Yes, I remember you handled it once before, the day I took it up into the town. Should that be enough for you to notice so small a difference when you had it in your hands again?'

'It was not that,' said Cadfael. 'It was you who made it clear to me. You knew the weight of it from carrying it, from living with it and handling it all the way from France. When she laid it in your hands you knew what to expect. Yet as you took it your hands rose. I saw it, and saw that you had recorded all

144

that it meant. For then you tilted it, this way and then that. And you know what you heard. That the box should be lighter by some small measure than when you last held it, that startled you as it startled me. That it should give forth the clinking of coin was no surprise to me, for we had just been told at chapter that it held five hundred and seventy silver pence. But I saw that it was a surprise to you, for you repeated the test. Why did you say nothing then?'

'There was no certainty,' said Elave, shaking his head. 'How could I be sure? I knew what I heard, but since last I had the box in my hands it has been opened, perhaps something not replaced when they put back what was in it, more wrappings, no longer needed ... Enough to change the weight, and let the coins within move, that were tight-packed before, and could not shift. I needed time to think. And if you had not come ...'

'I know,' said Cadfael, 'you would have put it out of your mind as of no importance, a mistaken memory. After all, you delivered your charge where it was sent, Fortunata had her money, what possible profit to waste time and thought over a morsel of weight and a few coins jingling? Especially for a man with graver matters on his mind. And you have just accounted for all, very sensibly. But now here am I, stirring the depths that were just beginning to settle. Son, I have just been handling that box again myself. I won't say I noted the difference in weight, except when it jarred you as it did. But what I do most clearly remember is how solid, how stable was that weight. Nothing moved in it when first I held it. It might have been a solid mass of wood in my hands. It is not so now. I doubt if any discarded wrappings of felt could quite have silenced the coins that are in it now, for I have just packed it again myself – six small felt bags, rolled up tightly and pressed in, and still I heard them chink when the box was taken up and carried. No, you were not mistaken. It is lighter than it was, and it has lost that solidity that formerly it had.'

Elave sat silent for a long moment, accepting what was set before him, but dubious of its sense or relevance. 'But I do not see,' he said slowly, 'of what use it is to know these things, even to think them, even to wonder. What bearing has it on anything? Even if it is all true, *why* should it be so? It's not worth solving so small a mystery, since no one is the better or the worse whether we fathom it or not.'

'Everything that is not what it seems, and not what it reasonably should be,' said Cadfael firmly, 'must have significance. And until I know what that significance is, in particular if it manifests itself in the middle of murder and malice, I cannot be content. Thank God, no one now supposes that you had any part in Aldwin's death, but *someone* killed him, and whatever his own faults and misdoings, worse was done to him, and he has a right to justice. I grant it was but natural that most people should take it as certain his sudden death had to do with you and the accusation he made against you. But now, with you out of the reckoning, is not that out of the reckoning, too? Who else in that quarrel had any cause to kill him? So is it not logic to look for another cause? Nothing to do with you and your troubles? But something, nevertheless, to do with your return here. Death came within days of your coming. And whatever is strange, whatever cannot be explained, during these few days since your return may indeed have a bearing.'

'And the box came with me,' said Elave, following this path to its logical ending. 'And here is something strange about the box, something that cannot be explained. Unless you will now tell me that you have an explanation for it?'

'A possible one, yes. For consider ... We have just been examining the box, emptied of its bags of pence, inside and out. And in the vellum lining of the base there are traces of gold leaf, powdered into a fine dust, but the light finds them. And on the deep ivory vellum there is a fine blue bloom, as on a plum. And I think, and so I know does Brother Anselm, though we have not yet spoken of it, that it is the delicate frettings of another vellum once in constant contact with it, and dyed purple. And pressed into a corner there was a fragment of purple vellum frayed from an end-tag such as we use on the spines of books in our chests in the library.'

'You are saying,' said Elave, watching him in bright-eyed speculation, 'that what the box contained at some time was a book – or books. A book that had formerly been kept among others in a chest. That could well be true, but need it mean anything to us, now? The thing is old, it could have been used in many ways since it was made. It could be a hundred years since it held a book.'

'So it could,' agreed Cadfael, 'but for this one thing. That both you and I handled it only five days ago, and have handled it again today, and found it to be lighter in weight, changed in balance, and filled with something that rings audibly when it is tilted or shaken. What I am saying, Elave, is that what it held, not a hundred years ago, but five short days ago, on the twentieth day of this very month of June, is not what it holds now, on the twenty-fifth.'

'A standard size,' said Brother Anselm, demonstrating with his hands on the desk before him. 'The skin folded to make eight leaves – it would fit the box exactly. Most probably the box was made for it.'

'But if they had been made together,' objected Cadfael, 'the book would not have been given the tabs at the spine. They would not have been needed.'

'That could well be, though the maker may have added them simply as common practice. But the box may have been made for it later. If the book was commissioned first, scribe and binder would finish it in the usual fashion. But if it was the kind of book it may well have been, by the traces left behind, the owner may very well have had a casket made for it to his own wishes, afterwards, to keep it from being rubbed by being drawn in and out from a chest among others of less value.'

Cadfael was smoothing out under his fingers the scrap of purple vellum, teasing out the fringe of gossamer fluff along the torn edge. Minute threads clung to his fingers, motes of bluish mist. 'I spoke to Haluin, who knows more about pigments and vellum than I shall ever know. I wish he had been here to see for himself. So does he! But he said what you have said. Purple is the imperial colour, gold on purple vellum should be a book made for an emperor. East or west, they both had such books made. Purple and gold were the imperial symbols.'

'They still are. And here we have the purple, and traces of the gold. In old Rome,' said Anselm, 'the Caesars used the same fashion, and were jealous of it. I doubt if any other dared so exalt himself. In Aachen or Byzantium, they've been known to follow the Caesars.'

'And from which empire, supposing we are right about this book and the box that contained it, did these works of art come? Can you read the signs?'

'You might do better than I can,' said Anselm. 'You have been in those parts of the world, as I have not. Read your own riddle.'

'The ivory was carved by a craftsman from Constantinople or near it, but it need not have been made there. There is traffic between the two courts, as there has been since Charles

147

the Great. Strange that the box brings the two together as it does, for the carving of the wood is not eastern. The wood itself I cannot fathom, but I think it must be from somewhere round the Middle Sea. Perhaps Italy? How all these materials and talents come together from many places to create so small and rare a thing!'

'And once it contained, perhaps, a smaller and rarer. And who knows who was the scribe who wrote – in gold throughout, do you think, on purple vellum? – whatever that text might be, or for what prince of Byzantium or Rome it was written? Or who was the painter who adorned it, and in which style, of the east or the west?'

Brother Anselm was gazing out across the sunny garth in a dream of treasure, the fashion of treasure that best pleased him, words and neums inscribed with loving care for the pleasure of kings, and ornamented with delicate elaborations of tendril and blossom.

'It may well have been a marvel,' he said fondly.

'I wonder,' said Cadfael, rather to himself than to any other, 'where it is now.'

Fortunata came into Jevan's shop in the early evening and found him putting his tools tidily away, and laying aside on his shelves the skin he had just folded, creamy white and fine-textured. Three folds had made of it a potential sheaf of eight leaves, but he had not yet trimmed the edges. Fortunata came to his shoulder and smoothed the surface with a forefinger.

'That would be the right size,' she said thoughtfully.

'The right size for many purposes,' said Jevan. 'But what made you say it? Right for what?'

'To make a book to fit my box.' She looked up at him with wide, clear hazel eyes. 'You know I went with Father to try and get them to release Elave, to live with us here until his case is heard? They wouldn't do it. But they took a great interest in the box. Brother Anselm, who keeps all the abbey books, wanted to examine it. Do you know, they think it must once have held a book. Because of the size being so right for a sheepskin folded three times. And the box being so fine, it must have been a very precious book. Do you think they could be right?'

'All things are possible,' said Jevan. 'I hadn't thought of it, but the size is certainly suggestive, now you speak of it. It

148

would indeed make a splendid case for a book.' He looked down into her grave face with his familiar dark smile. 'A pity it had lost its contents before Uncle William happened on it in Tripoli, but I daresay it had been through a great many changes of use and fortune by then. Those are troubled regions. Easier to plant a kingdom there for Christendom than to maintain it.'

'Well, I'm glad,' said Fortunata, 'that it was good silver coin in the box when it reached me, rather than some old book. I can't read, what use would a book be to me?'

'A book would have its value, too. A high value if it was well penned and painted. But I'm glad you're content with what you have, and I hope it will bring you what you want.'

She was running a hand along a shelf, and frowning at the faint fur of dust she found on her palm. Just as the monks had smoothed at the lining of the box, and found something significant in whatever minute residue it left upon the skin. She had caught the tiny flashes of gold in the sunlight, but the rest she had not understood. She studied her own hand, and wiped away the almost imperceptible velvety dust. 'It's time I cleaned your rooms for you,' she said. 'You keep everything so neatly, but it docs need dusting.'

'Whenever you wish!' Jevan took a detached look about the room, and agreed placidly: 'It does build up, even here with the finished membranes there's a special dust. I live in it, I breathe it, so it slips my notice. Yes, dust and polish if you want to.'

'It must be much worse in your workshop,' she said, 'with all the scraping of the skins, and going back and forth to the river, coming in with muddy feet, and then the skins, when you bring them first to soak, and all the hair ... It must smell, too,' she said, wrinkling her nose at the very thought.

'Not so, my lady!' Jevan laughed at her fastidious countenance. 'Conan cleans my workshop for me as often as it needs it, and makes a good job of it, too. I could even teach him the trade, if he was not needed with the sheep. He's no fool, he knows a deal already about the making of vellum.'

'But Conan is shut up in the castle,' she reminded him seriously. 'The sheriff is still hunting for anyone who can show just where he went and what he did before he went out to the pastures, that day that Aldwin was killed. You don't believe, do you, that he really could kill?'

'Who could not,' said Jevan indifferently, 'given the time

and the place? But no, not Conan. They'll let him go in the end. He'll be back. It won't hurt him to sweat for a few days. And it won't hurt my workshop to wait a while for its next cleaning. Now, madam, are you ready for supper? I'll shut the shop, and we'll go in.'

She was paying no attention. Her eyes were roaming the length of his shelves, and the rack where the largest finished membranes were draped, cut and trimmed to order into the great bifolia intended for some massive lectern Bible. These she passed by to dwell upon the eight-leaved gatherings of the size that fitted her box.

'Uncle, you have some books this same size, haven't you?'

'It's the most usual,' he said. 'Yes, the best thing I have is of that measure. It was made in France. God knows how it ever found its way to the abbey fair here in Shrewsbury. Why did you ask?'

'Then it would fit into my box. I'd like you to have it. Why not? If it's so fine, and has a value, it should stay in the household, and I'm unlettered, and have no book to put in it, and besides,' she said, 'I'm happy with my dowry, and grateful to Uncle William for it. Let's try it, after supper. Show me your books again. I may not be able to read, but they're beautiful to look at.'

Jevan stood looking down at her from his lean height, solemn and still. Thus motionless, everything about him seemed a little more elongated than usual, like a saint carved into the vertical moulding of a church porch, from his narrow, scholarly face to the long-toed shoes on his thin, sinewy feet, and the lean, clever, adept's hands. His deep eyes searched her face. He shook his head at such rash and thoughtless generosity.

'Child, you should not so madly give away everything you have, before you know the value of it, or what need you may have of it in the future. Do nothing on impulse, you may pay for it with regret.'

'No,' said Fortunata. 'Why should I regret giving a thing for which I have no use to someone who will make good and proper use of it? And dare you tell me that you don't want it?' Certainly his black eyes were glittering, if not with covetousness, with unmistakeable longing and pleasure. 'Come to supper, and afterwards we'll try how they match together. And I'll get Father to mind my money for me.'

The French breviary was one of seven manuscripts Jevan had acquired over the years of his dealings with churchmen and other patrons. When he lifted the lid of the chest in which he kept them Fortunata saw them ranged side by side, spines upward, leaning towards one side because he had not quite enough as yet to fill the space neatly. Two had fading titles in Latin inscribed along the spine, one was in a cover dyed red, the rest had all originally been bound in ivory leather drawn over thin wooden boards, but some were old enough to have mellowed into the pleasant pale brown of the lining of her box. She had seen them several times before, but had never paid them such close attention. And there at head and foot of every spine were the little rounded tongues of leather for lifting them in and out.

Jevan drew out his favourite, its binding still almost virgin white, and opened it at random, and the brilliant colours sprang out as if they were just freshly applied, a right-hand border the length of the page, very narrow and delicate, of twining leaves and tendrils and flowers, the rest of the page written in two columns, with one large initial letter, and five smaller ones to open later paragraphs, each one using the letter as a frame for vivid miniatures of flower and fern. The precision of the painting was matched by the limpid lucidity of the blues and reds and golds and greens, but the blues in particular filled and satisfied the eyes with a translucent coolness that was pure pleasure.

'It's in such mint condition,' said Jevan, stroking the smooth binding lovingly, 'that I fancy it was stolen, and brought well away from the place where it belonged before the merchant dared sell it. This is the beginning of the Common of the Saints, hence the large initial. See the violets, and how true their colour is!'

Fortunata opened her box on her knees. The colour of the lining blended softly with the paler colour of the breviary's binding. The book fitted comfortably within. When the lid was closed on it the soft clinging of the lining held the book secure.

'You see?' she said. 'How much better that it should have a use! And truly it does seem that this is the purpose for which it was made.'

There was room for the box within the chest. Jevan closed that lid also over his library, and kneeled for a moment with

151

both long hands pressed upon the wood, caressing and reverent. 'Very well! At least you may be sure it will be valued.' He rose to his feet, his eyes still lingering upon the chest that held his treasure, a shadowy private smile of perfect contentment playing round his lips. 'Do you know, chick, that I've never locked this before? Now I have your gift within it I shall keep it locked for safety.'

They turned towards the door together, his hand on her shoulder. At the head of the stairs that went down into the hall she halted, and turned her face up to him suddenly. 'Uncle, you know you said Conan had learned a great deal about your business, through helping you there sometimes? Would he know what value to set on books? Would he recognise it, if by chance he lit on one of immense value?'

Chapter Twelve

N THE twenty-sixth day of June Fortunata rose
early, and with her first waking thought recalled
that it was the day of Aldwin's funeral. It was taken
for granted that the entire household would attend,
so much was owed to him, for many reasons, years of service,
undistinguished but conscientious, years of familiarity with his
harmless, disconsolate figure about the place, and the pity and
the vague sense of having somehow failed him, now that he
had come to so unexpected an end. And the last words she had
ever said to him were a reproach! Deserved, perhaps, but now,
less reasonably, reproaching her.

Poor Aldwin! He had never made the most of his blessings,
always feared their loss, like a miser with his gold. And he had
done a terrible thing to Elave in his haunting fear of being
discarded. But he had not deserved to be stabbed from behind
and cast into the river, and she had him somehow on her
conscience in spite of her anxiety and dread for Elave, whom
he had injured. On this of all mornings he filled Fortunata's
mind, and drove her on along a road she was reluctant to take.
But if justice is to be denied to the inadequate, grudging and
sad, to whom then is it due?

Early as she was, it seemed that someone else was earlier.
The shop would remain closed all this day, shuttered and dim,
so there was no occasion for Jevan to be up so early, but he had
risen and gone out before Fortunata came down into the hall.

'He's off to his workshop,' said Margaret, when Fortunata

asked after him. 'He has some fresh skins to put into the river to soak, but he'll be back in good time for poor Aldwin's funeral. Were you wanting him?'

'No, nothing that won't wait,' said Fortunata. 'I missed him, that's all.'

She was glad that the household was fully occupied with the preparations for one more memorial gathering, so soon after the first, the evening of Uncle William's wake when this whole cycle of misfortune had begun. Margaret and the maid were busy in the kitchen, Girard, as soon as he had broken his fast, was out in the yard arranging Aldwin's last dignified transit to the church he had neglected in life. Fortunata went into the shuttered shop, and without more light than filtered through the joints of the shutters, began swiftly and silently to search along the shelves among the array of uncut skins, tools, every corner of a neat, sparsely furnished room. Everything was open to view. She had scarcely expected to find anything alien in here, and did not spend much time on it. She closed the door again upon the shadowy interior, and went back into the empty hall, and up the staircase to Jevan's bedchamber, over the entry from the street.

Perhaps he had forgotten that she had known from infancy where everything in this house was kept, or overlooked the fact that even those details which had never interested her before might be of grave importance now. She had not yet given him any cause to reflect on such matters, and she was praying inwardly at this moment that she never need give him cause. Whatever she did now, she was going to feel guilt, but that she could bear, since she must. The haunting uncertainty she could not bear.

Never before, Jevan had said, had he troubled to lock up his manuscripts, never until her precious dower box was laid among them. And that might well have been a light, affectionate gesture of praise and thanks to flatter her, but for the fact that he had indeed turned the key on her gift when he was alone in the room at night. She knew it, even before she laid hand to the lid to raise it, and found it locked. Now, if he had kept his keys on his person when he left the house, she could go no further along this fearful road. But he had seen no need for that, for they were there in their usual place, on a hook inside the chest where his clothes were kept, in a corner of the room. Her hand shook as she selected the smallest, and metal grated acidly against metal before she could insert it in the lock of the book-chest.

She raised the lid, and kneeled motionless beside the chest, gripping the carved edge with both hands, so hard that her fingers stiffened and ached with tension. It needed only one glance, not the long, dismayed stare she fixed upon the interior, the serried spines upturned, the vacant space at one end. There was no dark casket there, no great-eyed, round-browed ivory saint returning her wide stare. Whitest of the pale spines, cheek by jowl with its one red-dyed companion, Jevan's treasured French breviary, bought from some careful thief or trader in stolen goods at Saint Peter's Fair a couple of years ago, rested in its accustomed place among the others, deprived of its new and sumptuous casket.

The book remained, the box into which it fitted so harmoniously had been removed, and Fortunata could think of only one reason, and only one place where it could have gone.

She closed the lid in a sudden spurt of haste and panic, and turned the key, and a tress of her hair caught in the fretted edge of the lock, and she tugged it loose as she rose, in a fever to escape from this room, and take refuge elsewhere among ordinary events and innocent people, from the knowledge she wished she had let lie, but now could not unknow, and the path on to which she had stepped hoping it would fade from under her feet, and now must follow to its end.

Aldwin was carried to his burial at mid-morning, escorted by Girard of Lythwood and all his household, and guided into the next world with all solemnity by Father Elias, satisfied now of his parishioner's credentials and relieved of all his former doubts. Fortunata stood beside Jevan at the graveside, and felt the counter-currents of pity and horror tearing her mind between them as his sleeve brushed hers. She had watched him make one among those carrying the bier, scatter a handful of earth into the grave, and gaze down into the dark pit with austere and composed face as the clods fell dully and covered the dead. A life lived in discouragement and pessimism might not seem much to lose, but when it is snatched away by murder the offence and the deprivation show as monstrous.

So there went Aldwin out of this world, which had never seen fit to content him, and home went Girard and his family, having done their duty by their unfortunate dependent. They were all quiet at table, but the gap Aldwin had left was narrow at best, and would soon close up like a trivial wound, to leave no scar.

Fortunata cleared away the dishes, and went into the kitchen to help wash the pots after dinner. She could not be sure whether she was delaying what she knew she must do out of care to arouse no special interest in her movements, or out of desperate longing not to do it at all. But in the end she could not leave it unfinished. She might yet be agonising needlessly. There might be a good answer, even now, and if she did not finish what she had begun she might never find it out. Truth is a terrible compulsion.

She crossed the yard and slipped unnoticed into the shuttered shop. The key of the Frankwell workshop was dangling in its proper place, where Jevan had hung it openly and serenely when he returned from his early morning expedition. Fortunata took it down, and hid it in the bodice of her gown.

'I'm going down to the abbey,' she said, looking in at the hall door, 'to see if they'll let me see Elave again. Or at least to find out if anything has happened yet. The bishop must surely send a message any day now, Coventry is not so far.'

No one objected, no one offered to go with her. No doubt they felt that after the morning's preoccupation with death it would be the best thing in the world for her to go out into the summer afternoon, and turn her thoughts, however anxious they might be, towards life and youth.

Since only the eyes of the shop, blind and shuttered now, looked out upon the street, the house windows being all in the upright of the L and looking out upon the long strip of yard and garden, no one saw her emerge from the passageway and turn, not left towards the town gate and the abbey, but right, towards the western bridge and the suburb of Frankwell.

Brother Cadfael, not usually given to hesitation, had spent the entire morning and an hour of the early afternoon pondering the events of the previous day, and trying to determine how much of what was troubling his mind was knowledge, and how much was wild speculation. Certainly at some stage Fortunata's box had contained a book, and by the traces left it had been so used for a very considerable time, to leave that faint lavender bloom on the lining, and a frayed, wafer-thin wisp of purple leather trapped in a corner between lining and wood. Gold leaf is applied over glue, and then burnished, and though the sheets are too frail and fine to be handled safely out in the cloister, or in any trace of wind, properly finished gilding is very durable. It would take much use and frequent lifting in and out of a well-fitted container, to fret away even those few infinitesimal grains of gold. The more he thought of it the more he felt sure that somewhere there was a book meant for this casket, and that they had kept company together for a century or more. If they had parted long ago, the book perhaps stolen, raided away into paynim hands, even destroyed, then what had been the nature of the dowry old William had sent to his fosterdaughter? For he was certain, as Elave was now certain, that it had not been those six felt bags of silver pence.

And supposing it had indeed still been the book, secure in its beautiful coffin, carried across half the world unhandled and unread, for its value to a girl when she had reached marriageable age? Value as something to be sold, and sold shrewdly, to bring in the best profit. Books have another value, to those who have fallen for ever and wholly in love with them. There are those who would cheat for them, steal for them, lie for them, even if then they could never show nor boast of their treasures to any other creature. Kill for them? It was not impossible.

But that was surely looking far beyond the present case, for where was the connection? Who threatened? Who stood in the way? Not a barely literate clerk, who certainly cared not at all about exquisite manuscripts worked long ago by consummate artists.

Abruptly, and somewhat to his own surprise, for he was unaware of the intention forming, Cadfael stopped fretting out small weeds from between his herb beds, put away his hoe, and went to look for Brother Winfrid, weeding by hand in the vegetable garden.

'Son, I have an errand to do, if Father Abbot allows. I should be back before Vespers, but if I come late, see everything in order and close up my workshop for me before you go.'

Brother Winfrid straightened up to his full brawny country height for a moment to acknowledge his orders, with one large fist full of the greenery he had uprooted. 'I will. Is there anything within needs a stir?'

'Nothing. You can take your ease when you are finished here.' Not that he was likely to take that literally. Brother Winfrid had so much energy in him that it had to find constant outlet, or it would probably split him apart. Cadfael clapped him on the shoulder, left him to his vigorous labours, and went off in search of Abbot Radulfus.

The abbot was in his office, poring over the cellarer's accounts, but he put them aside when Cadfael asked audience, and gave his full attention to the petitioner.

'Father,' said Cadfael, 'has Brother Anselm told you what we discovered yesterday concerning the box that was brought back from the east for the girl Fortunata? And what, with reservations, we concluded from examining it?'

'He has,' said the abbot. 'I would trust Anselm's judgement on such matters, but it is still speculation. It does seem likely that there was such a book. A great pity it should be lost.'

'Father, I am not sure that it is lost. There is reason to believe that what came to England in that box was not the money that is in it now. There was a difference of weight and balance. So says the young man who brought it from the east, and so say I, also, for I handled it on the same day he delivered it to Girard of Lythwood's house. I think,' said Cadfael vehemently, 'that what we have noted should also be reported to the sheriff.'

'You believe,' said Radulfus, eyeing him gravely, 'that it may have some bearing on the only case I know of that Hugh Beringar now has in hand? But that is a case of murder. What can a book, present or absent, have to say regarding that crime?'

'When the clerk was killed, Father, was it not taken as proven by most men that the young man he had injured had killed him in revenge? Yet we know now it was not so. Elave never harmed him. And who else had cause to move against the man's life in the matter of that accusation he made? No one. I have come to believe that the cause of his death had nothing to do with his denunciation of Elave. Yet it does still seem that it had something to do with Elave himself, with his coming home to Shrewsbury. Everything that has happened has happened since that return. Is it not possible, Father, that it has to do with what he brought back to that house? A box that changes in weight, and one day handles like a solid carving of wood, and a few days later rings with silver coins. This in itself is strange. And whatever is strange within and around that household, where the dead man lived and worked for years, may have a bearing.'

'And should be taken into account,' concluded the abbot, and sat pondering what he had heard for some minutes in silence. 'Very well, so be it. Yes, Hugh Beringar should know of it. What he may make of it I cannot guess. God knows I can make nothing of it myself, not yet, but if it can shed one gleam of light to show the way a single step towards justice, yes, he must know. Go to him now, if you wish. Take whatever time may be needed, and I pray it may be used to good effect.'

Cadfael found Hugh, not at his own house by Saint Mary's, but at the castle. He was just striding across the outer ward in a preoccupied haste that curiously managed to indicate both buoyancy and irritation as Cadfael came up the ramp from the street, and in through the deep tunnel of the gate-tower. Hugh checked and turned at once to meet him.

'Cadfael! You come very timely, I've news for you.'

'And so have I for you,' said Cadfael, 'if mine can be called news. But for what it may be worth, I think you should have it.'

'And Radulfus agreed? So there must be substance in it. Come within, and let's exchange what we have,' said Hugh, and led the way forthwith towards the guardroom and anteroom in the gate-tower, where they could be private. 'I was about to go in and see our friend Conan,' he said with a somewhat wry smile, 'before I turn him loose. Yes, that's my news. It's taken a time to fill in all the comings and goings of his day, but we've dredged up at last a cottar at the edge of Frankwell who knows him, and saw him going up the pastures to his flock well before Vespers that afternoon. There's no way he could have killed Aldwin, the man was alive and well a good hour later.'

Cadfael sat down slowly, with a long, breathy sigh. 'So he's out of it, too! Well, well! I never thought him a likely murderer, I confess, but certainty, that's another matter.'

'Neither did I think him a likely murderer,' agreed Hugh ruefully, 'but I grudge him the days it's cost us to prise out his witnesses for him, and the fool so sick with fright he could barely remember the very acquaintances he'd passed on his way through Frankwell. And still lying, mark you, when his wits worked at all. But clean he is, and soon he'll be on his way back to his work, free as a bird. I wish Girard joy of him!' said Hugh disgustedly. He leaned his elbows on the small table between them, and held Cadfael eye to eye. 'Will you credit it? He swore he'd seen nothing of Aldwin after the girl's reproof sent the poor devil off in a passion of guilt to try and retrieve what he'd done – until he knew we'd found out about the hour or so they spent together in the alehouse. Then he admitted that, but swore that was the end of it. No such thing, as it turned out. It was one of the eager hounds baying along the Foregate after Elave who told us the next part of the story. He saw the pair of them cross over the bridge and come along the road towards the abbey with Conan's arm persuasively about Aldwin's shoulders, and Conan talking fast and urgently into Aldwin's ear. Until they both saw and heard the hunt in full cry! Frightened them out of their wits, he says, you'd have thought it was them the hounds were coursing. They went to ground among the trees so fast nothing showed but their scuts. I fancy that was what put an end once and for all to Aldwin's intention of going to the abbey with his bad conscience. Who knows, after the young priest confessed him he might have got his courage back, if ... Only today has Conan admitted that he went after him a second time. They were both a shade drunk, I expect. But finally he did go out to his flock, when he was certain Aldwin was far too frightened to involve himself further.'

'So you've lost your best suspect,' said Cadfael thoughtfully.

'The only one I had. And not sorry, so far as the fool himself is concerned, that he should turn out to be blameless. Well, short of murder, at least,' Hugh corrected himself. 'But contenders were thin on the ground from the start. And what follows now?'

'What follows,' said Cadfael, 'is that I tell you what I've come to tell you, for with even Conan removed from the field it becomes more substantial even than I thought. And then, if you agree, we might drain Conan dry of everything he knows, to the last drop, before you turn him loose. I can't be sure, even, that anyone has so much as mentioned to you the box that Elave brought home for the girl, by way of dowry? From the old man, before he died in France?'

'Yes,' said Hugh wonderingly, 'it was mentioned. Jevan told me, by way of accounting for Conan's wanting to get rid of Elave. He liked the daughter, did Conan, in a cool sort of way, but he began to like her much better when she had a dowry to bring with her. So says Jevan. But that's all I know if it. Why? How does the box have any bearing on the murder?'

'I have been baffled from the start,' said Cadfael, 'by the absence of motive. Revenge, said everyone, pointing the finger at Elave, but when that was blown clear away by young Father Eadmer, what was left? Conan may have been eager to prevent Aldwin from withdrawing his denunciation, but even that was thin enough, and now you tell me that's gone, too. Who had

160

anything against Aldwin so grievous as to be worth even a clout in a quarrel, let alone murder? It was hard enough to see the poor devil at all, let alone resent him. He had nothing worth coveting, had done no great harm to anyone until now. No wonder suspects were thin on the ground. Yet he stood in someone's way, or menaced someone, surely, whether he knew it or not. So since his betrayal of Elave was not the cause of his death, I began to look more closely at all the affairs of the household to which both men were attached, however loosely, every detail, especially anything that was new, this outbreak being so sudden and so dire. All was quiet enough until Elave came home. The only thing but himself he brought into that house was Fortunata's box. And even at first sight it was no ordinary box. So when Fortunata brought it to the abbey, thinking to use the money in it to procure Elave's release, I asked if we could examine it more closely. And this, Hugh, this is what we found.'

He told it scrupulously, in every detail of the gold and purple, the change in its weight, the possible and disturbing change in its contents. Hugh listened without comment to the end. Then he said slowly: 'Such a thing, if indeed it did enter that house, might well be enough to tempt any man.'

'Any who understood its value,' said Cadfael. 'Either in money, or for its own rare sake.'

'And before all, it would have to be a man who had opened the box, and seen what was there. Before it was made known to them all. Do we know whether it was opened at once, when the boy delivered it? Or how soon after?'

'That,' said Cadfael, 'I do not know. But you have one in hold who may know. One who may even know where it was laid by, who went near it, what was said about it, through those few days, as Elave could not know at all, not being there. Why do we not question Conan once more, before you set him free?'

'Bearing in mind,' Hugh warned, 'that this, too, may blow away in the wind. It may all along have been coins within there, but better packed.'

'English coin, and in such quantity?' said Cadfael, catching at a thread he had not considered, but finding it frail. 'At the end of such a journey, and committed to her from France? But if he sent her money at all, it must needs be English money. He could have been holding it in reserve for such a purpose, once he began to be a sick man. No, there's nothing certain,

161

everything slips through the fingers.'

Hugh rose decisively. 'Come, let's go and see what can be wrung out of Master Conan, before I let him slip through mine.'

Conan sat in his stone cell, and eyed them doubtfully and slyly from the moment they entered. He had a slit window on the air, a hard but tolerable bed, ample food and no work, and was just getting used to the fact, at first surprising, that no one was interested in using him roughly, but for all that he was uneasy and anxious whenever Hugh appeared. He had told so many lies in his efforts to distance himself from suspicion of the murder that he had difficulty in remembering now exactly what he had said, and was wary of trapping himself in still more tangled coils.

'Conan, my lad,' said Hugh, walking in upon him breezily, 'there's still a little matter in which you can be of help to me. You know most of what goes on in Girard of Lythwood's house. You know the box that was brought for Fortunata from France. Answer me some questions about it, and let's have no more lies this time. Tell me about the box. Who was there when it first came into the house?

Uneasy at this or any diversion he could not understand, Conan answered warily: 'There was Jevan, Dame Margaret, Aldwin and me. And Elave! Fortunata wasn't there, she came in later.'

'Was the box opened then?'

'No, the mistress said it should wait until Master Girard came home.' Chary of words until he understood the drift, Conan added nothing more.

'So she put it away, did she? And you saw where, did you not? Tell us!'

He was growing ever more uneasy. 'She put it away in the press, on a high shelf. We all saw it!'

'And the key, Conan? The key was with it? And were you not curious about it? Did you not want to see what was in it? Didn't your fingers begin to itch before nightfall?'

'I never meddled with it!' cried Conan, alarmed and defensive. 'It wasn't me who pried into it. I never went near it.'

So easy it was! Hugh and Cadfael exchanged a brief glance of astonished gratification. Ask the right question, and the road ahead opens before you. They closed in almost fondly on the sweating Conan.

'Then who was it?' Hugh demanded.

'Aldwin! He pried into everything. He never took things,'

162

said Conan feverishly, desperate to point the bolts of suspicion away from himself at all costs, 'but he couldn't bear not knowing. He was always afraid there was something brewing against him. *I* never touched it, but *he* did.'

'And how do you know this, Conan?' asked Cadfael.

'He told me, afterwards. But I heard them, down in the hall.'

'And when was it you heard *them* – down in the hall?'

'That same night.' Conan drew breath, beginning to be somewhat reassured again, since nothing of all this seemed to be pointing in his direction, after all. 'I went to bed, and left Aldwin down in the kitchen, but I wasn't asleep. I never heard him come into the hall, but I did hear Jevan suddenly shout down at him from the top of the stairs, "What are you doing there?" and then Aldwin, down below, all in a hurry, said he'd left his penknife in the press, and he'd be needing it in the morning. And Jevan says take it, then, and get to bed, and give over disturbing other people. And Aldwin came up in haste, with his tail between his legs. And I heard Jevan go on down into the hall and cross to the press, and I think he locked it and took the key away, for it was locked next morning. I asked Aldwin later what he'd been up to, and he said he only wanted to have a look inside, and he had the box open, and then had to shut and lock it again in a hurry, and try to hide what he was about, when Jevan shouted at him.'

'And *did* he see what was in it?' asked Cadfael, already foreseeing the answer, and tasting its bitter irony.

'Not he! He pretended at first he had, but he wouldn't tell me what it was, and in the end he had to admit he never got a glimpse. He'd barely raised the lid when he had to close it again in a hurry. It got him nothing!' said Conan, almost with satisfaction, as if he had scored over his fellow in some way by that wasted curiosity.

It got him his death, thought Cadfael, with awful certainty. And all for nothing! He never had time to see what the box held. Perhaps no one had then seen it. Perhaps it was that prying inquisitiveness that set off another man's quickening curiosity, fatal to them both.

'Well, Conan,' said Hugh, 'you may take heart and think yourself lucky. There's a man from the Welsh side of the town can swear to it you were on your way to Girard's fold well before Vespers, the night Aldwin was killed. You're clear of blame. You can be off home when you choose, the door's open.'

'And he did not even see it,' said Hugh, as they recrossed the outer ward side by side.

'But there was one who believed he had. And looked for himself,' said Cadfael, 'and was lost. Fathoms deep! And in one more day, or two, three at the most, Girard would be home, the box would be opened, what was in it would be known to all, and would be Fortunata's. Girard is a shrewd merchant, he would get for her the highest sum possible – not that it would approach its worth. But if he did not himself know where best to sell it, he would know where to ask. If it was what I begin to believe, the sum left her in its place would not have bought one leaf.'

'And only one life stood in the way, to threaten betrayal,' said Hugh. 'Or so it seemed! And all for nothing, the poor wretch never did have time to see what should have been there to be seen when the box was opened. Cadfael, my mind misgives me – yesterday, when Anselm examined that box, gold leaf, purple dye and all, Girard and the girl were present? How if one of them proved sharp enough to think as we are thinking? Having gone so far, could a man stop short now, if the same danger threatened his gains all over again?'

It was a new and disturbing thought. Cadfael checked for an instant in midstride, shaken into considering it.

'I think Girard never gave it much thought. The girl – I would not say! She is deeper than she seems, and she it is who has so much at stake. And she's young and kind, and sudden undeserved death has never before come so near her. I wonder! Truly I wonder! She did pay close attention, missing nothing, saying little. Hugh, what will you do?'

'Come!' said Hugh, making up his mind. 'You and I will go and visit the Lythwood household. We have pretext enough. They have buried their murdered man this morning, I have released one suspect from their retinue this afternoon, and I am still bent on finding a murderer. No need for one member rather than another to be wary of my probing, as yet, not until I have filled up the score of that day's movements for him as I took so long to do for Conan. At least we'll take note here and now of where the girl is, until you or I can talk with her again, and make sure she does nothing to draw danger upon herself.'

At about the same time that Hugh and Cadfael set out from the castle, Jevan of Lythwood had occasion to go up to his chamber, to discard and fold away the best cotte he had worn for Aldwin's funeral, and put on the lighter and easier coat in which he worked. He seldom entered the room without casting a pleased, possessive glance at the chest which held his books, and so he did now. The sunlight, declining from the zenith into the golden, sated hours of late afternoon, came slanting in by the south-facing window, gilded a corner of the lid and just reached the metal plate of the lock. Something gossamer-fine fluttered from the ornate edge, appearing and disappearing as it stirred in an air not quite motionless. Four or five long hairs, dark but bright, showing now and then a brief scintillation of red. But for the light, which just touched them against shadow, they would have been invisible.

Jevan saw them and stood at gaze, his face unchanging. Then he went to take the key from its place, and unlocked the chest and raised the lid. Nothing within was disturbed. Nothing was changed but those few sunlit filaments that stirred like living things, and curled about his fingers when he carefully detached them from the fretted edge in which they were caught.

In thoughtful silence he closed and locked the chest again, and went down into the shuttered shop. The key of his workshop upriver, on the right bank of the Severn well clear of the town, was gone from its hook.

He crossed the yard and looked in at the hall, where Girard was busy over the accounts Aldwin had left in arrears, and Margaret was mending a shirt at the other end of the table.

'I'm going down to the skins again,' said Jevan. 'There's something I left unfinished.'

Chapter Thirteen

HE WELCOME at Girard's house was all the warmer because Conan had arrived home only a quarter of an hour earlier, ebullient with relief and none the worse for his few days' incarceration, and Girard, a practical man, was disposed to let the dead bury their dead, once the living had seen to it that they got their dues and were seen off decently into a better world. What was left of his establishment seemed now to be clear of all aspersions, and could proceed about its business without interference.

Two members, however, were missing.

'Fortunata?' said Margaret in answer to Cadfael's enquiry. 'She went out after dinner. She said she was going to the abbey, to try to see Elave again, or at least to find out if anything had happened yet in his case. I daresay you'll be meeting her on the way down, but if not, you'll find her there.'

That was a load lifted from Cadfael's mind, at least. Where better could she be, or safer? 'Then I'd best be on my way home,' he said, pleased, 'or I shall be outstaying my leave.'

'And I came hoping to pick your brother's brains,' said Hugh. 'I've been hearing a great deal about this box of your daughter's, and I'm curious to see it. I'm told it may have been made to hold a book, at one time. I wondered what Jevan thought of that. He knows everything about the making of books, from the raw skin to the binding. I should like to consult him when he has time to spare. But perhaps I might see the box?'

They were quite happy to tell him what they could. There was no foreboding, no tremor in the house. 'He's away to his workshop just now,' said Girard. 'He was down there this morning, but he said he'd left something unfinished. He'll surely be back soon. Come in and wait a while, and he'll be here. The box? I doubt it's locked away until he comes. Fortunata gave it to him last night. If it's meant to hold a book, she says, Uncle Jevan is the man who has books, let me give him the box. And he's using it for the one he most values, as she wanted. He'll be pleased to show it to you. It is a very fine thing.'

'I won't trouble you now, if he's not here,' said Hugh. 'I'll look in later, I'm close enough.'

They took their leave together, and Hugh went with Cadfael as far as the head of the Wyle. 'She gave him the box,' said Hugh, frowning over a puzzle. 'What should that mean?'

'Bait,' said Cadfael soberly. 'Now I do believe she has been following the same road my mind goes. But not to prove – rather to disprove if she can. But at all costs needing to *know*. He is her close and valued kin, but she is not one who can shut her eyes and pretend no wrong has ever been done. Yet still we may both be wrong, she as well as I. Well, at the worst, she is safe enough if she's at the abbey. I'll go and find her there. And as for the other one ...'

'The other one,' said Hugh, 'leave to me.'

Cadfael walked in through the arch of the gatehouse into a scene of purposeful activity. It seemed he had arrived on the heels of an important personage, to whose reception the hierarchies of the house were assembling busily. Brother Porter had come in a flurry of skirts to take one bridle, Brother Jerome was contending with a groom for another one, Prior Robert was approaching from the cloister at his longest stride, Brother Denis hovered, not yet certain whether the newcomer would be housed in the guest hall or with the abbot. A flutter of brothers and novices hung at a respectful distance, ready to run any errands that might arise, and three or four of the schoolboys, sensibly withdrawn out of range of notice and censure, stood frankly staring, all eyes and ears.

And in the middle of this flurry of arrival stood Deacon Serlo, just dismounted from his mule and shaking out the skirts of his gown. A little dusty from the ride, but as rounded and pink-cheeked and wholesome as ever, and decidedly happier

167

now that he had brought his bishop with him, and could leave all decisions to him with a quiet mind.

Bishop Roger de Clinton was just alighting from a tall roan horse, with the vigour and spring of a man half his age. For he must, Cadfael thought, be approaching sixty. He had been bishop for fourteen years, and wore his authority as easily and forthrightly as he did his plain riding clothes, and with the same patrician confidence. He was tall, and his erect bearing made him appear taller still. A man austere, competent, and of no pretensions because he needed none, there was something about him, Cadfael thought, of the warrior bishops who were becoming a rare breed these days. His face would have done just as well for a soldier as for a priest, hawk-featured, direct and resolute, with penetrating grey eyes that summed up as rapidly and decisively as they saw. He took in the whole scene about him in one sweeping glance, and surrendered his bridle to the porter as Prior Robert bore down on him, all reverence and welcome.

They moved off together towards the abbot's lodging, and the group broke apart gradually, having lost its centre. The horses were eased of their saddle-bags and led away to the stables, the hovering brothers dispersed about their various businesses, the children drifted off in search of other amusement until they should be rounded up for their early supper. And Cadfael thought of Elave, who must have heard, distantly across the court, the sounds that heralded the coming of his judge. Cadfael had seen Roger de Clinton only twice before, and had no means of knowing in what mood and what mind he came to this vexed cause. But at least he had come in person, and looked fully capable of wresting back the responsibility for his diocese and its spiritual health from anyone who presumed to trespass on his writ.

Meantime, Cadfael's immediate business was to find Fortunata. He approached the porter with his enquiry. 'Where am I likely to find Girard of Lythwood's daughter? They told me at the house she would be here.'

'I know the girl,' said the porter, nodding. 'But I've seen nothing of her today.'

'She told them at home she was coming down here. Soon after dinner, so the mother told me.'

'I've neither seen nor spoken to her, and I've been here most of the time since noon. An errand or two to do, but I was only a matter of minutes away. Though she may have come in while my back was turned. But she'd need to speak to someone in authority. I think she'd have waited here at the gate until I came.'

Cadfael would have thought so, too. But if she'd caught sight of the prior as she waited, or Anselm, or Denis, she might very well have accosted one of them with her petition. Cadfael sought out Denis, whose duties kept him most of the time around the court, and within sight of the gate, but Denis had seen nothing of Fortunata. She was acquainted now with Anselm's little kingdom in the north walk, she might have made her way there, seeking for someone she knew. But Anselm shook his head decidedly, no, she had not been there. Not only was she not to be found within the precinct now, but it seemed she had not set foot in it all day.

The bell for Vespers found Cadfael hovering irresolute over what he ought to do, and reminded him sternly of his obligations to the vocation he had accepted of his own free will, and sometimes reproached himself for neglecting. There are more ways of approaching a problem than by belligerent action. The mind and the will have also something to say in the unending combat. Cadfael turned towards the south porch and joined the procession of his brothers into the dim, cool cavern of the choir, and prayed fervently for Aldwin, dead and buried in his piteous human imperfection, and for William of Lythwood, come home contented and shriven to rest in his own place, and for all those trammelled and tormented by suspicion and doubt and fear, the guilty as well as the innocent, for who needs succour more? Whether he was building a fantastic folly round a book which might not even exist, or confronting a serious peril for any who blundered on too much knowledge, one crime was hard and clear as black crystal, someone had taken the sad, inoffensive life of Aldwin the clerk, of whom the one man he had injured had said honestly: 'Everything he has said that I said, I *did* say.' But someone else, to whom he had done nothing, had slipped a dagger between his ribs from behind and killed him.

Cadfael emerged from Vespers consoled, but not the less aware of his own responsibilities. It was still full daylight, but with the slanting evening radiance about it, and the stillness of the air that seemed to dim all colours into a diaphanous pearly sheen. There remained one enquiry he could still make, before going further. It was just possible that Fortunata, grown dubious of venturing to ask admittance to Elave so soon after a

169

first visit, had simply asked someone at the gate, in the porter's brief absence, to carry a message to the prisoner, nothing to which any man could raise objection, merely to remind him his friends thought of him, and beg him to keep up his courage. It might not mean anything that Cadfael had not encountered her on her way home, she might already have been back in the town, and used the time to some other purpose before returning home. At least he would have a word with the boy, and satisfy himself he was anxious to no purpose.

He took the key from where it hung in the porch, and went to let himself into the cell. Elave swung round from his little desk, and turned a frowning face because he had been narrowing his eyes and knitting his brows in the dimming light over one of Augustine's more humane and ecstatic sermons. The apparent cloud cleared as soon as he left poring over the cramped minuscule of the text. Other people feared for him, but it seemed to Cadfael that Elave himself was quite free from fear, and had not shown even as restive in his close confinement.

'There's something of the monk in you,' said Cadfael, speaking his thoughts aloud. 'You may end up under a cowl yet.'

'Never!' said Elave fervently, and laughed aloud at the notion.

'Well, perhaps it would be a waste, seeing what other ideas you have for the future. But you have the mind for it. Travelling the world or penned in a stone cell, neither of them upsets your balance. So much the better for you! Has anyone thought to tell you that the bishop's come? In person! He pays you a compliment, for Coventry's nearer the turmoil than we are here, and he needs to keep a close eye on his church there, so time given to your case is a mark of your importance. And it may be a short time, for he looks a man who can make up his mind briskly.'

'I heard the to-do about someone arriving,' said Elave. 'I heard the horses on the cobbles. But I didn't know who it might be. Then he'll be wanting me soon?' At Cadfael's questioning glance he smiled, though seriously enough. 'I'm ready. I want it, too. I've made good use of my time here. I've found that even this Augustine went through many changes of mind over the years. You could take some of his early writings, and they say the very opposite of what he said in old age. That, and a dozen changes between. Cadfael, did you ever think

170

what a waste it would be if you burned a man for what he believed at twenty, when what he might believe and write at forty would be hailed as the most blessed of holy writ?'

'That is the kind of argument to which the most of men never listen,' said Cadfael, 'otherwise they would baulk at taking any life. You haven't been visited today, have you?'

'Only by Anselm. Why?'

'Nor had any message from Fortunata?'

'No. Why?' repeated Elave with sharper urgency, seeing Cadfael frown. 'All's well with her, I trust?'

'So I trust also,' agreed Cadfael, 'and so it should be. She told her family she was coming down to the abbey to ask if she could see you again, or get word of any progress in your case, that's why I asked. But no one has seen her. She hasn't been here.'

'And that troubles you,' said Elave sharply. 'Why should it matter? What is it you have in mind? Is there some threat to her? Are you *afraid* for her?'

'Let's say I should be glad to know that she's safe at home. As surely she must be. Afraid, no! But you must remember there is a murderer loose among us, and close to that household, and I would rather she kept to home and safe company than go anywhere alone. But as for today, I left Hugh Beringar keeping a close watch on the house and all who stir in and out of it, so set your mind at rest.'

They had neither of them been paying any attention to the passing sounds without, the brief ring of hooves distant across the court, the rapid exchange of voices, short and low, and then the light feet coming at an impetuous walk. It startled them both when the door of the cell was flung open before a gust of evening air and the abrupt entry of Hugh Beringar.

'They told me I should find you here,' he said, high and breathless with haste. 'They say the girl is *not* here, and has not been since yesterday. Is that true?'

'She has not come home?' said Cadfael, aghast.

'Nor she nor the other. The dame's beginning to be anxious. I thought best to come down and fetch the girl home myself if she was still here, but now I find she has not been here, and I know she is not at home, for I'm fresh come from there. So long away, and not where she said she'd be!'

Elave clutched at Cadfael's arm, shaking him vehemently in his bewilderment and alarm. 'The other? What other? What is happening? Are you saying she may be in danger?'

171

Cadfael fended him off with a restraining arm, and demanded of Hugh: 'Have you sent to the workshop?'

'Not yet! She might have been here, and safe enough. Now I'm going there myself. Come with me! I'll see you excused to Father Abbot afterwards.'

'I will well!' said Cadfael fervently, and was starting for the door, but Elave hung upon him desperately, and could not be shaken off.

'You *shall* tell me! What other? What man? Who is it threatens her? The workshop ... whose?' And on the instant he knew, and moaned the name aloud: 'Jevan! The book – you believe in it ... You think it was *he* ...?' He was on his feet, hurling himself at the open doorway, but Hugh stood solidly in his way, braced between the jambs.

'Let me go! I *will* go! Let me out to go to her!'

'Fool!' said Hugh brusquely, 'don't make things worse for yourself. Leave this to us, what more could you do than we can and will? Now, with the bishop already here, see to your own weal, and trust us to take care of hers.' And he shifted aside enough to order Cadfael, with a jerk of his head: 'Out, and fit the key!' and forthwith gripped Elave struggling in his arms, and bore him back to trip him neatly with a heel and tip him onto his bed. By the time he had sprung again like a wildcat, Hugh was outside the door, Cadfael had the key in the lock, and Elave thudded against the timber with a bellow of rage and despair, still a prisoner.

They heard him battering at the door and shouting wild appeals after them as they made for the gatehouse. They would surely hear him right across the court and into the guest-hall, all the windows being open to the air.

'I sent to saddle up a horse for you,' said Hugh, 'as soon as I heard she was not here. I can think of nowhere else she might have gone, and seeing he went back there ... Has she been searching? Did he find out?'

The porter had accepted the sheriff's orders as if they came from the abbot himself, and was already leading a saddled pony up from the stable yard at a brisk trot.

'We'll go straight through the town, it's quicker than riding round.'

The thunderous battering on the cell door had already ceased. Elave's voice was silent, but the silence was more daunting than the fury had been. Elave nursed his forces and bided his time.

'I pity whoever opens that door again tonight,' said Cadfael breathlessly, reaching for the rein. 'And within the hour someone will have to take him his supper.'

'You'll be back with better news by then, God willing,' said Hugh, and swung himself into the saddle and led the way out to the Foregate.

Between the bells that signalled the offices of the horarium, Elave's timepiece was the light, and he could judge accurately the passing of another clear day by those he had already spent in this narrow room. He knew, as soon as he drew breath and steeled himself into silence, that it could not be long now before the novice who brought his food would come with his wooden platter and pitcher, expecting nothing more disturbing than the courteous reception to which he had become accustomed, from a prisoner grimly resigned to patience, and too just to blame a young brother under orders for his predicament. A big, strapping young man they had chosen for the duty, with a guileless face and a friendly manner. Elave wished him no ill and would do him none if he could help it, but whoever stood between him and the way to Fortunata must look out for himself.

Yet the very arrangement of the cell was advantageous. The window and the desk beneath it were so situated that the opening of the door partly obscured them from anyone entering, until the door was closed again, and the natural place for the novice to set down his tray was on the end of the bed. Visit by visit he had lost all wariness, having had no occasion for it thus far, and his habit was to walk in blithely, pushing the door wide open with elbow and shoulder, and go straight to the bed to lay down his burden. Only then would he close the door and set his broad back to it, and pass the time of morning or evening companionably until the meal was done.

Elave withdrew from the indignity of shouting appeals that no one would heed or answer, and settled down grimly to wait for the footsteps to which he had grown used. His nameless novice had a giant's stride and a weighty frame, and the slap of his sandals on the cobbles was more of a hearty clout. There was no mistaking him, even if the narrow lancet of window had not afforded a glimpse of the wiry brown ring of his tonsure passing by before he turned the corner and reached the door. And there he had to balance his tray on one hand while he turned the key. Ample time for Elave to be motionless behind

173

the door when the young man walked in as guilelessly as ever, and made straight for the bed.

The smallness of the space caused Elave to collide sidelong with the unsuspecting boy and send him reeling to the opposite wall but even so the prisoner was round the door and out into the court, and running like a hare for the gatehouse, before anyone in sight realised what had happened. After him came the novice, with longer legs and a formidable turn of speed, and a bellow that alerted the porter, and fetched out brothers, grooms and guests like a swarm of bees, from hall and cloister and stableyard. Those quickest to comprehend and most willing to join any pursuit converged upon Elave's flying figure. Those less active drew in more closely to watch. And it seemed that the first shouted alarm had reached even the abbot's lodging, and brought out Radulfus and his guest in affronted dignity to suppress the commotion.

There had been from the first a very poor prospect of success. Yet even when four or five scandalised brothers had run to mass in Elave's path and pinion him between them, he drove the whole reeling group almost to the arch of the gate before they hung upon him so heavily that he was dragged to a standstill. Writhing and struggling, he was forced to his knees, and fell forward on his face on the cobbles, winded and sobbing for breath.

Above him a voice said, quite dispassionately: 'This is the man of whom you told me?'

'This is he,' said the abbot.

'And thus far he has given no trouble, threatened none, made no effort to escape?'

'None,' said Radulfus, 'and I expected none.'

'Then there must be a reason,' said the equable voice. 'Had we not better examine what it can be?' And to the captors, who were still distrustfully retaining their grip on Elave as he lay panting: 'Let him rise.'

Elave braced his hands against the cobbles and got to his knees, shook his bruised head dazedly, and looked up from a pair of elegant riding-boots, by way of plain dark chausses and cotte to a strong, square, masterful face, with a thin, aquiline nose, and grey eyes that were bent steadily and imperturbably upon the dishevelled hair and soiled face of his reputed heretic. They looked at each other with intent and fascinated interest, judge and accused, taking careful stock of a whole field of faith and error, justice and injustice, across which, with all its

174

quicksands and pitfalls, they must try to meet.

'You are Elave?' said the bishop mildly. 'Elave, why run away now?'

'I was not running away, but towards!' said Elave, drawing wondering breath. 'My lord, there's a girl in danger, if things are as I fear. I learned of it only now. And I brought her into peril! Let me but go to her and fetch her off safe, and I'll come back, I swear it. My lord, I love her, I want her for my wife ... If she is threatened I must go to her.' He had got his breath back now, he reached forward and gripped the skirt of the bishop's cotte, and clung. An incredulous hope was springing up within him, since he was neither repelled nor avoided. 'My lord, my lord, the sheriff is gone to try and find her, he will tell you afterwards, what I say is true. But she is mine, she is part of me and I of her, and I must go to her. My lord, take my word, my most sacred word, my oath that I will return to face my judgement, whatever it may be, if only you will loose me for these few hours of this night.'

Abbot Radulfus took two paces back from this encounter, very deliberately, and with so strong a suggestion of command that all those standing by also drew off silently, still watching wide-eyed. And Roger de Clinton, who could make up his mind about a man in a matter of moments, reached a hand to grip Elave strongly by the hand and raise him from the ground, and stepping with an authoritative gesture from between Elave and the gate, said to the porter: 'Let him go!'

The workshop where Jevan of Lythwood treated his sheepskins lay well beyond the last houses of the suburb of Frankwell, solitary by the right bank of the river, at the foot of a steep meadow backed by a ridge of trees and bushes higher up the slope. Here the land rose, and the water, even at its summer level, ran deep, and with a rapid and forceful current, ideal for Jevan's occupation. The making of vellum demanded an unfailing supply of water, for the first several days of the process running water, and this spot where the Severn ran rapidly provided perfect anchorage for the open wooden frames covered with netting, in which the raw skins were fastened, so that the water could flow freely down the whole length of them, day and night, until they were ready to go into the solution of lime and water in which they would spend a fortnight, before being scraped clean of all remaining hair, and another fortnight afterwards to complete the long bleaching.

Fortunata was familiar with the processes which produced at last the thin, creamy-white membranes of which her uncle was so justly proud. But she wasted no time on the netted cages in the river. No one would hide anything of value there, no matter how many folds of cerecloth were wrapped round it for protection. A faint drift of a fleshy odour from the soaking skins made her nostrils quiver as she passed, but the current was fast enough to disperse any stronger stench. Within the workshop the fleshy taint mingled with the sharp smell from the lime tanks, and the more acceptable scent of finished leather.

She turned the key in the lock, and went in, taking the key in with her and closing the door. It was heavy and dark within there, having been closed since morning, but she did not dare open the shutters that would let in light directly on to Jevan's great table, where he cleaned, scraped and pumiced his skins. Everything must appear closed and deserted. There were no houses near, no path passing close by. And surely now she had time enough, and no need for haste. What was no longer in the house must be here. He had no other place so private and so his own.

She knew the layout of the place, where the tanks of lime lay, one for the first soaking when the skins came from the river, one for the second, after both sides had been scraped clean of hair and traces of flesh. The final rinsing was done in the river, before the membranes were stretched over a frame and dried in the sun, and subjected to repeated and arduous cleanings with pumice and water. Jevan had taken in the single frame in use on his morning visit; the skin stretched over it felt smooth and warm to the touch.

She waited some minutes to allow her eyes to grow used to the dimness. A little light filtered in where the shutters joined. The roof was of thick straw thatch, sunwarmed, sagging a little between the supporting beams, and the air was heavy to stifling.

Jevan's place of work was meticulously kept, but it was also overfilled, with all the tools of his trade, his lime tanks, nets in reserve for the river cages, piles of skins at various stages of manufacture, the drying frames, and racks of his knives, pumice, cloths for rubbing. He kept also a little oil lamp, in case he needed to finish some process in a failing light, and a box with flint and tinder, charred cloth and touchwood and sulphur-tipped spunks for kindling it. Fortunata began her

176

search by what light came in through the shutters. The lime tanks could be disregarded, but they were so placed as to shroud one end of the workshop in darkness, and behind them lay the long shelf piled with skins still at varied stages of their finishing. Easy enough to use those to shroud a relatively small box, it could lie between them with the untrimmed edges draped to hide it. It took her a long time to go through them all, for they had to be laid aside in scrupulous order, to be restored just as she found them, all the more if she was in error, and there was still nothing to find but the box. But it was far too late to believe in that. If it had been true, why hide it, why remove it from its place in the chest, and leave his breviary stripped of its splendid covering?

The faint, furry dust danced in the thin chink of late sunlight, and tickled her throat and nostrils as she disturbed skin after skin. One pile was gradually stacked back into place, the second began to be stripped down, fold by fold, but there was nothing there but sheepskins. When that was done, the light was failing, for the sun had moved westward and vacated the chink in the shutters. She needed the lamp in order to see into the dark corners of the room, where two or three wooden chests housed a miscellany of offcuts, faulty pieces worth saving for smaller uses, and the finished gatherings of leaves ready for use, from a few great bifolia to the little, narrow, sixteen-leaf foldings used for small grammars or schooling texts. She was well aware that Jevan did not lock these. The workshop itself was locked up when vacant, and vellum was not a common temptation to theft. If one of the chests was locked now, that very fact would be significant.

It took her a little time to get the touchwood to nurse a spark, and kindle grudgingly into a tiny flame, enough to set to the wick of the lamp. She carried it to the line of chests and set it on the lid of the middle one, to shed its light within when she opened the first. If there was nothing alien here, there was nowhere else to look, the racks of tools stood open to view, the solid table was empty, but for the key of the door, which she had laid down there.

She had reached the third chest, in which the waste cuts and trimmings of vellum were tumbled, but here, too, all was as it should be. She had searched everywhere and found nothing.

She was on her knees on the beaten earth floor, lowering the lid, when she heard the door begin to open. The faint creak of the hinges froze her into stillness, her breath held. Then, very

177

slowly, she closed the chest.

'You have found nothing,' said Jevan's voice behind her, low and mild. 'You will find nothing. There is nothing to find.'

Chapter Fourteen

ORTUNATA braced her hands upon the chest on which she leaned, and came slowly to her feet before she turned to face him. In the yellow gleam of the lamp she saw his face in white bone highlights and deep hollows of shadow, perfectly motionless, betraying nothing. And yet it was too late for dissembling, they had both betrayed themselves already, she by whatever sign she had inadvertently left at home to warn him, and this present search, he by following her here. Too late by far to pretend there was nothing to hide, nothing to answer, nothing to be accounted for. Too late to attempt to reconstruct the simple trust she had always had in him. He knew it was gone, as she knew now, beyond doubt, that there was reason for its going.

She sat down on the chest she had just closed, and set the lamp safely apart on the one beside it. And since silence seemed even more impossible than speech, she said simply: 'I wondered about the box. I saw that it was gone from its place.'

'I know,' he said. 'I saw the signs you left for me. I thought you had given me the box. Am I still to account for whatever I do with it?'

'I was curious,' she said. 'You were going to use it for the best of your books. I wondered that it had gone out of favour in one day. But perhaps you have found a better,' she said deliberately, 'to take its place.'

He shook his head, advancing into the room the few steps that took him to the corner of the table where she had laid

179

down the key. That was the moment when she was quite sure, and something withered in her memories of him, forcing her, like a wounded plant, in urgent haste towards maturity. The lamp showed his face arduously smiling, but it was more akin to a spasm of pain. 'I don't understand you,' he said. 'Why must you meddle secretly? Could you not have asked me whatever you wanted to know?'

His hand crept almost stealthily to the key. He drew back into the shadows by the door, and without taking his eyes from her, felt behind him with a grating fumble for the lock, and locked them in together.

It seemed to Fortunata then that she would do well to be a little afraid, but all she could feel was a baffled sadness that chilled her to the heart. She heard her own voice saying: 'Had Aldwin meddled secretly? Was that what ailed him?'

Jevan braced his shoulders back against the door, and stood staring at her with stubborn forbearance, as though dealing with someone unaccountably turned idiot, but his consciously patient smile remained fixed and strained, like a convulsion of agony.

'You are talking in riddles,' he said. 'What has this to do with Aldwin? I can't guess what strange fancy you've got into your head, but it is an illusion. If I choose to show the gem you gave me to a friend who would appreciate it, does that mislead you into thinking I have somehow misprised or misused it?'

'Oh, no!' said Fortunata in the flat tone of helpless despair. 'It will not do! Today you have been nowhere but here, not alone. If there had been no more than that, you would have taken book and all to show, you would have said what you were about. And you would not have followed me here! It was a mistake! You should have waited. I've found nothing. But by your coming I do know now there is something here to be found. Why else should you trouble what I did?' A sudden gust of rage took her at his immovable and self-deceiving attempt at condescension, which struggled and failed to diminish her. 'Why do we keep pretending?' she cried. 'What is the use? If I had known I would have *given* you the book, or taken your price for it if that was what you wanted. But now there's murder, murder, murder in between us, and there's no turning back or putting that away out of mind. And you know it as well as I. Why do we not speak openly? We cannot stay here for ever, unable to go forward or back. Tell me, what *are* we to do now?'

But that was what neither he nor she could answer. Her hands were tied like his, they were suspended in limbo together, and neither of them could cut the cord that fettered them. He would have to kill, she would have to denounce, before either of them could ever be free again, and neither of them could do it, and neither of them, in the end, would be able to refrain. There was no answer. He drew deep breath, and uttered something like a groan.

'You meant that? You could forgive me for robbing you?'

'Without a thought! What you took from me I can do without. But what you took from Aldwin there's no replacing, and no one who is not Aldwin has the right to forgive it.'

'How do you know,' he demanded with abrupt ferocity, 'that I ever did any harm to Aldwin?'

'Because if you had not you would have denied it here and now, in defiance of what I may believe I know. Oh, why, why? But for that I could have held my tongue. For you I would have! But what had Aldwin ever done, to come by such a death?'

'He opened the box,' said Jevan starkly, 'and looked inside. No one else knew. When it was opened before us all he would have blabbed it out. Now you have it! An inquisitive fool who walked in my way, and he could have betrayed me, and I should have lost it ... lost it for ever ... It was the box, the box that made me marvel. And he was before me, and had seen what afterwards I saw ... and coveted!'

Long, heavy silences had broken the low, furious thread of this speech, as if for minutes at a time he forgot where he was, and what manner of audience he was addressing. Outside, the light was gently dimming. Within, the lamp began to burn lower. It seemed to Fortunata that they had been there together for a very long time.

'I had only until Girard came home. I took it that very night, and put what I had in its place. I did not want to cheat you of all, I paid what I had ... But then there was Aldwin. When could he ever keep to himself anything he knew? And my brother on his way home ...'

Another haunted silence, in which he began to stir from his post by the door, moving restlessly the length of the room, past where she sat almost forgotten, silent and still.

'When he went running back after Elave, that day, I had almost grown reconciled. My word against his! A risk ... but almost I came to terms with it. Even now – do you see it? – all

181

this is my word against yours, if you so choose!' He said it without emphasis, almost indifferently. But he had remembered her again, a danger like the other. His unquiet prowling drove him back to the table. He ran the hand that was not clutching the key along the rack of his knives, in a kind of absent caress for a profession he had enjoyed and at which he had excelled.

'In the end it was pure chance. Can you believe that? Chance that I had the knife ... It was no lie, I came out here to work that afternoon. I had been using a knife – this knife ...'

Time and silence hung for a long while as he took it from the rack and drew it slowly out of its leather sheath, running long fingers down the thin, sharp blade.

'I had the sheath strapped to my belt, I forgot and left it there when I locked up to go home. And I thought I would go on through the town and go to Vespers at Holy Cross, seeing it was the day of Saint Winifred's translation ...'

He turned to look at her, darkly and intently, she sitting there slender and still on the chest beside the lamp, her grave eyes fixed unwaveringly on him. Just once he saw her glance down briefly at the knife in his hand. He turned the blade thoughtfully to catch the light. Now how easily he could end her, take the prize for which he had killed, and set out towards the west, as many and many a wanted man had done from here before him. Wales was not far, fugitives crossed that border both ways at need. But more is needed than mere opportunity. Time was passing, and it seemed this deadlock must last for ever, in a kind of self-created purgatory.

' ... I came late, they were all within, I heard the chanting. And then he came out from the little door that leads to the priest's room! If he had not, I should have gone into the church, and there would have been no death. Do you believe that?'

Once again he had remembered her fully, as the niece of whom he had been humanly fond. And this time he wanted a reply, there was hunger in the very vibration of his voice.

'Yes,' she said, 'I do believe it.'

'But he came. And seeing he turned towards the town, to go home, I changed my mind. It happens in a moment in a breath, and everything is changed. I fell in beside him and went with him. There was no one to see, they were all in the church. And I remembered the knife – this knife! It was very simple ... nothing unseemly ... He was just newly confessed and shriven, as near content as ever I knew him. At the head of the path down to the riverside I slid it into him, and drew him away in my arm down through the bushes, down to the boat under the bridge. It was still almost full daylight then, I hid him there until dark. So there was no one left to betray me.'

'Except yourself,' she said, 'and now me.'

'And you will not,' said Jevan. 'You cannot ... any more than I can kill you ...'

This time the silence was longer and even more strained, and the close, stifling air within the room dulled Fortunata's senses. It was as if they had shut themselves for ever into a closed world where no one else could come, to shatter the tension between them and set them free to move again, to act, to go forward or back. Jevan began once more to pace the floor, turning and twisting at every few steps as though intense pain convulsed him. It went on for a long time, before he suddenly halted, and lowering with a long sigh the hands that still gripped the knife and key, went on as though only a second had passed since he last spoke:

' ... and yet in the end one of us will have to give way. There is no one else to deliver us.'

He had barely uttered it when a fist banged briskly at the door, and Hugh Beringar's voice called loudly and cheerfully: 'Are you within there, Master Jevan? I saw your light through the shutters. I brought your kin some good news a while ago, but you weren't there to hear it. Open the door and hear it now!'

For one shocked moment Jevan froze where he stood. She felt him stiffen into ice, but his rigor lasted no longer than the flicker of an eyelid, before he heaved himself out of it with a contortion of effort like a man plucking up the weight of the world, and summoned up from somewhere the most matter-of-fact of voices to call back an answer.

'One moment only! I'm just finishing here.'

He was at the door and turning the key as silently and softly as a cat moves. She had risen to her feet, but had not moved from her place, uncertain what he meant to do, but filled with a kind of passive wonder that kept her from making any move of her own. He gripped her by the arm with his left hand, sliding his arm through hers to hold her close and fondly by the wrist, close as a lover or an affectionate father. There was never a word said of threatening or pleading, no request for her silence and submission. Perhaps he was already sure of it, if she was not. But she watched him turn the naked knife he held in his right hand, so that the blade lay along his forearm, and the sleeve concealed it. His long fingers were competent and assured on the shaped haft. He drew her with him to the door, and she went unresisting. With the hand that nursed the knife he set the door wide open, and led her out with him on to the green meadow, into the gentle, cloudless evening light that from within had seemed to be ultimate darkness.

'Good news is always welcome,' he said, confronting Hugh at a few yards' distance with an open and untroubled countenance, from which he had banished the brief, icy pallor by force of will. 'I should have heard it soon – we're bound for home now. My niece has been sweeping and tidying my workshop for me. You need not have gone out of your way for me, my lord, but it was gracious in you.'

'I am not out of my way,' said Hugh. 'We were close, and your brother said you would be here. The matter is, I've set your shepherd free. A liar Conan may be, but a murderer he is not. Every part of his day is accounted for at last, and he's back home and clear of blame. As well you should hear it from me, you may well have been wondering yourself, after all the lies he told, how deep he was mired in this business.'

'Then does this mean,' asked Jevan calmly, 'that you have found the real murderer?'

'Not yet,' said Hugh, with an equally confident and deceptive face, 'though it narrows the field. You'll be glad to get your man back. And he's mortal glad to be back, I can tell you. I suppose that affects your brother's side of the business rather than yours; but according to Conan he has been known to help you with the skins sometimes.' He had advanced to the door of the workshop, and was peering curiously within, into a cavern dimly lit by the little glow-worm lamp, still burning on the lid of the chest. The yellow gleam faded in the light flooding in through the wide open door. Hugh's eyes roamed with an inquisitive layman's interest over the great table under the shuttered windows, the chests and the lime tanks, and arrived at the long rack of knives ranged along the wall, knives for dressing, for fleshing, for scraping, for trimming.

And one of the sheaths empty.

Cadfael, standing a little apart with the horses, between the belt of trees that curved round close to the river on his left

184

hand and the open slope of meadow on his right, had a brightly lit view of the exterior of the workshop, the grassy slope, and the three figures gathered outside the open door. The sun was low, but not yet sunk behind the ridge of bushes, and the slanting westward light picked out detail with golden, glittering clarity, and found every point from which it could reflect. Cadfael was watching intently, for from this retired position he might see things hidden from Hugh, who stood close. He did not like the way Jevan was clasping Fortunata's arm, holding her hard against his side. That embrace, uncharacteristic of so cool and self-sufficient a person as Jevan of Lythwood, Hugh certainly would not have missed. But had he seen, as Cadfael had, in one ruby-red shaft from the setting sun, and for one instant only, the steel of the knife flashing from under the cuff of Jevan's right sleeve?

There was nothing strange in the girl's appearance, except perhaps the unusual stillness of her face. She had nothing to say, made no motion of fear or distrust, was not uneasy at being held so, or if she was, there was no discerning it in her bearing. But she knew, quite certainly, what Jevan had in his other hand.

'So this is where you perform your mysteries,' Hugh was saying, advancing curiously into the workshop. 'I've often wondered about your craft. I know the quality of what you produce, I've seen it in use, but how the leaves come by that whiteness, seeing what the raw hides are like, I've never understood.'

Like any inquisitive stranger, he was prowling about the room, probing into corners, but avoiding the rack of knives, since the gap would be too obvious to be missed if he went near it and made no comment. He was tempting Jevan, if he felt any anxiety or had things to hide within, to loose his hold on the girl and follow, but Jevan never relaxed his grip, only drew Fortunata with him to the doorway, and followed no further. And now indeed that strained and tethered movement began to seem sinister, and how to break the link began to seem a matter of life and death. Cadfael moved a little nearer, leading the horses.

Hugh had emerged from the hut again, still at gaze, still curious. He passed by the close-linked pair and went down towards the edge of the bank, where the netted cages were moored in the river. Jevan followed, but still retaining the girl's arm, cramped into the hollow of his side. Woman walks on the

185

left, so that her man's right arm may be free to defend her, whether with fist or sword. Jevan held Fortunata so fast on his left in order that she might be within instant reach of his knife, if this matter ended past hope. Or was the knife for himself?

Elave had come, as the riders had, through the town, in by one bridge, out by the other, running, after the first frenzy, no longer like a demented man, but steadily, at a pace and rhythm he knew he could maintain. From past years he knew exactly the quickest path beyond the suburb, upriver to the curve where the current had carved its bed deep and fast. When he came over the ridge, and was able to halt and look down towards the solitary workshop in the meadow, withdrawn far enough up the slope to evade even the thaw-water spate unless in a very bad year, he lingered in cover among the trees to take in the scene below, and get his breath back while he assessed it.

And there they were, just outside the door of the workshop, which was in the upstream end of the hut, to prolong the evening light from the west, as the wide opening in the inland, south-facing wall admitted it through the main part of the day. He could see the two netted frames in the water by the way the surface eddies span; they lay slightly downstream, where the raised bank afforded firm anchorage. Behind the linked figures of Jevan and Fortunata the door of the hut stood wide open, in a deceptive suggestion of honesty, as the linked arms of uncle and niece presented a travesty of affection. In all the years of her childhood, never had Jevan handled and petted the girl freely, as Girard would do by his nature. This was a different kind of man, private, self-sufficient, not given to touching or being touched, not effusive in his likings. He had been a kind uncle to her in his cool, teasing way, surely he had loved her, but never thus. It was not love that joined them now. What had she become? His hostage? His protection, for a short while if no more? No, if she had nothing to reveal against him, and he was sure of her, what need to clasp her so close? She could have stood apart, and helped him all the better to an appearance of normality, to fend off the sheriff at least for today. He held fast to her because he was not sure of her, he had to remind her by his grip that if she spoke the wrong word he could avenge himself.

Elave crept round in the cover of the trees, which swept in a long, thinning curve down towards the Severn, upstream of the hut, and shrank into scrub and bushes perhaps fifty paces from

186

the bank. He was nearer now, he could hear the sound of voices but not what was said. Between him and the group at the door stood Brother Cadfael with the horses, for the time being holding off from a nearer approach. And it was all a play, Elave saw that now, a play to preserve the face of normality between all these people. Nothing must shatter it; a too open word, a threatening move might precipitate disaster. The very voices were casual, light and current, like acquaintances exchanging the day's trivial news in the street.

He saw Hugh go into the workshop, and saw that Jevan did not loose his hold of Fortunata to follow him, but stood immovably without. He saw the sheriff emerge again, animated and smiling, brushing past the pair of them and waving Jevan with him towards the river, but when they followed him they moved as one. Then Cadfael stirred himself abruptly and led the horses down the slope to join them, suddenly treading close on Jevan's heels as it seemed, but Jevan never turned his head or relaxed his hold. And Fortunata all this time went silently where she was led, with a still and wary face.

What they needed, what they were trying to achieve, was a diversion, anything that would break that mated pair apart, enable Hugh to pluck the girl away from the man, unhurt. Once robbed of her, Jevan could be dealt with. But they were only two, and he was well aware of both of them, and could so contrive as to keep them both at arm's length and beyond. As long as he held Fortunata by the arm he was safe, and she in peril, and no one could afford to demolish the pretence that everything was as it always was.

But he, Elave, could! Of him Jevan was not aware, and against him he could not be on guard. And there must be something that would shatter his pretence and startle his hand from its attendant shield, and leave him defenceless. Only there would be no more than one chance.

A last long, red ray of the setting sun before it sank pierced the veil of bushes, and at once paled the small yellow glow from within the hut, which Elave had all this time seen without seeing, and glittered for one instant at the wrist of Jevan's right hand. Elave recognised at once fire and steel, and knew why Hugh held off so patiently. Knew, also, what he was about to do. For the whole group with the led horses, had moved downstream towards the netted cages where skins swayed and writhed in the current. A few yards more, and he could put the

187

bulk of the workshop between him and them as he crossed the meadow to the open door.

Hugh Beringar was doing the talking, pretending interest in the processes involved in vellum-making, trying to occupy Jevan's attention to such an extent that he should relax his vigilance. Cadfael ranged distractingly close with the horses, but Jevan never looked round. He had surely left the door of the hut open and the lamp burning to force the sheriff to draw off in the end, mount and ride away, and leave the tolerant craftsman to close up his affairs for the night. Hugh was just as set on outstaying even this relentless patience. And while they were deadlocked there, standing over the bank of the Severn, here was one free agent who could act, and only one.

Elave broke cover and ran, using the hut as shield, headlong for the open doorway and the dim interior, and caught up the lamp. The thatch of the roof was old, dried from a fine summer, bellying loosely between its supporting beams. He set the flame of the lamp to it in two places, over the long table where the draught from the shutters would fan it, and again close to the doorway as he backed out again. Outside he plucked out the burning wick and flung it up on the slope of the roof, and the remaining oil after it. The breeze that often stirred at sunset after a still day was just waking from the west, and caught at the small spurt of flame, sending a thin, sinuous serpent of fire up the roof. Inside the hut he heard what sounded like a giant's gusty sigh, and flames exploded and licked from truss to truss along the thatch between the rafters. Elave ran, not back into the cover of the bushes, but round to the shutters on the landward side of the hut, and gripped and tore at the best hold he could get on the boards until one panel gave and swung clear, and billowing smoke gushed out first, and after it tall tongues of flame as the air fanned the fire within. He sprang back, and stood off to see the fearful thing he had done, as smoke billowed and flame soared above the roof.

Cadfael was the first to see, and cry an alarm: 'Fire! Look, your hut's afire!'

Jevan turned his head, perhaps only half believing, and saw what Cadfael had seen. He uttered one awful scream of despair and loss, flung Fortunata away from him so suddenly and roughly that she almost fell, flung off the knife he held to quiver upright in the turf, and ran frenziedly straight for the hut. Hugh yelled after him: 'Stop! You can do nothing!' and

188

ran after, but Jevan heeded nothing but the tower of fire and smoke, dimming the sunset against which he saw it, and blackening the rose and pale gold of the sky. Round to the far wall of the workshop he ran headlong, and in through the drifting smoke that filled the doorway.

Elave, rounding the corner of the building just in time to confront him face to face, beheld a horrified mask with open, screaming mouth and frantic eyes, before Jevan plunged without pause into the choking darkness within. Elave even grasped at his sleeve to halt him from such madness, and Jevan turned on him and hurled him off with a blow in the face, sending him reeling as a spurt of flame surged between them and drove them apart. Stumbling backwards and falling in the tufted grass, Elave saw the drifting smoke momentarily coiled aside in an eddy of wind. He was staring full into the open doorway, and could not choose but see what happened within.

Jevan had blundered heedless through the smoke, and clambered on to the long table, and was stretching up with both arms plunged to the elbow in the burning thatch, that dangled in swags above his head, reaching for something secreted there. He had it, he tugged wildly to bring it down into his arms, moaning and writhing at the pain of his burned hands. Then it seemed that half the disturbed thatch collapsed in a great explosion of flame on top of him, and he vanished in a dazzling rose of fire and a long howl of anguish and rage.

Elave clawed his way up from the ground and lunged forward with arms over his face to shield him. Hugh came up breathless and baulked in the doorway, as the heat drove them both back, coughing and retching for clean air. And suddenly a blackened figure burst out between them, trailing a comet's tail of smoke and sparks, his clothing and hair on fire, something muffled and shapeless hugged protectively and passionately in his arms. He was keening in a thin wail, like wind in winter in door and chimney. They sprang to intercept him and try to beat out the flames, but he was too sudden and too swift. Down the slope of the grass he went, a living torch, and leaped far out into the mid-current. The Severn hissed and spat, and Jevan was gone, swept downstream past his own nets and skins, past Fortunata, rigid and mute with shock in Cadfael's arms, down this free-flowing reach of the river, to drift ashore somewhere in the slower stretches and lower water where the Severn encircled the town.

Fortunata saw him pass, turning with the current, very soon

189

lost to sight. He was not swimming. Both arms embraced fiercely the swathed burden for which he had killed and now was dying.

It was over. There was nothing now to be done for Jevan of Lythwood, nothing for his blackened and blazing property but to let it burn out. There was nothing near enough to catch fire from it, only the empty field. What mattered now, to Hugh as to Cadfael, was to get these two shocked and inarticulate souls safely back into a real world among familiar things, even if for one of them it must be a return to a household horrified and bereaved, and for the other to a stone cell and a threatened condemnation. Here and now, all Fortunata could say, over and over again, was: 'He would not have hurt me – he would not!' and at last, after many such repetitions, almost inaudibly: '*Would he*?' And nothing as yet could be got out of Elave but the horrified protest: 'I never wanted that! How could I know? How could I know? I never wished him that!' And at last, in a kind of fury against himself, he said: 'And we do not even know he is guilty of anything, even now we do not know!'

'Yes,' said Fortunata then, quickening out of her icy numbness. 'I do know! He told me.'

But that was a story she was not yet able to tell fully, nor would Hugh allow her to waste present time on it, for she was cold with an unnatural cold from within, and he wanted her home.

'See to the lad, Cadfael, and get him back where his bishop wants him, before his truancy is added to the charges against him. I'll take the lady back to her mother.'

'The bishop knows I'm gone,' said Elave, rousing himself to respond, with a great heave of his shoulders that still could not shrug off the stunning load they carried. 'I begged him, and he gave me leave.'

'Did he so?' said Hugh, surprised. 'Then the more credit to him and to you. I have hopes of such a bishop.' He was up into the saddle with a vigorous spring, and reaching down a hand to Fortunata. His favourite rawboned grey would never notice the slight extra weight. 'Hand her up, boy ... that's it, your foot on mine. And now be wise, leave all till tomorrow. What more needs to be done, I'll do.' He had shed his coat to wrap round the girl's shoulders, and settled her securely in his arm. 'Tomorrow, Cadfael, I'll be early with the abbot. Doubtless we shall all meet before the day's out.'

190

They were gone, away at a canter up the slope of the field, turning their backs on the blaze that was already settling down into a blackened, smouldering heap of roofless timber, and the netted sheepskins weaving and swaying in the sharp current, while the water under the opposite bank lay smooth and almost still.

'And we'll be on our way, too,' said Cadfael, gathering the pony's rein, 'for there's nothing any man can do more here. All's done now, and by the same token, might have been much worse done. Here, you ride and I'll walk with you, and we'll just make our way quietly home.'

'*Would* he have harmed her?' Elave asked after long silence, when they were threading the highroad through the thriving houses and shops of Frankwell and approaching the western bridge.

'How can we know, when she herself cannot be certain? God's providence decreed that he should not. That must be enough for us. And you were his instrument.'

'I have been the death of his brother for Girard,' said Elave. 'How can he but blame me? What better could I expect from him now?'

'Would it have been better for Girard if his brother had lived to be hanged?' asked Cadfael. 'And his name blown about in the scandal of it? No, leave Girard to Hugh. He's a man of sense, he'll not hold it against you. You sent him back a daughter, he won't grudge her to you when the time comes.'

'I never killed a man before.' Elave's voice was weary and reflective. 'In all those miles we travelled, and with dangers, and fights enough along the way, I doubt if I ever drew blood.'

'You did not kill him, and must not claim more than your due. His own actions killed him.'

'Do you think he may have dragged himself ashore somewhere? Living? *Could* he live? After that?'

'All things are possible,' said Cadfael. But he remembered the arms in their smouldering sleeves clamped fast over the thing Jevan had snatched from the fire, the long body swept past beneath the water without struggle or sound, and he had not much doubt what would be found next day, somewhere in the circuit of the town.

Over the bridge and through the streets the pony paced placidly, and at the descent of the Wyle he snuffed the evening air and his pace grew brisker, scenting his stable and the comforts of home.

191

When they entered the great court, the brothers had just come out from Compline. Abbot Radulfus emerged from the cloister to cross to his own lodging, with his distinguished guests one on either side. They came at the right moment to see a brother of the house leading in, on one of the abbey's ponies, the prisoner accused of heresy, and released on his parole some three hours earlier. The rider was soiled and blackened by smoke, his hands and his hair at the temples somewhat scorched by fire, a circumstance he had not so far noticed, but which rendered the whole small procession a degree more outrageous in Canon Gerbert's eyes. Brother Cadfael's calm acceptance of this unseemly spectacle only redoubled the offence. He helped Elave to dismount, patted him encouragingly on the back, and ambled off to the stables with the pony, leaving the prisoner to return to his cell of his own volition, even gladly, as if he were indeed coming home. This was no way to hold an alleged heretic. Everything about the procedures here in the abbey of Saint Peter and Saint Paul scandalised Canon Gerbert.

'Well, well!' said the bishop, unshaken, even appreciative. 'Whatever else the young man may be, he's a man of his word.'

'I marvel,' said Gerbert coldly, 'that your lordship should ever have taken such a risk. If you had lost him it would have been a grave dereliction, and a great injury to the Church.'

'If I had lost him,' said the bishop, unmoved, 'he would have lost more and worse. But he comes back as he went, intact!'

Chapter Fifteen

ROTHER CADFAEL asked audience with the abbot early next morning, to recount all that had happened, and was glad to meet Hugh arriving just as he himself was leaving. Hugh's session with Abbot Radulfus lasted longer. There was much to tell, and still much to do, for nothing had yet been seen of Jevan of Lythwood, dead or alive, since he had leaped into the Severn a lighted torch, his hair erected and ablaze. For Radulfus, too, the day's business was of grave importance. Roger de Clinton abhorred time wasted, and was needed in Coventry, and it was his intention to make an end, one way or another, at this morning's chapter, and be off back to his restless and vulnerable city.

'Oh, yes, and I have brought and delivered to Canon Gerbert,' said Hugh, rising to take his leave, 'the latest report from Owain's borders. Earl Ranulf has come to terms for the time being, it suits Owain to keep the peace with him for a while. The earl will be back in Chester by tonight. No doubt the canon will be relieved to be able to continue his journey.'

'No doubt,' said the abbot. He did not smile, but even in two bare syllables there was a tone of satisfaction in his voice.

Elave came to his trial shaven, washed clean of his smoky disfigurement, and provided, by Brother Denis' good offices, with a clean shirt and a decent coat in exchange for his scorched and unsightly one. It was almost as if the community

193

had grown so accustomed to him during his few day's stay, and so completely lost all inclination to regard him as in any way perilous or to be condemned, that they were united in wishing him to present the most acceptable appearance possible, and make the most favourable impression, in a benevolent conspiracy which had come into being quite spontaneously.

'I have been taking advice,' said the bishop briskly, opening the assembly, 'concerning the ordinary human record of this young man, from some who know him well and have had dealings with him, as well as what I have observed with my own eyes in this short while. And let no man present feel that the probity or otherwise of a man's common behaviour has nothing to do with such a charge as heresy. There is authority in scripture: By their fruits you may know them. A good tree cannot bring forth bad fruit, nor a bad tree good fruit. So far as anyone has been able to inform me, this man's fruits would seem to bear comparison with what most of us can show. I have heard of none that could be called rotten. Bear that in mind. It is relevant. As to the exact charges brought against him, that he has said certain things which go directly against the teachings of the Church ... Let someone now rehearse them to me.'

Prior Robert had written them down, and delivered them with a neutral voice and impartial countenance, as if even he had felt how the very atmosphere within the enclave had changed towards the accused.

'My lord, in sum, there are four heads: first, that he does not believe that children who die unbaptised are doomed to reprobation. Second, as a reason for that, he does not believe in original sin, but holds that the state of newborn children is the state of Adam before his fall, a state of innocence. Third, that he holds that a man can, by his own acts, make his own way towards salvation, which is held by the Church to be a denial of divine grace. Fourth, that he rejects what Saint Augustine wrote of predestination, that the number of the elect is already chosen and cannot be changed, and all others are doomed to reprobation. For he said rather that he held with Origen, who wrote that in the end all men would be saved, since all things came from God, and to God they must return.'

'And those four heads are all that matter?' said the bishop thoughtfully.

'They are, my lord.' ·

194

'And how do you say, Elave? Have you been misreported in any of these counts?'

'No, my lord,' said Elave firmly. 'I hold by all of those. Though I never named this Origen, for I did not then know the name of the elder who wrote what I accepted and still believe.'

'Very well! Let us consider the first head, your defence of those infants who die unbaptised. You are not alone in having difficulty in accepting their damnation. In doubt, go back to Holy Writ. That cannot be wrong. Our Lord,' said the bishop, 'ordered that children should be allowed to come to him freely, for of such, he said, is the kingdom of heaven. To the best of my reading, he never asked first whether they were baptised or not before he took them up in his arms. Heaven he certainly allotted to them. But tell me, then, Elave, what value *do* you see in infant baptism, if it is not the sole way to salvation?'

'It is a welcome into the Church and into life, surely,' said Elave, uncertain as yet of his ground and of his judge, but hopeful. 'We come innocent, but such a membership and such a blessing is to help us keep our innocence.'

'To speak of innocence at birth is to bring us to the second count. It is part of the same thinking. You do not believe that we come into the world already rotten with the sin of Adam?'

Pale, obstinate and unrelenting, Elave said: 'No, I do not believe it. It would be unjust. How can God be unjust? By the time we are grown we have enough to bear with our own sins.'

'Of all men,' agreed the bishop with a rueful smile, 'that is certainly true. Saint Augustine, who has been mentioned here, regarded the sin of Adam as perpetuated in all his heirs. It might be well to give a thought to what the sin of Adam truly was. Augustine held it to be the fleshly act between man and woman, and considered it the root and origin of all sin. There is here another disputable point. If this in every case is sin, how comes it that God instructed his first-made creatures to be fruitful and multiply and people the earth?'

'It is nevertheless a more blessed course to refrain,' said Canon Gerbert coldly but carefully, for Roger de Clinton was on his own ground, noble, and highly regarded.

'Neither the act nor abstention from the act is of itself either good or bad,' said the bishop amiably, 'but only in respect of its purpose, and the spirit in which it is undertaken. What was your third head, Father Prior?'

'The question of free will and divine grace,' said Robert. 'And namely, whether a man can of his free will choose right

195

instead of wrong, and whether by so doing he can proceed one step towards his own salvation. Or whether nothing can avail of all he does, however virtuous, but only by divine grace.'

'As to that, Elave,' said the bishop, looking at the resolute face that fronted him with such intent and sombre eyes, 'you may speak your mind. I am not trying to trap you, I desire to know.'

'My lord,' said Elave, picking his way with deliberation, 'I do believe we have been given free will, and can and must use it to choose between right and wrong, if we are men and not beasts. Surely it is the least of what we owe, to try and make our way towards salvation by right action. I never denied divine grace. Surely it is the greatest grace that we are given this power to choose, and the strength to make right use of it. And see, my lord, if there is a last judgement, it will not and cannot be of God's grace, but of what every man has done with it, whether he buried his talent or turned it to good profit. It is for our own actions we shall answer, when the day comes.'

'So thinking,' said the bishop, eyeing him with interest, 'I see that you can hardly accept that the roll of the elect is already made up, and the rest of us are eternally lost. If that were true, why strive? And strive we do. It is native to man to have an aim, and labour towards it. And God he knows, better than any, that grace and truth and uprightness are as good aims as any. What else is salvation? It is no bad thing to feel obliged to earn it, and not wait to be given it as alms to a beggar, unearned.'

'These are mysteries for the wise to ponder, if anyone dare,' said Gerbert in chill disapproval, but somewhat abstractedly, too, for a part of his mind was already preoccupied with the journey on to Chester, and the subtle diplomacy he must have at his finger-ends when he got there. 'From one obscure even among the laity it is presumptuous.'

'It was presumptuous of Our Lord to argue with the doctors in the temple,' said the bishop, 'seeing he was human boy as well as God, and in both kinds true to that nature. But he did it. We doctors in the temple nowadays do well to recall how vulnerable we are.' And he sat back in his stall, and regarded Elave very earnestly for some minutes. 'My son,' he said then, 'I find no fault with you for venturing to use wits which, I'm sure you would say, are also the gift of God, and meant for use, not to be buried profitless. Only take care to remember that you are also subject to error, and vulnerable after your own kind as I after mine.'

'My lord,' said Elave, 'I have learned it all too well.'

'Not so well, I hope, as to bury your talent now. It is better to cut too deep a course than to stagnate and grow foul. One test only I require, and that is enough for me. If you believe, in all good faith, the words of the creed, in the sight of this assembly and of God, recite it for me now.'

Elave had begun to glow as brightly as the sun slanting across the floor of the chapter-house. Without further invitation, without an instant's thought, he began in a voice loud, clear and joyful: 'I believe in one God, the Father, the ruler of all men, the maker of all things visible and invisible ...'

For this belonged in the back of his mind untouched since childhood, learned from his first priestly patron, whom he loved and who could do no wrong for him, and with whom he had chanted it regularly and happily for years without ever questioning what it meant, only feeling what it meant to the gentle teacher he adored and imitated. This was his faith for once not chiselled out for himself, but received, rather an incantation than a declaration of belief. After all his doubts and probings and rebellions, it was his innocence and orthodoxy that set the seal on his deliverance.

He was just ending, in triumph, knowing himself free and vindicated, when Hugh Beringar came quietly into the chapter-house, with a bundle wrapped in thick swathes of waxed cloth under his arm.

'We found him,' said Hugh, 'lodged under the bridge, caught up by the chain that used to moor a boat mill there, years ago. We have taken his body home. Girard knows everything we could tell him. With Jevan's end this whole matter can end. He owned to murder before he died. There is no need to publish to the world what would further injure and distress his kin.'

'None,' said Radulfus.

There were seven of them gathered together in Brother Anselm's corner of the north walk, but Canon Gerbert was not among them. He had already shaken off the dust of this questionably orthodox abbey from his riding-boots, mounted a horse fully recovered from his lameness and eager for exercise, and set off for Chester, with his body servant and his grooms, and no doubt was already rehearsing what he would have to say to Earl Ranulf, and how much he could get from him without promising anything of substance in return. But the bishop, once having heard of what Hugh carried, and the vicissitudes through which it had passed, had the human curiosity to wait and see for himself the final outcome. Here with him were Anselm, Cadfael, Hugh, Abbot Radulfus, and Elave and Fortunata, silent, hand in hand though they dissembled the clasp reticently between their bodies in this august company. They were still a little dazed with too sudden and too harsh experience, and not yet fully awake to this equally abrupt and bewildering release from tension.

Hugh had delivered his report in few words. The less said now of that death, the better. Jevan of Lythwood was gone, taken from the Severn under the same arch of the same bridge where he had hidden his own dead man until nightfall. In time Fortunata would remember him as she had always known him, an ordinary uncle, kind if not demonstrative. Some day it would cease to matter that she still could not be certain whether he would indeed have killed her, as he had killed one witness already, rather than give up what in the end he had valued more than life. It was the last irony that Aldwin, according to Conan, had never managed to see what was within the box. Jevan had killed to no purpose.

'And this,' said Hugh, 'was still in his arms, lodged fast against the stone of the pier.' It lay now upon Anselm's work-table, still shedding a few drops of water as the wrappings were stripped away. 'It belongs, as you know, to this lady, and she has asked that it be opened here, before you, my lords, as witnesses knowledgeable in such works as may be found within.'

He was unfolding layer after layer as he spoke. The outermost, scorched and frayed into holes, had already been discarded, but Jevan had given his treasure every possible protection, and by the time the last folds were stripped away the box lay before them immaculate, untouched by fire or water, the ornate key still in the lock. The ivory lozenge stared up at them with immense Byzantine eyes from beneath the great round forehead that might have been drawn with compasses, before the rich hair was carved, and the beard, and the lines of age and thought. The coiling vines gleamed, refracting light from polished edges. Now at last they all hesitated to turn the key and open the lid.

It was Anselm who at length set hands to it and opened it. From both sides they leaned to gaze. Fortunata and Elave drew close, and Cadfael made room for them. Who had a better right?

The lid rose on the binding of purple dyed vellum, bordered with a rich tracery of leaves, flowers and tendrils in gold, and bearing in the centre, in a delicate framework of gold, a fellow to the ivory on the box. The same venerable face and majestic brow, the same compelling eyes gazing upon eternity, but this one was carved on a smaller scale, not a head but a half-length, and held a little harp in his hands.

With reverent care Anselm tilted the box, and supported the book on his palm as he slid it out on to the table.

'Not a saint,' he said, 'except that they often showed him with a halo. This is King David, and surely what we have here is a psalter.'

The purple vellum of the binding was stretched over thin boards, and the first gathering of the book, and the last, when Anselm opened it, were also of gold on purple. The rest of the leaves were of very fine, smooth finish and almost pure white. There was a frontispiece painting of the psalmist playing and singing, enthroned like an emperor, and surrounded by musicians earthly and heavenly. The vibrant colours sprang ringing from the page, as brilliantly as the sounds the royal minstrel was plucking from his strings. Here was no powerful, massive Byzantine block colouring, classic and monumental, but sinuous, delicate, graceful shapes, as pliant and ethereal as the pattern of vines that surrounded the picture. Everything rippled and twined, and was elegantly elongated. Opposite, on a skin side smooth as silk, the title page was lined out in golden uncials. But on the following leaf, which was the dedication page, the penmanship changed to a neat, fluent, round hand.

'This is not eastern,' said the bishop, leaning to look more closely.

'No. It is Irish minuscule, the insular script.' Anselm's voice grew more reverent and awed as he turned page after page, into the ivory whiteness of the main part of the book, where the script had abandoned gold for a rich blue-black, and the numerals and initials flowered in exquisite colours, laced and bordered with all manner of meadow flowers, climbing roses, little herbers no bigger than a thumbnail, where birds sang in branches hardly thicker than a hair, and shy animals leaned out from the cover of blossoming bushes. Tiny, perfect women sat reading on turfed seats under bowers of eglantine. Golden fountains played into ivory basins, swans sailed on crystal rivers, minute ships ventured oceans the size of a tear.

In the last gathering of the book the leaves reassumed their

199

imperial purple, the final exultant psalms were again inscribed in gold, and the psalter ended with a painted page in which an empyrean of hovering angels, a paradise of haloed saints, and a transfigured earth of redeemed souls all together obeyed the psalmist, and praised God in the firmament of his power, with every instrument of music known to man. And all the quivering wings, all the haloes, all the trumpets and psalteries and harps, the stringed instruments and organs, the timbrels and the loud cymbals were of burnished gold, and the denizens of heaven and paradise and earth alike were as sinuous and ethereal as the tendrils of rose and honeysuckle and vine that intertwined with them, and the sky above them as blue as the irises and periwinkles under their feet, until the tips of the angels' wings melted into a zenith all blinding gold, in which the ultimate mystery vanished from sight.

'This is a wonder!' said the bishop. 'Never have I seen such work. This is beyond price. Where can such a thing have been produced? Where was there art the match of this?'

Anselm turned back to the dedication page, and read aloud slowly from the golden Latin:

Made at the wish of Otto, King and Emperor, for the marriage of his beloved son, Otto, Prince of the Roman Empire, to the most Noble and Gracious Theofanu, Princess of Byzantium, this book is the gift of His Most Christian Grace to the Princess. Diarmaid, monk of Saint Gall, wrote and painted it.

'Irish script and an Irish name,' said the abbot. 'Gallus himself was Irish, and many of his race followed him there.'

'Including one,' said the bishop, 'who created this most precious and marvellous thing. But the box, surely, was made for it later, and by another Irish artist. Perhaps the same hand that made the ivory on the binding also made the second one for the casket. Perhaps she brought such an artist to the west in her train. It is a marriage of two cultures indeed, like the marriage it celebrated.'

'They were in Saint Gall,' said Anselm, scholar and historian, regarding with love but without greed the most beautiful and rare book he was ever likely to see. 'The same year the prince married they were there, son and father both. It is recorded in the chronicle. The young man was seventeen, and knew how to value manuscripts. He took several away with him from the library. Not all of them were ever returned. Is it any wonder that a man who loved books, once having set eyes on this, should covet it to the edge of madness?'

Cadfael, silent and apart, took his eyes from the pure, clear colours laid on, almost two hundred years since, by a steady hand and a loving mind, to watch Fortunata's face. She stood with Elave close and watchful at her shoulder, and Cadfael knew that the boy had her by the hand still in the shelter of their bodies, as fast as ever Jevan had held her by the arm when she was the only frail barrier he had against betrayal and ruin. She gazed and gazed at the beautiful thing William had sent her as dowry, and her eyes were hooded and her lips set in a pale, still face.

No fault of Diarmaid, the Irish monk of Saint Gall, who had poured his loveliest art into a gift of love, or at least a gift for marriage, the loftiest of the age, a mating of empires! No fault of his that this exquisite thing had brought about two deaths, and bereaved as well as endowed the bride to whom it was sent. Was it any wonder that such a perfect thing could corrupt a hitherto blameless lover of books to covet, steal and kill?

Fortunata looked up at last, and found the bishop's eyes upon her, across the table and its radiant burden.

'My child,' he said, 'you have here a most precious gift. If it pleases you to sell it, it will provide you with a rich dowry indeed, but take good advice before you part with it, and keep it safe. Abbot Radulfus here would surely hold it in trust for you, if you wish it, and see that you are properly counselled when you come to deal with a buyer. Though I must tell you that in truth it would be impossible to put a price on it fit for what is priceless.'

'My lord,' said Fortunata, 'I know what I want to do with it. I cannot keep it. It is beautiful, and I shall always remember it and be glad that I've seen it. But as long as it remains with me I shall find it a bitter reminder, and it will seem to me somehow spoiled and wronged. Nothing ugly should ever have touched it. I would rather that it should go with you. In your church treasury it will be pure again, and blessed.'

'I understand your revulsion,' said the bishop gently, 'after all that has happened, and I feel the justice of your grief for a thing of beauty and grace misused. But if that is truly what you wish, then you must accept what the library of my see can pay you for the book, though I must tell you I have not its worth to spend.'

201

'No!' Fortunata shook her head decidedly. 'Money has been paid for it once, money must not be paid for it again. If it has no price, no price must be given for it, but I may give it, and suffer no loss.'

Roger de Clinton, himself a man of decision, recognised as strong a resolution confronting him and, moreover, respected and approved it. But in conscience he reminded her considerately: 'The pilgrim who brought it half across the world, and sent it to you as a dowry, he also has a right to have his wishes honoured. And his wish was that this gift should be yours – no one's else.'

She acknowledged it with an inclination of her head, very seriously. 'But having given it, and made it mine, he would have held that it was mine, to give again if I pleased, and would never have grudged it. Especially,' said Fortunata firmly, 'to you and the Church.'

'But also he wished his gift to be used to ensure you a good marriage and a happy life,' said the bishop.

She looked back at him steadily and earnestly, with Elave's hand in hers, and Elave's face at her shoulder matching the look. 'That it has already done,' said Fortunata. 'The best of what he sent me I am keeping.'

By mid-afternoon they were all gone. Bishop de Clinton and his deacon, Serlo, were on their way back to Coventry, where one of Roger's predecessors in office had transferred the chief seat of his diocese, though it was still more often referred to as Lichfield than as Coventry, and both churches considered themselves as having cathedral status. Elave and Fortunata had returned together to the distracted household by Saint Alkmund's church, where now the body of the slayer lay on the same trestle bier in the same outhouse where his victim had lain, and Girard, who had buried Aldwin, must now prepare to bury Jevan. The great holes torn in the fabric of a close-knit household would gradually close and heal, but it would take time. Doubtless the women would pray just as earnestly for both the slayer and the slain.

With the bishop, carefully and reverently packed in his saddle-roll, went Princess Theofanu's psalter. How it had ever made its way back to the east, to some small monastery beyond Edessa, no one would ever know, and some day, perhaps two hundred years on, someone would marvel how it had travelled from Edessa to the library of Coventry, and that would also remain a mystery. Books are more durable than their authors, but at least the Irish monk Diarmaid had secured his own immortality.

Even the guest-hall was almost empty. The festival was over, and those who had lingered for a few days more were now finishing whatever business they had in Shrewsbury, and packing up to leave. The midsummer lull between Saint Winifred's translation and Saint Peter's fair provided convenient time for harvesting the abbey cornfields, beyond the vegetable gardens of the Gaye, where ears were already whitening towards ripeness. The seasons kept their even pace. Only men came and went, acted and refrained, untimely.

Brother Winfrid, content in his labours, was clipping the overgrown hedge of box, and whistling as he worked. Cadfael and Hugh sat silent and reflective on the bench against the north wall of the herb-garden, grown a little somnolent in the sun, and the lovely languor that comes after stress has spent itself. The colours of the roses in the distant beds became the colours of Diarmaid's rippling borders, and the white butterfly on the dim blue flower of fennel was changed into a little ship on an ocean no bigger than a pearl.

'I must go,' said Hugh for the third time, but made no move to go.

'I hope,' said Cadfael at last, stirring with a sigh, 'we have heard the last of the word heresy. If we must have episcopal visitations, may they all turn out as well. With another man it might have ended in anathema.' And he asked thoughtfully: 'Was she foolish to part with it? I have it in my eyes still. Almost I can imagine a man coveting it to death, his own or another's. The very colours could burn into the heart.'

'No,' said Hugh, 'she was not foolish, but very wise. How could she have ever have sold it? Who could pay for such a thing, short of kings? No, in enriching the diocese she enriches herself.'

'For that matter,' said Cadfael, after a long, contented silence, 'he did pay her a fair price for it. He gave Elave back to her, free and approved. I wouldn't say but she may have got the better of the bargain, after all.'

The Potter's Field

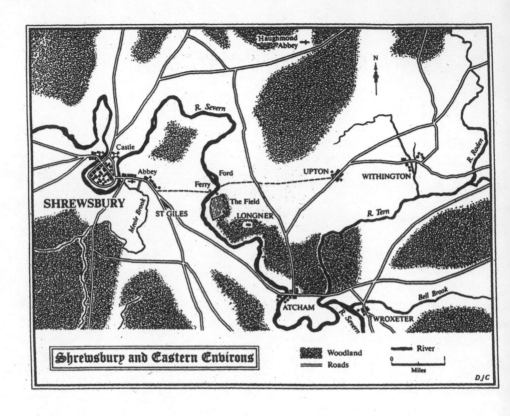

Shrewsbury and Eastern Environs

Woodland
Roads
River
0 Miles

Haughmond Abbey
N
R. Severn
Castle
Abbey
Ford
Ferry
UPTON
WITHINGTON
R. Roden
SHREWSBURY
Meole Brook
ST GILES
The Field
LONGNER
R. Tern
Bell Brook
ATCHAM
R. Severn
WROXETER

DJC

Chapter One

AINT PETER'S Fair of that year, 1143, was one week past, and they were settling down again into the ordinary routine of a dry and favourable August, with the corn harvest already being carted into the barns, when Brother Matthew the cellarer first brought into chapter the matter of business he had been discussing for some days during the Fair with the prior of the Augustinian priory of Saint John the Evangelist, at Haughmond, about four miles to the north-east of Shrewsbury. Haughmond was a FitzAlan foundation, and FitzAlan was out of favour and dispossessed since he had held Shrewsbury castle against King Stephen, though rumour said he was back in England again from his refuge in France, and safe with the Empress's forces in Bristol. But many of his tenants locally had continued loyal to the king, and retained their lands, and Haughmond flourished in their patronage and gifts, a highly respectable neighbour with whom business could be done to mutual advantage at times. This, according to Brother Matthew, was one of the times.

'The proposal for this exchange of land came from Haughmond,' he said, 'but it makes good sense for both houses. I have already set the necessary facts before Father Abbot and Prior Robert, and I have here rough plans of the two fields in question, both large and of comparable quality. The one which this house owns lies some mile and a half beyond Haughton, and is bounded on all sides by land gifted to

207

Haughmond Priory. Clearly it will advantage them to add this piece to their holdings, for economy in use and the saving of time and labour in going back and forth. And the field which Haughmond wishes to exchange for it is on the hither side of the manor of Longner, barely two miles from us but inconveniently distant from Haughmond. Clearly it is good sense to consider this exchange. I have viewed the ground, and the bargain is a fair one. I recommend that we should accept.'

'If this field is on the hither side of Longner,' said Brother Richard, the sub-prior, who came from a mile or so beyond the manor and knew the outlines of the land, 'how does it lie with regard to the river? Is it subject to flooding?'

'No. It has the Severn along one flank, yes, but the bank is high, and the meadow climbs gradually from it to a headland and a windbreak of trees and bushes along the ridge. It is the field of which Brother Ruald was tenant until some fifteen months ago. There were two or three small claypits along the river bank, but I believe they are exhausted. The field is known as the Potter's Field.'

A slight ripple of movement went round the chapter-house, as all heads turned in one direction, and all eyes fastened for one discreet moment upon Brother Ruald. A slight, quiet, grave man, with a long, austere face, very regular of feature, of an ageless, classical comeliness, he still went about the devout hours of the day like one half withdrawn into a private rapture, for his final vows were only two months old, and his desire for the life of the cloister, recognised only after fifteen years of married life and twenty-five of plying the potter's craft, had burned into an acute agony before he gained admittance and entered into peace. A peace he never seemed to leave now, even for a moment. All eyes might turn on him, and his calm remained absolute. Everyone here knew his story, which was complex and strange enough, but that did not trouble him. He was where he wanted to be.

'It is good pasture,' he said simply. 'And could well be cultivated, if it is needed. It lies well above any common floodline. The other field, of course, I do not know.'

'It may be a little greater,' said Brother Matthew judicially, contemplating his parchments with head on one side, measuring with narrowed eyes. 'But at that distance we are spared time and labour. I have said, I judge it a fair exchange.'

'The Potter's Field!' said Prior Robert, musing. 'It was such a field that was bought with the silver of Judas's betrayal, for

208

the burial of strangers. I trust there can be no ill omen in the name.'

'It was only named for my craft,' said Ruald. 'Earth is innocent. Only the use we make of it can mar it. I laboured honestly there, before I knew whither I was truly bound. It is good land. It may well be better used than for a workshop and kiln such as mine. A narrow yard would have done for that.'

'And access is easy?' asked Brother Richard. 'It lies on the far side of the river from the highroad.'

'There is a ford a little way upstream, and a ferry even nearer to the field.'

'That land was gifted to Haughmond only a year ago, by Eudo Blount of Longner,' Brother Anselm reminded them. 'Is Blount a partner to this exchange? He made no demur? Or has he yet been consulted?'

'You will remember,' said Brother Matthew, patiently competent at every point, as was his way, 'that Eudo Blount the elder died early this year at Wilton, in the rearguard that secured the king's retreat. His son, also Eudo, is now lord of Longnor. Yes, we have talked with him. He has no objection. The gift is Haughmond's property, to be used to Haughmond's best advantage, which manifestly this exchange serves well. There is no obstacle there.'

'And no restriction as to the use we in our turn may make of it?' demanded the prior acutely. 'The agreement will be on the usual terms? That either party may make whatever use it wishes of the fields? To build, or cultivate, or keep as pasture, at will?'

'That is agreed. If we want to plough, there is no bar.'

'It seems to me,' said Abbot Radulfus, casting a long glance around at the attentive faces of his flock, 'that we have heard enough. If anyone has any other point to raise, do so now, by all means.'

In the considering silence that followed many eyes turned again, mildly expectant, to the austere face of Brother Ruald, who alone remained withdrawn and unconcerned. Who should know better the qualities of that field where he had worked for so many years, or be better qualified to state whether they would be doing well in approving the proposed exchange? But he had said all he had to say, in duty bound, and felt no need to add another word. When he had turned his back upon the world and entered into his desired vocation, field and cottage and kiln and kin had vanished for him. He never spoke of his former life, probably he never thought of it. All those years he had been astray and far from home.

'Very well!' said the abbot. 'Clearly both we and Haughmond gain by the exchange. Will you confer with the prior, Matthew, and draw up the charter accordingly, and as soon as a day can be fixed we will see it witnessed and sealed. And once that is done, I think Brother Richard and Brother Cadfael might view the ground, and consider its most profitable use.'

Brother Matthew rolled up his plans with a brisk hand and a satisfied countenance. It was his part to keep a strict eye upon the property and funds of the house, to reckon up land, crops, gifts and legacies in the profits they could bring to the monastery of Saint Peter and Saint Paul, and he had assessed the Potter's Field with professional shrewdness, and liked what he saw.

'There is no other business?' asked Radulfus.

'None, Father!'

'Then this chapter is concluded,' said the abbot, and led the way out of the chapter-house into the sunbleached August grasses of the cemetery.

Brother Cadfael went up into the town after Vespers, in the cooling sunlight of a clear evening, to sup with his friend Hugh Beringar, and visit his godson Giles, three and a half years old, long and strong and something of a benevolent tyrant to the entire household. In view of the sacred duty such a sponsor has towards his charge, Cadfael had leave to visit the house with reasonable regularity, and if the time he spent with the boy was occupied more often in play than in the serious admonitions of a responsible godparent, neither Giles nor his own parents had any complaint to make.

'He pays more heed to you,' said Aline, looking on with smiling serenity, 'than he does to me. But he'll tire you out before you can do as much for him. Well for you it's near his bedtime.'

She was as fair as Hugh was black, primrose-fair, and fine-boned, and a shade taller than her husband. The child was built on the same long, slender lines, and flaxen like her. Some day he would top his father by a head. Hugh himself had foretold it, when first he saw his newborn heir, a winter child, come with the approach of Christmas, the finest of gifts for the festival. Now at three years old he had the boisterous energy of

210

a healthy pup, and the same whole-hearted abandonment to sleep when energy was spent. He was carried away at length in Aline's arms to his bed, and Hugh and Cadfael were left to sit down companionably together over their wine, and look back over the events of the day.

'Ruald's field?' said Hugh, when he heard of the morning's business at chapter. 'That's the big field the near side of Longner, where he used to have his croft and his kiln? I remember the gift to Haughmond, I was a witness to it. Early October of last year, that was. The Blounts were always good patrons to Haughmond. Not that the canons ever made much use of that land when they had it. It will do better in your hands.'

'It's a long time since I passed that way close,' said Cadfael. 'Why is it so neglected? When Ruald came into the cloister there was no one to take over his craft, I know, but at least Haughmond put a tenant into the cottage.'

'So they did, an old widow woman, what could she do with the ground? Now even she is gone, to her daughter's household in the town. The kiln has been looted for stone, and the cottage is falling into decay. It's time someone took the place over. The canons never even bothered to take the hay crop in, this year, they'll be glad to get it off their hands.'

'It suits both sides very well,' said Cadfael thoughtfully. 'And young Eudo Blount at Longner has no objection, so Matthew reports. Though the prior of Haughmond must have asked his leave beforehand, since the gift came from his father in the first place. A pity,' he said ruefully, 'the giver is gone to his maker untimely, and isn't here to say a word for himself in the matter.'

Eudo Blount the elder, of the manor of Longner, had left his lands in the charge of his son and heir only a few weeks after making the gift of the field to the priory, and gone in arms to join King Stephen's army, then besieging the Empress and her forces in Oxford. That campaign he had survived, only to die a few months later in the unexpected rout of Wilton. The king, not for the first time, had underestimated his most formidable opponent, Earl Robert of Gloucester, miscalculated the speed at which the enemy could move, and ridden with only his vanguard into a perilous situation from which he had extricated himself safely only by virtue of a heroic rearguard action, which had cost the king's steward, William Martel, his liberty, and Eudo Blount his life. Stephen, in honour bound, had paid a high price to redeem Martel. No one, in this world, could ransom back Eudo Blount. His elder became lord of Longner in his place. His younger son, Cadfael recalled, a novice at the abbey of Ramsey, had brought his father's body home for burial in March.

'A fine, tall man he was,' Hugh recalled, 'no more than two or three years past forty. And handsome! There's neither of his lads can match him. Strange how the lot falls. The lady's some years older, and sick with some trouble that's worn her to a shadow and gives her no rest from pain, yet she lingers on here, and he's gone. Does she ever send to you for medicines? The lady of Longner? I forget her name.'

'Donata,' said Cadfael. 'Donata is her name. Now you mention it, there was a time when her maid used to come for draughts to help her with the pain. But not for a year or more now. I thought she might have been on the mend, and felt less need of the herbs. Little enough I could ever do for her. There are diseases beyond any small skill of mine.'

'I saw her when they buried Eudo,' said Hugh, gazing sombrely out through the open hall door at the summer dusk gathering blue and luminous above his garden. 'No, there's no remission. So little flesh she has between her skin and bone, I swear the light shone through her hand when she raised it, and her face grey as lavender, and shrunken into deep lines. Eudo sent for me when he made up his mind to go to Oxford, to the siege. I did wonder how he could bear to leave her in such case. Stephen had not called him, and even if he had, there was no need for him to go himself. His only due was an esquire, armed and mounted, for forty days. Yet he saw his affairs in order, made over his manor to his son, and went.'

'It may well be,' Cadfael said, 'that he could no longer bear to stay, and look on daily at a distress he could neither prevent nor help.'

His voice was very low, asked Aline, re-entering the hall at that moment, did not hear the words. The very sight of her, radiantly content in her fulfilment, happy wife and mother, banished all such thoughts, and caused them both to shake off in haste all trace of a solemnity that might have cast a shadow on her serenity. She came to sit with them, her hands for once empty, for the light was too far gone for sewing or even spinning, and the warm, soft evening too beautiful to be banished by lighting candles.

'He's fast asleep. He was nodding over his prayers. But still he could rouse enough to demand his story from Constance. He'll have heard no more than the first words, but custom is custom. And I want my story, too,' she said, smiling at Cadfael, 'before I let you leave us. What is the news with you, there at the abbey? Since the fair I've got no further afield than Saint Mary's for Mass. Do you find the fair a success this year? There were fewer Flemings there, I thought, but some excellent cloths, just the same. I bought well, some heavy Welsh woollen for winter gowns. The sheriff,' she said, and made an impish face at Hugh, 'cares nothing what he puts on, but I won't have my husband go threadbare and cold. Will you believe, his best indoor gown is ten years old, and twice relined, and still he won't part with it?'

'Old servants are the best,' said Hugh absently. 'Truth to tell, it's only habit sends me looking for it, you may clothe me new, my heart, whenever you wish. And for what else is new, Cadfael tells me there's an exchange of lands agreed between Shrewsbury and Haughmond. The field they call the Potter's Field, by Longner, will come to the abbey. In good time for the ploughing, if that's what you decide, Cadfael.'

'It may well be,' Cadfael conceded. 'At least on the upper part, well clear of the river. The lower part is good grazing.'

'I used to buy from Ruald,' said Aline rather ruefully. 'He was a good craftsman. I still wonder – what was it made him leave the world for the cloister, and all so suddenly?'

'Who can tell?' Cadfael looked back, as now he seldom did, to the turning-point of his own life, many years past. After all manner of journeying, fighting, endurance of heat and cold and hardship, after the pleasures and the pains of experience, the sudden irresistible longing to turn about and withdraw into quietness remained a mystery. Not a retreat, certainly. Rather an emergence into light and certainty. 'He never could explain it or describe it. All he could say was that he had had a revelation of God, and had turned where he was pointed, and come where he was called. It happens. I think Radulfus had his doubts at first. He kept him the full term and over in his novitiate. His desire was extreme, and our abbot suspects extremes. And then, the man had been fifteen years married, and his wife was by no means consenting. Ruald left her everything he had to leave, and all of it she scorned. She fought his resolve for many weeks, but he would not be moved. After he was admitted among us she did not stay long in the croft, or avail herself of anything he had left behind for her. She went

213

away, only a few weeks later, left the door open and everything in its place, and vanished.'

'With another man, so all the neighbours said,' Hugh remarked cynically.

'Well,' said Cadfael reasonably, 'her own had left her. And very bitter she was about it, by all accounts. She might well take a lover by way of revenge. Did ever you see the woman?'

'No,' said Hugh, 'not that I recall.'

'I have,' said Aline. 'She helped at his booth on market days and at the fair. Not last year, of course, last year he was in the cloister and she was already gone. There was a lot of talk about Ruald's leaving her, naturally, and gossip is never very charitable. She was not well liked among the market women, she never went out of her way to make friends, never let them close to her. And then, you see, she was very beautiful, and a stranger. He brought her from Wales, years ago, and even after years she spoke little English, and never made any effort to be anything but a stranger. She seemed to want no one but Ruald. No wonder if she was bitter when he abandoned her. The neighbours said she turned to hating him, and claimed she had another lover and could do without such a husband. But she fought for him to the end. Women turn for ease to hate, sometimes, when love leaves them nothing but pain.' She had mused herself into another woman's anguish with unwonted gravity; she shook off the image with some dismay. 'Now *I* am the gossip! What will you think of me? And it's all a year past, and surely by now she's reconciled. No wonder if she took up her roots – they were shallow enough here, once Ruald was gone – and went away home to Wales without a word to a soul. With another man, or alone, what does it matter?'

'Love,' declared Hugh, at once touched and amused, 'you never cease to be a wonder to me. How did you ever come to know so much about the case? And feel so hotly about it?'

'I've seen them together, that was enough. From across a fairground stall it was plain to be seen how fond and wild she was. And you men,' said Aline, with resigned tolerance, 'naturally see the man's rights first, when he sets his heart on doing what he wants, whether it's entering the cloister or going off to war, but I'm a woman, and I see how deeply wronged the wife was. Had she no rights in the matter? And did you ever stop to think – *he* could have his freedom to go and become a monk, but his going didn't confer freedom on *her*. She could not take another husband; the one she had, monk or no, was

214

still alive. Was that fair? Almost,' avowed Aline roundly, 'I hope she did go with a lover, rather than have to live and endure alone.'

Hugh reached a long arm to draw his wife to him, with something between a laugh and a sigh. 'Lady, there is much in what you say, and this world is full of injustice.'

'Still I suppose it was not Ruald's fault,' said Aline, relenting. 'I daresay he would have released her if he could. It's done, and I hope, wherever she is, she has some comfort in her life. And I suppose if a man really is overtaken by an act of God there's nothing he can do but obey. It may even have cost him almost as much. What kind of brother has he made, Cadfael? Was it really something that could not be denied?'

'Truly,' said Cadfael, 'it seems that it was. The man is wholly devoted. I verily believe he had no choice.' He paused reflectively, finding it hard to discover the appropriate words for a degree of self-surrender which was impossible to him. 'He has now that entire security that cannot be moved by well or ill, since to his present state everything is well. If martyrdom was demanded of him now, he would accept it with the same serenity as bliss. Indeed it would be bliss, he knows nothing less. I doubt if he gives a thought to any part of that life he led for forty years, or the wife he knew and abandoned. No, Ruald had no choice.'

Aline was regarding him steadily with her wide iris eyes, that were so shrewd in their innocence. 'Was it like that for you,' she asked, 'when your time came?'

'No, I had a choice. I made a choice. It was even a hard choice, but I made it, and I hold to it. I am no such elect saint as Ruald.'

'Is that a saint?' asked Aline. 'It seems to me all too easy.'

The charter of the exchange of lands between Haughmond and Shrewsbury was drawn up, sealed and witnessed in the first week of September. Some days later Brother Cadfael and Brother Richard the sub-prior went to view the new acquisition, and consider its future use to the best advantage of the abbey. The morning was misty when they set out, but by the time they had reached the ferry just upsteam from the field the sun was already coming through the haze, and their sandalled feet left dark tracks through the dewy grass above the shore. Across the river the further bank rose, sandy and steep, undercut here and there by the currents, and levelling

215

off into a narrow plain of grass, with a rising edge of bushes and trees beyond. When they stepped from the boat they had some minutes of walking along this belt of pasture, and then they stood at the corner of the Potter's Field, and had the whole expanse obliquely before them.

It was a very fair place. From the sandy escarpment of the river bank the slope of grass rose gradually towards a natural headland of bush and thorn and a filigree screen of birch trees against the sky. Backed into this crest in the far corner the shell of the empty cottage squatted, its garden unfenced and running wild into the embracing wildness of the unreaped grass. The crop Haughmond had not found worth his while to garner was bleaching into early autumn pallor, having ripened and seeded weeks earlier, and among the whitened standing stems all manner of meadow flowers still showed, harebell and archangel, poppy and daisy and centaury, with the fresh green shoots of new grass just breaking through the roots of the fading yield. Under the headland above, tangles of bramble offered fruit just beginning to blacken from red.

'We could still cut and dry this for bedding,' said Brother Richard, casting a judicial eye over the wild expanse, 'but would it be worth the labour? Or we could leave it to die down of itself, and plough it in. This land has not been under the plough for generations.'

'It would be heavy work,' said Cadfael, viewing with pleasure the sheen of sunlight on the distant white trunks of the birch trees on the ridge.

'Not so heavy as you might think. The soil beneath is good, friable loam. And we have a strong ox-team, and the field has length enough to get a team of six into the yoke. We need a deep, broad furrow for the first ploughing. I would recommend it,' said Brother Richard, secure in the experience of his farming stock, and set off up the field to the crest, by the same rural instinct keeping to the headland instead of wading through the grass. 'We should leave the lower strip for pasture, and plough this upper level.'

Cadfael was of the same mind. The field they had parted with, distant beyond Haughton, had been best left under stock; here they could very well take a crop of wheat or barley, and turn the stock from the lower pasture into the stubble afterwards, to manure the land for the next year. The place pleased him, and yet had an undefined sadness about it. The remnants of the garden fence, when they reached it, the

216

tangled growth in which herb and weed contended for root and light and space, the doorless doorway and shutterless window, all sounded a note of humanity departed and human occupation abandoned. Without the remnants this would have been a scene wholly placid, gentle and content. But it was impossible to look at the deserted croft without reflecting that two lives had been lived there for fifteen years, joined in a childless marriage, and that of all the thoughts and feelings they had shared not a trace now remained here. Nor to note the bare, levelled site from which every stone had been plundered, without recalling that a craftsman had laboured here at loading his kiln and firing it, where now the hearth was barren and cold. There must surely have been human happiness here, satisfaction of the mind, fulfilment of the hands. There had certainly been grief, bitterness and rage, but only the detritus of that past life clung about the spot now, coldly, indifferently melancholy.

Cadfael turned his back upon the corner which had once been inhabited, and there before him lay the sweep of meadow, gently steaming as the sun drew off the morning mist and dew, and the sharp, small colours of the flowers brightened among the seeding grasses. Birds skimmed the bushes of the headland and flickered among the trees of the crest, and the uneasy memory of man was gone from the Potter's Field.

'Well, what's your judgement?' asked Brother Richard.

'I think we should do well to sow a winter crop. Deep-plough now, then do a second ploughing, and sow winter wheat, and some beans with it. So much the better if we can get some marl on to it for the second ploughing.'

'As good a use as any,' agreed Richard contentedly, and led the way down the slope towards the curve and glimmer of the river under its miniature cliffs of sand. Cadfael followed, the dry grasses rustling round his ankles in long, rhythmic sighs, as if for a tragedy remembered. As well, he thought, break the ground up there as soon as maybe, and get the soil to bear. Let's have young corn greening over where the kiln was, and either pull down the cottage or put a live tenant into it, and see to it he clears and tends the garden. Either that, or plough up all. Better forget it ever was a potter's croft and field.

In the first days of October the abbey's plough team of six oxen, with the heavy, high-wheeled plough, was brought over by the ford, and cut and turned the first sod in Ruald's field.

217

They began at the upper corner, close to the derelict cottage, and drove the first furrow along beneath the ridge, under the strong growth of bushes and brambles that formed the headland. The ox-driver urged his team, the oxen lumbered stolidly ahead, the coulter bit deep through turf and soil, the ploughshare sheared through the matted roots, and the furrow-board heaved the sod widely away like a sullenly breaking wave, turning up black soil and the strong scent of the earth. Brother Richard and Brother Cadfael had come to see the work begun, Abbot Radulfus had blessed the plough, and every augury was good. The first straight furrow drove the length of the field, brightly black against the autumnal pallor of the grasses, and the ploughman, proud of his skill, swung his long team in a swooping curve to bring them about as neatly as possible on the return course. Richard had been right, the soil was not so heavy, the work would go briskly.

Cadfael had turned his back on the work, and stood in the gaping doorway of the cottage, gazing into the empty interior. A full year ago, after the woman had shaken off the dust of this place from her feet and walked away from the debris of her life to look for a new beginning elsewhere, all the movable belongings of Ruald's marriage had been removed, with the consent of his overlord at Longner, and given to Brother Ambrose the almoner, to be shared among his petitioners according to their needs. Nothing remained within. The hearthstone was still soiled with the last cold ashes, and leaves had been blown into corners and silted there into nesting-places for the hibernating hedge-pig and the dormouse. Long coils of bramble had found their way in at the vacant window from the bushes outside, and a branch of hawthorn nodded in over his shoulder, half its leaves shed, but starred with red berries. Nettle and groundsel had rooted and grown in the crevices of the flooring. It takes a very short time for earth to seal over the traces of humankind.

He heard the distant shout from across the field, but thought nothing of it but that the driver was bawling at his team, until Richard caught at his sleeve and said sharply into his ear: 'Something's amiss, over there! Look, they've stopped. They've turned up something – or broken something – Oh, surely not the coulter!' He had flashed easily into vexation. A plough is a costly machine, and an iron-shod coulter on new and untried ground might well be vulnerable.

Cadfael turned to stare towards the spot where the team had

halted, at the far edge of the field where the tangle of bushes rose. They had taken the plough close, making the fullest use possible of the ground, and now the oxen stood still and patient in their harness, only a few yards advanced into the new furrow, while teamster and ploughman were stooped with their heads together over something in the ground. And in a moment the ploughman came springing to his feet and running headlong for the cottage, arms pumping, feet stumbling in the tufted grasses.

'Brother ... Brother Cadfael ... Will you come? Come and see! There's something there ...'

Richard had opened his mouth to question, in some irritation at so incoherent a summons, but Cadfael had taken a look at the ploughman's face, startled and disquieted, and was off across the field at a trot. For clearly this something, whatever it might be, was as unwelcome as it was unforeseen, and of a nature for which higher authority would have to take the responsibility. The ploughman ran beside him, blurting distracted words that failed to shed much light.

'The coulter dragged it up – there's more underground, no telling what ...'

The teamster had risen to his feet and stood waiting for them with hands dangling helplessly.

'Brother, we could take no charge here, there's no knowing what we've come on.' He had led the team a little forward to leave the place clear and show what had so strangely interrupted the work. Close under the slight slope of the bank which marked the margin of the field, with broom brushes leaning over the curve of the furrow, where the plough had turned, the coulter had cut in more deeply, and dragged along the furrow after it something that was not root or stem. Cadfael went on his knees, and stooped close to see the better. Brother Richard, shaken at last by the consternation that had rendered his fellows inarticulate and now chilled them into silence, stood back and watched warily, as Cadfael drew a hand along the furrow, touching the long threads that had entangled the coulter and been drawn upward into the light of day.

Fibres, but fashioned by man. Not the sinewy threads of roots gouged out of the bank, but half rotted strands of cloth, once black, or the common dark brown, now the colour of the earth, but still with enough nature left in them to tear in long, frayed rags when the iron ripped through the folds from which

219

they came. And something more, drawn out with them, perhaps from within them, and lying along the furrow for almost the length of a man's forearm, black and wavy and fine, a long thick tress of dark hair.

Chapter Two

ROTHER CADFAEL returned alone to the abbey, and asked immediate audience of Abbot Radulfus.

'Father, something unforseen sends me back to you in this haste. I would not have troubled you for less, but in the Potter's Field the plough has uncovered something which must be of concern both to this house and to the secular law. I have not yet gone further. I need your sanction to report this also to Hugh Beringar, and if he so permits, to pursue what as yet I have left as we found it. Father, the coulter has brought into daylight rags of cloth and a coil of human hair. A woman's hair, or so it seems to me. It is long and fine, I think it has never been cut. And, Father, it is held fast under the earth.'

'You are telling me,' said Radulfus, after a long and pregnant pause, 'that it is still rooted in a human head.' His voice was level and firm. There were few improbable situations he had not encountered in his more than fifty years. If this was the first of its kind, it was by no means the gravest he had ever confronted. The monastic enclave is still contained within and contingent upon a world where all things are possible. 'In this unconsecrated place there is some human creature buried. Unlawfully.'

'That is what I fear,' said Cadfael. 'But we have not gone on to confirm it, wanting your leave and the sheriff's attendance.'

'Then what have you done? How have you left things there in the field?'

221

'Brother Richard is keeping watch at the place. The ploughing continues, but with due care, and away from the spot. There seemed no need,' he said reasonably, 'to delay it. Nor would we want to call too much attention to what is happening there. The ploughing accounts for our presence, no one need wonder at seeing us busy there. And even if it proves true, this may be old, very old, long before our time.'

'True,' said the abbot, his eyes very shrewd upon Cadfael's face, 'though I think you do not believe in any such grace. To the best that I know from record and charter, there never at any time was church or churchyard near that place. I pray God there may be no more such discoveries to be made, one is more than enough. Well, you have my authority, do what needs to be done.'

What needed to be done, Cadfael did. The first priority was to alert Hugh, and ensure that the secular authority should be witness to whatever followed. Hugh knew his friend well enough to cast no doubts, ask no questions, and waste no time in demur, but at once had horses saddled up, taking one sergeant of the garrison with him to rise messenger should he be needed, and set off with Cadfael for the ford of Severn and the Potter's Field.

The plough team was still at work, lower down the slope, when they rode along the headland to the spot where Brother Richard waited by the bank of broom bushes. The long, attenuated, sinuous S-shapes of the furrows shone richly dark against the thick, matted pallor of the meadow. Only this corner under the headland had been left virgin, the plough drawn well aside after the first ominous turn. The scar the coulter had left ended abruptly, the long, dark filaments drawn along the groove. Hugh stooped to look, and to touch. The threads of cloth disintegrated under his fingers, the long strands of hair curled and clung. When he lifted them tentatively they slid through his hold, still rooted in earth. He stood back, and stared down sombrely into the deep scar.

'Whatever you've found here, we'd best have it out. Your ploughman was a little too greedy for land, it seems. He could have spared us trouble if he'd turned his team a few yards short of the rise.'

But it was already too late, the thing was done and could not be covered again and forgotten. They had brought spades with them, a mattock to peel off, with care, the matted root-felt of long undisturbed growth, and a sickle to cut back the overhanging broom that hampered their movements and had partially hidden this secret burial place. Within a quarter of an hour it became plain that the shape beneath had indeed the length of a grave, for the rotted shreds of cloth appeared here and there in alignment with the foot of the bank, and Cadfael abandoned the spade to kneel and scoop away earth with his hands. It was not even a deep grave, rather this swathed bundle had been laid in concealment under the slope, and the thick sod restored over it, and the bushes left to veil the place. Deep enough to rest undisturbed, in such a spot; a less efficient plough would not have turned so tightly as to reach it, nor the coulter have driven deep enough to penetrate it.

Cadfael felt along the exposed swathes of black cloth, and knew the bones within. The long tear the coulter had made slit the side distant from the bank from middle to head, where it had dragged out with the threads the tress of hair. He brushed away soil from where the face should be. Head to foot, the body was swathed in rotting woollen cloth, cloak or brychan, but there was no longer any doubt that it was a human creature, here laid underground in secret. Unlawfully, Radulfus had said. Buried unlawfully, dead unlawfully.

With their hands they scooped away patiently the soil that shrouded the unmistakable outline of humanity, worked their way cautiously beneath it from either side, to ease it out of its bed, and hoisted it from the grave to lay it upon the grass. Light, slender and fragile it rose into light, to be handled with held breath and careful touch, for at every friction the woollen threads crumbled and disintegrated. Cadfael eased the folds apart, and turned back the cloth to lay bare the withered remains.

Certainly a woman, for she wore a long, dark gown, ungirdled, unornamented, and strangely it seemed that the fullness of the skirt had been drawn out carefully into orderly folds, still preserved by the brychan in which she had been swathed for burial. The face was skeletal, the hands that emerged from the long sleeves were mere bone, but held in shape by her wrappings. Traces of dried and shrunken flesh showed at the wrists and at her bared ankles. The one last recollection of abundant life left to her was the great crown of black, braided hair, from which the one disordered coil had been drawn out by the coulter from beside her right temple. Strangely, she had clearly been stretched out decently for burial, her hands drawn up and crossed on her breast. More strangely still they were clasped upon a crude cross, made from two trimmed sticks bound together with a strip of linen cloth.

Cadfael drew the edges of the rotting cloth carefully back over the skull, from which the dark hair burgeoned in such strange profusion. With the death's-head face covered she became even more awe-inspiring, and they drew a little back from her, all four, staring down in detached wonder, for in the face of such composed and austere death, pity and horror seemed equally irrelevant. They did not even feel any will to question, or admit to notice, what was strange about her burial, not yet; the time for that would come, but not now, not here. First, without comment or wonder, what was needful must be completed.

'Well,' said Hugh drily, 'what now? Does this fall within my writ, Brothers, or yours?'

Brother Richard, somewhat greyer in the face than normally, said doubtfully: 'We are on abbey land. But this is hardly in accordance with law, and law is your province. I don't know what the lord abbot will wish, in so strange a case.'

'He will want her brought back to the abbey,' said Cadfael with certainty. 'Whoever she may be, however long buried unblessed, it's a soul to be salved, and Christian burial is her due. We shall be bringing her from abbey land, and to abbey land he'll want her returned. When,' said Cadfael with deliberation, 'she has received what else is her due, if that can ever be determined.'

'It can at least be attempted,' said Hugh, and cast a considering glance along the bank of broom bushes and round the gaping pit they had cut through the turf. 'I wonder is there anything more to be found here, put in the ground with her. Let's at least clear a little further and deeper, and see.' He stooped to draw the disintegrated brychan again round the body, and his very touch parted threads and sent motes of dust floating into the air. 'We shall need a better shroud if we're to carry her back with us, and a litter if she's to be carried whole and at rest, as we see her. Richard, take my horse and ride back to the lord abbot, tell him simply that we have indeed found a body buried here, and send us litter and decent covering to get her home. No need for more, not yet. What more do we know? Leave any further report until we come.'

'I will so!' agreed Brother Richard, so warmly that his relief was plain. His easy-going nature was not made for such discoveries, his preference was for an orderly life in which all things behaved as they should, and spared him too much exertion of body or mind. He made off with alacrity to where Hugh's raw-boned grey stood peacefully cropping the greener turf under the headland, heaved a sturdy foot into the stirrup, and mounted. There was nothing the matter with his horsemanship but recent lack of practice. He was a younger son from a knightly family, and had made the choice between service in arms and service in the cloister at only sixteen. Hugh's horse, intolerant of most riders except his master, condescended to carry this one along the headland and down into the water-meadow without resentment.

'Though he may spill him at the ford,' Hugh allowed, watching them recede towards the river, 'if the mood takes him. Well, let's see what's left us to find here.'

The sergeant was cutting back deeply into the bank, under the rustling broom brushes. Cadfael turned from the dead to descend with kilted habit into her grave, and cautiously began to shovel out the loose loam and deepen the hollow where she had lain.

'Nothing,' he said at last, on his knees upon a floor now packed hard and changing to a paler colour, the subsoil revealing a layer of clay. 'You see this? Lower, by the river, Ruald had two or three spots where he got his clay. Worked out now, they said, at least where they were easy to reach. This has not been disturbed, in longer time than she has lain here. We need go no deeper, there is nothing to find. We'll sift around the sides a while, but I doubt not this is all.'

'More than enough,' said Hugh, scouring his soiled hands in the thick, fibrous turf. 'And not enough. All too little to give her an age or a name.'

'Or a kinship or a home, living,' Cadfael agreed sombrely, 'or a reason for dying. We can do no more here. I have seen what there is to be seen of how she was laid. What remains to be done can better be done in privacy, with time to spare, and trusted witnesses.'

It was an hour more before Brother Winfrid and Brother Urien came striding along the headland with their burden of brychans and litter. Carefully they lifted the slender bundle of bones, folded the rugs round them and covered them decently from sight. Hugh's sergeant was dismissed, back to the garrison at the castle. In silence and on foot the insignificant funeral cortège of the unknown set off for the abbey.

'It is a woman,' said Cadfael, reporting in due course to Abbot Radulfus in the privacy of the abbot's parlour. 'We have bestowed her in the mortuary chapel. I doubt if there is anything about her that can ever be recognised by any man, even if her death is recent, which I take to be unlikely. The gown is such as any cottage wife might wear, without ornament, without girdle, once the common black, now drab. She wears no shoes, no jewellery, nothing to give her a name.'

'Her face …?' wondered the abbot, but dubiously, expecting nothing.

'Father, her face is now the common image. There is nothing left to move a man to say: This is wife, or sister, or any woman ever I knew. Nothing, except, perhaps, that she had a wealth of dark hair. But so have many women. She is of moderate height for a woman. Her age we can but guess, and that very roughly. Surely by her hair she was not old, but I think she was no young girl, either. A woman in her prime, but between five-and-twenty and forty who can tell?'

'Then there is nothing singular about her at all? Nothing to mark her out?' said Radulfus.

'There is the manner of her burial,' said Hugh. 'Without mourning, without rites, put away unlawfully in unconsecrated ground. And yet – Cadfael will tell you. Or if you so choose, Father, you may see for yourself, for we have left her lying as we found her.'

'I begin to see,' said Radulfus with deliberation, 'that I must indeed view this dead woman for myself. But since so much has been said, you may tell me what it is that outdoes in strangeness the circumstances of her secret burial. And yet …?'

'And yet, Father, she was laid out straight and seemly, her hair braided, her hands folded on her breast, over a cross banded together from two sticks from a hedgerow or a bush. Whoever put her into the ground did so with some show of reverence.'

'The worst of men, so doing, might feel some awe,' said Radulfus slowly, frowning over this evidence of a mind torn two ways. 'But it was a deed done in the dark, secretly. It implies a worse deed, also done in the dark. If her death was natural, without implication of guilt to any man, why no priest, no rites of burial? You have not so far argued, Cadfael, that

226

this poor creature was killed as unlawfully as she was buried, but I do so argue. What other reason can there be for laying her underground in secrecy, and unblessed? And even the cross her grave-digger gave her, it seems, was cut from hedgerow twigs, never to be known as any man's property, to point a finger at the murderer! For from what you say, everything that might have given her back her identity was removed from her body, to keep a secret a secret still, even now that the plough has brought her back to light and to the possibility of grace.'

'It does indeed seem so,' Hugh said gravely, 'but for the fact that Cadfael finds no mark of injury upon her, no bone broken, nothing to show how she died. After so long in the ground, a stroke from dagger or knife might escape finding, but we've seen no sign of such. Her neck is not broken, nor her skull. Cadfael does not think she was strangled. It is as if she had died in her bed – even in her sleep. But no one would then have buried her by stealth and hidden everything that marked her out from all other women.'

'No, true! No one would so imperil his own soul but for desperate reasons.' The abbot brooded some moments in silence, considering the problem which had fallen into his hands thus strangely. Easy enough to do right to the wronged dead, as due to her immortal soul. Even without a name prayers could be said for her and Mass sung; and the Christian burial once denied her, and the Christian grave, these could be given at last. But the justice of this world also clamoured for recognition. He looked up at Hugh, one office measuring the other. 'What do you say, Hugh? Was this a murdered woman?'

'In the face of what little we know, and of the much more we do not know,' said Hugh carefully, 'I dare not assume that she is anything else. She is dead, she was thrust into the ground unshriven. Until I see reason for believing better of the deed, I view this as murder.'

'It is clear to me, then,' said Radulfus, after a moment's measuring silence, 'that you do not believe she has been long in her grave. This is no infamy from long before our time, or nothing need concern us but the proper amendment of what was done wrong to her soul. The justice of God can reach through centuries, and wait its time for centuries, but ours is helpless outside our own generation. How long do you judge has passed since she died?'

'I can but hazard, and with humility,' said Cadfael. 'It may

227

have been no more than a year, it may have been three or four, even five years, but no more than that. She is no victim from old times. She lived and breathed only a short time ago.'

'And I cannot escape her,' said Hugh wryly.

'No. No more than I can.' The abbot flattened his long, sinewy hands abruptly on his desk, and rose. 'The more reason I must see her face to face, and acknowledge my duty towards her. Come let's go and look at our demanding guest. I owe her that, before we again commit her to the earth, with better auguries this time. Who knows, there may be something, some small thing, to call the living woman to mind, for someone who once knew her.'

It seemed to Cadfael, as he followed his superior out across the great court and in at the southern porch to the cloister and the church, that there was something unnatural in the way they were all avoiding one name. It had not yet been spoken, and he could not choose but wonder who would be the first to utter it, and why he himself had not already preciptated the inevitable. It could not go unspoken for much longer. But in the meantime, as well the abbot should be the first to assay. Death, whether old or new, could not disconcert him.

In the small, chilly mortuary chapel candles burned at head and foot of the stone bier, on which the nameless woman was laid, with a linen sheet stretched over her. They had disturbed her bones as little as possible in examining the remains for some clue to the means of her death, and composed them again as exactly as they could when that fruitless inspection was over. So far as Cadfael could determine, there was no mark of any injury upon her. The odour of earth clung heavy about her in the enclosed space, but the cold of stone tempered it, and the composure and propriety of her repose overcame the daunting presence of old death, thus summarily exposed again to light, and the intrusion of eyes.

Abbot Radulfus approached her without hesitation, and drew back the linen that covered her, folding it practically over his arm. He stood for some minutes surveying the remains narrowly, from the dark, luxuriant hair to the slender, naked bones of the feet, which surely the small secret inhabitants of the headland had helped to bare. At the stark white bone of her face he looked longest, but found nothing there to single her out from all the long generations of her dead sisters.

'Yes. Strange!' he said, half to himself. 'Someone surely felt tenderness towards her, and respected her rights, if he felt he dared not provide them. One man to kill, perhaps, and another to bury? A priest, do you suppose? But why cover up her death, if he had no guilt in it? Is it possible the same man both killed and buried her?'

'Such things have been known,' said Cadfael.

'A lover, perhaps? Some fatal mischance, never intended? A moment of violence, instantly regretted? But no, there would be no need to conceal, if that were all.'

'And there is no trace of violence,' said Cadfael.

'Then how did she die? Not from illness, or she would have been in the churchyard, shriven and hallowed. How else? By poison?'

'That is possible. Or a stab wound that reached her heart may have left no trace now in her bones, for they are whole and straight, never deformed by blow or fracture.'

Radulfus replaced the linen cloth, smoothing it tidily over her. 'Well, I see there is little here a man could match with a living face or a name. Yet I think even that must be tried. If she has been here, living, within the past five years, then someone has known her well, and will know when last she was seen, and have marked her absence afterwards. Come,' said the abbot, 'let us go back and consider carefully all the possibilities that come to mind.'

It was plain to Cadfael then that the first and most ominous possibility had already come to the abbot's mind, and brought deep disquiet with it. Once they were all three back in the quiet of the parlour, and the door shut against the world, the name must be spoken.

'Two questions wait to be answered,' said Hugh, taking the initiative. 'Who is she? And if that cannot be answered with certainty, then who may she be? And the second: Has any woman vanished from these parts during these last few years, without word or trace?'

'Of one such,' said the abbot heavily, 'we certainly know. And the place itself is all too apt. Yet no one has ever questioned that she went away, and of her own choice. That was a hard case for me to accept, as the wife never accepted it. Yet Brother Ruald could no more be barred from following his soul's bent than the sun from rising. Once I was sure of him, I had no choice. To my grief, the woman never was reconciled.'

So now the man's name had been spoken. Perhaps no one even recalled the woman's. Many within the walls could never have set eyes on her, or heard mention of her until her husband had his visitation and came to stand patiently at the gates and demand entry.

'I must ask your leave,' said Hugh, 'to have him view this body. Even if she is indeed his wife, truly he may not be able to say so now with any certainty, yet it must be asked of him that he make the assay. The field was theirs, the croft there was her home after he left it.' He was silent for a long moment, steadily eyeing the abbot's closed and brooding face. 'After Ruald entered here, until the time when she is said to have gone away with another man, was he ever at any time sent back there? There were belongings he gave over to her, there could be agreements to be made, even witnessed. Is he known to have met with her, after they first parted?'

'Yes,' said Radulfus at once. 'Twice in the first days of his novitiate he did visit her, but in company with Brother Paul. As master of the novices Paul was anxious for the man's peace of mind, no less than for the woman's, and tried his best to bring her to acknowledge and bless Ruald's vocation. Vainly! But with Paul he went, and with Paul he returned. I know of no other occasion when he could have seen or spoken with her.'

'Nor ever went out to field work or any other errand close to that field?'

'It is more than a year,' said the abbot reasonably. 'Even Paul would be hard put to it to say where Ruald served in all that time. Commonly, during his novitiate he would always be in company with at least one other brother, probably more, whenever he was sent out from the enclave to work. But doubtless,' he said, returning Hugh's look no less fixedly, 'you mean to ask the man himself.'

'With your leave, Father, yes.'

'And now, at once?'

'If you permit, yes. It will not yet be common knowledge what we have found. Best he should be taken clean, with no warning, and knowing no need for deception. In his own defence,' said Hugh emphatically, 'should he later find himself in need of defence.'

'I will send for him,' said Radulfus. 'Cadfael, will you find him, and perhaps, if the sheriff sees fit, bring him straight to the chapel? As you say, let him come to the proof in innocence, for his own sake. And now I remember,' said the abbot, 'a thing he himself said when first this exchange of land was mooted. Earth is innocent, he said. Only the use we make of it mars it.'

Brother Ruald was the perfect example of obedience, the aspect of the Rule which had always given Cadfael the most trouble. He had taken to heart the duty to obey instantly any order given by a superior as if it were a divine command, 'without half-heartedness or grumbling', and certainly without demanding 'Why?' which was Cadfael's first instinct, tamed now but not forgotten. Bidden by Cadfael, his elder and senior in vocation, Ruald followed him unquestioning to the mortuary chapel, knowing no more of what awaited him than that abbot and sheriff together desired his attendance.

Even on the threshold of the chapel, suddenly confronted by the shape of the bier, the candles, and Hugh and Radulfus conferring quietly on the far side of the stone slab, Ruald did not hesitate, but advanced and stood awaiting what should be required of him, utterly docile and perfectly serene.

'You sent for me, Father.'

'You are a man of these parts,' said the abbot, 'and until recently well acquainted with all of your neighbours. You may be able to help us. We have here, as you see, a body found by chance, and none of us here can by any sign set a name to the dead. Try if you can to do better. Come closer.'

Ruald obeyed, and stood faithfully staring upon the shrouded shape as Radulfus drew away the linen in one sharp motion, and disclosed the rigidly ordered bones and the fleshless face in its coils of dark hair. Certainly Ruald's tranquility shook at the unexpected sight, but the waves of pity, alarm and distress that passed over his face were no more than ripples briefly stirring a calm pool, and he did not turn away his eyes, but continued earnestly viewing her from head to foot, and again back to the face, as if by long gazing he could build up afresh in his mind's eye the flesh which had once clothed the naked bone. When at last he looked up at the abbot it was in mild wonder and resigned sadness.

'Father, there is nothing here that any man could recognise and name.'

'Look again,' said Radulfus. 'There is a shape, a height, colouring. This was a woman, someone must once have been near to her, perhaps a husband. There are means of recognition, sometimes, not dependent on features of a face. Is there nothing about her that stirs any memory?'

There was a long silence while Ruald in duty repeated his

careful scrutiny of every rag that clothed her, the folded hands still clasping the improvised cross. Then he said, with a sorrow rather at disappointing the abbot than over a distant death: 'No, Father. I am sorry. There is nothing. Is it so grave a matter? All names are known to God.'

'True,' said Radulfus, 'as God knows where all the dead are laid, even those hidden away secretly. I must tell you, Brother Ruald, where this woman was found. You know the ploughing of the Potter's Field was to begin this morning. At the turn of the first furrow, under the headland and partly screened by bushes, the abbey plough team turned up a rag of woollen cloth and a lock of dark hair. Out of the field that once was yours, the lord sheriff has disinterred and brought home here this dead woman. Now, before I cover her, look yet again, and say if there is nothing cries out to you what her name should be.'

It seemed to Cadfael, watching Ruald's sharp profile, that only at this moment was its composure shaken by a tremor of genuine horror, even of guilt, though guilt without fear, surely not for a physical death, but for the death of an affection on which he had turned his back without ever casting a glance behind. He stooped closer over the dead woman, staring intently, and a fine dew of sweat broke out on his forehead and lip. The candlelight caught its sheen. This final silence lasted for long moments, before he looked up pale and quivering, into the abbot's face.

'Father, God forgive me a sin I never understood until now. I do repent what now I find a terrible lack in me. There is nothing, nothing cries out to me. I feel nothing in beholding her. Father, even if this were indeed Generys, my wife Generys, I should not know her.'

Chapter Three

N THE abbot's parlour, some twenty minutes later, he had regained his calm, the calm of resignation even to his own shortcomings and failures, but he did not cease to accuse himself.

'In my own need I was armed against hers. What manner of man can sever an affection half a lifetime long, and within the year feel nothing? I am ashamed that I could stand by that bier and look upon the relics of a woman, and be forced to say: I cannot tell. It may be Generys, for all I know. I cannot see why it should, or how it could so happen, but nor can I say: It is not so. Nothing moved in me from the heart. And for the eyes and the mind, what is there now in those bones to speak to any man?'

'Except,' said the abbot austerely, 'inasmuch as it speaks to all men. She was buried in unconsecrated ground, without rites, secretly. It is but a short step to the conclusion that she came by her death in a way equally secret and unblessed, at the hands of man. She requires of me due if belated provision for her soul, and from the world justice for her death. You have testified, and I believe it, that you cannot say who she is. But since she was found on land once in your possession, by the croft from which your wife departed, and to which she has never returned, it is natural that the sheriff should have questions to ask you. As he may well have questions to ask of many others, before the matter is resolved.'

'That I do acknowledge,' said Ruald meekly, 'and I will

233

answer whatever may be put to me. Willingly and truthfully.'

And so he did, even with sorrowful eagerness, as if he wished to flagellate himself for his newly realised failings towards his wife, in rejoicing in his own fulfilment while she tasted only the poison of bitterness and deprivation.

'It was right that I should go where I was summoned, and do what it was laid on me to do. But that I should embrace my joy and wholly forget her wretchedness, that was ill done. Now the day is come when I cannot even recall her face, or the way she moved, only the disquiet she has left with me, too long unregarded, now come home in full. Wherever she may be, she has her requital. These six months past,' he said grievously, 'I have not even prayed for her peace. She has been clean gone out of mind, because I was happy.'

'You visited her twice, I understand,' said Hugh, 'after you were received here as a postulant.'

'I did, with Brother Paul, as he will tell you. I had goods which Father Abbot allowed me to give over to her, for her living. It was done lawfully. That was the first occasion.'

'And when was that?'

'The twenty-eighth day of May, of last year. And again we went there in the croft in the first days of June, after I had made up the sum I had from selling my wheel and tools and what was left of use about the croft. I had hoped that she might have become reconciled, and would give me her forgiveness and goodwill, but it was not so. She had contended with me all those weeks to keep me at her side as before. But that day she turned upon me with hatred and anger, scorned to touch any part of what was mine, and cried out at me that I might go, for she had a lover worth the loving, and every tenderness ever she had had for me was turned to gall.'

'She told you that?' said Hugh sharply. 'That she had another lover? I know that was the gossip, when she left the cottage and went away secretly. But you had it from her own lips?'

'Yes, she said so. She was bitter that after she had failed to keep me at her side, neither could she now be rid of me and free in the world's eyes, for still I was her husband, a millstone about her neck, and she could not slough me off. But that should not prevent, she said, but she would take her freedom by force, for she had a lover, a hundred times my worth, and she would go with him, if he beckoned, to the ends of the earth. Brother Paul was witness to all,' said Ruald simply. 'He will tell you.'

'And that was the last time you saw her?'

234

'That was the last time. By the end of that month of June she was gone.'

'And since that time, have you ever been back to that field?'

'No. I have worked on abbey land, in the Gaye for the most part, but that field has only now become abbey land. Early in October, a year ago now, it was given to Haughmond. Eudo Blount of Longner, who was my overlord, made the gift to them. I never thought to see or hear of the place again.'

'Or of Generys?' Cadfael interjected mildly, and watched the lines of Ruald's thin face tighten in a brief spasm of pain and shame. And even these he would endure faithfully, mitigated and rendered bearable by the assurance of joy that now never deserted him. 'I have a question to ask,' said Cadfael, 'if Father Abbot permits. In all the years you spent with her, had you ever cause to complain of your wife's loyalty and fidelity, or the love she bore to you?'

Without hesitation Ruald said: 'No! She was always true and fond. Almost too fond! I doubt I ever could match her devotion. I brought her out of her own land,' said Ruald, setting truth before his own eyes and scarcely regarding those who overheard, 'into a country strange to her, where her tongue was alien and her ways little understood. Only now do I see how much more she gave me than I ever had it in me to repay.'

It was early evening, almost time for Vespers, when Hugh reclaimed the horse Brother Richard had considerately stabled, and rode out from the gatehouse into the Foregate, and for a moment hesitated whether to turn left, and make for his own house in the town, or right, and continue the pursuit of truth well into the dusk. A faint blue vapour was already rising over the river, and the sky was heavily veiled, but there was an hour or more of light left, time enough to ride to Longner and back and have a word with young Eudo Blount. Doubtful if he had paid any attention to the Potter's Field since it was deeded away to Haughmond, but at least his manor lay close to it, over the crest and in among the woodlands of his demesne, and someone among his people might almost daily have to pass that way. It was worth an enquiry.

He made for the ford, leaving the highway by the hospital of Saint Giles, and took the field path along the waterside, leaving the partially ploughed slope high on his left-hand side. Beyond the headland that bordered the new ploughland a gentle slope of woodland began above the water meadows, and in a cleared space within this belt of trees the manor of Longner stood, well clear of any flooding. The low undercroft was cut back into the slope, and stone steps led steeply up to the hall door of the living floor above. A groom was crossing the yard from the stable as Hugh rode in at the open gateway, and came blithely to take his bridle and ask his business with the master.

Eudo Blount had heard the voices below, and came out to his hall door to see who his visitor might be. He was already well acquainted with the sheriff of the shire, and greeted him warmly, for he was a young man cheerful and open by nature, a year established now in his lordship, and comfortable in his relationship with his own people and the ordered world around him. The burial of his father, seven months past now, and the heroic manner of his death, though a grief, had also served to ground and fortify the mutual trust and respect the new young lord enjoyed with his tenants and servants. The simplest villein holding a patch of Blount land felt a share in the pride due to Martel's chosen few who had covered the king's retreat from Wilton, and died in the battle. Young Eudo was barely twenty-three years old, and inexperienced, untravelled, as firmly bound to this soil as any villein in his holding, a big, comely, fair-skinned fellow with a shock of thick brown hair. The right management of a potentially prosperous manor, somewhat depleted in his grandfather's time, would be an absorbing joy to him, and he would make a good job of it, and leave it to his eventual heir richer than he had inherited it from his father. At this stage, Hugh recalled, this young man was only three months married, and the gloss of fulfilment was new and shiny upon him.

'I'm on an errand that can hardly be good news to you,' said Hugh without preamble, 'though no reason it should cause you any trouble, either. The abbey put in its plough team this morning in the Potter's Field.'

'So I've heard,' said Eudo serenely. 'My man Robin saw them come. I'll be glad to see it productive, though it's no business of mine now.'

'We're none of us overjoyed at the first crop it's produced,' said Hugh bluntly. 'The plough has turned up a body from under the headland. We have a dead woman in the mortuary chapel at the abbey – or her bones, at least.'

The young man had halted in the act of pouring wine for his

236

visitor, so abruptly that the pitcher shook and spilled red over his hand. He turned upon Hugh round, blue, astonished eyes, and stared open-mouthed.

'A dead woman? What, buried there? Bones, you say – how long dead then? And who can it be?'

'Who's to know that? Bones is all we have, but a woman it is. Or was once. Dead perhaps as long as five years, so I'm advised, but no longer, and perhaps much less. Have you ever seen strangers there, or anything happening to make a man take notice? I know you had no need to keep a watch on the place, it has been Haughmond's business for the past year, but since it's so close, some of your men may have noted if there were intruders about. You've no inkling of anything untoward?'

Eudo shook his head vehemently. 'I haven't been up there since my father, God rest him, gave the field to the priory. They tell me there have been vagabonds lying up there in the cottage now and then, during the fair or overnight last winter if they were travelling, but who or what I don't know. There was no harm ever reported or threatened, that I know of. This comes very strangely to me.'

'To all of us,' Hugh agreed ruefully, and took the offered cup. It was growing dim in the hall, and there was a fire already laid. Outside the open door the light showed faintly blue with mist, shot through with the faded gold of sunset. 'You never heard of any woman going astray from her home in these parts, these last few years?'

'No, none. My people live all around, they would have known, and it would have come to my ears soon enough. Or to my father's in his time. He had a good hold on everything that went on here, they brought everything to him, knowing he would not willingly let any man of his miscarry.'

'I know that for truth,' said Hugh heartily. 'But you'll not have forgotten, there was one woman who walked out of her house and went away without a word. And from that very croft.'

Eudo was staring at him again in open disbelief, great-eyed, even breaking into a broad grin at the very idea. 'Ruald's woman? You can't mean it! Everyone knew about her going, that was no secret. And do you truly mean it could be so recent? But even if it could, and this poor wench bones already, that's folly! Generys took herself off with another man, and small blame to her, when she found that if he was

237

free to follow his bent, she was still bound. We would have seen to it that she would not want, but that was not enough for her. Widows can wed again, but she was no widow. You can't surely believe, in good earnest, that this is *Generys* you have in the mortuary?'

'I am at a total loss,' Hugh admitted. 'But the place and the time and the way they tore themselves apart must make a man wonder. As yet there are but the few of us know of this, but in a little while it must out, and then you'll hear what every tongue will be whispering. Better if you should make enquiry among your own men for me, see if any of them has noted furtive things going on about that field, or doubtful fellows lurking in the cottage. Especially if any had women with them. If we can find some way of putting a name to the woman we shall be a long stride on the way.'

It seemed that Eudo had come to terms with the reality of death by this time, and was taking it seriously, though not as a factor which could or should be allowed to disturb the tenor of his own ordered existence. He sat thoughtfully gazing at Hugh over the wine cups, and considering the widening implications. 'You think this woman was done to death secretly? Could *Ruald* be in any real danger of such a suspicion? I cannot believe ill of him. Certainly I will ask among my fellows, and send you word if I find out anything of note. But had there been anything, surely it would have found its way to me before.'

'Nevertheless, do that service. A trifle that a man might let slip out of his mind lightly, in the ordinary way, could come to have a weighty meaning once there's a death in the matter. I'll be putting together all I can about Ruald's end of it, and asking questions of many a one besides. He has seen what we found,' said Hugh sombrely, 'and could not say yes or no to her, and no blame to him, for it would be hard indeed for any man, if he lived with her many years, to recognise her face now.'

'He cannot have harmed his wife,' Eudo avowed sturdily. 'He was already in the cloister, had been for three or four weeks, maybe more, while she was still there in the croft, before she went away. This is some other poor soul who fell foul of footpads, or some such scum, and was knifed or stabbed to death for the clothes she wore.'

'Hardly that,' said Hugh wryly. 'She was clothed decently, laid out straight, and her hands folded on her breast over a little rough cross, cut from a hedge. As for the manner of her death, there's no mark on her, no bone broken. There *may* have been a knife. Who's to tell, now? But she was buried with some care and respect. That's the strangeness of it.'

Eudo shook his head, frowning, over this growing wonder. 'As a priest might?' he hazarded doubtfully. 'If he found her dead? But then he would have cried it aloud, and had her taken to church, surely.'

'There are some,' said Hugh, 'will soon be saying, "As a husband might," if they were in bitter contention, and she drove him to violence first, and remorse afterwards. No, no need to fret yet for Ruald, he has been in the company of a host of brothers since before his wife was last seen whole and well. We'll be patchng together from their witness all his comings and goings since he entered his novitiate. And going back over the past few years in search of other women gone astray.' He rose, eyeing the gathering dusk outside the door. 'I'd best be getting back. I've taken too much of your time.'

Eudo rose with him, willing and earnest. 'No, you did right to look this way first. And I'll ask among my men, be sure. I still feel sometimes as though that field is my ground. You don't let go of land, even to the Church, without feeling you've left stray roots in it. I think I've stayed away from it to avoid despite, that it was left waste. I was glad to hear of the exchange, I knew the abbey would make better use of it. To tell the truth, I was surprised when my father made up his mind to give it to Haughmond, seeing the trouble they'd had turning it to account.' He had followed Hugh towards the outer door, to see his guest out and mounted, when he halted suddenly, and looked back at the curtained doorway in a corner of the great hall.

'Would you look in for a moment, and say a neighbourly word to my mother, Hugh, while you're here? She can't get out at all now, and has very few visitors. She hasn't been out of the door since my father's burial. If you'd look in for a moment, it would please her.'

'I will surely,' said Hugh, turning at once.

'But don't tell her anything about this dead woman, it would only upset her, land that was ours so lately, and Ruald being our tenant ... God knows she has enough to endure, we try to keep the world's ill news away from her, all the more when it comes so near home.'

'Not a word!' agreed Hugh. 'How is it with her since I saw her last?'

239

The young man shook his head. 'Nothing changes. Only day by day she grows a little thinner and paler, but she makes no complaint. You'll see. Go in to her!' His hand was at the curtain, his voice lowered, to be heard only by Hugh. Plainly he was reluctant to go in with the guest, his vigorous youth was uneasy and helpless in the presence of illness, he could be excused for turning his eyes away. As soon as he opened the door of the solar and spoke to the woman within, his voice became unnaturally gentle and constrained, as to a stranger difficult to approach, but to whom he owed affection. 'Mother, here's Hugh Beringar paying us a visit.'

Hugh passed by him, and entered a small room, warmed by a little charcoal brazier set on a flat slab of stone, and lit by a torch in a sconce on the wall. Close under the light the dowager lady of Longner sat on a bench against the wall, propped erect with rugs and cushions, and in her stillness and composure dominating the room. She was past forty-five and long, debilitating illness had aged her into a greyness and emaciation beyond her years. She had a distaff set up before her, and was twisting the wool with a hand that looked frail as a withered leaf, but was patient and competent as it teased out and twirled the strands. She looked up, at Hugh's entrance, with a startled smile, and let down the spindle to rest against the foot of the bench.

'Why, my lord, how good of you! It's a long time since I saw you last.' That had been at her husband's funeral, seven months past now. She gave him her hand, light as a windflower in his, and as cold when he kissed it. Her eyes, which were huge and dusky blue, and sunk deeply into her head, looked him over with measured and shrewd intelligence. 'Your office becomes you,' she said. 'You look well on responsibility. I am not so vain as to think you made the journey here to see me, when you have such weighty burdens on your time. Had you business with Eudo? Whatever brought you, a glimpse of you is very welcome.'

'They keep me busy,' he said, with considered reserve. 'Yes, I had business of a sort with Eudo. Nothing that need trouble you. And I must not stay to tire you too long, and with you I won't talk business. How are you? And is there anything you need, or any way I can serve you?'

'All my needs are met before I can even ask,' said Donata. 'Eudo is a good soul, and I'm lucky in the daughter he's brought me. I have no complaints. Did you know the girl is

240

already pregnant? And sturdy and wholesome as good bread, sure to get sons. Eudo has done well for himself. Perhaps I do miss the outside world now and then. My son is wholly taken up with making his manor worth a little more every harvest, especially now he looks forward to a son of his own. When my lord was alive, he looked beyond his own lands. I got to hear of every move up or down in the king's fortunes. The wind blew from wherever Stephen was. Now I labour behind the times. What *is* going on in the world outside?'

She did not sound to Hugh in need of any protection from the incursions of the outside world, near or far, but he stepped cautiously in consideration of her son's anxieties. 'In our part of it, very little. The Earl of Gloucester is busy turning the south-west into a fortress for the Empress. Both factions are conserving what they have, and for the moment neither side is for fighting. We sit out of the struggle here. Lucky for us!'

'That sounds,' she said, attentive and alert, 'as if you have very different news from elsewhere. Oh, come, Hugh, now you are here you won't deny me a little fresh breeze from beyond the pales of Eudo's fences? He shrouds me in pillows, but you need not.' And indeed it seemed to Hugh that even his unexpected company had brought a little wan colour to her fallen face, and a spark to her sunken eyes.

He admitted wryly: 'There's news enough from elsewhere, a little too much for the king's comfort. At St Albans there's been the devil to pay. Half the lords at court, it seems, accused the Earl of Essex of having traitorous dealings with the Empress yet again, and plotting the king's overthrow, and he's been forced to surrender his constableship of the Tower, and his castle and lands in Essex. That or the gallows, and he's by no means ready to die yet.'

'And he *has* surrendered them? That would go down very bitterly with such a man as Geoffrey de Mandeville,' she said, marvelling. 'My lord never trusted him. An arrogant, overbearing man, he said. He has turned his coat often enough before, it may very well be true he had plans to turn it yet again. It's well that he was brought to bay in time.'

'So it might have been, but once he was stripped of his lands they turned him loose, and he's made off into his own country and gathered the scum of the region about him. He's sacked Cambridge. Looted everything worth looting, churches and all, before setting light to the city.'

'Cambridge?' said the lady, shocked and incredulous. '*Dare*

241

he attack a city like Cambridge? The king must surely move against him. He cannot be left to pillage and burn as he pleases.'

'It will not be easy,' said Hugh ruefully. 'The man knows the Fen country like the lines of his hand, it's no simple matter to bring him to a pitched battle in such country.'

She leaned to retrieve the spindle as a movement of her foot set it rolling. The hand with which she recoiled the yarn was languid and translucent, and the eyelids half-lowered over her hollow eyes were marble-white, and veined like the petals of a snowdrop. If she felt pain, she betrayed none, but she moved with infinite care and effort. Her lips had the strong set of reticence and durability.

'My son is there among the fens,' she said quietly. 'My younger son. You'll remember, he chose to take the cowl, in September of last year, and entered Ramsey Abbey.'

'Yes, I remember. When he brought back your lord's body for burial, in March, I did wonder if he might have thought better of it by then. I wouldn't have said your Sulien was meant for a monk, from all I'd seen of him he had a good, sound appetite for living in the world. I thought six months of it might have changed his mind for him. But no, he went back, once that duty was done.'

She looked up at him for a moment in silence, the arched lids rolling back from still lustrous eyes. The faintest of smiles touched her lips and again faded. 'I hoped he might stay, once he was home again. But no, he went back. It seems there's no arguing with a vocation.'

It sounded like a muted echo of Ruald's inexorable departure from world and wife and marriage, and it was still ringing in Hugh's ears as he took his leave of Eudo in the darkening courtyard, and mounted and rode thoughtfully home. From Cambridge to Ramsey is barely twenty miles, he was reckoning as he went. Twenty miles, to the north-west, a little further removed from London and the head of Stephen's strength. A little deeper into the almost impenetrable world of the Fens, and with winter approaching. Let a mad wolf like de Mandeville once establish a base, islanded somewhere in those watery wastes, and it will take all Stephen's forces ever to flush him out again.

Brother Cadfael went up to the Potter's Field several times while the ploughing continued, but there were no more such unexpected finds to be made. The ploughman and his ox-herd had proceeded with caution at every turn under the bank, wary of further shocks, but the furrows opened one after another smooth and dark and innocent. The word kept coming to mind. Earth, Ruald had said, is innocent. Only the use we make of it can mar it. Yes, earth and many others things, knowledge, skill, strength, all innocent until use mars them. Cadfael considered in absence, in the cool, autumnal beauty of this great field, sweeping gently down from its ridge of bush and bramble and tree, hemmed on either side by its virgin headlands, the man who had once laboured here many years, and had uttered that vindication of the soil on which he laboured, and from which he dug his clay. Utterly open, decent and of gentle habit, a good workman and an honest citizen, so everyone who knew him would have said. But how well can man ever know his fellow-man? There were already plenty of very different opinions being expressed concerning Ruald, sometime potter, now a Benedictine monk of Shrewsbury. It had not taken long to change their tune.

For the story of the woman found buried in the Potter's Field had soon become common knowledge, and the talk of the district, and where should gossip look first but to the woman who had lived there fifteen years, and vanished without a word to anyone at the end of it? And where for the guilty man but to her husband, who had forsaken her for a cowl?

The woman herself, whoever she might be, was already reburied, by the abbot's grace, in a modest corner of the graveyard, with all the rites due to her but the gift of a name. Parochially, the situation of the whole demesne of Longner was peculiar, for it had belonged earlier to the bishops of Chester, who had bestowed all their local properties, if close enough, as outer and isolated dependencies of the parish of Saint Chad in Shrewsbury. But since no one knew whether this woman was a parishioner or a passing stranger, Radulfus had found it simpler and more hospitable to give her a place in abbey ground, and be done with one problem, at least, of the many she had brought with her.

But if she was finally at rest, no one else was.

'You've made no move to take him in charge,' said Cadfael to Hugh, in the privacy of his workshop in the herb garden, at the close of a long day. 'Nor even to question him hard.'

'No need yet,' said Hugh. 'He's safe enough where he is, if ever I should need him. He'll not move. You've seen for yourself, he accepts all as, at worst, a just punishment laid on him by God – oh, not necessarily for murder, simply for all the faults he finds newly in himself – or at best as a test of his faith and patience. If we all turned on him as guilty he would bear it meekly and with gratitude. Nothing would induce him to avoid. No, rather I'll go on piecing together all his comings and goings since he entered here. If ever it reaches the case where I have cause to suspect him in good earnest, I know where to find him.'

'And as yet you've found no such cause?'

'No more than I had the first day, and no less. And no other woman gone from where she should be. The place, the possible time, the contention between them, the anger, all speak against Ruald, and urge that this was Generys. But Generys was well alive after he was here within the enclave, and I have found no occasion when he could have met with her again, except with Brother Paul, as both have told us. Yet is it impossible that he should, just once, have been on some errand alone, and gone to her, against all orders, for I'm sure Radulfus wanted an end to the bitterness. The frame,' said Hugh, irritated and weary, 'is all too full of Ruald and Generys, and I can find no other to fit into it.'

'But you do not believe it,' Cadfael deduced, and smiled.

'I neither believe nor disbelieve. I go on looking. Ruald will keep. If tongues are wagging busily against him, he's safe within from anything worse. And if they wag unjustly, he may take it as Christian chastisement, and wait patiently for his deliverance.'

Chapter Four

N THE eighth day of October the morning began in a grey drizzle, hardly perceptible on the face, but wetting after a while. The working folk of the Foregate went about their business hooded in sacking, and the young man trudging along the highway past the horse-fair ground had his cowl drawn well forward over his forehead, and looked very much like any other of those obliged to go out this labouring morning despite the weather. The fact that he wore the Benedictine habit excited no attention. He was taken for one of the resident brothers on some errand between the abbey and Saint Giles, and on his way back to be in time for High Mass and chapter. He had a long stride, but trod as though his sandalled feet were sore, as well as muddy, and his habit was kilted almost to the knee, uncovering muscular, well-shaped legs, smooth and young, mired to the ankles. It seemed he must have walked somewhat further than to the hospital and back, and on somewhat less frequented and seemly roads than the Foregate.

He was moderately tall, but slender and angular in the manner of youth still not quite accomplished in the management of a man's body, as yearling colts are angular and springy, and to see such a youngster putting his feet down resolutely but tenderly, and thrusting forward with effort, struck Brother Cadfael as curious. He had looked back from the turn of the path into the garden on his way to his workshop, just as the young man turned in at the gatehouse wicket, and

245

his eye was caught by the gait before he noticed anything else about the newcomer. Belated curiosity made him take a second glance, in time to observe that the man entering, though manifestly a brother, had halted to speak to the porter, in the manner of a stranger making civil enquiry after someone in authority. Not a brother of this house, seemingly. And now that Cadfael was paying attention, not one that he knew. One rusty black habit is much like another, especially with the cowl drawn close against the rain, but Cadfael could have identified every member of this extensive household, choir monk, novice, steward or postulant, at greater distance than across the court, and this lad was none of them. Not that there was anything strange in that, since a brother of another house in the Order might very well be sent on some legitimate business here in Shrewsbury. But there was something about this visitor that set him apart. He came on foot: official envoys from house to house more often rode. And he had come on foot a considerable distance, to judge by his appearance, shabby, footsore and weary.

It was not altogether Cadfael's besetting sin of curiosity that made him abandon his immediate intent and cross the great court to the gatehouse. It was almost time to get ready for Mass, and because of the rain everyone who must venture out did so as briefly and quickly as possible and scurried back to shelter, so that there was no one else visible at this moment to volunteer to bear messages or escort petitioners. But it must be admitted that curiosity also had its part. He approached the pair at the gate with a bright eye and a ready tongue.

'You need a messenger, Brother? Can I serve?'

'Our brother here says he's instructed,' said the porter, 'to report himself first to the lord abbot, in accordance with his own abbot's orders. He has matter to report, before he can take any rest.'

'Abbot Radulfus is still in his lodging,' said Cadfael, 'for I left him there only a short while since. Shall I be your herald? He was alone. If it's so grave he'll surely see you at once.'

The young man put back the wet cowl from his head, and shook the drops that had slowly penetrated it from a tonsure growing somewhat long for conformity, and a crown covered with a strange fuzz of new growth, curly and of a dark, brownish gold. Yes, he had certainly been a long time on the way, pressing forward doggedly on foot from that distant cloister of his, wherever it might be. His face was oval, tapering slightly from a wide brow and wide-set eyes to a stubborn, probing jaw, covered at this moment by a fine golden down to match his unshaven crown. Weary and footsore he might be, but his long walk seemed to have done him no harm otherwise, for his cheeks had a healthy flush, and his eyes were of clear, light blue, and confronted Cadfael with a bright, unwavering gaze.

'I shall be glad if he will,' he said, 'for I do need to get rid of the dirt of travel, but I'm charged to unburden to him first, and must do as I'm bid. And yes, it's grave enough for the Order – and for me, though that's of small account,' he added, shrugging off with the moisture of his cowl and scapular the present consideration of his own problems.

'He may not think it so,' said Cadfael. 'But come, and we'll put it to the test.' And he led the way briskly down the great court towards the abbot's lodging, leaving the porter to retire into the comfort of his own lodge, out of the clinging rain.

'How long have you been on the road?' asked Cadfael of the young man limping at his elbow.

'Seven days.' His voice was low-pitched and clear, and matched every other evidence of his youth. Cadfael judged he could not yet be past twenty, perhaps not even so much.

'Sent out alone on so long an errand?' said Cadfael marvelling.

'Brother, we are all sent out, scattered. Pardon me if I keep what I have to say, to deliver first to the lord abbot. I would as soon tell it only once, and leave all things in his hands.'

'That you may do with confidence,' Cadfael assured him, and asked nothing further. The implication of crisis was there in the words, and the first note of desperation, quietly constrained, in the young voice. At the door of the abbot's lodging Cadfael let them both in without ceremony into the ante-room, and knocked at the half-open parlour door. The abbot's voice, preoccupied and absent, bade him enter. Radulfus had a folder of documents before him, and a long forefinger keeping his place, and looked up only briefly to see who entered.

'Father, there is here a young brother, from a distant house of our Order, come with orders from his own abbot to report himself to you, and with what seems to be grave news. He is here at the door. May I admit him?'

Radulfus looked up with a lingering frown, abandoning whatever had been occupying him, and gave his full attention

247

to this unexpected delivery.

'From what distant house?'

'I have not asked,' said Cadfael, 'and he has not said. His instructions are to deliver all to you. But he has been on the road seven days to reach us.'

'Bring him in,' said the abbot, and pushed his parchments aside on the desk.

The young man came in, made a deep reverence to authority, and as though some seal on his mind and tongue had been broken, drew a great breath and suddenly poured out words, crowding and tumbling like a gush of blood.

'Father, I am the bearer of very ill news from the abbey of Ramsey. Father, in Essex and the Fens men are become devils. Geoffrey de Mandeville has seized our abbey to be his fortress, and cast us out, like beggars on to the roads, those of us who still live. Ramsey Abbey is become a den of thieves and murderers.'

He had not even waited to be given leave to speak, or to allow his news to be conveyed by orderly question and answer, and Cadfael had barely begun to close the door upon the pair of them, admittedly slowly and with pricked ears, when the abbot's voice cut sharply through the boy's breathless utterance.

'Wait! Stay with us, Cadfael. I may need a messenger in haste.' And to the boy he said crisply: 'Draw breath, my son. Sit down, take thought before you speak, and let me hear a plain tale. After seven days, these few minutes will scarcely signify. Now, first, we here have had no word of this until now. If you have been so long afoot reaching us, I marvel it has not been brought to the sheriff's ears with better speed. Are you the first to come alive out of this assault?'

The boy submitted, quivering, to the hand Cadfael laid on his shoulder, and subsided obediently on to the bench against the wall. 'Father, I had great trouble in getting clear of de Mandeville's lines, and so would any other envoy have. In particular a man on horseback, such as might be sent to take the word to the king's sheriffs, would hardly get through alive. They are taking every horse, every beast, every bow or sword, from three shires, a mounted man would bring them down on him like wolves. I may well be the first, having nothing on me worth the trouble of killing me for it. Hugh Beringar may not know yet.'

The simple use of Hugh's name startled both Cadfael and

Radulfus. The abbot turned sharply to take a longer look at the young face confidingly raised to his. 'You know the lord sheriff here? How is that?'

'It is the reason – it is one reason – why I am sent here, Father. I am native here. My name is Sulien Blount. My brother is lord of Longner. You will never have seen me, but Hugh Beringar knows my family well.'

So this, thought Cadfael, enlightened, and studying the boy afresh from head to foot, this is the younger brother who chose to enter the Benedictine Order just over a year ago, and went off to become a novice at Ramsey in late September, about the time his father made over the Potter's Field to Haughmond Abbey. Now why, I wonder, did he choose the Benedictines rather than his family's favourite Augustinians? He could as well have gone with the field, and lived quietly and peacefully among the canons of Haughmond. Still, reflected Cadfael, looking down upon the young man's tonsure, with its new fuzz of dark gold within the ring of damp brown hair, should I quarrel with a preference that flatters my own choice? He liked the moderation and good sense of human kindliness of Saint Benedict, as I did. It was a little disconcerting that this comfortable reflection should only raise other and equally pertinent questions. Why all the way to Ramsey? Why not here in Shrewsbury?

'Hugh Beringar shall know from me, without delay,' said the abbot reassuringly, 'all that you can tell me. You say de Mandeville has seized Ramsey. When did this happen? And how?'

Sulien moistened his lips and put together, sensibly and calmly enough, the picture he had carried in his mind for seven days.

'It was the ninth day back from today. We knew, as all that countryside knew, that the earl had returned to lands which formerly were his own, and gathered together those who had served him in the past and all those living wild, or at odds with law, willing to serve him now in his exile. But we did not know where his forces were, and had no warning of any intent towards us. You know that Ramsey is almost an island, with only one causeway dryshod into it? It is why it was first favoured as a place of retirement from the world.'

'And undoubtedly the reason why the earl coveted it,' said Radulfus grimly. 'Yes, that we knew.'

'But what need had we ever had to guard that causeway?

249

And how could we, being brothers, guard it in arms even if we had known? They came in thousands,' said Sulien, clearly considering what he said of numbers, and meaning his words, 'crossed and took possession. They drove us out into the court and out from the gate, seizing everything we had but our habits. Some part of our enclave they fired. Some of us who showed defiance, though without violence, they beat or killed. Some who lingered in the neighbourhood though outside the island, they shot at with arrows. They have turned our house into a den of bandits and torturers, and filled it with weapons and armed men, and from that stronghold they go forth to rob and pillage and slay. No one for miles around has the means to till his fields or keep anything of value in his house. This is how it happened, Father, and I saw it happen.'

'And your abbot?' asked Radulfus.

'Abbot Walter is a valiant man indeed, Father. The next day he went alone into their camp and laid about him with a brand out of their fire, burning some of their tents. He has pronounced excommunication against them all, and the marvel is they did not kill him, but only mocked him and let him go unharmed. De Mandeville has seized all those of the abbey's manors that lie near at hand, and given them to his fellows to garrison, but some that lie further afield he has left unmolested, and Abbot Walter has taken most of the brothers to refuge there. I left him safe when I broke through as far as Peterborough. That town is not yet threatened.'

'How came it that he did not take you also with him?' the abbot questioned. 'That he would send out word to any of the king's liegemen I well understand, but why to this shire in particular?'

'I have told it everywhere as I came, Father. But my abbot sent me here to you for my own sake, for I have a trouble of my own. I have taken it to him, in duty bound,' said Sulien, with hesitant voice and lowered gaze, 'and since this disruption fell upon us before it could be resolved, he sent me here to submit myself and my burden to you, and take from you counsel or penance or absolution, whatever you may judge my due.'

'Then that is between us two,' said the abbot briskly, 'and can wait. Tell me whatever more you can concerning the scope of this terror in the Fens. We knew of Cambridge, but if the man now has a safe base in Ramsey, what places besides may be in peril?'

'He is but newly installed,' said Sulien, 'and the villages

nearby have been the first to suffer. There is no cottage too mean but they will wring some tribute out of the tenant, or take life or limb if he has nothing besides. But I do know that Abbot Walter feared for Ely, being so rich a prize, and in country the earl knows so well. He will stay among the waters, where no army can bring him to battle.'

This judgement was given with a lift of the head and a glint of the eye that bespoke rather the apprentice to arms than the monastic novice. Radulfus had observed it, too, and exchanged a long, mute glance with Cadfael over the young man's shoulder.

'So, we have it! If that is all you can furnish, let's see it fully delivered to Hugh Beringar at once. Cadfael, will you see that done? Leave Brother Sulien here with me, and send Brother Paul to us. Take a horse, and come back to us here when you return.'

Brother Paul, master of the novices, delivered Sulien again to the abbot's parlour in a little over half an hour, a different youth, washed clean of the muck of the roads, shaven, in a dry habit, his hair, if not yet properly trimmed of its rebellious down of curls, brushed into neatness. He folded his hands submissively before the abbot, with every mark of humility and reverence, but always with the same straight, confident stare of the clear blue eyes.

'Leave us, Paul,' said Radulfus. And to the boy, after the door had closed softly on Paul's departure: 'Have you broken your fast? It will be a while yet before the meal in the frater, and I think you have not eaten today.'

'No, Father, I set out before dawn. Brother Paul has given me bread and ale. I am grateful.'

'We are come, then, to whatever it may be that troubles you. There is no need to stand, I would rather you felt at ease, and able to speak freely. As you would with Abbot Walter, so speak with me.'

Sulien sat, submissive of orders, but still stiff within his own youthful body, unable quite to surrender from the heart what he offered ardently in word and form. He sat with straight back and eyes lowered now, and his linked fingers were white at the knuckles.

'Father, it was late September of last year when I entered Ramsey as a postulant. I have tried to deliver faithfully what I promised, but there have been troubles I never foresaw, and

251

things asked of me that I never thought to have to face. After I left home, my father went to join the king's forces, and was with him at Wilton. It may be all this is already known to you, how he died there with the rearguard, protecting the king's retreat. It fell to me to go and redeem his body and bring him home for burial, last March. I had leave from my abbot, and I returned strictly to my day. But ... It is hard to have two homes, when the first is not yet quite relinquished, and the second not yet quite accepted, and then to be forced to make the double journey over again. And lately there have also been contentions at Ramsey that have torn us apart. For a time Abbot Walter gave up his office to Brother Daniel, who was no way fit to step into his sandals. That is resolved now, but it was disruption and distress. Now my year of novitiate draws to an end, and I know neither what to do, nor what I want to do. I asked my abbot for more time, before I take my final vows. When this disaster fell upon us, he thought it best to send me here, to my brothers of the order here in Shrewsbury. And here I submit myself to your rule and guidance, until I can see my way before me plain.'

'You are no longer sure of your vocation,' said the abbot.

'No, Father, I am no longer sure. I am blown by two conflicting winds.'

'Abbot Walter has not made it simpler for you,' remarked Radulfus, frowning. 'He has sent you where you stand all the more exposed to both.'

'Father, I believe he thought it only fair. My home is here, but he did not say: Go home. He sent me where I may still be within the discipline I chose, and yet feel the strong pull of place and family. Why should it be made simple for me,' said Sulien, suddenly raising his wide blue stare, unwaveringly gallant and deeply troubled, 'so the answer at the end is the right one? But I cannot come to any decision, because the very act of looking back makes me ashamed.'

'There is no need,' said Radulfus. 'You are not the first, and will not be the last, to look back, nor the first nor the last to turn back, if that is what you choose. Every man has within him only one life and one nature to give to the service of God, and if there was but one way of doing that, celibate within the cloister, procreation and birth would cease, the world would be depeopled, and neither within nor without the Church would God receive worship. It behoves a man to look within himself, and turn to the best dedication possible those endowments he

252

has from his Maker. You do no wrong in questioning what once you held to be right for you, if now it has come to seem wrong. Put away all thought of being bound. We do not want you bound. No one who is not free can give freely.'

The young man fronted him earnestly in silence for some moments, eyes as limpidly light as harebells, lips very firmly set, searching rather his mentor than himself. Then he said with deliberation: 'Father, I am not sure even of my own acts, but I think it was not for the right reasons that I ever asked admission to the Order. I think that is why it shames me to think of abandoning it now.'

'That in itself, my son,' said Radulfus, 'may be good reason why the Order should abandon you. Many have entered for the wrong reasons, and later remained for the right ones, but to remain against the grain and against the truth, out of obstinacy and pride, that would be a sin.' And he smiled to see the boy's level brown brows draw together in despairing bewilderment. 'Am I confusing you still more? I do not ask why you entered, though I think it may have been to escape the world without rather than to embrace the world within. You are young, and of that outer world you have seen as yet very little, and may have misjudged what you did see. There is no haste now. For the present take your full place here among us, but apart from the other novices. I would not have them troubled with your trouble. Rest some days, pray constantly for guidance, have faith that it will be granted, and then choose. For the choice must be yours, let no one take it from you.'

'First Cambridge,' said Hugh, tramping the inner ward of the castle with long, irritated strides as he digested the news from the Fen country, 'now Ramsey. And Ely in danger! Your young man's right there, a rich prize that would be for a wolf like de Mandeville. I tell you what, Cadfael, I'd better be going over every lance and sword and bow in the armoury, and sorting out a few good lads ready for action. Stephen is slow to start, sometimes, having a vein of laziness in him until he's roused, but he'll have to take action now against this rabble. He should have wrung de Mandeville's neck while he had him, he was warned often enough.'

'He's unlikely to call on you,' Cadfael considered judicially, 'even if he does decide to raise a new force to flush out the wolves. He can call on the neighbouring shires, surely. He'll want men fast.'

253

'He shall have them fast,' said Hugh grimly, 'for I'll be ready to take the road as soon as he gives the word. True, he may not need to fetch men from the border here, seeing he trusts Chester no more than he did Essex, and Chester's turn will surely come. But whether or no, I'll be ready for him. If you're bound back, Cadfael, take my thanks to the abbot for his news. We'll set the armourers and the fletchers to work, and make certain of our horses. No matter if they turn out not to be needed, it does the garrison no harm to be alerted in a hurry now and then.' He turned towards the outer ward and the gatehouse with his departing friend, still frowning thoughtfully over this new complexity in England's already confused and troublous situation. 'Strange how great and little get their lives tangled together, Cadfael. De Mandeville takes his revenge in the east, and sends this lad from Longner scurrying home again here to the Welsh border. Would you say fate had done him any favour? It could well be. You never knew him until now, did you? He never seemed to me a likely postulant for the cloister.'

'I did gather,' said Cadfael cautiously, 'that he may not yet have taken his final vows. He said he came with a trouble of his own unresolved, that his abbot charged him bring with him here to Radulfus. It may be he's taken fright, now the time closes upon him. It happens! I'll be off back and see what Radulfus intends for him.'

What Radulfus had in mind for the troubled soul was made plain when Cadfael returned, as bidden, to the abbot's parlour. The abbot was alone at his desk by this time, the new entrant sent away with Brother Paul to rest from his long journey afoot and take his place, with certain safeguards, among his peers, if not of them.

'He has need of some days of quietude,' said Radulfus, 'with time for prayer and thought, for he is in doubt of his vocation, and truth to tell, so am I. But I know nothing of his state of mind and his behaviour when he conceived his desire for the cloister, and am in no position to judge how genuine were his motives then, or are his reservations now. It is something he must resolve for himself. All I can do is ensure that no further shadow or shock shall fall upon him, to distract his mind when most he needs a clear head. I do not want him perpetually reminded of the fate of Ramsey, nor, for that matter, upset by any talk of this matter of the Potter's Field. Let him have stillness and solitude to think out his own deliverance first. When he is ready to see me again, I have told Brother Vitalis to admit him at once. But in the meantime, it may be as well if you would take him to help you in the herb garden, apart from the brothers except at worship. In frater and dortoir Paul will keep a watchful eye on him, during the hours of work he will be best with you, who already know his situation.'

'I have been thinking,' said Cadfael, scrubbing reflectively at his forehead, 'that he knows Ruald is here among us. It was some months after Ruald's entry that this young fellow made up his mind for the cloister. Ruald was Blount's tenant lifelong, and close by the manor, and Hugh tells me this boy Sulien was in and out of that workshop from a child, and a favourite with them, seeing they had none of their own. He has not spoken of Ruald, or asked to see him? How if he seeks him out?'

'If he does, well. He has the right, and I do not intend to hedge him in for long. But I think he is too full of Ramsey and his own trouble to have any thought to spare for other matters as yet. He has not yet taken his final vows,' said Radulfus, pondering with resigned anxiety over the complex agonies of the young. 'All we can do is provide him a time of shelter and calm. His will and his acts are still his own. And as for this shadow that hangs over Ruald – what use would it be to ignore the threat? – if the relations between them were as Hugh says, that will be one more grief and disruption to the young man's mind. As well if he is spared it for a day or so. But if it comes, it comes. He is a man grown, we cannot take his rightful burdens from him.'

It was on the morning of the second day after his arrival that Sulien encountered Brother Ruald face to face at close quarters and with no one else by except Cadfael. At every service in church he had seen him among all the other brothers, once or twice had caught his eye, and smiled across the dim space of the choir, but received no more acknowledgement than a brief, lingering glance of abstracted sweetness, as if the older man saw him through a veil of wonder and rapture in which old associations had no place. Now they emerged at the same moment into the great court, converging upon the south door of the cloister, Sulien from the garden, with Cadfael ambling a yard or two behind him, Ruald from the direction of the infirmary. Sulien had a young man's thrusting, impetuous gait, now that his blistered feet were healed, and he rounded the corner of the tall box hedge so precipitately that the two almost collided, their sleeves brushing, and both halted abruptly and drew back a step in hasty apology. Here in the open, under a wide sky still streaked with trailers of primrose gold from a bright sunrise, they met like humble mortal men, with no veil of glory between them.

'Sulien!' Ruald opened his arms with a warm, delighted smile, and embraced the young man briefly cheek to cheek. 'I saw you in church the first day. How glad I am that you are here, and safe!'

Sulien stood mute for a moment, looking the older man over earnestly from head to foot, captivated by the serenity of his thin face, and the curious air he had of having found his way home, and being settled and content here as he had never been before, in his craft, in his cottage, in his marriage, in his community. Cadfael, holding aloof at the turn of the box hedge, with a shrewd eye on the pair of them, saw Ruald briefly as Sulien was seeing him, a man secure in the rightness of his choice, and radiating his unblemished joy upon all who drew near him. To one ignorant of any threat or shadow hanging over this man, he must seem the possessor of perfect happiness. The true revelation was that, indeed, so he was. A marvel!

'And you?' said Sulien, still gazing and remembering. 'How is it with you? You are well? And content? But I see that you are!'

'All is well with me,' said Ruald. 'All is very well, better than I deserve.' He took the young man by the sleeve and the pair of them turned together towards the church. Cadfael followed more slowly, letting them pass out of earshot. From the look of them, as they went, Ruald was talking cheerfully of ordinary things, as brother to brother. The occasion of Sulien's flight from Ramsey he knew, as the whole household knew it, but clearly he knew nothing as yet of the boy's shaken faith in his vocation. And just as clearly, he did not intend to say a word of the suspicion and possible danger that hung over his own head. The rear view of them, springy youth and patient, plodding middle age jauntily shoulder to shoulder, was like father and son in one craft on their way to work, and, fatherly, the elder wanted no part of his shadowed destiny to cloud the bright horizons of faith that beckoned his son.

*

'Ramsey will be recovered,' said Ruald with certainty. 'Evil will be driven out of it, though we may need long patience. I have been praying for your abbot and brothers.'

'So have I,' said Sulien ruefully, 'all along the way. I'm lucky to be out of that terror. But it's worse for the poor folk there in the villages, who have nowhere to run for shelter.'

'We are praying for them also. There will be a return, and a reckoning.'

The shadow of the south porch closed over them, and they halted irresolutely on the edge of separating, Ruald to his stall in the choir, Sulien to his obscure place among the novices, before Ruald spoke. His voice was still level and soft, but from some deeper well of feeling within him it had taken on a distant, plangent tone like a faraway bell.

'Did you ever hear word from Generys, after she left? Or do you know if any other did?'

'No, never a word,' said Sulien, startled and quivering.

'No, nor I. I deserved none, but they would have told me, in kindness, if anything was known of her. She was fond of you from a babe, I thought perhaps … I should dearly like to know that all is well with her.'

Sulien stood with lowered eyes, silent for a long moment. Then he said in a very low voice: 'And so should I, God knows how dearly!'

Chapter Five

T DID not please Brother Jerome that anything should be going on within the precinct of which he was even marginally kept in ignorance, and he felt that in the matter of the refugee novice from Ramsey not quite everything had been openly declared. True, Abbot Radulfus had made a clear statement in chapter concerning the fate of Ramsey and the terror in the Fens, and expressed the hope that young Brother Sulien, who had brought the news and sought refuge here, should be allowed a while of quietness and peace to recover from his experiences. There was reason and kindness in that, certainly. But everyone in the household, by now, knew who Sulien was, and could not help connecting his return with the matter of the dead woman found in the Potter's Field, and the growing shadow hanging over Brother Ruald's head, and wondering if he had yet been let into all the details of that tragedy, and what effect it would have on him if he had. What must he be thinking concerning his family's former tenant? Was that why the abbot had made a point of asking for peace and quietness for him, and seeing to it that his daily work should be somewhat set apart from too much company? And what would be said, what would be noted in the bearing of the two, when Sulien and Ruald met?

And now everyone knew that they had met. Everyone had seen them enter the church for Mass side by side, in quiet conversation, and watched them separate to their places without any noticeable change of countenance on either part, and go about their separate business afterwards with even step and unshaken faces. Brother Jerone had watched avidly, and was no wiser. That aggrieved him. He took pride in knowing everything that went on within and around the abbey of Saint Peter and Saint Paul, and his repuation would suffer if he allowed this particular obscurity to go unprobed. Moreover, his status with Prior Robert might feel the draught no less. Robert's dignity forbade him to point his own aristocratic nose into every shadowy corner, but he expected to be informed of what went on there, just the same. His thin silver brows might rise, with unpleasant implications, if he found his trusted source, after all, fallible.

So when Brother Cadfael sallied forth with a full scrip to visit a new inmate at the hospital of Saint Giles, that same afternoon, and to replenish the medicine cupboard there, leaving the herb garden to his two assistants, of whom Brother Winfrid was plainly visible digging over the depleted vegetable beds ready for the winter, Brother Jerome seized his opportunity and went visiting on his own account.

He did not go without an errand. Brother Petrus wanted onions for the abbot's table, and they were newly lifted and drying out in trays in Cadfael's store-shed. In the ordinary way Jerome would have delegated this task to someone else, but this day he went himself.

In the workshop in the herb garden the young man Sulien was diligently sorting beans dried for next year's seed, discarding those flawed or suspect, and collecting the best into a pottery jar almost certainly made by Brother Ruald in his former life. Jerome looked him over cautiously from the doorway before entering to interrupt his work. The sight only deepened his suspicion that things were going on of which he, Jerome, was insufficiently informed. For one thing, Sulien's crown still bore its new crop of light brown curls, growing more luxuriant every day, and presenting an incongruous image grossly offensive to Jerome's sense of decorum. Why was he not again shaven-headed and seemly, like all the brothers? Again, he went about his simple task with the most untroubled serenity and a steady hand, apparently quite unmoved by what he must have learned by now from Ruald's own lips. Jerome could not conceive that the two of them had walked together from the great court into the church before Mass, without one word being said about the murdered woman, found in the field once owned by the boy's father and tenanted by Ruald himself.

It was the chief subject of gossip, scandal and speculation, how could it be avoided? And this boy and his family might be a considerable protection to a man threatened with the charge of murder, if they chose to stand by him. Jerome, in Ruald's place, would most heartily have enlisted that support, would have poured out the story as soon as the chance offered. He took it for granted that Ruald had done the same. Yet here this unfathomable youth stood earnestly sorting his seed, apparently without anything else on his mind, even the tension and stress of Ramsey already mastered.

Sulien turned as the visitor's shadow fell within, and looked up into Jerome's face, and waited in dutiful silence to hear what was required of him. One brother was like another to him here as yet, and with this meagre little man he had not so far exchanged a word. The narrow, grey face and stooped shoulders made Jerome look older than he was, and it was the duty of young brothers to be serviceable and submissive to their elders.

Jerome requested onions, and Sulien went into the store-shed and brought what was wanted, choosing the soundest and roundest, since these were for the abbot's own kitchen. Jerome opened benevolently: 'How are you faring now, here among us, after all your trials elsewhere? Have you settled well here with Brother Cadfael?'

'Very well, I thank you,' said Sulien carefully, unsure yet of this solicitous visitor whose appearance was not precisely reassuring, nor his voice, even speaking sympathy, particularly sympathetic. 'I am fortunate to be here, I thank God for my deliverance.'

'In a very proper spirit,' said Jerome wooingly. 'Though I fear that even here there are matters that must trouble you. I wish that you could have come back to us in happier circumstances.'

'Indeed, so do I!' agreed Sulien warmly, still harking back in his own mind to the upheaval of Ramsey.

Jerome was encouraged. It seemed the young man might, after all, be in a mood to confide, if sympathetically prompted. 'I feel for you,' he said mellifluously. 'A shocking thing it must be, after such terrible blows, to come home to yet more ill news here. This death that has come to light, and worse, to know that it casts so black a shadow of suspicion upon a brother among us, and one well known to all your family—'

He was weaving his way so confidently into his theme that he

260

had not even noticed the stiffening of Sulien's body, and the sudden blank stillness of his face.

'Death?' said the boy abruptly. 'What death?'

Thus sharply cut off in full flow, Jerome blinked and gaped, and leaned to peer more intently into the young, frowning face before him, suspecting deception. But the blue eyes confronted him with a wide stare of such crystal clarity that not even Jerome, himself adept at dissembling and a cause of defensive evasion in others, could doubt the young man's honest bewilderment.

'Do you mean,' demanded Jerome incredulously, 'that Ruald has not told you?'

'Told me of what? Nothing of a death, certainly! I don't know what you mean, Brother!'

'But you walked with him to Mass this morning,' protested Jerome, reluctant to relinquish his certainty. 'I saw you come, you had some talk together ...'

'Yes, so we did, but nothing of ill news, nothing of a death. I have known Ruald since I could first run,' said Sulien. 'I was glad to meet him, and see him so secure in his faith, and so happy. But what is this you are telling me of a death? I beg you, let me understand you!'

Jerome had thought to be eliciting information, but found himself instead imparting it. 'I thought you must surely know it already. Our plough-team turned up a woman's body, the first day they broke the soil of the Potter's Field. Buried there unlawfully, without rites – the sheriff believes killed unlawfully. The first thought that came to mind was that it must be the woman who was Brother Ruald's wife when he was in the world. I thought you knew from him. Did he never say a word to you?'

'No, never a word,' said Sulien. His voice was level and almost distant, as though all his thoughts had already grappled with the grim truth of it, and withdrawn deep into his being, to contain and conceal any immediate consideration of its full meaning. His blue, opaque stare held Jerome at gaze, unwavering. 'That *it must be* – you said. Then it is not *known*? Neither he nor any can name the woman?'

'It would not be possible to name her. There is nothing left that could be known to any man. Mere naked bones is what they found.' Jerome's faded flesh shrank at the mere thought of contemplating so stark a reminder of mortality. 'Dead at least a year, so they judge. Maybe more, even as much as five years. Earth deals in many different ways with the body.'

261

Sulien stood stiff and silent for a moment, digesting this knowledge with a face still as a mask. At last he said: 'Did I understand you to say also that this death casts a black shadow of suspicion upon a brother of this house? You mean by that, on Ruald?'

'How could it be avoided?' said Jerome reasonably. 'If this is indeed she, where else would the law look first? We know of no other woman who frequented that place, we know that this one disappeared from there without a word to any. But whether living or dead, who can be certain?'

'It is impossible,' said Sulien very firmly. 'Ruald had been a month and more here in the abbey before she vanished. Hugh Beringar knows that.'

'And acknowledges it, but that does not make it impossible. Twice he visited her afterwards, in company with Brother Paul, to settle matters about such possessions as he left. Who can be sure that he never visited her alone? He was not a prisoner within the enclave, he went out with others to work at the Gaye, and elsewhere on our lands. Who can say he never left the sight of his fellows? At least,' said Jerome, with mildly malicious satisfaction in his own superior reasoning, 'the sheriff is busy tracing every errand Brother Ruald has had outside the gates during those early days of his novitiate. If he satisfies himself they never did meet and come to conflict, well. If not, he knows that Ruald is here, and will be here, waiting. He cannot evade.'

'It is foolishness,' said the boy with sudden quiet violence. 'If there were proof from many witnesses, I would not believe he ever harmed her. I should know them liars, because I know him. Such a thing he could not do. He *did not* do!' repeated Sulien, staring blue challenge-like daggers into Jerome's face.

'Brother, you presume!' Jerome drew his inadequate length to its tallest, though he was still topped by almost a head. 'It is sin to be swayed by human affection to defend a brother. Truth and justice are preferred before mere fallible inclination. In chapter sixty-nine of the Rule that is set down. If you know the Rule as you should, you know such partiality is an offence.'

It cannot be said that Sulien lowered his embattled stare or bent his head to this reproof, and he would certainly have been in for a much longer lecture if his superior's sharp ear had not caught, at that moment, the distant sound of Cadfael's voice, some yards away along the path, halting to exchange a few cheerful words with Brother Winfrid, who was just cleaning his

262

spade and putting away his tools. Jerome had no wish to see this unsatisfactory colloquy complicated by a third party, least of all Cadfael, who, upon consideration, might have been entrusted with this ill-disciplined assistant precisely in order to withdraw him from too much knowledge too soon. As well leave things as they stood.

'But you may be indulged,' he said, with hasty magnanimity, 'seeing this comes so suddenly on you, and at a time when you have already been sorely tried. I say no more!'

And forthwith he took a somewhat abrupt but still dignified leave, and was in time to be a dozen paces outside the door when Cadfael met him. They exchanged a brief word in passing, somewhat to Cadfael's surprise. Such brotherly civility in Jerome argued a slight embarrassment, if not a guilty conscience.

Sulien was collecting his rejected beans into a bowl, to be added to the compost, when Cadfael came into the workshop. He did not look round as his mentor came in. He had known the voice, as he knew the step.

'What did Jerome want?' Cadfael asked, with only mild interest.

'Onions. Brother Petrus sent him.'

No one below Prior Robert's status sent Brother Jerome anywhere. He kept his services for where they might reflect favour and benefit upon himself, and the abbot's cook, a red-haired and belligerent northerner, had nothing profitable to bestow, even if he had been well-disposed towards Jerome, which he certainly was not.

'I can believe Brother Petrus wanted onions. But what did Jerome want?'

'He wanted to know how I was faring, here with you,' said Sulien with deliberation. 'At least, that's what he asked me. And, Cadfael, you know how things are with me. I am not quite sure yet how I am faring, or what I ought to do, but before I commit myself either to going or staying, I think it is time I went to see Father Abbot again. He said I might, when I felt the need.'

'Go now, if you wish,' said Cadfael simply, eyeing with close attention the steady hands that swept the bench clear of fragments, and the head so sedulously inclined to keep the young, austere face in shadow. 'There's time before Vespers.'

Abbot Radulfus examined his petitioner with a detached and

tolerant eye. In three days the boy had changed in understandable ways, his exhaustion cured, his step now firm and vigorous, the lines of his face eased of their tiredness and strain, the reflection of danger and horror gone from his eyes. Whether the rest had resolved his problem for him was not yet clear, but there was certainly nothing indecisive in his manner, or in the clean jut of a very respectable jaw.

'Father,' he said directly. 'I am here to ask your leave to go and visit my family and my home. It is only fair that I should be equally open to influences from within and without.'

'I thought,' said Radulfus mildly, 'that you might be here to tell me that your trouble is resolved, and your mind made up. You have that look about you. It seems I am previous.'

'No, Father, I am not yet sure. And I would not offer myself afresh until I am sure.'

'So you want to breathe the air at Longner before you stake your life, and allow household and kin and kind to speak to you, as our life here has spoken. I would not have it otherwise,' said the abbot. 'Certainly you may visit. Go freely. Better, sleep again at Longner, think well upon all you stand to gain there, and all you stand to lose. You may need even more time. When you are ready, when you are certain, then come and tell me which way you have chosen.'

'I will, Father,' said Sulien. The tone was the one he had learned to take for granted in the year and more of his novitiate in Ramsey, submissive, dutiful and reverent, but the disconcerting eyes were fixed on some distant aim visible only to himself, or so it seemed to the abbot, who was as well versed in reading the monastic face as Sulien was in withdrawing behind it.

'Go then, at once if you wish.' He considered how long a journey afoot this young man had recently had to make, and added a concession. 'Take a mule from the stable, if you intend to leave now. The daylight will see you there if you ride. And tell Brother Cadfael you have leave to stay until tomorrow.'

'I will, Father!' Sulien made his reverence and departed with a purposeful alacrity which Radulfus observed with some amusement and some regret. The boy would have been well worth keeping, if that had truly been his bent, but Radulfus was beginning to judge that he had already lost him. He had been home once before, since electing for the cloister, to bring home his father's body for burial after the rout of Wilton, had stayed several days on that occasion, and still chosen to return

264

to his vocation. He had had seven months since then to reconsider, and this sudden urge now to visit Longner, with no unavoidable filial duty this time to reinforce it, seemed to the abbot significant evidence of a decision as good as made.

Cadfael was crossing the court to enter the church for Vespers when Sulien accosted him with the news.

'Very natural,' said Cadfael heartily, 'that you should want to see your mother and your brother, too. Go with all our goodwill and, whatever you decide, God bless the choice.'

His expectation, however, as he watched the boy ride out at the gatehouse, was the same that Radulfus had in mind. Sulien Blount was not, on the face of it, cut out for the monastic life, however hard he had tried to believe in his misguided choice. A night at home now, in his own bed and with his kin around him, would settle the matter.

Which conclusion left a very pertinent question twitching all through Vespers in Cadfael's mind. What could possibly have driven the boy to make for the cloister in the first place?

Sulien came back next day in time for Mass, very solemn of countenance and resolute of bearing, for some reason looking years nearer to a man's full maturity than when he had arrived from horrors and hardships, endured with all a man's force and determination. A youth, resilient but vulnerable, had spent two days in Cadfael's company; a man, serious and purposeful, returned from Longner to approach him after Mass. He was still wearing the habit, but his absurd tonsure, the crest of dark gold curls within the overgrown ring of darker brown hair, created an incongruous appearance of mockery, just when his face was at its gravest. High time, thought Cadfael, observing him with the beginning of affection, for this one to go back where he belongs.

'I am going to see Father Abbot,' said Sulien directly.

'So I supposed,' agreed Cadfael.

'Will you come with me?'

'Is that needful? What I feel sure you have to say is between you and your superior, but I do not think,' Cadfael allowed, 'that he will be surprised.'

'There is something more I have to tell him,' said Sulien, unsmiling. 'You were there when first I came, and you were the messenger he sent to repeat all the news I brought to the lord sheriff. I know from my brother that you have always access to Hugh Beringar's ear, and I know now what earlier I

265

did not know. I know what happened when the ploughing began, I know what was found in the Potter's Field. I know what everyone is thinking and saying, but I know it cannot be true. Come with me to Abbot Radulfus. I would like you to be by as a witness still. And I think he may need a messenger, as he did before.'

His manner was so urgent and his demand so incisive that Cadfael shrugged off immediate enquiry. 'As you and he wish, then. Come!'

They were admitted to the abbot's parlour without question. No doubt Radulfus had been expecting Sulien to seek an audience as soon as Mass was over. If it surprised him to find the boy bringing a sponsor with him, whether as advocate to defend his decision, or in mere meticulous duty as the mentor to whom he had been assigned in his probation, he did not allow it to show in face or voice.

'Well, my son? I hope you found all well at Longner? Has it helped you to find your way?'

'Yes, Father.' Sulien stood before him a little stiffly, his direct stare very bright and solemn in a pale face. 'I come to ask your permission to leave the Order and go back to the world.'

'That is your considered choice?' said the abbot in the same mild voice. 'This time you are in no doubt?'

'No doubt, Father. I was at fault when I asked admission. I know that now. I left duties behind, to go in search of my own peace. You said, Father, that this must be my own decision.'

'I say it still,' said the abbot. 'You will hear no reproach from me. You are still young, but a good year older than when you sought refuge within the cloister, and I think wiser. It is far better to do whole-hearted service in another field than remain half-hearted and doubting within the Order. I see you did not yet put off the habit,' he said, and smiled.

'No, Father!' Sulien's stiff young dignity was a little affronted at the suggestion. 'How could I, until I have your leave? Until you release me I am not free.'

'I do release you. I would have been glad of you, if you had chosen to stay, but I believe that for you it is better as it is, and the world may yet be glad of you. Go, with my leave and blessing, and serve where your heart is.'

He had turned a little towards his desk, where more mundane matters waited for his attention, conceiving that the audience was over, though without any sign of haste or dismissal: but Sulien held his ground, and the intensity of his gaze checked the abbot's movement, and made him look again, and more sharply, at the son he had just set free.

'There is something more you have to ask of us? Our prayers you shall certainly have.'

'Father,' said Sulien, the old address coming naturally to his lips, 'now that my own trouble is over, I find I have blundered into a great web of other men's troubles. At Longner my brother has told me what was spared me here, whether by chance or design. I have learned that when ploughing began on the field my father granted to Haughmond last year, and Haughmond exchanged for more convenient land with this house two months ago now, the coulter turned up a woman's body, buried there some while since. But not so long since that the manner, the time, the cause of her death can go unquestioned. They are saying everywhere that this was Brother Ruald's wife, whom he left to enter the Order.'

'It may be *said* everywhere,' the abbot agreed, fronting the young man with a grave face and drawn brows, 'but it is not *known* anywhere. There is no man can say who she was, no way of knowing, as yet, how she came by her death.'

'But that is not what is being said and believed outside these walls,' Sulien maintained sturdily. 'And once so terrible a find was made known, how could any man's mind escape the immediate thought? A woman found where formerly a woman vanished, leaving no word behind! What else was any man to think but that this was one and the same? True, they may all be in error. Indeed, they surely are! But as I heard it, that is the thought even in Hugh Beringar's mind, and who is to blame him? Father, that means that the finger points at Ruald. Already, so they have told me, the common talk has him guilty of murder, even in danger of his own life.'

'Gossip does not necessarily speak with any authority,' said the abbot patiently. 'Certainly it cannot speak for the lord sheriff. If he examines the movements and actions of Brother Ruald, he is but doing his duty, and will do as much by others, as the need arises. I take it that Brother Ruald himself has said no word of this to you, or you would not have had to hear it for the first time at home in Longner. If he is untroubled, need you trouble for him?'

'But, Father, that is what I have to tell!' Sulien flushed into ardour and eagerness. 'No one need be troubled for him. Truly, as you said, there is no man can say who this woman is, but here is one who can say with absolute certainty who she is *not*! For I have proof that Ruald's wife Generys is alive and well – or was so, at least, some three weeks ago.'

'You have seen her?' demanded Radulfus, reflecting back half-incredulously the burning glow of the boy's vehemence.

'No, not that! But I can do better than that.' Sulien plunged a hand deep inside the throat of his habit, and drew out something small that he had been wearing hidden on a string about his neck. He drew it over his head, and held it out to be examined in the palm of his open hand, still warm from his flesh, a plain silver ring set with a yellow stone such as were sometimes found in the mountains of Wales and the border. Of small value in itself, marvellous for what he claimed for it. 'Father, I know I have kept this unlawfully, but I promise you I never had it in Ramsey. Take it up, look within it!'

Radulfus gave him a long, searching stare before he extended a hand and took up the ring, turning it to catch the light on its inner surface. His straight black brows drew together. He had found what Sulien wanted him to find.

'G and R twined together. Crude, but clear – and old work. The edges are blunted and dulled, but whoever engraved it cut deep.' He looked up into Sulien's ardent face. 'Where did you get this?'

'From a jeweller in Peterborough, after we fled from Ramsey, and Abbot Walter charged me to come here to you. It was mere chance. There were some tradesmen in the town who feared to stay, when they heard how near de Mandeville was, and what force he had about him. They were selling and moving out. But others were stout-hearted, and meant to stay. It was night when I reached the town, and I was commended to this silversmith in Priestgate who would shelter me overnight. He was a stout man, who would not budge for outlaws or robbers, and he had been a good patron to Ramsey. His valuables he had hidden away, but among the lesser things in his shop I saw this ring.'

'And knew it?' said the abbot.

'From old times, long ago when I was a child. I could not mistake it, even before I looked for this sign. I asked him where and when it came into his hands, and he said a woman had brought it in only some ten days earlier, to sell, because, she said, she and her man thought well to move further away from the danger of de Mandeville's marauders, and were turning what they could into money to resettle them in safety

268

elsewhere. So were many people doing, those who had no great stake in the town. I asked him what manner of woman she was, and he described her to me, beyond mistaking. Father, barely three weeks ago Generys was alive and well in Peterborough.'

'And how did you acquire the ring?' asked Radulfus mildly, but with a sharp and daunting eye upon the boy's face. 'And why? You had then no possible reason to know that it might be of the highest significance here.'

'No, none.' The faintest flush of colour had crept upward in Sulien's cheeks, Cadfael noted, but the steady blue gaze was as wide and clear as always, even challenging question or reproof. 'You have returned me to the world, I can and will speak as one already outside these walls. Ruald and his wife were the close friends of my childhood, and when I was no longer a child that fondness grew and came to ripeness with my flesh. They will have told you, Generys was beautiful. What I felt for her touched her not at all, she never knew of it. But it was after she was gone that I thought and hoped, I admit vainly, that the cloister and the cowl might restore me my peace. I meant to pay the price faithfully, but you have remitted the debt. But when I saw and handled the ring I knew for hers, I wanted it. So simple it is.'

'But you had no money to buy it,' Radulfus said, in the same placid tone, withholding censure.

'He gave it to me. I told him what I have now told you. Perhaps more,' said Sulien, with a sudden glittering smile that lasted only an instant in eyes otherwise passionately solemn. 'We were but one night companions. I should never see him again, nor he me. Such a pair encountering confide more than ever they did to their own mothers. And he gave me the ring.'

'And why,' enquired the abbot as directly, 'did you not restore it, or at least show it, to Ruald and tell him that news, as soon as you met with him here?'

'It was not for Ruald I begged it of the silversmith,' said Sulien bluntly, 'but for my own consolation. And as for showing it, and telling him how I got it, and where, I did not know until now that any shadow hung over him, nor that there was a dead woman, newly buried here now, who was held to be Generys. I have spoken with him only once since I came, and that was for no more than a few minutes on the way to Mass. He seemed to me wholly happy and content, why should I hurry to stir old memories? His coming here was pain as well as

269

joy, I thought well to let his present joy alone. But now indeed he must know. It may be I was guided to bring back the ring, Father. I deliver it to you willingly. What I needed it has already done for me.'

There was a brief pause, while the abbot brooded over all the implications for those present and those as yet uninvolved. Then he turned to Cadfael. 'Brother will you carry my compliments to Hugh Beringar, and ask him to ride back with you and join us here? Leave word if you cannot find him at once. Until he has heard for himself, I think nothing should be said to any other, not even Brother Ruald. Sulien, you are no longer a brother of this house, but I hope you will remain as its guest until you have told your story over again, and in my presence.'

Chapter Six

UGH WAS at the castle, where Cadfael found him in the armoury, telling over the stores of steel, with the likelihood of a foray against the anarchy in Essex very much in mind. He had taken the omen seriously, and was bent on being ready at a day's notice if the king should call. But Hugh's provision for action was seldom wanting, and on the whole he was content with his preparations. He could have a respectable body of picked men on the road within hours when the summons came. There was no certainty that it would, to the sheriff of a shire so far removed from the devastated Fen country, but the possibility remained. Hugh's sense of order and sanity was affronted by the very existence of Geoffrey de Mandeville and his like.

He greeted Cadfael with somewhat abstracted attention, and went on critically watching his armourer beating a sword into shape. He was giving only the fringes of his mind to the abbot's pressing invitation, until Cadfael nudged him into sharp alertness by adding: 'It has to do with the body we found in the Potter's Field. You'll find the case is changed.'

That brought Hugh's head round sharply enough. 'How changed?'

'Come and hear it from the lad who changed it. It seems young Sulien Blount brought more than bad news back from the Fens with him. The abbot wants to hear him tell it again to you. If there's a thread of significance in it he's missed, he's certain you'll find it, and you can put your heads together afterwards, for it looks as if one road is closed to you. Get to horse and let's be off.'

But on the way back through the town and over the bridge into the Foregate he did impart one preliminary piece of news, by way of introduction to what was to follow. 'Brother Sulien, it seems, has made up his mind to return to the world. You were right in your judgement, he was never suited to be a monk. He has come to the same conclusion, without wasting too much of his youth.'

'And Radulfus agrees with him?' wondered Hugh.

'I think he was ahead of him. A good boy, and he did try his best, but he says himself he came into the Order for the wrong reasons. He'll go back to the life he was meant for, now. You may have him in your garrison before all's done, for if he's quitting one vocation he'll need another. He's not the lad to lie idle on his brother's lands.'

'All the more,' said Hugh, 'as Eudo is not long married, so in a year or two there may be sons. No place there for a younger brother, with the line secured. I might do worse. He looks a likely youngster. Well made, and a good long reach, and he always shaped well on a horse.'

'His mother will be glad to have him back, surely,' Cadfael reflected. 'She has small joy in her life, from what you told me; a son come home may do much for her.'

The likely youngster was still closeted with the abbot when Hugh entered the parlour with Cadfael at his heels. The two seemed to be very easy together, but for a slight sense of tension in the way Sulien sat, very erect and braced, his shoulders flattened against the panelling of the wall. His part here was still only half done; he waited, alert and wide-eyed, to complete it.

'Sulien here,' said the abbot, 'has something of importance to tell you, I thought best you should hear it directly from him, for you may have questions which have not occurred to me.'

'That I doubt,' said Hugh, seating himself where he could have the young man clear in the light from the window. It was a little past noon, and the brightest hour of an overcast day. 'It was good of you to send for me so quickly. For I gather this has to do with the matter of the dead woman. Cadfael has said nothing beyond that. I am listening, Sulien. What is it you have to tell?'

Sulien told his story over again, more briefly than before, but in much the same words where the facts were concerned.

272

There were no discrepancies, but neither was it phrased so exactly to pattern as to seem studied. He had a warm, brisk way with him, and words came readily. When it was done he sat back again with a sharp sigh, and ended: 'So there can be no suspicion now against Brother Ruald. When did he ever have ado with any other woman but Generys? And Generys is alive and well. Whoever it is you have found, it cannot be she.'

Hugh had the ring in his palm, the scored initials clear in the light. He sat looking down at it with a thoughtful frown. 'It was your abbot commended you to take shelter with this silversmith?'

'It was. He was known for a good friend to the Benedictines of Ramsey.'

'And his name? And where does his shop lie in the town?'

'His name is John Hinde, and the shop is in Priestgate, not far from the minster.' The answers came readily, even eagerly.

'Well, Sulien, it seems you have delivered Ruald from all concern with this mystery and death, and robbed me of one suspect, if ever the man really became suspect in earnest. He was never a very likely malefactor, to tell the truth, but men are men – even monks are men – and there are very few of us who could not kill, given the occasion, the need, the anger and the solitude. It was possible! I am not sorry to see it demolished. It seems we must look elsewhere for a woman lost. And has Ruald yet been told of this?' he asked, looking up at the abbot.

'Not yet.'

'Send for him now,' said Hugh.

'Brother,' said the abbot, turning to Cadfael, 'will you find Ruald and ask him to come?'

Cadfael went on his errand with a thoughtful mind. For Hugh this deliverance meant a setback to the beginning, and a distraction from the king's affairs at a time when he would much have preferred to be able to concentrate upon them. No doubt he had been pursuing a search for any other possible identities for the dead woman, but there was no denying that the vanished Generys was the most obvious possibility. But now with this unexpected check, at least the abbey of Saint Peter and Saint Paul could rest the more tranquilly. As for Ruald himself, he would be glad and grateful for the woman's sake rather than his own. The wholeness of his entranced peace, so far in excess of what most fallible human brothers could achieve, was a perpetual marvel. For him whatever God

273

decreed and did, for him or to him, even to his grief and humiliation, even to his life, was done well. Martyrdom would not have changed his mind.

Cadfael found him in the vaulted undercroft of the refectory, where Brother Matthew the cellarer had his most commodious stores. To him Ruald had been allotted, as a practical man whose skills were manual rather than scholarly or artistic. Summoned to the abbot's parlour, he dusted his hands, abandoned his inventory, reported his errand and destination to Brother Matthew in his little office at the end of the south range, and followed Cadfael in simple, unquestioning obedience. It was not for him to ask or to wonder, though in his present circumstances, Cadfael reflected, he might well feel his heart sink a little at the sight of the secular authority closeted side by side with the monastic, and both with austerely grave faces, and their eyes fixed upon him. If the vision of this double tribunal waiting for his entry did shake his serenity on the threshold of the parlour, there was no sign of it in his bearing or countenance. He made his reverence placidly, and waited to be addressed. Behind him, Cadfael closed the door.

'I sent for you, Brother,' said the abbot, 'because something has come to light, something you may recognise.'

Hugh held out the ring in his palm. 'Do you know this, Ruald? Take it up, examine it.'

It was hardly necessary, he had already opened his lips to answer at the mere sight of it in Hugh's hand. But obediently he took it, and at once turned it to bring the light sidewise upon the entwined initials cut crudely within. He had not needed it as identification, he wanted and accepted it gratefully as a sign both of remembered accord and of hope for future reconciliation and forgiveness. Cadfael saw the faint quiver of warmth and promise momentarily dissolve the patient lines of the lean face.

'I know it well, my lord. It is my wife's. I gave it to her before we married, in Wales, where the stone was found. How did it come here?'

'First let me be clear – you are certain this was hers? There cannot be another such?'

'Impossible. There could be other pairs having these initials, yes, but these I myself cut, and I am no engraver. I know every line, every irregularity, every fault in the work, I have seen the bright cuts dull and tarnish over the years. This I last saw on the hand of Generys. There is nothing more certain under the

274

sun. Where is she? Has she come back? May I speak with her?'

'She is not here,' said Hugh. 'The ring was found in the shop of a jeweller in the city of Peterborough, and the jeweller testified that he had bought it from a woman only some ten days previously. The seller was in need of money to help her to leave the town for a safer place to live, seeing the anarchy that has broken out there in the Fens. He described her. It would seem that she was indeed the same who was formerly your wife.'

The radiance of hope had made but a slow and guarded sunrise on Ruald's plain middle-aged face, but by this time every shred of cloud was dispersed. He turned on Abbot Radulfus with such shining eagerness that the light from the window, breaking now into somewhat pale sunrays, seemed only the reflection of his joy.

'So she is not dead! She is alive and well! Father, may I question further? For this is wonderful!'

'Certainly you may,' said the abbot. 'And wonderful it is.'

'My lord sheriff, how came the ring here, if it was bought and sold in Peterborough?'

'It was brought by one who recently came to this house from those parts. You see him here, Sulien Blount. You know him. He was sheltered overnight in his journey by the jeweller, and saw and knew the ring there in his shop. For old kindness,' said Hugh with deliberation, 'he wished to bring it with him, and so he has, and there you hold it in your hand.'

Ruald had turned to look steadily and long at the young man standing mute and still, a little apart, as though he wished to withdraw himself from sight, and being unable to vanish in so small a room, at least hoped to escape too close observance by being motionless, and closing the shutters over his too transparent face and candid eyes. A strange and searching look it was that passed between them, and no one moved or spoke to break its intensity. Cadfael heard within his own mind the questions that were not being asked: Why did you not show me the ring? If, for reasons I guess at, you were unwilling to do that, could you not at least have told me that you had had recent word of her, that she was alive and well? But all Ruald said, without turning away his eyes from Sulien's face, was: 'I cannot keep it. I have forsworn property. I thank God that I have seen it, and that he has pleased to keep Generys safe. I pray that he may have her in his care hereafter.'

'Amen!' said Sulien, barely audibly. The sound was a mere sigh, but Cadfael saw his taut lips quiver and move.

275

'It is yours to give, Brother, if not to keep,' said the abbot, watching the pair of them with shrewd eyes that weighed and considered, but refrained from judging. The boy had already confessed to him why he had obtained the ring, and why it was his intent to keep it. A small thing in itself, great in what it could accomplish, it had played its part, and was of no further significance. Unless, perhaps, in its disposal? 'You may bestow it where you think fit,' said Radulfus.

'If the lord sheriff has no further need of it,' said Ruald, 'I give it back to Sulien, who reclaimed it. He has brought me the best news I could have received, and that morsel of my peace of mind that even this house could not restore.' He smiled suddenly, the plain, long face lighting up, and held out the ring to Sulien. The boy advanced a hand very slowly, almost reluctantly, to receive it. As they touched, the vivid colour rose in his cheeks in a fiery flush, and he turned his face haughtily away from the light to temper the betrayal.

So that is how the case goes, Cadfael thought, enlightened. No questions asked because none are needed. Ruald must have watched his lord's younger son running in and out of his workshop and house almost since the boy was born, and seen him grow into the awkward pains of adolescence and the foreshadowing of manhood, and always close about the person of this mysterious and formidable woman, the stranger, who was no stranger to him, the one who kept her distance, but not from him, the being of whom every man said that she was very beautiful, but not for everyone was she also close and kind. Children make their way by right where others are not admitted. It touched her not at all, Sulien maintained, she never knew of it. But Ruald had known. No need now for the boy to labour his motives, or ask pardon for the means by which he defended what was precious to him.

'Very well,' said Hugh briskly, 'be it so. I have nothing further to ask. I am glad, Ruald, to see your mind set at rest. You, at least, need trouble no further over this matter, there remains no shadow of a threat to you or to this house, and I must look elsewhere. As I hear, Sulien, you have chosen to leave the Order. You will be at Longner for the present, should I need a word with you hereafter?'

'Yes,' said Sulien, still a little stiff and defensive of his own dignity. 'I shall be there when you want me.'

Now I wonder, thought Cadfael, as the abbot dismissed both Ruald and Sulien with a brief motion of benediction, and they went out together, what trick of the mind caused the boy to use the word 'when'? I should rather have expected '*if* you want me'. Has he a premonition that some day, for some reason, more will be demanded of him?

'It's plain he was in love with the woman,' said Hugh, when the three of them were left alone. 'It happens! Never forget his own mother has been ill some eight years, gradually wasting into the frail thing she is now. How old would this lad be when that began? Barely ten years. Though he was fond and welcome at Ruald's croft long before that. A child dotes on a kind and handsome woman many innocent years, and suddenly finds he has a man's stirrings in his body, and in his mind too. Then the one or the other wins the day. This boy, I fancy, would give his mind the mastery, set his love up on a pedestal – an altar, rather, if you'll allow me the word, Father – and worship her in silence.'

'So, he says, he did,' agreed Radulfus drily. 'She never knew of it. His words.'

'I am inclined to believe it. You saw how he coloured like a peony when he realised Ruald could see clean through him. Was he never jealous of his prize, this Ruald? The world seems to be agreed she was a great beauty. Or is it simply that he was used to having the boy about the place, and knew him harmless?'

'Rather, from all accounts,' Cadfael suggested seriously, 'he knew his wife immovably loyal.'

'Yet rumour says she told him she had a lover, at the last, when he was set on leaving her.'

'Not only rumour says so,' the abbot reminded them firmly. 'He says so himself. On the last visit he made to her, with Brother Paul to confirm it, she told him she had a lover better worth loving, and all the tenderness she had ever had for him, her husband, he himself had destroyed.'

'She said it,' agreed Cadfael. 'But was it true? Yet I recall she also spoke to the jeweller of herself and her man.'

'Who's to know?' Hugh threw up his hands. 'She might well strike out at her husband with whatever came to hand, true or false, but she had no reason to lie to the silversmith. The one thing certain is that our dead women is not Generys. And I can forget Ruald, and any other who might have had ado with Generys. I am looking for another woman, and another reason for murder.'

277

'Yet it sticks in my craw,' said Hugh, as he walked back towards the gatehouse with Cadfael at his side, 'that he did not blurt it out the second they met that the woman was alive and well. Who had a better right to know it, even if he had turned monk, than her husband? And what news could be more urgent to tell, the instant the boy clapped eyes on him?'

'He did not then know anything about a dead woman, nor that Ruald was suspected of anything,' Cadfael suggested helpfully, and was himself surprised at the tentative sound it had, even in his own ears.

'I grant it. But he did know, none better, that Ruald must have her always in his mind, wondering how she does, whether she lives or dies. The natural thing would have been to cry it out on sight: "No need to fret about Generys, she's well enough." It was all he needed to know, and his contentment would have been complete.'

'The boy was in love with her himself,' Cadfael hazarded, no less experimentally. 'Perhaps when it came to the point he grudged Ruald that satisfaction.'

'Does he seem to you a grudging person?' demanded Hugh.

'Let's say, then, his mind was still taken up with the sack of Ramsey and his escape from it. That was enough to put all lesser matters out of his mind.'

'The reminder of the ring came after Ramsey,' Hugh reminded him, 'and was weighty enough to fill his mind then.'

'True. And to tell the truth, I wonder about it myself. Who's to account for any man's reasoning under stress? What matters is the ring itself. She owned it; Ruald, who gave it to her, knew it instantly for hers. She sold it for her present needs. Whatever irregularities there may be in young Sulien's nature and actions, he did bring the proof. Generys is alive, and Ruald is free of all possible blame. What more do we need to know?'

'Where to turn next,' said Hugh ruefully.

'You have nothing more? What of the widow woman set up by Haughmond as tenant after Eudo made his gift to them?'

'I have seen her. She lives with her daughter in the town now, not far from the western bridge. She was there only a short while, for she had a fall, and her daughter's man fetched her away and left the place empty. But she left all in good order, and never saw nor heard anything amiss while she was

278

there, or any strangers drifting that way. It's off the highways. But there have been tales of travelling folk bedding there at times, mainly during the fair. Eudo at Longner promised to ask all his people if ever they'd noticed things going on up there without leave, but I've heard nothing to the purpose from him yet.'

'Had there been any rumours come to light there,' said Cadfael reasonably, 'Sulien would have brought them back with him, along with his own story.'

'Then I must look further afield.' He had had agents doing precisely that ever since the matter began, even though his own attention had certainly been, to some extent, distracted by the sudden alarming complication in the king's affairs.

'We can at least set a limit to the time,' Cadfael said consideringly. 'While the widow was living there it seems highly unlikely others would be up to mischief about the place. They could not use it as a cheap lodging overnight, it is well off any highway, so a chance passerby is improbable, and a couple looking for a quiet place for a roll in the grass would hardly choose the one inhabited spot in a whole range of fields. Once the tenant was out of the place it was solitary enough for any furtive purpose, and before ever she was installed by the canons ... What was the exact day when Generys walked away and left the cottage door wide and the ashes on the hearth?'

'The exact day, within three,' said Hugh, halting at the open wicket in the gate, 'no one knows. A cowman from Longner passed along the river bank on the twenty-seventh day of June, and saw her in the garden. On the last day of June a neighbour from over the north side of the ridge – the nearest neighbours they had, and those best part of a mile away – came round on her way to the ferry. None too direct a way, for that matter, but I fancy she had a nose for gossip, and was after the latest news on a tasty scandal. She found the door open and the place empty and the hearth cold. After that no one saw Ruald's wife again in these parts.'

'And the charter that gave the field to Haughmond was drawn up and witnessed early in October. Which day? You were a witness.'

'The seventh,' said Hugh. 'And the old smith's widow moved in to take care of the place three days later. There was work to be done before it was fit, there'd been a bit of looting done by then. A cooking pot or so, and a brychan from the bed, and the doorlatch broken to let the thieves in. Oh, yes, there had been visitors in and out of there, but no great damage up to then. It was later they scoured the place clean of everything worth removing.'

'So from the thirtieth of June to the tenth of October,' Cadfael reckoned, pondering, 'murder could well have been done up there, and the dead buried, and no one any the wiser. And when was it the old woman went away to her daughter in the town?'

'It was the winter drove her away,' said Hugh. 'About Christmas, in the frost, she had a fall. Lucky for her, she has a good fellow married to her girl, and when the hard weather began he kept a close eye on how she did, and when she was laid up helpless he fetched her away to the town to live with them. From that time the croft was left empty.'

'So from the beginning of this year it is also true that things mortal could have been done up there, and no witness. And yet,' said Cadfael, 'I think, truly I think, she had been in the ground a year and more, and put there when the soil was workable quickly and easily, not in the frosts. From spring of this year? No, it is too short a time. Look further back, Hugh. Some time between the end of June and the tenth of October of last year, I think, this thing was done. Long enough ago for the soil to have settled, and the root growth to have thickened and matted through the seasons. And if there were vagabonds making use of the cottage in passing, who was to go probing under the headland among the broom bushes? I have been thinking that whoever put her there foresaw that some day that ground might be broken for tillage, and laid her where her sleep should not be disturbed. A pace or two more cautious in the turn, and we should never have found her.'

'I am tempted,' admitted Hugh wryly, 'to wish you never had. But yes, you found her. She lived, and she is dead, and there's no escaping her, whoever she may be. And why it should be of so great import to restore her her name, and demand an account from whoever put her there in your field, I scarcely know, but there'll be small rest for you or me until it's done.'

It was a well-known fact that all the gossip from the countryside around, in contrast to that which seethed merrily within the town itself, came first into the hospital of Saint Giles, the better half of a mile away along the Foregate, at the eastern rim of the suburb. Those who habitually frequented that benevolent shelter were the rootless population of the roads: beggars, wandering labourers hoping for work, pickpockets and petty thieves and tricksters determined, on the contrary, to avoid work, cripples and sick men dependent on charity, lepers in need of treatment. The single crop they gathered on their travels was news, and they used it as currency to enlist interest. Brother Oswin, in charge of the hospice under the nominal direction of an appointed layman who rarely came to visit from his own house in the Foregate, had grown used to the common traffic in and out, and could distinguish between the genuine poor and unfortunate and the small, pathetic rogues. The occasional able-bodied fake feigning some crippling disability was a rarity, but Oswin was developing an eye even for that source of trouble. He had been Cadfael's helper in the herbarium for some time before graduating to his present service, and learned from him more skills than the mere mixing of lotions and ointments.

It was three days after Sulien's revelation when Cadfael put together the medicaments Brother Oswin had sent to ask for, and set off with a full scrip along the Foregate to replenish the medicine cupboard at Saint Giles, a regular task which he undertook every second or third week, according to the need. With autumn now well advanced, the people of the roads would be thinking ahead to the winter weather and considering where they could find patronage and shelter through the worst of it. The number of derelicts had not yet risen, but all those on the move would be making their plans to survive. Cadfael went without haste along the highway, exchanging greetings at open house doors, and taking some abstracted pleasure in the contemplation of children playing in the fitful sunshine, accompanied by their constant camp-followers, the dogs of the Foregate. His mood was contemplative, in keeping with the autumnal air and the falling leaves. He had put away from him for the moment all thoughts of Hugh's problem, and returned with slightly guilty zeal and devotion to the horarium of the monastic day and his own duties therein. Those small, gnawing doubts that inhabited the back of his mind were asleep, even if their sleep might be tenuous.

He reached the place where the road forked, and the long, low roof of the hospital rose beside the highway, beyond a gentle slope of grass and wattle fence, with the squat tower of its little church peering over all. Brother Oswin came out into the porch to meet him, as large, cheerful and exuberant as

281

ever, the wiry curls of his tonsure bristling from the low branches of the orchard trees, and a basket of the late, hard little pears on his arm, the kind that would keep until Christmas. He had learned to control his own vigorous body and lively mind since he had first come to assist Cadfael in the herb-garden, no longer broke what he handled or fell over his own feet in his haste and ardour to do good. Indeed, since coming here to the hospital he had quite exceeded all Cadfael's hopes. His big hands and strong arms were better adapted to lifting the sick and infirm and controlling the belligerent than to fashioning little tablets and rolling pills, but he was competent enough in administering the medicines Cadfael brought for him and had proved a sensible and cheerful nurse, never out of temper even with the most difficult and ungrateful of his patients.

They filled up the shelves of the medicine cupboard together, turned the key again upon its secrets, and went through into the hall. A fire was kept burning here, with November on the doorstep, and some of the guests too infirm to move about freely. Some would never leave this place until they were carried into the churchyard for burial. The able-bodied were out in the orchard, gleaning the latest of the harvest.

'We have a new inmate,' said Oswin. 'It would be well if you would take a look at him, and make sure I am using the right treatment. A foul old man, it must be said, and foul-mouthed, he came in so verminous I have him bedded in a corner of the barn, away from the rest. Even now that he's cleaned and new-clothed, I think better he should be kept apart. His sores may infect others. His malignancy would certainly do harm, he has a grudge against the whole world.'

'The whole world has probably done enough to him to earn it,' Cadfael allowed ruefully, 'but a pity to take it out on some even worse off than himself. There will always be the haters among us. Where did you get this one?'

'He came limping in four days ago. From his story, he's been sleeping rough around the forest villages, begging his food where he could, and as like as not stealing it when charity ran short. He says he got a few bits of work to do here and there during the fair, but I doubt it was picking pockets on his own account, for by the look of him no respectable merchant would care to give him work. Come and see!'

The hospice barn was a commodious and even comfortable

place, warm with the fragrance of the summer's hay and the ripe scent of stored apples. The foul old man, undoubtedly less foul in body than when he came, had his truckle bed installed in the most draught-proof corner, and was sitting hunched upon his straw pallet like a roosting bird, shaggy grey head sunk into once massive shoulders. By the malignant scowl with which he greeted his visitors, there had been no great change in the foulness of his temper. His face was shrunken and lined into a mask of suspicion and despite, and out of the pitted scars of half-healed sores small, malevolent, knowing eyes glittered up at them. The gown they had put on him was over-large for a body diminishing with age, and had been deliberately chosen, Cadfael thought, to lie loosely and avoid friction upon the sores that continued down his wrinkled throat and shoulders. A piece of linen cloth had been laid between to ease the touch of wool.

'The infection is somewhat improved,' said Oswin softly into Cadfael's ear. And to the old man, as they approached: 'Well, uncle, how do you feel this fine morning?'

The sharp old eyes looked up at them sidelong, lingering upon Cadfael. 'None the better,' said a voice unexpectedly full and robust to emerge from such a tattered shell, 'for seeing two of you instead of one.' He shifted closer on the edge of his bed, peering curiously. 'I know you,' he said, and grinned as though the realisation gave him, perhaps not pleasure, but an advantage over a possible opponent.

'Now you suggest it,' agreed Cadfael, viewing the raised face with equal attention, 'I think I also should recall seeing you somewhere. But if so, it was in better case. Turn your face to the light here, so!' It was the outbreak of sores he was studying, but he took in perforce the lines of the face, and the man's eyes, yellowish and bright in their nests of wrinkles, watched him steadily all the while he was examining the broken rash. Round the edges of the infection showed the faint, deformed crust of sores newly healed. 'Why do you complain of us, when you are warm and fed here, and Brother Oswin has done nobly for you? Your case is getting better, and well you know it. If you have patience for two or three weeks more, you can be rid of this trouble.'

'And then you'll throw me out of here,' grumbled the vigorous voice bitterly. 'I know the way of it! That's my lot in this world. Mend me and then cast me out to fester and rot again. Wherever I go it's the same. If I find a bit of a roof to

283

shelter me through the night, some wretch comes and kicks me out of it to take it for himself.'

'They can hardly do that here,' Cadfael pointed out placidly, restoring the protective linen to its place round the scrawny neck. 'Brother Oswin will see to that. You let him cure you, and give no thought to where you'll lie or what you'll eat until you're clean. After that it will be time to think on such matters.'

'Fine talk, but it will end the same. I never have any luck. All very well for you,' he muttered, glowering up at Cadfael, 'handing out crumbs in alms at your gatehouse, when you have plenty, and a sound roof over you, and good dry beds, and then telling God how pious you are. Much you care where us poor souls lay our heads that same night.'

'So that's where I saw you,' said Cadfael, enlightened. 'On the eve of the fair.'

'And where I saw you, too. And what did I get out of it? Bread and broth and a farthing to spend.'

'And spent it on ale,' Cadfael guessed mildly, and smiled. 'And where *did* you lay your head that night? And all the nights of the fair? We had as poor as you snug enough in one of our barns.'

'I'd as soon not lie inside your walls. Besides,' he said grudgingly, 'I knew of a place, not too far, a cottage, nobody living in it. I was there the last year, until that red-haired devil of a pedlar came with his wench and kicked me out of it. And where did I end? Under a hedge in the next field. Would he let me have even a corner by the kiln? Not he, he wanted the place to himself for his own cantrips with his wench. And then they fought like wild cats most nights, for I heard them at it.' He subsided into morose mutterings, oblivious of Cadfael's sudden intent silence. 'But I got it this year. For what it was worth! Small use it will be now, falling to pieces as it is. Whatever I touch rots.'

'This cottage,' said Cadfael slowly, 'that had also a kiln – where is it?'

'Across the river from here, close by Longner. There's no one working there now. Wrack and ruin!'

'And you spent the nights of the fair there this year?'

'It rains in now,' said the old man ruefully. 'Last year it was all sound and good, I thought to do well there. But that's my lot, always shoved out like a stray dog, to shiver under a hedge.'

'Tell me,' said Cadfael, 'of last year. This man who turned you out was a pedlar come to sell at the fair? He stayed there in that cottage till the fair ended?'

'He and the woman.' The old man had sharpened into the realisation that his information was here of urgent interest, and had begun to enjoy the sensation, quite apart from the hope of turning it to advantage. 'A wild, black-haired creature she was, every whit as bad as her man. Every whit! She threw cold water over me to drive me away when I tried to creep back.'

'Did you see them leave? The pair together?'

'No, they were still there when I went packman, with a fellow bound for Beiston who had bought more than he could manage alone.'

'And this year? Did you see this same fellow at this year's fair?'

'Oh yes, he was there,' said the old man indifferently. 'I never had any ado with him, but I saw him there.'

'And the woman still with him?'

'No, never a glimpse of her this year. Never saw him but alone or with the lads in the tavern, and who knows where he slept! The potter's place wouldn't be good enough for him now. I hear she was a tumbler and singer, on the road like him. I never did hear *her* name.'

The slight emphasis on the 'her' had not escaped Cadfael's ear. He asked, with a sense of lifting the lid from a jar which might or might not let loose dangerous revelations: 'But his you do know?'

'Oh, everybody about the booths and alehouses knows *his* name. He's called Britric, he comes from Ruiton. He buys at the city markets, and peddles his wares round all this part of the shire and into Wales. On the move, most times, but never too far afield. Doing well, so I heard!'

'Well,' said Cadfael on a long, slow breath, 'wish him no worse, and do your own soul good. You have your troubles, I don't doubt Britric has his, no easier or lighter. You take your food and your rest, and do what Brother Oswin bids, and your burden can soon be lightened. Let's wish as much to all men.'

The old man, squatting there observant and curious on his bed, watched them withdraw to the doorway. Cadfael's hand was on the latch when the voice behind them, so strangely resonant and full, called after them: 'I'll say this for him, his bitch was handsome, if she was cursed.'

285

Chapter Seven

O NOW they had it, a veritable name, a charm with which to prime memory. Names are powerful magic. Within two days of Cadfael's visit to Saint Giles, faithfully reported to Hugh before the end of the day, they had detail enough about the pedlar of Ruiton to fill a chronicle. Drop the name Britric into almost any ear about the market and the horse-fair ground, and mouths opened and tongues wagged freely. It seemed the only thing they had not known about him was that he had slept the nights of last year's fair in the cottage on the Potter's Field, then no more than a month abandoned, and in very comfortable shape still. Not even the neighbouring household at Longner had known that. The clandestine tenant would be off with his wares through the day, so would his woman if she had a living to make by entertaining the crowds, and they would have discretion enough to leave the door closed and everything orderly. If, as the old man declared, they had spent much of their time fighting, they had kept their battles withindoors. And no one from Longner had gone up the field to the deserted croft once Generys was gone. A kind of coldness and desolation had fallen upon the place, for those who had known it living, and they had shunned it, turning their faces away. Only the wretched old man hoping for a snug shelter for himself had tried his luck there, and been driven away by a prior and stronger claimant.

The smith's widow, a trim little elderly body with bright

round eyes like a robin, pricked up her ears when she heard the name of Britric. 'Oh, him, yes, he used to come round with his pack some years back, when I was living with my man at the smithy in Sutton. He started in a very small way, but he was regular round the villages, and you know a body can't be every week in the town. I got my salt from him. Doing well, he was, and not afraid to work hard, either, when he was sober, but a wild one when he was drunk. I remember seeing him at the fair last year, but I had no talk with him. I never knew he was sleeping the nights through up at the potter's croft. Well, I'd never seen the cottage myself then. It was two months later when the prior put me in there to take care of the place. My man was dead late that Spring, and I'd been asking Haughmond to find me some work to do. Smith had worked well for them in his time, I knew the prior wouldn't turn me away.'

'And the woman?' said Hugh. 'A strolling tumbler, so I'm told, dark, very handsome. Did you see him with her?'

'He did have a girl with him,' the widow allowed after a moment's thought, 'for I was shopping at the fishmonger's booth close by Wat's tavern, at the corner of the horse fair, the one day, and she came to fetch him away before, she said, he'd drunk all his day's gain and half of hers. That I remember. They were loud, he was getting cantankerous then in his cups, but she was a match for him. Cursed each other blind, they did, but then they went off together as close and fond as you please, and her holding him about the body from stumbling, and still scolding. Handsome?' said the widow, considering, and sniffed dubiously. 'Some might reckon so. A bold, striding, black-eyed piece, thin and whippy as a withy.'

'Britric was at this year's fair, too, so they tell me,' said Hugh. 'Did you see him?'

'Yes, he was here. Doing quite nicely in the world, by the look of him. They do say there's a good living to be made in pedlary, if you're willing to work at it. Give him a year or two more, and he'll be renting a booth like the merchants, and paying the abbey fees.'

'And the woman? Was she with him still?'

'Not that I ever saw.' She was no fool, and there was hardly a soul within a mile of Shrewsbury who did not know by this time that there was a dead woman to be accounted for, and the obvious answer, for some reason, was not satisfactory, since enquiry was continuing, and had even acquired a sharper edge.

'I was down into the Foregate only once during the three days, this year,' she said. 'There's others would be there all day and every day, they'll know. But I saw nothing of her. God knows what he's done with her,' said the widow, and crossed herself with matronly deliberation, standing off all evil omens from her own invulnerable virtue, 'but I doubt you'll find anyone here who set eyes on her since last year's Saint Peter's Fair.'

'Oh, yes, that fellow!' said Master William Rede, the elder of the abbey's lay stewards who collected their rents and their tolls due from merchants and craftsmen bringing their goods to the annual fair. 'Yes, I know the man you mean. A bit of a rogue, but I've known plenty worse. By rights he should be paying a small toll for selling here, he brings in as full a man-load as Hercules could have hefted. But you know how it is. A man who set up a booth for the three days, that's simple, you know where to find him. He pays his dues, and no time wasted. But a fellow who carries his goods on him, he sets eyes on you from a distance, and he's gone elsewhere, and you can waste more time chasing him than his small toll would be worth. Playing hoodman blind in and out of a hundred stalls, and all crowded with folk buying and selling, that's not for me. So he gets off scot-free. No great loss, and he'll come to it in time, his business is growing. I know no more about him than that.'

'Had he a woman with him this year?' Hugh asked. 'Dark, handsome, a tumbler and acrobat?'

'Not that I saw, no. There was a woman last year I noticed ate and drank with him, she could well be the one you mean. There were times I am sure she made him the sign when I came in sight, to make himself scarce. Not this year, though. He brought more goods this year, and I think you'll find he lay at Wat's tavern, for he needed somewhere to store them. You may learn more of him there.'

Walter Renold leaned his folded arms, bared and brawny, on the large cask he had just rolled effortlessly into position in a corner of the room, and studied Hugh across it with placid professional eyes.

'Britric, is it? Yes, he put up here with me through the fair. Came heavy laden this year, I let him put his bits and pieces in the loft. Why not? I know he slips his abbey dues, but the loss of his penny won't beggar them. The lord abbot doesn't cast too harsh an eye on the small folk. Not that Britric is small in any other way, mind you. A big lusty fellow, red-haired, a bit of a brawler sometimes, when he's drunk, but not a bad lad, take him all in all.'

'Last year,' said Hugh, 'he had a woman with him, or so I hear. I've good cause to know he was not lodging with you then, but if he did his drinking here you must have seen something of them both. You remember her?'

Wat was certainly remembering her already, with some pleasure and a great deal of amusement. 'Oh, her! Hard to forget, once seen. She could twist herself like a slip of willow, dance like a March lamb, and play on the little pipe. Easy to carry, better than a rebec unless you're a master. And she was the practical one, keeping a tight hold on the money they made between them. She talked of marriage, but I doubt she'd ever get him to the church door. Maybe she talked of it once too often, for he came alone this year round. Where he's left her there's no knowing, but she'll make her way wherever she is.'

That had a very bitter ring in Hugh's ear, considering the possibility he had in mind. Wat, it seemed, had not made the connection which had already influenced the widow's thinking. But before he could ask anything further Wat surprised him by adding simply: 'Gunnild, he called her. I never knew where she came from – I doubt if he knew it, either – but she's a beauty.'

That, too, had its strange resonance, when Hugh recalled the naked bones. More and more, in imagination, they took on the living aspect of this wild, sinuous, hardworking waif of the roads, darkly brilliant as the admiring gleam she could kindle in a middle-aged innkeeper's eyes after a year and more of absence.

'You have not seen her since, here or elsewhere?'

'How often am I elsewhere?' Wat responded good-humouredly. 'I did my roaming early. I'm content where I am. No, I've never set eyes on the girl again. Nor heard him so much as mention her name this year, now I come to think of it. For all the thought he seemed to be giving to last year's fancy,' said Wat tolerantly, 'she might as well be dead.'

'So there we have it,' said Hugh, summing up briskly for Cadfael in the snug privacy of the workshop in the herb garden. 'Britric is the one man we know to have made himself at home there in Ruald's croft. There may have been others, but none that we can learn of. Moreover, there was a woman with him, and their mating by all accounts tempestuous, she urging marriage on him, and he none too ready to be persuaded. More than a year ago, this. And this year not only does he come to the fair alone, but she is not seen there at all, she who gets her living at fairs and markets and weddings and such jollifications. It is not proof, but it requires answers.'

'And she has a name,' said Cadfael reflectively. 'Gunnild. But not a habitation. She comes from nowhere and is gone, nowhere. Well, you cannot but look diligently for them both, but he should be the easier to find. And as I guess, you already have all your people alerted to look out for him.'

'Both round the shire and over the border,' said Hugh flatly. 'His rounds, they say, go no further, apart from journeys to the towns to buy such commodities as salt and spices.'

'And here are we into November, and the season for markets and fairs over, but the weather still fairly mild and dry. He'll be still on his travels among the villages, but I would guess,' said Cadfael, pondering, 'not too far afield. If he still has a base in Ruiton, come the hard frosts and snow he'll be making for it, and he'll want to be within a reasonable few miles of it when the pinch comes.'

'About this time of year,' said Hugh, 'he remembers he has a mother in Ruiton, and makes his way back there for the winter.'

'And you have someone waiting there for his coming.'

'If luck serves,' said Hugh, 'we may pick him up before then. I know Ruiton, it lies barely eight miles from Shrewsbury. He'll time his journeys to bring him round by all those Welsh villages and bear east through Knockin, straight for home. There are many hamlets close-set in that corner, he can go on with his selling until the weather changes, and still be near to home. Somewhere there we shall find him.'

Somewhere there, indeed, they found him, only three days later. One of Hugh's sergeants had located the pedlar at work among the villages on the Welsh side of the border, and discreetly waited for him on the English side until he crossed and headed without haste for Meresbrook, on his way to Knockin and home. Hugh kept a sharp eye on his turbulent neighbours in Powys, and as he would tolerate no breach of English law on his own side of the border, so he was punctilious in giving them no occasion to complain that he trespassed against Welsh law on their side, unless they had first broken the tacit compact. His relations with Owain Gwynedd, to the north-west, were friendly, and well understood on either part, but the Welsh of Powys were ill-disciplined and unstable, not to be provoked, but not to be indulged if they caused him trouble without provocation. So the sergeant waited until his unsuspecting quarry crossed over the ancient dyke that marked the boundary, somewhat broken and disregarded in these parts but still traceable. The weather was still reasonably mild, and walking the roads not unpleasant, but it seemed that Britric's pack was as good as empty, so he was making for home ahead of the frosts, apparently content with his takings. If he had stocks at home in Ruiton, he could still sell to his neighbours and as far afield as the local hamlets.

So he came striding into the shire towards Meresbrook, whistling serenely and swinging a long staff among the roadside grasses. And short of the village he walked into a patrol of two light-armed men from the Shrewsbury garrison, who closed in on him from either side and took him by either arm, enquiring without excitement if he owned to the name of Britric. He was a big, powerful fellow half a head taller than either of his captors, and could have broken away from them had he been so minded, but he knew them for what they were and what they represented, and forbore from tempting providence unnecessarily. He behaved himself with cautious discretion, owned cheerfully to his name, and asked with disarming innocence what they wanted with him.

They were not prepared to tell him more than that the sheriff required his attendance in Shrewsbury, and their reticence, together with the stolid efficiency of their handling of him, might well have inclined him to think better of his co-operation and make a break for it, but by then it was too late, for two more of their company had appeared from nowhere to join them, ambling unhurriedly from the roadside, but both with bows slung conveniently to hand, and the look of men who knew how to use them. The thought of an arrow in the back did not appeal to Britric. He resigned himself to complying with necessity. A great pity, with Wales only a quarter of a mile behind. But if the worst came to the worst, their might be a better opportunity of flight later if he remained docile now.

They took him into Knockin, and for the sake of speed found a spare horse for him, brought him into Shrewsbury before nightfall, and delivered him safely to a cell in the castle. By that time he showed signs of acute uneasiness, but no real fear. Behind a closed and unrevealing face he might be weighing and measuring whatever irregularities he had to account for, and worrying about which of them could have come to light, but if so, the results seemed to bewilder rather than enlighten or alarm him. All his efforts to worm information out of his captors had failed. All he could do now was wait, for it seemed that the sheriff was not immediately on hand.

The sheriff, as it happened, was at supper in the abbot's lodging, together with Prior Robert and the lord of the manor of Upton, who had just made a gift to the abbey of a fishery on the River Tern, which bordered his land. The charter had been drawn up and sealed before Vespers, with Hugh as one of the witnesses. Upton was a crown tenancy, and the consent and approval of the king's officer was necessary to such transactions. The messenger from the castle was wise enough to wait patiently in the ante-room until the company rose from the table. Good news will keep at least as well as bad, and the suspect was safe enough within stone walls.

'This is the man you spoke of?' asked Radulfus, when he heard what the man had to say. 'The one who is known to have made free with Brother Ruald's croft last year?'

'The same,' said Hugh. 'And the only one I can hear of who *is* known to have borrowed free lodging there. And if you'll hold me excused, Father, I must go and see what can be got out of him, before he has time to get his breath and his wits back.'

'I am as concerned as you for justice,' the abbot avowed. 'Not so much that I want the life of this or any man, but I do want an accounting for the woman's. Of course, go. I hope we may be nearer the truth this time. Without it there can be no absolution.'

'May I borrow Brother Cadfael, Father? He first brought me word of this man, he knows best what the old fellow at Saint Giles said of him. He may be able to pick up details that would elude me.'

Prior Robert looked down his patrician nose at the suggestion, and thinned his long lips in disapproval. He considered that Cadfael was far too often allowed a degree of liberty outside the enclave that offended the prior's strict interpretation of the Rule. But Abbot Radulfus nodded thoughtful agreement.

'Certainly a shrewd witness may not come amiss. Yes, take him with you. I do know his memory is excellent, and his nose

292

for discrepancies keen. And he has been in this business from the beginning, and has some right, I think, to continue with it to the end.'

So it came about that Cadfael, coming from supper in the refectory, instead of going dutifully to Collations in the chapter-house, or less dutifully recalling something urgent to be attended to in his workshop, in order to avoid the dull, pedestrian reading of Brother Francis, whose turn it was, was haled out of his routine to go with Hugh up through the town to the castle, there to confront the prisoner.

He was as the old man had reported him, big, red-haired, capable of throwing out far more powerful intruders than a scabby old vagabond and, to an unprejudiced eye, a personable enough figure of a man to captivate a high-spirited and self-sufficient woman as streetwise as himself. At any rate for a time. If they had been together long enough to fall easily into fighting, he might well use those big, sinewy hands too freely and once too often, and find that he had killed without ever meaning to. And if ever he blazed into the real rage his bush of flaming hair suggested, he might kill with intent. Here in the cell where Hugh had chosen to encounter him, he sat with wide shoulders braced back against the wall, stiffly erect and alert, his face as stony as the wall itself, but for the wary eyes that fended off questions and questioners with an unwavering stare. A man, Cadfael judged, who had been in trouble before, and more than once, and coped with it successfully. Nothing mortal, probably, a deer poached here and there, a hen lifted, nothing that could not be plausibly talked out of court, in these somewhat disorganised days when in many places the king's foresters had little time or inclination to impose the rigours of forest law.

As for this present situation, there was no telling what fears, what speculations were going through his mind, how much he guessed at, or what feverish compilations of lies he was putting together against whatever he felt could be urged against him. He waited without protestations, so stiffly tensed that even his hair seemed to be erected and quivering. Hugh closed the door of the cell, and looked him over without haste.

'Well, Britric – that is your name? You have frequented the abbey fair, have you not, these past two years?'

'Longer,' said Britric. His voice was low and guarded, and unwilling to use more words than he need. 'Six years in all.' A small sidelong flicker of uneasy eyes took in Cadfael's habited figure, quiet in the corner of the cell. Perhaps he was recalling the tolls he had evaded paying, and wondering if the abbot had grown tired of turning a blind eye to the small defaulters.

'It's with last year we're concerned. Not so long past that your memory should fail you. The eve of Saint Peter ad Vincula, and the three days afterwards, you were offering your wares for sale. Where did you spend the nights?'

He was astray now, and that made him even more cautious, but he answered without undue hesitation: 'I knew of a cottage was left empty. They were talking of it in the market, how the potter had taken a fancy to be a monk, and his wife was gone, and left the house vacant. Over the river, by Longner. I thought it was no harm to take shelter there. Is that why I'm brought here? But why now, after so long? I never stole anything. I left all as I found it. All I wanted was a roof over me, and a place to lay down in comfort.'

'Alone?' asked Hugh.

No hesitation at all this time. He had already calculated that the same question must have been answered by others, before ever a hand was laid on him to answer for himself. 'I had a woman with me. Gunnild, she was called. She travelled the fairs and markets, entertaining for her living. I met her in Coventry, we kept together a while.'

'And when the fair here was over? Last year's fair? Did you then leave together, and keep company still?'

Britric's narrowed glance flickered from one face to the other, and found no helpful clue. Slowly he said: 'No. We went separate ways. I was going westward, my best trade is along the border villages.'

'And when and where did you part from her?'

'I left her there at the cottage where we'd slept. The fourth day of August, early. It was barely light when I started out. She was going east from there, she had no need to cross the river.'

'I can find no one in the town or the Foregate,' said Hugh deliberately, 'who saw her again.'

'They would not,' said Britric. 'I said, she was going east.'

'And you have never seen her since? Never made effort for old kindess' sake to find her again?'

'I never had occasion.' He was beginning to sweat, for whatever that might mean. 'Chance met, nothing more than that. She went her way, and I went mine.'

'And there was no falling out between you? Never a blow

294

struck? No loud disputes? Ever gentle and amiable together, were you, Britric? There are some report differently of you,' said Hugh. 'There was another fellow, was there not, had hoped to lie snug in that cottage? An old man you drove away. But he did not go far. Not out of earshot of the pair of you, when you did battle in the nights. A stormy partnership, he made it. And she was pressing you to marry her, was she not? And marriage was not to your mind. What happened? Did she grow too wearisome? Or too violent? A hand like yours over her mouth or about her throat could very easily quiet her.'

Britric had drawn his head hard back against the stone like a beast at bay, sweat standing on his forehead in quivering drops under the fall of red hair. Between his teeth he got out, in a voice so short of breath it all but strangled in his throat: 'This is mad ... mad ... I tell you, I left her there snoring, alive and lusty as ever she was. What is this? What are you thinking of me, my lord? What am I held to have done?'

'I will tell you, Britric, what I think you have done. There was no Gunnild at this year's fair, was there? Nor has she been seen in Shrewsbury since you left her in Ruald's field. I think you fell out and fought once too often, one of those nights, perhaps the last, and Gunnild died of it. And I think you buried her there in the night, under the headland, for the abbey plough to turn up this autumn. As it did! A woman's bones, Britric, and a woman's black hair, a mane of black hair still on the skull.'

Britric uttered a small, half-swallowed sound, and let out his breath in a great, gasping sigh, as if he had been hit in the breast with an iron first. When he could articulate, though in a strangled whisper understood rather by the shaping of his lips than by any sound, he got out over and over: 'No ... no ... no! Not Gunnild, no!'

Hugh let him alone until he had breath to make sense, and time to consider and believe, and reason about his own situation. For he was quick to master himself, and to accept, with whatever effort, the fact that the sheriff was not lying, that this was the reason for his arrest and imprisonment here, and he had better take thought in his own defence.

'I never harmed her,' he said at length, slowly and emphatically. 'I left her sleeping. I have never set eyes on her since. She was well alive.'

'A woman's body, Britric, a year at least in the ground. Black hair. They tell me Gunnild was black.'

'So she was. So she *is*, wherever she may be. So are many women along these borderlands. The bones you found cannot be Gunnild's.' Hugh had let slip too easily that all they had, virtually, was a skeleton, never to be identified by face or form. Now Britric knew that he was safe from too exact an accusing image. 'I tell you truly, my lord,' he said, with more insinuating care, 'she was well alive when I crept out and left her in the cottage. I won't deny she'd grown too sure of me. Women want to own a man, and that grows irksome. That was why I rose early, while she was deep asleep, and made off westward alone, to be rid of her without a screeching match. No, I never harmed her. This poor creature they found must be some other woman. It is not Gunnild.'

'What other woman, Britric? A solitary place, the tenants already gone, why should anyone so much as go there, let alone die there?'

'How could I know, my lord? I never heard of the place until the eve of the fair, last year. I know nothing about the neighbourhood that side of the river. All I wanted was a place to sleep snug.' He had himself well in hand now, knowing that no name could ever be confidently given to a mere parcel of female bones, however black the hair on her skull. That might not save him, but it gave him some fragile armour against guilt and death, and he would cling to it and repeat his denials as often and as tirelessly as he must. 'I never hurt Gunnild. I left her alive and well.'

'What did you know of her?' Cadfael asked suddenly, going off at so abrupt a tangent that for a moment Britric was thrown off-balance, and lost his settled concentration on simple denial. 'If you kept company for a while, surely you learned something of the girl, where she came from, where she had kin, the usual pattern of her travelling year. You say she is alive, or at least that you left her alive. Where should she be looked for, to prove as much?'

'Why, she never told much.' He was hesitant and uncertain, and plainly knew little about her, or he would have poured it out readily, as proof of his good intent towards the law. Nor had he had time to put together a neat package of lies to divert attention to some distant region where she might well be pursuing her vagabond living. 'I met her in Coventry. We came from there together, but she was close-mouthed. I doubt she went further south than that, but she never said where she was from, nor a word of any kinsfolk.'

296

'You said she was going east, after you left her. But how can you know that? She had not said so, and agreed to part there, or you need not have stolen away early to avoid her.'

'I spoke too loosely,' owned Britric, writhing. 'I own it. I believed – I believe – she would turn eastward, when she found me gone. Small use taking her singing and tumbling into Wales, not alone. But I tell you truly, I never harmed her. I left her alive.'

And that was his simple, stubborn answer to all further questions, that and the one plea he advanced between obstinate denials.

'My lord, deal fairly with me. Make it known that she is sought, have it cried in the town, ask travellers to carry the word wherever they go, that she should send word to you, and show she is still living. I have not lied to you. If she hears I am charged with her death she will come forward. I never harmed her. She will tell you so.'

'And so we will have her name put about, and see if she appears', agreed Hugh, when they had locked Britric in his stone cell and left him to his uneasy repose, and were walking back towards the castle gatehouse. 'But I doubt if a lady who lives Gunnild's style of life will be too eager to come near the law, even to save Britric's neck. What do you think of him? Denials are denials, worth very little by themselves. And he has something on his conscience, and something to do with that place and that woman, too. First thing he cries when we pin him to the place is: "I never stole anything. I left all as I found it." So I take it he did steal. When it came to the mention of Gunnild dead, then he took fright, until he realised I, like a fool, had let it out that she was mere bones. Then he knew how best to deal, and only then did he begin to plead that we seek her out. It looks and sounds well, but I think he knows she will never be found. Rather, he knows all too well that she *is* found, a thing he hoped would never happen.'

'And you'll keep him in hold?' asked Cadfael.

'Very surely! And go on following his traces wherever he's been since that time, and picking the brains of every inn-keeper or potman or village customer who's had to deal with him. There must be someone somewhere who can fill in an hour or two of his life – and hers. Now I have him I'll keep him until I know truth, one way or the other. Why? Have you a thing to add that has passed me by? I would not refuse any detail you may have in mind.'

'A mere thought,' said Cadfael abstractedly. 'Let it grow a day or two. Who knows, you may not have to wait too long for the truth.'

On the following morning, which was Sunday, Sulien Blount came riding in from Longner to attend Mass in the abbey church, and brought with him, shaken and brushed and carefully folded, the habit in which he had made his way home after the abbot dismissed him. In his own cotte and hose, linen shirt and good leather shoes, he looked, if anything, slightly less at ease than in the habit, so new was his release after more than a year of the novitiate. He had not yet regained the freedom of a young man's easy stride, unhampered by monastic skirts. Nor, strangely, did he look any the happier or more carefree for having made up his mind. There was a solemn set to his admirable jaw, and a silent crease of serious thought between his straight brows. The ring of hair that had grown over-long on his journey from Ramsey had been trimmed into tidiness, and the down of dark gold curls within it had grown into a respectable length to blend with the brown. He attended Mass with the same grave concentration he had shown when within the Order, delivered up the clothing he had abandoned, paid his reverences to Abbot Radulfus and Prior Robert, and went to find Brother Cadfael in the herb garden.

'Well, well!' said Cadfael. 'I thought you might be looking in on us soon. And how do you find things out in the world? You've seen no reason to change your mind?'

'No,' said the boy starkly, and for the moment had nothing more to say. He looked round the high-walled garden, its neat, patterned beds now growing a little leggy and bare with the loss of leaves, the bushy stems of thyme dark as wire. 'I liked it here, with you. But no, I wouldn't turn back. I was wrong to run away. I shall not make the same mistake again.'

'How is your mother faring?' asked Cadfael, divining that she might well be the insoluble grief from which Sulien had attempted flight. For the young man to live with the inescapable contemplation of perpetual pain and the infinitely and cruelly slow approach of lingering death might well be unendurable. For Hugh had reported her present condition very clearly. If that was the heart of it, the boy had braced himself now to make reparation, and carry his part of the load in the house, thereby surely lightening hers.

'Poorly,' said Sulien bluntly. 'Never anything else. But she never complains. It's as if she had some hungry beast for ever gnawing at her body from within. Some days are a little better than others.'

'I have herbs that might do something against the pain,' said Cadfael. 'Some time ago she did use them for a while.'

'I know. We have all told her so, but she refuses them now. She says she doesn't need them. All the same,' he said, warming, 'give me some, perhaps I may persuade her.'

He followed Cadfael into the workshop, under the rustling bunches of dried herbs hanging from the roof beams, and sat down on the wooden bench within while Cadfael filled a flask from his supply of the syrup he made from his eastern poppies, calmer of pain and inducer of sleep.

'You may not have heard yet,' said Cadfael, with his back turned, 'that the sheriff has a man in prison for the murder of the woman we thought was Generys, until you showed us that was impossible. A fellow named Britric, a pedlar who works the border villages, and bedded down in Ruald's croft last year, through Saint Peter's Fair.'

He heard a soft stir of movement at his back, as Sulien's shoulders shifted against the timber wall. But no word was said.

'He had a woman there with him, it seems, one Gunnild, a tumbler and singer entertaining at the fair-ground. And no one has seen her since last year's fair ended. A black-haired woman, they report her. She could very well be the poor soul we found. Hugh Beringar thinks so.'

Sulien's voice, a little clipped and quiet, asked: 'What does Britric say to that? He will not have admitted to it?'

'He said what he would say, that he left the woman there the morning after the fair, safe and well, and has not seen her since.'

'So he may have done,' said Sulien reasonably.

'It is possible. But no one has seen the woman since. She did not come to this year's fair, no one knows anything of her. And as I heard it, they were known to quarrel, even to come to blows. And he is a powerful man, with a hot temper, who might easily go too far. I would not like,' said Cadfael with intent, 'to be in his shoes, for I think the charge against him will be made good. His life is hardly worth the purchase.'

He had not turned until then. The boy was sitting very still, his eyes steady upon Cadfael's countenance. In a voice of

299

detached pity, not greatly moved, he said: 'Poor wretch! I daresay he never meant to kill her. What did you say her name was, this tumbler girl?'

'Gunnild. They called her Gunnild.'

'A hard life that must be, tramping the roads,' said Sulien reflectively, 'especially for a woman. Not so ill in the summer, perhaps, but what must they do in the winter?'

'What all the jongleurs do,' said Cadfael, practically. 'About this time of year they begin thinking of what manor is most likely to take them in for their singing and playing, over the worst of the weather. And with the Spring they'll be off again.'

'Yes, I suppose a corner by the fire and a dinner at the lowest table must be more than welcome once the snow falls,' Sulien agreed indifferently, and rose to accept the small flask Cadfael had stoppered for him. 'I'll be getting back now, Eudo can do with a hand about the stable. And I do thank you, Cadfael. For this and for everything.'

Chapter Eight

T WAS three days later that a groom came riding in at the gatehouse of the castle, with a woman pillion behind him, and set her down in the outer court to speak with the guards. Modestly but with every confidence she asked for the lord sheriff, and made it known that her business was important, and would be considered so by the personage she sought.

Hugh came up from the armoury in his shirt-sleeves and a leather jerkin, with the flush and smokiness of the smith's furnace about him. The woman looked at him with as much curiosity as he was feeling about her, so young and so unexpected was his appearance. She had never seen the sheriff of the shire before, and had looked for someone older and more defensive of his own dignity than this neat, lightly built young fellow in his twenties still, black-haired and black-browed, who looked more like one of the apprentice armourers than the king's officer.

'You asked to speak with me, mistress?' said Hugh. 'Come within, and tell me what you need of me.'

She followed him composedly into the small anteroom in the gatehouse, but hesitated for a moment when he invited her to be seated, as though her business must first be declared and accounted for, before she could be at ease.

'My lord, I think it is you who have need of me, if what I have heard is true.' Her voice had the cadences of the countrywoman, and a slight roughness and rawness, as though

301

in its time it had been abused by over-use or use under strain. And she was not as young as he had first thought her, perhaps around thirty-five years old, but handsome and erect of carriage, and moved with decorous grace. She wore a good dark gown, matronly and sober, and her hair was drawn back and hidden under a white wimple. The perfect image of a decent burgess's wife, or a gentlewoman's attendant. Hugh could not immediately guess where and how she fitted into his present preoccupations, but was willing to wait for enlightenment.

'And what is it you have heard?' he asked.

'They are saying about the market that you have taken a man called Britric into hold, a pedlar, for killing a woman who kept company with him for some while last year. Is it true?'

'True enough,' said Hugh. 'You have something to say to the matter?'

'I have, my lord!' Her eyes she kept half-veiled by heavy, long lashes, looking up directly into his face only rarely and briefly. 'I bear Britric no particular goodwill, for reasons enough, but no ill will, either. He was a good companion for a while, and even if we did fall out, I don't want him hung for a murder that was never committed. So here I am in the flesh, to prove I'm well alive. And my name is Gunnild.'

'And, by God, so it proved!' said Hugh, pouring out the whole unlikely story some hours later, in the leisure hour of the monastic afternoon in Cadfael's workshop. 'No question, Gunnild she is. You should have seen the pedlar's face when I brought her into his cell, and he took one long look at the decent, respectable shape of her, and then at her face closely, and his mouth fell open, he found her so hard to believe. But: "Gunnild!" he screeches, as soon as he gets his breath back. Oh, she's the same woman, not a doubt of it, but so changed it took him a while to trust his own eyes. And there was more than he ever told us to that early morning flight of his. No wonder he crept off and left her sleeping. He took every penny of her earnings with him as well as his own. I said he had something on his conscience, and something to do with the woman. So he had, he robbed her of everything she had of value, and a hard time she must have had of it through the autumn and into the winter, last year.'

'It sounds,' said Cadfael, attentive but unsurprised, 'as if their meeting today might well be another stormy one.'

'Well, he was so glad of her coming, he was all thanks and promises of redress, and fawning flattery. And she refuses to press the theft against him. I do believe he had thoughts of trying to woo her back to the wandering life, but she's having none of that. Not she! She calls up her groom, and he hoists her to the pillion, and away they go.'

'And Britric?' Cadfael reached to give a thoughtful stir to the pot he had gently simmering on the grid that covered one side of his brazier. The sharp, warm, steamy smell of horehound stung their nostrils. There were already a few coughs and colds among the old, frail brothers in Edmund's infirmary.

'He's loosed and away, very subdued, though how long that will last there's no knowing. No reason to hold him longer. We'll keep a weather eye on his dealings, but if he's beginning to prosper honestly – well, almost honestly! – he may have got enough wisdom this time to stay within the law. Even the abbey may get its tolls if he comes to next year's fair. But here are we, Cadfael, left with a history repeating itself very neatly and plausibly, to let loose not one possible murderer, but the second one also. Is that believable?'

'Such things have been known,' said Cadfael cautiously, 'but not often.'

'Do *you* believe it?'

'I believe it has happened. But that it has happened by chance, that has me in two minds. No,' Cadfael amended emphatically, 'more than two minds.'

'That one supposedly dead woman should come back to life, well and good. But the second also? And are we now to expect a third, if we can find a third to die or rise again? And yet we still have this one poor, offended soul waiting for justice, if not by another's death, at least by the grace and remembrance of a name. She *is* dead, and requires an accounting.'

Cadfael had listened with respect and affection to a speech which might as well have come from Abbot Radulfus, but delivered with a youthful and secular passion. Hugh did not often commit himself to indignation, at least not aloud.

'Hugh, did she tell you how and where she heard of Britric's being in your prison?'

'No more than vaguely. Rumoured about in the market, she said. I never thought,' said Hugh, vexed, 'to question more nearly.'

'And it's barely three days since you let it be known what he

303

was suspected of, and put out her name. News travels fast, but how far it should have reached in the time may be much to the point. I take it Gunnild has accounted for herself? For the change in fortunes? You have not told me, yet, where she lives and serves now.'

'Why, it seems that after a fashion Britric did her a favour when he left her penniless, there in Ruald's croft. It was August then, the end of the fair, no very easy way to pick up a profit, and she barely managed to keep herself through the autumn months, fed but with nothing saved, and you'll remember – God knows you should! – that the winter came early and hard. She did what the wandering players do, started early looking for a manor where there might be a place for a good minstrel through the worst of the winter. Common practice, but you gamble, and may win or do poorly!'

'Yes,' agreed Cadfael, rather to himself than to his friend, 'so I told him.'

'She did well for herself. She happened into the manor of Withington in the December snows. Giles Otmere holds it, a crown tenant these days, since FitzAlan's lands were seized, and he has a young family who welcome a minstrel over the Christmas feast, so they took her in. But better still, the young daughter is eighteen just turned, and took a liking to her, and according to Gunnild she has a neat hand with dressing hair, and is good with her needle, and the girl has taken her on as tirewoman. You should see the delicate pace of her now, and the maidenly manners. She's been profitable to her lady, and thinks the world of her. Gunnild will never go back to the roads and the fairgrounds now, she has too much good sense. Truly, Cadfael, you should see her for yourself.'

'Truly,' said Cadfael musingly, 'I think I should. Well, Withington is not far, not much beyond Upton, but unless Mistress Gunnild came into town for yesterday's market, or someone happened in at Withington with the day's news, rumour seems to have run through the grasses and across the river of its own accord. Granted it does fly faster than the birds at times, at least in town and Foregate, it takes a day or so to reach the outlying villages. Unless someone sets out in haste to carry it.'

'Brought home from market or blown on the wind,' said Hugh, 'it travelled as far as Withington, it seems. As well for Britric. I am left with no notion which way to look now, but better that than hound an innocent man. But I would be loath to give up, and let the thing go by default.'

'No need,' said Cadfael, 'to think in such terms yet. Wait but a few more days, and give your mind to the king's business meantime, and we may have one thread left to us yet.'

Cadfael made his way to the abbot's lodging before Vespers, and asked for an audience. He was a little deprecating in advancing his request, well aware of the licence often granted to him beyond what the Rule would normally countenance, but for once none too certain of what he was about. The reliance the abbot had come to place in him was in itself something of a burden.

'Father, I think Hugh Beringar will have been with you this afternoon, and told you what has happened concerning the man Britric. The woman who is known to have been in his company a year and more ago did indeed vanish from her usual haunts, but not by death. She has come forward to show that he has not harmed her, and the man is set free.'

'Yes,' said Radulfus, 'this I know. Hugh was with me an hour since. I cannot but be glad the man is innocent of murder, and can go his ways freely. But our responsibility for the dead continues, and our quest must go on.'

'Father, I came to ask leave to make a journey tomorrow. A few hours would suffice. There is an aspect of this deliverance that raises certain questions that need to be answered. I did not suggest to Hugh Beringar that he should undertake such an enquiry, partly because he has the king's business very much on his mind, but also because I may be wrong in what I believe, and if it proves so, no need to trouble him with it. And if it proves there is ground for my doubts,' said Cadfael very soberly, 'then I must lay the matter in his hands, and there leave it.'

'And am I permitted,' asked the abbot after a moment's thought, and with a shadowy and wry smile touching his lips briefly, 'to ask what these doubts may be?'

'I would as lief say nothing,' said Cadfael frankly, 'until I have the answers myself, yes or no. For if I am become a mere subtle, suspicious old man, too prone to see devious practices where none are, then I would rather not draw any other man into the same unworthy quagmire, nor levy false charges easier to publish than to suppress. Bear with me until tomorrow.'

'Then tell me one thing only,' said Radulfus. 'There is no cause, I trust, in this course you have in mind, to point again at Brother Ruald?'

305

'No, Father. It points away from him.'

'Good! I cannot believe any ill of the man.'

'I am sure he has done none,' said Cadfael firmly.

'So he at least can be at peace.'

'That I have not said.' And at the sharp and penetrating glance the abbot fixed upon him he went on steadily: 'All we within this house share the concern and grief for a creature laid astray in abbey land without a name or the proper rites of death and absolution. To that extent, until this is resolved, none of us can be at peace.'

Radulfus was still for a long moment, eyeing Cadfael closely; then he stirred abruptly out of his stillness, and said practically: 'Then the sooner you advance this argument the better. Take a mule from the stables, if the journey is somewhat long for going and returning in a day. Where is it you are bound? May I ask even so far?'

'No great distance,' said Cadfael, 'but it will save time if I ride. It is only to the manor of Withington.'

Cadfael set out next morning, immediately after Prime, on the six-mile ride to the manor where Gunnild had found her refuge from the chances and mischances of the road. He crossed by the ferry upstream from the Longner lands, and on the further side followed the little brook that entered the Severn there, with rising fields on either side. For a quarter of a mile he could see on his right the long crest of trees and bushes, on the far side of which lay the Potter's Field, transformed now into a plateau of new ploughland above, and the gentle slope of meadow below. What remained of the cottage would have been dismantled by now, the garden cleared, the site levelled. Cadfael had not been back to see.

The way was by open fields as far as the village of Upton, climbing very gently. Beyond, there was a well-used track the further two miles or more to Withington, through flat land, rich and green. Two brooks threaded their gentle way between the houses of the village, to merge on the southern edge and flow on to empty into the River Tern. The small church that sat in the centre of the green was a property of the abbey, like its neighbour at Upton, Bishop de Clinton's gift to the Benedictines some years back. On the far side of the village, drawn back a little from the brook, the manor lay within a low stockade, ringed with its barns and byres and stables. The undercroft was of timber beams, one end of the living floor of stone, which was standing open at this early working hour of the day, when baker and dairy-maid were likely to be running busily in and out.

Cadfael dismounted at the gate and led the mule at leisure into the yard, taking time to look about him. A woman-servant was crossing with a huge crock of milk from the byre to the dairy and halted at the sight of him, but went on about her business when a groom emerged from the stable and came briskly to take the mule's bridle.

'You're early abroad, Brother. How can we serve you? My master's ridden out towards Rodington already. Shall we send after him, if your errand's to him? Or if you have leisure to wait his return, you're welcome within. His door's always open to the cloth.'

'I'll not disrupt the order of a busy man's day,' said Cadfael heartily. 'I'm on a simple errand of thanks to your young mistress for her kindness and help in a certain vexed business, and if I can pay my compliments to the lady, I'll soon be on my way back to Shrewsbury. I don't know her name, for I hear your lord has a flock of children. The lady I want may well be the eldest, I fancy. The one who has a maid called Gunnild.'

By the practical way the groom received the name, Gunnild's place in this household was established and accepted, and if ever there had been whispers and grudges among the other maids over the transformation of a draggle-tailed tumbler into a favoured tirewoman, they were already past and forgotten, which was shrewd testimony to Gunnild's own good sense.

'Oh, ay, that's Mistress Pernel,' said the groom, and turned to call up a passing boy to take the mule from him and see him cared for. 'She's within, though my lady's gone with my lord, at least a piece of the way; she has business with the miller's wife at Rodington. Come within, and I'll call Gunnild for you.'

The to and fro of voices across the yard gave place, as they climbed the steps to the hall door, to shriller voices and a great deal of children's laughter, and two boys of about twelve and eight came darting out from the open doorway and down the steps in two or three leaps, almost bowling Cadfael over, and recovering with breathless yells to continue their flight towards the fields. They were followed in bounding haste by a small girl of five or six years, holding up her skirts in both plump hands and shrieking at her brothers to wait for her. The groom caught her up deftly and set her safely on her feet at the foot of the steps, and she was off after the boys at the fastest speed her short legs could muster. Cadfael turned for a moment on the steps to follow her flight. When he looked round again to continue mounting, an older girl stood framed in the doorway, looking down at him in smiling and wondering surprise.

Not Gunnild, certainly, but Gunnild's mistress. Eighteen, just turned, Hugh had said. Eighteen, and not yet married or, it seemed, betrothed, perhaps because of the modesty of her dowry and of her father's connections, but perhaps also because she was the eldest of this brood of lively chicks, and very valuable to the household. The succession was secured, with two healthy sons, and two daughters to provide for might be something of a tax on Giles Otmere's resources, so that there was no haste. With her gracious looks and evident warmth of nature she might need very little by way of dowry if the right lad came along.

She was not tall, but softly rounded and somehow contrived to radiate a physical brightness, as if her whole body, from soft brown hair to small feet, smiled as her eyes and lips smiled. Her face was round, the eyes wide-set and wide-open in shining candour, her mouth at once generously full and passionate, and resolutely firm, though parted at this moment in a startled smile. She had her little sister's discarded wooden doll in her hand, just retrieved from the floor where it had been thrown.

'Here is Mistress Pernel,' said the groom cheerfully, and drew back a step towards the yard. 'Lady, the good brother would like a word with you.'

'With me?' she said, opening her eyes wider still. 'Come up, sir, and welcome. Is it really me you want? Not my mother?'

Her voice matched the brightness she radiated, pitched high and gaily, like a child's, but very melodious in its singing cadences.

'Well, at least,' she said, laughing, 'we can hear each other speak, now the children are away. Come into the window-bench, and rest.'

The alcove where they sat down together had the weather shutter partially closed, but the lee one left open. There was almost no wind that morning, and though the sky was clouded over, the light was good. Sitting opposite to this girl was like facing a glowing lamp. For the moment they had the hall to themselves, though Cadfael could hear several voices in busy, braided harmony from passage and kitchen, and from the yard without.

'You are come from Shrewsbury?' she said.

'With my abbot's leave,' said Cadfael, 'to give you thanks for so promptly sending your maid Gunnild to the lord sheriff, to deliver the man held in prison on suspicion of causing her death. Both my abbot and the sheriff are in your debt. Their intent is justice. You have helped them to avoid injustice.'

'Why we could do no other,' she said simply, 'once we knew of the need. No one, surely, would leave a poor man in prison a day longer than was needful, when he had done no wrong.'

'And how did you learn of the need?' asked Cadfael. It was the question he had come to ask, and she answered it cheerfully and frankly, with no suspicion of its real significance.

'I was told. Indeed, if there is credit in the matter it is not ours so much as the young man's who told me of the case, for he had been enquiring everywhere for Gunnild by name, whether she had spent the winter of last year with some household in this part of the shire. He had not expected to find her still here, and settled, but it was great relief to him. All I did was send Gunnild with a groom to Shrewsbury. He had been riding here and there asking for her, to know if she was alive and well, and beg her to come forward and prove as much, for she was thought to be dead.'

'It was much to his credit,' said Cadfael, 'so to concern himself with justice.'

'It was!' she agreed warmly. 'We were not the first he had visited, he had ridden as far afield as Cressage before he came to us.'

'You know him by name?'

'I did not, until then. He told me he was Sulien Blount, of Longner.'

'Did he expressly ask for you?' asked Cadfael.

'Oh, no!' She was surprised and amused, and he could not be sure, by this time, that she was not acutely aware of the curious insistence of his questioning, but she saw no reason to hesitate in answering. 'He asked for my father, but Father was away in the fields, and I was in the yard when he rode in. It was only by chance that he spoke to me.'

At least a pleasant chance, thought Cadfael, to afford some unexpected comfort to a troubled man.

'And when he knew he had found the woman he sought, did he ask to speak with her? Or leave the telling to you?'

'Yes, he spoke with her. In my presence he told her how the pedlar was in prison, and how she must come forward and prove he had never done her harm. And so she did, willingly.'

309

She was grave now rather than smiling, but still open, direct and bright. It was evident from the intelligent clarity of her eyes that she had recognised some deeper purpose behind his interrogation, and was much concerned with its implications, but also that even in that recognition she saw no cause to withhold or prevaricate, since truth could not in her faith be a means of harm. So he asked the final question without hesitation: 'Did he ever have opportunity to speak with her alone?'

'Yes,' said Pernel. Her eyes, very wide and steady upon Cadfael's face, were a golden, sunlit brown, lighter than her hair. 'She thanked him and went out with him to the yard when he mounted and left. I was within with the children, they had just come in, it was near time for supper. But he would not stay.'

But she had asked him. She had liked him, was busy liking him now, and wondering, though without misgivings, what this monk of Shrewsbury might want concerning the movements and generosities and preoccupations of Sulien Blount of Longner.

'What they said to each other,' said Pernel, 'I do not know. I am sure it was no harm.'

'That,' said Cadfael, 'I think I may guess at. I think the young man may have asked her, when she came to the sheriff at the castle, not to mention that it was he who had come seeking her, but to say that she had heard of Britric's plight and her own supposed death from the general gossip. News travels. She would have heard it in the end, but not, I fear, so quickly.'

'Yes,' said Pernel, flushing and glowing, 'that I can believe of him, that he wanted no credit for his own goodness of heart. Why? Did she do as he wished?'

'She did. No blame to her for that, he had the right to ask it of her.'

Perhaps not only the right, but the need! Cadfael made to rise, to thank her for the time she had devoted to him, and to take his leave, but she put out a hand to detain him.

'You must not go without taking some refreshment in our house, Brother. If you will not stay and eat with us at midday, at least let me call Gunnild to bring us wine. Father bought some French wine at the summer fair.' And she was on her feet and across the width of the hall to the screen door, and calling, before he could either accept or withdraw. It was fair, he reflected. He had had what he wanted from her, ungrudging

310

and unafraid; now she wanted something from him. 'We need say nothing to Gunnild,' she said softly, returning. 'It was a harsh life she used to live, let her put it by, and all reminders of it. She has been a good friend and servant to me, and she loves the children.'

The woman who came in from the kitchen and pantry with flask and glasses was tall, and would have been called lean rather than slender, but the flow of her movements was elegant and sinuous still within the plain dark gown. The oval face framed by her white wimple was olive-skinned and suave, the dark eyes that took in Cadfael with serene but guarded curiosity and dwelt with almost possessive affection upon Pernel, were still cleanly set and beautiful. She served them handily, and withdrew from them discreetly. Gunnild had come into a haven from which she did not intend to sail again, certainly not at the invitation of a vagabond like Britric. Even when her lady married, there would be the little sister to care for, and perhaps, some day, marriage for Gunnild herself, the comfortable, practical marriage of two decent, ageing retainers who had served long enough together to know they can run along cosily for the rest of their days.

'You see,' said Pernel, 'how well worth it was to take her in, and how content she is here. And now,' she said, pursuing without conceal what most interested her, 'tell me about this Sulien Blount. For I think you must know him.'

Cadfael drew breath and told her all that it seemed desirable to him she should know about the sometime Benedictine novice, his home and his family, and his final choice of the secular world. It did not include any more about the history of the Potter's Field than the mere fact that it had passed by stages from the Blounts to the abbey's keeping, and had given up, when ploughed, the body of a dead woman for whose identity the law was now searching. That seemed reason enough for a son of the family taking a personal interest in the case, and exerting himself to extricate the innocent from suspicion, and accounted satisfactorily for the concern shown by the abbot and his envoy, this elderly monk who now sat in a window embrasure with Pernel, recounting briefly the whole disturbing history.

'And his mother is so ill?' said Pernel, listening with wide, sympathetic eyes and absorbed attention. 'At least how glad she must be that he has chosen, after all, to come home.'

'The elder son married in the summer,' said Cadfael, 'so

311

there is a young woman in the household to give her comfort and care. But yes, certainly she will be glad to have Sulien home again.'

'It is not so far,' Pernel mused, half to herself. 'We are almost neighbours. Do you think the lady Donata is ever well enough to want to receive visitors? If she cannot go out, she must sometimes be lonely.'

Cadfael took his leave with that delicate suggestion still in his ears, in the girl's warm, purposeful, buoyant voice, and with her bright and confident face before his eyes, the antithesis of illness, loneliness and pain. Well, why not? Even if she went rather in search of the young man who had touched her generous fancy than for such benefit as her vigour and charm could confer upon a withered gentlewoman, her presence might still do wonders.

He rode back through the autumnal fields without haste, and instead of turning in at the abbey gatehouse, went on over the bridge and into the town, to look for Hugh at the castle.

It was plain, as soon as he began to climb the ramp to the castle gatehouse, that something had happened to cause a tremendous stir within. Two empty carts were creaking briskly up the slope and in under the deep archway in the tower, and within, there was such bustle between hall, stables, armoury and stores, that Cadfael sat his mule unnoticed for many minutes in the midst of the to-ings and fro-ings, weighing up what he saw, and considering its inevitable meaning. There was nothing confused or distracted about it, everything was purposeful and exact, the ordered climax of calculated and well-planned preparations. He dismounted, and Will Warden, Hugh's oldest and most seasoned sergeant, halted for an instant in directing the carters through to the inner yard, and came to enlighten him.

'We're on the march tomorrow morning. The word came only an hour past. Go in to him, Brother, he's in the gate-tower.'

And he was gone, waving the teamster of the second cart through the arch to the inner ward, and vanishing after the cart to see it efficiently loaded. The supply column must be preparing to leave today, the armed company would ride after them at first light.

Cadfael abandoned his mule to a stable boy, and crossed to the deep doorway of the guardroom in the gate-tower. Hugh

312

rose from a littered table at sight of him, shuffled his records together and pushed them aside.

'It's come, as I thought it would. The king had to move against the man, for the saving of his own face he could no longer sit and do nothing. Though he knows as well as I do,' admitted Hugh, preoccupied and vehement, 'that the chances of bringing Geoffrey de Mandeville to pitched battle are all too thin. What, with his Essex supply lines secure even if the time comes when he can wring no more corn or cattle out of the Fens? And all those bleak levels laced with water, and as familiar to him as the lines of his own hand? Well, we'll do him what damage we can, perhaps bolt him in if we can't flush him out. Whatever the odds, Stephen has ordered his muster to Cambridge, and demanded a company of me for a limited time, and a company he shall have, as good as any he'll get from his Flemings. And unless he has the lightning fit on him – it takes him and us by surprise sometimes – we'll be in Cambridge before him.'

Having thus unburdened himself of his own immediate preoccupations, concerning which there was no particular haste, since everything had been taken care of in advance, Hugh took a more attentive look at his friend's face, and saw that King Stephen's courier had not been the only visitor with news of moment to impart.

'Well, well!' he said mildly. 'I see you have things on your mind, no less than his Grace the king. And here am I about to leave you hefting the load alone. Sit down and tell me what's new. There's time, before I need stir.'

Chapter Nine

HANCE HAD no part in it' said Cadfael, leaning his folded arms upon the table. 'You were right. History repeated itself for good reason, because the same hand thrust it where the same mind wanted it. Twice! It was in my mind, so I put it to the test. I took care the boy should know there was another man suspected of this death. It may even be that I painted Britric's danger blacker than it was. And behold, the lad takes to heart that true word I offered him, that the folk of the roads look round for a warm haven through the winter and off he goes, searching here and there about these parts, to find out if one Gunnild had found a corner by some manor fire. And this time, mark you, he had no possibility of knowing whether the woman was alive or dead, knowing nothing of her beyond what I had told him. He had luck, and he found her. Now, why, never having heard her name before, never seen her face, why should he bestir himself for Britric's sake?'

'Why,' agreed Hugh, eye to eye with him across the board, 'unless he knew, whatever else he did not know, that our dead woman was not and could not be this Gunnild? And how could he know that, unless he knows all too well who she really is? And what happened to her?'

'Or believes he knows,' said Cadfael cautiously.

'Cadfael, I begin to find your failed brother interesting. Let us see just what we have here. Here is this youngster who suddenly, so short a while after Ruald's wife vanished from her

314

home, chooses most unexpectedly to desert his own home and take the cowl, not close here where he's known, with you, or at Haughmond, the house and the order his family has always favoured, but far away at Ramsey. Removing himself from a scene now haunting and painful to him? Perhaps even dangerous? He comes home, perforce, when Ramsey becomes a robber's nest, and it may well be true that he comes now in doubt of his own wisdom in turning to the cloister. And what does he find here? That the body of a woman has been found, buried on lands that once pertained to his family demesne, and that the common and reasonable thought is that this is Ruald's lost wife, and Ruald her murderer. So what does he do? He tells a story to prove that Generys is alive and well. Distant too far to be easily found and answer for herself, seeing the state of that country now, but he has proof. He has a ring which was hers, a ring she sold in Peterborough, long after she was gone from here. Therefore this body cannot be hers.'

'The ring,' said Cadfael reasonably, 'was unquestionably hers, and genuine. Ruald knew it at once, and was glad and grateful beyond measure to be reassured that she's alive and well, and seemingly fairing well enough without him. You saw him, as I did. I am sure there was no guile in him, and no falsity.'

'So I believe, too. I do not think we are back to Ruald, though God knows we may be back with Generys. But see what follows! Next, a search throws up another man who may by all the signs be guilty of killing another vanished woman in that very place. And yet again Sulien Blount, when he hears of it so helpfully from you, continues to interest himself in the matter, voluntarily setting out to trace this woman also, and show that she is alive. And, by God, is lucky enough to find her! Thus delivering Britric as he delivered Ruald. And now tell me, Cadfael, tell me truly, what does all that say to you?'

'It says,' admitted Cadfael honestly, 'that whoever the woman may be, Sulien himself is guilty, and means to battle it out for his life, yes, but not at the expense of Ruald or Britric or any innocent man. And that, I think, would be in character for him. He might kill. He would not let another man hang for it.'

'That is how you read the omens?' Hugh was studying him closely, black brows obliquely tilted, and a wry smile curling one corner of his expressive mouth.

'That is how I read the omens.'

'But you do not believe it!'

It was a statement rather than a question, and voiced without

315

surprise. Hugh was well enough versed in Cadfael by now to discern in him tendencies of which he himself was still unaware. Cadfael considered the implications very seriously for a few moments of silence. Then he said judicially: 'On the face of it, it is logical, it is possible, it is even likely. If, after all, this is Generys, as now again seems all too likely, by common consent she was a very beautiful woman. Nearly old enough to be the boy's mother, true, and he had known her from infancy, but he himself as good as said that he fled to Ramsey because he found himself guiltily and painfully in love with her. It happens to many a green boy, to suffer his first disastrous experience of love for a woman long familiarly known, and loved in another fashion, a woman out of his generation and out of his reach. But how if there was more to it than mere flight to escape from insoluble problems and incurable pain? Consider the situation, when a husband she had loved and trusted was wrenching himself away from her as it were in blood, her blood, and yet leaving her bound and lonely! In her rage and bitterness at such a desertion a passionate woman might well have set herself to take revenge on all men, even the vulnerable young. Taken him up, comforted herself in his worshipping dog's eyes, and then cast him off. Such affronts the young in their first throes feel mortally. But the death may have been hers. Reason enough to fly from the scene and from the world into a distant cloister, out of sight even of the trees that sheltered her home.'

'It is logical,' said Hugh, echoing Cadfael's own words, 'it is possible, it is credible.'

'My only objection,' agreed Cadfael, 'is that I find I do not credit it. Nor cannot, for good sound reasons – simply do not.'

'Your reservations,' said Hugh philosophically, 'always have me reining in and treading very carefully. Now as ever! But I have another thought: How if Sulien had the ring in his possession all along, ever since he parted with Generys – living or dead? How if she herself had given it to him? Tossed away her husband's love gift in bitterness at his desertion, upon the most innocent and piteous lover she could ever have had. And she did say that she had a lover.'

'If he had killed her,' said Cadfael, 'would he have kept her token?'

'He might! Oh, yes, he very well might. Such things have been known, when love at its most devilish raises hate as another devil, to fight it out between them. Yes, I think he

316

would keep her ring, even through a year of concealing it from abbot and confessor and all, in Ramsey.'

'As he swore to Radulfus,' remarked Cadfael, suddenly reminded, 'that he did not. He could lie, I think, but would not lie wantonly, for no good reason.'

'Have we not attributed to him good reason enough for lying? Then, if all along he had the ring, the time came when it was urgent, for Ruald's sake, to produce it in evidence, with this false story of how he came by it. If indeed it is false. If I had proof it is not,' said Hugh, fretting at the frustration of chance, 'I could put Sulien almost – *almost* – out of my mind.'

'There is also,' said Cadfael slowly, 'the question of why he did not tell Ruald at once, when they met, that he had heard news of Generys in Peterborough, and she was alive and well. Even if, as he says, his intent was to keep the ring for himself, still he could have told the man what he must have known would come as great ease and relief to him. But he did not.'

'The boy did not know, then,' Hugh objected fairly, 'that we had found a dead woman, nor that any shadow lay over Ruald. He knew of no very urgent need to give him news of his wife, not until he heard the whole story at Longner. Indeed, he might well have thought it better to leave well alone, since the man is blessedly happy where he is.'

'I am not altogether sure,' Cadfael said slowly, peering back into the brief while he had spent with Sulien as helper in the herbarium, 'that he did now know of the case until he went home. The same day that he asked leave to visit Longner and see his family again, Jerome had been with him in the garden, for I met him as he left, and he was at once in haste, and a shade more civil and brotherly than usual. And I wonder now if something had not been said of a woman's bones discovered, and a man's reputation under threat. That same evening Sulien went to the lord abbot, and was given leave to ride to Longner. When he came back next day, it was to declare his intent to leave the Order, and to bring forth the ring and the story of how he got it.'

Hugh was drumming his fingers softly on the table, his eyes narrowed in thought. 'Which first?' he demanded.

'First he asked and obtained his dismissal.'

'Would it, you think, be easier, to a man usually truthful, to lie to the abbot after that than before?'

'You have thoughts not unlike mine,' said Cadfael glumly.

'Well,' said Hugh, shaking off present concerns from his

317

shoulders, 'two things are certain. The first, that whatever the truth about Sulien himself, this second deliverance is proven absolutely. We have seen and spoken with Gunnild. She is alive, and thriving, and very sensibly has no intent in the world to go on her travels again. And since we have no cause to connect Britric with any other woman, away he goes in safety, and good luck to them both. And the second certainty, Cadfael, is that the very fact of this second deliverance casts great doubt upon the first. Generys we have *not* seen. Ring or no ring, I am in two minds now whether we ever shall see her again. And yet, and yet – Cadfael does not credit it! Not as it stands, not as we see it now.'

'There is one more certainty,' Cadfael reminded him seriously, 'that you are bound away from here tomorrow morning, and the king's business will not wait, so our business here must. What, if anything, do you want done until you can take the reins again? Which, God willing, may not be too long.'

They had both risen at the sound of the loaded carts moving briskly out under the archway, the hollow sound of the wheels beneath the stone echoing back to them as from a cavern. A detachment of archers on foot went with the supplies on this first stage of their journey, to pick up fresh horses at Coventry, where the lances would overtake them.

'Say no word to Sulien or any,' said Hugh, 'but watch whatever follows. Let Radulfus know as much as you please, he knows how to keep a close mouth if any man does. Let young Sulien rest, if rest he can. I doubt if he'll sleep too easily, even though he has cleared the field of murderers for me, or hopes, believes, prays he has. Should I want him, when time serves, he'll be here.'

They went out together in the outer ward, and there halted to take leave. 'If I'm gone long,' said Hugh, 'you'll visit Aline?' There had been no mention, and would be none, of such small matters as that men get killed even in untidy regional skirmishes, such as the Fens were likely to provide. As Eudo Blount the elder had died in the rearguard after the messy ambush of Wilton, not quite a year ago. No doubt Geoffrey de Mandeville, expert at turning his coat and still making himself valuable and to be courted, would prefer to keep his devious options open by evading battle with the king's forces if he could, and killing none of baronial status, but he might not always be able to dictate the terms of engagement, even on his own watery ground. And Hugh was not a man to lead from behind.

'I will,' said Cadfael heartily. 'And God keep the both of you, yes, and the lads who're going with you.'

Hugh went with him to the gate, a hand on his friend's shoulder. They were much of a height, and could match paces evenly. Under the shadow of the archway they halted.

'One more thought has entered my mind,' said Hugh, 'one that has surely been in yours all this while, spoken or not. It's no very great distance from Cambridge to Peterborough.'

'So it has come!' said Abbot Radulfus sombrely, when Cadfael gave him the full report of his day's activities, after Vespers. 'The first time Hugh has been called on to join the king's muster since Lincoln. I hope it may be to better success. God grant they need not be absent about this business very long.'

Cadfael could not imagine that this confrontation would be over easily or quickly. He had never seen Ramsey, but Sulien's description of it, an island with its own natural and formidable moat, spanned by only one narrow causeway, defensible by a mere handful of men, held out little hope of an easy conquest. And though de Mandeville's marauders must sally forth from their fortress to do their plundering, they had the advantage of being local men, used to all the watery fastnesses in that bleak and open countryside, and able to withdraw into the marshes at any hostile approach.

'With November already here,' he said, 'and winter on the way, I doubt if more can be done than penning these outlaws into their own Fens, and at least limiting the harm they can do. By all accounts it's already more than enough for the poor souls who live in those parts. But, with the Earl of Chester our neighbour here, and so dubious in his loyalty, I fancy King Stephen will want to send Hugh and his men home again, to secure the shire and the border, as soon as they can be spared. He may well be hoping for a quick stroke and a quick death. I see no other end to de Mandeville now, however nimbly he may have learned to turn his coat. This time he has gone too far for any recovery.'

'Bleak necessity,' said Radulfus grimly, 'to be forced to wish for any man's death, but this one has been the death of so many others, souls humble and defenceless, and by such abominable means, I could find it in me to offer prayers for his ending, as a needful mercy to his neighbours. How else can

319

there ever be peace and good husbandry in those desolated lands? In the meantime, Cadfael, we are left for a while unable to move in the matter of this death nearer home. Hugh has left Alan Herbard as castellan in his absence?'

Hugh's deputy was young and ardent, and promised well. He had little experience as yet in managing a garrison, but he had hardened sergeants of the older generation at his back, to strengthen his hand if their experience should be needed.

'He has. And Will Warden will be keeping an ear open for any word that may furnish a new lead, though his orders, like mine, are to keep a still tongue and a placid face, and let sleeping dogs lie as long as they will. But you see, Father, how the very fact of this woman coming forward at Sulien's prompting, as she has, casts doubts on the story he first told us. Once, we said, yes, that's wholly credible, why question it? But twice, by the same hand, the same deliverance? No, that is not chance at work, nor can it be easily believed. No! Sulien will not suffer either Ruald or Britric to be branded as a murderer, and goes to great pains to prove it impossible. How can he be so certain of their innocence, unless he knows who is really guilty? Or at least, believes he knows?'

Radulfus looked back at him with an impenetrable countenance, and said outright what as yet neither Cadfael nor Hugh had put into words:

'*Or is himself the man!*'

'It is the first and logical thought that came to me,' Cadfael owned. 'But I found I could not admit it. The farthest I dare go as yet is to acknowledge that his behaviour casts great doubt on his ignorance, if not his innocence, of this death. In the case of Britric there is no question. This time it is not a matter of any man's bare word, the woman came forward in the flesh and spoke for herself. Living she is, fortunate and thankful she is, no one need look for her in the grave. It's at the first deliverance we must turn and look again. That Generys is still in this world alive, for that we have only Sulien's word. *She* has not come forward. *She* has not spoken. Thus far, all we have is hearsay. One man's word for the woman, the ring, and all.'

'From such small knowledge of him as I have,' said Radulfus, 'I do not think that Sulien is by nature a liar.'

'Neither do I. But all men, even those not by nature liars, may be forced to lie where they see overwhelming need. As I fear he did, to deliver Ruald from the burden of suspicion. Moreover,' said Cadfael confidently, harking back to the old

320

experience with fallible men outside this enclave, 'if they lie only for such desperate cause they will do it well, better than those who do it lightly.'

'You argue,' said Radulfus drily, but with the flicker of a private smile, 'as one who speaks from knowledge. Well, if one man's word is no longer acceptable without proof, I do not see how we can advance our enquires beyond your "thus far". As well we should let well alone while Hugh is absent. Say nothing to any man from Longner, nothing to Brother Ruald. In stillness and quietness whispers are heard clearly, and the rustle of a leaf has meaning.'

'And I have been reminded,' said Cadfael, rising with a gusty sigh to make his way to the refectory, 'by the last thing Hugh said to me, that it is not too far from Cambridge to Peterborough.'

The next day was sacred to Saint Winifred, and therefore an important feast in the abbey of Saint Peter and Saint Paul, though the day of her translation and installation on her present altar in the church, the twenty-second of June, was accorded greater ceremonial. A midsummer holiday provides better weather and longer daylight for processions and festivities than the third of November, with the days closing in and winter approaching.

Cadfael rose very early in the morning, long before Prime, took his sandals and scapular, and stole out from the dark dortoir by the night stars, where the little lamp burned all night long to light stumbling feet uncertain from sleep down into the church for Matins and Lauds. The long room, lined with its low partitions that separated cell from cell, was full of small human sounds, like a vault peopled with gentle ghosts, soft, sighing breath, the involuntary catch in the throat, close to a sob, that saluted a nostalgic dream, the uneasy stirring of someone half awake, the solid, contented snoring of a big body sleeping without dreams, and at the end of the long room the deep, silent sleeping of Prior Robert, worshipfully satisfied with all his deeds and words, untroubled by doubts, unintimidated by dreams. The prior habitually slept so soundly that it was easy to rise and slip away without fear of disturbing him. In his time, Cadfael had done it for less approved reasons than on this particular morning. So, possibly, had several of these innocent sleepers around him.

He went silently down the stairs and into the body of the

church, dark, empty and vast, lit only by the glow-worm lamps on the altars, minute stars in a vaulted night. His first destination, whenever he rose thus with ample time in hand, was always the altar of Saint Winifred, with its silver reliquary, where he stopped to exchange a little respectful and affectionate conversation with his countrywoman. He always spoke Welsh to her, the accents of his childhood and hers brought them into a welcome intimacy, in which he could ask her anything and never feel rebuffed. Even without his advocacy, he felt, her favour and protection would go with Hugh to Cambridge, but there was no harm in mentioning the need. It did not matter that Winifred's slender Welsh bones were still in the soil of Gwytherin, many miles away in North Wales, where her ministry had been spent. Saints are not corporeal, but presences, they can reach and touch wherever their grace and generosity desire.

It came into Cadfael's mind, on this particular morning, to say a word also for Generys, the stranger, the dark woman who was also Welsh, and whose beautiful, disturbing shadow haunted the imaginations of many others besides the husband who had abandoned her. Whether she lived out the remnant of her life somewhere far distant from her own country, in lands she had never thought to visit, among people she had never desired to know, or was lying now in that quiet corner of the cemetery here, removed from abbey land to lie in abbey land, the thought of her touched him nearly, and must surely stir the warmth and tenderness of the saint who had escaped a like exile. Cadfael put forward her case with confidence, on his knees on the lowest step of Winifred's altar, where Brother Rhun, when she had led him by the hand and healed his lameness, had laid his discarded crutches.

When he rose, the first faint pre-dawn softening of the darkness had grown into a pallid, pearly hint of light, drawing in the tall shapes of the nave windows clearly, and conjuring pillar and vault and altar out of the gloom. Cadfael passed down the nave to the west door, which was never fastened but in time of war or danger, and went out to the steps to look along the Foregate towards the bridge and the town.

They were coming. An hour and more yet to Prime, and only the first dim light by which to ride out, but he could already hear the hooves, crisp and rapid and faintly hollow on the bridge. He heard the change in their tread as they emerged upon the solid ground of the Foregate, and saw as it were an agitation of the darkness, movement without form, even before faint glints of lambent light on steel gave shape to their harness and brought them human out of the obscurity. No panoply, only the lance-pennants, two slung trumpets for very practical use, and the workmanlike light arms in which they rode. Thirty lances and five mounted archers. The remainder of the archers had gone ahead with the supplies. Hugh had done well by King Stephen, they made a very presentable company and numbered, probably, more than had been demanded.

Cadfael watched them pass, Hugh at the head on his favourite raw-boned grey. There were faces he knew among them, seasoned soldiers of the garrison, sons of merchant families from the town, expert archers from practice at the butts under the castle wall, young squires from the manors of the shire. In normal times the common service due from a crown manor would have been perhaps one esquire and his harness, and a barded horse, for forty days' service against the Welsh near Oswestry. Emergencies such as the present anarchy in East Anglia upset all normalities, but some length of service must have been stipulated even now. Cadfael had not asked for how many days these men might be at risk. There went Nigel Apsley among the lances, well-mounted and comely. That lad had made one tentative assay into treason, Cadfael remembered, only three years back, and no doubt was intent upon putting that memory well behind him by diligent service now. Well, if Hugh saw fit to make use of him, he had probably learned his lesson well, and was not likely to stray again. And he was a good man of his hands, athletic and strong, worth his place.

They passed, the drumming of their hooves dull on the packed, dry soil of the roadway, and the sound ebbed into distance along the wall of the enclave. Cadfael watched them until they almost faded from sight in the gloom, and then at the turn of the highway vanished altogether round the high precinct wall. The light came grudgingly, for the sky hung low in heavy cloud. This was going to be a dark and overcast day, possibly later a day of rain. Rain was the last thing King Stephen would want in the Fens, to reduce all land approaches and complicate all marshland paths. It costs much money to keep an army in the field, and though the king summoned numbers of men to give duty service this time, he would still be paying a large company of Flemish mercenaries, feared and

323

hated by the civilian population, and disliked even by the English who fought alongside them. Both rivals in the unending dispute for the crown made use of Flemings. To them the right side was the side that paid them, and could as easily change to the opposing party if they offered more; yet Cadfael in his time had known many mercenaries who held fast faithfully to their bargains, once struck, while barons and earls like de Mandeville changed direction as nimbly as weather-cocks for their own advantage.

They were gone, Hugh's compact and competent little company, even the last fading quiver and reverberation of earth under them stilled. Cadfael turned and went back through the great west door into the church.

There was another figure moving softly round the parish altar, a silent shadow in the dimness still lit only by the constant lamps. Cadfael followed him into the choir, and watched him light a twisted straw taper at the small red glow, and kindle the altar candles ready for Prime. It was a duty that was undertaken in a rota, and Cadfael had no idea at this moment whose turn this day might be, until he had advanced almost within touch of the man standing quietly, with head raised, gazing at the altar. An erect figure, lean but sinewy and strong, with big, shapely hands folded at his waist, and deepset eyes wide and fixed in a rapt dream. Brother Ruald heard the steady steps drawing near to him, but felt no need to turn his head or in any other way acknowledge a second presence. Sometimes he seemed almost unaware that there were others sharing this chosen life and this place of refuge with him. Only when Cadfael stood close beside him, sleeve to sleeve, and the movement made the candles flicker briefly, did Ruald look round with a sharp sigh, disturbed out of his dream.

'You are early up, Brother,' he said mildly. 'Could you not sleep?'

'I rose to see the sheriff and his company set out,' said Cadfael.

'They are gone already?' Ruald drew breath wonderingly, contemplating a life and a discipline utterly alien to his former or his present commitment. Half the life he could expect had been spent as a humble craftsman, for some obscure reason the least regarded among craftsmen, though why honest potters should be accorded such low status was a mystery to Cadfael. Now all the life yet remaining to him would be spent here in the devoted service of God. He had never so much as shot at

324

the butts for sport, as the young bloods of Shrewsbury's merchant families regularly did, or done combat with singlesticks or blunt swords at the common exercise-ground. 'Father Abbot will have prayers said daily for their safe and early return,' he said. 'And so will Father Boniface at the parish services.' He said it as one offering reassurance and comfort to a soul gravely concerned, but by something which touched him not at all. A narrow life his had been, Cadfael reflected, and looked back with gratitude at the width and depth of his own. And suddenly it began to seem to him as though all the passion there had been even in this man's marriage, all the blood that had burned in its veins, must have come from the woman.

'It is hoped,' he said shortly, 'that they come back as many as they have set out today.'

'So it is,' agreed Ruald meekly, 'yet they who take the sword, so it's written, will perish by the sword.'

'You will not find a good honest swordsman quarrelling with that,' said Cadfael. 'There are far worse ways.'

'That may well be true,' said Ruald very seriously. 'I do know that I have things to repent, things for which to do penance, fully as dreadful as the shedding of blood. Even in seeking to do what God required of me, did not I kill? Even if she is still living, there in the east, I took as it were the breath of life from her. I did not know it then. I could not even see her face clearly, to understand how I tore her. And here am I, unsure now whether I did well at all in following what I thought was a sacred beckoning, or whether I should not have forgone even this, for her sake. It may be God was putting me to the test. Tell me, Cadfael, you have lived in the world, travelled the world, known the extremes to which men can be driven, for good or ill. Do you think there was ever any man ready to forgo even heaven, to stay with another soul who loved him, in purgatory?'

To Cadfael, standing close beside him, this lean and limited man seemed to have grown taller and more substantial; or it might have been simply the growing strength and clarity of the light now gleaming in at every window, paling the candles on the altar. Certainly the mild and modest voice had never been so eloquent.

'Surely the range is so wide,' he said with slow and careful deliberation, 'that even that is possible. Yet I doubt if such a marvel was demanded of you.'

'In three days more,' said Ruald more gently, watching the flames he had lit burn tall and steady and golden, 'it will be Sailt Illtud's day. You are Welsh, you will know what is told of him. He had a wife, a noble lady, willing to live simply with him in a reed hut by the River Nadafan. An angel told him to leave his wife, and he rose up early in the morning, and drove her out into the world alone, thrusting her off, so we are told, very roughly, and went to receive the tonsure of a monk from Saint Dyfrig. I was not rough, yet that is my own case, for so I parted from Generys. Cadfael, what I would ask is, was that an angel who commanded it, or a devil?'

'You are posing a question,' said Cadfael, 'to which only God can know the answer, and with that we must be content. Certainly others before you have received the same call that came to you, and obeyed it. The great earl who founded this house and sleeps there between the altars, he, too, left his lady and put on the habit before he died.' Only three days before he died, actually, and with his wife's consent, but no need at this moment to say any word of that.

Never before had Ruald opened up the sealed places within him where his wife was hidden, even from his own sight, first by the intensity of his desire for holiness, then by the human fallibility of memory and feeling which had made it hard even to recall the lines of her face. Conversion had fallen on him like a stunning blow that had numbed all sensation, and now in due time he was coming back to life, remembrance filling his being with sharp and biting pain. Perhaps he never could have wrenched his heart open and spoken about her, except in this timeless and impersonal solitude, with no witness but one.

For he spoke as if to himself, clearly and simply, rather recalling than recounting. 'I had no intent to hurt her – Generys ... I could not choose but go, yet there are ways and ways of taking leave. I was not wise. I had no skills, I did not do it well. And I had taken her from her own people, and she content all these years with little reward but the man I am, and wanting nothing more. I can never have given her a tenth part, not a mere tithe, of all that she gave me.'

Cadfael was motionless, listening as the quiet voice continued its threnody. 'Dark, she was, very dark, very beautiful. Everyone would call her so, but now I see that none ever knew how beautiful, for to the world outside it was as if she went veiled, and only I ever saw her uncover her face. Or perhaps, to children ·– to them she might show herself unconcealed. We never had children, we were not so blessed. That made her tender and loving to those her neighbours bore. She is not yet past all hope of bearing children of her own. Who knows but with another man, she might yet conceive.'

'And you would be glad for her?' said Cadfael, so softly as not to break this thread.

'I would be glad. I would be wholly glad. Why should she continue barren, because I am fulfilled? Or bound, where I am free? I never thought of that when the longing came on me.'

'And do you believe she told you truth, the last time, saying that she had a lover?'

'Yes,' said Ruald, simply and without hesitation, 'I do believe. Not that she might not lie to me then, for I was crass and did her bitter offence, as now I understand, even by visiting her then I offended. I believe because of the ring. You remember it? The ring that Sulien brought back with him when he came from Ramsey.'

'I remember it,' said Cadfael.

The dormitory bell was just ringing to rouse the brothers for Prime. In some remote corner of their consciousness it sounded very faintly and distantly, and neither of them heeded it.

'It never left her finger, from the time I put it there. I would not have thought it could be eased over her knuckle, after so long. The first time that I visited her with Brother Paul I know she was wearing it as she always did. But the second time ... I had forgotten, but now I understand. It was not on her finger when I saw her the last time. She had stripped her marriage to me from her finger with the ring, and given it to someone else, as she stripped me from her life, and offered it to him. Yes, I believe Generys had a lover. One worth the loving, she said. With all my heart I hope he has proved so to her.'

327

Chapter Ten

HROUGHOUT THE ceremonies and services and readings of Saint Winifred's day a morsel of Cadfael's mind, persistent and unrepentant, occupied itself, much against his will, with matters which had nothing to do with the genuine adoration he had for his own special saint, whom he thought of always as she had been when her first brief life was so brutally ended: a girl of about seventeen, fresh, beautiful and radiant, brimming over with kindness and sweetness as the waters of her well brimmed always sparkling and pure, defying frost, radiating health of body and soul. He would have liked his mind to be wholly filled with her all this day, but obstinately it turned to Ruald's ring, and the pale circle on the finger from which Generys had ripped it, abandoning him as he had abandoned her.

It became even more clear that there had indeed been another man. With him she had departed, to settle, it seemed in Peterborough, or somewhere in that region, perhaps a place even more exposed to the atrocities of de Mandeville's barbarians. And when the reign of murder and terror began, she and her man had taken up their new, shallow roots, turned what valuables they had into money, and removed further from the threat, leaving the ring for young Sulien to find, and bring home with him for Ruald's deliverance. That, at least, was surely what Ruald believed. Every word he had spoken before the altar that morning bore the stamp of sincerity. So now much depended on the matter of forty miles or so between

Cambridge and Peterborough. Not such a short distance, after all, but if all went well with the king's business, and he thought fit soon to dispense with a force that could be better employed keeping an eye on the Earl of Chester, a passage by way of Peterborough would not greatly lengthen the way home.

And if the answer was yes, confirming every word of Sulien's story, then Generys was indeed still living, and not abandoned to loneliness, and the dead woman of the Potter's Field was still left adrift and without a name. But in that case, why should Sulien have stirred himself so resolutely to prove Britric, who was nothing to him, as innocent as Ruald? How could he have known, and why should he even have conceived the possibility, that the pedlar was innocent? Or that the woman Gunnild was alive, or even might be alive?

And if the answer was no, and Sulien had never spent the night with the silversmith in Peterborough, never begged the ring of him, but made up his story in defence of Ruald out of whole cloth, and backed it with a ring he had had in his possession all along, then surely he had been weaving a rope for his own neck while he was so busy unpicking someone else's bonds.

But as yet there was no answer, and no way of hastening it, and Cadfael did his best to pay proper attention to the office, but Saint Winifred's feast passed in distracted thought. In the days that followed he went about his work in the herbarium conscientiously but without his usual hearty concentration, and was taciturn and slightly absent-minded with Brother Winfrid, whose placidity of temperament and boyish appetite for work fortunately enabled him to ride serenely through other men's changes of mood without losing his own equilibrium.

Now that Cadfael came to consider the early part of the November calender, it seemed to be populated chiefly by Welsh saints. Ruald had reminded him that the sixth day was dedicated to Saint Illtud, who had obeyed his dictatorial angel with such alacrity, and so little consideration for his wife's feelings in the matter. No great devotion was paid to him in English houses, perhaps, but Saint Tysilio, whose day came on the eighth, had a rather special significance here on the borders of Powys, and his influence spilled over the frontier into the neighbouring shires. For the centre of his ministry was the chief church of Powys at Meifod, no great way into Wales, and the saint was reputed to have had military virtues as well as sacred, and to have fought on the Christian side at the battle of

Maserfield, by Oswestry, where the royal saint, Oswald, was captured and martyred by the pagans. So a measure of respect was paid to his feast day, and the Welsh of the town and the Foregate came to Mass that morning in considerable numbers. But for all that, Cadfael had hardly expected the attendance of one worshipper from further afield.

She rode in at the gatehouse, pillion behind an elderly groom, in good time before Mass, and was lifted down respectfully to the cobbles of the court by the younger groom who followed on a second stout horse, with the maid Gunnild perched behind him. Both women stood shaking out their skirts for a moment before they crossed demurely to the church, the lady before, the maid attentive and dutiful a pace behind her, while the grooms spoke a word or two to the porter, and then led away the horses to the stable yard. The perfect picture of a young woman conforming to every social sanction imposing rules upon her bearing and movements, with her maid for guardian and companion, and her grooms for escort. Pernel was ensuring that this venture out of her usual ambience should be too correct in every detail to attract comment. She might be the eldest of the brood at Withington, but she was still very young, and it was imperative to temper the natural directness and boldness with caution. It had to be admitted that she did it with considerable style and grace, and had an admirable abettor in the experienced Gunnild. They crossed the great court with hands folded and eyes cast down modestly, and vanished into the church by the south door without once risking meeting the gaze of any of these celibates who moved about court and cloister round them.

Now if she has in mind what I think she has, Cadfael reflected, watching them go, she will have need of all Gunnild's worldly wisdom to abet her own good sense and resolution. And I do believe the woman is devoted to her, and will make a formidable protective dragon if ever there's need.

He caught a brief glimpse of her again as he entered the church with the brothers, and passed through to his place in the choir. The nave was well filled with lay worshippers, some standing beside the parish altar, where they could see through to the high altar within, some grouped around the stout round pillars that held up the vault. Pernel was kneeling where the light, by chance, fell on her face through the opening from the lighted choir. Her eyes were closed, but her lips still. Her prayers were not in words. She looked very grave, thus austerely attired for church, her soft brown hair hidden within a white wimple, and the hood of her cloak drawn over all, for it was none too warm in the church. She looked like some very young novice nun, her round face more childlike than ever, but the set of her lips had a mature and formidable firmness. Close at her back Gunnild kneeled, and her eyes, though half veiled by long lashes, were open and bright, and possessively steady upon her lady. Woe betide anyone who attempted affront to Pernel Otmere while her maid was by!

After Mass Cadfael looked for them again, but they were hidden among the mass of people gathering slowly to leave by the west door. He went out by the south door and the cloisters, and emerged into the court to find her waiting quietly there for the procession of the brothers to separate to their various duties. It did not surprise him when at sight of him her face sharpened and her eyes brightened, and she took a single step towards him, enough to arrest him.

'Brother, may I speak with you? I have asked leave of the lord abbot.' She sounded practical and resolute, but she had not risked the least indiscretion, it seemed. 'I made so bold as to accost him just now, when he left,' she said. 'It seems that he already knew my name and family. That can only have been from you, I think.'

'Father Abbot is fully informed,' said Cadfael, 'with all the matter that brought me to visit you. He is concerned for justice, as we are. To the dead and to the living. He will not stand in the way of any converse that may serve that end.'

'He was kind,' she said, and suddenly warmed and smiled. 'And now we have observed all the proper forms, and I can breathe again. Where may we talk?'

He took them to his workshop in the herb garden. It was becoming too chilly to linger and converse outdoors, his brazier was alight but damped down within, and with the timber doors wide open, Brother Winfrid returning to the remaining patch of rough pre-winter digging just outside the enclosure wall, and Gunnild standing at a discreet distance within, not even Prior Robert could have raised his brows at the propriety of this conference. Pernel had been wise in applying directly to the superior, who already knew of the role she had played, and certainly had no reason to disapprove of it. Had she not gone far to save both a body and a soul? And she had brought the one, if not visibly the other, to show to him.

'Now,' said Cadfael, tickling the brazier to show a gleam of

331

red through its controlling turves, 'sit down and be easy, the both of you. And tell me what you have in mind, to bring you here to worship when, as I know, you have a church and a priest of your own. I know, for it belongs, like Upton, to this house of Saint Peter and Saint Paul. And your priest is a rare man and a scholar, as I know from Brother Anselm, who is his friend.'

'So he is,' said Pernel warmly, 'and you must not think I have not talked with him, very earnestly, about this matter.' She had settled herself decorously at one end of the bench against the wall of the hut, composed and erect, her face bright against the dark timber, her hood fallen back on her shoulders. Gunnild, invited by a smile and a gesture, glided out of shadow and sat down on the other end of the bench, leaving a discreet gap between the two of them to mark the difference in their status, but not too wide, to underline the depth of her alliance with her mistress. 'It was Father Ambrosius,' said Pernel, 'who said the word that brought me here on this day of all days. Father Ambrosius studied for some years in Brittany. You know, Brother, whose day we are celebrating?'

'I should,' said Cadfael, relinquising the bellows that had raised a red glow in his brazier. 'He is as Welsh as I am, and a close neighbour to this shire. What of Saint Tysilio?'

'But did you know that he is said to have gone over to Brittany to fly from a woman's persecution? And in Brittany they also tell of his life, like the readings you will hear today at Collations. But there they know him by another name. They call him Sulien.'

'Oh, no,' she said, seeing how speculatively Cadfael was eyeing her, 'I did not take it as a sign from heaven, when Father Ambrosius told me that. It was just that the name prompted me to act, where before I was only wondering and fretting. Why not on his day? For I think, Brother, that you believe that Sulien Blount is not what he seems, not as open as he seems. I have been thinking and asking about this matter. I think things are so inclining, that he may be suspect of too much knowledge, in this matter of the poor dead woman your plough team found under the headland in the Potter's Field. Too much knowledge, perhaps even guilt. Is it true?'

'Too much knowledge, certainly,' said Cadfael. 'Guilt, that is mere conjecture, yet there is ground for suspicion.' He owed her honesty, and she expected it.

'Will you tell me,' she said, 'the whole story? For I know only what is gossiped around. Let me understand whatever danger he may be in. Guilt or no, he would not let another man be blamed unjustly.'

Cadfael told her the whole of it, from the first furrow cut by the abbey plough. She listened attentively and seriously, her round brow furrowed with thought. She could not and did not believe any evil of the young man who had visited her for so generous a purpose, but neither did she ignore the reasons why others might have doubts of him. At the end she drew breath long and softly, and gnawed her lip for a moment, pondering.

'Do *you* believe him guilty?' she asked then, point blank.

'I believe he has knowledge which he has not seen fit to reveal. More than that I will not say. All depends on whether he told us the truth about the ring.'

'But Brother Ruald believes him?' she said.

'Without question.'

'And he has known him from a child.'

'And may be partial,' said Cadfael, smiling. 'But yes, he has more knowledge of the boy than either you or I, and plainly expects nothing less than truth from him.'

'And so would I. But one thing I wonder at,' said Pernel very earnestly. 'You say that you think he knew of this matter before he went to visit his home, though *he* said he heard of it only there. If you are right, if he heard it from Brother Jerome before he went to ask leave to visit Longner, why did he not bring forth the ring at once, and tell what he had to tell? Why leave it until the next day? Whether he got the ring as he said, or had it in his possession from long before, he could have spared Brother Ruald one more night of wretchedness. So gentle a soul as he seems, why should he leave a man to bear such a burden an hour longer than he need, let alone a day?'

It was the one consideration which Cadfael had had at the back of his mind ever since the occasion itself, but did not yet know what to make of it. If Pernel's mind was keeping in reserve the same doubt, let her speak for him, and probe beyond where he had yet cared to go. He said simply: 'I have not pursued it. It would entail questioning Brother Jerome, which I should be loath to do until I am more sure of my ground. But I can think of only one reason. For some motive of his own, he wished to preserve the appearance of having heard of the case only when he paid his visit to Longner.'

'Why should he want that?' she challenged.

333

'I suppose that he might well want to talk to his brother before he committed himself to anything. He had been away more than a year, he would want to ensure that his family was in no way threatened by a matter of which he had only just learned. Naturally he would be tender of their interests, all the more because he had not seen them for so long.'

To that she agreed, with a thoughtful and emphatic nod of her head. 'Yes, so he would. But I can think of another reason why he delayed, and I am sure you are thinking of it, too.'

'And that is?'

'That he had not got it,' said Pernel firmly, 'and could not show it, until he had been home to fetch it.'

She had indeed spoken out bluntly and fearlessly, and Cadfael could not but admire her singlemindedness. Her sole belief was that Sulien was clean of any shadow of guilt, her sole purpose to prove it to the world, but her confidence in the efficacy of truth drove her to go headlong after it, certain that when found it must be on her side.

'I know,' she said, 'I am making a case that may seem hurtful to him, but in the end it cannot be, because I am sure he has done no wrong. There is no way but to look at every possibility. I know you said that Sulien grew to love that woman, and said so himself, and if she did give her ring to another man, for spite against her husband, yes, it could have been to Sulien. But equally it could have been to someone else. And though I would not try to lift the curse from one man by throwing it upon another, Sulien was not the only young man close neighbour to the potter. Just as likely to be drawn to a woman every account claims was beautiful. If Sulien has guilty knowledge he cannot reveal, he could as well be shielding a brother as protecting himself. I cannot believe,' she said vehemently, 'that you have not thought of that possibility.'

'I have thought of many possibilities,' agreed Cadfael placidly, 'without much by way of fact to support any. Yes, for either himself or his brother he might lie. Or for Ruald. But only if he knows, as surely as the sun will rise tomorrow, that our poor dead lady is indeed Generys. And never forget, there is also the possibility, however diminished since his efforts for Britric, that he was *not* lying, that Generys *is* alive and well, somewhere there in the eastlands, with the man she chose to follow. And we may never, never know who was the dark-haired woman someone buried with reverence in the Potter's Field.'

'But you do not believe that,' she said with certainty.

'I think truth, like the burgeoning of a bulb under the soil, however deeply sown, will make its way to the light.'

'And there is nothing we can do to hasten it,' said Pernel, and heaved a resigned sigh.

'At present, nothing but wait.'

'And pray, perhaps?' she said.

Cadfael could not choose but wonder, none the less, what she would do next, for inaction would be unbearably irksome to her now that her whole energy was engaged for this young man she had seen only once. Whether Sulien had paid as acute attention to her there was no knowing, but it was in Cadfael's mind that sooner or later he would have to, for she had no intention of turning back. It was also in his mind that the boy might do a good deal worse. If, that is, he came out of this web of mystery and deceit with a whole skin and a quiet mind, something he certainly did not possess at present.

From Cambridge and the Fens there was no news. No one had yet expected any. But travellers from eastward reported that the weather was turning foul, with heavy rains and the first frosts of winter. No very attractive prospect for an army floundering in watery reaches unfamiliar to them but known to the elusive enemy. Cadfael bethought him of his promise to Hugh, by this time more than a week absent, and asked leave to go up into the town and visit Aline and his godson. The sky was overclouded, the weather from the east gradually moving in upon Shrewsbury in a very fine rain, hardly more than mist, that clung in the hair and the fibres of clothing, and barely darkened the slate-grey earth of the Foregate. In the Potter's Field the winter crop was already sown, and there would be cattle grazing the lower strip of pasture. Cadfael had not been back to see it with his own eyes, but with the inner eye he saw it very clearly, dark, rich soil soon to bring forth new life; green, moist turf and tangled briary headland under the ridge of bushes and trees. That it had once held an unblessed grave would soon be forgotten. The grey, soft day made for melancholy. It was pleasure and relief to turn in at the gate of Hugh's yard, and be met and embraced about the thighs by a small, boisterous boy yelling delighted greetings. Another month or so, and Giles would be four years old. He took a first grip on a fistful of Cadfael's habit, and towed him gleefully into the house. With Hugh absent, Giles was the man of the house, and well aware of all his duties and privileges. He made Cadfael free of the amenities of his manor with solemn dignity, seated him ceremoniously, and himself made off to the buttery to fetch a beaker of ale, bearing it back cautiously in both still-rounded, infantile hands, over-filled and in danger of spilling, with his primrose hair erect and rumpled, and the tip of his tongue braced in the corner of his mouth. His mother followed him into the hall at a discreet distance, to avoid upsetting either his balance or his dignity. She was smiling at Cadfael over her son's fair head, and suddenly the radiant likeness between them shone on Cadfael like the sun bursting out of clouds. The round, earnest face with its full childish cheeks, and the pure oval with its wide brow and tapered chin, so different and yet so similar, shared the pale, lustrous colouring and the lily-smooth skin, the refinement of feature and steadiness of gaze. Hugh is indeed a lucky man, Cadfael thought, and then drew in cautious breath on a superstitious prayer that such luck should stand by him still, wherever he might be at this moment.

If Aline had any misgivings, they were not allowed to show themselves. She sat down with him cheerfully as always, and talked of the matters of the household and the affairs at the castle under Alan Herbard, with her usual practical good sense; and Giles, instead of clambering into this godfather's lap as he might well have done some weeks previously, climbed up to sit beside him on the bench like a man and a contemporary.

'Yes,' said Aline, 'there is a bowman of the company has ridden in only this afternoon, the first word we've had. He got a graze in one skirmish they had, and Hugh sent him home, seeing he was fit to ride, and they had left changes of horses along the way. He will heal well, Alan says, but it weakens his drawing arm.'

'And how are they faring?' Cadfael asked. 'Have they managed to bring Geoffrey into the open?'

She took her head decisively. 'Very little chance of it. The waters are up everywhere, and it's still raining. All they can do is lie in wait for the raiding parties when they venture out to plunder the villages. Even there the king is at a disadvantage, seeing Geoffrey's men know every usable path, and can bog them down in the marshes only too easily. But they have picked off a few such small parties. It isn't what Stephen wants, but it's all he can get. Ramsey is quite cut off, no one can hope to fetch them out of there.'

336

'And this tedious business of ambush and waiting,' said Cadfael, 'wastes too much time. Stephen cannot afford to keep it up too long. Costly and ineffective as it is, he'll have to withdraw to try some other measure. If Geoffrey's numbers have grown so great, he must be getting supplies now from beyond the Fen villages. His supply lines might be vulnerable. And Hugh? He is well?'

'Wet and muddy and cold, I daresay,' said Aline, ruefully smiling, 'and probably cursing heartily, but he's whole and well, or was when his archer left him. That's one thing to be said for this tedious business, as you called it, such losses as there are have been de Mandeville's. But too few to do him much harm.'

'Not enough,' Cadfael said consideringly, 'to be worth the king's while for much longer. I think, Aline, you may not have to wait long to have Hugh home again.'

Giles pressed a little closer and more snugly into his godfather's side, but said nothing. 'And you, my lord,' said Cadfael, 'will have to hand over your manor again, and give account of your stewardship. I hope you have not let things get out of hand while the lord sheriff's been away.'

Hugh's deputy made a brief sound indicative of scorn at the very idea that his strict rule should ever be challenged. 'I am *good* at it,' he stated firmly. 'My father says so. He says I keep a tighter rein than he does. And use the spur more.'

'Your father,' said Cadfael gravely, 'is always fair and ungrudging even to those who excel him.' He was aware, through some alchemy of proximity and affection, of the smile Aline was not allowing to show in her face.

'Especially with the woman,' said Giles complacently.

'Now that,' said Cadfael, 'I can well believe.'

King Stephen's tenacity, in any undertaking, had always been precarious. Not want of courage, certainly, not even want of determination, caused him to abandon sieges after a mere few days and rush away to some more promising assault. It was rather impatience, frustrated optimism and detestation of being inactive that made him quit one undertaking for another. On occasion, as at Oxford, he could steel himself to persist, if the situation offered a reasonable hope of final triumph, but where stalemate was obvious he soon wearied and went off to fresh fields. In the wintry rains of the Fens anger and personal hatred kept him constant longer than usual, but his successes

337

were meagre, and it was borne in upon him by the last week of November that he could not hope to finish the work. Floundering in the quagmires of those bleak levels, his forces had certainly closed in with enough method and strength to compress de Mandeville's territory, and had picked off a fair number of his rogue troops when they ventured out on to drier ground, but it was obvious that the enemy had ample supplies, and could hold off for a while even from raiding. There was no hope of digging them out of their hole. Stephen turned to changed policies with the instant vigour he could find at need. He wanted his feudal levies, especially any from potentially vulnerable regions, such as those neighbour to the Welsh, or to dubious friends like the Earl of Chester, back where they were most useful. Here in the Fens he proposed to marshal an army rather of builders than soldiers, throw up a ring of hasty but well-placed strongpoints to contain the outlaw territory, compress it still further wherever they could, and menace Geoffrey's outside supply lines when his stores ran low. Manned by the experienced Flemish mercenaries, familiar with fighting in flat lands and among complex waterways, such a ring of forts could hold what had been gained through the winter, until conditions were more favourable to open manoeuvring.

It was nearing the end of November when Hugh found himself and his levy briskly thanked and dismissed. He had lost no men killed, and had only a few minor wounds and grazes to show, and was heartily glad to withdraw his men from wallowing in the quagmires round Cambridge and set out with them north-westward towards Huntingdon, where the royal castle had kept the town relatively secure and the roads open. From there he sent them on due west for Kettering, while he rode north, heading for Peterborough.

He had not paused to consider, until he rode over the bridge of the Nene and up into the town, what he expected to find there. Better, perhaps, to approach thus without expectations of any kind. The road from the bridge brought him up into the marketplace, which was alive and busy. The burgesses who had elected to stay were justified, the town had so far proved too formidable to be a temptation to de Mandeville while there were more isolated and defenceless victims to be found. Hugh found stabling for his horse, and went afoot to look for Priestgate.

338

The shop was there, or at least a flourishing silversmith's shop was there, open for business and showing a prosperous front to the world. That was the first confirmation. Hugh went in, and enquired of the young fellow sitting at work in the back of the shop, under a window that lit his workbench, for Master John Hinde. The name was received blithely, and the young man laid down his tools and went out by a rear door to call his master. No question of any discrepancy here, the shop and the man were here to be found, just as Sulien had left them when he made his way west from Ramsey.

Master John Hinde, when he followed his assistant in from his private quarters, was plainly a man of substance in the town, one who might well be a good patron to his favoured religious house, and on excellent terms with abbots. He was perhaps fifty, a lean, active, upright figure in a rich furred gown. Quick dark eyes in a thin, decisive face summed up Hugh in a glance.

'I am John Hinde. How can I help you?' The marks of the wearisome lurking in wet, windswept ambushes, and occasional hard riding in the open, were there to be seen in Hugh's clothes and harness. 'You come from the king's muster? We have heard he's withdrawing his host. Not to leave the field clear for de Mandeville, I hope?'

'No such matter,' Hugh assured him, 'though I'm sent back to take care of my own field. No, you'll be none the worse for our leaving, the Flemings will be between you and danger, with at least one strong-point well placed to pen them into their island. There's little more or better he could do now, with the winter coming.'

'Well, we live as candles in the breath of God,' said the silversmith philosophically, 'wherever we are. I've known it too long to be easily frightened off. And what's your need, sir, before you head for home?'

'Do you remember,' said Hugh, 'about the first or second day of October, a young monk sheltering here with you overnight? It was just after the sack of Ramsey, the boy came from there, commended to you, he said, by his abbot. Abbot Walker was sending him home to the brother house at Shrewsbury, to take the news of Ramsey with him along the way. You remember the man?'

'Clearly,' said John Hinde, without hesitation. 'He was just at the end of his novitiate. The brothers were scattering for safety. None of us is likely to forget that time. I would have

339

lent the lad a horse for the first few miles, but he said he would do better afoot, for they were all about the open countryside like bees in swarm then. What of him? I hope he reached Shrewsbury safely?'

'He did, and brought the news wherever he passed. Yes, he's well, though he's left the Order since, and returned to his brother's manor.'

'He told me then he was in doubts if he was on the right way,' agreed the silversmith. 'Walter was not the man to hold on to a youngster against his inclination. So what is it I can add, concerning this youth?'

'Did he,' asked Hugh deliberately, 'notice a particular ring in your shop? And did he remark upon it, and ask after the woman from whom you had bought it, only ten days or so earlier? A plain silver ring set with a small yellow stone, and bearing initials engraved within it? And did he beg it of you, because he had known the woman well from his childhood, and kept a kindness for her? Is any part of this truth?'

There was a long moment of silence while the silversmith looked back at him, eye to eye, with intelligent speculation sharpening the lean lines of his face. It is possible that he was considering retreat from any further confidence, for want of knowing what might result from his answers for a young man perhaps innocently entrammelled in some misfortune no fault of his own. Men of business learn to be chary of trusting too many too soon. But if so, he discarded the impulse of denial, after studying Hugh with close attention and arriving, it seemed, at a judgement.

'Come within!' he said then, with equal deliberation and equal certainty. And he turned towards the door from which he had emerged, inviting Hugh with a gesture of his hand. 'Come! Let me hear more. Now we have gone so far, we may as well go further together.'

Chapter Eleven

ULIEN HAD put off the habit, but the hourly order that went with it was not so easy to discard. He found himself waking at midnight for Matins and Lauds, and listening for the bell, and was shaken and daunted by the silence and isolation where there should have been the sense of many brothers stirring and sighing, a soft murmur of voices urging the heavy sleepers, and in the dimness at the head of the night stairs the glow of the little lamp to light them down safely to the church. Even the freedom of his own clothes sat uneasily on him still, after a year of the skirted gown. He had put away one life without being able to take up the old where he had abandoned it, and making a new beginning was unexpected effort and pain. Moreover, things at Longner had changed since his departure to Ramsey. His brother was married to a young wife, settled in his lordship, and happy in the prospect of an heir, for Jehane was pregnant. The Longner lands were a very fair holding, but not great enough to support two families, even if such sharing had ever promised well, and a younger son would have to work out an independent life for himself, as younger sons had always had to do. The cloister he had sampled and abandoned. His family bore with him tolerantly and patiently until he should find his way. Eudo was the most open and amiable of young men, and fond of his brother. Sulien was welcome to all the time he needed, and until he made up his mind Longner was his home, and glad to have him back.

341

But no one could quite be sure that Sulien was glad. He filled his days with whatever work offered, in the stables and byres, exercising hawk and hound, lending a hand with sheep and cattle in the fields, carting timber for fence repairs and fuel, whatever was needed he was willing and anxious to do, as though he had stored within him such a tension of energy that he must at all costs grind it out of his body or sicken with it.

Withindoors he was quiet company, but then he had always been the quiet one. He was gentle and attentive to his mother, and endured stoically hours of her anguished presence, which Eudo tended to avoid when he could. The steely control with which she put aside every sign of pain was admirable, but almost harder to bear than open distress. Sulien marvelled and endured with her, since there was nothing more he could do for her. And she was gracious and dignified, but whether she was glad of his company or whether it added one more dimension to her burden, there was no telling. He had always supposed that Eudo was her favourite and had the lion's share of her love. That was the usual order of things, and Sulien had no fault to find with it.

His abstraction and quietness were hardly noticed by Eudo and Jehane. They were breeding, they were happy, they found life full and pleasant, and took it for granted that a youth who had mistakenly wasted a year of his life on a vocation of which he had thought better only just in time, should spend these first weeks of freedom doing a great deal of hard thinking about his future. So they left him to his thoughts, accommodated him with the hard labour he seemed to need, and waited with easy affection for him to emerge into the open in his own good time.

He rode out one day in mid-November with orders to Eudo's herdsman in the outlying fields of Longner land to eastward, along the River Tern, almost as far afield as Upton, and having discharged his errand, turned to ride back, and then instead wheeled the horse again and rode on very slowly, leaving the village of Upton on his left hand, hardly knowing what it was he had in mind. There was no haste, all his own industry could not convince him that he was needed at home, and the day, though cloudy, was dry, and the air mild. He rode on, gradually drawing a little further from the river bank, and only when he topped the slight ridge which offered the highest point in these flat, open fields did he realise where he was heading. Before him, at no great distance, the roofs of Withington showed through a frail filigree of naked branches, and the

342

squat, square tower of the church just rose above the grove of low trees.

He had not realised how constantly she had been in his mind since his visit here, lodged deep in his memory, unobtrusive but always present. He had only to close his eyes now, and he could see her face as clearly as when she had first caught the sound of his horse's hooves on the hard soil of the courtyard, and turned to see who was riding in. The very way she halted and turned to him who was like a flower swaying in the lightest of winds, and the face she raised to him was open like a flower, without reserve or fear, so that at that first glance he had seemed to see deep into her being. As though her flesh, though rounded and full and firm, had been translucent from without and luminous from within. There had been a little pale sunshine that day, and it had gained radiance from her eyes, russet-gold eyes, and reflected light from her broad brow under the soft brown hair. She had smiled at him with that same ungrudging radiance, shedding warmth about her to melt the chill of anxiety from his mind and heart, she who had never set eyes on him before, and must not be made ever to see him or think of him again.

But he had thought of her, whether he willed it or not.

He had hardly realised now that he was still riding towards the further edge of the village, where the manor lay. The line of the stockade rose out of the fields, the steep pitch of the roof within, the pattern of field strips beyond the enclosure, a square plot of orchard trees, all gleaned and almost leafless. He had splashed through the first stream almost without noticing, but the second, so close now to the wide-open gate in the manor fence, caused him to baulk suddenly and consider what he was doing, and must not do, had no right to do.

He could see the courtyard within the stockade, and the elder boy carefully leading a pony in decorously steady circles, with the small girl on its back. Regularly they appeared, passed and vanished, to reappear at the far rim of their circle and vanish again, the boy giving orders importantly, the child with both small fists clutched in the pony's mane. Once Gunnild came into view for a moment, smiling, watching her youngest charge, astride like a boy, kicking round bare heels into the pony's fat sides. Then she drew back again to clear their exercise ground, and passed from his sight. With an effort, Sulien came to himself, and swung away from them towards the village.

And there she was, coming towards him from the direction of the church, with a basket on her arm under the folds of her cloak, and her brown hair braided in a thick plait and tied with a scarlet cord. Her eyes were on him. She had known him before ever he was aware of her, and she approached him without either hastening or lingering, with confident pleasure. Just as he had been seeing her with his mind's eye a moment earlier, except that then she had worn no cloak, and her hair had been loose about her shoulders. But her face had the same open radiance, her eyes the same quality of letting him into her heart.

A few paces from where he had reined in she halted, and they looked at each other for a long moment in silence. Then she said: 'Were you really going away again, now that you've come? Without a word? Without coming in?'

He knew that he ought to claw out of some astute corner of his mind wit enough and words enough to show that his presence here had nothing to do with her or his former visit, some errand that would account for his having to ride by here, and make it urgent that he should be on his way home again without delay. But he could not find a single word, however false, however rough, to thrust her away from him.

'Come and be acquainted with my father,' she said simply. 'He will be glad, he knows why you came before. Of course Gunnild told him, how else do you think she got horse and groom to bring her into Shrewsbury, to the sheriff? None of us need ever go behind my father's back. I know you asked her to leave you out of it with Hugh Beringar, and so she did, but in this house we don't have secrets, we have no cause.'

That he could well believe. Her nature spoke for her sire, a constant and carefree inheritance. And though he knew it was none the less incumbent upon him to draw away from her to avoid her and leave her her peace of mind, and relieve her parents of any future grief on her behalf, he could not do it. He dismounted, and walked with her, bridle in hand and still mute and confounded, in at the gate of Withington.

Brother Cadfael saw them in church together at the sung Mass for Saint Cecilia's day, the twenty-second of November. It was a matter for conjecture why they should choose to attend here at the abbey, when they had parish churches of their own. Perhaps Sulien still kept a precarious fondness for the Order he had left, for its stability and certainty, not to be found in the world outside, and still felt the need to make contact with it from time to time, while he reorientated his life. Perhaps she wanted Brother Anselm's admired music, especially on this day of all the saints' days. Or perhaps, Cadfael reflected, they found this a convenient and eminently respectable meeting-place for two who had not yet progressed so far as to be seen together publicly nearer home. Whatever the reason, there they were in the nave, close to the parish altar where they could see through into the choir and hear the singing unmarred by the mute spots behind some of the massive pillars. They stood close, but not touching each other, not even the folds of a sleeve brushing, very still, very attentive, with solemn faces and wide, clear eyes. Cadfael saw the girl for once grave, though she still shone, and the boy for once eased and tranquil, though the shadow of his disquiet still set its finger in the small furrow between his brows.

When the brothers emerged after service Sulien and Pernel had already left by the west door, and Cadfael went to his work in the garden wondering how often they had met thus, and how the first meeting had come about, for though the two had never looked at each other or touched hands during worship, or given any sign of being aware each of the other's presence, yet there was something about their very composure and the fixity of their attention that bound them together beyond doubt.

It was not difficult, he found, to account for this ambivalent aura they carried with them, so clearly together, so tacitly apart. There would be no resolution, no solving of the dichotomy, until the one devouring question was answered. Ruald, who knew the boy best, had never found the least occasion to doubt that what he told was truth, and the simplicity of Ruald's acceptance of that certainty was Ruald's own salvation. But Cadfael could not see certainty yet upon either side. And Hugh and his lances and archers were still many miles away, their fortune still unknown, and nothing to be done but wait.

On the last day of November an archer of the garrison, soiled and draggled from the roads, rode in from the east, pausing first at Saint Giles to cry the news that the sheriff's levy was not far behind him, intact as it had left the town, apart from a few grazes and bruises, that the king's shire levies, those most needed elsewhere, were dismissed to their own garrisons at least for the winter, and his tactics changed from the attempt to

345

dislodge and destroy his enemy to measures to contain him territorially and limit the damage he could do his neighbours. A campaign postponed rather than ended, but it meant the safe return of the men of Shropshire to their own pastures. By the time the courier rode on into the Foregate the news was already flying ahead of him, and he eased his speed to cry it again as he passed, and answer some of the eager questions called out to him by the inhabitants. They came running out of their houses and shops and tofts, tools in hand, the women from their kitchens, the smith from his forge, Father Boniface from his room over the north porch of the abbey church, in a great buzz of relief and delight, passing details back and forth to one another as they had snatched them by chance from the courier's lips.

By the time the solitary rider was past the abbey gatehouse and heading for the bridge, the orderly thudding of hooves and the faint jingle of harness had reached Saint Giles, and the populace of the Foregate stayed to welcome the returning company. Work could wait for an hour or two. Even within the abbey pale the news was going round, and brothers gathered outside the wall unreproved, to watch the return. Cadfael, who had risen to see them depart, came thankfully to see them safely home again.

They came, understandably, a little less immaculate in their accoutrements then they had departed. The lance pennants were soiled and frayed, even tattered here and there, some of the light armour dinted and dulled, a few heads bandaged, one or two wrists slung for support, and several beards where none had been before. But they rode in good order and made a very respectable show, in spite of the travel stains and the mud imperfectly brushed out of their garments. Hugh had overtaken his men well before they reached Coventry, and made a sufficient halt there to allow rest and grooming to men and horses alike. The baggage carts and the foot bowmen could take their time from Coventry on, where the roads were open and good, and word of their safety had gone before them.

Riding at the head of the column, Hugh had discarded his mail to ride at ease in his own coat and cloak. He looked alert and stimulated, faintly flushed with pleasure from the hum and babel of relief and joy that accompanied him along the Foregate, and would certainly be continued through the town. Hugh would always make a wry mock of praise and plaudits, well aware of how narrowly they were separated from the rumblings of reproach that might have greeted him had he lost men, in however desperate an encounter. But it was human to take pleasure in knowing he had lost none. The return from Lincoln, almost three years ago, had not been like this; he could afford to enjoy his welcome.

At the abbey gatehouse he looked for Cadfael among the bevy of shaven crowns, and found him on the steps of the west door. Hugh said a word into his captain's ear, and drew his grey horse out of the line to rein in alongside, though he did not dismount. Cadfael reached up to the bridle in high content.

'Well, lad, this is a welcome sight if ever there was. Barely a scratch on you, and not a man missing! Who would want more?'

'What I wanted,' said Hugh feelingly, 'was de Mandeville's hide, but he wears it still, and devil a thing can Stephen do about it until we can flush the rat out of his hole. You've seen Aline? All's well there?'

'All's well enough, and will be better far when she sees your face in the doorway. Are you coming in to Radulfus?'

'Not yet! Now now! I must get the men home and paid, and then slip home myself. Cadfael, do something for me!'

'Gladly,' said Cadfael heartily.

'I want young Blount, and want him anywhere but at Longner, for I fancy his mother knows nothing about this business he's tangled in. She goes nowhere out to hear the talk, and the family would go out of their way to keep every added trouble from her. If they've said no word to her about the body you found, God forbid I should shoot the bolt at her now, out of the blue. She has grief enough. Will you get leave from the abbot, and find some means to bring the boy to the castle?'

'You've news, then!' But he did not ask what. 'An easier matter to bring him here, and Radulfus will have to hear, now or later, whatever it may be. He was one of us, he'll come if he's called. Radulfus can find a pretext. Concern for a sometime son. And no lie!'

'Good!' said Hugh. 'It will do! Bring him, and keep him until I come.'

He dug his heels into the grey, dappled hide, and Cadfael released the bridle. Hugh was away at a canter after his troop, towards the bridge and the town. Their progress could be followed by the diminishing sound of their welcome, a wave rolling into the distance, while the contented and grateful hum of voices here along the Foregate had levelled into a murmur

347

like bees in a flowering meadow. Cadfael turned back into the great court, and went to ask audience with the abbot.

It was not so difficult to think of a plausible reason for paying a visit to Longner. There was a sick woman there who at one time had made use of his skills at least to dull her pain, and there was the younger son newly returned, who had consented to take a supply of the same syrup, and try to persuade her to employ it again, after a long while of refusing all solace. To enquire after the mother's condition, while extending the abbot's fatherly invitation to the son, so recently in his care, should not strain belief. Cadfael had seen Donata Blount only once, in the days when she was still strong enough to go out and about and willing, then, to ask and take advice. Just once she had come to consult Brother Edmund, the infirmarer, and been led by him to Cadfael's workshop. He had not thought of that visit for some years, and during that time she had grown frailer by infinitely slow and wasting degrees, and was no longer seen beyond the courtyard of Longner, and seldom even there of late. Hugh was right, her menfolk had surely kept from her every ill thing that could add another care to the all-too-grievous burden she already bore. If she must learn of evil in the end, at least let it be only after proof and certainty, when there was no escape.

He remembered how she had looked, that sole time that ever he had set eyes on her, a woman a little taller than his own modest height, slender as a willow even then, her black hair already touched with some strands of grey, her eyes of a deep, lustrous blue. By Hugh's account she was now shrunk to a dry wand, her every movement effort, her every moment pain. At least the poppies of Lethe could procure for her some interludes of sleep, if only she would use them. And somewhere deep within his mind Cadfael could not help wondering if she abstained in order to invite her death the sooner and be free.

But what he was concerned with now, as he saddled the brown cob and set out eastwards along the Foregate, was her son, who was neither old nor ailing, and whose pains were of the mind, perhaps even of the soul.

It was early afternoon, and a heavy day. Clouds had gathered since morning, sagging low and blotting out distances, but there was no wind and no sign of rain, and once out of town and heading for the ferry he was aware of a weighty silence, oppressive and still, in which not even a leaf or a blade of grass moved to disturb the leaden air. He looked up towards the ridge of trees above the Potter's Field as he passed along the meadows. The rich dark ploughland was beginning to show the first faint green shadow of growth, elusive and fragile as a veil. Even the cattle along the river levels were motionless, as if they slept.

He came through the belt of tidy, well-managed woodland beyond the meadows, and up the slight slope of the clearing into the open gates of Longner. A stable boy came running to the cob's bridle, and a maidservant, crossing the yard from the dairy, turned back to enquire his business here, with some surprise and curiosity, as though unexpected visitors were very rare here. As perhaps they were, for the manor was off the main highways where travellers might have need of a roof for the night, or shelter in inclement weather. Those who came visiting here came with a purpose, not by chance.

Cadfael asked for Sulien, in the abbot's name, and she nodded acceptance and understanding, her civility relaxing into a somewhat knowing smile. Naturally the monastic orders do not much like letting go of a young man, once he has been in their hands, and it might be worth a solicitous visit, so soon after his escape, while judgement is still awkward and doubtful, to see if persuasion can coax him back again. Something of the sort she was thinking, but indulgently. It would do very well. Let her say as much to the servants of the household, and Sulien's departure at the abbot's summons would only confirm the story, perhaps even put the issue in doubt.

'Go in, sir, you'll find them in the solar. Go through, freely, you'll be welcome.'

She watched him climb the first steps to the hall door, before she herself made for the undercroft, where the wide cart-doors stood open and someone was rolling and stacking barrels within. Cadfael entered the hall, dim after the open courtyard, even dimmer by reason of the overcast day, and paused to let his eyes adjust to the change. At this hour the fire was amply supplied and well alight, but turfed down to keep it burning slowly until evening, when the entire household would be gathered within here and glad of both warmth and light. At present everyone was out at work, or busy in the kitchen and store, and the hall was empty, but the heavy curtain was drawn back from a doorway in the far corner of the room, and the door it shielded half open. Cadfael could hear voices from within the room, one a man's young and pleasantly low. Eudo

349

or Sulien? He could not be certain. And the woman's ... No, the women's, for these were two, one steady, deep, slow and clear in utterance, as though an effort was needed to form the words and give them sound; one young, fresh and sweet, with a candid fullness about it. That one Cadfael did recognise. So they had progressed this far, that somehow she or circumstances or fate itself had prevailed upon Sulien to bring her home. Therefore this must be Sulien in the solar with her.

Cadfael drew back the curtain fully, and rapped on the door as he opened it wide, pausing on the threshold. The voices had ceasd abruptly, Sulien's and Pernel's with instant recognition and instant reserve, the Lady Donata's with the slightly startled but gracious tolerance of her kind. Intruders here were few and surprising, but her durable, worn dignity would never be disrupted.

'Peace on all here!' said Cadfael. The words had come naturally, a customary bendiction, but he felt the instant stab of guilt at having used them, when he was all too conscious that what he brought them might be anything but peace. 'I am sorry, you did not hear me come. I was told to come through to you. May I enter?'

'Enter and be warmly welcome, Brother!' said Donata.

Her voice had almost more body than her flesh, even though it cost her effort and care to use it. She was installed on the wide bench against the far wall, under a single torch that spilled wavering light from its sconce over her. She was propped in cushions carefully piled to support her upright, with a padded footstool under her feet. The thin oval of her face was the translucent bluish colour of shadows in untrodden snow, lit by huge, sunken eyes of the deep, lustrous blue of bugloss. The hands that lay at rest on the pillows were frail as cobweb, and the body within her dark gown and brocaded bliaut little but skin and bone. But she was still the mistress here, and equal to her role.

'You have ridden from Shrewsbury? Eudo and Jehane will be sorry to have missed you, they have ridden over to Father Eadmer at Atcham. Sit here, Brother, close to me. The light's feeble. I like to see my visitor's faces, and my sight is not quite so sharp as it used to be. Sulien, bring a draught of ale for our guest. I am sure,' she said, turning upon Cadfael the thin, tranquil smile that softened the stoical set of her lips, 'that your visit must really be to my son. It is one more pleasure his return has brought me.'

Pernel said nothing at all. She was sitting at Donata's right hand, very quiet and still, her eyes upon Cadfael. It seemed to him that she was quicker even than Sulien to sense a deeper and darker purpose beyond this unexpected visit. If so, she suppressed what she knew, and continued composed and dutiful, the well-conditioned young gentlewoman being respectful and attentive to her elder. A first visit here? Cadfael thought so, by the slight tension that possessed both the young people.

'My name is Cadfael. Your son was my helper in the herb gardens at the abbey, for the few days he spent with us. I was sorry to lose him,' said Cadfael, 'but not sorry that he should return to the life he chose.'

'Brother Cadfael was an easy master,' said Sulien, presenting the cup to him with a somewhat strained smile.

'So I believe,' she said, 'from all that you have told me of him. And I do remember you, Brother, and the medicines you made for me, some years ago. You were so kind as to send a further supply by Sulien, when he came to see you. He has been persuading me to use the syrup. But I need nothing. You see I am very well tended, and quite content. You should take back the flask, others may need it.'

'It was one of the reasons for the visit,' said Cadfael, 'to enquire if you had found any benefit from the draught, or if there is anything besides that I could offer you.'

She smiled directly into his eyes, but all she said was: 'And the other reason?'

'The lord abbot,' said Cadfael, 'sent me to ask if Sulien will ride back with me and pay him a visit.'

Sulien stood fronting him with an inscrutable face, but betrayed himself for a second by moistening lips suddenly dry. 'Now?'

'Now.' The word fell too heavily, it needed leavening. 'He would take it kindly of you. He thought of your son,' said Cadfael, turning to Donata, 'for a short while as his son. He has not withdrawn that paternal goodwill. He would be glad to see and to know,' he said with emphasis, looking up again into Sulien's face, 'that all is well with you. There is nothing we want more than that.' And whatever might follow, that at least was true. Whether they could hope to have and keep what they wanted was another matter.

'Would an hour or two of delay be allowed me?' asked Sulien steadily. 'I must escort Pernel home to Withington.

351

Perhaps I should do that first.' Meaning, for Cadfael, who know how to interpret: It may be a long time before I come back from the abbey. Best to clear up all unfinished business.

'No need for that,' said Donata with authority. 'Pernel shall stay here with me over the night, if she will be so kind. I will send a boy over to Withington to let her father know that she is safe here with me. I have not so many young visitors that I can afford to part with her so soon. You go with Brother Cadfael, and we shall keep company very pleasantly together until you come back.'

That brought a certain wary gleam to Sulien's face and Pernel's. They exchanged the briefest of glances, and Pernel said at once: 'I should like that very much, if you'll really let me stay. Gunnild is there to take care of the children, and my mother, I'm sure, will spare me for a day.'

Was it possible, Cadfael wondered, that Donata, even in her own extremity, was taking thought for her younger son, and welcomed this first sign in him of interest in a suitable young woman? Mothers of strong nature, long familiar with their own slow deaths, may also wish to settle any unfinished business.

He had just realised what it was that most dismayed him about her. This wasting enemy that had greyed her hair and shrunk her to the bone had still not made her look old. She looked, rather, like a frail waif of a young girl, blighted, withered and starved in her April days, when the bud should just have been unfolding. Beside Pernel's radiance she was a blown wisp of vapour, the ghost of a child. Yet in this or any room she would still be the dominant.

'I'll go and saddle up, then,' said Sulien, almost as lightly as if he had been contemplating no more than a canter through the woods for a breath of air. He stooped to kiss his mother's fallen cheek, and she lifted a hand that felt like the flutter of a dead leaf's filigree skeleton as it touched his face. He said no farewells, to her or to Pernel. That might have spilled over into something betrayingly ominous. He went briskly out through the hall, and Cadfael made his own farewells as gracefully as he could, and hurried down to join him in the stables.

They mounted in the yard, and set out side by side without a word being spoken, until they were threading the belt of woodland.

'You will already have heard,' said Cadfael then, 'that Hugh Beringar and his levy came back today? Without losses!'

'Yes, we heard. I did grasp,' said Sulien, wryly smiling,

'whose voice it was summoning me. But it was well done to let the abbot stand for him. Where are we really bound? The abbey or the castle?'

'The abbey. So much was truth. Tell me, how much *does* she know?'

'My mother? Nothing. Nothing of murder, nothing of Gunnild, or Britric, or Ruald's purgatory. She does not know your plough team ever turned up a woman's body, on what was once our land. Eudo never said a word to her, nor has any other. You have seen her,' said Sulien simply. 'There is not a soul about her who would let one more grief, however small, be added to her load. I should thank you for observing the same care.'

'If that can be sustained,' said Cadfael, 'it shall. But to tell the truth, I am not sure that you have done her any service. Have you ever considered that she may be stronger than any one of you? And that in the end, to worse sorrow, she may have to know?'

Sulien rode beside him in silence for a while, his head was raised, his eyes fixed steadily ahead, and his profile, seen clearly against the open sky with its heavy clouds, pale and set with the rigidity of a mask. Another stoic, with much of his mother in him.

'What I most regret,' he said at last, with deliberation, 'is that I ever approached Pernel. I had no right. Hugh Beringar would have found Gunnild in the end, she would have come forward when she heard of the need, without any meddling. And now see what mischief I have done!'

'I think,' said Cadfael, with respectful care, 'that the lady played as full a part as you. And I doubt if she regrets it.'

Sulien splashed ahead of his companion into the ford. His voice came back to Cadfael's ears clear and resolute. 'Something may be done to undo what we have done. And as to my mother, yes, I have considered the ending. Even for that I have made provision.'

Chapter Twelve

N THE abbot's parlour the four of them were gathered after Vespers, with the window shuttered and the door fast closed against the world. They had had to wait for Hugh. He had a garrison to review, levies newly dismissed from feudal service to pay and discharge home to their families, a few wounded to see properly tended, before he could even dismount stiffly in his own courtyard, embrace wife and son, shed his soiled travelling clothes and draw breath at his own table. The further examination of a doubtful witness, however low his credit stood now, could wait another hour or two without disadvantage.

But after Vespers he came, eased and refreshed but weary. He shed his cloak at the door, and made his reverence to the abbot. Radulfus closed the door, and there was a silence, brief but deep. Sulien sat still and mute on the bench built against the panelled wall. Cadfael had drawn aside into the corner by the shuttered window.

'I must thank you, Father,' said Hugh, 'for providing us this meeting place. I should have been sorry to impose upon the family at Longner, and by all counts you have also an interest in this matter, as valid as mine.'

'We have all an interest in truth and justice, I trust,' said the abbot. 'Nor can I discard all responsibility for a son because he had gone forth into the world. As Sulien knows. Proceed as you choose, Hugh.'

He had made room for Hugh beside him behind his desk, cleared now of its parchments and the business of the day. Hugh accepted the place and sat down with a great sigh. He was still cramped from the saddle and had stiffening grazes newly healed, but he had brought back his company intact from the Fens, and that was achievement enough. What else he had brought back with him he was about to sift, and these three in company with him here were about to learn.

'Sulien, I need not remind you, or these who were witnesses, of the testimony you gave concerning Ruald's wife's ring, and how you came by it at the shop of John Hinde, in Priestgate, in Peterborough. Name and place I asked, and you told me. From Cambridge, when we were discharged from service, I went to Peterborough. Priestgate I found. The shop I found. John Hinde I found. I have talked to him, Sulien, and I report his testimony as I heard it from him. Yes,' said Hugh with deliberation, his eyes on Sulien's blanched but composed face, 'Hinde remembers you well. You did come to him with the name of Abbot Walter to commend you, and he took you in for a single night, and set you on your way home next day. That is truth. That he confirms.'

Recalling how readily Sulien had supplied the jeweller's name and the place where his shop was to be found, Cadfael had had little doubt of the truth of that part of the story. It had not seemed likely, then, that the rest of it would ever be tested. But Sulien's face continued as marble-blank as resolution could make it, and his eyes never left Hugh's face.

'But when I asked him of the ring, he asked, what ring was that? And when I pictured it to him, he was absolute that he had never seen such a ring, never bought that or anything else from such a woman as I described. So recent a transaction he could not possibly forget, even if he did not keep good records, as he does. He never gave you the ring, for he never had the ring. What you told us was a fabric of lies.'

The new silence fell like a stone, and seemed to be arrested in Sulien's braced stillness. He neither spoke nor lowered his eyes. Only the small, spasmodic movement of Rudulfus's muscular hand upon the desk broke the tension within the room. What Cadfael had foreseen from the moment he had conveyed the abbot's summons, and observed the set of Sulien's face as he received it, came as a shock to Radulfus. There was not much of human behaviour he had not encountered in his life. Liars he had known and dealt with, without surprise, but this one he had not expected.

'Yet you produced the ring,' Hugh continued steadily, 'and Ruald recognised and verified the ring. Since you did not get it from the silversmith, how did you come by it? One story you told is shown to be false. Now you have your chance to tell another and a truer. Not all liars have that grace. Now say what you have to say.'

Sulien opened his lips with a creaking effort, like one turning a key in a lock unwilling to respond.

'I already had the ring,' he said. 'Generys gave it to me. I have told the lord abbot, I tell you now, all my life long I held her in affection, deeper than I knew. Even as I grew a man, I never understood how that affection was changing, until Ruald deserted her. Her rage and grief made me to know. What moved her I hardly know. It may be she was avenging herself upon all men, even me. She did receive and make use of me. And she gave me the ring. It did not last long,' he said, without bitterness. 'I could not satisfy, green as I was. I was not Ruald, nor of sufficient weight to pierce Ruald to the heart.'

There was something strange, Cadfael thought, in his choice of words, as though at times the blood of passion did run in them, and at others they came with detached care, measured and contrived. Perhaps Radulfus had felt the same unease, for this time he did speak, impatient for plainer telling.

'Are you saying, my son, that you were this woman's lover?'

'No,' said Sulien. 'I am saying that I loved her, and she admitted me some small way into her grief, when she was in mortal need. If my torment was any ease to hers, that time was not wasted. If you mean, did she admit me even into her bed, no, that she never did, nor I never asked nor hoped for it. My significance, my usefulness, never came so high.'

'And when she vanished,' Hugh pursued with relentless patience, 'what did you know of that?'

'Nothing, no more than any other man.'

'What did you suppose had become of her?'

'My time,' said Sulien, 'was over by then, she had done with me. I believed what the world believed, that she had taken up her roots and fled the place that had become abhorrent to her.'

'With another lover?' Hugh asked evenly. 'The world believed so.'

'With a lover or alone. How could I know?'

'Truly! You knew no more than any other man. Yet when you came back here, and heard that we had found a woman's

356

body buried in the Potter's Field, you knew that it must be she.'

'I knew,' said Sulien with aching care, 'that it was the common belief that it must be. I did not know that it was.'

'True again! You had no secret knowledge, so equally you could not know that it was *not* Generys. Yet you felt it necessary at once to make up your lying story, and produce the ring she had given you, as you now say, in order to prove that she was well alive and far enough away to make confirmation hard, and to lift the shadow of suspicion from Ruald. Without respect to his guilt or innocence, for according to the account you give of yourself now, you did not know whether she was alive or dead, nor whether he had or had not killed her.'

'No!' said Sulien, with a sudden flush of energy and indignation that jerked his braced body forward from the pannelled wall. 'That I did know, because I know him. It is inconceivable that he could ever have harmed her. It is not in the man to do murder.'

'Happy the man whose friends can be so sure of him!' said Hugh drily. 'Very well, pass on to what followed. We had no cause to doubt your word then; you had proved, had you not, that Generys was alive? Therefore we looked about us for other possibilities, and found another woman who had frequented there, and not been seen of late. And behold, your hand is seen again moulding matters. From the moment you heard of the pedlar's arrest you began a hunt for some manor where the woman might have found a shelter through the winter, where someone might be able to testify to her being alive well after she parted from Britric. I doubt if you expected to find her still settled there, but I am sure you were glad of it. It meant you need not appear, she could come forward of her own accord, having heard there was a man charged with her murder. Twice, Sulien? Twice are we to accept your hand for the hand of God, with no more pressing motive than pure love of justice? Since you had so infallibly proved the dead woman could not be Generys, why should you be so sure she was not Gunnild? Two such rescues were one too many to be believed in. Gunnild's survival was proven, she came, she spoke, she was flesh and blood beyond doubt. But for the life of Generys we have only your word. And your word is shown to be false. I think we need look no further for a name for the woman we found. By denying her a name, you have named her.'

Sulien had shut his lips and clenched his teeth, as though he

357

would never speak another word. It was too late to deploy any more lies.

'I think,' said Hugh, 'that when you heard what the abbey plough had turned up out of the soil, you were never in a moment's doubt as to her name. I think you knew very well that she was there. And you were quite certain that Ruald was not her murderer. Oh, that I believe! A certainty, Sulien, to which only God can be entitled, who knows all things with certainty. Only God, and you, who knew all too well who the murderer was.'

'Child,' said Radulfus into the prolonged silence, 'if you have an answer to this, speak out now. If there is guilt on your soul, do not continue obdurate, but confess it. If not, then tell us what your answer is, for you have brought this suspicion upon yourself. To your credit, it seems that you would not have another man, be he friend or stranger, bear the burden of a crime not his to answer. That I should expect of you. But the lies are not worthy, not even in such a cause. Better by far to deliver all others, and say outright: I am the man, look no further.'

Silence fell again, and this time lasted even longer, so that Cadfael felt the extreme stillness in the room as a weight upon his flesh and a constriction upon his breath. Outside the window dusk had gathered in thin, low, featureless cloud, a leaden grey sucking out all colour from the world. Sulien sat motionless, shoulders braced back to feel the solid wall supporting him, eyelids half lowered over the dimmed blue of his eyes. After a long time he stirred, and raised both hands to press and flex with stiff fingers at his cheeks, as though the desperation in which he found himself had cramped even his flesh, and he must work the paralysing chill out of it before he could speak. But when he did speak, it was in a voice low, reasonable and persuasive, and confronted Hugh with the composure of one who had reached a decision and a stance from which he will not easily be shifted.

'Very well! I have lied, and lied again, and I love lies no more than you do, my lord. But if I make a bargain with you, I swear to you I shall keep it faithfully. I have not confessed to anything, yet. But I will give you my confession to murder, upon conditions!'

'Conditions?' said Hugh, with black brows obliquely raised in wry amusement.

'They need not limit in any degree what can be done to me,'

said Sulien, as gently as if he argued a sensible case to which all sane men must consent once they heard it. 'All I want is that my mother and my family shall suffer no dishonour and no disgrace by me. Why should not a bargain be struck even over matters of life and death, if it can spare all those who are not to blame, and destroy only the guilty?'

'You are offering me a confession,' said Hugh, 'in exchange for blanketing this whole matter in silence?'

The abbot had risen to his feet, a hand raised in indignant protest. 'There can be no bargaining over murder. You must withdraw, my son, you are adding insult to your offence.'

'No,' said Hugh, 'let him speak. Every man deserves a hearing. Go on, Sulien, what is it you are offering and asking?'

'Something which could very simply be done. I have been summoned here, where I chose to abandon my calling,' Sulien began in the same measured and persuasive voice. 'Would it be so strange if I should change yet again, and return to my vocation here as a penitent? Father Abbot here, I'm sure, could win me if he tried.' Radulfus was frowning at this moment in controlled disapproval, not of the misuse being made of his influence and office, but of the note of despairing levity which had crept into the young man's voice. 'My mother is in her death illness,' said Sulien, 'and my brother has an honoured name, like our father before us, a wife, and a child to come next year, and has done no wrong to any man, and knows of none. For God's sake leave them in peace, let them keep their name and reputation as clean as ever it was. Let them be told that I have repented of my recantation, and returned to the Order, and am sent away from here to seek out Abbot Walter, wherever he may be, submit myself to his discipline and earn my return to the Order. He would not refuse me, they will be able to believe it. The Rule allows the stray to return and be accepted even to the third time. Do this for me, and I will give you my confession to murder.'

'So in return for your confession,' said Hugh, begging silence of the abbot with a warning gesture of his hand, 'I am to let you go free, but back into the cloister?'

'I did not say that. I said let them believe that. No, do this for me,' said Sulien in heavy earnest, and paler than his shirt, 'and I will take my death however you may require it, and you may shovel me into the ground and forget me.'

'Without benefit of a trial?'

'What should I want with a trial? I want them to be left in

peace, to know nothing. A life is fair pay for a life, what difference can a form of words make?'

It was outrageous, and only a very desperate sinner would have dared advance it to a man like Hugh, whose grip on his office was as firm and scrupulous as it was sometimes unorthodox. But still Hugh sat quiet, fending off the abbot with a sidelong flash of his black eyes, and tapping the fingertips of one long hand upon the desk, as if seriously considering. Cadfael had an inkling of what he was about, but could not guess how he would set about it. The one thing certain was that no such abominable bargain could ever be accepted. To wipe a man out, murderer or no, in cold blood and in secret was unthinkable. Only an inexperienced boy, driven to the end of his tether, could ever have proposed it, or cherished the least hope that it could be taken seriously. This was what he had meant by saying that he had made provision. These children, Cadfael thought in a sudden blaze of enlightened indignation, how dare they, with such misguided devotion, do their progenitors such insult and offence? And themselves such grievous injury!

'You interest me, Sulien,' said Hugh at length, holding him eye to eye across the desk. 'But I need to know somewhat more about this death before I can answer you. There are details that may temper the evil. You may as well have the benefit of them, for your own peace of mind and mine, whatever happens after.'

'I cannot see the need,' said Sulien wearily but resignedly.

'Much depends on how this thing happened,' Hugh persisted. 'Was it a quarrel? When she rejected and shamed you? Even a mere unhappy chance, a struggle and a fall? For we do know by the manner of her burial, there under the bushes by Ruald's garden...' He broke off there, for Sulien had stiffened sharply and turned his head to stare. 'What is it?'

'You are confused, or trying to confuse me,' said Sulien, again withdrawing into the apathy of exhaustion. 'It was not there, you must know it. It was under the clump of broom bushes in the headland.'

'Yes, true, I had forgotten. Much has happened since then, and I was not present when the ploughing began. We do know, I was about to say, that you laid her in the ground with some evidence of respect, regret, even remorse. You buried a cross with her. Plain silver,' said Hugh, 'we could not trace it back to you or anyone, but it was there.'

Sulien eyed him steadily and made no demur.

'It leads me to ask,' Hugh pursued delicately, 'whether this

360

was not simply mischance, a disaster never meant to happen. For it may take no more than a struggle, perhaps flight, an angry blow, a fall, to break a woman's skull as hers was broken. She had no other broken bones, only that. So tell us, Sulien, how this whole thing befell, for it may go some way to excuse you.'

Sulien had blanched into a marble pallor, fending him off with a bleak and wary face. He said between his teeth: 'I have told you all you need to know. I will not say a word more.'

'Well,' said Hugh, rising abruptly, as though he had lost patience, 'I daresay it may be enough. Father, I have two archers with horses outside. I propose to keep the prisoner under guard in the castle for the present, until I have more time to proceed. May my men come in and take him? They have left their arms at the gate.'

The abbot had sat silent all this time, but paying very close attention to all that was said, and by the narrowed intelligence of his eyes in the austere face he had missed none of the implications. Now he said: 'Yes, call them in.' And to Sulien, as Hugh crossed to the door and went out: 'My son, however lies may be enforced upon us, or so we may think, there is in the end no remedy but truth. It is the one course that cannot be evil.'

Sulien turned his head, and the candle caught and illuminated the dulled blue of his eyes and the exhausted pallor of his face. He unlocked his lips with an effort. 'Father, will you keep my mother and my brother in your prayers?'

'Constantly,' said Radulfus.

'And my father's soul?'

'And your own.'

Hugh was at the parlour door again. The two archers of the garrison came in on his heels, and Sulien, unbidden, rose with the alacrity of relief from the bench, and went out between them without a word or a glance behind. And Hugh closed the door.

'You heard him,' said Hugh. 'What he knew he answered readily. When I took him astray he knew he could not sustain it, and would not answer at all. He was there, yes, he saw her buried. But he neither killed nor buried her.'

'I understood,' said the abbot, 'that you put to him points that would have betrayed him...'

'That did betray him,' said Hugh.

'But since I do not know all the details, I cannot follow precisely what you got out of him. Certainly there is the matter of exactly where she was found. That I grasped. He set you right. That was something he knew, and it bore out his story. Yes, he was a witness.'

'But not a sharer, not even a close witness,' said Cadfael. 'Not close enough to see the cross that was laid on her breast, for it was not silver, but made hastily out of two sticks from the bushes. No, he did not bury her, and he did not kill her, because if he had done so, with his bent for bearing the guilt, he would have set us right about her injuries – or want of them. You know, as I know, that her skull was not broken. She had no detectable injuries. If he had known how she died, he would have told us. But he did not know, and he was too shrewd to risk guessing. He may even have realised that Hugh was setting traps for him. He chose silence. What you do not say cannot betray you. But with eyes like those in his head, even silence cannot shield him. The lad is crystal.'

'I am sure it was truth,' said Hugh, 'that he was sick with love for the woman. He had loved her unquestioning, unthinking, like a sister or a nurse, from childhood. The very pity and anger he felt on her account when she was abandoned must have loosed all the strings of a man's passion in him. It must be true, I think, that she did lean on him then, and gave him cause to believe himself elect, while she still thought of him as a mere boy, a child of whom she was fond, offering her a child's comfort.'

'True, also,' the abbot wondered, 'that she gave him the ring?'

It was Cadfael who said at once: 'No.'

'I was still in some doubt,' said Radulfus mildly, 'but you say no?'

'One thing had always troubled me,' said Cadfael, 'and that is the manner in which he produced the ring. You'll recall, he came to ask you, Father, for leave to visit his home. He stayed there overnight, as you permitted, and on his return he gave us to understand that only from his brother, during that visit, had he learned of the finding of the woman's body, and the understandable suspicion it cast upon Ruald. And then he brought forth the ring, and told his story, which we had then no cause to doubt. But I believe that already, before he came to you to ask leave of absence, he had been told of the case. That was the very reason his visit to Longner became necessary. He had to go home because the ring was there, and he must get it before he could speak out in defence of Ruald. With lies, yes, because truth was impossible. We can be sure, now, that he knew, poor lad, who had buried Generys, and where she was laid. Why else should he take flight into the cloister, and so far distant, from a place where he could no longer endure to be?'

'There is no help for it,' said Radulfus reflectively, 'he is protecting someone else. Someone close and dear to him. His whole concern is for his kin and the honour of his house. Can it be his brother?'

Hugh said: 'No. Eudo seems to be the one person who has escaped. Whatever happened in the Potter's Field, not a shadow of it has ever fallen upon Eudo. He is happy, apart from his mother's sickness he has no cares, he is married to a pleasant wife, and looking forward hopefully to having a son. Better still, he is wholly occupied with his manor, with the work of his hands and the fruits of his soil, and seldom looks below, for the dark things that gnaw on less simple men. No, we can forget Eudo.'

'There were two,' said Cadfael slowly, 'who fled from Longner after Generys vanished. One into the cloister, one into the battlefield.'

'His father!' said Radulfus, and pondered in silence for a moment. 'A man of excellent repute, a hero who fought in the king's rearguard at Wilton, and died there. Yes, I can believe that Sulien would sacrifice his own life rather than see that record soiled and blemished. For his mother's sake, and his brother's, and the future of his brother's sons, no less than for his father's memory. But of course,' he said simply, 'we cannot let it lie. And now what are we to do?'

Cadfael had been wondering the same thing, ever since Hugh's springes had caused even obstinate silences to speak with such eloquence, and confirmed with certainty what had always been persistent in a corner of Cadfael's mind. Sulien had knowledge that oppressed him like guilt, but he carried no guilt of his own. He knew only what he had seen. But how much had he seen? Not the death, or he would have seized on every confirming detail, and offered it as evidence against himself. Only the burial. A boy in the throes of his first impossible love, embraced and welcomed into an all-consuming grief and rage, then put aside, perhaps for no worse reason than that Generys had cared for him deeply, and willed him not to be scorched and maimed by her fire more incurably than he already was, or else because another had taken his place, drawn irresistibly into the same furnace, one deprivation fused inextricably with another. For Donata was already, for several years, all too well acquainted with her interminable death, and Eudo Blount in his passionate and spirited prime as many years forced to be celibate as ever was priest or monk. Two starving creatures were fed. And one tormented boy spied upon them, perhaps only once, perhaps several times, but in any event once too often, feeding his own anguish with his jealousy of a rival he could not even hate, because he worshipped him.

It was conceivable. It was probable. Then how successful had father and son been in dissembling their mutual and mutually destructive obsession? And how much had any other in that house divined of the danger?

Yes, it could be so. For she had been, as everyone said, a very beautiful woman.

'I think,' said Cadfael, 'that with your leave, Father, I must go back to Longner.'

'No need,' said Hugh abstractedly. 'We could not leave the lady waiting all night without word, certainly, but I have sent a man from the garrison.'

'To tell her no more than that he stays here overnight? Hugh, the great error has been, throughout, telling her no more than some innocuous half-truth to keep her content and incurious. Or, worse, telling her nothing at all. Such follies are committed in the name of compassion! We must not let her get word of this! We must keep this trouble from her! Starving her courage and strength and will into a feeble shadow, as disease has eaten away her body. When if they had known and respected her as they should she could have lifted half the load from them. If she is not afraid of the monster thing with which she shares her life, there is nothing of which she can be afraid. It is natural enough,' he said ruefully, 'for the manchild to feel he must be his mother's shield and defence, but he does her no service. I said so to him as we came. She would far rather have scope to fulfil her own will and purpose and be shield and defence to him, whether he understands it or not. Better, indeed, if he never understands it.'

'You think,' said Radulfus, eyeing him sombrely, 'that she should be told?'

'I think she should have been told long ago everything there was to tell about this matter. I think she should be told, even

364

now. But I cannot do it, or let it be done if I can prevent. Too easily, as we came, I promised him that if the truth could still be kept from her, I would see it done. Well, if you have put off the hour for tonight, so be it. True, it is too late now to trouble them. But, Father, if you permit, I will ride back there early in the morning.'

'If you think it necessary,' said the abbot, 'by all means go. If it is possible now to restore her her son with the least damage, and salve her husband's memory for her without publishing any dishonour, so much the better.'

'One night,' said Hugh mildly, rising as Cadfael rose, 'cannot alter things, surely. If she has been left in happy ignorance all this time, and goes to bed this night supposing Sulien to have been detained here by the lord abbot without a shadow of ill, you may leave her to her rest. There will be time to consider how much she must know when we have reasoned the truth out of Sulien. It need not be mortal. What sense would it make now to darken a dead man's name?'

Which was good sense enough, yet Cadfael shook his head doubtfully even over these few hours of delay. 'Still, go I must. I have a promise to keep. And I have realised, somewhat late, that I have left someone there who has made no promises.'

Chapter Thirteen

ADFAEL SET out with the dawn, and took his time over the ride, since there was no point in arriving at Longner before the household was up and about. Moreover, he was glad to go slowly, and find time for thought, even if thought did not get him very far. He hardly knew whether to hope to find all as he had left it when he rode away with Sulien, or to discover this morning that he was already forsworn, and all secrecy had been blown away overnight. At the worst, Sulien was in no danger. They were agreed that he was guilty of nothing but suppressing the truth, and if the guilt in fact belonged to a man already dead, what need could there be to publish his blemish to the world? It was out of Hugh's writ or King Stephen's now, and no advocates were needed where next his case must be brought to the bar. All that could be said in accusation or extenuation was known to the judge already.

So all we need, Cadfael thought, is a little ingenuity in dealing with Sulien's conscience, and a little manipulating of truth in gradually laying the case to rest, and the lady need never know more or worse that she knew yesterday. Given time, gossip will tire of the affair, and turn to the next small crisis or scandal around the town, and they will forget at last that their curiosity was never satisfied, and no murderer ever brought to book.

And there, he realised, was where he came into headlong collision with his own unsatisfied desire to have truth, if not set out before the public eye, at least unearthed, recognised and acknowledged. How, otherwise, could there be real reconciliation with life and death and the ordinances of God?

Meantime, Cadfael rode through an early morning like any other November morning, dull, windless and still, all the greens of the fields grown somewhat blanched and dried, the filigree of the trees stripped of half their leaves, the surface of the river leaden rather than silver, and stirred by only rare quivers where the currents ran faster. But the birds were up and singing, busy and loud, lords of their own tiny manors, crying their rights and privileges in defiance of intruders.

He left the highroad at Saint Giles, and rode by the gentle, upland track, part meadow, part heath and scattered trees, that crossed the rising ground towards the ferry. All the bustle of the awaking Foregate, the creaking of carts, the barking of dogs and interlacing of many voices fell away behind him, and the breeze which had been imperceptible among the houses here freshened into a brisk little wind. He crested the ridge, between the fringing trees, and looked down towards the sinuous curve of the river and the sharp rise of the shore and the meadows beyond. And there he halted sharply and sat gazing down in astonishment and some consternation at the ferryman's raft in mid-passage below him. The distance was not so great that he could not distinguish clearly the freight it was carrying towards the near shore.

A narrow litter, made to stand on four short, solid legs, stood squarely placed in the middle of the raft to ride as steadily as possible. A linen awning sheltered the head of it from wind and weather, and it was attended on one side by a stockily built groom, and on the other by a young woman in a brown cloak, her head uncovered, her russet hair ruffled by the breeze. At the rear of the raft, where the ferryman poled his load through placid waters, the second porter held by a bridle a dappled cob that swam imperturbably behind. Indeed, he had to swim only in mid-stream, for the water here was still fairly low. The porters might have been servants from any local household, but the girl there was no mistaking. And who would be carried in litters over a mere few miles and in decent weather but the sick, the old, the disabled or the dead?

Early as it was, he had set out on this journey too late. The Lady Donata had left her solar, left her hall, left, God alone knew on what terms, her careful and solicitous son, and come forth to discover for herself what business abbot and sheriff in

Shrewsbury had with her second son, Sulien.

Cadfael nudged his mule out through the crest of trees, and started down the long slope of the track to meet them, as the ferryman brought his raft sliding smoothly in to the sandy level below.

Pernel left the porters leading the horse ashore and lifting the litter safely to land, and came flying to meet Cadfael as he dismounted. She was flushed with the air and her own haste and the improbable excitement of this most improbable expedition. She caught him anxiously but resolutely by the sleeve, looking up earnestly into his face.

'She wills it! She knows what she is doing! Why could they never understand? Did you know she has never been told anything of all this business? The whole household ... Eudo would have her kept in the dark, sheltered and wrapped in down. All of them, they did what he wanted. All out of tenderness, but what does she want with tenderness? Cadfael, there has been no one free to tell her the truth, except for you and me.'

'I was not free,' said Cadfael shortly. 'I promised the boy to respect his silence, as they have all done.'

'*Respect*!' breathed Pernel, marvelling. 'Where has been the respect for her? I met her only yesterday, and it seems to me I know her better than all these who move all day and every day under the same roof. You have seen her! Nothing but a handful of slender bones covered with pain for flesh and courage for skin. How dare any man look at her, and say of any matter, however daunting: We mustn't let this come to her ears, *she could not bear it*!'

'I have understood you,' said Cadfael, making for the strip of sand where the porters had lifted the litter ashore. 'You were still free, the only one.'

'One is enough! Yes, I have told her, everything I know, but there's more that I don't know, and she will have all. She has a purpose now, a reason for living, a reason for venturing out like this, mad as you may think it – better than sitting waiting for death.'

A thin hand drew back the lined curtain as Cadfael stooped to the head of the litter. The shell was plaited from hemp, to be light of weight and give with the movement, and within it Donata reclined in folded rugs and pillows. Thus she must have travelled a year and more ago, when she had made her last excursions into the world outside Longner. What prodigies of endurance it cost her now could hardly be guessed. Under the linen awning her wasted face showed livid and drawn, her lips blue-grey and set hard, so that she had to unlock them with an effort to speak. But her voice was still clear, and still possessed its courteous but steely authority.

'Were you coming to me, Brother Cadfael? Pernel supposed your errand might be to Longner. Be content, I am bound for the abbey. I understand that my son has involved himself in matters of moment both to the lord abbot and the sheriff. I believe I may be able to set the record straight, and see an account settled.'

'I will gladly ride back with you,' said Cadfael, 'and serve you in whatever way I can.'

No point now in urging caution and good sense upon her, none in trying to turn her back, none in questioning how she had eluded the anxious care of Eudo and his wife to undertake this journey. The fierce control of her face spoke for her. She knew what she was doing, no pain, no risk could have daunted her. Brittle energy had burned up in her as in a stirred fire. And a stirred fire was what she was, too long damped down into resignation.

'Then ride before, Brother,' she said, 'if you will be so good, and ask Hugh Beringar if he will come and join us at the abbot's lodging. We shall be slower on the road, you and he may be there before us. But not my son!' she added, with a lift of her head and a brief, deep spark in her eyes. 'Let him be! It is better, is it not, that the dead should carry their own sins, and not leave them for the living to bear?'

'It is better,' said Cadfael. 'An inheritance comes more kindly clear of debts.'

'Good!' she said. 'What is between my son and me may remain as it is until the right time comes. I will deal. No one else need trouble.'

One of her porters was busy rubbing down the cob's saddle and streaming hide for Pernel to remount. At foot pace they would be an hour yet on the way. Donata had sunk back in her pillows braced and still, all the fleshless lines of her face composed into stoic endurance. On her deathbed she might look so, and still never let one groan escape her. Dead, all the tension would have been wiped away, as surely as the passage of a hand closes the eyes for the last time.

Cadfael mounted his mule, and set off back up the slope,

heading for the Foregate and the town.

'She *knows*?' said Hugh in blank astonishment. 'The one thing Eudo insisted on, from the very day I went to him first, the one person he would not have drawn into so grim a business! The last thing you said yourself, when we parted last night, was that you were sworn to keep the whole tangle from her. And now you have *told* her?'

'Not I,' said Cadfael. 'But yes, she knows. Woman to woman she heard it. And she is making her way now to the abbot's lodging, to say what she has to say to authority both sacred and secular, and have to say it but once.'

'In God's name,' demanded Hugh, gasping, 'how did she contrive the journey? I saw her, not so long since, every movement of a hand tired her. She had not been out of the house for months.'

'She had not compelling reason,' said Cadfael. 'Now she has. She had no cause to fight against the care and anxiety they pressed upon her. Now she has. There is no weakness in her will. They have brought her these few miles in a litter, at cost to her, I know it, but it is what she would have, and I, for one, would not care to deny her.'

'And she may well have brought on her death,' Hugh said, 'in such an effort.'

'And if that proved so, would it be so ill an ending?'

Hugh gave him a long, thoughtful look, and did not deny it.

'What has she said, then, to you, to justify such a wager?'

'Nothing, as yet, except that the dead should carry their own sins, and not leave them a legacy to the living.'

'It is more than we have got out of the boy,' said Hugh. 'Well, let him sit and think a while longer. He had his father to deliver, she has her son. And all of this while sons and household and all have been so busy and benevolent delivering her. If she's calling the tune now, we may hear a different song. Wait, Cadfael, and make my excuses to Aline, while I go and saddle up.'

They had reached the bridge, and were riding so slowly that they seemed to be eking out time for some urgent thinking before coming to this conference, when Hugh said: 'And she would not have Sulien brought in to hear?'

'No. Very firmly she said: Not my son! What is between them, she said, let it rest until the right time. Eudo she knows she can manipulate, lifelong, if you say no word. And what point is there in publishing the offences of a dead man? He cannot be made to pay, and the living should not.'

'But Sulien she cannot deceive. He witnessed the burial. He knows. What can she do but tell him the truth? The whole of it, to add to the half he knows already.'

Not until then had it entered Cadfael's mind to wonder if indeed they knew, or Sulien knew, even the half of it. They were being very sure, because they thought they had discounted every other possibility, that what they had left was truth. Now the doubt that had waited aside presented itself suddenly as a world of unconsidered possibilities, and no amount of thought could rule out all. How much even of what Sulien knew was not knowledge at all, but assumption? How much of what he believed he had seen was not vision, but illusion?

They dismounted in the stable yard at the abbey, and presented themselves at the abbot's door.

It was the middle of the morning when they assembled at last in the abbot's parlour. Hugh had waited for her at the gatehouse, to ensure that she should be carried at once the length of the great court to the very door of Radulfus's lodging. His solicitude, perhaps, reminded her of Eudo, for when he handed her out among the tattered autumnal beds of the abbot's garden she permitted all with a small, tight but tolerant smile, bearing the too-anxious assiduities of youth and health with the hard-learned patience of age and sickness. She accepted the support of his arms through the ante-room where normally Brother Vitalis, chaplain and secretary, might have been working at this hour, and Abbot Radulfus took her hand upon the other side, and led her within, to a cushioned place prepared for her, with the support of the panelled wall at her back.

Cadfael, watching this ceremonious installation without attempting to take any part in it, thought that it had something of the enthronement of a sovereign lady about it. That might even amuse her, privately. The privileges of mortal sickness had almost been forced upon her, what she thought of them might never be told. Certainly she had an imperishable dignity, and a large and tolerant understanding of the concern and even unease she caused in others and must endure graciously. She had also, thus carefully dressed for an ordeal and a social visit,

371

a fragile and admirable elegance. Her gown was deep blue like her eyes, and like her eyes a little faded, and the bliaut she wore over it, sleeveless and cut down to either hip, was the same blue, embroidered in rose and silver at the hems. The whiteness of her linen wimple turned her drawn cheeks to a translucent grey in the light almost of noon.

Pernel had followed silently into the ante-room, but did not enter the parlour. She stood waiting in the doorway, her golden-russet eyes round and grave.

'Pernel Otmere has been kind enough to bear me company all this way,' said Donata, 'and I am grateful to her for more than that, but she need not be put to the weariness of listening to the long conference I fear I may be forcing upon you, my lords. If I may ask, first ... where is my son now?'

'He is in the castle,' said Hugh simply.

'Locked up?' she asked pointblank, but without reproach or excitement. 'Or on his parole?'

'He has the freedom of the wards,' said Hugh, and added no further enlightenment.

'Then, Hugh, if you would be kind enough to provide Pernel with some token that would let her in to him, I think they might spend the time more pleasantly together than apart, while we confer? Without prejudice,' she said gently, 'to any proceedings you may have in mind later.'

Cadfael saw Hugh's black, betraying brows twitch, and lift into oblique appreciation, and thanked God devoutly for an understanding rare between two so different.

'I will give her my glove,' said Hugh, and cast one sharp, enjoying glance aside at the mute girl in the doorway. 'No one will question it, no need for more.' And he turned and took Pernel by the hand, and went out with her.

Their plans had been made, of course, last night or this morning, in the solar at Longner where the truth came forth so far as truth was known, or on the journey at dawn, before they ever reached the ferry over Severn, where Cadfael had met them. A conspiracy of women had been hatched in Eudo's hall, that kept due consideration of Eudo's right and needs, of his wife's contented pregnancy, even as it nurtured and advanced Pernel Otmere's determined pursuit of a truth that would set Sulien Blount free from every haunted and chivalrous burden that weighed him down. The young one and the old one – old not in years, only in the rapidity of her advance upon death – they had come together like lodestone and metal, to compound their own justice.

Hugh came back into the room smiling, though the smile was invisible to all but Cadfael. A burden smile, none the less, for he, too, was in pursuit of a truth which might not be Pernel's truth. He closed the door firmly on the world without.

'Now, madam, in what particular can we be of service to you?'

She had composed herself into a settled stillness which could be sustained through a long conference. Without her cloak she made so slight a figure, it seemed a man could have spanned her body with his hands.

'I must thank you, my lords,' she said, 'for granting me this audience. I should have asked for it earlier, but only yesterday did I hear of this matter which has been troubling you both. My family are too careful of me, and their intent was to spare me any knowledge that might be distressing. A mistake! There is nothing more distressing than to find out, very late, that those who rearrange circumstances around you to spare you pain have themselves been agonising day and night. And needlessly, to no purpose. It is an indignity, would not you think, to be protected by people you know, in your own mind, to be more in need of protection than you have ever been, or ever will be? Still, it is an error of affection. I cannot complain of it. But I need no longer suffer it. Pernel has had the good sense to tell me what no one else would. But there are still things I do not know, since she did not yet know them herself. May I ask?'

'Ask whatever you wish,' said the abbot. 'In your own time, and tell us if you need to rest.'

'True,' said Donata, 'there is no haste now. Those who are dead are safe enough, and those still living and wound into this coil, I trust, are also safe. I have learned that my son Sulien has given you some cause to believe him guilty of this death which is come to judgement here. Is he still suspect?'

'No,' said Hugh without hesitation. 'Certainly not of murder. Though he has said, and maintains, and will not be persuaded to depart from it, that he is willing to confess to murder. And if need be, to die for it.'

She nodded her head slowly, unsurprised. The stiff fold of linen rustled softly against her cheeks. 'I thought it might be so. When Brother Cadfael here came for him yesterday, I knew nothing to make me wonder or question. I thought all was as it seemed, and that you, Father, had still some doubts whether he had not made a wrong decision, and should not be advised to think more deeply about abandoning his vocation. But when Pernel told me how Generys had been found, and how my son had set himself to prove Ruald blameless, by proving this could not in fact be Generys ... And then how he exerted himself, once again, to find the woman Gunnild alive ... Then I understood that he had brought inevitable suspicion upon himself, as one knowing far too much. So much wasted exertion, if only I had known! And he was willing to take that load upon him? Well, but it seems you have already seen through that pretence, with no aid from me. May I take it, Hugh, that you have been in Peterborough? We heard that you were newly back from the Fen country, and since Sulien was sent for so promptly after your return, I could not fail to conclude the two were connected.'

'Yes,' said Hugh, 'I went to Peterborough.'

'And you found that he had lied?'

'Yes, he had lied. The silversmith lodged him overnight, true. But he never gave him the ring, never saw the ring, never bought anything from Generys. Yes, Sulien lied.'

'And yesterday? Being found out in his lies, what did he tell you yesterday?'

'He said that he had the ring all along, that Generys had given it to him.'

'One lie leads to another,' she said with a deep sigh. 'He felt he had good cause, but there is never cause good enough. Always lies come to grief. I can tell you where he got the ring. He took it from a small box I keep in my press. There are a few other things in it, a pin for fastening a cloak, a plain silver torque, a ribbon ... All trifles, but they could have been recognised, and given her a name, even after years.'

'Are you saying,' asked Radulfus, listening incredulously to the quiet, detached tone of the voice that uttered such things, 'that these things were taken from the dead woman? That she is indeed Generys, Ruald's wife?'

'Yes, she is indeed Generys. I could have named her at once, if anyone had asked me. I would have named her. I do not deal in lies. And yes, the trinkets were all hers.'

'It is a terrible sin,' said the abbot heavily, 'to steal from the dead.'

'There was no such intent,' she said with unshakable calm. 'But without them, after no very long time, no one would be able to name her. As you found, no one was. But it was not my choice, I would not have gone to such lengths. I think it must have been when Sulien brought my lord's body back from Salisbury, after Wilton, and we buried him and set all his affairs and debts in order, that Sulien found the box. He would know the ring. When he needed his proof, to show that she still lived, then he came home and took it. Her possessions no one has ever worn or touched, otherwise. Simply, they are in safe keeping. I will readily deliver them up to you, or to anyone who has a claim. Until last night I had not opened the box since first it was laid there. I did not know what he had done. Neither did Eudo. He knows nothing about this. Nor ever shall.'

From his preferred corner, where he could observe without involvement, Cadfael spoke for the first time. 'I think, also, you may not yet know all you would wish to know about your son Sulien. Look back to the time when Ruald entered this house, abandoning his wife. How much did you know of what went on in Sulien's mind then? Did you know how deeply he was affected to Generys? A first love, the most desperate always. Did you know that in her desolation she gave him cause for a time to think there might be a cure for his? When in truth there was none?'

She had turned her head and fixed her gaunt dark eyes earnestly on Cadfael's face. And steadily she said: 'No, I did not know it. I knew he frequented their croft. So he had from a small child, they were fond of him. But if there was so extreme a change, no, he never said word or give sign. He was a secret child, Sulien. Whatever ailed Eudo I always knew, he is open as the day. Not Sulien!'

'He has told us that it was so. And did you know that because of this attachment he still went there, even when she had thought fit to put an end to his illusion? And that he was there in the dark,' said Cadfael with rueful gentleness, 'when Generys was buried?'

'No,' she said, 'I did not know. Only now had I begun to fear it. That or some other knowledge no less dreadful to him.'

'Dreadful enough to account for much. For why he made up his mind to take the cowl, and not here in Shrewsbury, but far away in Ramsey. What did you make of that, then?' asked Hugh.

'It was not so strange in him,' she said, looking into distance and faintly and ruefully smiling. 'That was something that could well happen to Sulien, he ran deep, and thought much. And then, there was a bitterness and a pain in the house, and I know he could not choose but feel it and be troubled. I think I was not sorry that he should escape from it and go free, even if it must be into the cloister. I knew of no worse reason. That he had been there, and seen – no, that I did not know.'

'And what he saw,' said Hugh after a brief and heavy silence, 'was his father, burying the body of Generys.'

'Yes,' she said. 'It must have been so.'

'We could find no other possibility,' said Hugh, 'and I am sorry to have to set it before you. Though I still cannot see what reason there could be, why or how it came about that he killed her.'

'Oh no!' said Donata. 'No, not that. He buried her, yes. But he did not kill her. Why should he? I see that Sulien believed it, and would not at any cost have it known to the world. But it was not like that.'

'Then who did?' demanded Hugh, confounded. 'Who was her murderer?'

'No one,' said Donata. 'There was no murder.'

Chapter Fourteen

UT OF the unbelieving silence that followed, Hugh's voice asked: 'If this was not murder, why the secret burial, why conceal a death for which there could be no blame?'

'I have not said,' Donata said patiently, 'that there was no blame. I have not said that there was no sin. It is not for me to judge. But murder there was none. I am here to tell you truth. The judgement must be yours.'

She spoke as one, and the only one, who could shed light on all that had happened, and the only one who had been kept in ignorance of the need. Her voice remained considerate, authoritative and kind. Very simply and clearly she set out her case, excusing nothing, regretting nothing.

'When Ruald turned away from his wife, she was desolated and despairing. You will not have forgotten, Father, for you must have been in grave doubt concerning his decision. She, when she found she could not hold him, came to appeal to my husband, as overlord and friend to them both, to reason with Ruald and try to persuade him he did terrible wrong. And truly I think he did his best for her, and again and again went to argue her case, and tried also, surely, to comfort and reassure her, that she should not suffer loss of house and living by reason of Ruald's desertion. My lord was good to his people. But Ruald would not be turned back from the way he had chosen. He left her. She had loved him out of all measure,' said Donata dispassionately, speaking pure truth, 'and in the same

377

measure she hated him. And all these days and weeks my lord had contended her right, but could not win it. He had never before been so often and so long in her company.'

A moment she paused, looking from face to face, presenting her own ruin with wide, illusionless eyes.

'You see me, gentlemen. Since that time I may, perhaps, have moved a few short paces nearer the grave, but the change is not so great. I was already what I am now. I had been so for some few years. Three at least, I think, since Eudo had shared my bed, for pity of me, yes, but himself in abstinence to starvation, and without complaint. Such beauty as I ever had was gone, withered away into this aching shell. He could not touch me without causing me pain. And himself worse pain, whether he touched or abstained. And she, you will remember if ever you saw her, she was most beautiful. What all men said, I say also. Most beautiful, and enraged, and desperate. And famished, like him. I fear I distress you, gentlemen,' she said, seeing them all three held in frozen awe at her composure and her merciless candour, delivered without emphasis, even with sympathy. 'I hope not. I simply wish to make all things plain. It is necessary.'

'There is no need to labour further,' said Radulfus. 'This is not hard to understand, but very hard to hear as it must be to tell.'

'No,' she said reassuringly, 'I feel no reluctance. Never fret for me. I owe truth to her, as well as to you. But enough, then. He loved her. She loved him. Let us make it brief. They loved, and I knew. No one else. I did not blame them. Neither did I forgive them. He was my lord, I loved him five-and-twenty years, and there was no remission because I was an empty shell. He was mine, I would not endure to share him.

'And now,' she said, 'I must tell something that had happened more than a year earlier. At that time I was using the medicines you sent me, Brother Cadfael, to ease my pain when it grew too gross. And I grant you the syrup of poppies does help, for a time, but after a while the charm fails, the body grows accustomed, or the demon grows stronger within.'

'It is true,' said Cadfael soberly. 'I have seen it lose its hold. And beyond a certain strength treatment cannot go.'

'That I understood. Beyond that there is only one cure, and we are forbidden to resort to that. None the less,' said Donata inexorably, 'I did consider how to die. Mortal sin, Father, I knew it, yet I did consider. Oh, never look aside at Brother

Cadfael, I would not have come to him for the means, I knew he would not give them to me if I did. Nor did I ever intend to give my life away easily. But I foresaw a time when the load would become more than even I could bear, and I wished to have some small thing about me, a little vial of deliverance, a promise of peace, perhaps never to use, only to keep as a talisman, the very touch of it consolation to me that at the worst … at the last extreme, there was left to me a way of escape. To know that was to go on enduring. Is that reproach to me, Father?'

Abbot Radulfus stirred abruptly out of a stillness so long sustained that he emerged from it with a sharp indrawn breath, as if himself stricken with a shadowy insight into her suffering.

'I am not sure that I have the right to pronounce. You are here, you have withstood that temptation. To overcome the lures of evil is all that can be required of mortals. But you make no mention of those other consolations open to the Christian soul. I know your priest to be a man of grace. Did you not allow him the opportunity to lift some part of your burden from you?'

'Father Eadmer is a good man and a kind,' said Donata with a thin, wry smile, 'and no doubt my soul has benefited from his prayers. But pain is here in the body, and has a very loud voice. Sometimes I could not hear my own voice say Amen! for the demon howling. Howbeit, rightly or wrongly, I did look about me for other aid.'

'Is this to the present purpose?' Hugh asked gently. 'For it cannot be pleasant to you, and God knows it must be tiring you out.'

'It is very much to the purpose. You will see. Bear with me, till I end what I have begun. I got my talisman,' she said. 'I will not tell you from whom. I was still able to go about, then, to wander among the booths at the abbey fair, or in the market. I got what I wanted from a traveller. By now she may herself be dead, for she was old. I have not seen her since, nor ever expected to. But she made for me what I wanted, one draught, contained in so small a vial, my release from pain and from the world. Tightly stoppered, she said it would not lose its power. She told me its properties, for in very small doses it is used against pain when other things fail, but in this strength it would end pain for ever. The herb is hemlock.'

'It has been known,' said Cadfael bleakly, 'to end pain for ever even when the sufferer never meant to surrender life. I do

379

not use it. Its dangers are too great. There is a lotion can be made to use against ulcers and swellings and inflammations, but there are other remedies safer.'

'No doubt!' said Donata. 'But the safety I sought was of a different kind. I had my charm, and I kept it always about me, and often I set my hand to it when the pain was extreme, but always I withdrew without drawing the stopper. As if the mere having it was buttress to my own strength. Bear with me, I am coming to the matter in hand. Last year, when my lord gave himself utterly to the love of Generys, I went to her cottage, at a time in the afternoon when Eudo was elsewhere about his manor. I took with me a flask of a good wine, and two cups that matched, and my vial of hemlock. And I proposed to her a wager.'

She paused only to draw breath, and ease slightly the position in which she had been motionless so long. None of her three hearers had any mind to break the thread now. All their presuppositions were already blown clean away in the wind of her chill detachment, for she spoke of pain and passion in tones level and quiet, almost indifferent, concerned only with making all plain past shadow of doubt.

'I was never her enemy,' she said. 'We had known each other many years, I felt for her rage and despair when Ruald abandoned her. This was not in hate or envy or despite. We were two women impossibly shackled together by cords of our rights in one man, and neither of us could endure the mutilation of sharing him. I set before her a way out of the trap. We would pour two cups of wine, and add to one of them the draught of hemlock. If it was I who died, then she would have full possession of my lord, and, God knows, my blessing if she could give him happiness, as I had lost the power to do. And if it was she who died, then I swore to her that I would live out my life to the wretched end unsparing, and never again seek alleviation.'

'And Generys agreed to such a bargain?' Hugh asked incredulously.

'She was as bitter, bold and resolute as I, and as tormented by having and not having. Yes, she agreed. I think, gladly.'

'Yet this was no easy thing to manage fairly.'

'With no will to cheat, yes, it was very easy,' she said simply. 'She went out from the room, and neither watched nor listened, while I filled the cups, evenly but that the one contained hemlock. Then I went out, far down the Potter's

Field, while she parted and changed the cups as she thought fit, and set the one on the press and the other on the table, and came and called me in and I chose. It was June, the twenty-eighth day of the month, a beautiful midsummer. I remember how the meadow grasses were coming into flower, I came back to the cottage with my skirts spangled with the silver of their seeds. And we sat down together, there within, and drank our wine, and were at peace. And afterwards, since I knew that the draught brought on a rigor of the whole body, from the extremities inward to the heart, we agreed between us to part, she to remain quiet where she was, I to go back to Longner, that whichever of us God – dare I say God, Father, or must I say only chance, or fate? – whichever of us was chosen should die at home. I promise you, Father, I had not forgotten God, I did not feel that he had stricken me from his book. It was as simple as where you have it written: of two, one shall be taken and the other left. I went home, and I span while I waited. And hour by hour – for it does not hurry – I waited for the numbness in the hands to make me fumble at the wool on the distaff, and still my fingers span and my wrist twisted, and there was no change in my dexterity. And I waited for the cold to seize upon my feet, and climb into my ankles, and there was no chill and no clumsiness, and my breath came without hindrance.'

She drew a deep, unburdened sigh, and let her head rest back against the panelling, eased of the main weight of the load she had brought them.

'You had won your wager,' said the abbot in a low and grieving voice.

'No,' said Donata, 'I had lost my wager.' And in a moment she added scrupulously: 'There is one detail I had forgotten to mention. We kissed, sisterly, when we parted.'

She had not done, she was only gathering herself to continue coherently to the end, but the silence lasted some minutes. Hugh got up from his place and poured a cup of wine from the flask on the abbot's table, and went and set it down on the bench beside her, convenient to her hand. 'You are very tired. Would you not like to rest a little while? You have done what you came to do. Whatever this may have been, it was not murder.'

She looked up at him with the benign indulgence she felt now towards all the young, as though she had lived not

381

forty-five years but a hundred, and seen all manner of tragedies pass and lapse into oblivion.

'Thank you, but I am the better for having resolved this matter. You need not trouble for me. Let me make an end, and then I will rest.' But to accommodate him she put out a hand for her cup, and seeing how even that slight weight made her wrist quiver, Hugh supported it while she drank. The red of the wine gave her grey lips, for a moment, the dew and flush of blood.

'Let me make an end! Eudo came home, I told him what we had done, and that the lot had failed to fall on me. I wanted no concealment, I was willing to bear witness truly, but he would not suffer it. He had lost her, but he would not let me be lost, or his honour, or his sons' honour. He went that night, alone, and buried her. Now I see that Sulien, deep in his own pit of grief, must have followed him to an assignation, and discovered him in a funeral rite. But my lord never knew it. Never a word was said of that, never a sign given. He told me how he found her, lying on her bed as if asleep. When the numbness began she must have lain down there, and let death come to her. Those small things about her that gave her a name and a being, those he brought away with him and kept, not secret from me. There were no more secrets between us two, there was no hate, only a shared grief. Whether he removed them for my sake, looking upon what I had done as a terrible crime, as I grant you a man might, and fearing what should fall on me in consequence, or whether he wanted them for himself, as all he could now keep of her, I never knew.

'It passed, as everything passes. When she was missed, no one ever thought to look sidelong at us. I do not know where the word began that she was gone of her own will, with a lover, but it went round as gossip does, and men believed it. As for Sulien, he was the first to escape from the house. My elder son had never had ado with Ruald or Generys, beyond a civil word if they passed in the fields or crossed by the ferry together. He was busy about the manor, and thinking of marriage, he never felt the pain within the house. But Sulien was another person. I felt his unease, before ever he told us he was set on entering Ramsey. Now I see he had better reason for his trouble than I had thought. But his going weighed yet more heavily on my lord, and the time came when he could not bear ever to go near the Potter's Field, or look upon the place where she had lived and died. He made the gift to Haughmond, to be rid of it, and when that was completed, he went to join King Stephen at Oxford. And what befell him afterwards you know.

'I have not asked the privilege of confession, Father,' she said punctiliously, 'since I want no more secrecy from those fit to judge me, whether it be the law or the Church. I am here, do as you see fit. I did not cheat her, living, it was a fair wager, and I have not cheated her now she is dead. I have kept my pledge. I take no palliatives now, whatever my state. I pay my forfeit every day of my remaining life, to the end. In spite of what you see, I am strong. The end may still be a long way off.'

It was done. She rested in quietness, and in a curious content that showed in the comparative ease of her face. Distantly from across the court the bell from the refectory sounded noon.

The king's officer and the representative of the Church exchanged no more than one long glance by way of consultation. Cadfael observed it, and wondered which of them would speak first, and indeed, to which of these two authorities the right of precedence belonged, in a case so strange. Crime was Hugh's business, sin the abbot's, but what was justice here, where the two were woven together so piteously as to be beyond unravelling? Generys dead, Eudo dead, who stood to profit from further pursuit? Donata, when she had said that the dead should carry their own sins, had counted herself among them. And infinitely slow as the approach of death had been for her, it must now be very near.

Hugh was the first to speak. 'There is nothing here,' he said, 'that falls within my writ. What was done, whatever its rights or wrongs, was not murder. If it was an offence to put the dead into the ground unblessed, he who did it is already dead himself, and what would it benefit the king's law or the good order of my shire to publish it to his dishonour now? Nor could anyone wish to add to your grief, or cause distress to Eudo's heir, who is innocent of all. I say this case is closed, unsolved, and so let it remain, to my reproach. I am not so infallible that I cannot fail, like any other man, and admit it. But there are claims that must be met. I see no help but we must make it public that Generys is Generys, though how she came to her death will never be known. She has the right to her name, and to have her grave acknowledged for hers. Ruald has the right to know that she is dead, and to mourn her duly. In time people will let the matter sink into the past and be forgotten. But for you there remains Sulien.'

'And Pernel,' said Donata.

'And Pernel. True, she already knows the half. What will you do about them?'

'Tell them the truth,' she said steadily. 'How else could they ever rest? They deserve truth, they can endure truth. But not my elder son. Leave him his innocence.'

'How will you satisfy him,' Hugh wondered practically, 'about this visit? Does he even know that you are here?'

'No,' she admitted with her wan smile, 'he was out and about early. No doubt he will think me mad, but when I return no worse than I set out, it will not be so hard to reconcile him. Jehane does know. She tried to dissuade me, but I would have my way, he cannot blame her. I told her I had it in mind to offer my prayers for help at Saint Winifred's shrine. And that I will make good, Father, with your leave, before I return. If,' she said, 'I am to return?'

'For my part, yes,' said Hugh. 'And to that end,' he said, rising, 'if the lord abbot agrees, I will go and bring your son to you here.'

He waited for the abbot's word, and it was long in coming. Cadfael could divine something, at least, of what passed in that austere and upright mind. To bargain with life and death is not so far from self-murder, and the despair that might lead to the acceptance of such a wager is in itself mortal sin. But the dead woman haunted the mind with pity and pain, and the living one was there before his eyes, relentlessly stoical in her interminable dying, inexorable in adhering to the penalty she had imposed upon herself when she lost her wager. And one judgement, the last, must be enough, and that was not yet due.

'So be it!' said Radulfus at last. 'I can neither condone nor condemn. Justice may already have struck its own balance, but where there is no certainty the mind must turn to the light and not the shadow. You are your own penance, my daughter, if God requires penance. There is nothing here for me to do, except to pray that all things remaining may work together for grace. There have been wounds enough, at all costs let us cause no more. Let no word be said, then, beyond these few who have the right to know, for their own peace. Yes, Hugh, if you will, go and bring the boy, and the young woman who has shed, it seems, so welcome a light among these grievous shadows. And, madam, when you have rested and eaten here in my house, we will help you into the church, to Saint Winifred's altar.'

'And it shall be my care,' said Hugh, 'to see that you get home safely. You do what is needed for Sulien and Pernel.

Father Abbot, I am sure, will do what is needful for Brother Ruald.'

'That,' said Cadfael, 'I will undertake, if I may.'

'With my blessing,' said Radulfus. 'Go, find him after dinner in the frater, and let him know her story ends in peace.'

All of which they did before the day was over.

They were standing under the high wall of the graveyard, in the furthest corner where modest lay patrons found a place, and stewards and good servants of the abbey and, under a low mound still settling and greening, the nameless woman orphaned after death and received and given a home by Benedictine compassion.

Cadfael had gone with Ruald after Vespers, in the soft rain that was hardly more than a drifting dew on the face, chill and silent. The light would not last much longer. Vespers was already at its winter hour, and they were alone here in the shadow of the wall, in the wet grass, with the earthy smells of fading foliage and autumnal melancholy about them. A melancholy without pain, an indulgence of the spirit after the passing of bitterness and distress. And it did not seem strange that Ruald had shown no great surprise at learning that this translated waif was, after all, his wife, had accepted without wonder that Sulien had concocted, out of mistaken concern for an old friend, a false and foolish story to disprove her death. Nor had he rebelled against the probability that he would never know how she had died, or why she had been buried secretly and without rites, before she was brought to this better resting-place. Ruald's vow of obedience, like all his vows, was carried to the ultimate extreme of duty, into total acceptance. Whatever was, was best to him. He did not question.

'What is strange, Cadfael,' he said, brooding over the new turf that covered her, 'is that now I begin to see her face clearly again. When first I entered here I was like a man in fever, aware only of what I had longed for and gained. I could not recall how she looked, it was as if she and all my life aforetime had vanished out of the world.'

'It comes of staring into too intense a light,' said Cadfael, dispassionately, for himself had never been dazzled. He had done what he had done in his right senses, made his choice, no easy choice, with deliberation, walked to his novitiate on broad bare feet treading solid earth, not been borne to it on clouds of bliss. 'A very fine experience in its way,' he said, 'but bad for

385

the sight. If you stare too long you may go blind.'

'But now I see her clearly. Not as I last saw her, not angry or bitter. As she always used to be, all the years we were together. And young,' said Ruald, marvelling. 'Everything I knew and did, aforetime, comes back with her, I remember the croft, and the kiln, and where every small thing had its place in the house. It was a very pleasant place, looking down from the crest to the river, and beyond.'

'It still is,' said Cadfael. 'We've ploughed it, and brushed back the headland bushes, and you might miss the field flowers, and the moths at midsummer when the meadow grasses ripen. But there'll be the young green starting now along the furrows, and the birds in the headlands just the same. Yes, a very fine place.'

They had turned to walk back through the wet grass towards the chapter-house, and the dusk was a soft blue-green about them, clinging moist in the half-naked branches of the trees.

'She would never have had a place in this blessed ground,' said Ruald, out of the shadow of his cowl, 'but that she was found in land belonging to the abbey, and without any other sponsor to take care of her. As Saint Illtud drove his wife out into the night for no offence, as I, for no offence in her, deserted Generys, so in the end God has brought her back into the care of the Order, and provided her an enviable grave. Father Abbot received and blessed what I misused and misprized.'

'It may well be,' said Cadfael, 'that our justice sees as in a mirror image, left where right should be, evil reflected back as good, good as evil, your angel as her devil. But God's justice, if it makes no haste, makes no mistakes.'

The Summer of The Danes

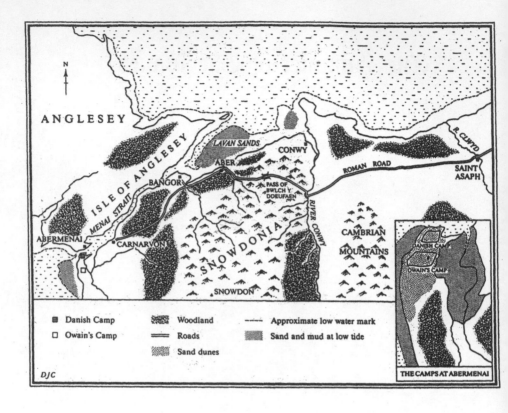

THE CAMPS AT ABERMENAI

Chapter One

HE EXTRAORDINARY events of that summer of 1144 may properly be said to have begun the previous year, in a tangle of threads both ecclesiastical and secular, a net in which any number of diverse people became enmeshed, clerics, from the archbishop down to Bishop Roger de Clinton's lowliest deacon, and the laity from the princes of North Wales down to the humblest cottager in the trefs of Arfon. And among the commonalty thus entrammelled, more to the point, an elderly Benedictine monk of the Abbey of Saint Peter and Saint Paul, at Shrewsbury.

Brother Cadfael had approached that April in a mood of slightly restless hopefulness, as was usual with him when the birds were nesting, and the meadow flowers just beginning to thrust their buds up through the new grass, and the sun to rise a little higher in the sky every noon. True, there were troubles in the world, as there always had been. The vexed affairs of England, torn in two by two cousins contending for the throne, had still no visible hope of a solution. King Stephen still held his own in the south and most of the east; the Empress Maud, thanks to her loyal half-brother, Robert of Gloucester, was securely established in the southwest and maintained her own court unmolested in Devizes. But for some months now there had been very little fighting between them, whether from exhaustion or policy, and a strange calm had settled over the country, almost peace. In the Fens the raging outlaw Geoffrey de Mandeville, every man's enemy, was still at liberty, but a liberty constricted by the king's new encircling fortresses, and increasingly vulnerable. All in all, there was room for some cautious optimism, and the very freshness and lustre of the Spring forbade despondency, even had despondency been among Cadfael's propensities.

So he came to chapter, on this particular day at the end of April, in the most serene and acquiescent of spirits, full of mild good intentions towards all men, and content that things should continue as bland and uneventful through the summer and into the autumn. He certainly had no premonition of any immediate change in this idyllic condition, much less of the agency by which it was to come.

As though compelled, half fearfully and half gratefully, to the same precarious but welcome quietude, the business at chapter that day was modest and aroused no dispute, there was no one in default, not even a small sin among the novices for Brother Jerome to deplore, and the schoolboys, intoxicated with the Spring and the sunshine, seemed to be behaving like the angels they certainly were not. Even the chapter of the Rule, read in the flat, deprecating tones of Brother Francis, was the 34th, gently explaining that the doctrine of equal shares for all could not always be maintained, since the needs of one might exceed the needs of another, and he who received more accordingly must not preen himself on being supplied beyond his brothers, and he that received less but enough must not grudge the extra bestowed on his brothers. And above all, no grumbling, no envy. Everything was placid, conciliatory, moderate. Perhaps, even, a shade on the dull side?

It is a blessed thing, on the whole, to live in slightly dull times, especially after disorder, siege and bitter contention. But there was still a morsel somewhere in Cadfael that itched if the hush continued too long. A little excitement, after all, need not be mischief, and does sound a pleasant counterpoint to the constant order, however much that may be loved and however faithfully served.

They were at the end of routine business, and Cadfael's attention had wandered away from the details of the cellarer's accounts, since he himself had no function as an obedientiary, and was content to leave such matters to those who had. Abbot Radulfus was about to close the chapter, with a sweeping glance around him to make sure that no one else was brooding over some demur or reservation, when the lay porter who

390

served at the gatehouse during service or chapter put his head in at the door, in a manner which suggested he had been waiting for this very moment, just out of sight.

'Father Abbot, there is a guest here from Lichfield. Bishop de Clinton has sent him on an errand into Wales, and he asks lodging here for a night or two.'

Anyone of less importance, thought Cadfael, and he would have let it wait until we all emerged, but if the bishop is involved it may well be serious business, and require official consideration before we disperse. He had good memories of Roger de Clinton, a man of decision and solid good sense, with an eye for the genuine and the bogus in other men, and a short way with problems of doctrine. By the spark in the abbot's eye, though his face remained impassive, Radulfus also recalled the bishop's last visit with appreciation.

'The bishop's envoy is very welcome,' he said, 'and may lodge here for as long as he wishes. Has he some immediate request of us, before I close this chapter?'

'Father, he would like to make his reverence to you at once, and let you know what his errand is. At your will whether it should be here or in private.'

'Let him come in,' said Radulfus.

The porter vanished, and the small, discreet buzz of curiosity and speculation that went round the chapterhouse like a ripple on a pond ebbed into anticipatory silence as the bishop's envoy came in and stood among them.

A little man, of slender bones and lean but wiry flesh, diminutive as a sixteen-year-old boy, and looking very much like one, until discerning attention discovered the quality and maturity of the oval, beardless face. A Benedictine like these his brothers, tonsured and habited, he stood erect in the dignity of his office and the humility and simplicity of his nature, as fragile as a child and as durable as a tree. His straw-coloured ring of cropped hair had an unruly spikiness, recalling the child. His grey eyes, formidably direct and clear, confirmed the man.

A small miracle! Cadfael found himself suddenly presented with a gift he had often longed for in the past few years, by its very suddenness and improbability surely miraculous. Roger de Clinton had chosen as his accredited envoy into Wales not some portly canon of imposing presence, from the inner hierarchy of his extensive see, but the youngest and humblest deacon in his household, Brother Mark, sometime of

391

Shrewsbury Abbey, and assistant for two fondly remembered years among the herbs and medicines of Cadfael's workshop.

Brother Mark made a deep reverence to the abbot, dipping his ebullient tonsure with a solemnity which still retained, until he lifted those clear eyes again, the slight echo and charm of absurdity which had always clung about the mute waif Cadfael first recalled. When he stood erect he was again the ambassador; he would always be both man and child from this time forth, until the day when he became priest, which was his passionate desire. And that could not be for some years yet, he was not old enough to be accepted.

'My lord,' he said, 'I am sent by my bishop on an errand of goodwill into Wales. He prays you receive and house me for a night or two among you.'

'My son,' said the abbot, smiling, 'you need here no credentials but your presence. Did you think we could have forgotten you so soon? You have here as many friends as there are brothers, and in only two days you will find it hard to satisfy them all. And as for your errand, or your lord's errand, we will do all we can to forward it. Do you wish to speak of it? Here, or in private?'

Brother Mark's solemn face melted into a delighted smile at being not only remembered, but remembered with obvious pleasure. 'It is no long story, Father,' he said, 'and I may well declare it here, though later I would entreat your advice and counsel, for such an embassage is new to me, and there is no one could better aid me to perform it faithfully than you. You know that last year the Church chose to restore the bishopric of Saint Asaph, at Llanelwy.'

Radulfus agreed, with an inclination of his head. The fourth Welsh diocese had been in abeyance for some seventy years, very few now living could remember when there had been a bishop on the throne of Saint Kentigern. The location of the see, with a foot either side the border, and all the power of Gwynedd to westward, had always made it difficult to maintain. The cathedral stood on land held by the earl of Chester, but all the Clwyd valley above it was in Owain Gwynedd's territory. Exactly why Archbishop Theobald had resolved on reviving the diocese at this time was not quite clear to anyone, perhaps not even the archbishop. Mixed motives of Church politics and secular manoeuvring apparently required a firmly English hold on this borderland, for the appointed man was a Norman. There was not much tenderness towards Welsh sensitivities in such a preferment, Cadfael reflected ruefully.

'And after his consecration last year by Archbishop Theobald, at Lambeth, Bishop Gilbert is finally installed in his see, and the archbishop wishes him to receive assurance he has the support of our own bishop, since the pastoral duties in those parts formerly rested in the diocese of Lichfield. I am the bearer of letters and gifts to Llanelwy on my lord's behalf.'

That made sense, if the whole intent of the Church was to gain a firm foothold well into Welsh land, and demonstrate that it would be preserved and defended. A marvel, Cadfael considered, that any bishop had ever contrived to manage so huge a see as the original bishopric of Mercia, successively shifting its base from Lichfield to Chester, back again to Lichfield, and now to Coventry, in the effort to remain in touch with as diverse a flock as ever shepherd tended. And Roger de Clinton might not be sorry to be quit of those border parishes, whether or not he approved the strategy which deprived him of them.

'The errand that brings you back to us, even for a few days, is dearly welcome,' said Radulfus. 'If my time and experience can be of any avail to you, they are yours, though I think you are equipped to acquit yourself well without any help from me or any man.'

'It is a weighty honour to be so trusted,' said Mark very gravely.

'If the bishop has no doubts,' said Radulfus, 'neither need you. I take him for a man who can judge very well where to place his trust. If you have ridden from Lichfield you must be in need of some rest and refreshment, for it's plain you set out early. Is your mount being cared for?'

'Yes, Father.' The old address came back naturally.

'Then come with me to my lodging, and take some ease, and use my time as you may wish. What wisdom I have is at your disposal.' He was already acutely aware, as Cadfael was, that this apparently simple mission to the newly made and alien bishop at Saint Asaph covered a multitude of other calculated risks and questionable issues, and might well send this wise innocent feeling his way foot by foot through a quagmire, with quaking turf on every hand. All the more impressive, then, that Roger de Clinton had placed his faith in the youngest and least of his attendant clerics.

'This chapter is concluded,' said the abbot, and led the way out. As he passed the visitor by, Brother Mark's grey eyes, at

393

liberty at last to sweep the assembly for other old friends, met Cadfael's eyes, and returned his smile, before the young man turned and followed his superior. Let Radulfus have him for a while, savour him, get all his news from him, and all the details that might complicate his coming journey, give him the benefit of long experience and unfailing commonsense. Later on, when that was done, Mark would find his own way back to the herb garden.

'The bishop has been very good to me,' said Mark, shaking off firmly the idea of any special preference being shown him in his selection for this mission, 'but so he is to all those close about him. There's more to this than favour to me. Now that he's set up Bishop Gilbert in Saint Asaph, the archbishop knows very well how shaky his position must be, and wants to make sure his throne is secured by every support possible. It was his wish – indeed his command – that our bishop should pay the new man this complimentary visit, seeing it's from his diocese most of Gilbert's new see has been lopped. Let the world see what harmony there is among bishops – even bishops who have had a third of their territory whipped from under their feet. Whatever Bishop Roger may be thinking of the wisdom of planting a Norman, with not a word of Welsh, in a see nine-tenths Welsh, he could hardly refuse the archbishop. But it was left to him how he carried out the order. I think he chose me because he does not wish to make too lavish and flattering a show. His letter is formal and beautifully executed, his gift is more than suitable. But I – I am a judicious half-measure!'

They were gathered in conference in one of the carrels of the north walk, where the Spring sunshine still reached slanting fingers of pale gold even in late afternoon, an hour or so before Vespers. Hugh Beringar had ridden down from his house in the town as soon as word of Brother Mark's arrival had reached him, not because the sheriff had any official business in this clerical embassage, but for the pleasure of seeing again a young man he held in affectionate remembrance, and to whom, in this present instance, he might be able to give some help and advice. Hugh's relations with North Wales were good. He had a friendly agreement with Owain Gwynedd, since neither of them trusted their mutual neighbour the earl of Chester, and they could accept each other's word without question. With Madog ap Meredith of Powis the sheriff had a more precarious relationship. The Shropshire border was constantly alert against sporadic and almost playful raids from beyond the dyke, though at this present time all was comparatively quiet. What the conditions of travel were likely to be on this ride to Saint Asaph, Hugh was the most likely man to know.

'I think you are too modest,' he said seriously. 'I fancy the bishop knows you well enough by now, if he's had you constantly about him, to have a very good opinion of your wit, and trusts you to step gently where a weightier ambassador might talk too much and listen too little. Cadfael here will tell you more than I can about Welsh feeling in Church matters, but I know where politics enter into it. You can be sure that Owain Gwynedd has a sharp eye on the doings of Archbishop Theobald in his domain, and Owain is always to be reckoned with. And only four years ago there was a new bishop consecrated in his own home diocese of Bangor, which is totally Welsh. There at least they did sanction a Welshman, one who at first refused to swear fealty to King Stephen or acknowledge the dominance of Canterbury. Meurig was no hero, and did finally give way and do both, and it cost him Owain's countenance and favour at the time. There was strong resistance to allowing him to take his seat. But they've come to terms and made up their differences since then, which means they'll certainly work together to keep Gwynedd from being wholly subservient to Theobald's influence. To consecrate a Norman now to Saint Asaph is a challenge to princes as well as prelates, and whoever undertakes a diplomatic mission there will have to keep a sharp eye on both.'

'And Owain at least,' Cadfael added shrewdly, 'will be keeping a sharp eye on what his people are feeling, and an ear open to what they are saying. It behoves Gilbert to do the same. Gwynedd has no mind to give way to Canterbury, they have saints and customs and rites of their own.'

'I have heard,' said Mark, 'that formerly, a long time ago, St David's was the metropolitan see of Wales, with its own archbishop not subject to Canterbury. There are some Welsh churchmen now who want that rule restored.'

Cadfael shook his head rather dubiously at that. 'Better not to look too closely into the past, we're hearing more of that claim the more the writ of Canterbury is urged on us. But certainly Owain will be casting his shadow over his new bishop, by way of a reminder he's in alien territory, and had better mind his manners. I hope he may be a wise man, and go gently with his flock.'

'Our bishop is very much in agreement with you,' said Mark,

'and I'm well briefed. I did not tell the whole of my errand in chapter, though I have told it to Father Abbot since. I have yet another letter and gift to deliver. I am to go on to Bangor – oh, no, this is certainly not at Archbishop Theobald's orders! – and pay the same courtesy to Bishop Meurig as to Bishop Gilbert. If Theobald holds that bishops should stand together, then Roger de Clinton's text is that the principle applies to Norman and Welsh alike. And we propose to treat them alike.'

The 'we', as applying to Mark in common with his illustrious superior, sounded an echoing chord in Cadfael's ears. He recalled just as innocent a presumption of partnership some years back, when this boy had been gradually emerging from his well-founded wariness of all men into warmth and affection, and this impulsive loyalty to those he admired and served. His 'we', then, had signified himself and Cadfael, as if they were two venturers keeping each the other's back against the world.

'More and more,' said Hugh appreciatively, 'I warm to this bishop of ours. But he's sending you even on this longer journey alone?'

'Not quite alone.' Brother Mark's thin, bright face flashed for an instant into a slightly mischievous smile, as though he had still some mysterious surprise up his sleeve. 'But *he* would not hesitate to ride across Wales alone, and neither would I. He takes it for granted the Church and the cloth will be respected. But of course I shall be glad of any advice you can give me about the best way. You know far better than I or my bishop what conditions hold good in Wales. I thought to go directly by Oswestry and Chirk. What do you think?'

'Things are quiet enough up there,' Hugh agreed. 'In any event, Madog, whatever else he may be, is a pious soul where churchmen are concerned, however he may treat the English laity. And for the moment he has all the lesser lads of Powis Fadog on a tight rein. Yes, you'll be safe enough that way, and it's your quickest way, though you'll find some rough upland riding between Dee and Clwyd.'

By the brightness and speculation of Mark's grey eyes he was looking forward to his adventure. It is a great thing to be trusted with an important errand when you are the latest and least of your lord's servants, and for all his awareness that his humble status was meant to temper the compliment, he was also aware how much depended on the address with which he discharged his task. He was meant not to flatter, not to exalt, but nevertheless to present in his person the real and formidable solidarity of bishop with bishop.

'Are there things I should know,' he asked, 'about affairs in Gwynedd? The politics of the Church must reckon with the politics of state, and I am ignorant about things Welsh. I need to know on what subjects to keep my mouth shut, and when to speak, and what it would be wise to say. All the more as I am to go on to Bangor. What if the court should be there? I may have to account for myself to Owain's officers. Even to Owain himself!'

'True enough,' said Hugh, 'for he usually contrives to know of every stranger who enters his territory. You'll find him approachable enough if you do encounter him. For that matter, you may give him my greetings and compliments. And Cadfael has met him, twice at least. A large man, every way! Just say no word of brothers! It may still be a sore point with him.'

'Brothers have been the ruin of Welsh princedoms through all ages,' Cadfael observed ruefully. 'Welsh princes should have only one son apiece. The father builds up a sound principality and a strong rule, and after his death his three or four or five sons, in and out of wedlock, all demand by right equal shares, and the law says they should have them. Then one picks off another, to enlarge his portion, and it would take more than law to stop the killing. I wonder, sometimes, what will happen when Owain's gone. He has sons already, and time enough before him to get more. Are they, I wonder, going to undo everything he's done?'

'Please God,' said Hugh fervently, 'Owain's going may not be for thirty years or more. He's barely past forty. I can deal with Owain, he keeps his word and he keeps his balance. If Cadwaladr had been the elder and got the dominance we should have had border war along this frontier year in, year out.'

'This Cadwaladr is the brother it's best not to mention?' Mark asked. 'What has he done that makes him anathema?'

'A number of things over the years. Owain must love him, or he would have let someone rid him of the pest long ago. But this time, murder. Some months ago, in the autumn of last year, a party of his closest men ambushed the prince of Deheubarth and killed him. God knows for what mad reason! The young fellow was in close alliance with him, and betrothed to Owain's daughter, there was no manner of sense in such an act. And for all Cadwaladr did not appear himself in the deed, Owain for one was in no doubt it was done on his orders. None of them would have dared, not of their own doing.'

Cadfael recalled the shock of the murder, and the swift and thorough retribution. Owain Gwynedd in outraged justice had sent his son Hywel to drive Cadwaladr bodily out of every furlong of land he held in Ceredigion, and burnt his castle of Llanbadarn, and the young man, barely past twenty, had accomplished his task with relish and efficiency. Doubtless Cadwaladr had friends and adherents who would give him at least the shelter of a roof, but he remained landless and outcast. Cadfael could not but wonder, not only where the offender was lurking now, but whether he might not end, like Geoffrey of Mandeville in the Fens, gathering the scum of North Wales about him, criminals, malcontents, natural outlaws, and preying on all law-abiding people.

'What became of this Cadwaladr?' asked Mark with understandable curiosity.

'Dispossession. Owain drove him out of every piece of land he had to his name. Not a toehold left to him in Wales.'

'But he's still at large, somewhere,' Cadfael observed, with some concern, 'and by no means the man to take his penalty tamely. There could be mischief yet to pay. I see you're bound into a perilous labyrinth. I think you should not be going alone.'

Hugh was studying Mark's face, outwardly impassive, but with a secretive sparkle of fun in the eyes that watched Cadfael so assiduously. 'As I recall,' said Hugh mildly, 'he said: "Not quite alone!" '

'So he did!' Cadfael stared into the young face that confronted him so solemnly, but for that betraying gleam in the eyes. 'What is it, boy, that you have not told us? Out with it! Who goes with you?'

'But I did tell you,' said Mark, 'that I am going on to Bangor. Bishop Gilbert is Norman, and speaks both French and English, but Bishop Meurig is Welsh, and he and many of his people speak no English, and my Latin would serve me only among the clerics. So I am allowed an interpreter. Bishop Roger has no competent Welsh speaker close to him or in his confidence. I offered a name, one he had not forgotten.' The sparkle had grown into a radiance that lit his face, and reflected not only light but enlightenment back into Cadfael's dazzled eyes. 'I have been keeping the best till last,' said Mark, glowing. 'I got leave to win my man, if Abbot Radulfus would sanction his absence. I have as good as promised him the loan will be for only ten days or so at the most. So how can I possibly miscarry,' asked Mark reasonably, 'if you are coming with me?'

It was a matter of principle, or perhaps of honour, with Brother Cadfael, when a door opened before him suddenly and unexpectedly, to accept the offer and walk through it. He did so with even more alacrity if the door opened on a prospect of Wales; it might even be said that he broke into a trot, in case the door slammed again on that enchanting view. Not merely a brief sally over the border into Powis, this time, but several days of riding, in the very fellowship he would have chosen, right across the coastal regions of Gwynedd, from Saint Asaph to Carnarvon, past Aber of the princes, under the tremendous shoulders of Moel Wnion. Time to talk over every day of the time they had been apart, time to reach the companionable silences when all that needed to be said was said. And all this the gift of Brother Mark. Wonderful what riches a man can bestow who by choice and vocation possesses nothing! The world is full of small, beneficent miracles.

'Son,' said Cadfael heartily, 'for such refreshment I'll be your groom along the way, as well as your interpreter. There's no way you or any man could have given me more pleasure. And did Radulfus really say I'm free to go?'

'He did,' Mark assured him, 'and the choice of a horse from the stables is yours. And you have today and tomorrow to make your preparations with Edmund and Winfrid for the days you're absent, and to keep the hours of the Office so strictly that even your errant soul shall go protected to Bangor and back.'

'I am wholly virtuous and regenerate,' said Cadfael with immense content. 'Has not heaven just shown it by letting me loose in Wales? Do you think I am going to risk disapprobation now?'

Since at least the first part of Mark's mission was meant to be public and demonstrative, there was no reason why every soul in the enclave should not take an avid interest in it, and there was no lack of gratuitous advice available from all sides as to how it could best be performed, especially from old Brother Dafydd in the infirmary, who had not seen his native cantref of

399

Duffryn Clwyd for forty years, but was still convinced he knew it like the palm of his ancient hand. His pleasure in the revival of the diocese was somewhat soured by the appointment of a Norman, but the mild excitement had given him a new interest in life, and he reverted happily to his own language, and was voluble in counsel when Cadfael visited him. Abbot Radulfus, by contrast, contributed nothing but his blessing. The mission belonged to Mark, and must be left scrupulously in his hands. Prior Robert forebore from comment, though his silence bore a certain overtone of disapproval. An envoy of his dignity and presence would have been more appropriate in the courts of bishops.

Brother Cadfael reviewed his medical supplies, committed his garden confidently to Brother Winfrid, and paid a precautionary visit to Saint Giles to ensure that the hospital cupboards were properly provided, and Brother Oswin in serene command of his flock, before he repaired to the stables to indulge in the pleasure of selecting his mount for the journey. It was there that Hugh found him early in the afternoon, contemplating with pleasure an elegant light roan with a cream-coloured mane, that leaned complacently to his caressing hand.

'Too tall for you,' said Hugh over his shoulder. 'You'd need a lift into the saddle, and Mark could never hoist you.'

'I am not yet grown so heavy nor so shrunken with age that I cannot scramble on to a horse,' said Cadfael with dignity. 'What brings you here again and looking for me?'

'Why, a good notion Aline had, when I told her what you and Mark are up to. May is on the doorstep already, and in a week or two at the most I should be packing her and Giles off to Maesbury for the summer. He has the run of the manor there, and it's better for him out of the town.' It was his usual custom to leave his family there until after the wool clip had been taken and the fields gleaned, while he divided his time between home and the business of the shire. Cadfael was familiar with the routine. 'She says, why should we not hasten the move by a week, and ride with you tomorrow, to set you on your way as far as Oswestry? The rest of the household can follow later, and we could have one day, at least, of your company, and you could bide the night over with us at Maesbury if you choose. What do you say?'

Cadfael said yes, very heartily, and so, when it was put to him, did Mark, though he declined, with regret, the offer of a night's lodging. He was bent on reaching Llanelwy in two days, and arriving at a civilised time, at the latest by mid-afternoon, to allow time for the niceties of hospitality before the evening meal, so he preferred to go beyond Oswestry and well into Wales before halting for the night, to leave an easy stage for the second day. If they could reach the valley of the Dee, they could find lodging with one of the churches there, and cross the river in the early morning.

So it seemed that everything was already accounted for, and there remained nothing to be done but go reverently to Vespers and Compline, and commit this enterprise like all others to the will of God, but perhaps also with a gentle reminder to Saint Winifred that they were bound into her country, and if she felt inclined to let her delicate hand cover them along the way, the gesture would be very much appreciated.

The morning of departure found a little cavalcade of six horses and a pack-pony winding its way over the westward bridge and out of the town, on the road to Oswestry. There was Hugh, on his favourite self-willed grey, with his son on his saddle-bow, Aline, unruffled by the haste of her preparations for leaving town, on her white jennet, her maid and friend Constance pillion behind a groom, a second groom following with the pack-pony on a leading rein, and the two pilgrims to Saint Asaph merrily escorted by this family party. It was the last of April, a morning all green and silver. Cadfael and Mark had left before Prime, to join Hugh and his party in the town. A shower, so fine as to be almost imperceptible in the air, had followed them over the bridge, where the Severn ran full but peaceful, and before they had assembled in Hugh's courtyard the sun had come out fully, sparkling on the leaves and grasses. The river was gilded in every ripple with capricious, scintillating light. A good day to be setting out, and no great matter why or where.

The sun was high, and the pearly mist of morning all dissolved when they crossed the river at Montford. The road was good, some stretches of it with wide grass verges where the going was comfortable and fast, and Giles demanded an occasional canter. He was much too proud to share a mount with anyone but his father. Once established at Maesbury the little pack-pony, sedate and goodhumoured, would become his riding pony for the summer, and the groom who led it his discreet guardian on his forays, for like most children who have

401

never seen cause to be afraid, he was fearless on horseback – Aline said foolhardy, but hesitated to issue warnings, perhaps for fear of shaking his confidence, or perhaps out of the certainty that they would not be heeded.

They halted at noon under the hill at Ness, where there was a tenant of Hugh's installed, to rest the horses and take refreshment. Before mid-afternoon they reached Felton, and there Aline and the escort turned aside to take the nearest way home, but Hugh elected to ride on with his friends to the outskirts of Oswestry. Giles was transferred, protesting but obedient, to his mother's arms.

'Go safely, and return safely!' said Aline, her primrose head pale and bright as the child's, the gloss of Spring on her face and the burnish of sunlight in her smile. And she signed a little cross on the air between them before she wheeled her jennet into the lefthand track.

Delivered of the baggage and the womenfolk, they rode on at a brisker pace the few miles to Whittington, where they halted under the walls of the small timber keep. Oswestry itself lay to their left, on Hugh's route homeward. Mark and Cadfael must go on northward still, but here they were on the very borderland, country which had been alternately Welsh and English for centuries before ever the Normans came, where the names of hamlets and of men were more likely to be Welsh than English. Hugh lived between the two great dykes the princes of Mercia had constructed long ago, to mark where their holding and writ began, so that no force should easily encroach, and no man who crossed from one side to the other should be in any doubt under which law he stood. The lower barrier lay just to the east of the manor, much battered and levelled now; the greater one had been raised to the west, when Mercian power had been able to thrust further into Wales.

'Here I must leave you,' said Hugh, looking back along the way they had come, and westward towards the town and the castle. 'A pity! I could gladly have ridden as far as Saint Asaph with you in such weather, but the king's officers had best stay out of Church business and avoid the crossfire. I should be loth to tread on Owain's toes.'

'You have brought us as far as Bishop Gilbert's writ, at any rate,' said Brother Mark, smiling. 'Both this church and yours of Saint Oswald are now in the see of Saint Asaph. Did you realise that? Lichfield has lost a great swathe of parishes here

402

in the northwest. I think it must be Canterbury policy to spread the diocese both sides the border, so that the line between Welsh and English can count for nothing.'

'Owain will have something to say to that, too.' Hugh saluted them with a raised hand, and began to wheel his horse towards the road home. 'Go with God, and a good journey! We'll look to see you again in ten days or so.' And he was some yards distant when he looked back over his shoulder and called after them: 'Keep him out of mischief! If you can!' But there was no indication to which of them the plea was addressed, or to which of them the misgiving applied. They could share it between them.

Chapter Two

'I AM TOO OLD,' Brother Cadfael observed complacently, 'to embark on such adventures as this.'

'I notice,' said Mark, eyeing him sidelong, 'you say nothing of the kind until we're well clear of Shrewsbury, and there's no one to take you at your word, poor aged soul, and bid you stay at home.'

'What a fool I should have been!' Cadfael willingly agreed.

'Whenever you begin pleading your age, I know what I have to deal with. A horse full of oats, just let out of his stall, and with the bit between his teeth. We have to do with bishops and canons,' said Mark severely, 'and they can be trouble enough. Pray to be spared any worse encounters.' But he did not sound too convinced. The ride had brought colour to his thin, pale face and a sparkle to his eyes. Mark had been raised with farm horses, slaving for the uncle who grudged him house-room and food, and he still rode farm fashion, inelegant but durable, now that the bishop's stable had provided him a fine tall gelding in place of a plodding farm drudge. The beast was nutbrown, with a lustrous copper sheen to his coat, and buoyantly lively under such a light weight.

They had halted at the crest of the ridge overlooking the lush green valley of the Dee. The sun was westering, and had mellowed from the noon gold into a softer amber light, gleaming down the stream, where the coils of the river alternately glimmered and vanished among its fringes of woodland. Still an upland river here, dancing over a rocky bed and conjuring rainbows out of its sunlit spray. Somewhere down there they would find a night's lodging.

They set off companionably side by side, down the grassy track wide enough for two. 'For all that,' said Cadfael, 'I never expected, at my age, to be recruited into such an expedition as this. I owe you more than you know. Shrewsbury is home, and I would not leave it for any place on earth, beyond a visit, but every now and then my feet itch. It's a fine thing to be heading home, but it's a fine thing also to be setting out from home, with both the going and the return to look forward to. Well for me that Theobald took thought to recruit allies for his new bishop. And what is it Roger de Clinton's sending him, apart from his ceremonial letter?' He had not had time to feel curiosity on that score until now. Mark's saddle-roll was too modest to contain anything of bulk.

'A pectoral cross, blessed at the shrine of Saint Chad. One of the canons made it, he's a good silversmith.'

'And the same to Meurig at Bangor, with his brotherly prayers and compliments?'

'No, Meurig gets a breviary, a very handsome one. Our best illuminator had as good as finished it when the archbishop issued his orders, so he added a special leaf for a picture of Saint Deiniol, Meurig's founder and patron. I would rather have the book,' said Mark, winding his way down a steep woodland ride and out into the declining sun towards the valley. 'But the cross is meant as the more formal tribute. After all, we had our orders. But it shows, do you not think, that Theobald knows that he's given Gilbert a very awkward place to fill?'

'I should not relish being in his shoes,' Cadfael admitted. 'But who knows, he may delight in the struggle. There are those who thrive on contention. If he meddles too much with Welsh custom he'll get more than enough of that.'

They emerged into the green, undulating meadows and bushy coverts along the riverside, the Dee beside them reflecting back orange gleams from the west. Beyond the water a great grassy hill soared, crowned with the man-made contours of earthworks raised ages ago, and under the narrow wooden bridge the Dee dashed and danced over a stony bed. Here at the church of Saint Collen they asked and found a lodging for the night with the parish priest.

On the following day they crossed the river, and climbed over the treeless uplands from the valley of the Dee to the valley of the Clwyd, and there followed the stream at ease the length of a bright morning and into an afternoon of soft showers and wilful gleams of sun. Through Ruthin, under the outcrop of red sandstone crowned with its squat timber fortress, and into the vale proper, broad, beautiful, and the fresh green of young foliage everywhere. Before the sun had stooped towards setting they came down into the narrowing tongue of land between the Clwyd and the Elwy, before the two rivers met above Rhuddlan, to move on together into tidal water. And there between lay the town of Llanelwy and cathedral of Saint Asaph, comfortably nestled in a green, sheltered valley.

Hardly a town at all, it was so small and compact. The low wooden houses clustered close, the single track led into the heart of them, and disclosed the unmistakable long roof and timber bell-turret of the cathedral at the centre of the village. Modest though it was, it was the largest building to be seen, and the only one walled in stone. A range of other low roofs crowded the precinct, and on most of them some hasty repairs had been done, and on others men were still busily working, for though the church had been in use, the diocese had been dormant for seventy years, and if there were still canons attached to this centre their numbers must have dwindled and their houses fallen into disrepair long ago. It had been founded, many centuries past, by Saint Kentigern, on the monastic principle of the old Celtic clas, a college of canons under a priest-abbot, and with one other priest or more among the members. The Normans despised the clas, and were busy disposing of all things religious in Wales to be subject to the Roman rite of Canterbury. Uphill work, but the Normans were persistent people.

But what was astonishing about this remote and rural community was that it seemed to be over-populated to a startling degree. As soon as they approached the precinct they found themselves surrounded by a bustle and purpose that belonged to a prince's llys rather than a church enclave. Besides the busy carpenters and builders there were men and women scurrying about with pitchers of water, armfuls of bedding, folded hangings, trays of new-baked bread and baskets of food, and one strapping lad hefting a side of pork on his shoulders.

'This is more than a bishop's household,' said Cadfael, staring

406

at all the activity. 'They are feeding an army! Has Gilbert declared war on the valley of Clwyd?'

'I think,' said Mark, gazing beyond the whirlpool of busy people to the gently rising hillside above, 'they are entertaining more important guests than us.'

Cadfael followed where Mark was staring, and saw in the shadow of the hills points of colour patterning a high green level above the little town. Bright pavilions and fluttering pennants spread across the green, not the rough and ready tents of a military encampment, but the furnishings of a princely household.

'Not an army,' said Cadfael, 'but a court. We've strayed into lofty company. Had we not better go quickly and find out if two more are welcome? For there may be business afoot that concerns more than staunch brotherhood among bishops. Though if the prince's officers are keeping close at Gilbert's elbow, a reminder from Canterbury may not come amiss. However cool the compliment!'

They moved forward into the precinct and looked about them. The bishop's palace was a new timber building, hall and chambers, and a number of new small dwellings on either side. It was the better part of a year since Gilbert had been consecrated at Lambeth, and clearly there had been hasty preparations to restore some semblance of a cathedral enclave in order to receive him decently. Cadfael and Mark were dismounting in the court when a young man threaded a brisk way to them through the bustle, and beckoned a groom after him to take their horses.

'Brothers, may I be of service?'

He was young, surely not more than twenty, and certainly not one of Gilbert's ecclesiastics, rather something of a courtier in his dress, and wore gemstones about a fine, sturdy throat. He moved and spoke with an easy confidence and grace, bright of countenance and fair in colouring, his hair a light, reddish brown. A tall fellow, with something about him that seemed to Cadfael elusively familiar, though he had certainly never seen him before. He had addressed them first in Welsh, but changed easily to English after studying Mark from head to foot in one brilliant glance.

'Men of your habit are always welcome. Have you ridden far?'

'From Lichfield,' said Mark, 'with a brotherly letter and gift for Bishop Gilbert from my bishop of Coventry and Lichfield.'

407

'He will be heartily glad,' said the young man, with surprising candour, 'for he may be feeling the need of reinforcements.' His flashing grin was mischievous but amiable. 'Here, let me get someone to bring your saddle-rolls after us, and I'll bring you where you can rest and take refreshment. It will be a while yet to supper.'

A gesture from him brought servants running to unstrap the pack-rolls and follow hard on the visitors' heels as the young man led them across the court to one of the new cells built out from the hall.

'I am without rights to command here, being a guest myself, but they have got used to me.' It was said with an assured and slightly amused confidence, as if he knew good reason why the bishop's circle should accommodate him, and was forbearing enough not to presume upon it too far. 'Will this suffice?'

The lodging was small but adequate, furnished with beds, bench and table, and full of the scent of seasoned wood freshly tooled. New brychans were piled on the beds, and the smell of good wool mingled with the newness of timber.

'I'll send someone with water,' said their guide, 'and find one of the canons. His lordship has been selecting where he can, but his demands come high. He's having trouble in filling up his chapter. Be at home here, Brothers, and someone will come to you.'

And he was gone, with his blithe long strides and springing tread, and they were left to settle and stretch at ease after their day in the saddle.

'Water?' said Mark, pondering this first and apparently essential courtesy. 'Is that by way of taking salt, here in Wales?'

'No, lad. A people that goes mostly afoot knows the value of feet and the dust and aches of travel. They bring water for us to bathe our feet. It is a graceful way of asking: Are you meaning to bide overnight? If we refuse it, we intend only a brief visit in courtesy. If we accept it, we are guests of the house from that moment.'

'And that young lord? For he's too fine for a servant, and certainly no cleric. A guest, he said. What sort of an assembly have we blundered into, Cadfael?'

They had left the door wide for the pleasure of the evening light and the animation to be viewed about the court. A girl came threading her way through the purposeful traffic with a long, striding grace in her step, bearing before her a pitcher in a bowl. The water-carrier was tall and vigorous. A braid of glassy blue-black hair thick as her wrist hung over her shoulder, and stray curls blew about her temples in the faint breeze. A pleasure to behold, Cadfael thought, watching her approach. She made them a deep reverence as she entered, and kept her eyes dutifully lowered as she served them, pouring water for them, unlatching their sandals with her own long, shapely hands, no servant but a decorous hostess, so surely in a position of dominance here that she could stoop to serve without at any point abasing herself. The touch of her hands on Mark's lean ankles and delicate, almost girlish feet brought a fiery blush rising from his throat to his brow, and then, as if she had felt it scorch her forehead, she did look up.

It was the most revealing of glances, though it lasted only a moment. As soon as she raised her eyes, a face hitherto impassive and austere was illuminated with a quicksilver sequence of expressions that came and passed in a flash. She took in Mark in one sweep of her lashes, and his discomfort amused her, and for an instant she considered letting him see her laughter, which would have discomforted him further; but then she relented, indulging an impulse of sympathy for his youth and apparent fragile innocence, and restored the gravity of her oval countenance.

Her eyes were so dark a purple as to appear black in shadow. She could not be more than eighteen years of age. Perhaps less, for her height and her bearing gave her a woman's confidence. She had brought linen towels over her shoulder, and would have made a deliberate and perhaps mildly teasing grace of drying Mark's feet with her own hands, but he would not let her. The authority that belonged not in his own small person but in the gravity of his office reached out to take her firmly by the hand and raise her from her knees. She rose obediently, only a momentary flash of her dark eyes compromising her solemnity. Young clerics, Cadfael thought, perceiving that he himself was in no danger, might have trouble with this one. For that matter, so might elderly clerics, if in a slightly different way.

'No,' said Mark firmly. 'It is not fitting. Our part in the world is to serve, not to be served. And from all we have seen, outside there, you have more than enough guests on your hands, more demanding than we would wish to be.'

At that she suddenly laughed outright, and clearly not at him, but at whatever thoughts his words had sparked in her mind. Until then she had spoken no word but her murmured greeting on the threshold. Now she broke into bubbling speech in Welsh, in a lilting voice that made dancing poetry of language.

'More than enough for his lordship Bishop Gilbert, and more than he bargained for! Is it true what Hywel said, that you are sent with compliments and gifts from the English bishops? Then you will be the most welcome pair of visitors here in Llanelwy tonight. Our new bishop feels himself in need of all the encouragement he can get. A reminder he has an archbishop behind him will come in very kindly, seeing he's beset with princes every other way. He'll make the most of you. You'll surely find yourselves at the high table in hall tonight.'

'Princes!' Cadfael echoed. 'And Hywel? Was that Hywel who spoke with us when we rode in? Hywel ab Owain?'

'Did you not recognise him?' she said, astonished.

'Child, I never saw him before. But his reputation we do know.' So this was the young fellow who had been sent by his father to waft an army across the Aeron and drive Cadwaladr headlong out of North Ceredigion with his castle of Llanbadarn in flames behind him, and had made a most brisk and workmanlike job of it, without, apparently, losing his composure or ruffling his curls. And he looking barely old enough to bear arms at all!

'I thought there was something about him I should know! Owain I have met, we had dealings three years back, over an exchange of prisoners. So he's sent his son to report on how Bishop Gilbert is setting about his pastoral duties, has he?' Cadfael wondered. Trusted in both secular and clerical matters, it seemed, and probably equally thorough in both.

'Better than that,' said the girl, laughing. 'He's come himself! Did you not see his tents up there in the meadows? For these few days Llanelwy is Owain's llys, and the court of Gwynedd, no less. It's an honour Bishop Gilbert could have done without. Not that the prince makes any move to curb or intimidate him, bar his simply being there, for ever in the corner of the bishop's eye, and 'ware of everything he does or says. The prince of courtesy and consideration! He expects the bishop to house only himself and his son, and provides for the rest himself. But tonight they all sup in hall. You will see, you came very opportunely.'

She had been gathering up the towels over her arm as she

talked, and keeping a sharp eye now and then on the comings and goings in the courtyard. Following such a glance, Cadfael observed a big man in a black cassock sailing impressively across the grass towards their lodging.

'I'll bring you food and mead,' said the girl, returning abruptly to the practical; and she picked up bowl and pitcher, and was out at the door before the tall cleric could reach it. Cadfael saw them meet and pass, with a word from the man, and a mute inclination of the head from the girl. It seemed to him that there was a curious tension between them, constrained on the man's part, coldly dutiful on the girl's. His approach had hastened her departure, yet the way he had spoken to her as they met, and in particular the way he halted yet again before reaching the lodging, and turned to look after her, suggested that he was in awe of her rather than the other way round, and she had some grievance she was unwilling to give up. She had not raised her eyes to look at him, nor broken the vehement rhythm of her gait. He came on more slowly, perhaps to reassemble his dignity before entering to the strangers.

'Goodday, Brothers, and welcome!' he said from the threshold. 'I trust my daughter has looked after your comfort well?'

That established at once the relationship between them. It was stated with considered clarity as if some implied issue was likely to come up for consideration, and it was as well it should be properly understood. Which might well be the case, seeing this man was undoubtedly tonsured, in authority here, and a priest. That, too, he chose to state plainly: 'My name is Meirion, I have served this church for many years. Under the new dispensation I am a canon of the chapter. If there is anything wanting, anything we can provide you, during your stay, you have only to speak, I will see it remedied.'

He spoke in formal English, a little hesitantly, for he was obviously Welsh. A burly, muscular man, and handsome in his own black fashion, with sharply cut features and a very erect presence, the ring of his cropped hair barely salted with grey. The girl had her colouring from him, and her dark, brilliant eyes, but in her eyes the spark was of gaiety, even mischief, and in his it gave an impression of faint uneasiness behind the commanding brow. A proud, ambitious man not quite certain of himself and his powers. And perhaps in a delicate situation now that he had become one of the canons attendant on a

411

Norman bishop? It was a possibility. If there was an acknowledged daughter to be accounted for, there must also be a wife. Canterbury would hardly be pleased. They assured him that the lodging provided them was in every way satisfactory, even lavish by monastic principles, and Mark willingly brought out from his saddle-roll Bishop Roger's sealed letter, beautifully inscribed and superscribed, and the little carved wood casket which held the silver cross. Canon Meirion drew pleased breath, for the Lichfield silversmith was a skilled artist, and the work was beautiful.

'He will be pleased and glad, of that you may be sure. I need not conceal from you, as men of the Church, that his lordship's situation here is far from easy, and any gesture of support is a help to him. If you will let me suggest it, it would be well if you make your appearance in form, when all are assembled at table, and there deliver your errand publicly. I will bring you into the hall as your herald, and have places left for you at the bishop's table.' He was quite blunt about it, the utmost advantage must be made of this ceremonious reminder not simply from Lichfield, but from Theobald and Canterbury, that the Roman rite had been accepted and a Norman prelate installed in Saint Asaph. The prince had brought up his own power and chivalry on one side, Canon Meirion meant to deploy Brother Mark, inadequate symbol though he might appear, upon the other.

'And, Brother, although there is no need for translation for the bishop's benefit, it would be good if you would repeat in Welsh what Deacon Mark may say in hall. The prince knows some English, but few of his chiefs understand it.' And it was Canon Meirion's determined intent that they should all, to the last man of the guard, be well aware of what passed. 'I will tell the bishop beforehand of your coming, but say no word as yet to any other.'

'Hywel ab Owain already knows,' said Cadfael.

'And doubtless will have told his father. But the spectacle will not suffer any diminution by that. Indeed, it's a happy chance that you came on this of all days, for tomorrow the royal party is leaving to return to Aber.'

'In that case,' said Mark, choosing to be open with a host who was certainly being open with them, 'we can ride on among his company, for I am the bearer of a letter also to Bishop Meurig of Bangor.'

The canon received this with a short pause for reflection, and

412

then nodded approvingly. He was, after all, a Welshman himself, even if he was doing his able best to hold on to favour with a Norman superior. 'Good! Your bishop is wise. It puts us on a like footing, and will please the prince. As it chances, my daughter Heledd and I will also be of the party. She is to be betrothed to a gentleman in the prince's service, who holds land in Anglesey, and he will come to meet us at Bangor. We shall be companions along the way.'

'Our pleasure to ride in company,' said Mark.

'I'll come for you as soon as they take their places at table,' the canon promised, well content, and left them to an hour of rest. Not until he was gone did the girl come back, bearing a dish of honey cakes and a jar of mead. She served them in silence, but made no move to go. After a moment of sullen thought she asked abruptly: 'What did he tell you?'

'That he and his daughter are bound for Bangor tomorrow, as we two are. It seems,' said Cadfael equably, and watching her unrevealing face, 'that we shall have a prince's escort as far as Aber.'

'So he does still own he is my father,' she said with a curling lip.

'He does, and why should he not profess it proudly? If you look in your mirror,' said Cadfael candidly, 'you will see very good reason why he should boast of it.' That coaxed a reluctant smile out of her. He pursued the small success: 'What is it between you two? Is it some threat from the new bishop? If he's bent on ridding himself of all the married priests in his diocese he has an uphill row to hoe. And your father seems to me an able man, one a new incumbent can ill afford to lose.'

'So he is,' she agreed, warming, 'and the bishop wants to keep him. His case would have been much worse, but my mother was in her last illness when Bishop Gilbert arrived, and it seemed she could not last long, so they waited! Can you conceive of it? Waiting for a wife to die, so that he need not part with her husband, who was useful to him! And die she did, last Christmas, and ever since then I have kept his house, cooked and cleaned for him, and thought we could go on so. But no, I am a reminder of a marriage the bishop says was unlawful and sacrilegious. In his eyes I never should have been born! Even if my father remains celibate the rest of his life, *I* am still here, to call to mind what he wants forgotten. Yes, *he*, not only the bishop! I stand in the way of his advancement.'

'Surely,' said Mark, shocked, 'you do him injustice. I am

413

certain he feels a father's affection for you, as I do believe you feel a daughter's for him.'

'It never was tested before,' she said simply. 'No one grudged us a proper love. Oh, he wishes me no ill, neither does the bishop. But very heartily they both wish that I may go somewhere else to thrive, so far away I shall trouble them no more.'

'So that is why they've planned to match you with a man of Anglesey. As far away,' said Cadfael ruefully, 'as a man could get and still be in North Wales. Yes, that would certainly settle the bishop's mind. But what of yours? Do you know the man they intend for you?'

'No, that was the prince's doing, and he meant it kindly, and indeed I take it kindly. No, the bishop wanted to send me away to a convent in England, and make a nun of me. Owain Gwynedd said that would be a wicked waste unless it was my wish, and asked me there in front of everyone in the hall if I had any mind to it, and very loudly and clearly I said no. So he proposed this match for me. His man is looking for a wife, and they tell me he's a fine fellow, not so young but barely past thirty, which is not so old, and good to look at, and well regarded. Better at least,' she said without great enthusiasm, 'than being shut up behind a grid in an English nunnery.'

'So it is,' agreed Cadfael heartily, 'unless your own heart drives you there, and I doubt that will ever happen to you. Better, too, surely, than living on here and being made to feel an outcast and a burden. You are not wholly set against marriage?'

'No!' she said vehemently.

'And you know of nothing against this man the prince has in mind?'

'Only that I have not chosen him,' she said, and set her red lips in a stubborn line.

'When you see him you may approve him. It would not be the first time,' said Cadfael sagely, 'that an intelligent matchmaker got the balance right.'

'Well or ill,' she said, rising with a sigh, 'I have no choice but to go. My father goes with me to see that I behave, and Canon Morgant, who is as rigid as the bishop himself, goes with us to see that we both behave. Any further scandal now, and goodbye to any advancement under Gilbert. I could destroy him if I so wished,' she said, dwelling vengefully on something she knew could never be a possibility, for all her anger and disdain. And from the evening light in the doorway she looked back to add: 'I can well live without him. Soon or late, I should have gone to a husband. But do you know what most galls me? That he should give me up so lightly, and be so thankful to get rid of me.'

Canon Meirion came for them as he had promised, just as the bustle in the courtyard was settling into competent quietness, building work abandoned for the day, all the domestic preparations for the evening's feast completed, the small army of servitors mustered into their places, and the household, from princes to grooms, assembled in hall. The light was still bright, but softening into the gilded silence before the sinking of the sun.

Dressed for ceremony, the canon was brushed and immaculate but plain, maintaining the austerity of his office, perhaps, all the more meticulously to smooth away from memory all the years when he had been married to a wife. Time had been, once, long ago in the age of the saints, when celibacy had been demanded of all Celtic priests, just as insistently as it was being demanded now by Bishop Gilbert, by reason of the simple fact that the entire structure of the Celtic Church was built on the monastic ideal, and anything less was a departure from precedent and a decline in sanctity. But long since even the memory of that time had grown faint to vanishing, and there would be just as indignant a reaction to the reimposition of that ideal as there must once have been to its gradual abandonment. For centuries now priests had lived as decent married men and raised families like their parishioners. Even in England, in the more remote country places, there were plenty of humble married priests, and certainly no one thought the worse of them. In Wales it was not unknown for son to follow sire in the cure of a parish, and worse, for the sons of bishops to take it for granted they should succeed their mitred fathers, as though the supreme offices of the Church had been turned into heritable fiefs. Now here came this alien bishop, imposed from without, to denounce all such practices as abominable sin, and clear his diocese of all but the celibate clergy.

And this able and impressive man who came to summon them to the support of his master had no intention of suffering diminution simply because, though he had buried his wife just in time, the survival of a daughter continued to accuse him.

415

Nothing against the girl, and he would see her provided for, but somewhere else, out of sight and mind.

To do him justice, he made no bones about going straight for what he wanted, what would work to his most advantage. He meant to exploit his two visiting monastics and their mission to his bishop's pleasure and satisfaction.

'They are just seated. There will be silence until princes and bishop are settled. I have seen to it there is a clear space below the high table, where you will be seen and heard by all.'

Do him justice, too, he was no way disappointed or disparaging in contemplating Brother Mark's smallness of stature and plain Benedictine habit, or the simplicity of his bearing; indeed he looked him over with a nod of satisfied approval, pleased with a plainness that would nevertheless carry its own distinction.

Mark took the illuminated scroll of Roger de Clinton's letter and the little carved casket that contained the cross in his hands, and they followed their guide across the courtyard to the door of the bishop's hall. Within, the air was full of the rich scent of seasoned timber and the resiny smoke of torches, and the subdued murmur of voices among the lower tables fell silent as the three of them entered, Canon Meirion leading. Behind the high table at the far end of the hall an array of faces, bright in the torchlight, fixed attentively upon the small procession advancing into the cleared space below the dais. The bishop in the midst, merely a featureless presence at this distance, princes on either side of him, the rest clerics and Welsh noblemen of Owain's court disposed alternately, and all eyes upon Brother Mark's small, erect figure, solitary in the open space, for Canon Meirion had stepped aside to give him the floor alone, and Cadfael had remained some paces behind him.

'My lord bishop, here is Deacon Mark, of the household of the bishop of Lichfield and Coventry, asking audience.'

'The messenger of my colleague of Lichfield is very welcome,' said the formal voice from the high table.

Mark made his brief address in a clear voice, his eyes fixed on the long, narrow countenance that confronted him. Straight, wiry steel-grey hair about a domed tonsure, a long, thin blade of a nose flaring into wide nostrils, and a proud, tight-lipped mouth that wore its formal smile somewhat unnervingly for lack of practice.

'My lord, Bishop Roger de Clinton bids me greet you

reverently in his name, as his brother in Christ and his neighbour in the service of the Church, and wishes you long and fruitful endeavour in the diocese of Saint Asaph. And by my hand he sends you in all brotherly love this letter, and this casket, and begs you accept them in kindness.'

All of which Cadfael took up, after the briefest of pauses for effect, and turned into ringing Welsh that brought an approving stir and murmur from his fellow-countrymen among the assembly.

The bishop had risen from his seat, and made his way round the high table to approach the edge of the dais. Mark went to meet him, and bent his knee to present letter and casket into the large, muscular hands that reached down to receive them.

'We accept our brother's kindness with joy,' said Bishop Gilbert with considered and gratified grace, for the secular power of Gwynedd was there within earshot, and missing nothing that passed. 'And we welcome his messengers no less gladly. Rise, Brother, and make one more honoured guest at our table. And your comrade also. It was considerate indeed of Bishop de Clinton to send a Welsh speaker with you into a Welsh community.'

Cadfael stood well back, and followed only at a distance on to the dais. Let Mark have all the notice and the attention, and be led to a place of honour next to Hywel ab Owain, who sat at the bishop's left. Was that Canon Meirion's doing, the bishop's own decision to make the most of the visit, or had Hywel had a hand in it? He might well be interested in learning more about what other cathedral chapters thought of the resurrection of Saint Kentigern's throne, and its bestowal on an alien prelate. And probing from him might be expected to find a more guileless response than if it came from his formidable father, and produce a more innocent and lavish crop. A first occasion, it might be, for Mark to say little and listen much.

Cadfael's own allotted place was much further from the princely centre, near the end of the table, but it gave him an excellent view of all the faces ranged along the seats of honour. On the bishop's right sat Owain Gwynedd, a big man every way, in body, in breadth of mind, in ability, very tall, exceeding by a head the average of his own people, and flaxen-hair by contrast with their darkness, for his grandmother had been a princess of the Danish kingdom of Dublin, more Norse than Irish, Ragnhild, a granddaughter of King Sitric Silk-Beard, and his mother Angharad had been noted for

417

her golden hair among the dark women of Deheubarth. On the bishop's left Hywel ab Owain sat at ease, his face turned towards Brother Mark in amiable welcome. The likeness was clear to be seen, though the son was of a darker colouring, and had not the height of the sire. It struck Cadfael as ironic that one so plainly signed with his father's image should be regarded by the cleric who sat beside him as illegitimate, for he had been born before Owain's marriage, and his mother, too, was an Irishwoman. To the Welsh a son acknowledged was as much a son as those born in marriage, and Hywel on reaching manhood had been set up honourably in south Ceredigion, and now, after his uncle's fall, possessed the whole of it. And very well capable, by his showing so far, of holding on to his own. There were three or four more Welshmen of Owain's party, all arranged turn for turn with Gilbert's canons and chaplains, secular and clerical perforce rubbing shoulders and exchanging possibly wary conversation, though now they had the open casket and its filigree silver cross as a safe topic, for Gilbert had opened it and set it on the board before him to be admired, and laid de Clinton's scroll beside it, doubtless to await a ceremonial reading aloud when the meal was drawing to its close.

Meantime, mead and wine were oiling the wheels of diplomacy, and by the rising babel of voices successfully. And Cadfael had better turn his attention to his own part in this social gathering, and begin to do his duty by his neighbours.

On his right hand he had a middle-aged cleric, surely a canon of the cathedral, well-fleshed and portly, but with a countenance of such uncompromising rectitude that Cadfael judged he might well be that Morgant whose future errand it was to see that both father and daughter conducted themselves unexceptionably on the journey to dispose of Heledd to a husband. Just such a thin, fastidious nose seemed suitable to the task, and just such chill, sharp eyes. But his voice when he spoke, and his manner to the guest, were gracious enough. In every situation he would be equal to events, and strike the becoming note, but he did not look as if he would be easy on shortcomings in others.

On Cadfael's left sat a young man of the prince's party, of the true Welsh build, sturdy and compact, very trim in his dress, and dark of hair and eye. A very black, intense eye, that focussed on distance, and looked through what lay before his gaze, men and objects alike, rather than at them. Only when

418

he looked along the high table, to where Owain and Hywel sat, did the range of his vision shorten, fix and grow warm in recognition and acknowledgement, and the set of his long lips soften almost into smiling. One devoted follower at least the princes of Gwynedd possessed. Cadfael observed the young man sidewise, with discretion, for he was worth study, very comely in his black and brooding fashion, and tended to a contained and private silence. When he did speak, in courtesy to the new guest, his voice was quiet but resonant, and moved in cadences that seemed to Cadfael to belong elsewhere than in Gwynedd. But the most significant thing about his person did not reveal itself for some time, since he ate and drank little, and used only the right hand that lay easy on the board under Cadfael's eyes. Only when he turned directly towards his neighbour, and rested his left elbow on the edge of the table, did it appear that the left forearm terminated only a few inches below the joint, and a fine linen cloth was drawn over the stump like a glove, and secured by a thin silver bracelet.

It was impossible not to stare, the revelation came so unexpectedly; but Cadfael withdrew his gaze at once, and forbore from any comment, though he could not resist studying the mutilation covertly when he thought himself unobserved. But his neighbour had lived with his loss long enough to accustom himself to its effect on others.

'You may ask, Brother,' he said, with a wry smile. 'I am not ashamed to own where I left it. It was my better hand once, though I could use both, and can still make shift with the one I have left.'

Since curiosity was understood and expected of him, Cadfael made no secret of it, though he was already hazarding a guess at the possible answers. For this young man was almost certainly from South Wales, far from his customary kin here in Gwynedd.

'I am in no doubt,' he said cautiously, 'that wherever you may have left it, the occasion did you nothing but honour. But if you are minded to tell me, you should know that I have carried arms in my time, and given and taken injury in the field. Where you admit me, I can follow you, and not as a stranger.'

'I thought,' sid the young man, turning black, brilliant eyes on him appraisingly, 'you had not altogether the monastic look about you. Follow, then, and welcome. I left my arm lying over my lord's body, the sword still in my hand.'

419

'Last year,' said Cadfael slowly, pursuing his own prophetic imaginings, 'in Deheubarth.'

'As you have said.'

'Anarawd?'

'My prince and my foster-brother,' said the maimed man. 'The stroke, the final stroke, that took his life from him took my arm from me.'

Chapter Three

OW MANY,' asked Cadfael carefully, after a
moment of silence, 'were with him then?'

'Three of us. On a simple journey and a short,
thinking no evil. There were eight of them. I am the
only one left who rode with Anarawd that day.' His voice was
low and even. He had forgotten nothing and forgiven nothing,
but he was in complete command of voice and face.

'I marvel,' said Cadfael, 'that you lived to tell the story. It
would not take long to bleed to death from such a wound.'

'And even less time to strike again and finish the work,' the
young man agreed with a twisted smile. 'And so they would
have done if some others of our people had not heard the
affray and come in haste. Me they left lying when they rode
away. I was taken up and tended after his murderers had run.
And when Hywel came with his army to avenge the slaying, he
brought me back here with him, and Owain has taken me into
his own service. A one-armed man is still good for something.
And he can still hate.'

'You were close to your prince?'

'I grew up with him. I loved him.' His black eyes rested
steadily upon the lively profile of Hywel ab Owain, who surely
had taken Anarawd's place in his loyalty, in so far as one man
can ever replace another.

'May I know your name?' asked Cadfael. 'And mine is, or in
the world it was, Cadfael ap Meilyr ap Dafydd, a man of
Gwynedd myself, born at Trefriw. And Benedictine though I

421

may be, I have not forgotten my ancestry.'

'Nor should you, in the world or out of it. And my name is Cuhelyn ab Einion, a younger son of my father, and a man of my prince's guard. In the old days,' he said, darkling, 'it was disgrace for a man of the guard to return alive from the field on which his lord was slain. But I had and have good reason for living. Those of the murderers whom I knew I have named to Hywel, and they have paid. But some I did not know. I keep the faces in mind, for the day when I see them again and hear the names that go with the faces.'

'There is also one other, the chief, who has paid only a blood-price in lands,' said Cadfael. 'What of him? Is it certain he gave the orders for this ambush?'

'Certain! They would never have dared, otherwise. And Owain Gwynedd has no doubts.'

'And where, do you suppose, is this Cadwaladr now? And has he resigned himself to the loss of everything he possessed?'

The young man shook his head. 'Where he is no one seems to know. Nor what mischief he has next in mind. But resigned to his loss? That I doubt! Hywel took hostages from among the lesser chiefs who served under Cadwaladr, and brought them north to ensure there should be no further resistance in Ceredigion. Most of them have been released now, having sworn not to bear arms against Hywel's rule or offer service again to Cadwaladr, unless at some time to come he should pledge reparation and be restored. There's one still left captive in Aber, Gwion. He's given his parole not to attempt escape, but he refuses to forswear his allegiance to Cadwaladr or promise peace to Hywel. A decent enough fellow,' said Cuhelyn tolerantly, 'but still devoted to his lord. Can I hold that against a man? But such a lord! He deserves better for his worship.'

'You bear no hatred against him?'

'None, there is no reason. He had no part in the ambush, he is too young and too clean to be taken into such a villainy. After a fashion, I like him as he likes me. We are two of a kind. Could I blame him for holding fast to his allegiance as I hold fast to mine? If he would kill for Cadwaladr's sake, so would I have done, so I did, for Anarawd. But not by stealth, in double force against light-armed men expecting no danger. Honestly, in open field, that's another matter.'

The long meal was almost at its end, only the wine and mead still circling, and the hum of voices had mellowed into a low, contented buzzing like a hive of bees drunken and happy among summer meadows. In the centre of the high table Bishop Gilbert had taken up the fine scroll of his letter and broken the seal, and was on his feet with the vellum leaf unrolled in his hands. Roger de Clinton's salutation was meant to be declaimed in public for its full effect, and had been carefully worded to impress the laity no less than the Celtic clergy, who might be most in need of a cautionary word. Gilbert's sonorous voice made the most of it. Cadfael, listening, thought that Archbishop Theobald would be highly content with the result of his embassage.

'And now, my lord Owain,' Gilbert pursued, seizing the mellowed moment for which he must have been waiting throughout the feast, 'I ask your leave to introduce a petitioner, who comes asking your indulgence for a plea on behalf of another. My appointment here gives me some right, by virtue of my office, to speak for peace, between individual men as between peoples. It is not good that there should be anger between brothers. Just cause there may have been at the outset, but there should be a term to every outlawry, every quarrel. I ask an audience for an ambassador who speaks on behalf of your brother Cadwaladr, that you may be reconciled with him as is fitting, and restore him to his lost place in your favour. May I admit Bledri ap Rhys?'

There was a brief, sharp silence, in which every eye turned upon the prince's face. Cadfael felt the young man beside him stiffen and quiver in bitter resentment of such a breach of hospitality, for clearly this had been planned deliberately without a word of warning to the prince, without any prior consultation, taking an unfair advantage of the courtesy such a man would undoubtedly show towards the host at whose table he was seated. Even had this audience been sought in private, Cuhelyn would have found it deeply offensive. To precipitate it thus publicly, in hall before the entire household, was a breach of courtesy only possible to an insensitive Norman set up in authority among a people of whom he had no understanding. But if the liberty was as displeasing to Owain as it was to Cuhelyn, he did not allow it to appear. He let the silence lie just long enough to leave the issue in doubt, and perhaps shake Gilbert's valiant self-assurance, and then he said clearly:

'At your wish, my lord bishop, I will certainly hear Bledri ap Rhys. Every man has the right to ask and to be heard. Without prejudice to the outcome!'

It was plain, as soon as the bishop's steward brought the petitioner into the hall, that he had not come straight from travel to ask for this audience. Somewhere about the bishop's enclave he had been waiting at ease for his entry here, and had prepared himself carefully, very fine and impressive in his dress and in his person, every grain of dust from the roads polished away. A tall, broad-shouldered, powerful man, black-haired and black-moustached, with an arrogant beak of a nose, and a bearing truculent rather than conciliatory. He swept with long strides into the centre of the open space fronting the dais, and made an elaborate obeisance in the general direction of prince and bishop. The gesture seemed to Cadfael to tend rather to the performer's own aggrandisement than to any particular reverence for those saluted. He had everyone's attention, and meant to retain it.

'My lord prince – my lord bishop, your devout servant! I come as a petitioner here before you.' He did not look the part, nor was his full, confident voice expressive of any such role.

'So I have heard,' said Owain. 'You have something to ask of us. Ask it freely.'

'My lord, I was and am in fealty to your brother Cadwaladr, and I dare venture to speak for his right, in that he goes deprived of his lands, and made a stranger and disinherited in his own country. Whatever you may hold him guilty of, I dare to plead that such a penalty is more than he has deserved, and such as brother should not visit upon brother. And I ask of you that measure of generosity and forgiveness that should restore him his own again. He has endured this despoiling a year already, let that be enough, and set him up again in his lands of Ceredigion. The lord bishop will add his voice to mine for reconciliation.'

'The lord bishop has been before you,' said Owain drily, 'and equally eloquent. I am not, and never have been, adamant against my brother, whatever follies he has committed, but murder is worse than folly, and requires a measure of penitence before forgiveness is due. The two, separated, are of no value, and where the one is not, I will not waste the other. Did Cadwaladr send you on this errand?'

'No, my lord, and knows nothing of my coming. It is he who suffers deprivation, and I who appeal for his right to be restored. If he has done ill in the past, is that good reason for shutting him out from the possibility of doing well in the

424

future? And what has been done to him is extreme, for he has been made an exile in his own country, without a toehold on his own soil. Is that fair dealing?'

'It is less extreme,' said Owain coldly, 'than what was done to Anarawd. Lands can be restored, if restoration is deserved. Life once lost is past restoration.'

'True, my lord, but even homicide may be compounded for a blood-price. To be stripped of all, and for life, is another kind of death.'

'We are not concerned with mere homicide, but with murder,' said Owain, 'as well you know.'

At Cadfael's left hand Cuhelyn sat stiff and motionless in his place, his eyes fixed upon Bledri, their glance lengthened to pierce through him and beyond. His face was white, and his single hand clenched tightly upon the edge of the board, the knuckles sharp and pale as ice. He said no word and made no sound, but his bleak stare never wavered.

'Too harsh a name,' said Bledri fiercely, 'for a deed done in heat. Nor did your lordship wait to hear my prince's side of the quarrel.'

'For a deed done in heat,' said Owain with immovable composure, 'this was well planned. Eight men do not lie in wait in cover for four travellers unsuspecting and unarmed, in hot blood. You do your lord's cause no favour by defending his crime. You said you came to plead. My mind is not closed against reconciliation, civilly sought. It is proof against threats.'

'Yet, Owain,' cried Bledri, flaring like a resinous torch, 'it behoves even you to weigh what consequences may follow if you are obdurate. A wise man would know when to unbend, before his own brand burns back into his face.'

Cuhelyn started out of his stillness, quivering, and was half rising to his feet when he regained control, and sank back in his place, again mute and motionless. Hywel had not moved, nor had his face changed. He had his father's formidable composure. And Owain's unshaken and unshakable calm subdued in a moment the uneasy stir and murmur that had passed round the high table and started louder echoes down in the floor of the hall.

'Am I to take that as threat, or promise, or a forecast of a doom from heaven?' asked Owain, in the most amiable of voices, but none the less with a razor edge to the tone that gave it piercing sweetness, and caused Bledri to draw back his head

425

a little as if from a possible blow, and for a moment veil the smouldering fire of his black eyes, and abate the savage tightness of his lips. Somewhat more cautiously he responded at last:

'I meant only that enmity and hatred between brothers is unseemly among men, and cannot but be displeasing to God. It cannot bear any but disastrous fruit. I beg you, restore your brother his rights.'

'That,' said Owain thoughtfully, and eyeing the petitioner with a stare that measured and probed beyond the words offered, 'I am not yet ready to concede. But perhaps we should consider of this matter at more leisure. Tomorrow morning I and my people set out for Aber and Bangor, together with some of the lord bishop's household and these visitors from Lichfield. It is in my mind, Bledri ap Rhys, that you should ride with us and be our guest at Aber, and on the way, and there at home in my llys, you may better develop your argument, and I better consider on those consequences of which you make mention. I should not like,' said Owain in tones of honey, 'to invite disaster for want of forethought. Say yes to my hospitality, and sit down with us at our host's table.'

It was entirely plain to Cadfael, as to many another within the hall, that by this time Bledri had small choice in the matter. Owain's men of the guard had fully understood the nature of the invitation. By his tight smile, so had Bledri, though he accepted it with every evidence of pleasure and satisfaction. No doubt it suited him to continue in the prince's company, whether as guest or prisoner, and to keep his eyes and ears open on the ride to Aber. All the more if his hint of dire consequences meant more than the foreshadowing of divine disapproval of enmity between brothers. He had said a little too much to be taken at his face value. And as a guest, free or under guard, his own safety was assured. He took the place that was cleared for him at the bishop's table, and drank to the prince with a discreet countenance and easy smile.

The bishop visibly drew deep breath, relieved that his well-meaning effort at peace-making had at least survived the first skirmish. Whether he had understood the vibrating undertones of what had passed was doubtful. The subtleties of the Welsh were probably wasted on a forthright and devout Norman, Cadfael reflected. The better for him, he could speed his departing guests, thus augmented by one, and console himself that he had done all a man could do to bring about

426

reconciliation. What followed, whatever it might be, was no responsibility of his.

The mead went round amicably, and the prince's harper sang the greatness and virtues of Owain's line and the beauty of Gwynedd. And after him, to Cadfael's respectful surprise, Hywel ab Owain rose and took the harp, and improvised mellifluously on the women of the north. Poet and bard as well as warrior, this was undoubtedly an admirable shoot from that admirable stem. He knew what he was doing with his music. All the tensions of the evening dissolved into amity and song. Or if they survived, at least the bishop, comforted and relaxed, lost all awareness of them.

In the privacy of their own lodging, with the night still drowsily astir outside the half-open door, Brother Mark sat mute and thoughtful on the edge of his bed for some moments, pondering all that had passed, until at last he said, with the conviction of one who has reviewed all circumstances and come to a firm conclusion: 'He meant nothing but good. He is a good man.'

'But not a wise one,' said Cadfael from the doorway. The night without was dark, without a moon, but the stars filled it with a distant, blue glimmer that showed where occasional shadows crossed from building to building, making for their rest. The babel of the day was now an almost-silence, now and then quivering to the murmur of low voices tranquilly exchanging goodnights. Rather a tremor on the air than an audible sound. There was no wind. Even the softest of movements vibrated along the cords of the senses, making silence eloquent.

'He trusts too easily,' Mark agreed with a sigh. 'Integrity expects integrity.'

'And you find it missing in Bledri ap Rhys?' Cadfael asked respectfully. Brother Mark could still surprise him now and then.

'I doubt him. He comes too brazenly, knowing once received he is safe from any harm or affront. And he feels secure enough in Welsh hospitality to threaten.'

'So he did,' said Cadfael thoughtfully. 'And passed it off as a reminder of heaven's displeasure. And what did you make of that?'

'He drew in his horns,' said Mark positively, 'knowing he had gone a step too far. But there was more in that than a

427

pastoral warning. And truly I wonder where this Cadwaladr is now, and what he is up to. For I think that was a plain threat of trouble here and now if Owain refused his brother's demands. Something is in the planning, and this Bledri knows of it.'

'I fancy,' said Cadfael placidly, 'that the prince is of your opinion also, or at least has the possibility well in mind. You heard him. He has given due notice to all his men that Bledri ap Rhys is to remain in the royal retinue here, in Aber, and on the road between. If there's mischief planned, Bledri, if he can't be made to betray it, can be prevented from playing any part in it, or letting his master know the prince has taken the warning, and is on his guard. Now I wonder did Bledri read as much into it, and whether he'll go to the trouble to put it to the test?'

'He did not seem to me to be put out of his stride,' said Mark doubtfully. 'If he did understand it so, it did not disquiet him. Can he have provoked it purposely?'

'Who knows? It may suit him to go along with us to Aber, and keep his eyes and ears open along the way and within the llys, if he's spying out the prince's dispositions for his master. Or for himself!' Cadfael conceded thoughtfully. 'Though what's the advantage to him, unless it's to put him safely out of the struggle, I confess I don't see.' For a prisoner who enjoys officially the status of a guest can come to no harm, whatever the issue. If his own lord wins, he is delivered without reproach, and if his captor is the victor he is immune just as surely, safe from injury in the battle or reprisals after it. 'But he did not strike me as a cautious man,' Cadfael owned, rejecting the option, though with some lingering reluctance.

A few threads of shadow still crossed the gathering darkness of the precinct, ripples on a nocturnal lake. The open door of the bishop's great hall made a rectangle of faint light, most of the torches within already quenched, the fire turfed down but still glowing, distant murmurs of movement and voices a slight quiver on the silence, as the servants cleared away the remnants of the feast and the tables that had borne it.

A tall, dark figure, wide-shouldered and erect against the pale light, appeared in the doorway of the hall, paused for a long moment as though breathing in the cool of the night, and then moved leisurely down the steps, and began to pace the beaten earth of the court, slowly and sinuously, like a man flexing his muscles after being seated a while too long. Cadfael opened the door a little wider, to have the shadowy movements in view.

'Where are you going?' asked Mark at his back, anticipating with alert intelligence.

'Not far,' said Cadfael. 'Just far enough to see what rises to our friend Bledri's bait. And how he takes it!'

He stood motionless outside the door for a long moment, drawing the door to behind him, to accustom his eyes to the night, as doubtless Bledri ap Rhys was also doing as he trailed his coat to and fro, nearer and nearer to the open gate of the precinct. The earth was firm enough to make his crisp, deliberate steps audible, as plainly he meant them to be. But nothing stirred and no one took note of him, not even the few servants drifting away to their beds, until he turned deliberately and walked straight towards the open gate. Cadfael had advanced at leisure along the line of modest canonical houses and guest lodgings, to keep the event in view.

With admirable aplomb two brisk figures heaved up into the gateway from the fields without, amiably wreathed together, collided with Bledri in mid-passage, and untwined themselves to embrace him between them.

'What, my lord Bledri!' boomed one blithe Welsh voice. 'Is it you? Taking a breath of air before sleeping? And a fine night for it!'

'We'll bear you company, willingly,' the second voice offered heartily. 'It's early to go to bed yet. And we'll see you safe to your own brychan, if you lose your way in the dark.'

'I'm none so drunk as to go astray,' Bledri acknowledged without surprise or concern. 'And for all the good company there is to be had in Saint Asaph tonight, I think I'll get to my bed. You gentlemen will be needing your sleep, too, if we're off with the morn tomorrow.' The smile in his voice was clear to be sensed. He had the answer he had looked for, and it caused him no dismay, rather a measure of amusement, perhaps even satisfaction. 'Goodnight to you!' he said, and turned to saunter back towards the hall door, still dimly lighted from within.

Silence hung outside the precinct wall, though the nearest tents of Owain's camp were not far away. The wall was not so high that it could not be climbed, though wherever a man mounted, there would be someone waiting below on the other side. But in any case Bledri ap Rhys had no intention of removing himself, he had merely been confirming his expectation that any attempt to do so would very simply and neatly be frustrated. Owain's orders were readily understood

429

even when obliquely stated, and would be efficiently carried out. If Bledri had been in any doubt of that, he knew better now. And as for the two convivial guards, they withdrew again into the night with an absence of pretence which was almost insulting.

And that, on the face of it, was the end of the incident. Yet Cadfael continued immobile and detachedly interested, invisible against the dark bulk of the timber buildings, as if he expected some kind of epilogue to round off the night's entertainment.

Into the oblong of dim light at the head of the steps came the girl Heledd, unmistakable even in silhouette by the impetuous grace of her carriage and her tall slenderness. Even at the end of an evening of serving the bishop's guests and the retainers of his household she moved like a fawn. And if Cadfael observed her appearance with impersonal pleasure, so did Bledri ap Rhys, from where he stood just side from the foot of the steps, with a startled appreciation somewhat less impersonal, having no monastic restraints to hold it in check. He had just confirmed that he was now, willing or otherwise, a member of the prince's retinue at least as far as Aber, and in all probability he already knew, since he was lodged in the bishop's own house, that this promising girl was the one who would be riding with the party at dawn. The prospect offered a hope of mild pleasure along the way, to pass the time agreeably. At the very least, here was this moment, to round off an eventful and enjoyable evening. She was descending, with one of the embroidered drapings of the high table rolled up in her arms, on her way to the canonical dwellings across the precinct. Perhaps wine had been spilled on the cloth, or some of the gilt threads been snagged by a belt buckle or the rough setting of a dagger hilt or a bracelet, and she was charged with its repair. He had been about to ascend, but waited aside instead, for the pleasure of watching her at ever closer view as she came down, eyes lowered to be sure of stepping securely. He was so still and she so preoccupied that she had not observed him. And when she had reached the third step from the ground he suddenly reached out and took her by the waist between his hands, very neatly, and swung her round in a half-circle, and so held her suspended, face to face with him and close, for a long moment before he set her quite gently on her feet. He did not, however, relinquish his hold of her.

It was done quite lightly and playfully, and for all Cadfael could see, which was merely a shadow play, Heledd received it without much trace of displeasure, and certainly none of alarm, once the surprise was past. She had uttered one small, startled gasp as he plucked her aloft, but that was all, and once set down she stood looking up at him eye to eye, and made no move to break away. It is not unpleasant to any woman to be admired by a handsome man. She said something to him, the words indistinguishable but the tone light and tolerant to Cadfael's ear, if not downright encouraging. And something he said in return to her, at the very least with no sign of discouragement. No doubt Bledri ap Rhys had a very good opinion of himself and his attractions, but it was in Cadfael's mind that Heledd, for all she might enjoy his attentions, was also quite capable of keeping them within decorous bounds. Doubtful if she was considering letting him get very far. But from this pleasurable brush with him she could extricate herself whenever she chose. They were neither of them taking it seriously.

In the event she was not to be given the opportunity to conclude it in her own fashion. For the light from the open doorway above was suddenly darkened by the bulk of a big man's body, and the abrupt eclipse cast the linked pair below into relative obscurity. Canon Meirion paused for a moment to adjust his vision to the night, and began to descend the steps with his usual selfconscious dignity. With the dwindling of his massive shadow renewed light fell upon Heledd's glossy hair and the pale oval of her face, and the broad shoulders and arrogant head of Bledri ap Rhys, the pair of them closely linked in what fell little short of an embrace.

It seemed to Brother Cadfael, watching with unashamed interest from his dark corner, that both of them were very well aware of the stormcloud bearing down on them, and neither was disposed to do anything to evade or placate it. Indeed, he perceived that Heledd softened by a hair the stiffness of her stance, and allowed her head to tilt towards the descending light and glitter into a bright and brittle smile, meant rather for her father's discomfort than for Bledri's gratification. Let him sweat for his place and his desired advancement! She had said that she could destroy him if she so willed. It was something she would never do, but if he was so crass, and knew so little of her, as to believe her capable of bringing about his ruin, he deserved to pay for his stupidity.

The instant of intense stillness exploded into a flurry of

movement, as Canon Meirion recovered his breath and came seething down the steps in a turmoil of clerical black, like a sudden thundercloud, took his daughter by the arm, and wrenched her firmly away from Bledri's grasp. As firmly and competently she withdrew herself from this new compulsion, and brushed the very touch of his hand from her sleeve. The dagger glances that must have strained through the dimness between sire and daughter were blunted by the night. And Bledri suffered his deprivation gracefully, without stirring a step, and very softly laughed.

'Oh, pardon if I have trespassed on your rights of warren,' he said, deliberately obtuse. 'I had not reckoned with a rival of your cloth. Not here in Bishop Gilbert's household. I see I have undervalued his breadth of mind.'

He was being provocative deliberately, of course. Even if he had had no notion that this indignant elder was the girl's father, he certainly knew that this intervention could hardly bear the interpretation he was placing upon it. But had not the impulse of mischief originated rather with Heledd? It did not please her that the canon should have so little confidence in her judgement as to suppose she would need help in dealing with a passing piece of impudence from this questionably welcome visitor. And Bledri was quite sufficiently accomplished in the study of women to catch the drift of her mild malice, and play the accomplice, for her gratification as readily as for his own amusement.

'Sir,' said Meirion with weighty and forbidding dignity, curbing his rage, 'my daughter is affianced, and shortly to be married. Here in his lordship's court you will treat her and all other women with respect.' And to Heledd he said brusquely, and with a sharp gesture of his hand towards their lodging under the far wall of the enclave: 'Go in, girl! The hour is late already, you should be withindoors.'

Heledd, without haste or discomposure, gave them a slight, curt inclination of her head to share between them, and turned and walked away. The rear view of her as she went was expressive, and disdainful of men in general.

'And a very fine girl, too,' said Bledri approvingly, watching her departure. 'You may be proud of your getting, Father. I hope you are marrying her to a man who'll appreciate beauty. The small courtesy of hefting the lass down the steps to level ground can hardly have blemished his bargain.' His clear, incisive voice had dwelt fondly on the word 'Father', well aware of the dual sting. 'Well, what the eye has not seen, the heart need not grieve, and I hear the bridegroom is well away in Anglesey. And no doubt you can keep a still tongue where this match is concerned.' The plain implication was there, very sweetly insinuated. No, Canon Meirion was exceedingly unlikely to make any move that could jeopardise his cleansed and celibate and promising future. Bledri ap Rhys was very quick on the uptake, and well informed about the bishop's clerical reforms. He had even sensed Heledd's resentment at being so ruthlessly disposed of, and her impulse to take her revenge before departing.

'Sir, you are a guest of prince and bishop, and as such are expected to observe the standards due to their hospitality.' Meirion was stiff as a lance, and his voice thinned and steely as a sword-blade. Within his well-schooled person there was a ferocious Welsh temper under arduous control. 'If you do not, you will rue it. Whatever my own situation, I will see to that. Do not approach my daughter, or attempt to have any further ado with her. Your courtesies are unwelcome.'

'Not, I think, to the lady,' said Bledri, with the most complacent of smiles implicit in the very tone of his voice. 'She has a tongue, and a palm, and I fancy would have been ready enough to use both if I had caused her any displeasure. I like a lass of spirit. If she grants me occasion, I shall tell her so. Why should she not enjoy the admiration she is entitled to, these few hours on the road to her marriage?'

The brief silence fell like a stone between them; Cadfael felt the air quiver with the tension of their stillness. Then Canon Meirion said, through gritted teeth and from a throat constricted with the effort to contain his rage: 'My lord, do not think this cloth I wear will prove any protection to you if you affront my honour, or my daughter's good name. Be warned, and keep away from her, or you shall have excellent cause to regret it. Though perhaps,' he ended, even lower and more malevolently, 'too brief time!'

'Time enough,' said Bledri, not noticeably disturbed by the palpable threat, 'for all the regretting I'm likely to do. It's something I've had small practice in. Goodnight to your reverence!' And he passed by Meirion so close their sleeves brushed, perhaps intentionally, and began to climb the steps to the hall door. And the canon, wrenching himself out of his paralysis of rage with an effort, composed his dignity about him as best he could, and stalked away towards his own door.

Cadfael returned to his own quarters very thoughtfully, and recounted the whole of this small incident to Brother Mark, who was lying wakeful and wide-eyed after his prayers, by some private and peculiar sensitivity of his own already aware of turbulent cross-currents trembling on the night air. He listened, unsurprised.

'How much, would you say, Cadfael, is his concern only for his own advancement, how much truly for his daughter? For he does feel guilt towards her. Guilt that he resents her as a burden to his prospects, guilt at loving her less than she loves him. A guilt that makes him all the more anxious to put her out of sight, far away, another man's charge.'

'Who can decipher any man's motives?' said Cadfael resignedly. 'Much less a woman's. But I tell you this, she would do well not to drive him too far. The man has a core of violence in him. I would not like to see it let loose. It could be a killing force.'

'And against which of them,' wondered Mark, staring into the dark of the roof above him, 'would the lightning be launched, if ever the storm broke?'

Chapter Four

HE PRINCE'S cortège mustered in the dawn, in a morning hesitant between sullenness and smiles. There was the moisture of a brief shower on the grasses as Cadfael and Mark crossed to the church for prayer before saddling up, but the sun was shimmering on the fine drops, and the sky above was the palest and clearest of blues, but for a few wisps of cloud to eastward, embracing the rising orb of light with stroking fingers. When they emerged again into the courtyard it was already full of bustle and sound, the baggage horses being loaded, the brave city of tents along the hillside above folded and on the move, and even the frail feathers of cloud dissolved into moist and scintillating radiance.

Mark stood gazing before him with pleasure at the preparations for departure, his face flushed and bright, a child embarking on an adventure. Until this moment, Cadfael thought, he had not fully realised the possibilities, the fascinations, even the perils of the journey he had undertaken. To ride with princes was no more than half the tale, somewhere there was a lurking threat, a hostile brother, a prelate bent on reforming a way of life which in the minds of its population needed no reform. And who could guess what might happen between here and Bangor, between bishop and bishop, the stranger and the native?

'I spoke a word in the ear of Saint Winifred,' said Mark, flushing almost guiltily, as though he had appropriated a patroness who by rights belonged to Cadfael. 'I thought we must be very close to her here, it seemed only gracious to let her know of our presence and our hopes, and ask her blessing.'

'If we deserve!' said Cadfael, though he had small doubt that so gentle and sensible a saint must look indulgently upon this wise innocent.

'Indeed! How far is it, Cadfael, from here to her holy well?'

'A matter of fourteen miles or so, due east of us.'

'Is it true it never freezes? However hard the winter?'

'It is true. No one has ever known it stilled, it bubbles always in the centre.'

'And Gwytherin, where you took her from the grave?'

'That lies as far south and west of us,' said Cadfael, and refrained from mentioning that he had also restored her to her grave in that same place. 'Never try to limit her,' he advised cautiously. 'She will be wherever you may call upon her, and present and listening as soon as you cry out your need.'

'That I never doubted,' said Mark simply, and went with a springy and hopeful step to put together his small belongings and saddle his glossy nutbrown gelding. Cadfael lingered a few moments to enjoy the bright bustle before him, and then followed more sedately to the stables. Outside the walls of the enclave Owain's guards and noblemen were already marshalling, their encampment vanished from the greensward, leaving behind only the paler, flattened patches which would soon spring back into lively green, and erase even the memory of their visitation. Within the wall grooms whistled and called, hooves stamped lively, muffled rhythms in the hard-packed earth, harness jingled, maidservants shrilled to one another above the general babel of male voices, and the faint dust of all this vigorous movement rose into the sunlight and shimmered in gilded mist overhead.

The company gathered as blithely as if they were going maying, and certainly so bright a morning invited to so pleasant a pastime. But there were certain graver reminders to be remarked as they mounted. Heledd made her appearance cloaked and ready, serene and demure of countenance, but with Canon Meirion keeping close on one side of her, with tight lips and downdrawn brows, and Canon Morgant on the other, equally tightlipped but with brows arched into uncompromising severity, and sharp eyes dwelling alternately on father and daughter, and with no very assured approval of either. And for all their precautions, at the last moment Bledri ap Rhys stepped between them and lifted the girl into the saddle with his own large and potentially predatory hands, with a courtesy so elaborate that it glittered into insolence: and, worse, Heledd accepted the service with as gracious an inclination of her head, and a cool, reserved smile, ambiguous between chaste reproof and discreet mischief. To take exception to the behaviour of either party would have been folly, so well had both preserved the appearance of propriety, but both canons perceptibly beheld the incident with raised hackles and darkening frowns if they kept their mouths shut.

Nor was that the only sudden cloud in this clear sky, for Cuhelyn, appearing already mounted in the gateway, too late to have observed any present cause for offence, sat his horse with drawn brows, while his intent eyes ranged the entire company within until he found Bledri, and there settled and brooded, a long-memoried man of intense passions, measuring an enemy. It seemed to Cadfael, surveying the scene with a thoughtful eye, that there would be a considerable weight of illwill and not a few grudges among the rich baggage of this princely party.

The bishop came down into the courtyard to take leave of his royal guests. This first encounter had passed off successfully enough, considering the strain he had put upon it by inviting Cadwaladr's envoy into conference. He was not so insensitive that he had not felt the momentary tension and displeasure, and no doubt he was drawing relieved breath now at having survived the danger. Whether he had the humility to realise that he owed it to the prince's forbearance was another matter, Cadfael reflected. And here came Owain side by side with his host, and Hywel at his back. At his coming the whole bright cortège quivered into expectant life, and as he reached for bridle and stirrup, so did they all. Too tall for me, eh, Hugh? Cadfael thought, swinging aloft into the roan's high saddle, with a buoyancy that set him up in a very gratifying conceit of himself. I'll show you whether I have lost my appetite for travel and forgotten everything I learned in the east before ever you were born.

And they were away, out of the wide-open gate and heading westward after the prince's lofty fair head, uncovered to the morning sun. The bishop's household stood to watch them depart, warily content with one diplomatic encounter successfully accomplished. Such threats as lingered uneasily from last night's exchanges cast their shadows on these

437

departing guests. Bishop Gilbert, if he had believed in them at all, could let them withdraw unchallenged, for they were no threat to him.

As those within the enclave emerged into the green track without, Owain's officers from the encampment fell into neat order about them, lining either flank, and Cadfael observed with interest but without surprise that there were archers among them, and two keeping their station a few yards behind Bledri ap Rhys's left shoulder. Given this particular guest's undoubted quickness of perception, he was equally aware of them, and just as clearly he had no objection to their presence, for in the first mile he did not let it inhibit him from changing his position two or three times to speak a civil word in Canon Morgant's ear, or exchange courtesies with Hywel ab Owain, riding close at his father's back. But he did not make any move to edge his way through the attendant file of guards. If they were keeping him in mind of his virtual captivity, so was he bent on assuring them that he was perfectly content, and had no intention of attempting to remove himself. Indeed, once or twice he looked to left and right to take the measure of the prince's unobtrusive efficiency, and seemed not unfavourably impressed by what he saw.

All of which was of considerable interest to an inquisitive man, even if at this stage it remained undecipherable. Put it away at the back of the mind, along with everything else of oddity value in this expedition, and the time would come when its meaning would be revealed. Meantime, here was Mark, silent and happy at his elbow, the road westward before him, and the sun bright on Owain's pennant of bright hair at the head of the column. What more could any man ask on a fine May morning?

They did not, as Mark had expected, bear somewhat northwards towards the sea, but made due west, over softly rolling hills and through well-treed valleys, by green trails sometimes clearly marked, sometimes less defined, but markedly keeping a direct line uphill and down alike, here where the lie of the land was open and the gradients gentle enough for pleasant riding.

'An old, old road,' said Cadfael. 'It starts from Chester, and makes straight for the head of Conwy's tidal water, where once, they say, there was a fort the like of Chester. At low tide, if you know the sands, you can ford the river there, but with the tide boats can ply some way beyond.'

'And after the river crossing?' asked Mark, attentive and glowing.

'Then we climb. To look westward from there, you'd think no track could possibly pass, but pass it does, up and over the mountains, and down at last to the sea. Have you ever seen the sea?'

'No. How could I? Until I joined the bishop's household I had never been out of the shire, not even ten miles from where I was born.' He was straining his eyes ahead as he rode now, with longing and delight, thirsty for all that he had never seen. 'The sea must be a great wonder,' he said on a hushed breath.

'A good friend and a bad enemy,' said Cadfael, beckoned back into old memories. 'Respect it, and it will do well by you, but never take liberties.'

The prince had set a steady, easy pace that could be maintained mile by mile in this undulating countryside, green and lush, patterned with hamlets in the valleys, cottages and church snugly huddled together, the fringe of cultivable fields a woven tapestry round them, and here and there solitary, scattered throughout the tref, the households of the free landowners, and no less solitary, somewhere among them, their parish church.

'These men live lonely,' said Mark, taking in the distinction with some wonder.

'These are the freeborn men of the tribe. They own their land, but not to do as they please with it, it descends by strict law of inheritance within the family. The villein villages till the soil among them, and pay their communal dues together, though every man has his dwelling and his cattle and his fair share of the land. We make sure of that by overseeing the distribution every so often. As soon as sons grow to be men they have their portion at the next accounting.'

'So no one there can inherit,' Mark deduced reasonably.

'None but the youngest son, the last to grow into a portion of his own. He inherits his father's portion and dwelling. His elder brothers by then will have taken wives and built houses of their own.' It seemed to Cadfael, and apparently to Mark also, a fair, if rough and ready, means of assuring every man a living and a place in which to live, a fair share of the work and a fair share of the profit of the land.

'And you?' asked Mark. 'Was this where you belonged?'

'Belonged and could not belong,' Cadfael acknowledged, looking back with some surprise at his own origins. 'Yes, I was born in just such a villein tref, and coming up to my fourteenth birthday and a slip of land of my own. And would you believe it now? – I did not want it! Good Welsh earth, and I felt nothing for it. When the wool merchant from Shrewsbury took a liking to me, and offered me work that would give me licence to see at least a few more miles of the world, I jumped at that open door as I've jumped at most others that ever came my way. I had a younger brother, better content to sit on one strip of earth lifelong. I was for off, as far as the road would take me, and it took me half across the world before I understood. Life goes not in a straight line, lad, but in a circle. The first half we spend venturing as far as the world's end from home and kin and stillness, and the latter half brings us back by roundabout ways but surely, to that state from which we set out. So I end bound by vow to one narrow place, but for the rare chance of going forth on the business of my house, and labouring at a small patch of earth, and in the company of my closest kin. And content,' said Cadfael, drawing satisfied breath.

They came over the crest of a high ridge before noon, and there below them the valley of the Conwy opened, and beyond, the ground rose at first gently and suavely, but above these green levels there towered in the distance the enormous bastions of Eryri, soaring to polished steel peaks against the pale blue of the sky. The river was a winding silver thread, twining a tortuous course through and over shoals of tidal mud and sand on its way northward up to the sea, its waters at this hour so spread and diminished that it could be forded without difficulty. And after the crossing, as Cadfael had warned, they climbed.

The first few green and sunny miles gave way to a rising track that kept company with a little tributary river, mounting steeply until the trees fell behind, and they emerged gradually into a lofty world of moorland, furze and heather, open and naked as the sky. No plough had ever broken the soil here, there was no visible movement but the ruffling of the sudden wind among the gorse and low bushes, no inhabitants but the birds that shot up from before the foremost riders, and the hawks that hung almost motionless, high in the air. And yet across this desolate but beautiful wilderness marched a perceptible causeway laid with stones and cushioned with rough grass, raised clear of the occasional marshy places, straddling the shallow pools of peat-brown water, making straight for the lofty wall of honed rock that seemed to Brother Mark utterly impenetrable. In places where the firm rock broke through the soil and gave solid footing, the raised sarn remained visible as a trodden pathway needing no ramp of stones, but always maintained its undeviating line ahead.

'Giants made this,' said Brother Mark in awe.

'Men made it,' said Cadfael. It was wide where it was clearly to be seen, wide enough for a column of men marching six abreast, though horsemen had to ride no more than three in line, and Owain's archers, who knew this territory well, drew off on either flank and left the paved way to the company they guarded. A road, Cadfael thought, made not for pleasure, not for hawking or hunting, but as a means of moving a great number of men from one stronghold to another as quickly as possible. It took small count of gradients, but set its sights straight ahead, deviating only where that headlong line was rankly impossible to maintain, and then only until the obstacle was passed.

'But through that sheer wall,' Mark marvelled, staring ahead at the barrier of the mountains, 'surely we cannot go.'

'Yes, you will find there's a gate through, narrow but wide enough, at the pass of Bwlch y Ddeufaen. We thread through those hills, keep this high level three or four more miles, and after that we begin to descend.'

'Towards the sea?'

'Towards the sea,' said Cadfael.

They came to the first decline, the first sheltered valley of bushes and trees, and in the heart of it bubbled a spring that became a lively brook, and accompanied them downhill gradually towards the coast. They had long left behind the rivulets that flowed eastward towards the Conwy; here the streams sprang sparkling into short, precipitous lives, and made headlong for the sea. And down with this most diminutive of its kind went the track, raised to a firm level above the water, at the edge of the cleft of trees. The descent became more gradual, the brook turned somewhat away from the path, and suddenly the view opened wide before them, and there indeed was the sea.

Immediately below them a village lay in its patterned fields, beyond it narrow meadowland melting into salt flats and shingle, and then the wide expanse of sea, and beyond that again, distant but clear in the late afternoon light, the coast of Anglesey stretched out northward, to end in the tiny island of

441

Ynys Lanog. From the shore towards which they moved the shallow water shimmered pale gold overlaid with aquamarine, almost as far as the eye could distinguish colour, for Lavan Sands extended the greater part of the way to the island shore, and only there in the distance did the sea darken into the pure, greenish blue of the deep channel. At the sight of this wonder about which he had dreamed and speculated all day long, Mark checked his horse for a moment, and sat staring with flushed cheeks and bright eyes, enchanted by the beauty and diversity of the world.

It happened that Cadfael turned his head to see where someone else had reined in at the same moment, perhaps in the same rapt delight. Between her two guardian canons Heledd had checked and sat staring before her, but her sights were raised beyond the crystal and gold of the shallows, beyond the cobalt channel to the distant shore of Anglesey, and her lips were austerely drawn, and her brows level and unrevealing. She looked towards her bridegroom's land, the man against whom she knew nothing, of whom she had heard nothing but good; she saw marriage advancing upon her all too rapidly, and there was such a baffled and resentful sadness in her face, and such an obstinate rejection of her fate, that Cadfael marvelled no one else felt her burning outrage, and turned in alarm to find the source of this intense disquiet.

Then as suddenly as she had halted she shook the rein, and set her horse to an impatient trot downhill, leaving her black-habited escort behind, and threaded a way deeper into the cavalcade to shake them off at least for a few rebellious moments.

Watching her vehement passage through the ranks of the prince's retinue, Cadfael absolved her of any deliberate intent in drawing close alongside Bledri's mount. He was simply there in her way, in a moment she would have passed by him. But there was intent enough in the opportunist alacrity with which Bledri reached a hand to her bridle, and checked her passage knee to knee with him, and in the intimate, assured smile he turned upon her as she yielded to the persuasion. There was, Cadfael thought, one instant when she almost shook him off, almost curled her lip with the tolerant mockery which was all she truly felt for him. Then with perverse deliberation she smiled at him, and consented to fall in beside him, in no hurry to free herself of the muscular hand that detained her. They rode on together in apparent amity, with matched pace and in easy talk together. The rear view of them suggested to Cadfael nothing more than a continuation of a somewhat malicious but enjoyable game on both parts, but when he turned his head cautiously to see what effect the incident had had upon the two canons of Saint Asaph it was all too plain that to them it implied something very different. If Meirion's drawn brows and rigid lips threatened storms towards Heledd and rage towards Bledri ap Rhys, equally they were stiff with apprehension of what must be going on behind the controlled but ominous rectitude of Morgant's fleshy countenance.

Ah, well! Two days more, and it should be over. They would be safely in Bangor, the bridegroom would cross the strait to meet them, and Heledd would be rapt away to that mist-blue shore beyond the faint gold and ice-blue of Lavan Sands. And Canon Meirion could draw breath in peace at last.

They came down to the rim of the salt flats and turned westward, with the quivering plane of the shallows reflecting glittering light on their right hand, and the green of field and copse on the left, rising terrace beyond terrace into the hills. Once or twice they plashed through tenuous streams trickling down through the salt marshes to the sea. And within the hour they were riding alongside the high stockade of Owain's royal seat and tref of Aber, and the porters and guards at the gates had seen the shimmer of their colours nearing, and cried their coming within.

From all the buildings that lined the walls of the great court of Owain's maenol, from stables and armoury and hall, and the array of guest dwellings, the household came surging to welcome the prince home, and make his visitors welcome. Grooms ran to receive the horses, squires came with pitchers and horns. Hywel ab Owain, who had distributed his hospitable attentions punctiliously during the journey, moving from rider to rider with civilities as his father's representative, and no doubt taking due note of all the undercurrents that drew taut between them, with his father's interests in mind, was the first out of the saddle, and went straight to take the prince's bridle, in an elegant gesture of filial respect, before ceding the charge to the waiting groom, and going to kiss the hand of the lady who had come out from the timber hall to welcome her lord home. Not his own mother! The two young boys who came leaping down the steps from the hall door after her were hers, lithe dark imps of about ten and seven years,

443

shrilling with excitement and with a flurry of dogs wreathing round their feet. Owain's wife was daughter to a prince of Arwystli, in central Wales, and her lively sons had her rich colouring. But an older youth, perhaps fifteen or sixteen, followed them more circumspectly down the steps, and came with authority and confidence straight to Owain, and was embraced with an affection there was no mistaking. This one had his father's fair hair deepened into pure gold, and his father's impressive male comeliness refined into a startling beauty. Tall, erect, with an athlete's grace of movement, he could not emerge into any company without being noticed, and even at a distance the brilliant northern blue of his eyes was as clear as if an inner sun shone through crystals of sapphire. Brother Mark saw him, and held his breath.

'*His* son?' he said in an awed whisper.

'But not hers,' said Cadfael. 'Another like Hywel.'

'There cannot be many such in this world,' said Mark, staring. Beauty in others he observed with a particular, ungrudging delight, having always felt himself to be the plainest and most insignificant of mortals.

'There is but one such, lad, as you know full well, for there is but one of any man that ever lived, black or fair. And yet,' owned Cadfael, reconsidering the uniqueness of the physical envelope if not of the inhabiting soul, 'we go close to duplicating this one, there at home in Shrewsbury. The boy's name is Rhun. You might look at our Brother Rhun, since Saint Winifred perfected him, and think one or the other a miraculous echo.'

Even to the name! And surely, thought Mark, recalling with pleasure the youngest of those who had been his brothers in Shrewsbury, this is how the pattern of a prince, the son of a prince, should look – and no less, a saint, the protégé of a saint. All radiance and clarity, all openness and serenity in the face. No wonder his father, recognising a prodigy, loves him better than all others.

'I wonder,' said Cadfael half to himself, unwittingly casting a shadow athwart Mark's contemplation of light, 'how *her* two will look upon him, when they're all grown.'

'It is impossible,' Mark said firmly, 'that they should ever wish him harm, even if land-greed and power-greed have sometimes turned brothers into enemies. This youth no one could hate.'

Close at his shoulder a cool, dry voice observed ruefully:

'Brother, I envy your certainty, but I would not for the world share it, the fall is too mortal. There is no one who cannot be hated, against whatever odds. Nor anyone who cannot be loved, against all reason.'

Cuhelyn had approached them unnoticed, threading a way through the stir of men and horses, hounds and servants and children. For all his black intensity, he was a very quiet man, unobtrusive in all his comings and goings. Cadfael turned in response to the unexpected observation, just in time to see the intent glance of the young man's shrewd eyes, presently fastened with a wry, indulgent warmth upon the boy Rhun, sharpen and chill as another figure passed between, and follow the transit with a fixity that suggested to Cadfael, at first, nothing more than detached interest, and in a matter of seconds froze into composed but indubitable hostility. Perhaps even more than hostility, a measure of restraint but implacable suspicion.

A young man of about Cuhelyn's years, and by no means unlike him in build and colouring, though thinner in feature and somewhat longer in the reach, had been standing a little apart, watching the bustle all around him, his arms folded and his shoulders leaned against the wall of the undercroft, as though this tumultuous arrival concerned him rather less than the rest of the household. From this detached stance he had moved suddenly, crossing between Cuhelyn and the linked pair, father and son, and cutting off the view of Rhun's radiant face. Something to be seen here certainly mattered to this young man, after all, someone had been sighted who meant more to him than clerics from Saint Asaph or the young noblemen of Owain's guard. Cadfael followed his vehement passage through the press, and saw him take one dismounting horseman by the sleeve. The very touch, the very encounter, that had drawn taut all the lines of Cuhelyn's countenance. Bledri ap Rhys swung about, face to face with the youth who accosted him, visibly recognised an acquaintance, and guardedly acknowledged him. No very exuberant welcome, but on both parts there was one momentary flash of warmth and awareness, before Bledri made his visage formally blank, and the boy accepted the suggestion, and began what seemed to be the most current of court civilities. No need, apparently, to pretend they did not know each other well enough, but every need to keep the acquaintance on merely courteous terms.

445

Cadfael looked along his shoulder, and briefly, at Cuhelyn's face, and asked simply: 'Gwion?'

'Gwion!'

'They were close? These two?'

'No. No closer than two must be who hold by the same lord.'

'That might be close enough for mischief,' said Cadfael bluntly. 'As you told me, your man has given his word not to attempt escape. He has not pledged himself to give up his allegiance beyond that.'

'Natural enough he should welcome the sight of another liegeman,' said Cuhelyn steadily. 'His word he will keep. As for Bledri ap Rhys, the terms of his sojourn with us *I* will see kept.' He shook himself briefly, and took each of them by an arm. The prince and his wife and sons were climbing the steps into the hall, the closest of their household following without haste. 'Come, Brothers, and let me be your herald here. I'll bring you to your lodging, and show you the chapel. Use it as you find occasion, and the prince's chaplain will make himself known to you.'

In the privacy of the lodgings alloted to them, backed into the shelter of the maenol wall, Brother Mark sat refreshed and thoughtful, looking back with wide grey eyes at all that had passed during this arrival in Aber. And at length he said: 'What most caused me to watch and wonder, was how like they were, those two – the young liegemen of Anarawd and of Cadwaladr. It is no mere matter of the same years, the same manner of body, the same make of face, it is the same passion within them. In Wales, Cadfael, this is another fashion of loyalty even than the bond the Normans hold by, or so it seems to me. They are on opposing sides, your Cuhelyn and this Gwion, and they could be brothers.'

'And as brothers should, and by times do not, they respect and like each other. Which would not prevent them from killing each other,' Cadfael admitted, 'if ever it came to a clash between their lords in the field.'

'That is what I feel to be so wrong,' said Mark, earnestly. 'How could either young man look at the other, and not see himself? All the more now that they have lived together in the same court, and admitted affection?'

'They are like twins, the one born left-handed, the other right-handed, at once doubles and opposites. They could kill without malice, and die without malice. God forbid,' said

Cadfael, 'it should ever come to that. But one thing is certain. Cuhelyn will be watching every moment his mirror image brushes sleeves with Bledri ap Rhys, and marking every word that passes between them, and every glance. For I think he knows somewhat more of Cadwaladr's chosen envoy than he has yet told us.'

At supper in Owain's hall there was good food and plenteous mead and ale, and harp music of the best. Hywel ab Owain sang, improvising upon the beauty of Gwynedd and the splendour of her history, and Cadfael's recalcitrant heart shed its habit for a half-hour, and followed the verses far into the mountains inland of Aber, and across the pale mirror of Lavan Sands to the royal burial-place of Llanfaes on Anglesey. In youth his adventurings had all looked eastward, now in his elder years eyes and heart turned westward. All heavens, all sanctuaries of the blessed lie to westward, in every legend and every imagination, at least for men of Celtic stock; a suitable meditation for old men. Yet here in the royal llys of Gwynedd Cadfael did not feel old.

Nor did it seem that his senses were in the least dulled or blunted, even as he rejoiced in his dreams, for he was sharp enough to detect the moment when Bledri ap Rhys slid an arm about Heledd's waist as she served him with mead. Nor did he miss the icy rigidity of Canon Meirion's face at the sight, or the deliberation with which Heledd, well aware of the same maledictory stare, forbore from freeing herself immediately, and said a smiling word in Bledri's ear, which might as well have been a curse as a compliment, though there was no doubt how her father interpreted it. Well, if the girl was playing with fire, whose fault was that? She had lived with her sire many loyal, loving years, he should have known her better, well enough to trust her. For Bledri ap Rhys she had no use at all but to take out her grievance on the father who was in such haste to get rid of her.

Nor did it appear, on reflection, that Bledri ap Rhys was seriously interested in Heledd. He made the gesture of admiration and courtship almost absentmindedly, as though by custom it was expected of him, and though he accompanied it with a smiling compliment, he let her go the moment she drew away, and his gaze went back to a certain young man sitting among the noblemen of the guard at a lower table. Gwion, the last obstinate hostage, who would not forswear his absolute

447

fealty to Cadwaladr, sat silent among his peers, and enemies, some of whom, like Cuhelyn, had become his friends. Throughout the feast he kept his own counsel, and guarded his thoughts, and even his eyes. But whenever he looked up at the high table, it was upon Bledri ap Rhys that his glance rested, and twice at least Cadfael saw them exchange a brief and brilliant stare, such as allies might venture to convey worlds of meaning where open speech was impossible.

Those two will somehow get together in private, Cadfael thought, before this night is out. And for what purpose? It is not Bledri who so passionately seeks a meeting, though he has been at liberty and is suspect of having some secret matter to impart. No, it is Gwion who wants, demands, relies upon reaching Bledri's ear. It is Gwion who has some deep and urgent purpose that needs an ally to reach fulfilment. Gwion who has given his word not to leave Owain's easy captivity. As Bledri ap Rhys has not done.

Well, Cuhelyn had vouched for Gwion's good faith, and pledged a constant watch upon Bledri. But it seemed to Cadfael that the llys was large enough and complex enough to provide him with a difficult watch, if those two were resolved to elude him.

The lady had remained with her children in private, and had not dined in hall, and the prince also withdrew to his own apartments early, having been some days absent from his family. He took his most beloved son with him, and left Hywel to preside until his guests chose to retire. With every man now free to change his place, or go out to walk in the fresh air of the late evening, there was considerable movement in the hall, and in the noise of many conversations and the music of the harpers, in the smoke of the torches and the obscurity of the shadowy corners, who was to keep a steady eye upon one man among so many? Cadfael marked the departure of Gwion from among the young men of the household, but still Bledri ap Rhys sat in his modest place towards the foot of the high table, serenely enjoying his mead – but in moderation, Cadfael noted – and narrowly observing everything that passed about him. He appeared to be cautiously impressed by the strength and strict order of the royal household, and the numbers, discipline and confidence of the young men of the guard.

'I think,' said Brother Mark softly into Cadfael's ear, 'we might have the chapel to ourselves if we go now.'

It was about the hour of Compline. Brother Mark would not

rest if he neglected the office. Cadfael rose and went with him, out from the doorway of the great hall into the cool and freshness of the night, and across the inner ward to the timber chapel against the outer wall. It was not yet fully dark nor very late, the determined drinkers still in hall would not end their gathering yet, but in the shadowy passages between the buildings of the maenol those who had duties about the place moved without haste, and quietly, going about their usual tasks in the easy languor of the end of a long and satisfactory day.

They were still some yards from the door of the chapel when a man emerged from it, and turned along the row of lodgings that lined the wall of the ward, to disappear into one of the narrow passages behind the great hall. He did not pass them close, and he might have been any one of the taller and elder of the frequenters of Owain's court. He was in no haste, but going tranquilly and a little wearily to his night's rest, yet Cadfael's mind was so persistently running upon Bledri ap Rhys that he was virtually certain of the man's identity, even in the deepening dusk.

He was quite certain when they entered the chapel, dimly lit by the rosy eye of the constant lamp on the altar, and beheld the shadowy outline of a man kneeling a little aside from the small pool of light. He was not immediately aware of them, or at least seemed not to be, though they had entered without any great care to preserve silence; and when they checked and hung back in stillness to avoid interrupting his prayers he gave no sign, but continued bowed and preoccupied, his face in shadow. At length he stirred, sighed and rose to his feet, and passing them by on his way out, without surprise, he gave them: 'Goodnight, Brothers!' in a low voice. The small red eye of the altar lamp drew his profile on the air clearly, but only for a moment; long enough, however, to show plainly the young, intense, brooding features of Gwion.

Compline was long over, and midnight past, and they were peacefully asleep in their small, shared lodging, when the alarm came. The first signs, sudden clamour at the main gate of the maenol, the muted thudding of hooves entering, the agitated exchange of voices between rider and guard, passed dreamlike and distant through Cadfael's senses without breaking his sleep, but Mark's younger ear, and mind hypersensitive to the excitement of the day, started him awake even before the murmur of voices rose into loud orders, and

449

the men of the household began to gather in the ward, prompt but drowsy from the rushes of the hall and the many lodgings of the maenol. Then what was left of the night's repose was shattered brazenly by the blasting of a horn, and Cadfael rolled from his brychan on to his feet, wide-awake and braced for action.

'What's afoot?'

'Someone rode in. In a hurry! Only one horseman!'

'They would not rouse the court for a little thing,' said Cadfael, clawing on his sandals and making for the door. The horn blared again, echoes ricocheting between the buildings of the prince's llys, and blunting their sharp edges against walls. In the open ward the young men came thronging in arms to the call, and the hum of many voices, still pitched low in awe of the night, swelled into a wordless, muted bellowing like a stormy tide flowing. From every open doorway a thread of light from hastily kindled lamps and candles spilled into the dark, conjuring here and there a recognisable face out of the crowd. A jaded horse, hard-ridden, was being led with drooping head towards the stables, and his rider, heedless of the many hands that reached to arrest him and the many voices that questioned, was thrusting a way through the press towards the great hall. He had barely reached the foot of the steps when the door above him opened, and Owain in his furred bed-gown came out, large and dark against the light from within, the squire who had run to arouse him with news of the coming close at his shoulder.

'Here am I,' said the prince, loud and clear and wide awake. 'Who's come wanting me?' As he moved forward to the edge of the steps the light from within fell upon the messenger's face, and Owain knew him. 'You, is it, Goronwy? From Bangor? What's your news?'

The messenger scarcely took time to bend his knee. He was known and trusted, and ceremony was waste of precious moments. 'My lord, early this evening one came with word from Carnarvon, and I have brought that word here to you as fast as horse can go. About Vespers they sighted ships westward off Abermenai, a great fleet in war order. The seamen say they are Danish ships from the kingdom of Dublin, come to raid Gwynedd and force your hand. And that Cadwaladr, your brother, is with them! He has brought them over to avenge and restore him, in your despite. The fealty he could not keep for love he has bought with promised gold.'

450

Chapter Five

ITHIN OWAIN'S writ the invasion of disorder might bring about momentary consternation, but could not hope to create disorder in its turn. His mind was too quick and resolute ever to entertain chaos. Before the muted roar of anger and resentment had circled the ward the captain of the prince's guard was at his elbow, awaiting his orders. They understood each other too well to need many words.

'This report is certain?' Owain asked.

'Certain, my lord. The messenger I had it from saw them himself from the dunes. Too distant then to be sure how many ships, but no question whence they come, and small doubt why. It was known he had fled to them. Why come back in such force but for a reckoning?'

'He shall have one,' said Owain composedly. 'How long before they come to land?'

'My lord, before morning surely. They were under sail, and the wind is steady from the west.'

For the length of a deep breath Owain considered. Perhaps a quarter of the horses in his stables had been ridden far, though not hard, the previous day, and as many of his armed men had made that journey, and sat merry in hall late into the night. And the ride that faced them now would be urgent and fast.

'Short time,' he said, musing, 'to raise even the half of Gwynedd, but we'll make sure of reserves, and collect every man available between here and Carnarvon as we go. Six

451

couriers I want, one to go before us now, the others to carry my summons through the rest of Arlechwedd and Arfon. Call them to Carnarvon. We may not need them, but no harm in making certain.' His clerks accepted the expected word, and vanished with commendable calm to prepare the sealed writs the couriers would bear to the chieftains of two cantrefs before the night was over. 'Now, every man who bears arms,' said Owain, raising his voice to carry to the containing walls and echo back from them, 'get to your beds and take what rest you can. We muster at first light.'

Cadfael, listening on the edge of the crowd, approved. Let the couriers, by all means, ride out by night, but to move the disciplined host across country in the dark was waste of time that could better be used in conserving their energy. The fighting men of the household dispersed, if reluctantly; only the captain of Owain's bodyguard, having assured himself of his men's strict obedience, returned to his lord's side.

'Get the women out of our way,' said Owain over his shoulder. His wife and her ladies had remained above in the open doorway of the hall, silent but for an agitated whispering among the younger maids. They departed uneasily and with many a glance behind, rather curious and excited than alarmed, but they departed. The princess had as firm a hold over her own household as Owain over his fighting men. There remained the stewards and elder counsellors, and such menservants as might be needed for any service, from armoury, stables, stores, brewhouse and bakehouse. Armed men also had needs, beyond their brands and bows, and the addition of some hundreds to a garrison meant a supply train following.

Among the smaller group now gathered about the prince Cadfael noted Cuhelyn, by the look of him fresh from his bed, if not from sleep, for he had thrown on his clothes in haste, he who was wont to appear rather elegantly presented. And there was Hywel, alert and quiet at his father's side. And Gwion, attentive and still, standing a little apart, as Cadfael had first seen him, as though he held himself always aloof from the concerns of Owain and Gwynedd, however honourably he acknowledged them. And Canon Meirion and Canon Morgant, for once drawn together in contemplating a crisis which had nothing to do with Heledd, and held no direct threat against either of them. They were onlookers, too, not participators. Their business was to get the reluctant bride

safely to Bangor and her bridegroom's arms, and there were no
Danish ships as near as Bangor, nor likely to be. Heledd had
been safely disposed of for the night with the princess's
women, and no doubt was gossiping excitedly with them now
over what might well seem to her an almost welcome diversion.

'So this,' said Owain into the comparative silence that waited
on his decree, 'is the dire consequence Bledri ap Rhys had in
mind. He knew, none so well, what my brother had planned.
He gave me fair warning. Well, let him wait his turn, we have
other work to do before morning. If he's secure in his bed, he'll
keep.'

The chosen couriers to his vassal princes were reappearing
cloaked for the night ride, and up from the stables the grooms
came leading the horses saddled and ready for them. The
leader came almost at a trot, led by the head groom, and the
man was in some measured excitement, poured out in a breath
before ever he came to a halt.

'My lord, there's a horse gone from the stables, and harness
and gear with him! We checked again, wanting to provide you
the best for the morning. A good, young roan, no white on
him, and saddle-cloth, saddle, bridle and all belonging to him.'

'And the horse he rode here – Bledri ap Rhys? His own
horse that he brought to Saint Asaph with him?' Hywel
demanded sharply. 'A deep grey, dappled lighter down his
flanks? Is he still there?'

'I know the one, my lord. No match for this roan. Still jaded
from yesterday. He's still there. Whoever the thief was, he
knew how to choose.'

'And meant good speed!' said Hywel, burning. 'He's gone,
surely. He's gone to join Cadwaladr and his Irish Danes at
Abermenai. How the devil did he ever get out of the gates?
And with a horse!'

'Go, some of you, and question the watch,' Owain ordered,
but without any great concern, and without turning to see who
ran to do his bidding. The guards on all the gates of his maenol
were men he could trust, as witness the fact that not one of
them had come running here from his post, however acute the
curiosity he might be feeling about the audible turmoil
continuing out of his sight. Only here at the main gate, where
the messenger from Bangor had entered, had any man stirred
from his duty, and then only the officer of the guard. 'There's
no way of locking a man in,' reflected Owain philosophically,
'if he has his vigour and is determined to get out. Any wall ever

built can be climbed, for a high enough cause. And he is to the last degree my brother's man.' He turned again to the tired messenger. 'In the dark a wise traveller would keep to the roads. Did you meet with any man riding west as you rode east here to us?'

'No, my lord, never a one. Not since I crossed the Cegin, and those were men of our own, known to me, and in no hurry.'

'He'll be far out of reach now, but let's at least start Einion off on his tracks with my writ. Who knows? A horse can fall lame, ridden hard in the dark, a man can lose his way in lands not his own. We may halt him yet,' said Owain, and turned to meet the steward who had run to see how watch was kept on the postern gates of the llys. 'Well?'

'No man challenged, no man passed. They know him now by sight, stranger though he may be. However he broke loose, it was not by the gates.'

'I never thought it,' the prince agreed sombrely. 'They never yet kept any but a thorough watch. Well, send out the couriers, Hywel, and then come to me within, to my private chamber. Cuhelyn, come with us.' He looked round briefly as his messengers mounted. 'Gwion, this is no fault nor concern of yours. Go to your bed. And keep your parole in mind still. Or take it back,' he added drily, 'and bide under lock and key while we're absent.'

'I have given it,' said Gwion haughtily, 'I shall keep it.'

'And I accepted it,' said the prince, relenting, 'and trust to it. There, go, what is there for you to do here?'

What, indeed, Cadfael thought wryly, except grudge us all the freedom he has denied himself? And the instant thought came, that Bledri ap Rhys, that fiery advocate so forward to excuse his lord and threaten in his name, had given no parole, and had, almost certainly, had very private and urgent conference with Gwion in the chapel of the llys only a matter of hours ago, and was now away to rejoin Cadwaladr at Abermenai, with much knowledge of Owain's movements and forces and defences. Gwion had never promised anything except not to escape. Within the walls he might move at will, perhaps his freedom extended even to the tref that lay outside the gate. For that he had pledged his own consent to detention. No one had promised as much for Bledri ap Rhys. And Gwion had made no pretence of his steely loyalty to Cadwaladr. Could he be blamed as recreant if he had helped his

454

unexpected ally to break out and return to his prince? A nice point! Knowing, if only at second hand from Cuhelyn, Gwion's stubborn and ferocious loyalty, he might well have warned his captors over and over of the limits he set on his parole, and the fervour with which he would seize any opportunity of serving the master he so obstinately loved, even at this remove.

Gwion had turned, slowly and hesitantly, to accept his dismissal, but then halted, stood with bent head and irresolute step, and in a moment gathered himself abruptly, and strode away instead towards the chapel; from the open door the faint red spark drew him like a lodestone. And what had Gwion to pray for now? A successful landing for Cadwaladr's Danish mercenaries, and a rapid and bloodless accommodation between brothers rather than a disastrous war? Or some repair to his own peace of mind? Fiercely upright, he might consider even his loyalty a sin where some unavoidable infringement of his oath was concerned. A complicated mind, sensitive to any self-reproach, however venial the sin.

Cuhelyn, who perhaps understood him best, and most resembled him, had watched him go with a thoughtful frown, and even taken a couple of impulsive steps to follow him before thinking better of the notion, and turning back to Owain's side. Prince and captains and counsellors mounted the steps to the great hall and the private apartments, and vanished purposefully within. Cuhelyn followed without another glance behind, and Cadfael and Mark, and a few hovering servants and retainers, were left in an almost empty ward, and the silence came down after clamour, and the dark stillness after a turmoil of movement. Everything was known and understood, everything was in hand, and would be dealt with competently.

'And there is no part in it for us,' Brother Mark said quietly at Cadfael's shoulder.

'None, except to saddle up tomorrow and ride on to Bangor.'

'Yes, that I must,' Mark agreed. There was a curious note of unease and regret in his voice, as if he found it almost a dereliction of his humanity to remove himself at this crisis in pursuit of his own errand, and leave all things here confounded and incomplete. 'I wonder, Cadfael ... The watch on the gates, all the gates, were they thought enough? Do you suppose a watch was set on the man himself, even here within, or was it enough that the walls held him? No man stood guard over the door of his lodging, or followed him from hall to his bed?'

'From the chapel to his bed,' Cadfael amended, 'if any man had that charge. No, Mark, we watched him go. There was no one treading on his heels.' He looked across the ward, to the alley into which Bledri had vanished when he came from the chapel. 'Are we not taking too much for granted, all of us? The prince has more urgent matters on his hands, true, but should not someone confirm what we have all leaped to believe?'

Gwion emerged slowly and silently from the open doorway of the chapel, drawing the door to after him, so that the tiny gleam of red vanished. He came somewhat wearily across the ward, seemingly unaware of the two who stood motionless and mute in the shadows, until Cadfael stepped forward to intercept him, mildly seeking information from one who might be expected to be able to supply it: 'A moment! Do you know in which of the many lodgings here this Bledri ap Rhys slept overnight?' And as the young man halted abruptly, turning on him a startled and wary face: 'I saw you greet him yesterday when we rode in, I thought you might know. You must have been glad to have some talk with an old acquaintance while he was here.'

For some reason the protracted interval of silence was more eloquent than what was finally said in reply. It would have been natural enough to answer at once: 'Why do you want to know? What does it matter now?' seeing that lodging must be empty, if the man who had slept there had fled in the night. The pause made it plain that Gwion knew well enough who had walked in upon him in the chapel, and was well aware that they must have seen Bledri departing. He had time to think before he spoke, and what he said was: 'I *was* glad, to set eyes on a man of my own tribe. I have been here hostage more than half a year. They will have told you as much. The steward had given him one of the lodgings against the north wall. I can show you. But what difference does it make now? He's gone. Others may blame him,' he said haughtily, 'but not I. If I had been free, I would have done as he did. I never made secret of where my fealty lay. And lies still!'

'God forbid anyone should condemn a man for keeping faith,' agreed Cadfael equably. 'Did Bledri have his chamber to himself?'

'He did.' Gwion hoisted his shoulders, shrugging off an interest it seemed he did not understand, but accepted as meaning something to these wandering Benedictines if it meant nothing to him. 'There was none sharing it with him, to prevent his going, if that is what you mean.'

456

'I was wondering, rather,' said Cadfael deprecatingly, 'whether we are not assuming too much, just because a horse is missing. If his lodging was in a remote corner of the wards, with many a wall between, may he not have slept through this whole uproar, and be still snoring in all innocence? Since he lay alone, there was no one to wake him, if he proved so sound a sleeper.'

Gwion stood staring, eye to eye with him, his thick dark brows raised. 'Well, true enough, but for the horn call a man with enough drink in him might have slept through it all. I doubt it, but if you feel the need to see for yourself ... It's not on my way, but I'll show you.' And without more words he set off into the passage between the rear of the great hall and the long timber range of the storehouse and armoury. They followed his brisk figure, shadowy in the dimness, through towards the long line of buildings in the shelter of the outer wall.

'The third door was his.' It stood just ajar, no gleam of light showing in the crack. 'Go in, Brothers, and see for yourselves. But by the look of it you'll find him gone, and all his gear with him.'

The range of small rooms was built in beneath the watch-platform along the outer wall, and shadowed deeply by its overhang. Cadfael had seen only one stairway to the platform, broad and easy of access but in full view of the main gate. Moreover, it would not be easy to descend on the outer side, unless with a long rope, for the fighting gallery projected outward from the wall, and there was a ditch below. Cadfael set a hand to the door and pushed it open upon darkness. His eyes, by this time accustomed to the night and such light as the clear but moonless sky provided, were at once blind again. There was no movement, and no sound within. He set the door wide, and advanced a step or two into the small chamber.

'We should have brought a torch,' said Mark, at his shoulder.

No need for that, it seemed, to show that the room was empty of life. But Gwion, tolerant of these exigent visitors, offered from the threshold: 'The brazier will be burning in the guardhouse. I'll bring a light.'

Cadfael had made another step within, and all but stumbled as his foot tangled soundlessly with some shifting fold of soft material, as though a rumpled brychan had been swept from bed to floor. He stooped and felt forward into the rough weave

457

of cloth, and found something of firmer texture within it. A fistful of sleeve rose to his grip, the warmth and odour of wool stirred on the air, and an articulated weight dangled and swung as he lifted it, solid within the cloth. He let it rest back again gently, and felt down the length of it to a thick hem, and beyond that, the smooth, lax touch of human flesh, cooling but not yet cold. A sleeve indeed, and an arm within it, and a large, sinewy hand at the end of the arm.

'Do that,' he said over his shoulder. 'Bring a light. We are going to need all the light we can get.'

'What is it?' asked Mark, intent and still behind him.

'A dead man, by all the signs. A few hours dead. And unless he has grappled with someone who stood in the way of his flight, and left him here to tell the tale, who can this be but Bledri ap Rhys?'

Gwion came running with a torch, and set it in the sconce on the wall, meant only to hold a small lantern. In such confined rooms a torch would never normally be permitted, but this was crisis. The sparse contents of the chamber sprang sharply outlined from the dark, a rumpled bench bed against the rear wall, the brychans spilled over and dangling to the floor, the impression of a long body still discernible indenting the cover of the straw mattress. On a shelf beside the bed-head, convenient to the guest's hand, a small saucer-lamp stood. Not quenched, for it had burned out and left only a smear of oil and the charred wick. Beneath the shelf, half-unfolded, lay a leather saddle-roll, and dropped carelessly upon it a man's cotte and chausses and shirt, and the rolled cloak he had not needed on the journey. And in the corner his riding-boots, one overturned and displaced, as if a foot had kicked it aside.

And between the bed and the doorway, sprawled on his back at Cadfael's feet, arms and legs flung wide, head propped against the timber wall, as though a great blow had lifted and hurled him backwards, Bledri ap Rhys lay with eyes half-open, and lips drawn back from his large, even teeth in a contorted grin. The skirts of his gown billowed about him in disorder, the breast had fallen open wide as he fell, and beneath it he was naked. In the flickering of the torch it was hard to tell whether the darkened blotch on his left jaw and cheek was shadow or bruise, but there was no mistaking the gash over his heart, and the blood that had flowed from it down into the folds of cloth under his side. The dagger that had inflicted the wound had been as quickly withdrawn, and drawn out the life after it.

Cadfael went down on his knees beside the body, and gently turned back the breast of the woollen gown to reveal the wound more clearly to the quivering light. Gwion, behind him in the doorway and hesitant to enter, drew deep breath, and let it out in a gusty sob that caused the flame to flicker wildly, and what seemed a living shudder passed over the dead face.

'Be easy,' said Cadfael tolerantly, and leaned to close the half-open eyes. 'For he is easy enough now. Well I know, he was of your allegiance. And I am sorry!'

Mark stood quiet and still, staring down in undismayed compassion. 'I wonder had he wife and children,' he said at last. Cadfael marked the first focus of one fledgling priest's concern, and approved it. Christ's first instinct might have been much the same. Not: 'Unshriven, and in peril!' not even: 'When did he last confess and find absolution?' but: 'Who will care for his little ones?'

'Both!' said Gwion, very low. 'Wife and children he has. I know. I will deal.'

'The prince will give you leave freely,' said Cadfael. He rose from his knees, a little stiffly. 'We must go, all, and tell him what has befallen. We are within his writ and guests in his house, all, not least this man, and this is murder. Take the torch, Gwion, and go before, and I will close the door.'

Gwion obeyed this alien voice without question, though it had no authority over him but what he gave of his own free will. On the threshold he stumbled, for all he was holding the light. Mark took his arm until he had his balance again, and as courteously released him as soon as his step was secure. Gwion said no word, made no acknowledgement, as Mark needed none. He went before like a herald, torch in hand, straight to the steps of the great hall, and lit them steadily within.

'We were all in error, my lord,' said Cadfael, 'in supposing that Bledri ap Rhys had fled your hospitality. He did not go far, nor did he need a horse for the journey, though it is the longest a man can undertake. He is lying dead in the lodging where your steward housed him. From all we see there, he never intended flight. I will not say he had slept. But he had certainly lain in his bed, and certainly put on his gown over his nakedness when he rose from it, to encounter whoever it may have been who walked in upon his rest. These two with me here have seen what I have seen, and will bear it out.'

459

'It is so,' said Brother Mark.

'It is so,' said Gwion.

Round Owain's council table in his private apartment, austerely furnished, the silence lasted long, every man among his captains frozen into stillness, waiting for the prince's reaction. Hywel, standing at his father's shoulder, in the act of laying a parchment before him, had halted with the leaf half-unrolled in his hands, his eyes wide and intent upon Cadfael's face.

Owain said consideringly, rather digesting than questioning the news thus suddenly laid before him: 'Dead. Well!' And in a moment more: 'And how did this man die?'

'By a dagger in the heart,' said Cadfael with certainty..

'From before? Face to face?'

'We have left him as we found him, my lord. Your own physician may see him just as we saw him. As I think,' said Cadfael, 'he was struck a great blow that hurled him back against the wall, so that he fell stunned. Certainly whoever struck him down faced him, this was confrontation, no assault from behind. And no weapon, not then. Someone lashed out with a fist, in great anger. But then he was stabbed as he lay. His blood has run down and gathered in the folds of his gown under his left side. There was no movement. He was out of his senses when he was stabbed. By someone!'

'The same someone?' wondered Owain.

'Who can tell? It is probable. It is not certain. But I doubt he would have lain helpless more than a matter of moments.'

Owain spread his hands upon the table before him, pushing aside the parchments scattered there. 'You are saying that Bledri ap Rhys has been murdered. Under my roof. In my charge, however he may have come there, friend or enemy, to all intent he was a guest in my house. This I will not abide.' He looked beyond Cadfael, at Gwion's sombre face. 'You need not fear that I will value my honest enemy's life at less than any man of my own,' he said in generous reassurance.

'My lord,' said Gwion, very low, 'that I never doubted.'

'If I must go after other matters now,' said Owain, 'yet he shall have justice, if by any means I can ensure it. Who last saw the man, living?'

'I saw him leave the chapel, late,' said Cadfael, 'and cross towards his own lodging. So did Brother Mark, who was with me. Beyond that I cannot say.'

'At that time,' said Gwion, his voice a little hoarse with

460

constraint, 'I was in the chapel. I talked with him. I was glad to see a face I knew. But when he left I did not follow.'

'Enquiry shall be made,' said Owain, 'of all the servants of the house, who would be the last wakeful about the maenol. See to it, Hywel. If any had occasion to pass there, and saw either Bledri ap Rhys, or any man going or coming late about his door, bring the witness here. We muster at first light, but we have yet a few hours before dawn. If this thing can be resolved before I go to deal with my brother and his Danes, so much the better.'

Hywel departed on the word, laying his leaf of vellum down on the table, and plucking a couple of men out of the council to speed the search. There was to be no rest that night for the menservants, stewards and maids of Owain's court, none for the members of his bodyguard, or the young men who followed him in arms. Bledri ap Rhys had come to Saint Asaph intending mischief, threatening mischief, and the cost had fallen on his own head, but the echoes would spread outward like ripples from a stone flung into a pool, and scarify the lives of all here until murder was paid for.

'The dagger that was used,' said Owain, returning to his quest like a hawk stooping. 'It was not left in the wound?'

'It was not. Nor have I examined the wound so closely that I dare guess what manner of blade it had. Your own men, my lord, will be able to hazard that as well as I. Better,' said Cadfael, 'since even daggers change with years, and I am long out of the practice of arms.'

'And the bed, you say, had been slept in. At least lain in. And the man had made no preparation for riding, and left no sign he ever intended flight. It was not so vital a matter that I should set a man to watch him through the night. But there is yet another mystery here,' said the prince. 'For if he did not make away with one of our horses, who did? There is no question but the beast is gone.'

It was a point that Cadfael, in his preoccupation with Bledri's death, had not even considered. Somewhere at the back of his mind he had felt the nagging and elusive misgiving that something else would have to be investigated before the night was over, but in the brief instants when he ventured to turn and attempt to see it clearly, it had vanished from the corner of his eye. Suddenly confronted with the puzzle that had eluded him, he foresaw a lengthy and careful numbering of every soul in the maenol to find the one, the only one, lost

461

without trace. Someone else would have to undertake that, for there could be no delay in the prince's dawn departure.

'It is in your hands, my lord,' he said, 'as are we all.'

Owain flattened a large and shapely hand upon the table before him. 'My course is set, and cannot be changed until Cadwaladr's Dublin Danes are sent back to their own land with clipped ears, if it comes to that. And you, Brothers, have your own way to go, in less haste than my way, but not to be delayed, either. Your bishop is entitled to as strict service as princes expect. Let us by all means consider, in what time we have left, which among us may have done murder. Then, if it must be left behind for another time, yet it shall not be forgotten. Come, I'll see for myself how this ill matter looks, and then we'll have the dead cared for, and see due reparation made to his kin. He was no man of mine, but he did me no wrong, and such right as I may I'll do to him.'

They rejoined the gathering in the council chamber the better part of an hour later. By then the body of Bledri ap Rhys was decently bestowed in the chapel, in the charge of the prince's chaplain, and there was no more to be learned from the sparse furnishings of the room where he had died. No weapon remained to speak, even the flow of his blood was meagre, and left small trace behind, the stab wound being neat, narrow and precise. It is not difficult to make a clean and exact job of stabbing to the heart a man already laid senseless to your hand. Bledri could scarcely have felt death remove him from the world.

'He was not a man to be greatly loved, I fancy,' Owain said as they crossed once more to the hall. 'Many here must have resented him, for he came arrogantly enough. It might take no more than a quarrelsome encounter, after that, to make a man lash out on impulse. But to kill? Would any man of mine take it so far, when I had made him my guest?'

'It would need a very angry man,' Cadfael owned, 'to go so far in your despite. But it takes only an instant to strike, and less than an instant to forget all caution. He had made himself a number of enemies, even in the short time we all rode together.' Names were to be suppressed at all cost, but he was thinking of the blackly murderous glare of Canon Meirion, beholding Bledri's familiarity with his daughter, and the consequent threat to a career the good canon had no intention of risking.

'An open quarrel would be no mystery,' said Owain. 'That I could have resolved. Even if it came to a death, a blood price would have paid it, the blame would not have been all one way. He did provoke hatred. But to follow him to his bedchamber and hale him out of his bed? It is a very different matter.'

They passed through the hall and entered the council chamber. Every eye turned upon them as they came in. Mark and Gwion had waited with the rest. They stood close together, silent, as though the very fact of discovering a death together had linked them in a continuing fellowship that set them apart from the captains round the council table. Hywel was back before his father, and had brought with him one of the kitchen servants, a shaggy dark boy a little puffy with sleep, but bright-eyed again with reviving wakefulness now that he knew of a sudden death, and had something, however small, to impart concerning it.

'My lord,' said Hywel, 'Meurig here is the latest I could find to pass by the lodgings where Bledri ap Rhys was housed. He will tell you what he saw. He has not yet told it, we waited for you.'

The boy spoke up boldly enough. It seemed to Cadfael that he was not altogether convinced of the importance of what he had to say, though it pleased him well enough to be here declaring it. Its significance he was content to leave to the princes.

'My lord, it was past midnight before I finished my work, and went through the passage there to my bed. There was no one about then, I was among the last. I did not see a soul until I came by the third door in that range, where they tell me now this Bledri ap Rhys was lodged. There was a man standing in the doorway, looking into the room, with the latch in his hand. When he heard me coming he closed the door, and went away along the alley.'

'In haste?' asked Owain sharply. 'Furtively? In the dark he could well slip away unrecognised.'

'No, my lord, no such matter. Simply, he drew the door to, and walked away. I thought nothing of it. And he took no care not to be seen. He said a goodnight to me as he went. As though he had been seeing a guest safe to his bed – one none too steady on his feet, or too sure of his way, it might be.'

'And you answered him?'

'Surely, my lord.'

'Now name him,' said Owain, 'for I think you knew him well enough to call him by name then.'

'My lord, I did. Every man in your court of Aber has got to know him and value him by now, though he came as a stranger when first the lord Hywel brought him from Deheubarth. It was Cuhelyn.'

A sharp, indrawn breath hissed round the table. All heads turned, and all eyes fixed upon Cuhelyn, who sat apparently unmoved at finding himself suddenly the centre of marked and loaded attention. His thick dark brows had risen in mild surprise, even a trace of amusement.

'That is true,' he said simply. 'That I could have told you, but for all I knew or know now there could have been others there after me. As certainly there was one. The last to see him, living, no question. But that was not I.'

'Yet you offered us no word of this,' the prince pointed out quietly. 'Why not?'

'True, I did none too well there. It came a little too close to home for comfort,' said Cuhelyn. 'I opened my mouth once to say it, and shut it again with nothing said. For sober truth is that I did have the man's death in mind, and for all I never touched him nor went in to him, when Brother Cadfael told us he lay dead, I felt the finger of guilt cold on my neck. But for solitude, and chance, and this lad coming along when most he was needed, yes, I might have been Bledri's murderer. But I am not, thanks be to God!'

'Why did you go there, and at that hour?' asked Owain, giving no sign whether he believed or disbelieved.

'I went there to confront him. To kill him in single combat. Why at that hour? Because the hatred had taken hours to come to the boil within me, and only then had I reached the length of killing. Also, I think, because I wished to make it clear past doubt that no other man was drawn into my quarrel, and no other could be accused even of knowing what I did.' Cuhelyn's level voice remained quiet and composed still, but his face had tightened until pale lines stood clear over the cheekbones and round the lean, strong angle of his jaw.

Hywel said softly, filling and easing the pause: 'A one-armed man against a seasoned warrior with two?'

Cuhelyn looked down indifferently at the silver circlet that secured the linen cover over the stump of his left arm. 'One arm or two, the end would have been the same. But when I

464

opened his door, there he lay fast asleep. I heard his breathing, long and placid. Is it fair dealing to startle a man out of his sleep and challenge him to the death? And while I stood there in the doorwy, Meurig here came along. And I drew the door closed again, and went away, and left Bledri sleeping. Not that I gave up my purpose,' he said, rearing his head fiercely. 'Had he been living when the morning came, my lord, I meant to challenge him openly of his mortal offence, and call him to battle for his life. And if you gave me countenance, to kill him.'

Owain was staring upon him steadily, and visibly probing the mind that fashioned this bitter speech and gave it such passionate force. With unshaken calm he said: 'So far as is known to me, the man had done me no grave offence.'

'Not to you, my lord, beyond his arrogance. But to me, the worst possible. He made one among the eight that set upon us from ambush, and killed my prince at my side. When Anarawd was murdered, and this hand was lopped, Bledri ap Rhys was there in arms. Until he came into the bishop's hall I did not know his name. His face I have never forgotten. Nor never could have forgotten, until I had got Anarawd's price out of him in blood. But someone else has done that for me. And I am free of him.'

'Say to me again,' Owain commanded, when Cuhelyn had made an end of this declaration, 'that you left the man living, and have no guilt in his death.'

'I did so leave him. I never touched him, his death is no guilt of mine. If you bid me, I will swear it on the altar.'

'For this while,' said the prince gravely, 'I am forced to leave this matter unresolved until I come back from Abermenai with a more urgent matter settled and done. But I still need to know who did the thing you did not do, for not all here have your true quarrel against Bledri ap Rhys. And as I for my part take your word, there may be many who still doubt you. If you give your word to return with me, and abide what further may be found out, till all are satisfied, then come with me. I need you as I may need every good man.'

'As God sees me,' said Cuhelyn. 'I will not leave you, for any reason, until you bid me go. And the happier, if you never do so bid me.'

The last and most unexpected word of a night of the unexpected lay with Owain's steward, who entered the council chamber just as the prince was rising to dismiss his officers, sufficiently briefed for the dawn departure. Provision was already made for the rites

465

due to the dead. Gwion would remain at Aber, according to his oath, and had pledged his services to send word to Bledri's wife in Ceredigion, and conduct such necessary duties for the dead man as she demanded. A melancholy duty, but better from a man of the same allegiance. The morning muster was planned with precision, and order given for the proper provision due to the bishop of Lichfield's envoy on his way to Bangor, while the prince's force pursued the more direct road to Carnarvon, the old road that had linked the great forts by which an alien people had kept their footing in Wales, long ago. Latin names still clung to the places they had inhabited, though only priests and scholars used them now; the Welsh knew them by other names. It was all prepared, to the last detail. Except that somehow the missing horse had been lost yet again, slipping through the cracks between greater concerns into limbo. Until Goronwy ab Einion came in with the result of a long and devious enquiry into the total household within the llys.

'My lord, the lord Hywel set me a puzzle, to find the one person who should be here, and is not. Our own household of retainers and servants I thought well to leave aside, why should any among them take to his heels? My lord, the princess's waiting woman knows the roll of her maids perfectly, and any guests who are women are her charge. There is one girl who came in your train yesterday, my lord, who is gone from the place allotted to her. She came here with her father, a canon of Saint Asaph, and a second canon of that diocese travelled with them. We have not disturbed the father as yet. I waited for your word. But there is no question, the young woman is gone. No one has seen her since the gates were closed.'

'God's wounds!' swore Owain, between laughter and exasperation. 'It was true what they told me! The dark lass that would not be a nun in England – God keep her, why should she, a black Welshwoman as ever was! – and said yes to Ieuan ab Ifor as a blessed relief by comparison – do you tell me she has stolen a horse and made off into the night before the guard shut us in? The devil!' he said, snapping his fingers. 'What is the child's name?'

'Her name is Heledd,' said Brother Cadfael.

Chapter Six

O QUESTION, Heledd was gone. No hostess here, with duties and status, but perhaps the least among the arriving guests, she had held herself aloof from the princess's waiting-woman, keeping her own counsel and, as it seemed, waiting her own chance. No more reconciled to the prospect of marriage with the unknown bridegroom from Anglesey than to a conventual cell among strangers in England, Heledd had slipped through the gates of Aber before they closed at night, and gone to look for some future of her own choosing. But how had she abstracted also a horse, saddled and bridled, and a choice and fleet horse into the bargain?

The last that anyone had seen of her was when she left the hall with an empty pitcher, barely halfway through the prince's feast, leaving all the nobility busy at table, and her father still blackly scowling after her as she swung the screen curtain closed behind her. Perhaps she had truly intended to refill the pitcher and return to resume replenishing the Welsh drinking horns, if only to vex Canon Meirion. But no one had seen her since that moment. And when the first light came, and the prince's force began to muster in the wards, and the bustle and clamour, however purposeful and moderate, would certainly bring out all the household, who was to tell the good canon that his daughter had taken flight in the darkness from the cloister, from marriage, and from her sire's very imperfect love and care for her?

Such an unavoidable task Owain chose not to delegate. When the light from the east tipped the outer wall of the maenol, and the ward began to fill with horse and groom and man-at-arms and archer roused and ready, he sent to summon the two canons of Saint Asaph to the gatehouse, where he waited with one shrewd eye on the ranks mustering and mounting, and one on a sky and light that promised good weather for riding. No one had forestalled him with the bad news; so much was plain from Canon Meirion's serene, assured face as he strode across the ward with a civil good-morning already forming on his lips, and a gracious benediction ready to follow it as soon as the prince should mount and ride. At his back, shorter-legged and more portly and selfconscious of bearing, Canon Morgant hugged his ponderous dignity about him, and kept a noncommittal countenance.

It was not Owain's way to beat about bushes. Time was short, business urgent, and what mattered was to make such provision as was now possible to repair what had gone awry, both with threats from an obdurate brother and peril to a lost daughter.

'There is news in the night,' said the prince briskly, as soon as the two clerics drew close, 'that will not please your reverences, and does not please me.'

Cadfael, watching from beside the gate, could detect no disquiet in Canon Meirion's face at this opening. No doubt he thought it referred only to the threat of the Danish fleet, and possibly the flight of Bledri ap Rhys, for the two clerics had gone to their beds before that supposed flight changed to a death. But either would come rather as a relief and satisfaction to him, seeing that Bledri and Heledd between them had given him cause to tremble for his future career, with Canon Morgant storing up behind his austere forehead every unbecoming look and wanton word to report back to his bishop. By his present bearing, Meirion knew of nothing worse, nothing in the world to disturb his complacency now, if Bledri was either fled or dead.

'My lord,' he began benignly, 'we were present to hear of the threat to your coast. It will surely be put off without harm ...'

'Not that!' said Owain bluntly. 'This concerns yourself. Sir, your daughter has fled in the night. Sorry I am to say it, and to leave you to deal with the case in my absence, but there's no help. I have given orders to the captain of my garrison here to give you every aid in searching for her. Stay as long as you need to stay, make use of my men and my stables as best serves. I and all who ride with me will be keeping a watch and asking news of her westward direct to Carnarvon. So, I trust, will Deacon Mark and Brother Cadfael on their ride to Bangor. Between us we should cover the country to westward. You ask and search round Aber and eastward, and south if need be, though I think she would not venture the mountains alone. I will return to the search as soon as I may.'

He had proceeded thus far uninterrupted only because Canon Meirion had been struck mute and amazed at the very first utterance, and stood staring with round eyes and parted lips, paling until the peaks of his sharp cheekbones stood out white under the straining skin. Utter consternation stopped the breath in his throat.

'My daughter!' he repeated slowly at last, the words shaped almost without sound. And then in a hoarse wheeze: 'Gone? My daughter loose alone, and these sea-raiders abroad in the land?'

At least, thought Brother Cadfael approvingly, if she could be here to hear it, she would know that he has some real care for her. His first outcry is for her safety, for once his own advancement is forgotten. If only for a moment!

'Half the width of Wales from here,' said Owain stoutly, 'and I'll see to it they come no nearer. She knows better than to ride into their arms. This girl you bred is no fool.'

'But headstrong!' Meirion lamented, his voice recovered and loud with anguish. 'Who knows what risk she might not venture? And if she has fled me now, she will still hide from me. This I never foresaw, that she could feel so driven and so beset.'

'I say again,' said Owain firmly, 'use my garrison, my stables, my men as you will, send out after news of her, for surely she cannot be far. As for the ways to westward, we will watch for her as we go. But go we must. You well know the need.'

Meirion drew himself back a little, erect at his tallest, and shook his broad shoulders.

'Go with God, my lord, you can do no other. My girl's life is but one, and many depend upon you. She shall be my care. I dread I have not served her turn lately as well as I have served my own, or she would never have left me so.'

And he turned, with a hasty reverence, and strode away towards the hall, so precipitately that Cadfael could see him clambering fiercely into his boots and marching down to the stable to saddle his horse, and away to question everyone in the village outside the walls, in search of the dark daughter he had gone to some pains to despatch into distance, and now was all afire to recover. And after him, still silent, stonily expressionless, potentially disapproving, went Canon Morgant, a black recording angel.

They were more than a mile along the coastal track towards Bangor before Brother Mark broke his deep and thoughtful silence. They had parted from the prince's force on leaving Aber, Owain bearing south-west to take the most direct road to Carnarvon, while Cadfael and Mark kept to the shore, with the shining, pallid plain of the shallows over Lavan Sands reflecting the morning light on their right hand, and the peaks of Eryri soaring one above another on their left, beyond the narrow green lowlands of the coast. Over the deep channel beyond the sands, the shores of Anglesey were bright in sunlight.

'Did he know,' Mark wondered aloud suddenly, 'that the man was dead?'

'He? Meirion? Who can tell? He was there among the rest of us when the groom cried out that a horse was missing, and Bledri was held to have taken him and made off to his master. So much he knew. He was not with us when we looked for and found the man dead, nor present in the prince's counsel. If the pair of them were safe in their beds they cannot have heard the news until this morning. Does it signify? Dead or fled, the man was out of Meirion's way, and could scandalise Morgant no longer. Small wonder he took it so calmly.'

'That is not what I meant,' said Mark. 'Did he know of his own knowledge? Before ever another soul knew it?' And as Cadfael was silent, he pursued hesitantly: 'You had not considered it?'

'It had crossed my mind,' Cadfael admitted. 'You think him capable of killing?'

'Not in cool blood, not by stealth. But his blood is not cool, but all too readily heated. There are some who bluster and bellow, and rid their bile that way. Not he! He contains it, and it boils within him. It is likelier far to burst forth in action than in noise. Yes, I think him capable of killing. And if he did confront Bledri ap Rhys, he would meet only with provocation and disdain there. Enough to make for a violent end.'

470

'And could he go from that ending straight to his bed, in such unnerving company, and keep his countenance? Even sleep?'

'Who says that he slept? He had only to be still and quiet. There was nothing to keep Canon Morgant wakeful.'

'I return you another question,' said Cadfael. 'Would Cuhelyn lie? He was not ashamed of his purpose. Why, then, should he lie about it when it came to light?'

'The prince believes him,' said Mark, thoughtfully frowning.

'And you?'

'Any man may lie, not even for very grave reason. Even Cuhelyn may. But I do not think he would lie to Owain. Or to Hywel. He has given his second fealty, as absolute as the first. But there is another question to be asked concerning Cuhelyn. No, there are two. Had he told anyone what he knew about Bledri ap Rhys? And if he would not lie to Hywel, who had salved him and brought him to an honourable service, would he lie *for* him? For if he did tell anyone that he recognised Bledri as one among his prince's murderers, it would be Hywel. Who had no better reason to love the perpetrators of that ambush than had Cuhelyn himself.'

'Or any man who went with Hywel to drive Cadwaladr out of Ceredigion for Anarawd's sake,' agreed Cadfael resignedly, 'or any who took bitter offence at hearing Bledri so insolent on Cadwaladr's behalf in hall that night, spitting his threats into Owain's face. True, a man is dead who was well-hated, living, and took no keep to be anything better than hated. In a crowded court where his very presence was an affront, is it any wonder if he came by a short ending? But the prince will not let it rest.'

'And we can do nothing,' said Mark, and sighed. 'We cannot even look for the girl until I have discharged my errand.'

'We can ask,' said Cadfael.

And ask they did, at every hamlet and dwelling along the way, whether a young woman had not ridden past by this road, a dark Welsh girl on a young roan, all of one colour. A horse from the prince's stables would not go unremarked, especially with a lone girl in the saddle. But the day wore on, and the sky clouded gently and cleared again, and they drew into Bangor by mid-afternoon; but no one could give them word of Heledd, Meirion's daughter.

*

Bishop Meurig of Bangor received them as soon as they had threaded their way through the streets of the town to his cathedral enclave, and announced themselves to his archdeacon. It seemed that here everything was to be done briskly and briefly, with small respect to the planned and public ceremony Bishop Gilbert had preferred. For here they were by many miles nearer to the threat of Danish raiders, and very sensibly taking such precautions as were possible to cope with them if they should penetrate so far. Moreover, Meurig was native Welsh, at home here, and had no need of the cautious dispositions Gilbert felt necessary to secure his position. It might be true that he had proved at first a disappointment to his prince, by succumbing to Norman pressure and submitting to Canterbury, but stoutly Welsh he remained, and his resistance, if diverted, must still be proceeding by more subtle ways. At least he did not seem to Cadfael, when they were admitted to his presence in private, the kind of man to compromise his Welshness and his adherence to the ways of the Celtic Church without a long and doughty rearguard action.

The bishop was not at all like his fellow of Saint Asaph. Instead of the tall, dignified Gilbert, selfconsciously patrician and austere without, and uneasily insecure within, here was a small, round, bustling cleric in his forties, voluble of speech but very much to the point, rapid of movement and a little dishevelled and shaggy, with a sharp eye and a cheerfully bouncing manner, like a boisterous but businesslike hound on a scent. His pleasure in the very fact of their coming on such an errand was made very plain, and outweighed even his delight in the breviary Mark had brought him, though clearly he had an eye for a handsome script, and turned the leaves with lovingly delicate movements of thick, strong fingers.

'You will have heard already, Brothers, of the threat to our shores, so you will understand that here we are looking to our defences. God grant the Norsemen never get ashore, or no further than the shore, but if they should, we have a town to keep, and churchmen must turn to like the rest. For that reason we observe at present little state or ceremony, but I trust you will be my guests for a day or two before you need return with my letters and compliments to your bishop.'

It was for Mark to respond to this invitation, which was offered warmly enough, but with a vaguely preoccupied look in the bishop's shrewd eyes. At least a part of his mind was away

472

scanning the waterfront of his town, where the brief mudflat between the tides gave place to the narrowing neck of the strait. Fifteen miles or more to the western end at Abermenai, but the smaller shallow-draught ships, oared by twenty rowers, could cover that distance rapidly. A pity the Welsh had never really taken to the seas! And Bishop Meurig had his flock to consider, and no amenable temper to let them suffer anything his vigour could prevent. He would not be sorry to pack his visitors from England off back to Lichfield, and have his hands free. Hands that looked quite capable of turning to the sword or the bow whenever the need arose.

'My lord,' said Brother Mark, after a brief thoughtful hesitation, 'I think we should leave tomorrow, if that does not cause you too much inconvenience. Much as I would like to linger, I have pledged myself to a prompt return. And even beyond that, the party with which we rode from Saint Asaph included a young woman who should have come here to Bangor with us, under Owain Gwynedd's protection, but now, bereft of that protection, since the prince perforce has hurried on to Carnarvon, she has unwisely ridden out from Aber alone, and somewhere has lost her way. They are seeking for her from Aber. But since we have come as far as Bangor, if I may justify the delay even of one day, or two, I should like to spend them searching for her in these parts also. If you will grant me leave to make use of so short a delay, we will spend it for the lady's benefit, and you, I know, will be making use of every moment for the better keep of your own people.'

A good speech, Cadfael approved, one that gives nothing away of what lies behind Heledd's flight, thereby sparing her reputation and this good prelate's very proper concern. He interpreted it carefully, improvising a little where memory faltered, since Mark had allowed him no pause between the lines. The bishop nodded instant comprehension, and demanded practically: 'Did the lady know of this threat from Dublin?'

'No,' said Mark, 'the messenger from Carnarvon came only later. She cannot have known.'

'And she is somewhere abroad between Aber and here, and alone? I wish I had more men to send out after her,' said Meurig, frowning, 'but we have already sent on to Carnarvon all the fighting men who can be spared, to join the prince there. Such as are left we may need here.'

'We do not know,' Cadfael said, 'which way she rode. She

may be well behind us to the east, for all we know, and safe enough. But if we can do no more, we can divide on the ride back, and enquire everywhere after her.'

'And if she has by now heard of the peril,' Mark added eagerly, 'and very wisely looks for safe shelter, are there in these regions any houses of religious women, where she might take refuge?'

This also Cadfael translated, though he could have given a general answer to it himself, without troubling the bishop. The Church in Wales had never run to nunneries, as even conventual life for men had never been on the same monastic pattern as in England. Instead of the orderly, well-regulated house of sisters, with a recognised authority and a rule, here there might arise, in the most remote and solitary wilderness, a small wattled oratory, with a single, simple saint living within it, a saint in the old dispensation, without benefit of Pope or canonisation, who grew a few vegetables and herbs for her food, and gathered berries and wild fruit, and came to loving terms with the small beasts of the warren, so that they ran to hide in her skirts when they were hunted, and neither huntsmen nor horn could urge on the hounds to do the lady affront, or her little visitors harm. Though Cadfael had to admit, on reflection, that the Dublin Danes might not observe a proper respect to such unaccustomed evidences of sanctity.

The bishop shook his head. 'Our holy women do not gather in communities, like yours, but set up their cells in the wilds, alone. Such anchoresses would not settle near a town. More likely far to withdraw into the mountains. There is one we know of here, who has her hermitage by this same Menai water, some miles west from here, beyond the narrows. But as soon as we heard of this threat from the sea I sent to warn her, and bring her in here to shelter. And she had the good sense to come, and make no demur about it. God is the first and best defence of lone women, but I see no virtue in leaving all to him. I want no martyrs within my domain, and sanctity is small protection.'

'Then her cell is left empty,' said Mark, and sighed. 'But if this girl should have ridden so far, and failed to find a friend at need, where next might she turn?'

'Inland, surely, into the cover of woodland. I know of no defensible holding close by, but these raiders, if they land, would not go far from their ships. Any house in Arfon would take a girl in. Though the nearest and themselves most at risk,'

474

he added simply, 'may well have drawn off into the hills themselves. Your fellow here knows how lightly we can vanish at need.'

'I doubt she can have gone far ahead of us,' said Cadfael, pondering possibilities. 'And for all we know she may have her own plans, and know very well where to run. At least we can ask wherever we touch on the way back.' There was always the chance, too; that Canon Meirion had already found his daughter, closer to the royal seat at Aber.

'I can have prayers said for her safety,' said the bishop briskly, 'but I have sheep of my own to fold, and cannot, however willingly I would, go searching after one stray. At least, Brothers, rest this night over, before you take to the roads again, and may you ride safely and get good word of the young woman you seek.'

Bishop Meurig might be preoccupied with guarding his extended household, but he did not let that interfere with his hospitality. His table was well-supplied, his meat and mead ample and well-prepared, and he did not let his guests depart next morning without rising at dawn to see them off. It was a limpid, moist morning, after some fitful showers in the night, and the sun came up glistening and radiant, gilding the shallows to eastward.

'Go with God!' said the bishop, solid and square in the gateway of his precinct, as though he would hold it single-handed against all comers. His complimentary letters were already bestowed in Mark's saddle-roll, together with a small flask of gilded glass filled with the cordial he made from his own honey, and Cadfael carried before him a basket with a day's supply of food for six men rather than two. 'Come safely back to your bishop, on whom be God's blessing, and to your convent, Brother Cadfael, where his grace surely prevails. I trust some day we may meet again.'

Of the peril now threatening he certainly went in no awe. When they looked back from the street he was bustling purposefully across the open court, head foremost and lowered, like a small, determined bull not yet belligerent but certainly not to be trifled with.

They had emerged from the edges of the town on to the highroad, when Mark reined in, and sat his horse mute and thoughtful, looking first back along the road towards Aber,

475

and then westward towards the invisible sinuous curves of the narrow strait that separated Anglesey from Arfon. Cadfael drew in beside him, and waited, knowing what was on his friend's mind.

'Could she have passed beyond this point? Ought we not to go on westward? She left Aber hours before us. How long, I wonder, before she got word of the coming of the Danes?'

'If she rode through the night,' said Cadfael, 'she was not likely to hear of it until morning, there would be no one abroad to warn her. By morning she could be well to the west, and if she intended by her flight to evade her marriage, she would not come near Bangor, for there she was to meet her husband. Yes, you are right, she might by this be well to westward, and into danger. Nor am I sure she would turn back even if she knew of it.'

'Then what are we waiting for?' demanded Mark simply, and turned his horse towards the west.

At the church of Saint Deiniol, several miles south-west from Bangor and perhaps two miles from the strait, they got word of her at last. She must have kept to the old, direct road, the same Owain and his host would take, but hours ahead of them. The only puzzle was why it had taken her so long to reach that point, for when they enquired of the priest there was no hesitation, but yes, she had lighted down here to ask directions only late the previous evening, about Vespers.

'A young woman on a light roan, and all alone. She asked her way to the cell of Nonna. Due west from here it lies, in the trees near the water. I offered her shelter for the night, but she said she would go to the holy woman.'

'She would find the cell deserted,' said Cadfael. 'Bishop Meurig feared for the anchoress, and sent to bring her into Bangor. From which direction did the girl ride in?'

'Down out of the forests, from the south. I did not know,' said the priest, distressed, 'that she would find the place empty. I wonder, poor child, what she would do? There would still be time enough for her to find refuge in Bangor.'

'That I doubt she would do,' said Cadfael. 'If she came to the cell only so late, she might well bide the night over there, rather than risk moving by darkness.' He looked at Mark, in no doubt already what that young man would be thinking. On this journey Mark had the governance, not for the world would Cadfael have robbed him of it by word or act.

'We will go and look for her at the hermitage,' said Mark

476

firmly, 'and if she is not there, we will separate and try whatever tracks seem most likely to offer her refuge. In these lowland pastures there must be homesteads she may have tried.'

'Many will have taken advice,' the priest suggested, shaking his head dubiously. 'In a few weeks they would have been moving their herds and flocks into the uplands, even without this threat. Some may have moved early, rather than risk being plundered.'

'We can but make the assay,' said Mark stoutly. 'If need be, we'll take to the hills ourselves in search of her.'

And forthwith he made a brisk reverence to their informant, and wheeled his horse and set off due west, straight as an arrow. The priest of Saint Deiniol looked after him with raised brows and an expression half amused and half solicitous, and shook his head doubtfully.

'Would that young man be seeking the girl out of the goodness of his heart? Or for himself?'

'Even for that young man,' Cadfael said cautiously, 'I would not presume to say anything is impossible. But it comes as near as makes no matter. Any creature in peril of death or harm, be it man, woman, plough horse, or Saint Melangell's hare, could draw him through moss or quicksand. I knew I should never get him back to Shrewsbury while Heledd was astray.'

'You are turning back here yourself?' the priest demanded drily.

'Small chance! If he is bound to her, fellow-voyager to his fellow, so am I to him. I'll get him home!'

'Well, even if his concern for her is purer than dew,' said the priest with conviction, 'he had best take heed to his vows when he does find her. For she's a bonny black maid as ever I saw. I was glad of my evening years when I dared bid her shelter the night over in my house. And thankful when she would not. And that lad is at the best of the morning, tonsure or no tonsure.'

'The more reason I should go after him,' agreed Cadfael. 'And my thanks to you for the good word. For all the good words! I'll see them strictly delivered when I overtake him.'

'Saint Nonna,' said Cadfael didactically, threading the woodland belt that spread more than a mile inland from the strait, 'was the mother of Saint David. She has many sacred wells about the country, that give healing, especially to the

477

eyes, even to curing blindness. This holy woman must have chosen to name herself after the saint.'

Brother Mark pursued his determined way along the narrow ride, and said nothing. On either hand the trees glittered in moist sunlight after the early morning showers, mixed woodland sufficiently open to let in the radiance of early afternoon, sufficiently close to be ridden in single file, and all just coming into the first full leaf, young and fresh and full of birds. Every Spring is the only Spring, a perpetual astonishment. It bursts upon a man every year, thought Cadfael, contemplating it with delight in spite of all anxieties, as though it had never happened before, but had just been shown by God how to do it, and tried, and found the impossible possible.

Ahead of him in the worn grass of the ride Mark had halted, staring ahead. Between the trees, here thinning, open light shone before them, at a little distance still, but now not very far, and shimmering with reflected gleams from water. They were nearing the strait. And on Mark's left hand a narrow footway twined in among the trees to a low-roofed hut some yards aside from the path.

'This is the place.'

'And she was here,' said Cadfael. The wet grass, unshaken on either side by the wind, had retained the soft dew of rain that dimmed its new green to a silver grey, but through it a horse had certainly passed, leaving his darker trail, and brushing before him the tips of new growth, for the passage to the cell was very narrow. The ride in which they had halted was in regular use, they had not thought to examine it as they rode. But here between the encroaching bushes a horse had certainly passed since the rain. And not inward, but outward. A few young shoots had been broken at the tip, leaning towards the open ride, and the longer grasses darkened by hooves clearly showed the direction in which they had been brushed in passing. 'And is gone,' said Cadfael, 'since the morning.'

They dismounted, and approached the cell on foot. Built little and low, and one room only, for a woman who had almost no needs at all, beyond her small stone-built altar against one wall, and her plain straw pallet against another, and her small cleared space of garden behind for vegetables and herbs. Her door was drawn to, but had no lock to be seen without, and no bar within, only a latch that any wayfarer could lift and enter. The place was empty now. Nonna had obeyed the bishop's expressed wish, and allowed herself to be escorted into shelter

478

in Bangor, how willingly there was no knowing. If she had had a guest here in her absence, the guest too was gone. But in a patch of clear turf between the trees the grass had been grazed, and hooves had ranged on a long tether, leaving their traces before the rain fell, for drops still hung on the grasses, unshaken. And in one place the beast had left his droppings, fresh and moist still, but already cold.

'She passed the night here,' said Cadfael, 'and with the morning she left. After the rain she left. Which way, who knows! She came to Llandeiniolen from inland, out of the hills and through the forest, so the priest said. Had she some place of refuge in mind up there, some kinsman of Meirion's who might take her in? And did she find that place, too, already deserted, and think of the anchoress as her next hope? It would account for why it took her so long to get here. But as for where she is gone now, how can we tell?'

'She knows by now of the danger from the sea,' said Mark. 'Surely she would not go on westward into such a peril? But back towards Bangor and her marriage? She has already risked much to evade it. Would she make her way back to Aber, and her father? That would not deliver her from this marriage, if she is so set against it.'

'She would not do it,' said Cadfael, 'in any case. Strange as it may be, she loves her father as much as she hates him. The one is the reflection of the other. She hates him because her love is far stronger than any love he has for her, because he is so ready and willing to give her up, to put her way by any means possible, so that she may no longer cast a cloud over his reputation and his advancement. Very clearly she declared herself once, as I remember.'

'As I remember also,' said Mark.

'Nevertheless, she will do nothing to harm him. The veil she refused. This marriage she accepted only for his sake, as the lesser evil. But when chance offered, she fled that, too, and chose rather to remove herself from blocking his light than to let others scheme to remove her. She has taken her own life into her own hands, prepared to face her own risks and pay her own debts, leaving him free. She will not now go back on that resolve.'

'But he is not free,' said Mark, putting a finger regretfully on the centre of the convoluted core of pain in this seemingly simple relationship of sire and daughter. 'He is aware of her now in absence as he never was when she waited on him dutifully every day, present and visible. He will have no peace until he knows she is safe.'

'So,' said Cadfael, 'we had better set about finding her.'

Out on the ride, Cadfael looked back through the screen of trees towards the sparks of quivering water beyond which lay the Anglesey shore. A slight breeze had arisen, and fluttered the bright green leaves into a scintillating curtain, but still the fleeting reflections of water flashed brighter still through the folds. And something else, something that appeared and vanished as the branches revealed and hid it again, but remained constant in the same place, only seeming to rock up and down as if afloat and undulating with a tide. A fragment of bright colour, vermilion, changing shape with the movement of its frame of leaves.

'Wait!' said Cadfael, halting. 'What is that?'

Not a red that was to be found in nature, certainly not in the late Spring, when the earth indulges itself only with delicate tones of pale gold and faint purple and white against the virgin green. This red had a hard, impenetrable solidity about it. Cadfael dismounted, and turned back towards it, threading the trees in cover until he came to a raised spot where he could lie warily invisible himself, but see clear through the edge of the woodland three hundred paces or more down to the strait. A green level of pasture and a few fields, one dwelling, no doubt forsaken now, and then the silver-blue glitter of the water, here almost at its narrowest, but still half a mile wide. And beyond, the rich, fertile plain of Anglesey, the cornfield of Wales. The tide was flowing, the stretch of shingle and sand under the opposite coast half exposed. And riding to anchor, close inshore below the bank of trees in which Cadfael stood, a long, lean boat, dragon-headed fore and aft, dipped and rose gently on the tide, central sail lowered, oars shipped, a cluster of vermilion shields draped along its low flank. A lithe serpent of a ship, its mast lowered aft from its steppings, clearing the gaunt body for action, while it swayed gently to its moorings like a sleeping lizard, graceful and harmless. Two of its crew, big, fair-headed, one with plaited braids either side his neck, idled on its narrow rear deck, above the oarsmen's benches. One, naked, swam lazily in mid-strait. But Cadfael counted what he took to be oar-ports in the third strake of the hull, twelve of them in this steerboard side. Twelve pairs of oars, twenty-four rowers, and more crew beside these three left on

480

guard. The rest could not be far.

Brother Mark had tethered the horses, and made his way down to Cadfael's shoulder. He saw what Cadfael had seen, and asked no questions.

'That,' said Cadfael, low-voiced, 'is a Danish keel from Dublin!'

Chapter Seven

HERE WAS NOT a word more said between them. By consent they turned and made their way back in haste to the horses, and led them away inland by the woodland track, until they were far enough from the shore to mount and ride. If Heledd, after her night in the hermitage, had seen the coming of this foraging boat with its formidable complement of warriors, small wonder she had made haste to remove herself from their vicinity. And small doubt but she would withdraw inland as quickly and as far as she could, and once at a sufficient distance she would make for the shelter of a town. That, at least, was what any girl in her right senses would do. Here she was midway between Bangor and Carnarvon. Which way would she take?

'One ship alone,' said Mark at last, where the path widened and made it possible for two to ride abreast. 'Is that good sense? Might they not be opposed, even captured?'

'So they might at this moment,' Cadfael agreed, 'but there's no one here to attempt it. They came by night past Carnarvon, be sure, and by night they'll slip out again. This will be one of the smallest and the fastest in their fleet; with more than twenty armed rowers aboard there's nothing we have could keep them in sight. You saw the building of her, she can be rowed either way, and turn in a flash. The only risk they take is while the most of the company are ashore, foraging, and that they'll do by rushes, fast ashore and fast afloat again.'

'But why send one small ship out alone? As I have heard

tell,' said Mark, 'they raid in force, and take slaves as well as plunder. That they cannot do by risking a single vessel.'

'This time,' said Cadfael, considering, 'it's no such matter. If Cadwaladr has brought them over, then he's promised them a fat fee for their services. They're here to persuade Owain he would be wise to restore his brother to his lands, and they expect to get well paid for doing it, and if it can be done cheaply by the threat of their presence, without the loss of a man in battle, that's what they'll prefer, and Cadwaladr will have no objection, provided the result is the same. Say he gets his way and returns to his lands, he has still to live beside his brother for the future, why make relations between them blacker than they need be? No, there'll be no random burning and killing, and no call to take bondmen, not unless the bargain turns sour.'

'Then why this foray by a single ship so far along the strait?' Mark demanded reasonably.

'The Danes have to feed their force, and it's not their way to carry their own provisions when they're heading for a land they can just as well live off at no cost. They know the Welsh well enough by now to know we live light and travel light, and can shift our families and our stock into the mountains at a few hours' notice. Yonder little ship has wasted no time in making inland from Abermenai as soon as it touched shore, to reach such hamlets as were late in hearing the news, or slow in rounding up their cattle. They'll be off back to their fellows tonight with a load of good carcasses amidships, and whatever store of flour and grain they've been able to lay their hands on. And somewhere along these woods and fields they're about that very business this moment.'

'And if they meet with a solitary girl?' Mark challenged. 'Would they refrain from doing unnecessary offence even then?'

'I would not speak for any man, Dane or Welsh or Norman, in such a case,' Cadfael admitted. 'If she were a princess of Gwynedd, why, she'd be worth far more intact and well treated than violated or misused. And if Heledd was not born royal, yet she has a tongue of her own, and can very well make it plain that she is under Owain's protection, and they'll be answerable to him if they do her offence. But even so ...'

They had reached a place where the woodland track divided, one branch bearing still inland but inclining to the west, the other bearing more directly east.

'We are nearer Carnarvon than Bangor,' Cadfael reckoned, halting where the roads divided. 'But would she know it? What now, Mark? East or west?'

'We had best separate,' Mark said, frowning over so blind a decision. 'She cannot be very far. She would have to keep in cover. If the ship must return this night, she might find a place to hide safely until they are gone. Do you take one way, and I the other.'

'We cannot afford to lose touch,' Cadfael warned seriously. 'If we part here it must be only for some hours, and here we must meet again. We are not free to do altogether as we choose. Go towards Carnarvon, and if you find her, see her safely there. But if not, make your way back here by dusk, and so will I. And if I find her by this lefthand way, I'll get her into shelter wherever I may, if it means turning back to Bangor. And at Bangor I'll wait for you, if you fail of meeting me here by sunset. And if I fail you, follow and find me there.'

A makeshift affair, but the best they could do, with so limited a time, and an inescapable duty waiting. She had left the cell by the shore only that morning, she would have had to observe caution and keep within the woodland ways, where a horse must go slowly. No, she could not be far. And at this distance from the strait, surely she would keep to a used path, and not wind a laborious way deep in cover. They might yet find and bring her here by nightfall, or conduct her into safety somewhere, rendezvous here free of her, and be off thankfully back to England.

Mark looked at the light and the slight decline of the sun from the zenith. 'We have four hours or more,' he said, and turned his horse westward briskly, and was off.

Cadfael's track turned east on a level traverse for perhaps half a mile, occasionally emerging from woodland into open pasture, and affording glimpses of the strait through the scattered trees below. Then it turned inland and began to climb, though the gradient here was not great, for this belt of land on the mainland side partook to some extent of the rich fertility of the island before it reared aloft into the mountains. He went softly, listening, and halting now and again to listen more intently, but there was no sign of life but for the birds, very busy about their Spring occupations and undisturbed by the turmoil among men. The cattle and sheep had been driven up higher into the hills, into guarded folds; the raiders would find only the few stragglers here, and perhaps would venture no further along the strait. The news must be ahead of them now wherever they touched, they would have made their most profitable captures already. If Heledd had turned this way, she might be safe enough from any further danger.

He had crossed an open meadow and entered a higher belt of woodland, bushy and dappled with sunbeams on his left hand, deepening into forest on his right, when a grass snake, like a small flash of silver-green lightning, shot across the path almost under his horse's hooves to vanish in deeper grass on the other side, and the beast shied for an instant, and let out a muted bellow of alarm. Somewhere off to the right, among the trees, and at no great distance, another horse replied, raising an excited whinny of recognition. Cadfael halted to listen intently, hoping for another call to allow him to take a more precise reading of the direction, but the sound was not repeated. Probably whoever was in refuge there, well aside from the path, had rushed to soothe and cajole his beast into silence. A horse's neighing could carry all too far along this rising hillside.

Cadfael dismounted, and led his beast in among the trees, taking a winding line towards where he thought the other voyager must be, and halting at every turn to listen again, and presently, when he was already deep among thick growth, he caught the sudden rustling of shaken boughs ahead, quickly stilled. His own movements, however cautious, had certainly been heard. Someone there in close concealment was waiting for him in ambush.

'Heledd!' said Cadfael clearly.

Silence seemed to become even more silent.

'Heledd? Here am I, Brother Cadfael. You can be easy, here are no Dublin Danes. Come forth and show yourself.'

And forth she came, thrusting through the bushes to meet him, Heledd indeed, with a naked dagger ready in her hand, though for the moment she might well have forgotten that she held it. Her gown was creased and soiled a little with the debris of bushes, one cheek was lightly smeared with green from bedding down in moss and grasses, and the mane of her hair was loose round her shoulders, here in shadow quite black, a midnight cloud. But her clear oval face was fiercely composed, just easing from its roused readiness to do battle, and her eyes, enormous in shade, were purple-black. Behind her among the trees he heard her horse shift and stamp, uneasy here in these unknown solitudes.

485

'It *is* you,' she said, and let the hand that held the knife slip down to her side with a great, gusty sigh. 'How did you find me? And where is Deacon Mark? I thought you would be off home before now.'

'So we would,' agreed Cadfael, highly relieved to find her in such positive possession of herself, 'but for you running off into the night. Mark is a mile or more from us on the road to Carnarvon, looking for you. We parted where the roads forked. It was guesswork which way you would take. We came seeking you at Nonna's cell. The priest told us he'd directed you there.'

'Then you've seen the ship,' said Heledd, and hoisted her shoulders in resignation at the unavoidable. 'I should have been well aloft into the hills by now to look for my mother's cousins up among the sheep-huts, the ones I hoped to find still in their lowland homestead, if my horse had not fallen a little lame. I thought best to get into cover and rest him until nightfall. And now we are two,' she said, and her smile flashed in shadow with recovering confidence, 'three if we can find your little deacon. And now which way should we make? Come with me over the hills, and you can find a safe way back to the Dee. For I am not going back to my father,' she warned, with a formidable flash of her dark eyes. 'He's rid of me, as he wanted. I mean him no ill, but I have not escaped them all only to go back and be married off to some man I have never seen, nor to dwindle away in a nunnery. You may tell him, or leave word with someone else to let him know, that I am safe with my mother's kinsmen, and he can be content.'

'You are going into the first safe shelter we can find,' said Cadfael firmly, moved to a degree of indignation he could not have felt if he had found her distressed and in fear. 'Afterwards, once this trouble is over, you may have your life and do what you will with it.' It seemed to him, even as he said it, that she was capable of doing with it something original and even admirable, and if it had to be in the world's despite, that would not stop her. 'Can your beast go?'

'I can lead him, and we shall see.'

Cadfael took thought for a moment. They were midway between Bangor and Carnarvon here, but once returned to the westward track by which Mark had set out, the road was more direct to Carnarvon, and by taking it they would eventually rejoin Mark. Whether he had gone on into the town, or turned back to return to the crossroads meeting place by dusk, along that pathway they would meet him. And in a city filled with Owain's fighting men there would be no danger. A force hired to threaten would not be so mad as to provoke the entire armies of Gwynedd. A little looting, perhaps, pleasant sport carrying off a few stray cattle and a few stray villagers, but they were not such fools as to bring out Owain's total strength against them in anger.

'Bring him out to the path,' said Cadfael. 'You may ride mine, and I'll walk yours.'

There was nothing in the glittering look she gave him to reassure him that she would do as he said, and nothing to disquiet him with doubts. She hesitated only an instant, in which the silence of the windless afternoon seemed phenomenally intense, then she turned and parted the branches behind her, and vanished, shattering the silence with the rustling and thrashing of her passage through deep cover. In a few moments he heard the horse whinny softly, and then the stirring of the bushes as girl and horse turned to thread a more open course back to him. And then, astonishingly high, wild and outraged, he heard her scream.

The instinctive leap forward he made to go to her never gained him so much as a couple of paces. From either side the bushes thrashed, and hands reached to clutch him by cowl and habit, pin his arms and bring him up erect but helpless, straining against a grip he could not break, but which, curiously, made no move to do him any harm beyond holding him prisoner. Suddenly the tiny open glade was boiling with large, bare-armed, fair-haired, leather-girt men, and out of the thicket facing him erupted an even larger man, a young giant, head and shoulders above Cadfael's sturdy middle height, laughing so loudly that the hitherto silent woods rang and re-echoed with his mirth, and clutching in his arms a raging Heledd, kicking and struggling with all her might, but making small impression. The one hand she had free had already scored its nails down her captor's cheek, and was tugging and tearing in his long flaxen hair, until he turned and stooped his head and took her wrist in his teeth and held it. Large, even, white teeth that had shone as he laughed, and now barely dented Heledd's smooth skin. It was astonishment, neither fear nor pain, that caused her suddenly to lie still in his arms, crooked fingers gradually unfolding in bewilderment. But when he released her to laugh again, she recovered her rage, and struck out at him furiously, pounding her fist vainly against his broad breast.

487

Behind him came a grinning boy about fifteen years old, leading Heledd's horse, which went a little tenderly on one foreleg. At sight of a second such prize tethered and shifting uneasily in the fringe of the trees, the boy let out a whoop of pleasure. Indeed, the entire mood of the marauding company seemed good-humoured and ebullient rather than menacing. There were not so many of them as at first they had seemed, by reason of their size and their exuberantly animal presence. Two, barrel-chested and moustached, with hair in straw-coloured braids down either cheek, held Cadfael pinioned by the arms. A third had taken the roan's bridle, and was fondling the long blazed brow and creamy mane. But somewhere out on the open ride there were others, Cadfael heard them moving and talking as they waited. The marvel was that men so massive could move so softly to close round their quarry. The horses, calling to each other, had alerted the returning foragers, and led them to this unexpected gain. A monastic, a girl, by her mount and dress a girl of quality, and two good horses.

The young giant was surveying his gains very practically over Heledd's unavailing struggles, and Cadfael noted that though he was casually rough with his captive, he was not brutal. And it seemed that Heledd had realised as much, and gradually abandoned her resistance, knowing it vain, and surprised into quietness by the fact there was no retaliation.

'*Saeson*?' demanded the giant, eyeing Cadfael with curiosity. He already knew that Heledd was Welsh enough, she had been reviling him in the language until she ran out of breath.

'Welsh!' said Cadfael. 'Like the lady. She is daughter to a canon of Saint Asaph, and under the protection of Owain Gwynedd.'

'He keeps wildcats?' said the young man, and laughed again, and set her down on her feet in one lithe movement, but kept a fast hold on the girdle of her gown, twisted in his large fist to tighten and secure it. 'And he'll want this one back without a hair missing? But the lady slipped her leash, seemingly, or what's she doing here with no bodyguard but a monk of the Benedictines?' He spoke a loose mixture of Erse, Danish and Welsh, very well able to make himself understood in these parts. Not all the centuries of fitful contact between Dublin and Wales had been by way of invasion and rapine, a good many marriages had been made between the princedoms, and a fair measure of honest commerce been profitable to both parties.

Probably this youth had a measure of Norman French in his tongue, no less. Even Latin, for very likely Irish monks had had him in school. He was plainly a young man of consequence. Also, happily, of a very open and cheerful humour, by no means inclined to waste what might turn out a valuable asset. 'Bring the man,' said the young fellow, returning briskly to business, 'and keep him fast. Owain has a respect for the black habit, even if the Celtic clas suits him best. If it comes to bargaining, holiness fetches a good price. I'll see to the girl.'

They sprang to obey him, as light of heart, it seemed, as their leader, and all in high content with their foraging. When they emerged with their captives into the open ride, the two horses led along behind them, it was easy to see what reason they had for being in high feather. There were four more of them waiting there, all afoot, and burdened with two long poles loaded down with slaughtered carcases and slung sacks, the plunder of scattered folds, stray corners of grazing, and even the forest itself, for there was venison among the booty. A fifth man had improvised a wooden yoke for his shoulders, to carry two balanced wineskins. This must be one of at least two shore parties, Cadfael judged, for the little ship carried twelve pairs of oars aside from other crew. It was guesswork how many the Danish force would muster in full, but they would not go short for a day or so.

He went where he was propelled, not entirely out of the sensible realisation that he was no match at all for one of the brawny warriors who held him, let alone two, not even because, though he might break away himself, he could do nothing to take Heledd with him. Wherever they were bound, useful hostages, he might still be able to afford her some protection and companionship. He had already given up any idea that she was likely to come to any great harm. He had done no more than confirm something already understood when he urged that she was valuable; and this was not total war, but a commercial expedition, to achieve the highest profit at the least expenditure.

There was some redistribution of the booty they had amassed, Heledd's lame horse being called into service to carry a part of the load. They were notably brisk and neat in their movements, balancing the weight and halting short of overburdening a valuable beast. Among themselves they fell back into their own Norse tongue, though the likelihood was that all these young, vigorous warriors had been born in the kingdom of Dublin, and their fathers before them, and had a broad understanding of the Celtic languages that surrounded their enclave, and dealt freely with them in war and peace. At the end of this day of raiding they had an eye to the sun, and but for this foray after the alarm the horses had sounded, they were losing no time.

Cadfael had wondered how their leader would dispose of the one sound horse, and fully expected he would claim the privilege of riding for himself. Instead, the young man ordered the boy into the saddle, the lightest weight among them, and swung Heledd up before him and into arms even at fifteen years brawny enough to make her struggles ineffective once her hands were securely bound by her own girdle. But she had understood by this time that resistance would be both useless and undignified, and suffered herself to be settled against the boy's broad chest without deigning to struggle. By the set of her face she would be waiting for the first chance of escape, and keeping all her wits and strength in reserve until the moment offered. She had fallen silent, shutting lips and teeth upon anger or fear, and keeping a taut, brooding dignity, but what was brewing behind that still face there was no knowing.

'Brother,' said the young man, turning briskly upon Cadfael, still pinned between his guards, 'if you value the lass, you may walk beside her without a hand on you. But I warn you, Torsten will be close behind, and he can throw a lance to split a sapling at fifty paces, so best keep station.' He was grinning as he issued the warning, already assured that Cadfael had no intention of making off and leaving the girl in captivity. 'Forward now, and fast,' he said cheerfully, and set the pace, and the entire party fell into file down the ride, and so did Cadfael, close alongside his own roan horse, with a hand at the rider's stirrup-leather. If Heledd needed the fragile reassurance of his presence, she had it; but Cadfael doubted the need. She had made no move since she was hoisted aloft, except to stir and settle more comfortably on her perch, and the very tension of her face had softened into a thoughtful stillness. Every time Cadfael raised his eyes to take a fresh look at her he found her more at ease in this unforeseen situation. And every time, her eyes were dwelling in speculaion upon the fair head that topped all the rest, stalking before them with erected crest and long blond locks stirring in the light breeze.

Downhill at a brisk pace, through woodland and pasture, until the first silvery glints of water winked at them through the last belt of trees. The sun was dipping gently towards the west, gilding the ripples drawn by the breeze along the surface, when they emerged upon the shore of the strait, and the crewmen left on guard launched a shout of welcome, and brought the dragon-ship inshore to take them aboard.

Brother Mark, returning empty-handed from his foray westward to keep the rendezvous at the crossroads before sunset, heard the passing of a company of men, swift and quiet though they were, crossing his track some little way ahead, going downhill towards the shore. He halted in cover until they had passed, and then followed cautiously in the same direction, intending only to make sure they were safely out of sight and earshot before he pushed on to the meeting place. It so happened that the line he followed downhill among the trees inclined towards the course of their open ride, and brought him rapidly closer, so that he drew back and halted again, this time catching glimpses of them between the branches of bushes now almost in full summer leaf. A tall youth, flaxen hair, his head floating past like a blown primrose but high as a three-year-spruce, a led horse, loaded, two men with a pole slung on their shoulders, and animal carcases swinging to their stride. Then, unmistakably, he saw Heledd and the boy pass by, a pair entwined and afloat six feet from the ground, the horse beneath them only implied by the rhythm of their passing, for the branches swung impenetrable between at that moment, leaving to view only a trudging tonsure beside them, russet brown almost wholly salted with grey. A very small clue to the man who wore it, but all Mark needed to know Brother Cadfael.

So he had found her, and these much less welcome strangers had found them both, before they could slip away thankfully into some safe refuge. And there was nothing Mark could do about it but follow them, far enough at least to see where they were taken, and how they were handled, and then make sure that the news was carried where there were those who could take their loss into account, and make plans for their recovery.

He dismounted and left his horse tethered, the better to move swiftly and silently among the trees. But the shout that presently came echoing up from the ship caused him to discard caution and emerge into the open, hurrying downhill to find a spot from which he could see the waters of the strait, and the steersman bringing his craft close in beneath the grassy bank, at a spot where it was child's play to leap aboard over the low

491

rim into the rowers' benches in the waist of the vessel. Mark saw the tide of fierce, fair men flow inboard, coaxing the loaded packhorse after them, and stowing their booty under the tiny foredeck and in the well between the benches. In with them went Cadfael, perforce, and yet it seemed to Mark that he went blithely where he was persuaded. Small chance to avoid, but another man would have been a shade less apt and adroit about it.

The boy on horseback had kept his firm hold of Heledd until the flaxen-haired young giant, having seen his men embarked, reached up and hoisted her in his arms, as lightly as if she had been a child, and leaped down with her between the rowers' benches, and setting her down there on her feet, stretched up again to the bridle of Cadfael's horse, and coaxed him aboard with a soft-spoken cajolery that came up strangely to Mark's ears. The boy followed, and instantly the steersman pushed off strongly from the bank, the knot of men busy bestowing their plunder dissolved into expert order at the oars, and the lean little dragon-ship surged out into midstream. She was in lunging motion before Mark had recovered his wits, sliding like a snake southwestward towards Carnarvon and Abermenai, where doubtless her companions were now in harbour or moored in the roads outside the dunes. She did not have to turn, even, being double-ended. Her speed could get her out of trouble in any direction; even if she was sighted off the town Owain had nothing that could catch her. The rapidity with which she dwindled silently into a thin, dark fleck upon the water left Mark breathless and amazed.

He turned to make his way back to where his horse was tethered, and set out in resolute haste westward towards Carnarvon.

Plumped aboard into the narrow well between the benches, and there as briskly abandoned, Cadfael took a moment to lean back against the boards of the narrow after-deck and consider their situation. Relations between captors and captives seemed already to have found a viable level, at surprisingly little cost in time or passion. Resistance was impracticable. Discretion recommended acceptance to the prisoners, and made it possible for their keepers to be about the more immediate business of getting their booty safely back to camp, without any stricter enforcement than a rapidly moving vessel and a mile or so of water on either side provided. No one laid hand on Cadfael once they were embarked. No one paid any further attention to Heledd, braced back defensively into the stern-post, where the young Dane had hoisted her, with knees drawn up and skirts hugged about her in embracing arms. No one feared that she would leap overboard and strike out for Anglesey; the Welsh were not known as notable swimmers. No one had any interest in doing either of them affront or injury; they were simple assets to be retained intact for future use.

To test it further, Cadfael made his way the length of the well amidships, between the stowed loot of flesh and provisions, paying curious attention to the details of the lithe, long craft, and not one oarsman checked in the steady heave and stretch of his stroke, or turned a glance to note the movement at his shoulder. A vessel shaped for speed, lean as a greyhound, perhaps eighteen paces long and no more than three or four wide. Cadfael reckoned ten strakes a side, six feet deep amidships, the single mast lowered aft. He noted the clenched rivets that held the strakes together. Clincher-built, shallow of draught, light of weight for its strength and speed, the two ends identical for instant manoeuvring, an ideal craft for beaching close inshore in the dunes of Abermenai. No use for shipping more bulky freight; they would have brought cargo hulls for that, slower, more dependent on sail, and shipping only a few rowers to get them out of trouble in a calm. Square-rigged, as all craft still were in these northern waters. The two-masted, lateen-rigged ships of the unforgotten midland sea were still unknown to these Norse seafarers.

He had been too deeply absorbed in these observations to realise that he himself was being observed just as shrewdly and curiously by a pair of brilliant ice-blue eyes, from under thick golden brows quizzically cocked. The young captain of this raiding party had missed nothing, and clearly knew how to read this appraisal of his craft. He dropped suddenly from the steersman's side to meet Cadfael in the well.

'You know ships?' he demanded, interested and surprised at so unlikely a preoccupation in a Benedictine brother.

'I did once. It's a long time now since I ventured on water.'

'You know the sea?' the young man pursued, shining with pleased curiosity.

'Not this sea. Time was when I knew the middle sea and the eastern shores well enough. I came late to the cloister,' he explained, beholding the blue eyes dilate and glitter in

493

delighted astonishment, a deeper spark of pleasure and recognition warming within them.

'Brother, you put up your own price,' said the young Dane heartily. 'I would keep you to know better. Seafaring monks are rare beasts, I never came by one before. How do they call you?'

'My name is Cadfael, a Welsh-born brother of the abbey of Shrewsbury.'

'A name for a name is fair dealing. I am Turcaill, son of Turcaill, kinsman to Otir, who leads this venture.'

'And you know what's in dispute here? Between two Welsh princes? Why put your own breast between their blades?' Cadfael reasoned mildly.

'For pay,' said Turcaill cheerfully. 'But even unpaid I would not stay behind when Otir puts to sea. It grows dull ashore. I'm no landsman, to squat on a farm year after year, and be content to watch the crops grow.'

No, that he certainly was not, nor of a temper to turn to cloister and cowl even when the adventures of his youth were over. Splendidly fleshed, glittering with animal energy, this was a man for marriage and sons, and the raising of yet more generations of adventurers, restless as the sea itself, and ready to cleave their way into any man's quarrel for gain, at the fair cost of staking their own lives.

He was away now, with a valedictory clap on Cadfael's shoulder, steady of stride along the lunging keel, to swing himself up beside Heledd on the after-deck. The light, beginning to fade into twilight now, still showed Cadfael the disdainful set of Heledd's lips and the chill arching of her brows as she drew the hem of her skirt aside from the contamination even of an enemy touch, and turned her head away, refusing him the acknowledgement of a glance.

Turcaill laughed, no way displeased, sat down beside her, and took out bread from a pouch at his belt. He broke it in his big, smooth young hands, and offered her the half, and she refused it. Unoffended, still laughing, he took her right hand by force, folded his offering into the palm, and shut her left hand hard over it. She could not prevent, and would not compromise her mute disdain by a vain struggle. But when he forthwith got up and left her so, without a glance behind, to do as she pleased with his gift, she neither hurled it into the darkening water of the strait nor bit into its crust by way of acceptance, but sat as he had left her, cradling it between her palms and gazing after his oblivious flaxen head with a narrow and calculating stare, the significance of which Cadfael could not read, but which at once intrigued and disquieted him.

In the onset of night, in a dusk through which they slid silently and swiftly in midstream, only faint glimmers of phosphorescence gilding the dip of the oars, they passed by the shore-lights of Owain's Carnarvon, and emerged into a broad basin shut off from the open sea only by twin rolling spits of sand-dunes, capped with a close growth of bushes and a scattering of trees. Along the water the shadowy shapes of ships loomed, some with stepped masts, some lean and low like Turcaill's little serpent. Spaced along the shore, the torches of the Danish outposts burned steadily in a still air, and higher towards the crest glowed the fires of an established camp.

Turcaill's rowers leaned to their last long stroke and shipped their oars, as the steersman brought the ship round in a smooth sweep to beach in the shallows. Over the side went the Danes, hoisting their plunder clear, and plashing up from the water to solid ground, to be met by their fellows on guard at the rim of the tide. And over the side went Heledd, plucked up lightly in Turcaill's arms, and this time making no resistance, since it would in any case have been unavailing, and she was chiefly concerned with preserving her dignity at this pass.

As for Cadfael himself, he had small choice but to follow, even if two of the rowers had not urged him over the side between them, and waded ashore with a firm grip on his shoulders. Whatever chances opened before him, there was no way he could break loose from this captivity until he could take Heledd with him. He plodded philosophically up the dunes and into the guarded perimeter of the camp, and went where he was led, well assured that the guardian circle had closed snugly behind him.

Chapter Eight

ADFAEL AWOKE TO the pearl-grey light of earliest dawn, the immense sweep of open sky above him, still sprinkled at the zenith with paling stars, and the instant recollection of his present situation. Everything that had passed had confirmed that they had little to fear from their captors, at least while they retained their bargaining value, and nothing to hope for in the way of escape, since the Danes were clearly sure of the efficiency of their precautions. The shore was well watched, the rim of the camp securely guarded. There was no need, within that pale, to keep a constant surveillance on a young girl and an elderly monastic. Let them wander at will, it would not get them out of the circle, and within it they could do no harm.

Cadfael recalled clearly that he had been fed, as generously as the young men of the guard who moved about him, and he was certain that Heledd, however casually housed here, had also been fed, and once left to her own devices, unobserved, would have had the good sense to eat what was provided. She was no such fool as to throw away her assets for spite when she had a fight on her hands.

He was lying, snugly enough, in the lee of a windbreak of hurdles, in a hollow of thick grass, his own cloak wrapped about him. He remembered Turcaill tossing it to him as it was unrolled from his small belongings as the horse was unloaded. Round him a dozen of the young Danish seamen snored at ease. Cadfael arose and stretched, and shook the sand from his

496

habit. No one made any move to intercept him as he made for the higher ground to look about him. The camp was alive, the fires already lit, and the few horses, including his own, watered and turned on to the greener sheltered levels to landward, where there was better pasture. Cadfael looked in that direction, towards the familiar solidity of Wales, and made his way unhindered through the midst of the camp to find a high spot from which he could see beyond the perimeter of Otir's base. From the south, and after a lengthy march round the tidal bay that bit deep to southward, Owain must come if he was ever to attack this strongpoint by land. By sea he would be at a disadvantage, having nothing to match the Norse longships. And Carnarvon seemed a long, long way from this armed camp.

The few sturdy tents that housed the leaders of the expedition had been pitched in the centre of the camp. Cadfael passed by them closely, and halted to mark the men who moved about them. Two in particular bore the unmistakable marks of authority, though curiously the pair of them together struck a discordant note, as if their twin authorities might somehow be at cross-purposes. The one was a man of fifty years or more, thickset, barrel-chested, built like the bole of a tree, and burned by the sun and the spray and the wind to a reddish brown darker than the two braids of straw-coloured hair that framed his broad countenance, and the long moustaches that hung lower than his jaw. He was bare-armed to the shoulder but for leather bands about his forearms and thick gold bracelets at his wrists.

'Otir!' said Heledd's voice softly in Cadfael's ear. She had come up behind him unnoticed, her steps silent in the drifting sand, her tone wary and intent. She had more here to contend with than a good-humoured youngster whose tolerant attitude might not always serve her turn. Turcaill was a mere subordinate here; this formidable man before them could overrule all other authorities. Or was it possible that even his power might suffer checks? Here was this second personage beside him, lofty of glance and imperious of gesture, by the look of him not a man to take orders tamely from any other being.

'And the other?' asked Cadfael, without turning his head.

'That is Cadwaladr. It was no lie, he has brought these long-haired barbarians into Wales to wrest back his rights from the Lord Owain. I know him, I have seen him before. The Dane I heard called by his name.'

A handsome man, this Cadwaladr, Cadfael reflected, approving the comeliness of the shape, if doubtful of the mind within.

497

This man was not so tall as his brother, but tall enough to carry his firm and graceful flesh well, and he moved with a beautiful ease and power beside the squat and muscular Dane. His colouring was darker than Owain's, thick russet hair clustered in curls over a shapely head, and dark, haughty eyes well set beneath brows that almost met, and were a darker brown than his hair. He was shaven clean, but had acquired some of the clothing and adornments of his Dublin hosts during his stay with them, so that it would not have been immediately discernible that here was the Welsh prince who had brought this entire expedition across the sea to his own country's hurt. He had the reputation of being hasty, rash, wildly generous to friends, irreconcilably bitter against enemies. His face bore out everything that was said of him. Nor was it hard to imagine how Owain could still love his troublesome brother, after many offences and repeated reconciliations.

'A fine figure of a man,' said Cadfael, contemplating this perilous presence warily.

'If he did as handsomely,' said Heledd.

The chieftains had withdrawn eastward towards the strait, the circle of their captains surrounding them. Cadfael turned his steps, instead, still southward, to get a view of the land approach by which Owain must come if he intended to shut the invaders into their sandy beachhead. Heledd fell in beside him, not, he judged, because she was in need of the comfort of his or any other company, but because she, too, was curious about the circumstances of their captivity, and felt that two minds might make more sense of them than one alone.

'How have you fared?' asked Cadfael, eyeing her closely as she walked beside him, and finding her composed, self-contained and resolute of lip and eye. 'Have they used you well, here where there are no women?'

She curled a tolerant lip and smiled. 'I needed none. If there's cause I can fend for myself, but as yet there's no cause. I have a tent to shelter me, the boy brings me food, and what else I want they let me go abroad and get for myself. Only if I go too near the eastern shore they turn me back. I have tried. I think they know I can swim.'

'You made no attempt when we were no more than a hundred yards offshore,' said Cadfael, with no implication of approval or disapproval.

'No,' she agreed, with a small, dark smile, and added not a word more.

'And even if we could steal back our horses,' he reflected philosophically, 'we could not get out of this armed ring with them.'

'And mine is lame,' she agreed again, smiling her private smile.

He had had no opportunity, until now, to ask her how she had come by that horse in the first place, somehow stealing him away out of the prince's stables while the feast was at its height, and before any word was brought from Bangor to alert Owain to the threat from Ireland. He asked her now. 'How came it that you ever came into possession of this horse you call yours so briskly?'

'I found him,' said Heledd simply. 'Saddled, bridled, tethered among the trees not far from the gatehouse. Better than ever I expected, I took it for a good omen and was thankful I had not to go wandering through the night afoot. But I would have done it. I had no thought of it when I went out to refill the pitcher, but out in the courtyard I thought, why go back? There was nothing left in Llanelwy I could keep, and nothing in Bangor or Anglesey that I wanted. But there must be something for me, somewhere in the world. Why should I not go and find it, if no one else would get it for me? And while I was standing there in shadow by the wall, the guards on the gate were not marking me, and I slipped out behind their backs. I had nothing, I took nothing, I would have walked away so, and never complained. It was my choice. But in the trees I found this horse, saddled and bridled and ready for me, a gift from God that I could not refuse. If I have lost him now,' she said very solemnly, 'it may be he has brought me where I was meant to be.'

'A stage on your journey, it may be,' said Cadfael, concerned, 'but surely not the end. For here are you and I, hostages in a very questionable situation, and you I take to be a lass who values her freedom highly. We have yet to get ourselves out of captivity, or wait here for Owain to do it for us.' He was revolving in some wonder what she had told him, and harking back to all that had happened in Aber. 'So there was this beast, made ready for riding and hidden away outside the enclave. And if heaven meant him for you, there was someone else who intended a very different outcome when he saddled him and led him out into the woods. Now it seems to me that Bledri ap Rhys did indeed mean to escape to his lord with word of all the prince's muster and strength. The means of

499

flight was ready outside the gate for him. And yet he was found naked in his bedchamber, no way prepared for riding. You have set us a riddle. Did he go to his bed to wait until the llys was well asleep? And was killed before the favourable hour? And how did he purpose to leave the maenol, when every gate was guarded?'

Heledd was studying him intently along her shoulder, brows knitted together, only partially understanding, but hazarding very alert and intelligent guesses at what was still obscure to her. 'Do you tell me Bledri ap Rhys is dead? Killed, you said. That same night? The night I left the llys?'

'You did not know? It was after you were gone, so was the news that came from Bangor. No one has told you since?'

'I heard of the coming of the Danes, yes, that news was everywhere from the next morning. But I heard nothing of any death, never a word.'

No, it would not be news of crucial importance, like the invasion from Ireland, tref would not spread it to tref and maenol to maenol as Owain's couriers had spread word of the muster to Carnarvon. Heledd was frowning over the belated news, saddened by any man's death, especially one she had known briefly, even made use of, in her own fashion, to plague a father who wronged her affection.

'I am sorry,' she said. 'He had such life in him. A waste! Killed, you think, to prevent his going? One more warrior for Cadwaladr, and with knowledge of the prince's plans to make him even more welcome? Then *who*? Who could have found out, and made such dreadful shift to stop him?'

'That there's no knowing, nor will I hazard guesses where they serve no purpose. But soon or late, the prince will find him out. The man was in a sense his guest, he will not let the death go unavenged.'

'You foretell another death,' said Heledd, with forceful bitterness. 'What does that amend?'

And to that there was no answer that would not raise yet further questions, probing all the obscure corners of right and wrong. They walked on together, to a higher point near the southern rim of the armed camp, unhindered, though they were observed with brief, curious interest by many of the Danish warriors through whose lines they passed. On the hillock, clear of the sparse trees, they halted to survey the ground all about them.

Otir had chosen to make his landfall not on the sands to the north of the strait, where the coast of Anglesey extended into a broad expanse of dune and warren, none too safe in high tides, and terminating in a long bar of shifting sand and shingle, but to the south, where the enclosing peninsula of land stood higher and dryer, sheltered a deeper anchorage, and afforded a more defensible campsite, as well as more rapid access to the open sea in case of need. That it fronted more directly the strong base of Carnarvon, where Owain's forces were mustered in strength, had not deterred the invader. The shores of his chosen encampment were well manned, the landward approach compact enough to afford a formidable defence under assault, and a broad bay of tidal water separated it from the town. Several rivers drained into this bight, Cadfael recalled, but at low tide they would be mere meandering streaks of silver in a treacherous waste of sand, not lightly to be braved by an army. Owain would have to bring his forces far round to the south to approach his enemy on safe ground. With some six or seven miles of marching between himself and Owain, and with a secure ground base already gained, no doubt Cadwaladr felt himself almost invulnerable.

Except that the six or seven miles seemed to have shrunk to a single mile during the night. For when Cadfael topped the ridge of bushes, and emerged with a clear view well beyond the rim of the camp to southward, the open sea just glimmering with morning light on his right hand, the pallid shallow waters and naked sands of the bay to his left, he caught in the distance, spaced across the expanse of dune and field and scrubland, an unmistakable shimmer of arms and faint sparkle of coloured tents, a wall ensconced overnight. The early light picked out traces of movement like the quiver of a passing wind rippling a cornfield, as men passed purposefully to and fro about their unhurried business of fortifying their chosen position. Out of range of lance or bow, Owain had brought up his army under cover of darkness to seal off the top of this peninsula, and pen the Danish force within it. There was to be no time wasted. Thus forehead to forehead, like two rival rams measuring each other, one party or the other must open the business in hand without delay.

It was Owain who opened dealings, and before the morning was out, while the Danish chiefs were still debating the appearance of his host so close to their boundaries, and what action he might have in mind now that he was there. It was unlikely that they had any qualms about their own security, having swift access to the open sea at need, and ships the Welsh could not match, and doubtless, thought Cadfael, discreetly, drawn back from the knot of armed men gathered now on the knoll, they were also speculating as to how strong a garrison he had left to hold Carnarvon, and whether it would be worth staging a raid by water upon the town if the prince attempted any direct assault here. As yet they were not persuaded that he would risk any such costly action. They stood watching the distant lines narrowly, and waited. Let him speak first. If he was already minded to receive his brother into favour again, as he had done several times before, why make any move to frustrate so desirable a resolution?

It was mid-morning, and a pale sun high, when two horsemen were seen emerging from a slight dip in the sandy levels between the two hosts. Mere moving specks as yet, sometimes lost in hollows, then breasting the next rise, making steadily for the Danish lines. There were barely half a dozen dwellings in all that stretch of dune and warren, since there was little usable pasture and no good ploughland, and doubtless those few settlements had been evacuated in the night. Those two solitary figures were the sole inhabitants of a no-man's-land between armies, and as it appeared, charged with opening negotiations to prevent a pointless and costly collision. Otir waited for their nearer approach with a face wary but content, Cadwaladr with braced body and tense countenance, but foreseeing a victory. It was in the arrogant spread of his feet bestriding Welsh ground, and the lofty lift of his head and narrowing of his eyes to view the prince's envoys.

Still at the limit of the range of lance or arrow, the second rider halted and waited, screened by a thin belt of trees. The other rode forward to within hailing distance, and there sat his horse, looking up at the watchful group on the hillock above him.

'My lords,' the hail came up to them clearly, 'Owain Gwynedd sends his envoy to deal with you on his behalf. A man of peace, unarmed, accredited by the prince. Will you receive him?'

'Let him come in,' said Otir. 'He shall be honourably received.'

The herald withdrew to a respectful distance. The second rider spurred forward towards the rim of the camp. As he drew near it became apparent that he was a small man, slender and young, and rode with more purpose than grace, as if he had dealt rather with farm horses than elegant mounts for princes and their ambassadors. Nearer still, and Cadfael, watching as ardently as any from the crest of the dunes, drew deep breath and let it out again in a great sigh. The rider wore the rusty black habit of the Benedictines, and showed the composed and intent young face of Brother Mark. A man of peace indeed, messenger of bishops and now of princes. No doubt in the world but he had begged this office for himself, none that he had urged upon the prince the practicality of making use of one whose motives could hardly be suspected, who had nothing to gain or lose but his own freedom, life and peace of mind, no axe to grind, no profit to make, no lord to placate in this world, Welsh, Danish, Irish or any other. A man whose humility could move like a charmed barrier between the excesses of other men's pride.

Brother Mark reached the edge of the camp, and the guards stood aside to let him pass. It was the young man Turcaill, twice Mark's modest size, who stepped forward hospitably to take his bridle, as he lighted down and set out briskly to climb the slight slope to where Otir and Cadwaladr waited to greet him.

In Otir's tent, crammed to the entrance with the chief among his forces, and every other man who could get a toehold close to the threshold, Brother Mark delivered himself of what he had come to say, partly on his own behalf, partly on behalf of Owain Gwynedd. Aware by instinct of the common assumption among these freebooters that they had rights in the counsels of their leaders, he let his voice ring out to reach the listeners crowding close outside the tent. Cadfael had made it his business to secure a foothold near enough to hear what passed, and no one had raised any objection to his presence. He was a hostage here, concerned after his own fashion as they were after theirs. Every man with a stake in the venture exercised his free right to guard his position.

'My lords,' said Brother Mark, taking his time to find the right words and give them their due emphasis, 'I have asked to undertake this embassage because I am not involved upon any part in this quarrel which brings you into Wales. I bear no arms, and I have nothing to gain, but you and I and every man here have much, all too much, to lose if this dispute ends in needless bloodshed. If I have heard many words of blame upon either

503

side, here I use none. I say only that I deplore enmity and hatred between brothers as between peoples, and hold that all disputes should be resolved without the shedding of blood. And for the prince of Gwynedd, Owain ap Griffith ap Cynan, I say what he has instructed me to say. This quarrel holds good between two men only, and all others should hold back from a cause which is not theirs. Owain Gwynedd bids me say that if Cadwaladr his brother has a grievance, let him come and discuss it face to face, in guaranteed safety to come and to return.'

'And I am to take his word for that, without security?' Cadwaladr demanded. But by the guarded gleam in his eyes he was not displeased with this approach.

'As you know very well that you can,' said Mark simply.

Yes, he knew it. Every man there knew it. Ireland had had dealings with Owain Gwynedd many times before this, and not always by way of contention. He had kin over there who knew his value as well as it was known in Wales. Cadwaladr's face had a glossy look of contained pleasure, as though he found this first exchange more than encouraging. Owain had taken warning, seeing the strength of the invading force, and was preparing to be conciliatory.

'My brother is known for a man of his word,' he conceded graciously. 'He must not think that I am afraid to meet him face to face. Certainly I will go.'

'Wait a little, wait a little!' Otir shifted his formidable bulk on the bench where he sat listening. 'Not so fast! This issue may well have arisen between two men, but there are more of us in it now, invited in upon terms to which I hold, and to which I will hold you, my friend. If you are content to let go your assets on any man's word, without security, I am not willing to let go mine. If you leave here to enter Owain's camp and submit yourself to Owain's persuasion or Owain's compulsion, then I require a hostage for your safe return, not a hollow promise.'

'Keep me,' said Brother Mark simply. 'I am willing to remain as surety that Cadwaladr shall go and come without hindrance.'

'Were you so charged?' Otir demanded, with some suspicion of the efficacy of such an exchange.

'No. But I offer it. It is your right, if you fear treachery. The prince would not deny you.'

Otir eyed the slight figure before him with a cautious degree of approval, but remained sceptical. 'And does the prince place on you, Brother, an equal value with his own kinsman and enemy? I think I might be tempted to secure the one bird in hand, and let the other fly or founder.'

'I am in some sort Owain's guest,' said Mark steadily, 'and in some sort his courier. The value he sets on me is the value of his writ and his honour. I shall never be worth more than I am as you see me here.'

Otir let loose a great bellow of laughter, and struck his palms together. 'As good an answer as I need. Stay, then, Brother, and be welcome! You have a brother here already. Be free of my camp, as he is, but I warn you, never venture too near the rim. My guards have their orders. What I have taken I keep, until it is fairly redeemed. When the lord Cadwaladr returns, you have due leave to go back to Owain, and give him such answer as we two here see fit.'

It was, Cadfael thought, a deliberate warning to Cadwaladr, as well as to Mark. There was no great trust between these two. If Otir required a surety that Cadwaladr would come back unmolested, it was certainly not simply out of concern for Cadwaladr's safety, but rather taking care of Otir's own bargain. The man was his investment, to be guarded with care, but never, never, to be wholly trusted. Once out of sight, who knew what use so rash a princeling would make of whatever advantage circumstances offered him?

Cadwaladr rose and stretched his admirable body with sleek, pleasurable assurance. Whatever reservations others might have, he had interpreted his brother's approach as wholly encouraging. The threat to the peace of Gwynedd had been shrewdly assessed, and Owain was ready to give ground, by mere inches it might be, but sufficient to buy off chaos. And now all he, Cadwaladr, had to do was go to the meeting, behave himself seemly before other eyes, as he knew well how to do with grace, and in private surrender not one whit of his demands, and he would regain all, every yardland that had been taken from him, every man of his former following. There could be no other ending, when Owain spoke so softly and reasonably at the first advance.

'I go to my brother,' he said, grimly smiling, 'and what I bring back with me shall be to your gain as well as mine.'

Brother Mark sat with Cadfael in a hollow of the sand dunes overlooking the open sea, in the clear, almost shadowless light of afternoon. Before them the swathes of sand, sculptured by sea winds, went rolling down in waves of barren gold and coarse, tenacious grass to the water's edge. At a safe depth offshore seven of Otir's ships rode at anchor, four of them cargo hulls, squat and sturdy, capacious enough to accommodate a wealth of plunder if it came to wresting their price out of Gwynedd by force, the other three the largest of his longships. The smaller and faster vessels all lay within the mouth of the bay, where there was safe anchorage at need, and comfortable beaching inshore. Beyond the ships to westward the open, silvery water extended, mirroring a pallid, featureless blue sky, but dappled in several places by the veiled gold of shoals.

'I knew,' said Mark, 'that I should find you here. But I would have come, even without that inducement. I was on my way back to the meeting-place when they passed by. I saw you prisoners, you and the girl. The best I could do was make for Carnarvon, and carry that tale to Owain. He has your case well in mind. But what else he has in his mind, with this meeting he has sought, I do not know. It seems you have not fared so badly with these Danes. I find you in very good heart. I confess I feared for Heledd.'

'There was no need,' Cadfael said. 'It was plain we had our value for the prince, and he would not suffer us to go unransomed, one way or another. They do not waste their hostages. They have a reward promised, they are bent on earning it as cheaply as possible, they'll do nothing to bring out the whole of Gwynedd angry and in arms, not unless the whole venture turns sour on them. Heledd has been offered no affront.'

'And has she told you what possessed her to run from us at Aber, and how she contrived to leave the llys? And the horse she rode – for I saw it led along with the raiders, and that was good harness and gear from the prince's stable – how did she come by her horse?'

'She found it,' said Cadfael simply, 'saddled and bridled and tethered among the trees outside the walls, when she slipped out at the gate behind the backs of the guards. She says she would have fled afoot, if need had been, but there was the beast ready and waiting for her. And what do you make of that? For I am sure she speaks truth.'

Mark gave his mind to the question very gravely for some minutes. 'Bledri ap Rhys?' he hazarded dubiously. 'Did he indeed intend flight, and make certain of a mount while the gates were open, during the day? And some other, suspicious of

506

his stubborn adherence to his lord, prevented the departure? But there was nothing to show that he ever thought of leaving. It seemed to me that the man was well content to be Owain's guest, and have Owain's hand cover him from harm.'

'There is but one man who knows the truth,' said Cadfael, 'and he has good reason to keep his mouth shut. But for all that, truth will out, or the prince will never let it rest. So I said to Heledd, and the girl says in reply: "You foretell another death. How does that amend anything?" '

'She says well,' agreed Mark sombrely. 'She has better sense than most princes and many priests. I have not yet seen her, here within the camp. Is she free to move as she pleases, within limits, like you?'

'You may see her this moment,' said Cadfael, 'if you please to turn your head, and look down to the right there, where the spit of sand juts out into the shallows yonder.'

Brother Mark turned his head obediently to follow where Cadfael pointed. The tongue of sand, tipped with a ridge of coarse blond grass to show that it was not quite submerged even at a normal high tide, thrust out into the shallows on their right like a thin wrist and hand, straining towards the longer arm that reached southward from the shores of Anglesey. There was soil enough on its highest point to support a few scrub bushes, and there a minute outcrop of rock stood up through the soft sand. Heledd was walking without haste along the stretched wrist towards this stony knuckle, at one point plashing ankle-deep through shallow water to reach it; and there she sat down on the rock, gazing out to sea, towards the invisible and unknown coast of Ireland. At this distance she appeared very fragile, very vulnerable, a small, slender, solitary figure. It might have been thought that she was withdrawing herself as far as possible from her captors, in a hapless defence against a fate she had no means of escaping in the body. Alone by the sea, with empty sky above her, and empty ocean before her, at least her mind sought a kind of freedom. Brother Cadfael found the picture deceptively appealing. Heledd was shrewdly aware of the strength, as well as the weakness, of her situation, and knew very well that she had little to fear, even had she been inclined to fear, which decidedly she was not. She knew, also, how far she could go in asserting her freedom of movement. She could not have approached the shores of the enclosed bay without being intercepted long before this. They knew she could swim. But this outer beach offered her no possibility of escape. Here she could wade through the shallows, and no one would lift a finger to prevent. She was hardly likely to strike out for Ireland, even if there had not been a flotilla of Danish ships offshore. She sat very still, her bare arms wreathed about her knees, gazing westward, but with head so alertly erect that even at this distance she seemed to be listening intently. Gulls wheeled and cried above her. The sea lay placid, sunlit, for the moment complacent as a cat. And Heledd waited and listened.

'Did ever creature seem more forlorn!' Brother Mark wondered, half aloud. 'Cadfael, I must speak with her as soon as may be. In Carnarvon I have seen her bridegroom. He came hotfoot from the island to join Owain, she should know that she is not forsaken. This Ieuan is a decent, stalwart man, and will put up a good fight for his bride. Even if Owain could be tempted to leave the girl to her fate here – and that is impossible! – Ieuan would never suffer it. If he had to venture for her with no forces but his own small following, I am sure he would never give up. Church and prince have offered her to him, and he is afire for her.'

'I do believe,' Cadfael said, 'that they have found her a good man, with all the advantages but one. A fatal lack! He is not of her choosing.'

'She might do very much worse. When she meets him, she may be wholly glad of him. And in this world,' Mark reflected ruefully, 'women, like men, must make the best of what they can get.'

'With thirty years and more behind her,' said Cadfael, 'she might be willing to settle for that. At eighteen – I doubt it!'

'If he comes in arms to carry her away – at eighteen that might weigh with her,' Mark observed, but not with entire conviction in his tone.

Cadfael had turned his head and was looking back towards the crest of the dunes, where a man's figure had just breasted the rise and was descending towards the beach. The long, generous stride, the exuberant thrust of the broad shoulders, the joyous carriage of the flaxen head, bright in the sun, would have given him a name even at a greater distance.

'I would not wager on the issue,' said Cadfael cautiously. 'And even so, he comes a little late, for someone else has already come in arms and carried her away. That issue, too, is still in doubt.'

The young man Turcaill erupted into Brother Mark's view

only as he drew towards the spit of sand, and scorning to go the whole way to walk it dryshod, waded cheerfully through the shallows directly to where Heledd sat. Her back remained turned towards him, but doubtless her ears were pricked.

'Who is that?' demanded Mark, stiffening at the sight.

'That is one Turcaill, son of Turcaill, and if you saw us marched away to his ship, you must have seen that lofty head go by. It can hardly be missed, he tops the rest of us by the length of it.'

'That is the man who made her prisoner?' Mark was frowning down at Heledd's minute island, where still she maintained her pretence at being unaware of any intruder into her solitude.

'It was you said it. He came in arms and carried her away.'

'What does he want with her now?' Mark wondered, staring.

'No harm. He's subject to authority here, but even aside from that, no harm.' The young man had emerged in a brief flurry of spray beside Heledd's rock, and dropped with large, easy grace into the sand at her feet. She gave him no acknowledgement, unless it could be considered an acknowledgement that she turned a little away from him. Whatever they may have said to each other could not be heard at such a distance, and it was strange that Cadfael should suddenly feel certain that this was not the first time Heledd had sat there, nor the first time that Turcaill had coiled his long legs comfortably into the sand beside her.

'They have a small private war going on,' he said placidly. 'They both take pleasure in it. He loves to make her spit fire, and she delights in flouting him.'

A children's game, he thought, a lively battle that passes the time pleasantly for both of them, all the more pleasantly because neither of them need take it seriously. By the same token, neither need we take it seriously.

It occurred to him afterwards that he was breaking his own rule, and wagering on an issue that was still in doubt.

Chapter Nine

N THE ABANDONED farmstead where Owain had set up his headquarters, a mile from the edge of Otir's camp, Cadwaladr set forth the full tale of his grievances, with some discretion because he spoke in the presence not only of his brother, but of Hywel, against whom he felt perhaps the greatest and most bitter animosity, and of half a dozen of Owain's captains besides, men he did not want to alienate if he could keep their sympathy. But he was incapable of damping down his indignation throughout the lengthy tale, and the very reserve and tolerance with which they listened to him aggravated his burning resentment. By the end of it he was afire with his wrongs, and ready to proceed to what had been implied in every word, the threat of open warfare if his lands were not restored to him.

Owain sat for some minutes silent, contemplating his brother with a countenance Cadwaladr could not read. At length he stirred, without haste, and said calmly: 'You are under some misapprehension concerning the state of the case, and you have conveniently forgotten a small matter of a man's death, for which a price was exacted. You have brought here these Danes of Dublin as a means of forcing my hand. Not even by a brother is my hand so easily forced. Now let me show you the reality. The boot is on the other foot now. It is no longer a matter of you saying to me: give me back all my lands, or I will let loose these barbarians on Gwynedd until you do. Now hear me saying to you: You brought this host here, now

510

you get rid of them, and then you may – I say *may!* – be given back what was formerly yours.'

It was by no means what Cadwaladr had hoped for, but he was so sure of his fortune with such allies that he could not refrain from putting the best construction upon it. Owain meant more and better than he was yet prepared to say. Often before he had proved pliant towards his younger brother's offences, so he would again. In his own way he was already declaring an alliance to defy and expel the foreign invaders. It could not be otherwise.

'If you are ready to receive and join with me ...' he had begun, for his high temper mildly and civilly, but Owain cut him off without mercy.

'I have declared no such intent. I tell you again, get rid of them, and only then shall I consider restoring you to your right in Ceredigion. Have I even said that I promise you anything? It rests with you, and not solely upon this present ground, whether you ever rule in Wales again. I promise you nothing, no help in sending these Danes back across the sea, no payment of any kind, no trucc unless or until *I* choose to make truce with them. They are your problem, not mine. I may have, and reserve, my own quarrel with them for daring to invade my realm. But now any such consideration is in abeyance. Your quarrel with them, if you dismiss their help now, is your problem.'

Cadwaladr had flushed into angry crimson, his eyes hot with incredulous rage. 'What is this you are demanding of me? How do you expect me to deal with such a force? Unaided? What do you want me to do?'

'There is nothing simpler,' said Owain imperturbably. 'Keep the bargain you made with them. Pay them the fee you promised, or take the consequences.'

'And that is all you have to say to me?'

'That is all I have to say. But you may have time to think what further may be said between us if you show sense. Stay here overnight by all means,' said Owain, 'or return when you will. But you will get no more from me, while there's a Dane uninvited on Welsh ground.'

It was so plainly a dismissal, and Owain so unremittingly the prince rather than the brother, that Cadwaladr rose tamely and went out from the presence shocked and silent. But it was not in his nature to accept the possibility that his endeavours had all come to nothing. Within his brother's compact and well-planned camp he was received and acknowledged as both guest and kin, sacred and entitled to the ultimate in courtesy on the one ground, treated with easy familiarity on the other. Such usage only confirmed his native optimism and reassured his arrogant self-confidence. What he had heard was the surface that covered a very different reality. There were many among Owain's chiefs who kept a certain affection for this troublesome prince, however sorely that affection had been tried in the past, and however forthrightly they condemned the excesses to which his lofty temper drove him. How much greater, he reflected, at Owain's campaign table and in Owain's tent overnight, was the love his brother bore him. Time and again he had flouted it, and been chastened, even cast out of all grace, but only for a while. Time and again Owain had softened towards him, and taken him back brotherly into the former inescapable affection. So he would again. Why should this time be different?

He rose in the morning certain that he could manipulate his brother as surely as he had always done before. The blood that held them together could not be washed away by however monstrous a misdeed. For the sake of that blood, once the die was cast, Owain would do better than he had said, and stand by his brother to the hilt, against whatever odds.

All Cadwaladr had to do was cast the die that would force Owain's hand. The result was never in doubt. Once deeply embroiled, his brother would not desert him. A less sanguine man might have seen these calculations as providing only a somewhat suspect wager. Cadwaladr saw the end result as certainty.

There were some in the camp who had been his men before Hywel drove him out of Ceredigion. He reckoned their numbers, and felt a phalanx at his back. He would not be without advocates. But he used none of them at this juncture. In the middle of the morning he had his horse saddled, and rode out of Owain's encampment without taking any formal leave, as though to return to the Danes, and take up his bargaining with them with as little loss of cattle or gold or face as possible. Many saw him go with some half-reluctant sympathy. So, probably, did Owain himself, watching the solitary horseman withdraw across open country, until he vanished into one of the rolling hollows, to reappear on the further slope already shrunken to a tiny, anonymous figure alone in the encroaching waste of blown sand. It was

512

something new in Cadwaladr to accept reproof, shoulder the burden laid on him, and go back without complaint to do the best he could with it. If he maintained this unexpected grace, it would be well worth a brother's while to salvage him, even now.

The reappearance of Cadwaladr, sighted before noon from the guard-lines covering Otir's landward approach, excited no surprise. He had been promised freedom to go and to return. The watch, captained by the man Torsten, he who was reputed to be able to split a sapling at fifty paces, sent word inward to Otir that his ally was returning, alone and unmolested, as he had been promised. No one had expected any other development; they waited only to hear what reception he had had, and what terms he was bringing back from the prince of Gwynedd.

Cadfael had been keeping a watchful eye on the approaches since morning, from a higher spot well within the lines, and at the news that Cadwaladr had been sighted across the dunes Heledd came curiously to see for herself, and Brother Mark with her.

'If his crest is high,' Cadfael said judicially, 'when he gets near enough for us to take note, then Owain has in some degree given way to him. Or else he believes he can prevail on him to give way with a little more persuasion. If there is one deadly sin this Cadwaladr will never fall by, it is surely despair.'

The lone horseman came on without haste into the sparse veil of trees on a ridge at some distance from the rim of the camp. Cadwaladr was as good a judge of the range of arrow or lance as most other men, for there he halted, and sat his horse in silence for some minutes. The first ripple of mild surprise passed through the ranks of Otir's warriors at this delay.

'What ails him?' wondered Mark at Cadfael's shoulder. 'He has his freedom to come and go. Owain has made no move to hold him, his Danes want him back. Whatever he brings with him. But it seems to me his crest is high enough. He may as well come in and deliver his news, if he has no cause to be ashamed of it.'

Instead, the distant rider sent a loud hail echoing over the folds of the dunes to those listening at the stockade. 'Send for Otir! I have a message to him from Gwynedd.'

'What can this be?' asked Heledd, puzzled. 'So he might well

513

have, why else did he go to parley? Why deliver it in a bull's bellow from a hundred paces distance?'

Otir came surging over the ridge of the camp with a dozen of his chiefs at his heels, Turcaill among them. From the mouth of the stockade he sent back an answering shout: 'Here am I, Otir. Bring your message in with you, and welcome.' But if he was not by this time mulling over many misgivings and doubts in his own mind, Cadfael thought, he must be the only man present still sure of his grip on the expedition. And if he was, he chose for the moment to dissemble them, and wait for enlightenment.

'This is the message I bring you from Gwynedd,' Cadwaladr called, his voice deliberate, high and clear, to be heard by every man within the Danish lines. 'Be off back to Dublin, with all your host and all your ships! For Owain and Cadwaladr have made their peace, Cadwaladr will have his lands back, and has no more need of you. Take your dismissal, and go!'

And on the instant he wheeled his horse, and spurred back into the hollows of the dunes at a gallop, back towards the Welsh camp. A great howl of rage pursued him, and two or three opportunist arrows, fitted on uneasy suspicion, fell harmlessly into the sand behind him. Further pursuit was impossible, he had the wings of any horse the Danes could provide, and he was off back to his brother in all haste, to make good what he had dared to cry aloud. They watched him vanish and reappear twice in his flight, dipping and rising with the waves of the dunes, until he was a mere speck in the far distance.

'Is this possible?' marvelled Brother Mark, shocked and incredulous. 'Can he have turned the trick so lightly and easily? Would Owain countenance it?'

The clamour of anger and disbelief that had convulsed the Danish freebooters sank with ominous suddenness into the contained and far more formidable murmur of understanding and acceptance. Otir gathered his chiefs about him, turned his back on the act of treachery, and went striding solidly up the dunes to his tent, to take counsel what should follow. There was no wasting time on denunciation or threat, and there was nothing in his broad brown countenance to give away what was going on behind the copper forehead. Otir beheld things as they were, not as he would have wished them. He would never be hesitant in confronting realities.

'If there's one thing certain,' said Cadfael, watching him pass by, massive, self-contained and perilous, 'it is that there goes one who keeps his own bargains, bad or good, and will demand as much from those who deal with him. With or without Owain, Cadwaladr had better watch his every step, for Otir will have his price out of him, in goods or in blood.'

No such forebodings troubled Cadwaladr on his ride back to his brother's camp. When he was challenged at the outer guard he drew rein long enough to reassure the watch blithely: 'Let me by, for I am as Welsh as you, and this is where I belong. We have common cause now. I will be answerable to the prince for what I have done.'

To the prince they admitted, and indeed escorted him, unsure of what lay behind this return, and resolute that he should indeed make good his purpose to Owain before he spoke with any other. There were enough of his old associates among the muster, and he had a way of retaining devotion long after it was proven he deserved none. If he had brought the Danes here to threaten Gwynedd, he might now have conspired with them in some new and subtle measure to get his way. And Cadwaladr stalked into the presence in their midst with a slight, disdainful smile for their implied distrust, as always convinced by the arguments of his own sanguine mind, and sure of his dominance.

Owain swung about from the section of the stockade that his engineers were reinforcing, to stare and frown at sight of his brother, so unexpectedly returned. A frown as yet only of surprise and wonder, even concern that something unforeseen might have prevented Cadwaladr's freedom of movement.

'You back again? What new thing is this?'

'I am come to myself,' said Cadwaladr with assurance, 'and have returned where I belong. I am as Welsh as you, and as royal.'

'It is high time you remembered it,' said Owain shortly. 'And now you are here, what is it you intend?'

'I intend to see this land freed of Irishman and Dane, as I am instructed is your wish also. I am your brother. Your forces and mine are one force, must be one force. We have the same interests, the same needs, the same aims ...'

Owain's frown had gathered and darkened on his brow into a thundercloud, as yet mute, but threatening. 'Speak plainly,' he said, 'I am in no mood to go roundabout. What have you done?'

'I have flung defiance at Otir and all his Danes!' Cadwaladr was proud of his act, and assured he could make it acceptable, and fuse into one the powers that would enforce it. 'I have bidden them board and up sail and be off home to Dublin, for you and I together are resolute to drive them from our soil, and they had best accept their dismissal and spare themselves a bloody encounter. I was at fault ever to bring them here. If you will, yes, I repent of it. Between you and me there is no need of such harsh argument. Now I have dismissed and spurned their bought services. We will rid ourselves of every last man of them. If we are at one, they will not dare stand against us …'

He had progressed thus far in an ever-hastening torrent of words, as if desperate to convince rather himself than Owain. Misgivings had made their stealthy way into his mind almost without his knowledge, by reason of the chill stillness of his brother's face, and the grimly silent set of his mouth below the unrelenting frown. Now the flow of eloquence flagged and faltered, and though Cadwaladr drew deep breath and took up the thread again, he could no longer recover the former conviction. 'I have still a following, I will do my part. We cannot fail, they have no firm foothold, they will be caged in their own defences, and swept into the sea that brought them here.'

This time he let fall the very effort of speech. There was even a silence, very eloquent to the several of Owain's men who had ceased their work on the defences to listen with a free tribesman's interest, and without any dissembling. There was never born a Welshman who would not speak his mind bluntly even to his prince.

'What is there,' Owain wondered aloud, to the sky above him and the soil below, 'persuades this man still that my words do not mean what they seem to mean in sane men's ears? Did I not say you get no more from me? Not a coin spent, not a man put at risk! This devilment of your own making, my brother, it was for you to unmake. So I said, so I meant and mean.'

'And I have gone far to do it!' Cadwaladr flared, flushing red to the brows. 'If you will do your part as heartily we are done with them. And who is put at risk? They dare not put it to the test of battle. They will withdraw while there's time.'

'And you believe I would have any part in such a betrayal? You made an agreement with these freebooters, now you break it as lightly as blown thistledown, and look to me to praise you for it? If your word and troth is so light, at least let

516

me weight it with my black displeasure. If it were for that alone,' said Owain, abruptly blazing, 'I would not lift a finger to save you from your folly. But there is worse. Who is put at risk, indeed! Have you forgotten, or did you never condescend to understand, that your Danes hold two men of the Benedictine habit, one of them willing hostage for your good faith, which now all men see was not worth a bean, let alone a good man's liberty and life. Yet more, they also hold a girl, one who was in my retinue and in my care, even if she chose to venture to leave it and make shift alone. For all these three I stand responsible. And all these three you have abandoned to whatever fate your Otir may determine for his hostages, now that you have spited, cheated and imperilled him at the cost of your own honour. This is what you have done! Now I will undo such part of it as I can, and you may make such terms as you can with the allies you have cheated and discarded.'

And without pause for any rejoinder, even had his brother retained breath enough to speak, Owain flung away from him to call to the nearest of his men: 'Send and saddle me my horse! Now, and hasten!'

Cadwaladr came to his senses with a violent convulsion, and sprang after him to catch him by the arm. 'What will you do? Are you mad? There's no choice now, you are committed as deep as I. You cannot let me fall!'

Owain plucked himself away from the unwelcome hold, thrusting his brother to arm's length in brief and bitter detestation. 'Leave me! Go or stay, do as you please, but keep out of my sight until I can bear the very look and touch of you. You have not spoken for me. If you have so represented the matter, you lied. If a hair of the young deacon's head has been harmed, you shall answer for it. If the girl has suffered any insult or hurt, you shall pay the price of it. Go, hide yourself, think on your own hard case, for you are no brother nor ally of mine; you must carry your own follies to their deserved ending.'

It was not more than two hours past noon when another solitary horseman was sighted from the camp on the dunes, riding fast and heading directly for the Danish perimeter. One man alone, coming with manifest purpose, and making no cautious halt out of range of weapons, but posting vehemently towards the guards, who stood watching his approach with eyes narrowed to weigh up his bearing and accoutrements, and guess at his intent. He wore no mail, and bore no visible arms.

'No harm in him,' said Torsten. 'What he wants he'll tell us, by the cut of him. Go tell Otir we have yet another visitor coming.'

It was Turcaill who carried the message, and delivered it as he interpreted it. 'A man of note by his beast and his harness. Fairer-headed than I am, he could be a man of our own, and big enough. My match, if I'm a judge. He might even top me. By this he's close. Shall we bring him in?'

Otir gave no more than a moment to considering it. 'Yes, let him come. A man who spurs straight in to me man to man is worth hearing.'

Turcaill went back jauntily to the guardpost, in time to see the horseman rein in at the gate, and light down empty-handed to speak for himself. 'Go tell Otir and his peers that Owain ap Griffith ap Cynan, prince of Gwynedd, asks admittance to speech with them.'

There had been very serious and very composed and deliberate consultation in Otir's inner circle of chieftains since Cadwaladr's defiance. They were not men of a temper to accept such treachery, and make the best of their way tamely out of the trap in which it had left them. But whatever they had discussed and contemplated in retaliation suddenly hung in abeyance when Turcaill, grinning and glowing with his astonishing embassage, walked in upon their counsels to announce:

'My lords, here on the threshold is Owain Gwynedd in his own royal person, asking speech with you.'

Otir had a sense of occasion that needed no prompting. The astonishment of this arrival he put by in an instant, and rose to stride to the open flap of his tent and bring in the guest with his own hand to the trestle table round which his captains were gathered.

'My lord prince, whatever your word, your self is welcome. Your line and your reputation are known to us, your forebears on your grandmother's side are close kin to kin of ours. If we have our dissensions, and have fought on opposing sides before now, and may again, that is no bar but we may meet in fair and open parley.'

'I expect no less,' said Owain. 'You I have no cause otherwise to love, since you are here upon my ground uninvited, and for no good purpose towards me. I am not come to exchange compliments with you, nor to complain of you, but to set right what may be misunderstood between us.'

518

'Is there such misunderstanding?' asked Otir with dry good humour. 'I had thought our situation must be clear enough, for here I am, and here are you acknowledging freely that here I have no right to be.'

'That, as at this moment,' said Owain, 'we may leave to be resolved at another time. What may have misled you is the visit my brother Cadwaladr paid you this morning.'

'Ah, that!' said Otir, and smiled. 'He is back in your encampment, then?'

'He is back. He is back, and I am here, to tell you – I could even say, to warn you – that he did not speak for me. I knew nothing of his intent. I thought he had come back to you just as he left you, still your ally, still hostile to me, still a man of his word and bound to you. It was not with my will or leave that he discarded you, and with you the sacred worth of his word. I have not made peace with him, nor will I make war with him against you. He has not won back the lands I took from him, for good reason. The bargain he made with you he must abide as best he may.'

They were steadily gazing at him, and from him to one another, about the table, waiting to be enlightened, and withholding judgement until the mists cleared.

'I am slow to see, then, the purpose of this visit,' said Otir civilly, 'however much pleasure the company of Owain Gwynedd gives me.'

'It is very simple,' said Owain. 'I am here to lay claim to three hostages you hold in your camp. One of them, the young deacon Mark, willingly remained to ensure the safe return of my brother, who has now made that return impossible, and left the boy to answer for it. The other two, the girl Heledd, a daughter of a canon of Saint Asaph, and the Benedictine Brother Cadfael of the abbey of Shrewsbury, were captured by this young warrior who conducted me in to you, when he raided for provisions far up the Menai. I came to ensure that no harm should come to any of these, by reason of Cadwaladr's abandonment of his agreement. They are no concern of his. They are all three under my protection. I am here to offer a fair ransom for them, no matter what may follow between your people and mine. My own responsibilities I will discharge honourably. Cadwaladr's are nothing to do with me. Exact from him what he owes you, not from any of these three innocent people.'

Otir did not openly say: 'So I intend!' but he smiled a tight and relishing smile that spoke just as clearly for him. 'You may well interest me,' he said, 'and I make no doubt we could agree upon a fair ransom, between us. But for this while you must hold me excused if I reserve all my assets. When I have given consideration to all things, then you shall know whether, and at what price, I am willing to sell your guests back to you.'

'At least, then,' said Owain, 'give me your pledge that they shall come back to me unharmed when I do recover them – whether by purchase or by capture.'

'I do not spoil what I may wish to sell,' agreed Otir. 'And when I collect what is due to me, it will be from the debtor. That I promise you.'

'And I take your word,' said Owain. 'Send to me when you will.'

'And there is no more to be said between us two?'

'As yet,' said Owain, 'there is nothing more. All your choices you have reserved. So do I reserve mine.'

Cadfael left the place where he had stood motionless and quiet, in the lee of the tent, and followed down through the mute ranks of the Danes as they drew aside to give the prince of Gwynedd clear passage back to his waiting horse. Owain mounted and rode, without haste now, more certain of his enemy than ever he had been since boyhood of his brother. When the fair head, uncovered to the sun, had twice dipped from sight and reappeared again, and was dwindling into a distant speck of pale gold in the distance, Cadfael turned back along the fold of the dunes, and went to look for Heledd and Mark. They would be together. Mark had taken upon himself, somewhat diffidently, the duty of keeping a guardian eye upon the girl's privacy. She might shake him off at will when she did not want him; when if ever she did want him, he would be within call. Cadfael had found it oddly touching how Heledd bore with this shy but resolute attendance, for she used Mark as an elder sister might, considerate of his dignity and careful never to open upon him the perilous weaponry she had at her disposal in dealing with other men, and sometimes had been known to indulge for her own pleasure no less than in hurt retaliation against her father. For there was no question but this Heledd, with her gown frayed at the sleeve and crumpled by sleeping in a scooped hollow of sand lined with grass, and her hair unbraided and loose about her shoulders in a mane of darkness burnished into blue highlights by the sun, and her feet as often as not bare in the warm sand and the cool shallows along the seaward shore, was perceptibly closer to pure beauty than she had ever been before, and could have wreaked havoc in most young men's lives here had she been so minded. Nor was it wholly in her own defence that she went about the camp so discreetly, suppressing her radiance, and avoided contact with her captors but for the young boy who waited on her needs and Turcaill, to whose teasing company she had become accustomed, and whose shafts she took passing pleasure in returning.

There was a bloom upon Heledd in these days of captivity, a summer gloss that was more than the sheen of the sun on her face. It seemed that now that she was a prisoner, however easy was her captivity within its strict limits, and had accepted her own helplessness, now that all action and all decisions were denied her she had abandoned all anxiety with them, and was content to live in the passing day and look no further. More content than she had been, Cadfael thought, since Bishop Gilbert came to Llanelwy, and set about reforming his clergy while her mother was on her deathbed. She might even have suffered the extreme bitterness of wondering whether her father was not looking forward to the death that would secure him his tenure. There was no such cloud upon her now, she radiated a warmth that seemed to have no cares left in the world. What she could not influence she had settled down to experience and survive, even to enjoy.

They were standing among the thin screen of trees on the ridge when Cadfael found them. They had seen Owain arrive, and they had climbed up here to watch him depart. Heledd was still staring wide-eyed and silent after the last glimpse of the prince's bright head, lost now in distance. Mark stood always a little apart from her, avoiding touch. She might treat him sisterly, but Cadfael wondered at times whether Mark felt himself in danger, and kept always a space between them. Who could ensure that his own feelings should always remain brotherly? The very concern he felt for her, thus suspended between an uncertain past and a still more questionable future, was a perilous pitfall.

'Owain will have none of it,' Cadfael announced practically. 'Cadwaladr lied. Owain has set the matter straight. His brother must work out his own salvation or damnation unaided.'

'How do you know so much?' asked Mark mildly.

'I took care to be close. Do you think a good Welshman would neglect his interests where the contrivances of his betters are concerned?'

'I had thought a good Welshman never acknowledged any betters,' said Mark, and smiled. 'You had your ear to the leather of the tent?'

'For your benefit no less. Owain has offered to buy us all three out of Otir's hold. And Otir, if he has held back from coming to terms at once, has promised us life and limb and this degree of freedom until he comes to a decision. We have nothing worse to fear.'

'I was not in any fear,' said Heledd, still gazing thoughtfully southward. 'Then what comes next, if Owain has left his brother to his fate?'

'Why, we sit back and wait, here where we are, until either Otir decides to accept his price for us, or Cadwaladr somehow scrapes together whatever fool sum in money and stock he promised his Danes.'

'And if Otir cannot wait, and decides to cut his fee by force out of Gwynedd?' Mark wondered.

'That he will not do, unless some fool starts the killing and forces his hand. I exact my dues, he said, from the debtor who owes them. And he means it, not now simply out of self-interest, but out of a very deep grudge against Cadwaladr, who has cheated him. He will not bring Owain and all his power into combat if by any means he can avoid it and still get his profit. And he is as able to make his own dispositions,' said Cadfael shrewdly, 'as any other man, and for all I can see, better than most. Not only Owain and his brother are calling the shots here, Otir may well have a trick or two of his own up his sleeve.'

'I want no killing,' said Heledd peremptorily, as though she gave orders by right to all men presently in arms. 'Not for us, not for them. I would rather continue here prisoner than have any man brought to his death. And yet,' she said grieving, 'I know it cannot go on thus deadlocked, it must end somehow.'

It would end, Cadfael reflected, unless some unforeseen disaster intervened, in Otir's acceptance of Owain's ransom for his captives, most probably after Otir had dealt, in whatever fashion he saw fit, with Cadwaladr. That score would rank first in his mind, and be tackled first. He had no obligation now to his sometime ally, that compact had been broken once for all. Cadwaladr might go into exile, once he had paid his dues, or go on his knees to his brother and beg back his lands. Otir owed him nothing. And since he had all his following to pay, he would not refuse the additional profit of Owain's ransom.

522

Heledd would go free, back to Owain's charge. And there was a man now in Owain's muster who was waiting to claim her on her return. A good man, so Mark said, presentable to the eye, well-thought of, a man of respectable lands, in good odour with the prince. She might do very much worse.

'There is no cause in the world,' said Mark, 'why it should not end for you in a life well worth the cherishing. This Ieuan whom you have never seen is wholly disposed to receive and love you, and he is worth your acceptance.'

'I do believe you,' she said, for her almost submissively. But her eyes were steady upon a far distance over the sea, where the light of air and the light of water melted into a shimmering mist, indissoluble and mysterious, everything beyond hidden in radiance. And Cadfael wondered suddenly if he was not, after all, imagining the conviction in Brother Mark's voice, and the womanly grace of resignation in Heledd's.

Chapter Ten

URCAILL CAME DOWN from conference in Otir's tent towards the shore of the sheltered bay, where his lithe little dragon-ship lay close inshore, its low sides mirrored in the still water of the shallows. The anchorage at the mouth of the Menai was separated from the broad sandy reaches of the bay to southward by a long spit of shingle, beyond which the water of two rivers and their tributaries wound its way to the strait and the open sea, in a winding course through the waste of sands. Turcaill stood to view the whole sweep of land and water, the long stretch of the bay extending more than two miles to the south, pale gold shoals and sinuous silver water, the green shore of Arfon beyond, rolling back into the distant hills. The tide was flowing, but it would be two hours or more yet before it reached its highest, and covered all but a narrow belt of salt marsh fringing the shore of the bay. By midnight it would be on the turn again, but full enough to float the little ship with its shallow draught close inshore. Inland of the saltings there would, if luck held, be scrub growth that would give cover to a few skilled and silent men moving inland. Nor would they have far to go. Owain's encampment must span the waist of the peninsula. Even at its narrowest point it might be as much as a mile across, but he would have pickets on either shore. Fewer and less watchful, perhaps, on the bay shore, since attack by ship was unlikely that way. Otir's larger vessels would not attempt to thread the shoals. The Welsh would be concentrating their watch on the sea to westward.

Turcaill was whistling to himself, very softly and content-edly, as he scanned a sky just deepening into dusk. Two hours yet before they could set out, and with the evening clouds had gathered lightly over the heavens, a grey veil, not threatening rain, but promising cover against too bright a night. From his outer anchorage he would have to make a detour round the bar of shingle to the mouth of the river to reach the clear channel, but that would add only some quarter of an hour to the journey. Well before midnight, he decided blithely, we can embark.

He was still happily whistling when he turned back to return to the heart of the camp and consider on the details of his expedition. And there confronting him was Heledd, coming down from the ridge with her long, springy stride, the dark mane of her hair swaying about her shoulders in the breeze that had quickened with evening, bringing the covering of cloud. Every encounter between them was in some sense a confrontation, bringing with it a racing of the blood on both sides, curiously pleasurable.

'What are you doing here?' he asked, the whistle breaking off short. 'Were you thinking of escaping across the sands?' He was mocking her, as always.

'I followed you,' she said simply. 'Straight from Otir's tent, and off with you this way, and eyeing the sky and the tide and that snake-ship of yours. I was curious.'

'The first time ever you were curious about me or anything I did,' he said cheerfully. 'Why now?'

'Because suddenly I see you head-down on a hunt, and I cannot but wonder what mischief you're about this time.'

'No mischief,' said Turcaill. 'Why should there be?' He was regarding her, as they walked back slowly together, with somewhat narrower attention than he gave to their usual easy skirmishing, for it seemed to him that she was at least half serious in her probing, even in some way anxious. Here in her captivity, between two armed camps, a solitary woman might well scent mischief, the killing kind, in every move, and fear for her own people.

'I am not a fool,' said Heledd impatiently. 'I know as well as you do that Otir is not going to let Cadwaladr's treason go unavenged, nor let his fee slip through his fingers. He's no such man! All this day he and all his chiefs have had their heads together over the next move, and now suddenly you come bursting out shining with the awful delight you fool men feel in plunging headfirst into a fight, and you try to tell me there's nothing in the wind. *No mischief!*'

'None that need trouble you,' he assured her. 'Otir has no quarrel with Owain or any of Owain's host, they have cast off Cadwaladr to untie his own knots and pay his own debts, why should we want to provoke worse? If the promised price is paid, we shall be off to sea and trouble you no more.'

'A good riddance that will be,' said Heledd sharply. 'But why should I trust you and your fellows to manage things so well? It needs only one chance wounding or killing, and there'll be blazing warfare, and a great slaughter.'

'And since you are so sure I'm deep in this mischief you foresee ...'

'The very instrument of it,' she said vehemently.

'Then can you not trust *me* to bring it to a good end?' He was laughing at her again, but with a degree of almost apprehensive delicacy.

'You least of all,' she said with vicious certainty. 'I know you, you have a lust after danger, there's nothing so foolhardy but you would dare it, and bring down everything in a bloody battle on all of us.'

'And you, being a good Welshwoman,' said Turcaill, wryly smiling, 'fear for your Gwynedd, and all those men of Owain's host camped there barely a mile from us.'

'I have a bridegroom among them,' she reminded him smartly, and set her teeth with a snap.

'So you have. I will not forget your bridegroom,' Turcaill promised, grinning. 'At every step I take, I will think on your Ieuan ab Ifor, and draw in my hand from any stroke that may bring him into peril of battle. There's no other consideration could so surely curb any rashness of mine as the need to see you married to a good, solid *uchelwr* from Anglesey. Will that content you?'

She had turned to look at him intently, her great eyes purple-black and unwaveringly earnest. 'So you are indeed bound on some mad foray for Otir! You have as good as said so.' And as he did not make any protest or attempt to deny it further: 'Make good what you have promised me, then. Take good care! Come back without hurt to any. I would not have even you come to harm.' And meeting the somewhat too bright intelligence of the blue eyes, she added with a toss of her head, but with a little too much haste for the disdainful dignity

526

at which she aimed: 'Let alone my own countrymen.'

'And foremost of all your countrymen, Ieuan ab Ifor,' Turcaill agreed with a solemn face: but she had already turned her back on him and set off with erected head and vehement stride towards the sheltered hollow where her own small tent was placed.

Cadfael arose from his chosen nest in the lee of the squat salt bushes wakeful and restless for no good reason, left Mark already sleeping, and dropped his cloak beside his friend, for the night was warm. It was at Mark's insistence that they lay always within call of Heledd's tent, though not so close as to offend her independent spirit. Cadfael had small doubt by this time of her safety within the Danish enclave. Otir had given his orders, and no man of his following was likely to take them lightly, even if their minds had not been firmly fixed upon more profitable plunder than one Welsh girl, however tempting. Adventurers, Cadfael had noted throughout his own early life of adventure, were eminently practical people, and knew the value of gold and possessions. Women came much lower down in the scale of desirable loot.

He looked towards where her low windbreak lay, and all was dark and silent there. She must be asleep. For no comprehensible reason, sleep eluded him. The sky bore a light covering of cloud, through which only a star here and there showed faintly. There was no wind, and tonight there would be no moon. The cloud might well thicken by morning, even bring rain. At this midnight hour the stillness was profound, even oppressive, the darkness over the dunes shading away both east and west into a very faint impression of lambent light from the sea, now almost at its fullest tide. Cadfael turned eastward, where the line of guards was more lightly manned, and he was less likely to excite any challenge by being up and about in the dead of night. There were no fires, except those turfed down in the heart of the camp to burn slowly till morning, and no torches to prick through the darkness. Otir's watchmen relied on their night eyes. So did Brother Cadfael. Shapes grew out of shapelessness gradually, even the curves and slopes of the dunes were dimly perceptible. It was strange how a man could be so solitary in the midst of thousands, as if solitude could be achieved at will, and how one to all intents and purposes a prisoner could feel himself freer than his captors, who went hampered by their numbers and chained by their discipline.

He had reached the crest of the ridge above the anchorage, where the lighter and faster Danish ships lay snugly between the open sea and the strait. A wavering line of elusive light, appearing and vanishing as he watched, lipped the shore, and there within its curve they lay, so many lean, long fishes just perceptible as darker flecks briefly outlined by the stroking of the tide. They quivered, but did not stir from their places. Except for one, the leanest and smallest. He saw it creep out from its anchorage so softly that for a moment he thought he was imagining the forward surge. Then he caught the dip of the oars, pinpricks of fire, gone almost before he could realise what they were. No sound came up to him from the distance, even in this nocturnal stillness and silence. The least and probably fastest of the dragon-ships was snaking out into the mouth of the Menai, heading eastward into the channel.

Another foraging expedition? If that was the intent, it would make good sense to take to the strait by night, and lie up somewhere well past Carnarvon to begin their forays ashore before dawn. The town would certainly have been left well garrisoned, but the shores beyond were still open to raiding, even if most of the inhabitants had removed their stock and all their portable goods into the hills. And what was there among the belongings of a good Welshman that was not portable? With ease they could abandon their homesteads if need arose, and rear them again when the danger was over. They had been doing it for centuries, and were good at it. Yet these nearest fields and settlements had already been looted once, and could not be expected to go on providing food for a small army. Cadfael would have expected rather that they would prefer combing the soft coast southward from the open sea, Owain's muster notwithstanding. Yet this small hunter set off silently into the strait. In that direction lay only the long passage of the Menai, or, alternatively, she could be meaning to round the bar of shingle and turn south into the bay by favour of this high tide. Unlikely, on the face of it, though so small a fish could find ample draught for some hours yet, until the tide was again well on the ebb towards its lowest. A larger craft, Cadfael reflected thoughtfully, would never venture there. Could that in itself be the reason why this one was chosen, and despatched alone? Then for what nocturnal purpose?

'So they're gone,' said Heledd's voice behind him, very softly and sombrely.

She had come up at his shoulder soundlessly, barefoot in the sand still warm from the day's sunlight. She was looking down to the shore as he was, and her gaze followed the faintly luminous single stroke of the longship's wake, withdrawing rapidly eastward. Cadfael turned to look at her, where she stood composed and still, the cloud of her long hair about her.

'*So they're gone!* Had you wind of it beforehand? It does not surprise you!'

'No,' she said, 'it does not surprise me. Not that I know anything of what is in their minds, but there has been something brewing all day since Cadwaladr so spited them as he did. What they are planning for him I do not know, and what it may well mean for all the rest of us I dare not guess, but surely nothing good.'

'That is Turcaill's ship,' said Cadfael. It was already so far lost in the darkness that they could follow it now only with the mind's eye. But it would not yet have reached the end of the shingle bar.

'So it would be,' she said. 'If there's mischief afoot, he must be in it. There's nothing Otir could demand of him, however mad, but he would plunge into it headfirst, joyfully, with never a thought for the consequences.'

'And you have thought of the possible consequences,' Cadfael deduced reasonably, 'and do not like them.'

'No,' she said vehemently, 'I do not like them! There could be battle and slaughter if by some foul chance he kills a man of Owain's. It needs no more to start such a blaze.'

'And what makes you think he is going anywhere near Owain's men, to risk such a chance?'

'How should I know what the fool has in mind?' she said impatiently. 'What troubles me is what he may bring down on the rest of us.'

'I would not so readily score him down as a fool,' said Cadfael mildly. 'I would have reckoned him as shrewd in the wits as he is an able man of his hands. Whatever he's about, judge it when he returns, for it's my belief he'll come back successful.' He was careful not to add: 'So leave fretting over him!' She would have denied any such concern, though now with less ferocity than once she would have attempted. Best leave well alone. However she might hope to deceive others, Heledd was not the girl to be able to deceive herself.

And away there to the south in Owain's camp was the man she had never yet seen, Ieuan ab Ifor, not much past thirty, which is not all that old, well thought of by his prince, holder of

529

good lands, and personable to the beholder's eye, possessed of every asset but one, and invisible and negligible without it. He was not the man she had chosen.

'Tomorrow will show,' said Heledd, with relentless practicality. 'We had best go get our sleep, and be ready for it.'

They had rounded the tip of the shingle bar, and kept well out in the main channel as they turned southward into the bay. Once well within, they could draw inshore and keep a watch on the coastline for the first outlying pickets of Owain's camp. Turcaill's boy Leif kneeled on the tiny foredeck, narrowing his eyes attentively upon the shore. He was fifteen years old, and spoke the Welsh of Gwynedd, for his mother had been snatched from this same north-western coast at twelve years old, on a passing Danish raid, and had married a Dane of the Dublin kingdom. But she had never forgotten her language, and had spoken it always with her son, from the time that he learned to speak at all. A half-naked boy in the high summer, Leif could go among the Welsh trefs and the fishing villages here and pass for one of their own, and his talent for acquiring information had brought in beforehand a useful harvest.

'Cadwaladr has kept in touch always with those who hold by him,' Leif had reported cheerfully, 'and there are some among his brother's muster now would go with him if he attempted some act of his own. And I hear them say he has sent word south from Owain's camp to his men in Ceredigion. What word nobody knows, whether to come and join him in arms, or whether to be ready to put together money and cattle if he is forced to pay what he promised us. But if a messenger comes asking for him he'll think it no harm, rather to his gain.'

And there was more to be told, the fruit of much attentive listening. 'Owain will not have him close to him. He keeps a few of his own about him now, and has made his base at the southern edge of the camp, in the corner nearest the bay. There if news comes for him from his old lands, he can let the messenger in and Owain need not know. For he'll play one hand against the other however his vantage lies,' said Leif knowingly.

There was no arguing with that. Everyone who knew Cadwaladr knew it for truth. If the Danes had been slow to realise it, they knew it now. And Leif could be the messenger as well as any other. At fourteen a Welsh boy becomes a man, and is acknowledged as a man.

The ship drew in cautiously closer to shore. Outlines of dune and shingle and scattered bushes showed as denser or paler bulks in the dark, slipping by on their right hand. And presently the outer fringe of the Welsh camp became perceptible rather by the lingering intimations of humanity, the smoke of fires, the resinous odours of newly split wood in the lengths of stockade, even the mingled, murmurous sounds of such activity as persisted into the night, than by anything seen or clearly heard. The steersman brought his barque still closer, wary of the undulations of marsh grass beneath the placid surface of the shallows, until they should have passed the main body of the camp, and drawn alongside that southern corner where Cadwaladr was reputed to have set up his camp within the camp, drawing about him men of his old following, whose adherence to his brother remained less reliable than to their former prince. More than one fashion of messenger could make contact with him there, and other tidings reach him besides the gratifying news that his lavish generosity was still remembered by some, and himself still held in respect as lord and prince, to whom old fealty was due. He could still be reminded, not only of privileges, but of responsibilities owing, and debts unpaid.

The line of the shore receded from them, dipping westward, and closed with them again gradually as they slid past. The faint warmth and stir that was not quite sound, but only some primitive sensitivity to the presence of other human creatures, unseen, unheard, watchful and potentially hostile, fell behind then into the empty silence of the night.

'We are past,' said Turcaill softly into the steersman's ear. 'Lay us inshore.'

The oars dipped softly. The lithe little ship slid smoothly in among the tufted grasses, and touched bottom as gently as a feather lighting. Leif swung his legs over the side, and dropped into the shallows. There was firm sand under his bare feet, and the water reached barely halfway to his knee. He looked back along the line of the shore where they had passed, and even over the darkened camp there still hung a faint glow over from the day.

'We're close. Wait till I bring word.'

He was gone, winding his way in through the salt grasses and the straggle of scrub to the lift of the dunes beyond, narrow here, and soon rising into rough pasture, and then into good fields. His slight shape melted into the soft, dense darkness.

He was back within a quarter of an hour, sliding out of the night as silently as a wisp of mist before they were prepared for his return, though they had waited without impatience, with ears pricked for any alien sound. Leif waded through the salt bush and the shallow water cold round his legs, and reached to hold by the ship's side and whisper in an excited hiss: 'I have found him! And close! He has a man of his own on the guardpost. Nothing simpler than to come to him in secret from this side. Here they expect no attack by land, he can go and come as he pleases, and so can some who would liefer do his bidding than Owain's.'

'You have not been within?' demanded Turcaill. 'Past the guard?'

'No need! Someone else found the way there not a moment ahead of me, coming from the south. I was in the bushes, close enough to hear him challenged. He had but to open his mouth, whoever he is, and he was welcome within. And I saw where he was led. He's fast within Cadwaladr's tent with him now, and even the guard sent back to his watch. There's none inside there now but Cadwaladr and his visitor, and only one guard between us and the pair of them.'

'Are you sure Cadwaladr is there?' demanded Torsten, low-voiced. 'You cannot have seen him.'

'I heard his voice. I waited on the man from the time we left Dublin,' said the boy firmly. 'Do you think I do not know the sound of him by now?'

'And you heard what was said? This other – did he name him?'

'No name! "You!" he said, loud and clear, but no name. But he was surprised and glad, more than glad of him. You may take the pair of them, once the guard is silenced, and let the man himself tell you his name.'

'We came for one,' said Turcaill, 'and with one we'll go back. And no killing! Owain is out of this quarrel, but he'll be in fast enough if we do murder on one of his men.'

'But won't stir for his brother?' marvelled Leif, half under his breath.

'What should he fear for his brother? Not a scratch upon Cadwaladr, bear in mind! If he pays his proper ransom he gets his leave to go, as whole as when he hired us. Owain knows it better than any. No need to have it said. Over with you, then, and we'll be out with the tide.'

Their plans had been made beforehand; and if they had

taken no count of this unexpected traveller from the south, they could very simply be adapted to accommodate him. Two men alone together in a tent conveniently close to the rim of the camp offered an easy target, once the guard was put out of action. Cadwaladr's own man, in his confidence and in whatever schemes he had in mind, must take his chance of rough handling, but need come to no permanent harm.

'I will take care of the guard,' said Torsten, first to slip over the side to where Leif waited. Five more of Turcaill's oarsmen followed their leader into the salt marsh and across the sandy beach. The night received them silently and indifferently, and Leif went before, retracing his own path from cover to sparse cover towards the perimeter of the camp. In the shelter of a straggling cluster of low trees he halted, peering ahead between the branches. The line of the defences was perceptible ahead merely as a more solid and rigid darkness where every other shadow was sinuous and elusive. But Cadwaladr's liegeman could be seen against the gap which was the gate he guarded, as he paced back and forth across it, head and shoulders clear against the sky. A big man, and armed, but casual in his movements, expecting no alarm. Torsten watched the leisurely patrol for some minutes, marked its extent, and slipped sidelong among the trees to be behind its furthest eastward point, where bushes approached to within a few yards of the stockade, and a man could draw close without being heard or seen.

The guard was whistling softly to himself as he turned in the soft sand, and Torsten's sinewy left arm took him hard around body and arms, and the right clamped a palm hard over his mouth and cut off the whistle abruptly. He groped frantically upward to try and grip the arm that was gagging him, but could not reach high enough, and his struggles to kick viciously backward cost him his balance and did no harm to Torsten, who swung him off his feet and dropped bodily over him into the sand, holding him face-down. By that time Turcaill was beside them, ready to thrust a fold of woollen cloth into the man's mouth as soon as he was allowed to raise himself, and empty it splutteringly of sand and grass. They wound him head and shoulders in his own cloak, and bound him fast hand and foot. There they bestowed him safely enough, if none too comfortably, among the bushes, and turned their attention to the rim of the camp. There had been no outcry, and there was no stirring within the fences. Somewhere about the prince's tents there would be men wakeful and alert, but here at the remotest corner, deliberately chosen by Cadwaladr for his own purposes, there was no one at hand to turn back retribution from him.

Only Turcaill and Torsten and two others followed Leif as he padded softly in through the unguarded gate, and along the stockade towards the remembered spot where he had caught the unmistakable, authoritative tones of Cadwaladr's voice, raised in astonished pleasure as he recognised his midnight visitor. The lines of the camp ended here, in stillness and silence, the invaders moved as shadows among shadows. Leif pointed, and said no word. There was no need. Even in a military camp Cadwaladr would have his rank heeded and his comforts attended to. The tent was ample, proof against wind and weather, and no doubt as well supplied within. At the edges of the flap that shielded its entrance fine lines of light showed, and on the still air of the night lowered voices made a level, confidential murmur, too soft for words. The messenger from the south was still there with his prince, their heads together over tidings brought and plans to be hatched.

Turcaill set his hand to the tent-flap, and waited until Torsten, with his drawn dagger in his hand, had circled the tent to find a rear seam where the skins were sewn together. Thin leather thongs or greased cord, either could be cut with a sharp enough blade. The light within, by the steady way it burned and its low source, must be a simple wick in a small dish of oil, set perhaps on a stool or a trestle. Bodies moving outside would show no outline, while Torsten as he selected his place, could sense rather than see the vague bulks of the two within. Close indeed, attentive, absorbed, expecting no interruption.

Turcaill whipped aside the tent-flap and plunged within so fast, and with two others so hard on his heels, that Cadwaladr had no time to do more than leap to his feet in indignant alarm, his mouth open to vent his outrage, before there was a drawn dagger at his throat, and princely anger at being rudely interrupted changed instantly into frozen understanding and devout and quivering stillness. He was a foolhardy man, but of excellently quick perceptions, and his foolhardiness did not extend so far as to argue with a naked blade when his own hands were empty. It was the man who sat beside him on the well-furnished brychan who sprang to the attack, lunging upward at Turcaill's throat. But behind him Torsten's knife had sliced down the leather thongs that bound the skins of the

534

tent together, and a great hand took the stranger by the hair, and dragged him backwards. Before he could rise again he was swathed in the coverings of the bed and held fast by Turcaill's men.

Cadwaladr stood motionless and silent, well aware of the steel just pricking his throat. His fine black eyes were glittering with fury, his teeth set with the effort of restraint, but he made no move as the companion he had welcomed with pleasure was trussed into helplessness, in spite of his struggles, and disposed of almost tenderly on his lord's bed.

'Make no sound,' said Turcaill, 'and come to no harm. Cry out, and my hand may slip. There is a little matter of business Otir wishes to discuss with you.'

'This you will rue!' said Cadwaladr through his teeth.

'So I may,' Turcaill agreed accommodatingly, 'but not yet. I would offer you the choice between walking or being dragged, but there's no putting any trust in you.' And to his two oarsmen he said: 'Secure him!' and drew back his hand to sheathe the dagger he held.

Cadwaladr was not quick enough to seize the one instant when he might have cried out loudly and raised a dozen men to his aid. As the steel was withdrawn he did open his mouth to call on his own, but a rug from the brychan was flung over his head, and a broad hand clamped it smotheringly into his open mouth. The only sound that emerged was a strangled moan, instantly crushed. He lashed out then with fists and feet, but the harsh woollen cloth was wound tightly about him, and bound fast.

Outside the tent Leif stood sentinel with pricked ears, and wide eyes sweeping the dark spaces of the camp for any movement that might threaten their enterprise, but all was still If Cadwaladr had desired and ordered private and undisturbed converse with his visitor, he had done Turcaill's work for him very thoroughly. No one stirred. In the copse where they had left the guard the last of their party came looming out of the dark to join them, and laughed softly at sight of the burden they carried between them, slung by the ropes that pinioned him.

'The guard?' asked Turcaill in a whisper.

'Well alive, and muttering curses. And we'd best be aboard before they find he's missing and come looking for him.'

'And the other one?' Leif ventured to ask softly, as they wound their way back from cover to cover towards the beach and the saltings. 'What have you done with him?'

'Left him to his rest,' said Turcaill.

'You said no killing!'

'And there's been none. Not a scratch on him, you can be easy. Owain has no cause for feud against us more than he had from the moment we set foot on his soil.'

'And we still don't know,' marvelled Leif, padding steadily along beside him into the moist fringe left by the receding tide, 'who the other one was, and what he was doing there. You may yet wish you'd secured him while you could.'

'We came for one, and we're taking back one. All we wanted and needed,' said Turcaill.

The crew left aboard reached to hoist Cadwaladr over into the well between the benches, and help their fellows after. The steersman leaned upon his heavy steerboard, the inshore rowers thrust off with their oars, poling the little ship quite lightly and smoothly back along the furrow she had ploughed in the sand, until she rode clear and lifted joyously into the ebb of the tide.

Before dawn they delivered their prize, with some pride, to an Otir who had just roused from sleep, but came bright-eyed and content to the encounter. Cadwaladr emerged from his stifling wrappings flushed and tousled and viciously enraged, but containing his bitter fury within an embattled silence.

'Had you trouble by the way?' asked Otir, eyeing his prisoner with shrewd satisfaction. Unmarked, unblooded, extracted from among his followers without trampling his formidable brother's toes, or harming any other soul. A mission very neatly accomplished, and one that should be made to show a profit.

'None,' said Turcaill. 'The man had prepared his own fall, withdrawing himself so to the very rim, and planting a man of his own on guard. Not for nothing! I fancy he has been looking for word from his old lands, and made shift to keep a door open. For I doubt he'll get any sympathy from Owain, or expects any.'

At that Cadwaladr did open his mouth, unlocking his set teeth with an effort, for it was doubtful if he himself quite believed what he was about to say. 'You misread the strength of the Welsh blood-tie. Brother will hold by brother. You have brought Owain down on you with all his host, and so you will discover.'

536

'As brother held by brother when you came hiring Dublin men to threaten *your* brother with warfare,' said Otir, and laughed briefly and harshly.

'You will see,' said Cadwaladr hotly, 'what Owain will venture for my sake.'

'So we shall, and so will you. I doubt you'll find less comfort in it than we shall. He has given both you and me fair notice that your quarrel is not his quarrel, and you must pay your own score. And so you shall,' said Otir with glossy satisfaction, 'before you set foot again outside this camp. I have you, and I'll keep you until you pay me what you promised. Every coin, every calf, or the equal in goods we will have out of you. That done, you may go free, back to your lands or beggarly into the world again, as Owain pleases. And I warn you, never again look to Dublin for help, we know now the worth of your word. And that being so,' he said, thoughtfully plying his massive jowls in a muscular fist, 'we'll make sure of you, now that we have you!' He turned upon Turcaill, who stood by watching this encounter with detached interest, his own part already done. 'Give him in charge to Torsten to keep, but see him tethered. We know all too well his word and oath are no bond to him, so we may rightly use other means. Put chains on him, and see him watched and kept close.'

'You dare not!' Cadwaladr spat on a hissing breath, and made a convulsive movement to launch himself against his judge, but ready hands plucked him back with insulting ease, and held him writhing and sweating between his grinning guards. In the face of such casual and indifferent usage his boiling rage seemed hardly more than a turbulent child's tantrum, and burned itself out inevitably into the cold realisation that he was helpless, and must resign himself to the reversion of his fortunes, for he could do nothing to change it.

'Pay what you owe us, and go,' said Otir with bleak simplicity. And to Torsten: 'Take him away!'

537

Chapter Eleven

WO MEN OF Cuhelyn's company, making the complete rounds of the southern rim of the encampment, found the remotest gate unguarded in the early hours of the morning, and reported as much to their captain. If he had been any other than Cuhelyn this early check upon the defences would not have been ordered in the first place. To him the presence within Owain's camp of Cadwaladr, tolerated if not accepted, was deep offence, not only for the sake of Anarawd dead, but also for the sake of Owain living. Nor had Cadwaladr's proceedings within the camp been any alleviation of the suspicion and detestation in which Cuhelyn bore him. Retirement into this remote corner might have been interpreted by others as showing a certain sensitivity to the vexation the sight of him must cause his brother. Cuhelyn knew him better, an arrogant creature blind to other men's needs and feelings. And never to be trusted, since all his acts were reckless and unpredictable. So Cuhelyn had made it his business, with nothing said to any other, to keep a close eye upon Cadwaladr's movements, and the behaviour of those who gathered about him. Where they mustered, there was need of vigilance.

The defection of a guard brought Cuhelyn to the gate in haste, before the lines were astir. They found the missing man lying unhurt but wound up like a roll of woollen cloth among the bushes not far from the fence. He had contrived to loosen the cord that bound his hands, though not yet enough to free them, and had worked the folds of cloth partly loose from his mouth. The muffled grunts that were all he could utter were enough to locate him as soon as the searchers reached the trees. Released, he came stiffly to his feet, and reported from swollen lips what had befallen him in the night.

'Danes – five at least – They came up from the bay. There was a boy could be Welsh showed them the way ...'

'Danes!' Cuhelyn echoed, between wonder and enlightenment. He had expected devilment of some kind from Cadwaladr, was it now possible that this meant devilment aimed against Cadwaladr, instead? The thought gave him some sour amusement, but he did not yet quite believe in it. This could still be mischief of another kind, Dane and Welshman regretting their severance and compounding their differences secretly to act together in Owain's despite.

He set off in haste to Cadwaladr's tent, and walked in without ceremony. A rising breeze blew in his face, flapping the severed skins behind the brychan. The swaddled figure on the bed heaved and strained, uttering small animal sounds. This second bound victim confounded all possible notions that might account for the first. Why should a party of Danes, having made its way clandestinely here to Cadwaladr, next proceed to bind and silence him, and then leave him here to be found and set free as inevitably as the sun rises? If they came to enter into renewed conspiracy with him, if they came to secure him hostage for what he owed them, either way it made no sense. So Cuhelyn was reflecting bewilderedly as he untied the ropes that pinioned arms and legs, plucking the knots loose with grim patience with his single hand, and unwound the twisted rugs from about the heaving body. A hand scored by the rope came up gropingly as it was freed, and plucked back the last folds from a shock head of disordered dark hair, and a face Cuhelyn knew well.

Not Cadwaladr's imperious countenance, but the younger, thinner, more intense and sensitive face of Cuhelyn's mirror twin, Gwion, the last hostage from Ceredigion.

They came to Owain's headquarters together, the one not so much shepherding the other as deigning to walk behind him, the other stalking ahead to make it plain to all viewers that he was not being driven, but going in vehement earnest where he wished to go. The air between them vibrated with the animosity that had never existed between them until this

539

moment, and by its very intensity and pain could not endure long. Owain saw it in the stiff set of their bodies and the arduous blankness of their faces when they entered his presence and stood side by side before him, awaiting his judgement.

Two dark, stern, passionate young men, the one a shade taller and leaner, the other a shade sturdier and with colouring of a less vivid darkness, but seen thus shoulder to shoulder, quivering with tension, they might indeed have been twin brothers. The glaring difference was that one of them was lopped of half a limb, and that by an act of blazing treachery on the part of the lord the other served and worshipped. But that was not what held them counterpoised in this intensity of anger and hostility, so strange to both of them, and causing them both such indignant pain.

Owain looked from the one grim face to the other, and asked neutrally of both: 'What does this mean?'

'It means,' said Cuhelyn, unlocking his set teeth, 'that this man's word is worth no more than his master's. I found him trussed up and gagged in Cadwaladr's tent. The why and how he must tell you, for I know nothing more. But Cadwaladr is gone, and this man left, and the guard who kept the lines there says that Danes came up from the bay in the night, and left him, too, bound among the bushes to open a way within. If all this to-do has a meaning, he must deliver it, not I. But I know, and so do you, my lord, better than any, that he gave his oath not to attempt flight from Aber, and he has broken his oath and befouled his bond.'

'Scarcely to his own gain,' said Owain, and forbore to smile, eyeing Gwion's face marked by the harsh folds of the brychan, his black hair tangled and erected, and the swollen lips bruised by the gag. And to the young man so grimly silent and defiantly braced he said mildly: 'And how do you say, Gwion? Are you forsworn? Dishonoured, with your oath in the mire?'

The misshapen lips parted, and shook for a moment with the recoil from tension. So low as to be barely audible, Gwion said remorselessly: 'Yes.'

It was Cuhelyn who twisted a little aside, and averted his eyes. Gwion fixed his black gaze on Owain's face, and drew deeper breath, having freely owned to the worst.

'And why did you so, Gwion? I have known you some while now. Read me your riddle. Truly I left you work to do in Aber, in the matter of Bledri ap Rhys dead. Truly I had your parole.

So much we all know. Now tell me how it came that you so belied yourself as to abandon your troth.'

'Let it lie!' said Gwion, quivering. 'I did it! Let me pay for it.'

'Nevertheless, tell it!' said Owain with formidable quietness. 'For I will know!'

'You think I will use excuses in my own defence,' said Gwion. His voice had steadied and firmed into a calm of utter detachment, indifferent to whatever might happen to him. He began gropingly, as if he himself had never until now probed the complexities of his own behaviour, and was afraid of what he might find. 'No, what I have done I have done, I do not excuse it, it *is* shameful. But I saw shame every way, and no choice but to accept and bear the lesser shame. No, wait. This is not for me to say. Let me tell it as I did it. You left it to me to send back Bledri's body to his wife for burial, and to convey to her the news of how he died. I thought I might without offence do her the grace of facing her, and bringing him to her myself, intending a return to my captivity – if I can so call that easy condition I had with you, my lord. So I went to her in Ceredigion, and there we buried Bledri. And there we talked of what Cadwaladr your brother had done, bringing a Danish fleet to enforce his right, and I came to see that both for you and for him, and for all Gwynedd and Wales, the best that could be was that you two should be brought together, and together send the Danes empty-handed back to Dublin. The thought did not come from me,' he said meticulously. 'It came from the old, wise men who have outlived wars and come to reason. I was, I am, Cadwaladr's man, I can be no other. But when they had shown me that for his very sake there must be peace made between you two brothers, then I saw as they saw. And I made cause with such of his old captains as I could in such haste, and gathered a force loyal to him, but intent on the reconciliation I also desired to see. And I broke my oath,' said Gwion with brutal vehemence. 'Whether our fine plans had succeeded or failed, I tell you openly, I would have fought for him. Against the Danes, joyfully. What business had they making such a bargain? Against you, my lord Owain, with a very heavy heart, but if it came to it, I would have done it. For he is my lord, and I serve no other. So I did not go back to Aber. I brought a hundred good fighting men of my own mind to deliver to Cadwaladr, whatever use it might be his intent to make of them.'

541

'And you found him in my camp,' said Owain, and smiled. 'And half of your design seemed to be already done for you, and our peace made.'

'So I thought and hoped.'

'And did you find it so? For you have talked with him, have you not, Gwion? Before the Danes came up from the bay, and took him with them a prisoner, and left you behind? Was he of your mind?'

A brief contortion shook Gwion's dark face. 'They came, and they have taken him. I know no more than that. Now I have told you, and I am in your hands. He is my lord, and if you will have me to fight under you I will yet be of service to him, but if you deny me that, you have the right. I thought on him beleaguered, and my heart could not stand it. Nevertheless, as I have given him my fealty, so now I have given for him even my honour, and I know all too well I am utterly the worse by its loss. Do as you see fit.'

'Do you tell me,' said Owain, studying him narrowly, 'that he had no time to tell you how things stand between us two? If I will have you to fight under me, you say! Why, so I might and not the worst man ever I had under my banner, if I had fighting in mind, but while I can get what I aim at without fighting, I have no such matter in mind. What makes you think I may be about to sound the onset?'

'The Danes have taken your brother!' protested Gwion, stammering and suddenly at a loss. 'Surely you mean to rescue him?'

'I have no such intent,' said Owain bluntly. 'I will not lift a finger to pluck him out of their hands.'

'What, when they have snatched him hostage because he has made his peace with you?'

'They have snatched him hostage,' said Owain, 'for the two thousand marks he promised them if they would come and hammer me into giving him back the lands he forfeited.'

'No matter, no matter what it is they hold against him, though that cannot be the whole! He is your brother, and in enemy hands, he is in peril of his life! You cannot leave him so!'

'He is in no peril at all of the least harm,' said Owain, 'if he pays what he owes. As he will. They will keep him as tenderly as their own babes, and turn him loose without a scratch on him when they have loaded his cattle and goods and gear to the worth he promised them. They do not want outright war any

542

more than I do, provided they get their dues. And they know that if they maim or kill my brother, then they *will* have to deal with me. We understand each other, the Danes and I. But put my men into the field to pull him out of the mire he chose for himself? No! Not a man, not a blade, not a bow!'

'This I cannot believe!' said Gwion, staring wide-eyed.

'Tell him, Cuhelyn, how this contention stands,' said Owain, leaning back with a sigh from such irreconcilable and innocent loyalty.

'My lord Owain offered his brother parley, without prejudice,' said Cuhelyn shortly, 'and told him he must get rid of his Danes before there could be any question of his lands being given back to him. And there was but one way to send them home, and that was to pay what he had promised. The quarrel was his, and he must resolve it. But Cadwaladr believed he knew better, and if he forced my lord's hand, my lord would have to join with him, to drive the Danes out by battle. And he would have to pay nothing! So he delivered defiance to Otir, and bade him be off back to Dublin, for that Owain and Cadwaladr had made their peace, and would drive them into the sea if they did not up anchor and go. In which,' said Cuhelyn through his teeth, and with his eyes fierce and steady and defiant upon Owain, who after all was brother to this devious man, and might recoil from too plain speaking, 'he lied. There was no such peace, and no such alliance. He lied, and he broke a solemn compact, and looked to be praised and approved for it! Worse, by such a cheat he left in peril three hostages, two monks and a girl taken by the Danes. Over them my lord has spread his hand, offering a fair price for their ransom. But for Cadwaladr he will not lift a finger. And now you know,' he said fiercely, 'why the Danes have sent by night to fetch him away, and why they have dealt fairly by you, who have committed no offence against them. They have shed no blood, harmed no man of my lord's following. From Cadwaladr they have a debt to collect. For even to Danes a prince of the Welsh people should keep his word.'

All this he delivered in a steady, deliberate voice, and yet at a white heat of outrage that kept Gwion silent to the end.

'All that Cuhelyn tells you is truth,' said Owain.

Gwion opened stiff lips to say hollowly: 'I do believe it. Nevertheless, he is still your brother and my lord. I know him rash and impulsive. He acts without thought. I cannot therefore abjure my fealty, if you can renounce your blood.'

'That,' said Owain with princely patience, 'I have not done. Let him keep his word to those he brought in to recover his right for him, and deliver my Welsh soil from an unwanted invader, and he is my brother as before. But I would have him clean of malice and false dealing, and I will not put my seal to those things he has done which dishonour him.'

'I can make no such stipulation,' said Gwion with a wry and painful smile, 'nor set any such limit to my allegiance. I am forsworn myself, even in this his fellow. I go with him wherever he goes, even into hell.'

'You are in my mercy,' said Owain, 'and I have not hell in mind for you or him.'

'Yet you will not help him now! Oh, my lord,' pleaded Gwion hotly, 'consider what men will say of you, if you leave a brother in the hands of his enemies.'

'Barely a week ago,' said Owain with arduous patience, 'these Danes were his friends and comrades in arms. If he had not mistaken me and cheated them out of their price they would be so still. If I pass over his treachery to them, I will not pass over his gross and foolish misreading of me. I do not like being taken for a man who will look kindly on oath-breakers, and men who go back shamefully on bargains freely made.'

'You condemn me no less than him,' said Gwion, writhing.

'You at least I understand. Your treason comes of too immovable a loyalty. It does you no credit,' said Owain, wearying of forbearance, 'but it will not turn away your friends from you.'

'I am in your mercy, then. What will you do with me?'

'Nothing,' said the prince. 'Stay or go, as you please. We will feed and house you as we did at Aber, if you want to stay, and wait out his fortune. If not, go when and where you please. You are his man, not mine. No one will hinder you.'

'And you no longer ask for my submission?'

'I no longer value it,' said Owain, and rose with a motion of his hand to dismiss them both from his presence.

They went out together, as they had entered, but once out of the farmstead Cuhelyn turned away, and would have departed brusquely and without a word, if Gwion had not caught him by the arm.

'He damns me with his mercy! He could have had my life, or loaded me with the chains I have earned. Do you, too, avert your eyes from me? Had it been otherwise, had it been Owain

544

himself, or Hywel, beleaguered among enemies, would not you have set your fealty to him above even your word, and gone to him forsworn if need were?'

Cuhelyn had pulled up as abruptly as he had turned away. His face was set. 'No. I have never given my fealty but to lords absolute in honour themselves, and demanding as much of those who serve them. Had I done as you have done, and brought the dishonour as a gift to Hywel, he would have struck me down and cast me out. Cadwaladr, I make no doubt, welcomed and was glad of you.'

'It was a hard thing to do,' said Gwion with the solemnity of despair. 'Harder than dying.'

But Cuhelyn had already plucked himself free, with fastidious care, and was striding away through the camp just stirring into life with the morning light.

Among Owain's men Gwion felt himself an exile and an outcast, even though they accepted his presence in their midst without demur, and took no pains to avoid or exclude him. Here he had no function. His hands and skills did not belong to this lord, and to his own lord he could not come. He passed through the lines withdrawn and mute, and from a hillock within the northern perimeter of the encampment he stood for a long time peering towards the distant dunes where Cadwaladr was a prisoner, a hostage for two thousand marks' worth in stock and money and goods, the hire of a Danish fleet.

Within his vision the fields in the distance gave way to the first undulations of sand, and the scattered trees dwindled into clusters of bushes and scrub. Somewhere beyond, perhaps even in chains after his recapture, Cadwaladr brooded and waited for help which his brother coldly withheld. No matter what the offence, not the breaking of his pledged word, not even the murder of Anarawd, if indeed such guilt touched him, nothing could justify for Gwion Owain's abandonment of his brother. His own breach of faith in leaving Aber Gwion saw as unforgivable, and had no blame for those who condemned it, but there was nothing Cadwaladr had done or could do that would have turned his devout vassal from revering and following him. Once given and accepted, fealty was for life.

And he could do nothing! True, he had leave to depart if he so wished, and also true, he had a company of a hundred good fighting men bivouacked not many miles away, but what was that against the numbers the Danes must have, and the

545

defences they had secured? An ill-considered attempt to storm their camp and free Cadwaladr might only cost him his life, or, more likely, cause the Danes to up anchor and put to sea, where they could not be matched, and take their prisoner away with them, back to Ireland, out of reach of any rescue.

The distant prospect afforded him no enlightenment, and no glimmer of a way forward towards the liberation of his lord. It grieved him that Cadwaladr, who had already lost so much, should be forced to pay out what remained to him in treasury and stock to buy his liberty, without even the certainty that he might recover his lost lands, for which the sum demanded of him had been promised in the first place. Even if Owain was right, and the Danes intended him no harm provided the debt was paid, the humiliation of captivity and submission would gnaw like an ulcer in that proud spirit. Gwion grudged Otir and his men every mark of their fee. It might be said that Cadwaladr should never have invoked alien aid against a brother, but such impetuous and flawed impulses had always threatened Cadwaladr's wisdom, and men who loved him had borne with them as with the perilous cantrips of a valiant and foolhardy child, and made the best of the resultant chaos. It was not kind or just to withdraw now, when most it was needed, the indulgence which had never before failed him.

Gwion moved on along the ridge, still straining his eyes towards the north. A fringe of trees crowned the crest, squat and warped by the salt air, and leaning inland from the prevailing wind. And there beyond their uneven line, still and sturdy and himself rooted as a tree, a man stood and stared towards the unseen Danish force as Gwion was staring. A man perhaps in his middle thirties, square-built and muscular, the first fine salting of grey in his brown hair, his eyes, over-shadowed beneath thick black brows, fixed darkly upon the sand-moulded curves of the naked horizon. He went unarmed, and bare of breast and arms in the sunlight of the morning, a powerful body formidably still in his concentration on distance. Though he heard Gwion's step in the dry grass beneath the trees, and it was plain that he must have heard it, he did not turn his head or stir from his fixed surveillance for some moments, until Gwion stood within touch of him. Even then he stirred and turned about only slowly and indifferently.

'I know,' he said, as though they had been aware of each other for a long time. 'Gazing will bring it no nearer.'

It was Gwion's own thought, worded very aptly, and it took

546

the breath out of him for a moment. Warily he asked: 'You, too? What stake have you over there among the Danes?'

'A wife,' said the other man, with a brief, dry force that needed no more words to express the enormity of his deprivation.

'A wife!' echoed Gwion uncomprehendingly. 'By what strange chance ...' What was it Cuhelyn had said, of three hostages left in peril after Cadwaladr's defection and defiance, two monks and a girl taken by the Danes? Two monks and a girl had set out from Aber in Owain's retinue. To fall victim in the first place to Cadwaladr's mercenaries, and then to be left to pay the price of Cadwaladr's betrayal, if the minds of the Danes ran to vengeance? Oh, the account was growing long, and Owain's obduracy became ever easier to understand. But Cadwaladr had not thought, he never thought before, he acted first and regretted afterwards, as by now he must be regretting everything he had done since he made the first fatal mistake of fleeing to the kingdom of Dublin for redress.

Yes, the girl – Gwion remembered the girl. A black-browed beauty, tall, slender, and mute, serving wine and mead about the prince's table without a smile, except occasionally the malicious and grieving smile with which she plagued the cleric they said was her father, reminding him on what thin ice he walked, and how she could shatter it under him if she so pleased. That story had been whispered around the llys from ostler to maid to armourer to page, and come early to the ears of the last hostage from Ceredigion, who alone could observe all these goings-on with an indifferent eye, since Gwynedd was not home to him, and Owain was not his lord, nor Gilbert of Saint Asaph his bishop. The same girl? She had been on her way, he recalled, to match with a man of Anglesey in Owain's service.

'You are that Ieuan ab Ifor,' he said, 'who was to marry the canon's daughter.'

'I am that same,' said Ieuan, bending thick black brows at him. 'And who are you, who know my name and what I'm doing here? I have not seen you among the prince's liegemen until now.'

'For reason enough. I am not his liegeman. I am Gwion, the last of the hostages he brought from Ceredigion. My allegiance was and is to Cadwaladr,' said Gwion starkly, and watched the slow fire kindle and glow in the sharp eyes that watched him. 'For good or ill, I am his man, but I would far rather it should be for good.'

'It is his doing,' said Ieuan, smouldering, 'that Meirion's daughter is left captive among these sea-pirates. Such good as ever came from him you may measure within the cup of an acorn, and like an acorn feed it to the pigs. He brings barbarian raiders into Gwynedd, and then goes back on his bargain, and takes to his heels into safety, leaving innocent hostages to bear the brunt of Otir's rage. He has been as dire a curse to his own best kin as he was to Anarawd, whom he had done to death.'

'Take heed not to go too far in his dispraise,' said Gwion, but in weariness and grief rather than indignation, 'for I may not hear him miscalled.'

'Oh, be easy! God knows I cannot hold it against any man that he stands by his prince, but God send you a better prince to stand by. You may forgive him all, no matter how he shames you, but do not ask me to forgive him for abandoning my bride to whatever fate the Danes keep for her.'

'The prince has declared her in his protection,' said Gwion, 'as I have heard only an hour ago. He has offered fair ransom for her and for the two monks who came from England, and warned to the value he sets on her safe-keeping.'

'The prince is here,' said Ieuan grimly, 'and she is there, and they have lost their grip on the one they would liefer have in hold. Other captives may find themselves serving in his place.'

'No,' said Gwion, 'you mistake. Whatever rancour you may have against him, be content! This past night they have sent a ship into the bay, and put men ashore to break their way into the camp to his tent. They have taken Cadwaladr prisoner back with them, to pay his own ransom or suffer his own fate. No need for another victim, they have the chosen one fast in their hands.'

Ieuan's rough brows, the most expressive thing about him, knotted abruptly into a ruled line of suspicion and disbelief, and then, confronted by Gwion's unwavering gaze, released their black tension into open bewilderment and wonder.

'You are deceived, that cannot be ...'

'It is truth.'

'How do you know it? Who has told you?'

'There was no need for any man to tell me,' said Gwion. 'I was there with him when they came. I saw it. Four of Otir's Danes burst in by night. Him they took, me they left bound and muted, as they had left the guard who kept the gate. Here I have still the grazes of the cords with which they tied me. See!'

They had scored his wrist deep in his efforts to break free; there was no mistaking rope-burns. Ieuan beheld them with a long, silent stare, assessing and accepting.

'So that is why you said to me: "You, too?" Now I know without asking what stake you have over there among the Danes. Hold me excused if I say plainly that your grief is no grief to me. What may fall upon him he has brought down on his own head. But what has my girl done to deserve the peril in which he left her? If his capture delivers her, I am right glad of it.'

Since there was no arguing with that, Gwion was silent.

'If I had but a dozen of my own mind,' Ieuan pursued, rather to himself than to any other, 'I would bring her off myself, against every Dane Dublin can ship over into Gwynedd. She is mine, and I will have her.'

'And you have not even seen her yet,' said Gwion, shaken by the sudden convulsion of passion in a man so contained and still.

'Ah, but I have seen her. I have been within a stone-throw of their stockade undetected, and can do as much again. I saw her within there, on a crest of the dunes, looking south, looking for the deliverance no one sends her. She is more than they told me. As lissome and bright as steel, and moves like a fawn. I would venture for her alone, but that I dread to be her death before ever I could break through to her.'

'I would as much for my lord,' said Gwion, grown quiet and intent, for this bold and fervent lover had started a vein of hope within him. 'If Cadwaladr is nothing to you, and your Heledd hardly more to me, yet if we put our heads and our forces together we may both benefit. Two is better than one alone.'

'But still no more than two,' said Ieuan. But he was listening.

'Two is but the beginning. Two now may be more in a few days. Even if they break my lord into paying his ransom, it will take some days to bring in and load his cattle, and put together what remains in silver coin.' He drew closer, his voice lowered to be heard only by Ieuan, if any other should pass by. 'I did not come here alone. From Ceredigion I have collected and led some hundred men who still hold by Cadwaladr. Oh, not for the purpose we have in mind at this moment. I was certain that there would be peace made between brothers, and they would combine to drive out the Danes, and I brought my lord at least a fair following to fight for him side by side with those who fight for Owain. I would not have him go free and living only by his brother's grace, but at the head of a company of his own men. I came ahead of them to carry him the news, only to find that Owain has abandoned him. And now the Danes have taken him.'

Ieuan's face had resumed its impassive calm, but behind the wide brow and distant gaze a sharp mind was busy with the calculation of chances hitherto unforeseen. 'How far distant are your hundred men?'

'Two days' march. I left my horse, and a groom who rode with me, a mile south and came alone to find Cadwaladr. Now Owain has cast me free of him into the world to stay or go, I can return within the hour to where I left my man, and send him to bring the company as fast as men afoot can march.'

'There are some within here,' said Ieuan, 'would welcome a venture. A few I can persuade, some will need no persuasion.' He rubbed large, powerful hands together softly, and shut the fingers hard on an invisible weapon. 'You and I, Gwion, will talk further of this. And before this day is out, should you not be on your way?'

Chapter Twelve

T WAS WELL past noon when Torsten again produced his prisoner, chained and humbled and choked with spleen, before Otir. Cadwaladr's handsome lips were grimly set, and his black eyes burning with rage all the more bitter for being under iron control. For all his protestations, he knew as well as any that Owain would not now relent from the position he had taken up. The time for empty hopes was past, and reality had engulfed him and brought him to bay. There was no point in holding out, since eventual submission was inevitable.

'He has a word for you,' said Torsten, grinning. 'He has no appetite for living in chains.'

'Let him speak for himself,' said Otir.

'I will pay you your two thousand marks,' said Cadwaladr. His voice came thinly through gritted teeth, but he had himself well in hand. 'You leave me no choice, since my brother uses me unbrotherly.' And he added, testing such shallows as were left to him in this flood of misfortune: 'You will have to allow me a few days at liberty to have such a mass of goods and gear collected together, for it cannot all be in silver.'

That brought a gust of throaty laughter from Torsten, and an emphatic jerk of the head from Otir. 'Oh, no, my friend! I am not such a fool as to trust you yet again. You do not stir one step out of here, nor shed your fetters, until my ships are loading and ready for sea.'

'How, then, do you propose I should effect this matter of

551

ransom?' demanded Cadwaladr with a savage snarl. 'Do you expect my stewards to render up my cattle to you, and my purse, simply at your orders?'

'I will use an agent I can trust,' said Otir, unperturbed now by any flash of anger or defiance from a man so completely in his power. 'If, that is, he will act for you even in this affair. That he approves it we already know, you better than any of us. What you will do, before I let you loose even within my guard, is to render up your small seal – I know you have it about you, you would not stir without it – and give me a message so worded that your brother will know it could come only from you. I will deal with a man I can trust, no matter how things stand between us, friend or enemy. Owain Gwynedd, if he will not buy you out of bondage, will not stint to welcome the news that you intend to pay your debts honourably, nor refuse you his aid to see due reparation made. Owain Gwynedd shall do the accounting between you and me.'

'He will not do it!' flared Cadwaladr, stung. 'Why should he believe that I have given you my seal of my own will, when you could as well have stripped me and taken it from me? No matter what message I might send, how can he trust, how can he be sure that I send it of my own free will, and not wrung from me with your dagger at my throat, under the threat of death?'

'He knows me by now well enough,' said Otir drily, 'to know that I am not so foolish as to destroy what can and shall be profitable to me. But if you doubt it, very well, we will send him one he will trust, and the man shall take due orders from you in your very person, and bear witness to Owain that he has so taken them, and that he saw you whole and in your right mind. Owain will know truth by the bearer of it. I doubt he can take pleasure in the sight of you, not yet. But he'll so far prove your brother as to put together your price in haste, once he knows you've chosen to honour your debts. He wants me gone, and go I will when I have what I came for, and he may have you back and welcome.'

'You have not such a man in your muster,' said Cadwaladr with a curling lip. 'Why should he trust any man of yours?'

'Ah, but I have! No man of mine, nor of Owain's, nor of yours, his service falls within quite another writ. One that offered himself freely as guarantor for your safe return when you left here to go and parley with your brother. Yes, and one that you left to his fate and my better sense when you tossed your defiance in my face and turned tail for your life back to a brother who despised you for it.' Otir watched the prince's dark face flame into scarlet, and took dour satisfaction in having stung him.

'Hostage for you he was, out of goodwill, and now you are returned indeed, though in every manner of illwill, and I have no longer any claim to keep him here. And he's the man shall go as your envoy to Owain, and in your name bid him plunder such means and valuables as you have left, and bring your ransom here.' He turned to Torsten, who had stood waiting in high and obvious content through these exchanges. 'Go and find that young deacon from Lichfield, the bishop's lad, Mark, and ask him to come here to me.'

Mark was with Brother Cadfael when the word reached him, gathering dry and fallen twigs for their fire from among the stunted trees along the ridge. He straightened up with his load gathered into the fold of a wide sleeve, and stared at the messenger in mild surprise, but without any trace of alarm. In these few days of nominal captivity he had never felt himself a captive, or in any danger or distress, but neither had he ever supposed that he was of any particular interest or consequence to his captors beyond what bargaining value his small body might have.

Like a curious child he asked, wide-eyed: 'What can your captain want with me?'

'No harm,' said Cadfael. 'For all I can see, these Irish Danes have more of the Irish than the Dane in them after all this time. Otir strikes me as Christian as most that habit in England or Wales, and a good deal more Christian than some.'

'He has a thing for you to do,' said Torsten, goodnaturedly grinning, 'that comes as a benefit to us all. Come and hear it for yourself.'

Mark piled his gathered fuel close to the hearth they had made for themselves of stones in their sheltered hollow of sand, and followed Torsten curiously to Otir's open tent. At the sight of Cadwaladr, rigidly erect in his chains and taut as a bowstring, Mark checked and drew breath, astonished. It was the first intimation he had had that the turbulent fugitive was back within the encampment, and to see him here fettered and at bay was baffling. He looked from captive to captor, and saw Otir grimly smiling and obviously in high content. Fortune was busy overturning all things for sport.

553

'You sent for me,' said Mark simply. 'I am here.'

Otir surveyed with an indulgent eye and some surprisingly gentle amusement this slight youth, who spoke here for a Church that Welsh and Irish and the Danes of Dublin all alike acknowledged. Some day, when a few more years had passed, he might even have to call this boy 'Father'! 'Brother' he might call him already.

'As you see,' said Otir, 'the lord Cadwaladr, for whom you stood guarantor that he should go and come again without hindrance, has come back to us. His return sets you free to leave us. If you will do an errand for him to his brother Owain Gwynedd, you will be doing a good deed for him and for us all.'

'You must tell me what that is,' said Mark. 'But I have not felt myself deprived of my freedom here. I have no complaint.'

'The lord Cadwaladr will tell you himself,' said Otir, and his satisfied smile broadened. 'He has declared himself ready to pay the two thousand marks he promised to us for coming to Abermenai with him. He desires to send word to his brother how this is to be done. He will tell you.'

Mark regarded with some doubt Cadwaladr's set face and darkly smouldering eyes. 'Is this true?'

'It is.' The voice was strong and clear, if it grated a little. Since there was no help for it, Cadwaladr accepted necessity, if not with grace, at least with the recovered remnant of his dignity. 'I am required to pay for my freedom. Very well, I choose to pay.'

'It is truly your own choice?' Mark wondered doubtfully.

'It is. Beyond what you see, I am not threatened. But I am not free until the ransom is paid, and the ships loaded for sea, and therefore I cannot go myself to see my cattle rounded up and driven, nor draw on my treasury for the balance. I want my brother to manage all for me, and as quickly as may be. I will send him my authority by you, and my seal by way of proof.'

'If it is what you wish,' said Mark, 'yes, I will bear your message.'

'It is what I wish. If you tell him you had it from my own lips, he will believe you.' His lips at that moment were drawn thin with the hard-learned effort to keep the bitterness and fury caged within, but his mind was made up. There could be revenges later, there could be another repayment to be made in requital of this one, but now what he needed was his freedom. He slid out his private seal from a pocket in his sleeve, and held it out, not to Otir, who sat watching with a glittering grin, but to Mark. 'Take my brother this, tell him you had it from my hand, and ask him to hasten what I need.'

'I will, faithfully,' said Mark.

'Then ask him for my sake to send to Llanbadarn, to Rhodri Fychan, who was my steward, and will be my steward again if ever I regain what is mine. What is left of my treasury he will know where to find, and at my orders, witnessed by my seal, he will deliver it over. If the sum is not enough, what is lacking must be made up in cattle. Rhodri knows where my stock are bestowed in safe charge. There are still herds kept for me, more than enough. Two thousand marks is the sum. Ask my brother to make haste.'

'I will,' said Mark simply, and began by himself making all haste. It was he who took an ambassador's leave of them, rather than acknowledging his own dismissal from Otir's presence. A brisk reverence and a brief farewell, and he was already on his way, and for some reason the space within the tent and about it looked curiously empty by the removal of his small, slight figure.

He went on foot; the distance was barely more than a mile. Within the halfhour he would be delivering his message to Owain Gwynedd, and setting in motion the events which were to restore Cadwaladr his freedom, if not his lands, and remove from Gwynedd the threat of war, and the oppressive presence of an alien army.

The only pause he made before leaving was to impart to Cadfael the errand on which he was sent.

Brother Cadfael came very thoughtfully to where Heledd was stirring the sleeping fire in the stone hearth, to prepare food for the evening meal. His mind was full of what he had just learned, but he could not help remarking how well this vagrant life in a military camp suited her. She had taken the sun graciously, her skin was a golden bronze, with an olive bloom upon it, suave and infinitely becoming to her dark hair and eyes, and the rich red of her mouth. She had never in her life been so free as she was now in her captivity. The gloss of it was about her like cloth of gold, and it mattered not at all that her sleeve was torn, and the hem of her gown soiled and frayed.

'There's news that could be good for us all,' said Cadfael, watching her neat movements with pleasure. 'Not only did Turcaill come back safely from his midnight foray, it seems he brought back Cadwaladr with him.'

555

'I know,' said Heledd, and stilled her busy hands for a moment, and stared into the fire and smiled. 'I saw them come back, before dawn.'

'And you never said word?' But no, she would not, not yet, not to anyone. That would be to reveal more than she was yet ready to reveal. How could she say that she had risen before the sun, to watch for the little ship's safe return? 'I've scarcely seen you today. No harm had come of whatever they were up to, that was all that mattered. Why, what follows? How is it so good for us all?'

'Why, the man has come to his senses, and agreed to pay these Danes what he promised them. Mark has just been sent off to commission Owain, in his brother's name, and with his brother's seal for surety, to collect and pay his ransom. Otir will take it and go, and leave Gwynedd in peace.'

Now she had indeed turned to pay due attention to what he was saying, with raised brows and sharply arrested hands. 'He has given in? Already? He will pay?'

'I have it from Mark, and Mark is already on his way. Nothing could be surer.'

'And they will go!' she said, a mere murmur within her still lips. She drew up her knees and folded her arms about them, and sat gazing before her, neither smiling nor frowning, only coolly and resolutely assessing these changed prospects for good and evil. 'How long, do you think, Cadfael, it will take to bring cattle up here by the drove roads from Ceredigion?'

'Three days at the least,' said Cadfael, and watched her put away that factor in the methodical recesses of her mind, to be kept in the reckoning.

'Three days at the most, then,' she said, 'for Owain will make all haste to be rid of them.'

'And you will be glad to be free,' said Cadfael, probing gently into regions where truth had at least two faces, and he could not be sure which one was turned towards him, and which was turned way.

'Yes,' she said, 'I shall be glad!' And she looked beyond him into the grey-blue, shifting surface of the sea, and smiled.

Gwion had reached the guard-post, the same by which his lord had been abducted, without hindrance, and was in the very act of stepping over the threshold when the guard barred his way with a braced lance, and challenged him sharply: 'Are not you Gwion, Cadwaladr's liegeman?'

Gwion owned to it, bewildered rather than alarmed. No doubt they were keeping a closer watch on this gate, after last night's incursion, and this sentry did not know Owain's mind, and had no intention of incurring blame by allowing either entry or exit unquestioned. 'I am. The prince has given me leave to stay or go, as I choose. Ask Cuhelyn. He will tell you so.'

'I have later news for you,' said the guard, unmoving. 'For the prince has only a short while since asked that you be sought, if you were still within the pale, and sent back to him.'

'I never knew him change his mind in such a fashion,' protested Gwion distrustfully. 'He made it plain he set no store on me, and did not care a pin whether I stayed or departed. Nor whether I lived or died, for that matter.'

'Nevertheless, it seems he has a use for you yet. No harm, if he never threatened any. Go and see. He wants you. I know no more than that.'

There was no help for it. Gwion turned back towards the squat roof of the farmstead, his mind a turmoil of unprofitable speculations. Owain could not possibly have got wind of what was still at best only a vague intent, hardly a plan at all, though he had spent a long time with Ieuan ab Ifor over the detail of numbers and means, and all that Ieuan had gathered concerning the layout of the Danish camp. Too long a time, as it now appeared. He should have left at once, before there could be any question of detaining him. By this time he could have despatched his groom south to bring up the promised force, and been back within the stockade here before ever he was missed. Planning could have waited. Now it was too late, he was trapped. Yet nothing was quite lost. Owain could not know. No one knew but Gwion himself and Ieuan, and Ieuan had not yet spoken a word to any of those stalwarts he knew of who would welcome a venture. That recruitment was still to come. Then what Owain wanted of him could have nothing to do with their half-formed enterprise.

He was still feverishly recording and discarding possibilities when he entered the low-beamed hall of the farm, and made his stiff and wary reverence to the prince across the rough trestle table.

Hywel was there, close at his father's shoulder, and two more of the prince's trusted captains stood a little apart, witnesses in some business which remained inexplicable to Gwion. For the only other person in the room was the meagre

557

little deacon from Lichfield, in his rusty black habit, his spiky ring of straw-coloured hair growing stubbornly every way, his grey eyes as always wide, direct and tranquil. They looked at Gwion, and Gwion turned his head away, as though he feared they might see too deeply into his mind if he met them fully. He found even the benevolent regard of such eyes unnerving. But what could this little cleric have to do with any matter between Owain and Cadwaladr and the Danish interlopers? Yet if the business in hand here was something entirely different, what could it have to do with him, and what need to recall him?

'It's well that you have not left us, Gwion,' said Owain, 'for after all there is a thing you can do for me, and therewith also for your lord.'

'That I would certainly do, and gladly,' said Gwion, but as yet withholding belief.

'Deacon Mark here is newly come from Otir the Dane,' said the prince, 'who holds my brother and your lord prisoner. He has brought word from Cadwaladr that he has agreed to pay the sum he promised, and buy himself out of debt and out of bondage.'

'I cannot believe it!' said Gwion, blanched to the lips with shock. 'I will not believe it, unless I hear him say so, freely and openly.'

'Then you and I are of one mind,' said Owain drily, 'for I also had hardly expected him to see sense so soon. You have good cause to know my mind in this matter. I would rather my brother should be a man of his word, and pay what he promises. But neither would I accept from another mouth the instruction that will beggar him. Otir deals fairly. From my brother's mouth you cannot hear his will made plain, he will not be free until his debt is paid. But you may hear it from Brother Mark, who received it in trust from him, and will testify that he spoke it firmly and with intent, being whole of his body and in his right mind.'

'I do testify,' said Mark. 'He has been prisoner only this one day. He is fettered, but further than that no hand has been laid on him, and no threat made against his body or his life. He says so, and I believe it, as no violence has ever been offered to me or to those others hostage with the Danes. He told me what was to be done. And he delivered to me with his own hand his seal, as authority for the deed, and I have delivered it to the prince, according to Cadwaladr's orders.'

'And the purport of his message? Be kind enough to repeat it,' the prince requested courteously. 'I would not have Gwion fear that I have in any degree prompted you, or put twisted words into your mouth.'

'Cadwaladr entreats the lord Owain, his brother,' said Mark, fixing his dauntingly clear eyes upon Gwion's face, 'to send with all haste into Llanbadarn, to Rhodri Fychan, who was his steward, and who knows where his remaining treasury is bestowed, and to tell him that his lord requires the despatch to Abermenai of money and stock to the value of two thousand marks, to be delivered to the Danish force under Otir, as promised to them as the agreement in Dublin. And to that end he has sent his seal for guarantee.'

There was a long silence after the clear, mild voice ended this recital, while Gwion stood motionless and mute, struggling with the fury of denial and despair and anger within him. It was not possible that so proud and intolerant a soul as Cadwaladr should have submitted, and so quickly. And yet men, even the most arrogant and hot-headed of men, do value their lives and liberty high, and will buy them back even with humiliation and shame when the threat comes close, and congeals from imagination into reality. But first to dare defy and discard his Danes, and then to grovel to them and scrape together their price in undignified haste – that was unworthy. Had he but waited a few days, there should have been another ending. His own men were so near, and would not have let him lie in chains for long, even if brother and all had deserted him. God, let me have two days yet, prayed Gwion behind his dark, closed face, and I will fetch him off by force, and he shall call off his bailiffs and take back his property, and be Cadwaladr again, erect as he always was.

'This charge,' Owain was saying, somewhere at the extreme edge of Gwion's consciousness, a voice from the distance, or from deep within, 'I intend to fulfil with all haste, as he asks, the quicker to redeem his person together with his good name. My son Hywel rides south at once. But since you are here, Gwion, and all your heart's concern is his service, you shall ride with Hywel's escort, and your presence will be a further guarantee to Rhodri Fychan that this is indeed Cadwaladr's voice speaking, and those who serve him are bound to obey. Will you go?'

'I will go.'

What else could he say? It was already decreed. It was

559

another way of discarding him, but with a sop to his implacable loyalty. In the name of that loyalty he must now assist in stripping his lord of a great part of what possessions remained to him, when only a short while ago he had been in high heart, setting out to bring an army to Cadwaladr's rescue, without this ignominy and loss. But: 'I will go,' said Gwion, swallowing necessity whole. There might still be an opportunity to make contact with his waiting muster, before ever the Danish ships loaded and raised anchor with their booty, and sailed in triumph for Dublin.

They set out within the hour, Hywel ab Owain, Gwion, and an escort of ten men-at-arms, well-mounted, and with authority to commandeer fresh remounts along the way. Whatever Owain's feelings now towards his brother, he did not intend him to remain long a prisoner – or, perhaps a defaulting debtor. There was no knowing which of the two mattered more.

The three days predicted by Cadfael passed in brisk activity elsewhere, but in the two opposed camps they dragged and were drawn out long, like a held breath. Even the watch kept upon the stockades grew a shade lax, expecting no attack now that the issue was near its resolution without the need of fighting. Only Ieuan ab Ifor still fretted at the waiting, and bore in mind always that such negotiations might collapse in failure, prisoners remain prisoners, debts unpaid, marriages delayed beyond bearing. And as the hours passed he spoke privately to this one and that one among his younger and more headstrong friends, rehearsed for them the safe passage he had made twice by night at low tide along the shingle and sand to spy out the Danish defences, and how there was a place where approach from the sea was possible in reasonable cover of scrub and trees. Cadwaladr might have submitted, but these young hot-heads of Wales had not. Bitterly they resented it that invaders from Ireland should not only sail home without losses, but even with a very substantial profit to show for their incursion. But was it not already too late, now that it was known Hywel had gone south with orders to bring back and pay over the sum Otir demanded and Cadwaladr had conceded?

By no means, said Ieuan. For Gwion was gone with them, and somewhere between here and Ceredigion Gwion had brought up a hundred men who would fight for Cadwaladr. None of these had consented to let his lord be plundered of two thousand marks, or be made to grovel before the Dane. They would not stomach it, even if Cadwaladr had been brought so low as to submit to it. Ieuan had spoken with Gwion before he left in Hywel's party. On the way south, if chance offered, he would break away from his companions and go to join his waiting warriors. On the way north again, if he was watched too suspiciously on the way south, even Hywel would be content with him for his part in dealing with Rhodri Fychan at Llanbadarn, and no one would be paying too much heed to what he did. Somewhere along the drove roads he could break away and ride ahead. One dark night was all they would need, with the tide out and their numbers thus reinforced, and Heledd and Cadwaladr would be snatched out of bondage, and Otir could take to the seas for his life, and go back empty-handed to Dublin.

There were not wanting a number of wild young men in Owain's following whose instincts leaned rather to fighting out every issue to a bloody conclusion than to manipulating a way out of impasse without loss of life. There were a few who said openly that Owain was wrong to abandon his brother to pay his dues alone. Oaths were meant to be kept, yes, but the tensions of blood and kinship could put even oaths out of mind. So they listened, and the thought of bursting in through the Danish fences, sweeping Otir and his men into their ships at the edge of the sword and driving them out to sea began to have a powerful appeal. They were weary of sitting here inactive day after day. Where was the glory in bargaining a way out of danger with money and compromise?

The image of Heledd burned in Ieuan's memory, the dark girl poised against the sky on a hillock of the dunes. Twice he had seen her there, watched the long, lissome stride and the proudly carried head. She had a fiery grace even in stillness. And he could not believe, he could not convince himself, that such a woman, one alone in a camp full of men, could continue to the end unviolated, uncoveted. It was against mortal nature. Whatever Otir's authority, someone would defy it. And now his most haunting fear was that when they had loaded their plunder, so tamely surrendered, and were raising anchor to sail for home, they would carry Heledd away with them, as they had carried many a Welsh woman in the past, to be slave to some Dublin Dane for the rest of her life.

He would not have bestirred himself as he did for Cadwaladr, to whom he owed nothing but ill. But for sheer hostility to the invaders, and for the recovery of Heledd, he would have dared the assault with only his own small band of like-minded heroes, if need arose. But better far if Gwion could return in time with his hundred. So for the first day, and the second, Ieuan waited with arduous patience, and kept watch southward for any sign.

In Otir's camp the days of waiting passed slowly but confidently, perhaps too confidently, for there was certainly some relaxation of the strict watch they had kept. The square-rigged cargo ships, with their central wells ready for loading, were brought inshore, to be easily beached when the time came, and only the small, fast dragon-boats remained within the enclosed harbourage. Otir had no reason to doubt Owain's good faith, and as an earnest of his own had removed Cadwaladr's chains, though Torsten stayed attentive at the prisoner's elbow, ready for any rash move. Cadwaladr they did not trust, they knew him now too well.

Cadfael watched the passing of the hours and kept an open mind. There was still room for things to go wrong, though there seemed no particular reason why they should do so. It was simply that when two armed bands were brought together so closely in confrontation, it needed only a spark to set light to the otherwise dormant hostility between them. Waiting could make even the stillness seem ominous, and he missed Mark's serene company. What engaged his attention most during this interlude was the behaviour of Heledd. She went about the simple routine she had devised here for her living without apparent impatience or anticipation, as if everything was predetermined, and already accepted, and there was nothing for her to do about any part of it, and nothing in it either to delight or trouble her. She was, perhaps, more silent than usual, but with no implication of tension or distress, rather as if words would be wasted on matters already assured. It might have suggested nothing better than resignation to a fate she could not influence, but there was no change in the summer gloss that had turned her comeliness into beauty, or the deep, burnished lustre of her iris eyes as they surveyed the ribbon of the shingle beach, and the swaying of the ships offshore under the urging of the changing tides. Cadfael did not follow her too assiduously, nor watch her too closely. If she had secrets, he did not want to know them. If she wanted to confide, she would. If there was anything she needed from him, she would demand it. And of her safety here he was assured. All these

562

restless young men wanted now was to load their ships and take their profits home to Dublin, well out of an engagement that might have ended in disaster, given so doubled-edged a partner.

Thus in either camp the second day drew to a close.

Faced with the authority of Hywel ab Owain, the grudging and stiff-necked testimony of Gwion, who so clearly hated having to admit his lord's capitulation, and holding Cadwaladr's seal in his hand, Rhodri Fychan on his own lands in Ceredigion found no reason to question further the instructions he was given. He accepted with a shrug the necessity, and delivered to Hywel the greater part of the two thousand marks in coin. It made some heavy loads for a number of sumpter horses which were likewise contributed as part of the ransom price. And the rest, he said resignedly, could be rounded up from grazing land close to the northern border of Ceredigion, near the crossing into Gwynedd, in Cadwaladr's swart, sturdy cattle, moved there when this same Hywel drove him out of his castle and fired it after him, more than a year ago. His own herdsmen had grazed them there on his behalf ever since he had been driven out.

It was at Gwion's own suggestion that he was commissioned to ride northward again ahead of his companions, and get this herd of cattle, slow-moving as they would be, in motion towards Abermenai at once. The horsemen would easily overtake them after they had loaded the silver, and no time would be wasted on the return journey. A groom of Rhodri's household rode with him, glad of the outing, to bear witness that they had the authority of Cadwaladr himself, through his steward, to cut out some three hundred head of cattle from his herds and drive them northward.

It was all and more than he could have hoped for. Travelling south he had had no opportunity to withdraw himself or make any preparation for his escape. Now with his face to the north again everything fell into his hand. Once he had set out across the border of Gwynedd, with herd and drovers in brisk motion behind him, nothing could have been easier than to detach himself and ride ahead, on the pretext of giving due notice to Otir to prepare his ships to receive them, and leave them to follow to Abermenai at the best speed they could make.

It was the morning of the second day, very early, when he set forth, and evening when he reached the camp where he had left his hundred like-minded companions living off the country about them, and by this little more popular with their neighbours than such roving armies usually are, and themselves glad to be on the move again.

It seemed wise to wait until morning before marching. They lay in a sheltered place in open woodland, aside from the roads. One more night spent here, and they could be on their way with the first light, for from now on they could move only at a fast foot pace, and even by forced marches foot soldiers cannot outpace the horsemen. Cadwaladr's drovers must rest their travelling herd overnight, there was no fear of being overtaken by them. Gwion slept his few hours with a mind content that he had done all a man could do.

In the night, on the highroad half a mile from their camp, Hywel and his mounted escort passed by.

Chapter Thirteen

ROTHER CADFAEL walked the crest of the dunes in the early evening of the third day, and saw the Danish cargo ships beached in the shallows below him, and the line of men, stripped half-naked to wade from shore to ships, ferrying the barrels of silver pence aboard, and stowing them under foredeck and afterdeck. Two thousand marks within those small, heavy containers. No, somewhat less, for by all accounts the sumpter horses and certain cattle were to go with them as part of Otir's fee. For Hywel was back from Llanbadarn before noon, and by all accounts the drovers would not be far behind.

Tomorrow it would all be over. The Danes would raise anchor and sail for home, Owain's force would see them off Welsh soil, and then return to Carnarvon, and from there disperse to their homes. Heledd would be restored to her bridegroom, Cadfael and Mark to their duties left behind and almost forgotten in England. And Cadwladr? By this time Cadfael was sure that Cadwaladr would be restored to some degree of power and certain of his old lands, once this matter was put by. Owain could not for ever hold out against his blood. Moreover, after every dismay and exasperation his brother had cost him, always Owain hoped and believed that there would be a change, a lesson learned, a folly or a crime regretted. So there was, but briefly. Cadwaladr would never change.

Down on the steel-grey shingle Hywel ab Owain stood to

watch the loading of the treasure he had brought from Llanbadarn. There was no haste, doubtful if they could put the beasts aboard until the morrow, even if they reached here before night. Down there on neutral ground Dane and Welshman brushed shoulders amicably, content to part with debts paid and no blood shed. The affair had almost become a matter of marketing. That would not suit the wildest of Owain's clansmen. It was to be hoped he had them all well in hand, or there might be fighting yet. They did not like to see silver being bled away from Wales into Dublin, even if it was silver pledged, a debt of honour. But steadily the small barrels passed from man to man, the sunbrowned backs bending and swaying, the muscular arms extending the chain from beach to hold. About their bared legs the shallow water plashed in palest blues and greens over the gold of sand, and the sky above them was blue almost to whiteness, with a scatter of whiter clouds diaphanous as feathers. A radiant day in a fine, settled summer.

From the stockade Cadwaladr was also watching the shipment of his ransom, with his stolid shadow Torsten at his shoulder. Cadfael had observed them, withdrawn a little to his right, Torsten placidly content, Cadwaladr stormy-browed and grim, but resigned to his loss. Turcaill was down there aboard the nearest of the ships, hoisting the barrels in under the afterdeck, and Otir stood with Hywel, surveying the scene benignly.

Heledd came over the crest, and made her way down through the scrub and the salt grasses to stand at Cadfael's side. She looked down at the activities stretching out from beach to ship, and her face was calm and almost indifferent. 'There are still the cattle to get aboard,' she said. 'A rough voyage it will be for them. They tell me that crossing can be terrible.'

'In such fine weather,' said Cadfael, matching her tone, 'they'll have an easy passage.' No need to ask from which of them she had that information.

'By tomorrow night,' she said, 'they'll be gone. A good deliverance for us all.' And her voice was serene and even fervent, and her eyes followed the movements of the last of the porters as he waded ashore, bright water flashing about his ankles. Turcaill stood on the after-deck for some moments, surveying the result of their labours, before he swung himself over the side and came surging through the shallows, driving blue of water and white of spray before him, and looking up, saw Heledd as blithely looking down from her high place, and flung back his lofty flaxen head to smile at her with a dazzle of white teeth, and wave a hand in salute.

Among the men-at-arms who stood at Hywel's back to see the money safely bestowed Cadfael had observed one, thickset and powerful and darkly comely, who was also looking up towards the ridge. His head was and remained tilted back, and his eyes seemed to Cadfael to be fixed upon Heledd. True, one woman among a camp of Danish invaders might well draw the eye and the interest of any man, but there was something about the taut stillness and the intent and sustained pose that made him wonder. He plucked at Heledd's sleeve.

'Girl, there's one below there, among the lads who brought the silver – you see him? On Hywel's left! – who is staring upon you very particularly. Do you know him? By the cut of him he knows you.'

She turned to look where he indicated, gave a moment to considering the face so assiduously raised to her, and shook her head indifferently.

'I never saw him before. How can he know me?' And she turned back to watch Turcaill cross the beach and pause to exchange civilities with Hywel ab Owain and his escort, before marshalling his own men back up the slope of the dunes towards the stockade. He passed before Ieuan ab Ifor without a glance, and Ieuan merely shifted his stance a little to recover the sight of Heledd on the dunes above him, as Turcaill's fair head cut her off from him in passing.

During those vital night watches, Ieuan ab Ifor had taken care to be captain of the guard on the westward gate of Owain's camp, and to have a man of his own on watch through the night hours. Towards midnight of that third night Gwion had brought his muster by forced marches to within sight of Owain's stockade, and there diverted them to the narrow belt of shingle exposed by the low tide, to pass by undetected. He himself made his way silently to the guard-post, and from its shadow Ieuan slid out to meet him.

'We are come,' said Gwion in a whisper. 'They are down on the shore.'

'You come late,' hissed Ieuan. 'Hywel is here before you. The silver is already loaded aboard their ships, they are waiting only for the cattle.'

567

'How can that be?' demanded Gwion, dismayed. 'I rode ahead from Llanbadarn. The only halt I made was the few hours of sleep we took last night. We marched before dawn this morning.'

'And in those few hours of the night Hywel overtook and passed you by, for he was here by mid-morning. And come tomorrow morning the herd will be here and loading. Late to save anything but a beggarly life for Cadwaladr as Owain's almsman instead of Otir's prisoner.' For Cadwaladr he did not grieve overmuch, except as his plight had strengthened the case for a rescue which could at the same time deliver Heledd.

'Not too late,' said Gwion, burning up like a stirred fire. 'Bring your few, and make haste! The tide is low and still ebbing. We have time enough!'

They had been ready every night for the signal, and they came singly, silently and eagerly, evading notice and question. Glissading down the suave slopes of the dunes, and across the belt of shingle to the moist, firm sand beyond, where their feet made no sound. More than a mile to go between the camps, but an hour left before the tide would be at its lowest, and ample time to return. There was a lambent light from the water, a shifting but gentle light that was enough for their purposes, the white edges of every ripple showing the extent of the uncovered sand. Ieuan led, and they followed him in a long line, silent and furtive under the dykes of Owain's defences, and on into the no-man's-land beyond. Before them, anchored offshore after their loading, the Danish cargo ships rode darkly swaying against the faint luminosity of the waves, and the comparative pallor of the sky. Gwion checked at sight of them.

'These have the silver already stored? We could reclaim it,' he said in a whisper. 'They'll have only holding crews aboard overnight.'

'Tomorrow!' said Ieuan with brusque authority. 'A long swim, they lie in deep water. They could pick us off one by one before ever we touched. Tomorrow they'll lay them inshore again to load the beasts. There are enough among Owain's muster who grudge so much as a penny to the pirates; if we start the onset they'll follow, the prince will have no choice but to fight. Tonight we take back my woman and your lord. Tomorrow the silver!'

In the small hours of the morning Cadfael awoke to a sudden clamour of voices bellowing and lurs blaring, and started up from his nest in the sand still dazed between reality and dreaming, old battles jerked back into mind with startling vividness, so that he reached blindly for a sword before ever he was steady on his feet, and aware of the starry night above and the cool rippling of the sand under his bare feet. He groped about him to pluck Mark awake before he recalled that Mark was no longer beside him, but back in Owain's retinue, out of reach of whatever this sudden threat might be. Over to his right, from the side where the open sea stretched away westward to Ireland, the acid clashing of steel added a thin, ferocious note to the baying of fighting men. Confused movements of struggle and alarm shook the still air in convulsive turmoil between sand and sky, as though a great stormwind had risen to sweep away men without so much as stirring the grasses they trod. The earth lay still, cool and indifferent, the sky hung silent and calm, but force and violence had come up from the sea to put an end to humanity's precarious peace.

Cadfael ran in the direction from which the uproar drifted fitfully to his ears. Others, starting out of their beds on the landward side of the encampment, were running with him, drawing steel as they ran, all converging on the seaward fences, where the clamour of battle had moved inward upon them, as though the stockade had been breached. In the thick of the tangle of sounds rose Otir's thunderous voice, marshalling his men. And I am no man of his, thought Cadfael, astounded but still running headlong towards the cry, why should I go looking for trouble? He could have been holding off at a safe distance, waiting to see who had staged what was plainly a determined attack, and how it prospered for Dane or Welshman, before assessing its import for his own wellbeing, but instead he was making for the heart of the battle as fast as he could, and cursing whoever had chosen to tear apart what could have been an orderly resolution of a dangerous business.

Not Owain! Of that he was certain. Owain had brought about a just and sensible ending, he would neither have originated nor countenanced a move calculated to destroy his achievement. Some hot-blooded youngsters envenomed with hatred of the Dane, or panting for the glory of warfare! Owain might reserve his quarrel with the alien fleet that invaded his land uninvited, he might even choose to exert himself to thrust them out when all other outstanding business was settled, but he would never have thrown away his own patient work in

569

procuring the clearing of the ground. Owain's battle, had it ever come to it, as it yet might, would have been direct, neat and workmanlike, with no needless killing.

He was near to the heave and strain of close infighting now, he could see the line of the stockade broken here and there by the heads and shoulders of struggling men, and a great gap torn in the barrier where the attackers had forced their way in unobserved, between guard-posts. They had not penetrated far, and Otir already had a formidable ring of steel drawn about them, but on the fringes, in the darkness and in such confusion, there was no knowing friend from enemy, and a few of the first through the gap might well be loose within the camp.

He was rubbing shoulders with the outer ring of Danes, who were thrusting hard to shift the whole intruding mass back through the stockade and down to the sea, when someone came running behind him, light and fast, and a hand clutched at his arm, and there was Heledd, her face a pale, startled oval, starry in the dark, lit by wide, blazing eyes.

'What is it? Who are they? They are mad, mad ... What can have set them on?'

Cadfael halted abruptly, drawing her back out of the press and clear of random steel. 'Fool girl, get back out of here! Are you crazed? Get well away until this is over. Do you want to be killed?'

She clung to him, but held her ground sturdily, more excited than afraid. 'But why? Why should any of Owain's do such mischief, when all was going so well?'

The struggling mass of men, too closely entangled to allow play to steel, reeled their way, and some among them losing balance and footing, the mass broke apart, several fell, and one at least was trampled, and let out breath in a wheezing groan. Heledd was torn away from Cadfael's grasp, and uttered a brief and angry scream. It cut through the din on a piercing, clear note, and even in the stress of battle turned heads in abrupt astonishment to stare in her direction. She had been flung aside so sharply that she would have fallen, if an arm had not taken her about the waist and dragged her clear as the shift of fighting surged towards her. Cadfael was borne the opposite way for a moment, and then Otir's rallying cry drew the Danish circle taut, and their driving weight bore the attackers backwards, and compressed them into the breach they had made in the stockade, cramming them through it in disorder. A dozen lances were hurled after them, and they broke and drew off down the slope of the dunes towards the shore.

A handful of the young Danes, roused and eager, would have pursued the retreating attackers down the dunes, but Otir called them sharply to order. There were wounded already, if none dead, why risk more? They came reluctantly, but they came. There might·be a time to take revenge for an act virtually of treachery, when agreement, if not sworn and sealed, had amounted almost to truce. But this was the time rather to salvage what was damaged, and sharpen once again a watchfulness grown slack as the need seemed to diminish.

In the comparative stillness and quiet they set about picking up the fallen, salving minor wounds, repairing the breach in the stockade, all in grim silence but for the few words needed. Under the broken fence three men lay dead, the foremost of the defenders overwhelmed by numbers before help could reach them. A fourth they picked up bleeding from a lance-thrust meant for his heart, but diverted through the shoulder. He would live, but he might lack the muscular power of his left arm for the rest of his life. Of minor gashes and grazes there were many, and the man who had been trampled spat blood from injuries within. Cadfael put by all other considerations, and went to work with the rest in the nearest shelter by torchlight, with whatever linen and medicines they could provide. They had experience of wounds, and were knowledgeable in treating them, if their treatment was rough and ready. The boy Leif fetched and carried, awed and excited by this burst of violence by night. When all was done that could be done Cadfael sat back with a sigh, and looked round at his nearest neighbour. He was looking into the ice-blue eyes and unwontedly sombre face of Turcaill. The young man had blood on his cheek from a graze, and blood on his hands from the wounds of his friends.

'Why?' said Turcaill. 'What was there to gain? It was as good as finished. Now they have their dead or wounded, too, I saw men being carried or dragged when they broke and ran. What was it made it worth their while to break in here?'

'I think,' said Cadfael, rubbing a hand resignedly over his tired eyes, 'they came for Cadwaladr. He still has a following, as rash as the man himself. They may well have thought to pluck him out of your keeping even in Owain's despite. What else do you hold of such value to them that they should risk their lives for it?'

'Why, the silver he's already paid,' said Turcaill practically. 'Would they not have made for that?'

'So they well may,' Cadfael admitted. 'If they have made a bid for the one, they may do as much for the other.'

'When we lay the ships inshore again tomorrow,' Turcaill's brillint eyes opened wide in thought. 'I will say so to Otir: the man they can have, and good riddance, but the ransom is fairly ours, and we'll keep it.'

'If they are in good earnest,' said Cadfael, 'they have still to do battle for both. For I take it Cadwaladr is still safely in Torsten's keeping?'

'And in chains again. And sat out this foray with a knife at his throat. Oh, they went away empty-handed,' said Turcaill with dour satisfaction. And he rose, and went to join his leader, in conference over his three dead. And Cadfael went to look for Heledd, but did not find her.

'These we take back with us for funeral,' said Otir, brooding darkly over the bodies of his men. 'You say that these who came by night were not sent by Owain. It is possible, but how can we tell? Certainly I had believed him a man of his word. But what is rightfully ours we will make shift to keep, against Owain or any other. If you are right, and they came for Cadwaladr, then they have but one chance left to win away both the man and his price. And we will be before them, with the ships and the sea at our backs, with masts stepped and ready for sail. The sea is no friend to them as it is to us. We'll stand armed between them and the shore, and we shall see if they will dare in daylight what they attempted in the night.'

He gave his orders clearly and briefly. By morning the encampment would be evacuated, the Danish ranks drawn up in battle array on the beach, the ships manoeuvred close to take the cattle aboard. If they came, said Otir, then Owain was in good faith, and the raiders were not acting on his orders. If they did not come, then all compacts were broken, and he and his force would put to sea and raid ashore at some unguarded coast to take for themselves the balance of the debt, and somewhat over for three lives lost.

'They will come,' said Turcaill. 'By its folly alone, this was not Owain's work. And he delivered you the silver by his own son's hand. And so he will the cattle. And what of the monk and the girl? There was a fair price offered for them, but that deal you never accepted. Brother Cadfael has earned his freedom tonight, and it's late now to haggle over his worth.'

'We will leave supplies for him and for the girl, they may stay safe here until we are gone. Owain may have them back as whole as when they came.'

'I will tell them so,' said Turcaill, and smiled.

Brother Cadfael was making his way towards them through the disrupted camp at that moment, between the lines soon to be abandoned. He came without haste, since there was nothing to be done about the news he carried, it was a thing accomplished. He looked from the three bodies laid decently straight beneath their shrouding cloaks to Otir's dour face, and thence full at Turcaill.

'We spoke too soon. They did not go away empty-handed. They have taken Heledd.'

Turcaill, whose movements in general were constant and flowed like quicksilver, was abruptly and utterly still. His face did not change, only his startling eyes narrowed a little, as if to look far into distance, beyond this present time and place. The last trace of his very private smile lingered on his lips.

'How came it,' he said, 'that she ever drew near such a fray? No matter, she would be sure to run towards what was forbidden or perilous, not away from it. You are sure, Brother?'

'I am sure. I have been looking for her everywhere. Leif saw her plucked out of the mêlée, but cannot say by whom. But gone she is. I had her beside me until we were flung apart, shortly before you drove them back through the stockade. Whoever he was who had her by the waist, he has taken her with him.'

'It was for her they came!' said Turcaill with conviction.

'It was for her one at least came. For I think,' said Cadfael, 'this must be the man to whom Owain had promised her. There was one close to Hywel, yesterday when you were loading the silver, could not take his eyes off her. But I did not know the man, and I thought no more of it.'

'She is safe enough, then, and free already,' said Otir, and made no more of it. 'And so are you, Brother, if you so please, but I would remain apart until we are gone, if I were you. For none of us knows what more may be intended for the morning. No need for you to put yourself between Dane and Welshman in arms.'

Cadfael heard him without hearing, though the words and their import came back to him later. He was watching Turcaill

573

so closely that he had no thought to spare for whatever his own next moves should be. The young man had stirred easily and naturally out of his momentary stillness. He drew breath smoothly as ever, and the last of the smile lingered as a spark in his light, bright eyes after it had left his lips. There was nothing to be read in that face, beyond the open, appreciative amusement which was his constant approach to Heledd, and that vanished instantly when he looked down again at the night's losses.

'It's well she should be out of today's work,' he said simply. 'There's no knowing how it will end.'

And that was all. He went about the business of striking camp and arming for action like all the rest. In the darkness they stripped such tents and shelters as they had, and moved the lighter longships from the harbour in the mouth of the bay round into the open sea to join the larger vessels and provide an alert and mobile guard for their crews and cargo. The sea was their element, and fought on their side, even to the fresh breeze that quivered through the stillness before dawn. With sails up and filled, even the slower ships could put out to sea rapidly, safe from attack. But not without the cattle! Otir would not go without the last penny of his due.

And now there was nothing for Cadfael to do, except walk the crest of the dunes among the deserted fires and discarded debris of occupation, and watch the Danish force pack, muster and move methodically down through the scrub grass towards the ships rocking at anchor.

And they will go! Heledd had said, serious but neither elated nor dismayed. They were as good as gone already, and glad to be on their way home. Now if it was indeed Ieuan ab Ifor who had inspired that nocturnal attack, perhaps after all there was no man exerting himself on behalf of Cadwaladr, neither for his person and prestige nor for his possessions, and there would be no further confrontation, on the beach or in the sea, but only an orderly departure, perhaps even with a cool exchange of civilities between Welsh and Danish by way of leave-taking. Ieuan had come for his promised wife, and had what he wanted. No need for him to stir again. But how had he persuaded so many to follow him? Men who had nothing to gain, and had gained nothing. Some, perhaps, who had lost their lives to help him to a marriage.

The lithe little dragon-ship stole round silently into the open sea, and took station, riding well inshore. Cadfael went down a little way towards the strip of shingle, and saw the beach now half dry, half glistening under the lapping of the waves, and empty until the head of the Danish line reached it, and turned southward along the strand, a darker line in a darkness now lightening slowly towards the dove-grey of pre-dawn. The withdrawing raiders had made haste away to the deserted fields and sparse woodland between the camps, into some measure of cover. There were places where the shore route would be too dangerous now, with the tide flowing, though Cadfael felt certain they had come that way. Better and faster to move inland with their wounded and their prize, to reach their own camp dryshod.

Cadfael put a ridge of salt-stunted bushes between himself and the wind, which was freshening, scooped a comfortable hole in the sand, and sat down to wait.

In the soft light of the morning, just after sun-up, Gwion arrayed his hundred men, and the few of Ieuan's raising who remained with them, in a hollow between the dunes, out of sight of the shore, with a sentry keeping watch on the crest above. There was mist rising from the sea, a diaphanous swirl of faint blue over the shore, which lay in shadow, while westward the surface of the water was already bright, flecked with the white shimmer of spray in the steady breeze. The Danes, drawn up in open ranks, lined the edge of the sea, waiting immovably and without impatience for Owain's herdsmen to bring them Cadwaladr's cattle. Behind them the cargo ships had been brought in to beach lightly in the shallows. And there, in the midst of the Danes, was Cadwaladr himself, no longer shackled but still prisoner, defenceless among his armed enemies. Gwion had gone himself to the top of the ridge to look upon him, and the very sight was like a knife in his belly.

He had failed miserably in all that he had tried to do. Nothing had been gained, there stood his lord, humbled at the hands of the Danes, exposed to the scorn of his brother, not even assured of regaining a single foot of land at that brother's hands after all this bitter undertaking. Gwion gnawed ceaselessly at his own frustration, and found it sour in his mouth. He should not have trusted Ieuan ab Ifor. The man had been concerned only with his woman, and with that prize in his arms he had not stayed, as Gwion had wanted to stay, to attempt a second achievement. No, he was away with her,

575

stifling her cries with a hand over her mouth, until he could hiss in her ear, well away from the Danes in their broken stockade, that she should not be afraid, for he meant her only good, for he was her man, her husband, come at risk to fetch her out of danger, and with him she was safe, and would be safe for ever … Gwion had heard him, totally taken up with his gains, and with no care at all for other men's losses. So the girl was out of bondage, but Cadwaladr, sick with humiliation and rage, must come under guard to be handed over for a price to the brother who discarded and misprized him.

It was not to be borne. There was still time to cut him out clean from the alien array before Owain could come to savour the sight of him a prisoner. Even without Ieuan, gone with his bruised and bewildered woman and the dozen or so of his recruits who had preferred to steal back into camp and lick their wounds, there were enough stout fighting men here to do it. Wait, though, wait until the herd and their escort came. For surely once the attack was launched, others would see the right of it, and follow. Not even Hywel, if Hywel was again the prince's envoy, would be able to call off his warriors once they had seen Danish blood flow. And after Cadwaladr, the ships. Once the gate was cast down, the Welsh would go on to the end, take back the silver, drive Otir and his pirates into the sea.

The waiting was long, and seemed longer, but Otir never moved from his station before his lines. They had lowered their guard once, they would not do so again. That was the missed opportunity, for now there could be no second surprise. Even in Hywel, even in Owain himself, they would not again feel absolute trust.

The lookout on the crest reported back regularly and monotonously, no change, no movement, no sign yet of the dust of the herd along the sandy track. It was more than an hour past sunrise when he called at last: 'They are coming!' And then they heard the lowing of the cattle, fitful and sleepy on the air. By the sound of them, fed and watered, and on the move again after at least a few hours of the night for rest.

'I see them. A good half-company, advancing aside and before the drovers, out of the dust. Hywel has come in force. They have sighted the Danes …' That sight might well give them pause, they would not have expected to see the full force of the invaders drawn up in battle array for the loading of a few hundred head of stock. But they came on steadily, at the pace

576

of the beasts. And now the foremost rider could be seen clearly, very tall in the saddle, bare-headed, fair as flax. 'It is not Hywel, it is Owain Gwynedd himself!'

On his hillock above the deserted camp Cadfael had seen the sun shine on that fair head, and even at that distance knew that the prince of Gwynedd had come in person to see the Norseman leave his land. He made his way slowly closer, looking down towards the impending meeting on the shore.

In the hollow between the dunes Gwion drew up his lines, and moved them a little forward, still screened by the curving waves of sand the wind had made and the tenacious grasses and bushes had partially clothed and secured in place.

'How close now?' Even in Owain's despite he would venture. And those clansmen who were approaching at Owain's heels, who could not all be tame even to their prince's leash, must see the attack, and be close enough to take fire from it in time, and drive the onslaught home with their added numbers.

'Not yet within call, but close. A short while yet!'

Otir stood like a rock in the edge of the surf, solid legs well braced, watching the advance of the swart, stocky cattle and their escort of armed men. Light-armed, as a man would normally go about his business. No need to expect any treachery there. Nor did it seem likely that Owain had had any part in that ill-managed raid in the night, or had any knowledge of it. If he had taken action, it would have been better done.

'Now!' said the lookout sharply from above. 'Now, while they are all watching Owain. You have them on the flank.'

'Forward now!' Gwion echoed, and burst out of the sheltering slopes with a great roar of release and resolve, almost of exultation. After him the ranks of his companions surged headlong, with swords drawn and short lances raised aloft, a sudden glitter of steel as they emerged from shadow into sun. Out into clear view, and streaming down the last slope of sand into the shingle of the beach, straight for the Danish muster. Otir swung about, bellowing an alarm that brought every head round to confront the assault. Shields went up to ward off the first flung javelins, and the hiss of swords being drawn as one was flung into the air like a great indrawn breath. Then the first wave of Gwion's force hurtled into the Danish ranks and bore them backwards into their fellows by sheer weight, so that the whole battle lurched knee-deep into the surf.

577

Cadfael saw it from his high place, the impact and the clashing recoil as the ranks collided in a quivering shock, and heard the sudden clamour of voices shouting, and startled cattle bellowing. The Danes had so spaced their array that every man had room to use his right arm freely, and was quick to draw steel. One or two were borne down by the first impetuous collision, and took their attackers down into the sea with them in a confusion of spray, but most braced themselves and stood firm. Gwion had flung himself straight at Otir. There was no way to Cadwaladr now but over Otir's body. But the Dane had twice Gwion's weight, and three times his experience in arms. The thrusting sword clanged harshly on a raised and twisted shield, and was almost wrenched out of the attacker's grasp. Then all Cadfael could see was one struggling, heaving mass of Welshman and Dane, wreathed in shimmering spray. He began to make his way rapidly down on to the beach, with what intent he himself could hardly have said.

Echoing shouts arose from among the clansmen who marched at Owain's back, and a few started out of their ranks and began to run towards the mêlée in the shallows, hands on hilts in an instant, their intent all too plain. Cadfael could not wonder at it. Welshmen were already battling against an alien invader, there in full view. Welsh blood could not endure to stand aside, all other rights and wrongs went for nothing. They hallooed their partisan approval, and plunged into the boiling shallows. The reeling mass of entangled bodies heaved and strained, so closely locked together that on neither side could they find free room to do one another any great hurt. Not until the ranks opened would there be deaths.

A loud, commanding voice soared above the din of snarling voices and clanging steel, as Owain Gwynedd set spurs to his horse and rode into the edge of the sea, striking at his own too impetuous men with the flat of his sheathed sword.

'Back! Stand off! Get back to your ranks, and put up your weapons!'

His voice, seldom raised, could split the quaking air like thunder hard on the heels of lightning when he was roused. It was that raging trumpet-call rather than the battering blows that caused the truants to shrink and cower before him, and lean aside out of his path, plashing ashore in reluctant haste. Even Cadwaladr's former liegemen wavered, falling back from their hand-to-hand struggles. The two sides fell apart, and thrusts and sword-strokes that might have been smothered in the encroaching weight of wrestling bodies found room to wound before they could be restrained or parried.

It was over. They fell back to the solid shingle, swords and axes and javelins lowered, in awe of the icy glare of Owain's eyes, and the angry circling of his horse's stamping hooves in the surf, trampling out a zone of stillness between the combatants. The Danes held their ranks, some of them bloodied, none of them fallen. Of the attackers, two lay groping feebly out of the waves to lie limp in the sand. Then there was a silence.

Owain sat his horse, quieted now by a calming hand but still quivering, and looked down at Otir, eye to eye, for a long moment. Otir held his ground, and gave him back penetrating stare for stare. There was no need for explanation or protestation between them. With his own eyes Owain had seen.

'This,' he said at length, 'was not by my contrivance. Now I will know, and hear from his own mouth, who has usurped my rule and cast doubt on my good faith. Come forth and show yourself.'

There was no question but he already knew, for he had seen the charge launched out of hiding. It was, in some measure, generous to let a man stand fast by what he had done, and declare himself defiantly of his own will, in the teeth of whatever might follow. Gwion let fall the arm still raised, sword in hand, and waded forward from among his fellows. Very slowly he came, but not from any reluctance, for his head was erected proudly, and his eyes fixed on Owain. He plashed waveringly out of the surf, as little wave on following wave lapped at his feet and drew back. He reached the edge of the shingle, and a sudden rivulet of blood ran from his clenched lips and spattered his breast, and a small blot of red grew out of the padded linen of his tunic, and expanded into a great sodden star. He stood a moment erect before Owain, and parted his lips to speak, and blood gushed out of his mouth in a dark crimson stream. He fell on his face at the feet of the prince's horse, and the startled beast edged back from him, and blew a great lamenting breath over his body.

Chapter Fourteen

EE TO HIM!' said Owain, looking down impassively at the fallen man. Gwion's hands stirred and groped feebly in the polished pebbles, faintly conscious of touch and texture. 'He is not dead, have him away and tend him. I want no deaths, more than are already past saving.'

They made haste to do his bidding. Three of the front rank, and Cuhelyn the first of them, ran to turn Gwion gently on his back, to free his mouth and nostrils from the churned-up sand. They made a litter from lances and shields, and muffled him in cloaks to carry him aside. And Brother Cadfael turned from the shore unnoticed, and followed the litter into the shelter of the dunes. What he had on him by way of linen or salves was little enough, but better than nothing until they could get their wounded man to a bed and less rough and ready care.

Owain looked down at the pool of blackening blood in the shingle at his feet, and up into Otir's intent face.

'He is Cadwaladr's man, sworn and loyal. Nevertheless, he did wrong. If he has cost you men, you have paid him.' There were two of those who had followed Gwion lying in the edge of the tide, lightly rocked by the advancing waves. A third had got to his knees, and those beside him helped him to his feet. He trailed blood from a gashed shoulder and arm, but he was in no danger of death. Nor did Otir trouble to add to the toll the three he had already put on board ship, to sail home for burial. Why waste breath in complaint to this prince who

580

acknowledged and deserved no blame for an act of folly?

'I hold you to terms,' he said, 'such as we understood between us. No more, and no less. This is none of your doing, nor any choice of mine. They chose it, and what came of it has been between them and me.'

'So be it!' said Owain. 'And now, put up your weapons and load your cattle, and go, more freely than you came, for you came without my knowledge or leave. And to your face I tell you that if ever you touch here on my land again uninvited I will sweep you back into the sea. As for this time, take your fee and go in peace.'

'Then here I deliver your brother Cadwaladr,' said Otir as coldly. 'Into his own hands, not yours, for that was not in any bargain between you and me. He may go where he will, or stay, and make his own terms with you, my lord.' He turned about, to those of his men who still held Cadwaladr sick with gall between them. He had been made nothing, a useless stock, in a matter conducted all between other men, though he was at the heart and core of the whole conflict. He had been silent while other men disposed of his person, his means and his honour, and that with manifest distaste. He had no word to say now, but bit back the bitterness and anger that rose in his throat and seared his tongue, as his captors loosed him and stood well aside, opening the way clear for him to depart. Stiffly he walked forward on to the shore, towards where his brother waited.

'Load your ships!' said Owain. 'You have this one day to leave my land.'

And he wheeled his horse and turned his back, pacing at a deliberate walk back towards his own camp. The ranks of his men closed in orderly march and followed him, and the bruised and draggled survivors of Gwion's unblessed army took up their dead and straggled after, leaving the trampled and bloodied beach clear of all but the drovers and their cattle, and Cadwaladr alone, aloof from all men, stalking in a black, forbidding cloud of disgust and humiliation after his brother.

In the nest of thick grass where they had laid him, Gwion opened his eyes, and said in a fine thread of a voice, but quite clearly: 'There is something I must tell Owain Gwynedd. I must go to him.'

Cadfael was on his knees beside him, staunching with what linen he had to hand, padded beneath thick folds of brychans, the blood that flowed irresistibly from a great wound in the young man's side, under the heart. Cuhelyn, kneeling with Gwion's head in his lap, had wiped away the foam of blood from the open mouth and the sweat from the forehead already chill and livid with the unhurried approach of death. He looked up at Cadfael, and said almost silently: 'We must carry him back to the camp. He is in earnest. He must go.'

'He is going nowhere in this world,' said Cadfael as quietly. 'If we lift him, he will die between our hands.'

Something resembling the palest and briefest of smiles, yet unquestionably a smile, touched Gwion's parted lips. He said, in the muted tones they had used over him: 'Then Owain must come to me. He has more time to spare than I have. He will come. It is a thing he will wish to know, and no one else can tell him.'

Cuhelyn drew back the tangle of black hair that lay damp on Gwion's brow, for fear it should discomfort him now, when all comfort was being rapt away all too quickly. His hand was steady and gentle. There was no hostility left. There was room for none. And in their opposed fashion they had been friends. The likeness was still there, each of them peered into a mirror, a darkening mirror and a marred image.

'I'll ride after him. Be patient. He will come.'

'Ride fast!' said Gwion, and shut his mouth upon the distortion of the smile.

On his feet already, and with a hand stretched to his horse's bridle, Cuhelyn hesitated. 'Not Cadwaladr? Should he come?'

'No,' said Gwion, and turned his face away in a sharp convulsion of pain. Otir's last defensive parry, never meant to kill, had struck out just as Owain thundered his displeasure and split the ranks apart, and Gwion had dropped his levelled sword and his guard, and opened his flank to the steel. No help for it now, it was done and could not be undone.

Cuhelyn was gone, in faithful haste, sending the sand spraying from his horse's hooves until he reached the upland meadow grass and left the dunes behind. There was no one more likely to make passionate haste to do Gwion's errand than Cuhelyn, who for a brief time had lost the ability to see in his opposite his own face. That also was past.

Gwion lay with closed eyes, containing whatever pain he felt. Cadfael did not think it was great, he had already almost slipped out of its reach. Together they waited. Gwion lay very still, for stillness seemed to slow the bleeding and conserve the life in him, and life he needed for a while yet. Cadfael had water beside him in Cuhelyn's helmet, and bathed away the beads of sweat that gathered on his patient's forehead and lip, cold as dew.

From the shore there was no more clamour, only the brisk exchanges of voices, and the stir of men moving about their business unhindered now and intent, and the lowing and occasional bellowing of cattle as they were urged through the shallows and up the ramps into the ships. A rough, uncomfortable voyage for them in the deep wells amidships, but a few hours and they would be on green turf again, good grazing and sweet water.

'Will he come?' wondered Gwion, suddenly anxious.

'He will come.'

He was coming already, in a moment more they heard the soft thudding of hooves, and in from the shore came Owain Gwynedd, with Cuhelyn at his back. They dismounted in silence, and Owain came to look down at the young, spoiled body, not too closely yet, for fear even dulling ears should be sharp enough to overhear what was not meant to be overheard.

'Can he live?'

Cadfael shook his head and made no other reply.

Owain dropped into the sand and leaned close. 'Gwion ... I am here. Spare to make many words, there is no need.'

Gwion's black eyes, a little dazzled by the mounting sun, opened wide and knew him. Cadfael moistened the lips that opened wryly, and laboured to articulate. 'Yes, there is need. I have a thing I must say.'

'For peace between us two,' said Owain, 'I say again, there is no need of words. But if you must, I am listening.'

'Bledri ap Rhys ...' began Gwion, and paused to draw breath. 'You require to know who killed him. Do not hold it against any other. I killed him.'

He waited, with resigned patience, for disbelief rather than outcry, but neither came. Only a considering and accepting silence that seemed to last a long while, and then Owain's voice, level and composed as ever, saying: 'Why? He was of your own allegiance, my brother's man.'

'So he had been,' said Gwion, and was shaken by a laugh that contorted his mouth and sent a thin trickle of blood running down his jaw. Cadfael leaned and wiped it away. 'I was glad when he came to Aber. I knew what my lord was about. I longed to join him, and I could and would have told him all I knew of your forces and movements. It was fair. I had told you I was wholly and for ever your brother's man, you knew my mind. But I could not go, I had given my word not to leave.'

'And had kept your word,' said Owain. 'So far!'

'But Bledri had given no such word. He could go, as I could not. So I told him all that I had learned in Aber, what strength you could raise, how soon you could be in Carnarvon, everything my lord Cadwaladr had to know for his defence. And I took a horse from the stables before dark, while the gates were open, and tethered it among the trees for him. And like a fool I never doubted but Bledri would be true to his salt. And he listened to all, and never said word, letting me believe he was of my mind!'

'How did you hope to get him out of the llys, once the gates were closed?' asked Owain, as mildly as if he questioned of some ordinary daily duty.

'There are ways ... I was in Aber a long time. Not everyone is always careful with keys. But in the waiting time he was noting all things within your court, and he could count as well as I, and weigh chances as sharply, while he so carried himself as to put all suspicion of his intent out of mind. What I thought was his intent!' Gwion said bitterly. His voice failed him for a moment, but he gathered his strength and resumed doggedly: 'When I went to tell him it was time to go, and see him safely away, he was naked in his bed. Without shame he told me he was going nowhere, he was no such fool, having seen for himself your power and your numbers. He would lie safe in Aber and watch which way the wind blew, and if it blew for Owain Gwynedd, then he was Owain's man. I called to mind his fealty, and he laughed at me. And I struck him down,' said Gwion through bared teeth. 'And then, since he would not, I knew if I was to keep faith with Cadwaladr I must break faith with you, and go in Bledri's place. And since he had so turned his coat, I knew that I must kill him, for to make his way with you he would certainly betray me. And before he had his wits again I stabbed him to the heart.'

Some quivering tension in his body relaxed, and he drew and breathed out a great sigh. He had done already almost all that truth required of him. The rest was very little burden.

'I went to find the horse, and the horse was gone. And then the messenger came, and there was no more I could do. Everything was in vain. I had done murder for nothing! What it

584

was entrusted to me to do for Bledri ap Rhys, whom I killed, that I did, for penance. And what came of it you know already. But it is just!' he said, rather to himself than to any other, but they heard it: 'He died unshriven, and so must I.'

'That need not be,' said Owain with detached compassion. 'Bear with this world a little while longer, and my priest will be here, for I sent word for him to come.'

'He will come late,' said Gwion, and closed his eyes.

Nevertheless, he was still living when Owain's chaplain came in obedient haste to take a dying man's last confession and guide his failing tongue through his last act of contrition. Cadfael, in attendance to the end, doubted if the penitent heard the words of the absolution, for after it was spoken there was no response, no quiver of the drained face or the arched lids that veiled the black, intense eyes. Gwion had said his last word to the world, and of what might come to pass in the world he was entering he had no great fear. He had lived long enough to rest assured of the absolution he most needed, Owain's forbearance and forgiveness, never formally spoken, but freely given.

'Tomorrow,' said Brother Mark, 'we must be on our way home. We have outstayed our time.'

They were standing together at the edge of the fields outside Owain's camp, looking out over the open sea. Here the dunes were only a narrow fringe of gold above the descent to the shore, and in subdued afternoon sunlight the sea stretched in cloudy blues, deepening far out into a clear green, and the long, drowned peninsula of shoals shone pale through the water. In the deep channels between, the Danish cargo ships were gradually dwindling into toy boats, dark upon the brightness, bearing out on a steady breeze under sail, for their own Dublin shore. And beyond, the lighter longships, smaller still, drove eagerly for home.

The peril was past, Gwynedd delivered, debts paid, brothers brought together again, if not yet reconciled. The affair might have turned out hugely bloodier and more destructive. Nevertheless, men had died.

Tomorrow, too, the camp at their backs would be dismantled of its improvised defences, the husbandman would come back to his farmhouse, bringing his beasts with him, and return imperturbably to the care of his land and his stock, as his forebears had done time after time, giving ground pliably

585

for a while to marauding enemies they knew they could outwait, outrun and outlast. The Welsh, who left their expendable homesteads for the hills at the approach of an enemy, left them only to return and rebuild.

The prince would take his muster back to Carnarvon, and thence dismiss those whose lands lay here in Arfon and Anglesey, before going on to Aber. Rumour said he would suffer Cadwaladr to return with him, and those who knew them best added that Cadwaladr would soon be restored to possession of some part, at least, of his lands. For in spite of all, Owain loved his younger brother, and could not shut him out of his grace much longer.

'And Otir has his fee,' said Mark, pondering gains and losses.

'It was promised.'

'I don't grudge it. It might have cost far more.'

And so it might, though two thousand marks could not buy back the lives of Otir's three young men, now being borne back to Dublin for burial, nor those few of Gwion's following picked up dead from the surf, nor Bledri ap Rhys in his chill, calculating faithlessness, nor Gwion himself in his stark, destructive loyalty, the one as fatal as the other. Nor could all these lost this year call into life again Anarawd, dead last year in the south, at Cadwaladr's instigation, if not at his hands.

'Owain has sent a courier to Canon Meirion in Aber,' said Mark, 'to put his mind at rest for his daughter. By this he knows she is here safe enough, with her bridegroom. The prince sent as soon as Ieuan brought her into camp last night.'

His tone, Cadfael thought, was carefully neutral, as though he stood aside and withheld judgement, viewing with equal detachment two sides of a complex problem, and one that was not his to solve.

'And how has she conducted herself here in these few hours?' asked Cadfael. Mark might study to absent himself from all participation in these events, but he could not choose but observe.

'She is altogether dutiful and quiet. She pleases Ieuan. She pleases the prince, for she is as a bride should be, submissive and obedient. She was in terror, says Ieuan, when he snatched her away out of the Danish camp. She is in no fear now.'

'I wonder,' said Cadfael, 'if submissive and obedient is as Heledd should be. Have we ever known her to be so, since she came from Saint Asaph with us?'

'Much has happened since then,' said Mark, thoughtfully smiling. 'It may be she has had enough of venturing, and is not sorry to be settling down to a sensible marriage with a decent man. You have seen her. Have you seen any cause to doubt that she is content?'

And in truth Cadfael could not say that he had observed in her bearing any trace of discontent. Indeed, she went smilingly about the work she found for herself, waited upon Ieuan serenely and deftly, and continued to distil about her a kind of lustre that could not come from an unhappy woman. Whatever was in her mind, and held in reserve there with deep and glossy satisfaction, it certainly did not disquiet or distress her. Heledd viewed the path opening before her with unmistakable pleasure.

'Have you spoken with her?' asked Mark.

'There has been no occasion yet.'

'You may essay now, if you wish. She is coming this way.'

Cadfael turned his head, and saw Heledd coming striding lightly along the crest of the ridge towards them, with purpose in her step, and her face towards the north. Even when she halted beside them, it was only for a moment, checked in flight like a bird hovering.

'Brother Cadfael, I'm glad to see you safe. The last I knew of you was when they swept us apart, by the breach in the stockade.' She looked out across the sea, where the ships had shrunk into black splinters upon scintillating water. All along the line of them her glance followed. She might have been counting them. 'They got off unhindered, then, with their silver and their cattle. Were you there to see?'

'I was,' said Cadfael.

'They never did me offence,' she said, looking after their departing fleet with a slight, remembering smile. 'I would have waved them away home, but Ieuan did not think it safe for me.'

'As well,' said Cadfael seriously, 'for it was not entirely a peaceful departure. And where are you going now?'

She turned and looked at them full, and her eyes were wide and innocent and the deep purple of irises. 'I left something of mine up there in the Danish camp,' she said. 'I am going to find it.'

'And Ieuan lets you go?'

'I have leave,' she said. 'They are all gone now.'

They were all gone, and it was safe now to let his hard-won

587

bride return to the deserted dunes where she had been a prisoner for a while, but never felt herself in bondage. They watched her resume her purposeful passage along the edge of the fields. There was barely a mile to go.

'You did not offer to go with her,' said Mark with a solemn face.

'I would not be so crass. But give her a fair start,' said Cadfael reflectively, 'and I think you and I might very well go after her.'

'You think,' said Mark, 'we might be more welcome company on the way back?'

'I doubt,' Cadfael admitted, 'whether she is coming back.'

Mark nodded his head by way of acknowledgement, unsurprised. 'I had been wondering myself,' he said.

The tide was on the ebb, but not yet so low as to expose the long, slender tongue of sand that stretched out like a reaching hand and wrist towards the coast of Anglesey. It showed pale gold beneath the shallows, here and there a tuft of tenacious grass and soil breaking the surface. At the end of it, where the knuckles of the hand jutted in an outcrop of rock, the stunted salt bushes stood up like rough, crisp hair, their roots fringed with the yellow of sand. Cadfael and Mark stood on the ridge above, and looked down as they had looked once before, and upon the same revelation. Repeated, it made clear all the times, all the evenings, when it had been repeated without witnesses. They even drew back a little, so that the shape of them might be less obtrusive on the skyline, if she should look up. But she did not look up. She looked down into the clear water, palest green in the evening light, that reached almost to her knees, as she trod the narrow golden path towards the seagirt throne of rock. She had her skirts, still frayed and soiled from travel and from living wild, gathered up in her hands, and she leaned to watch the cold, sweet water quivering about her legs, and breaking their lissome outlines into a disembodied tremor, as though she floated rather than waded. She had pulled all the pins from her hair; it hung in a black, undulating cloud about her shoulders, hiding the oval face stooped to watch her steps. She moved like a dancer, slowly, with languorous grace. For whatever tryst she had here she came early, and she knew it. But because there was no uncertainty, time was a grace, even waiting would be pleasure anticipated.

Here and there she halted, to be still, to let the water settle

588

and be still around her feet, and then she would lean to watch the tremulous ardour of her face shimmering as each wave ebbed back into the sea. A very gentle tide, with hardly any wind now. But Otir's ships under sail were more than halfway to Dublin by this hour.

On the throne of rock she sat down, wringing the water from the hem of her gown, and looked across the sea, and waited, without impatience, without doubts. Once, in this place, she had looked immeasurably lonely and forsaken, but that had been illusion, even then. Now she looked like one in serene possession of all that lay about her, dear companion to the sea and the sky. The orb of the sun was declining before her, due west, gilding her face and body.

The little ship, lean and dark and sudden, came darting down from the north, surging out of the concealment of the rising shoreline beyond the sandy warrens across the strait. Somewhere up-coast it had lain waiting off Anglesey until the sunset hour. There had been, thought Cadfael, watching intently, no compact, no spoken tryst at all. They had had no time to exchange so much as a word when she was snatched away. There had been only the inward assurance to keep them constant, that the ship would come, and that she would be there waiting. Body and blood, they had been superbly sure, each of the other. No sooner had Heledd recovered her breath and accepted the fact of her innocent abduction than she had come to terms with events, knowing how they must and would end. Why else had she gone so serenely about passing the waiting time, disarming suspicion, even putting herself out, who knows how ruefully, to give Ieuan ab Ifor some brief pleasure before he was to pay for it with perpetual loss. In the end Canon Meirion's daughter knew what she wanted, and was ruthless in pursuing it, since no one among her menfolk and masters showed any sign of helping her to her desire.

Small, serpentine and unbelievably swift, oars driving as one, Turcaill's dragon-ship swooped inshore, but held clear of beaching. It hung for a moment still, oars trailed, like a bird hovering, and Turcaill leaped over the side and came wading waist-deep towards the tiny island of rock. His flaxen hair shone almost red in the crimson descent of the sun, a match for Owain Gwynedd's, as dominant and as fair. And Heledd, when they turned their eyes again on her, had risen and walked into the sea. The tension of the ebbing tide drew her with it, skirts floating. Turcaill came up glistening out of the deeper

589

water. They met midway, and she walked into his arms, and was swung aloft against his heart. There was no great show, only a distant, brief peal of mingled laughter rising on the air to the two who stood watching. No need for more, there had never been any doubt in either of these sea creatures as to the inevitable ending.

Turcaill had turned his back, and was striding through the surf back to his ship, with Heledd in his arms, and the tide, receding more rapidly as the sun declined, gave back before him in iridescent fountains of spray, minor rainbows wreathing his naked feet. Lightly he hoisted the girl over the low side of his dragon, and swung himself after. And she, as soon as she had her footing, turned to him and embraced him. They heard her laughter, high and wild and sweet, thinner than a bird's song at this distance, but piercing and clear as a carillon of bells.

All the long, sinuous bank of oars, suspended in air, dipped together. The little serpent heeled and sped, creaming spray, round into the clear passage between the sandy shoals, already showing golden levels beneath the blue, but more than deep enough yet for this speedy voyager. She sped away end-on, small and ever smaller, a leaf carried on an impetuous current, borne away to Ireland, to Dublin of the Danish kings and the restless seafarers. And a fitting mate Turcaill had carried away with him, and formidable progeny they would breed between them to master these uneasy oceans in generations to come.

Canon Meirion need not fret that his daughter would ever reappear to imperil his status with his bishop, his reputation or his advancement. Love her as he might, and wish her well as he probably did, he had desired heartily that she should enjoy her good fortune elsewhere, out of sight if not out of mind. He had his wish. Nor need he agonise, thought Cadfael, watching that resplendent departure, over her happiness. She had what she wanted, a man of her own choosing. By that she would abide, wise or unwise by her father's measure. She measured by other means, and was not likely to suffer any regrets.

The small black speck, racing home, was barely visible as a dot of darkness upon a bright and glittering sea.

'They are gone,' said Brother Mark, and turned and smiled. 'And we may go, too.'

They had overstayed their time. Ten days at the most, Mark had said, and Brother Cadfael would be returned safe and sound to his herb garden and his proper work among the sick. But perhaps Abbot Radulfus and Bishop de Clinton would regard the truant days as well spent, considering the outcome. Even Bishop Gilbert might be highly content to keep his able and energetic canon, and have Meirion's inconvenient daughter safely oversea, and his scandalous marriage forgotten. Everyone else appeared well content to have so satisfactory a settlement of what might well have been a bloody business. What mattered now was to return to the level sanity of daily living, and allow old grudges and animosities to fade gradually into the obscurity of the past. Yes, Cadwaladr would be restored, on probation, Owain could not totally discard him. But not wholly restored, and not yet. Gwion, who by any measure had been the loser, would be decently buried, with no very great acknowledgement of his loyalty from the lord who had bitterly disappointed him. Cuhelyn would remain here in Gwynedd, and in time surely be glad that he had not had to do murder with his own hands to see Anarawd avenged, at least upon Bledri ap Rhys. Princes, who can depute other hands to do their less savoury work for them, commonly escape all temporary judgements, but not the last.

And Ieuan ab Ifor would simply have to resign himself to losing a delusory image of a submissive wife, a creature Heledd could never become. He had barely seen or spoken with her, his heart could scarcely be broken at losing her, however his dignity might be bruised. There were pleasant women in Anglesey who could console him, if he did but look about him here at home.

And she ... she had what she wanted, and she was where she wanted to be, and not where others had found it convenient to place her. Owain had laughed when he heard of it, though considerately he had kept a grave face in Ieuan's presence. And there was one more waiting in Aber who would have the last word in the story of Heledd.

The last word, when Canon Meirion had heard and digested the tale of his daughter's choice, came after a deep-drawn breath of relief for her safety at least – or was it for his own deliverance?

'Well, well!' said Meirion, knotting and unknotting his long hands. 'There is a sea between.' True, and there was relief for both of them in that. But then he continued: 'I shall never see her again!' and there was as much of grief in it as of satisfaction. Cadfael was always to be in two minds about Canon Meirion.

They came to the border of the shire in the early evening of the second day, and on the principle that it was as well to be hanged for a sheep as a lamb, turned aside to pass the night with Hugh at Maesbury. The horses would be grateful for the rest, and Hugh would be glad to hear at first hand what had passed in Gwynedd, and how the Norman bishop was rubbing along with his Welsh flock. There was also the pleasure of spending a few placid hours with Aline and Giles, in a domesticity all the more delightful to contemplate because they had forsworn it for themselves, along with the world outside the Order.

Some such unguarded remark Cadfael made, sitting contentedly by Hugh's hearth with Giles on his knees. And Hugh laughed at him.

'You, forswear the world? And you just back from gallivanting to the farthest western edge of Wales? If they manage to keep you within the pale for more than a month or two, even after this jaunt, it will be a marvel. I've known you restless after a week of strict observance. Now and again I've wondered if some day you wouldn't set out for Saint Giles, and end up in Jerusalem.'

'Oh, no, not that!' said Cadfael, with serene certainty. 'It's true, now and again my feet itch for the road.' He was looking deep into himself, where old memories survived, and remained, after their fashion, warming and satisfying, but of the past, never to be repeated, no longer desirable. 'But when it comes down to it,' said Cadfael, with profound content, 'as roads go, the road home is as good as any.'

The Complete Brother Cadfael series by Ellis Peters

1. A Morbid Taste for Bones	£7.99	12. The Raven in the Foregate	£5.99
2. One Corpse Too Many	£8.99	13. The Rose Rent	£5.99
3. Monk's-Hood	£7.99	14. The Hermit of Eyton Forest	£9.99
4. Saint Peter's Fair	£7.99	15. The Confession of	
5. The Leper of Saint Giles	£7.99	Brother Haluin	£9.99
6. The Virgin in the Ice	£7.99	16. The Heretic's Apprentice	£9.99
7. The Sanctuary Sparrow	£9.99	17. The Potter's Field	£9.99
8. The Devil's Novice	£7.99	18. The Summer of the Danes	£7.99
9. Dead Man's Ransom	£9.99	19. The Holy Thief	£9.99
10. The Pilgrim of Hate	£6.99	20. Brother Cadfael's Penance	£7.99
11. An Excellent Mystery	£9.99		

The prices shown above are correct at time of going to press. However, the publishers reserve the right to increase prices on covers from those previously advertised, without further notice.

───────────────── sphere ─────────────────

Please allow for postage and packing: **Free UK delivery.**
Europe: add 25% of retail price; Rest of World: 45% of retail price.

To order any of the above or any other Sphere titles, please call our credit card orderline or fill in this coupon and send/fax it to:

Sphere, PO Box 121, Kettering, Northants NN14 4ZQ
Fax: 01832 733076   Tel: 01832 737526
Email: aspenhouse@FSBDial.co.uk

☐ I enclose a UK bank cheque made payable to Sphere for £ . .
☐ Please charge £ . . . . to my Visa/Delta/Maestro

Expiry Date ☐☐☐☐   Maestro Issue No. ☐☐

NAME (BLOCK LETTERS please) . . . .

ADDRESS . . . .

. . . .

. . . .

Postcode . . . . Telephone . . . .

Signature . . . .

Please allow 28 days for delivery within the UK. Offer subject to price and availability.